MAN'S BOOK

WIND
ALONG THE WASTE
Ewart Brookes

★

PHYLLIS
E. V. Cunningham

★

DEATH OF A TOM
Douglas Warner

ODHAMS BOOKS LIMITED
LONG ACRE, LONDON

S.1263.S
MADE AND PRINTED IN
GREAT BRITAIN BY ODHAMS (WATFORD) LTD.
WATFORD, HERTS.

CONTENTS

WIND ALONG THE WASTE

Ewart Brookes

Into this Universe, and why not knowing,
Nor whence, like Water willy-nilly flowing;
And out of it, as Wind along the waste,
I know not whither, willy-nilly blowing.

Rubá'iyát of Omar Khayyám

*"Wind Along the Waste" is published by
Jarrolds Publishers (London) Ltd.*

The Author

Ewart Brookes, of Welsh-American parentage, was born in Swansea only a few hundred yards from the sea and the docks—and ships. Almost inevitably he was destined to add to his family's two hundred years of sea-faring history. But, after an arduous apprenticeship, he found that the shipping depression had created a glut of junior officers. He turned to the pen and eventually became a newspaperman, first with a local paper in Swansea, then with the North-cliffe Newspapers in Bristol and eventually in Fleet Street.

In the last war he served briefly with destroyers until the Dunkirk evacuation, after which he captained a minesweeper at Dover and later was given a larger command in Western Approaches. He came back to an uneasy peace with the rank of Commander, a Distinguished Service Cross and a Mention-in-Dispatches.

From his experience as a mine-sweeping officer he wrote the best-seller *Proud Waters*, and since then a succession of sea stories have rolled from his pen.

CHAPTER ONE

THE tall grandfather clock, set flush against the wall, slowly measured off the inexorable passing of time. Through a long narrow glass panel set in the body of the clock the broad brass disc at the end of the pendulum could be seen swinging over an impeccable arc.

The subdued noise from the clock was not a definite tock. It was more of a soft thud at the end of each end of the arc, as if it merely wished to draw attention in a quiet, discreet way, without sharply defined fuss, that another second of time had been noted and had been allowed to pass.

The man at the table sat curiously immobile except for his hands. A few inches from the edge of the table rested a squat, square tin of dark tobacco. Flanking it, almost touching it, was a box of matches. The hand holding the generously bowled pipe clasped it so that the bowl was held securely, with the little finger of the grasping hand barely touching the edge of the table. Methodically his fingers flickered out until they touched the tin of tobacco. He teased out a portion of tobacco and firmly pressed it into the bowl with a stubby forefinger.

It was a simple operation but one which had taken him weeks of learning. At first he had been impatient and much tobacco had fallen to the floor until he had learned that economy of movement was an essential for the unseeing.

Many times he had knocked things over, many times he had burned his hand until he learned that the blind never grab at anything. They tentatively, almost delicately, explore the black spaces until they have trained their fingers to be their eyes.

The bowl charged and pressed down until it was three-quarters full, his fingers sought for and found the box of matches. Heat was his guide. He had learned, too, in those first few weeks to tell the difference between the sound of a match which lit from the sound of one that failed to ignite.

At first he had burned his fingers fumbling uncertainly with flaming match for the bowl of his pipe. When he had finally made contact and the satisfying smoke was being drawn into his lungs he learned another lesson. The blind never completely fill a bowl of a pipe. All his life, until his sight had left him, the final ceremony of starting a pipe was the careful shepherding of errant, glowing shreds of tobacco back into the bowl. He had learned that at the expense of charred clothes and furniture. There had been a gentle slapping hand near him and a soft voice.

"You're trying to set yourself on fire, my dear."

With the bowl three-quarters charged the heat-expanding tobacco still remained confined in the bowl.

A new pipe, one with a larger bowl, had been slowly broken in until he could assess to within half a minute how long it would last.

Buller Cleeve was blind and was learning to see again. Learning to see with his fingers and with his ears. Things he had touched all his life and things he had seen all his life without them registering themselves in his mind took on a new significance. Simple things. He could sit in his high-back chair now and could tell how far off completing her washing up of dishes his wife would be. Although his wide, staring deep-blue eyes saw nothing, he could trace each movement she made in the kitchen. He could tell to within a few seconds when she would walk through the door of the kitchen and would say: "Well, that lot's done. I'll make a pot of tea when you get the boys on."

Then her chair would creak and the wicker lid of her basket would answer with a softer squeak and he knew that she would be sorting out a holed sock or a shirt without a button. All those things he had learned to see by listening.

First the cutlery would jangle musically and would be dropped into the knife drawer. Then the dishes and finally the pots, each one placed on a shelf above the sink with a decisive clink. And lastly the plug in the sink would be pulled and the water would rush away noisily, freed from its labours.

He cupped his fingers over the bowl with a cunning little gap between the fingers to increase the draught and he listened.

The grandfather clock made a soft sound, almost as if it were gutturally clearing its throat. In sixty seconds, one minute of time, it would break out into a sonorous jangle of sound—seven strokes, each a decisive note at first then merging into a deeper chorus until the last and seventh note. Gradually the noise would die away, almost with reluctance, until there was only a faint hum. The clock had been striking for him for his forty years of married life, but it was only after he had lost his eyesight that he had noticed how long after the last note had been struck did sound still remain. He had once tried to time the decreasing sound but had failed to detect the finally passing whisper.

One minute to go.

His hand moved certainly to his left until his wrist touched the small table at his side, lifted and as certainly fingered a knob on the radio set. He clicked it once, listened carefully until a subdued, tenuous thread of life told him the set was working. Then he leaned back in his chair, cocked an ear as the water gurgled musically down the waste pipe. Her feet shuffled softly across the kitchen floor and from the doorway she spoke.

"Well, that lot's done. I'll make a pot of tea when you get the boys on."

Buller Cleeve smiled softly.

"Coming up, dear. Want to make a guess?"

She smiled. "I'll guess Ben. He's always impatient."

"We'll see."

A thick forefinger caressed the knurled knob of the set and adjusted the tuning.

A faint jumble of voices came from the set, thinly, like voices heard from another room through closed doors. Again the finger delicately stroked the knob and a voice came from the set with startling clearness.

"How you making out, Ben?"

"Sam's up first," she whispered.

Another voice cut in.

"Lousy. I've been scratching around that Ragusson Bank all day. Four hauls and I wouldn't feed it to a mangy bloody dog."

"Careful," warned the first voice, the overtones loaded with laughter. "The Old Man's listening. Any bad language and he'll put you across his knee."

Buller Cleeve chuckled as he listened. Blind as he was he could picture the scene. Ben would be standing legs apart, flexing them to the roll of his trawler. Sam would be lounging sprawled out in the wireless room. He could almost see the wink passing between Sam and the radio operator.

Sam took up the legend.

"Talking of dogs. If it's dogs you want I've got a million tons. I could do better with a bit of string, a hook and a worm fishing in the New Cut at low tide."

Ben chuckled. "Nowt there but eels, boy. What do you figure the weather's going to do?"

"Won't get any worse. I wish it would blow up for a day or so. It would take that Bogey Man off my stern. He's been sitting on me since last night."

Buller Cleeve sat upright in his chair. He could see the chart, he knew the area like the back of his hand. A triangular problem set itself before him.

Ben had dolefully announced that he had been scratching around the Ragusson Bank all day with beggarly results. Sam had contributed that the Icelandic Fishery Protection ship, the Bogey Man, had been shadowing him all day.

Ben was fishing thirty miles from the coast. Sam was nearer, fishing on or near the disputed twelve-miles limit the Icelandic authorities were trying to impose.

Buller Cleeve listened intently.

Sam continued his narrative. "He's making me nervous. He comes bobbing out of the west all the time. For the few boxes I've got it isn't worth it. I think I'll move east a bit."

"The stuff I'm getting will do for the manure factory," Ben went on with a chuckle. "I'll bet he's sitting there burning holes in the carpet and guessing good and hard."

Buller Cleeve shook with silent laughter.

"And Ma's trying to darn those socks you left home. They looked like a chewed-up cod end to me."

Mrs Cleeve thrust a hand into a well-darned sock and smiled softly.

A kettle whistled shrilly from the kitchen and she made tea in a large, brown china pot, placed milk and sugar on the tray and softly laid it on the table near her husband's elbow. He moved a hand until the heat of the pot identified its position for him.

His fingers closed around the handle, the back of the other hand rested against the side of the cup, thumb upraised until it touched the spout of the teapot. He tilted it, judging by sound.

Anxiously his wife watched, then her face relaxed as he laid the pot down again. The cup was full to within half an inch. She marvelled as she had never ceased to marvel at that performance. Only once had she ever offered to pour it for him. The outburst had shocked her. But she still watched.

Buller listened.

"I'll bet it's thick and black and the spoon stands up in it." Ben chuckled.

"Could paint a ship's bottom with it," Sam added. "Like the stuff I'm drinking now."

"Me, too," Ben said.

Buller Cleeve sucked in a generous mouthful of hot tea. His tongue, made tender by the strong tobacco, coiled slightly and he blew sharply, gustily.

"I'm blowing mine," Ben said.

"I'm fanning mine with my hat, all refined like."

A duet of chuckles came from the radio set.

"Hey, Ben. I can hear old Charlie Bates wheezing away. How's the asthma, Charlie?"

A hoarse voice cut in with a rasping laugh.

"Got just the medicine for it in my hand right now. Out of a square bottle. I been listening. Scratching around for dogs, are you? Pity your Old Man didn't teach you a bit about fishing. Wonder to me you ain't all in the grubber chopping firewood for a living.

Buller Cleeve listened intently, a smile flickering around the corners of his mouth. Charlie Bates and he had been friends all their lives. It was Charlie Bates who had journeyed to London with him, who had sat on the edge of a chair in the consultant's room while that knowledgeable man had examined Buller Cleeve and had somewhat brusquely informed him that in a matter of weeks his life would be eternal darkness.

It was Charlie Bates who had stayed ashore with him for two trips and had fought him to a standstill when Buller, writhing in mental agony, had wanted to walk over the end of the quay.

Buller listened.

"Never did have no sense, either of you," Charlie rasped. "You, Ben, I stood for you when you was christened. Bellowing your head off you was, and you with a leaking stern gland. And Sam wasn't a lot better 'cept that he squeaked instead of crying. I hate to think of you two boys going home in debt. If I see you I'll spare you a couple of boxes of hake." There was a pause. "Might even make it a box or two of haddock."

Buller fingered his lip. The problem had become four-sided instead of triangular.

"I'm hopping it now. Just about to make another haul," Charlie concluded. "I fish, not waste time."

"So long, Charlie," Ben said.

"So long, Charlie," Sam's voice sounded solemn. After a few seconds of silence he continued. "Pity about poor Old Charlie. Flogging the dead horse two trips out of three."

Ben picked up the narrative.

"Yeah. Of course if he was given a decent trawler instead of that sea-going scrap-yard he might make a living."

"And something like a crew instead of a bunch of cripples he has to ship each trip."

Buller Cleeve's face squeezed up into a myriad wrinkles. He knew, as did his sons, that Charlie Bates was the best trawler skipper sailing under the Red Ensign. He hand-picked his crews and had steadfastly declined newly launched diesel-engined trawlers twice the size of his veteran *Southern Star*.

"Stink-boxes, throbbing like toothache," Charlie had said disdainfully. "Worse than them Junker-engined Belgian ditch-crawlers. Gimme steam and a few good firemen every time."

Charlie Bates had grieved for four days when the Admiralty had commandeered *Southern Star* for minesweeping, had been drunk for three more and finally had lied and wangled until the day came when, in square-rig uniform, and a collar and tie, he had stalked aboard *Southern Star* as skipper in command, spent half an hour looking around his beloved ship and about the same time in a verbal assessment of naval officers who could not bring a trawler alongside without denting plates and bending the stern. He touched flights of florid oratory which held three senior officers in awed, entranced admiring silence. When he had finished a grizzled captain asked a commander: "Did he repeat himself?" And received the answer: "Not once, sir, A spectacular performance."

Charlie had swept mines in *Southern Star* through the long years. His triumphs were *Southern Star*'s triumphs. Her griefs were his, as when a Stuka scored a near miss which left her with two foot of water in the engine and deepening very minute. Charlie nursed her in while his Geordie Chief Engineman kept a pump going by a succession of miracles. And Charlie grieved with her and made himself a thorn in the side of the dock-yard manager until *Southern Star* was repaired and restored to the sea.

The manager never knew how close he was to extermination when he had said: "It would have been better to let this rattle-trap sink out of the way. It's taking time, money and men away from important work to mess about with her."

All that Buller Cleeve knew, as did his sons Ben and Sam.

Buller Cleeve leaned forward until his ear was close to the loudspeaker of the radio set and listened intently. Through the background of static and mysterious cacophony of noise he heard that for which he was listening. A long-drawn-out, almost sepulchral wheezing sound. Charlie Bates was refusing to be drawn, but was listening—and laughing. And Buller Cleeve laughed with him.

Ben's voice cut across the spluttering silence. It was an innocent query.

"How about a trip up to London this time in, Sam?"

"Can do. We can see Arsenal play, have a look around the town and come back on Sunday."

"That's a date."

Buller did a simple calculation in his mind, leaned forward and said: "The boys will be home Friday week, Mother. Afternoon tide."

She had never grasped the simple code barely concealed in fragments of innocent conversation over the air and had sometimes marvelled when Buller was describing in detail when trawlers would return, what sort of catch they had made, and roughly what prices their haul would bring.

It was enough for her that he could do so. Finding out filled his black life.

She watched him, a smile crinkling his face as he fingered the knob, slowly bringing in voices, some harsh, some soft, some foreign and some English, as trawlers, using the trawler band of the wireless, spoke to one another and to their owners.

Although virtually imprisoned by darkness, he was living it with them, he was talking to them in his mind; he was with them, battling out the same problems of merciless weather, the mysterious absence of fish; coping with the endless task of catching enough—and more—to offset the expenses of the trip, the wages, the coal, the food and the general overheads.

It had been his life from the day he had sailed in a trawler skippered by his father, sailed as a decky learner and no favours asked or given.

In those days a trip to the Faroes or Iceland had been an epic voyage, most of the trawling had been done on the Dogger Banks, or around Rockall, that bleak, unlighted spear of stone off the north-west coast of Scotland.

Buller's father had been one of the half fishermen, half explorers who had courageously thrust north and east of Iceland, to the White Sea, to Bear Island, fighting a succession of screaming gales to arrive back with secrets in their hearts of places where the fish were twenty-fathom thick on the bottom, a new-found respect for wind and sea in their souls—and the firemen scraping the bottom of the bunkers for enough coal to get her home with a haul which made history.

Buller had grown up with it, had matured with it. He had sat for and earned his Second Hand's ticket. He was Mate of a trawler. Then he became skipper, competing with his ageing father but drawing on the older man's knowledge and guile freely.

There had been the night when the then primitive radio set had come on laboriously tapping out a message, a staccato call for help. A trawler was overwhelmed. The sea was claiming its own. The doomed ship was forty miles away from Buller's but he had slammed her into mountains of white-fanged seas through the night. And he been too late. It was his father's ship.

Buller had kept his grief to himself and talked of that night to nobody, but his crew talked in awed whispers of their ten-hour slam when Buller, hands locked tightly around the spokes of the wheel, had driven, coaxed and cursed her—only to be too late.

Only to Charlie Bates had he once confided: "If I marry and have sons I'll drown 'em in a tub before they'll become fishermen."

And he had married, with Charlie Bates standing half a shoulder behind him, strangling in a hard collar, while he had promised to love and cherish the woman of his choice.

And in due course she had presented him with two sons. Ben the elder, a replica of his father, squat, square, with a head set deeply between thick shoulders. With blue eyes which could sparkle or could take on the glint of ice.

When Samuel was on the way Buller's wife had secretly longed for a girl and had concealed her disappointment when a second son was born. Possibly that had imposed some pre-natal influence on the child. Samuel was finer-featured, appeared to be softer material until people realized that whereas Ben was the heavy club, the battering ram, Samuel was the chilled, tempered steel.

Buller had tried to fight tradition. In the short spells he had spent at home he had heard his growing boys talk of trawlers, of good hauls and bad hauls. He had seen them arrive home grubby from playing around the fish docks. He had tried—and failed—and had finally capitulated. First they had sailed with him in their holidays and had been enthralled.

But on one thing Buller had been adamant. They must have an education. What he had learned in laborious still watches, his lips soundlessly and slowly shaping the problems, they must learn in school.

Neither of them had been brilliant, but had run high in the

crowd and Buller had glowed the day he arrived home to find that their siege campaign against a scholarship had been successful. For the next five years or so they would attend the local grammar school.

Charlie Bates had been sceptical.

"You may think you're hiding 'em away by sending 'em to that school. But fishermen they were born and fishermen they'll be. You'll see."

Buller had slowly nodded.

"Maybe. But answer me this, Charlie Bates. How old were you when you got your Mate's ticket? I'll tell you. Same age as me. And like me you could just about write your name and read little words. Six weeks ashore we both did with a fellow cramming it into us like stuffing a duck. Why, even now when you write your name it looks like a drunken decky learner has been scrabbling around with a handful of waste dipped in a paint-pot. What do you read? Same as me. Kids' comics and such like and why? I'm asking you why? Because you can't read anything else, the words are too big. But my boys will be able to read, and able to figure. And maybe in that five years or so they'll learn that there's something else besides fishing. Earning money like horses and spending it like asses."

"Maybe," Charlie Bates had grunted.

And both of them had been right.

The Cleeve boys had left school and within minutes of arriving home on their last day had thrown aside their school-caps and had announced, without bravado, without question, that they wished to go to sea, wished to sail on trawlers.

Ben, the older, had been the first.

When Buller had heard it he had built up enough ammunition for a stormy scene, but his wife had demolished that in a few quiet moments as they lay in bed.

"If you stop him and force him into a job he doesn't like he'll be unhappy all his life. I don't want him to go, but let him find his own feet, my dear," she had said softly. "Maybe after a few trips he'll change his mind. After all, he has only been with you on holiday trips. Promise me you won't storm at him."

And Buller had promised.

Ben had sailed as a decky learner with Charlie Bates for his first trip and had found that while ashore Charlie was his godfather and his father's friend, at sea he was a hard taskmaster and there would be no favours. It had been a tough, exacting run and the thoughtful look in Ben's eyes had not escaped Charlie Bates.

The *Southern Star* was two hours from home when Charlie had asked: "Had enough?"

Ben had surveyed his new callouses, his scarred hands and had dug back into recent memories.

"I earned my keep, didn't I?" Ben had asked.

Charlie had nodded. "Yes, no question of that."

"Want me next trip?"

Charlie's face had relaxed. "Why not? We sail again Thursday night."

The grizzled, inarticulate man at the wheel had watched the little scene. When Ben had left the wheelhouse he grunted.

"Another mug."

"Mug yourself, Shorty," Charlie had snapped. "You'll be glad to ship with him in three or four years' time. There's a good skipper in that boy."

"Still a mug. Anybody as sails ten yards from the quay on a trawler is a mug."

"Maybe."

And Sam, impatiently scanning the fleeting days left of his school career, had followed suit. Ben had shipped with his father and Sam had followed his footsteps on the *Southern Star* to learn from a master. And because they had received some education those things which had been a trial and a tribulation to acquire by their father came easy to them.

Before Ben was twenty-three, Sam a year younger, they both had their skipper's tickets and a trawler-owner, without benevolence, had given them trawlers to command. Not new ships, but older ones, which had neither the range nor the capacity of the trawlers similar to their father's. But they had fished, and they had competed fiercely with each other, neither giving nor asking quarter. Their friendly, if keen, rivalry became a by-word in a fishing port where rivalry was a foundation stone.

The owner had smiled quietly to himself and in due course had backed his judgement so that they came to larger commands and found themselves competing with their own father and Charlie Bates and other top skippers to whom the sea bottom from North Cape to Bear Island and beyond was an open book, but an open book zealously guarded.

And each had developed in his own individual way. Ben, short, squat, like a young bull, rode roughshod over life. He had a lashing tongue which could make men squirm and curse him under their breaths. He could drive them until weariness filled their lives and tears of mingled misery and rage were burning the backs of their eyes.

Sam was the exact opposite. Nobody ever heard him raise his voice. Analyse what he said and it was innocuous. But hear it and the whisper of the sharp edge could be heard, the faint ring of steel, tempered hard and cutting cleanly but painfully.

Ashore they were inseparable, with a love for each other like David and Jonathan. They drank but sparingly and then only sociably. There was no reason for them to seek oblivion in drink, nor to seek courage.

Sometimes, within an hour or two of arriving in port, they would be expensively dressed and in the express train bound for London. For twenty-four hours of the flesh-pots. They did the rounds of the theatres and in this, too, there was an unspoken, tacit agreement that each would have his choice. Sam preferred the deeper material, a play or a film with a problem or a message. For Ben it was the flashing lights, the revue, dancing girls and the hard brightness.

After a show they would have a meal at an expensive hotel or club. Ben's bull shoulders and bright-blue eyes would cause a quickening of the pulse in suave, polished women who sought no deeper than an elemental, brutal response. A look at his deeply tanned face, his eyes and at the way he carried himself would cause them to look again at their pallid, languid escorts—with increasing distaste.

The more thoughtful would linger on Sam. There was the lithe, tensile strength they wished to know. The faultless spring of tempered steel with more than a hint of some of the tempering heat remaining there in lasting passion.

And Ben and Sam dallied, laughed and passed on their way, leaving shallow scars which soon healed over.

Each had reacted differently, in their own way, when they had heard that for their father the rest of his life would be darkness.

Buller first began to suspect that all was not well with his eyes when he found the small figures on the chart blurring as he peered at them. For a while he accepted it as a penalty of middle age and secretly kept in his waistcoat pocket a small magnifying glass which he used when nobody was looking.

Then one night, as he leaned against the wheelhouse door, he glanced at the brass clock screwed to the bulkhead. The face was opaque, formless. He could not see the hands.

"What time do you make it?" He casually poised the question to the man at the wheel.

A quick glance and the man had answered.

"'Bout time we were seeing outer-ledge buoy," Buller had added.

The man had peered at him. Outer-ledge buoy was flashing bravely less than a mile ahead.

"There she is, Skipper. Right on the stem."

Buller had screwed up his eyes, thrust forward his head. He could not see it. It was as if he was staring into a thin mist, with every outline diffused.

A tongue had swiftly licked his dry lips.

"So it is."

As casually, he had described the symptoms to a doctor who had sat him in a chair, peered through a small glass at him, while a bead of light pinned each eye.

"Um . . . yes . . . I'm only a general practitioner of course, Cleeve. I would advise you to see a specialist. The best man for this is . . ." and he had written a name on a piece of paper. "I'll write a letter for you. And, Cleeve," the doctor had leaned back in his chair, "I can tell you now that no doctor would pass you in a Board of Trade eyesight test." Briskly he had concluded: "See that man. He's the best in the country."

The appointment had been made and the doctor furnished the company with a confidential report that in his opinion Skipper Cleeve was rapidly going blind.

Charlie Bates announced baldly that he was taking a trip off but that it was not a licence for some smart Alec of a young skipper to bash about the *Southern Star*. And with an unaccustomed collar and tie on he had journeyed with Buller Cleeve to hear the verdict.

Buller's wife, in her way, had softly, gently, comforted him in the still hours of the night, the hours when a man, no matter how strong, is a weakling when grief strikes him. She had held him to her, felt him rigid and trembling, had heard the deep racking sobs burst from him.

Charlie Bates's part had been more physical, more brutal even. Twice he had fought Buller to a standstill when the stricken man had tried to end it swiftly.

The second time they had stood at the end of a pier. Charlie describing the trawlers slipping into the harbour, salt-crusted and rusted. He had sensed what was in Buller's mind. He dropped his restraining hand.

"Go ahead. Two steps and you make a hole in the water. And that's your lot, Buller boy. That'll end it for you. And the boys, Ben and Sam? Always people pointing saying: 'They're Cleeve's sons. The bloke who couldn't take it. Lost his sight and went off the end of the pier.' That's what people will say. Go ahead, Buller boy. Two steps and I won't make a move or a sound to stop you."

Charlie had stopped breathing and watched. Buller's shoulders had hunched, for a moment he had swayed and Charlie tensed to leap. Then Buller had turned.

"Let's go home, Charlie. It's going to be a long night."

Ben had raved. "Experts can be wrong. We're always hearing of it. Let's get another man. We'll take you to America, Dad. That's where the best men are. We'll show 'em. We'll get the best man in the world at the game."

Sam had been more thoughtful. When he and Ben were alone he said:

"Let's face it. Dad is going blind. He's practically that now. We've got to help him face it. We've got to fill his life somehow. Get him something to do."

"What? Doing what? Making bloody baskets? He's been a fisherman all his life."

The company doctor had sent a young woman to see Buller. To help him in arriving at a simple formula. To teach him the first elements; to teach him that blind people saw with their fingers and their ears. Her patience was inexhaustible. She taught him how to fill a pipe, how to pour himself a cup of tea, to listen for sounds which had significance. As they had talked on one occasion a trawler's steam whistle had hooted hoarsely.

"What does that mean, Mr Cleeve?" she had asked.

"Means he's turning to port, swinging to the left. Coming out of the inner basin, most likely. Sounds like one of Fraser's trawlers."

The whistle had sounded three short blasts.

"Going astern now. Somebody's got across his bow. He'll have to watch the tide on that knuckle. It's no place to start going astern."

She had chuckled, a soft musical sound.

"And you are seeing all that, Mr Cleeve. You are seeing it as if you were there. All the time sounds will tell you something, sounds you had never noticed before will mean something to you. Now listen."

And they had listened together intently. He had described for her things he could hear, the heavy clang of a riveting hammer in the dockyard, the sudden, staccato roar of lorry engines as they pulled away from the fish wharf and breasted the steep hill outside.

Buller had been interested.

"Now, miss. You tell me what you see and I'll tell you what I can hear."

There had been a pause.

"I'm afraid we'll have to listen together, Mr Cleeve. You see, I've always been blind."

Mrs Cleeve had left them and had gone into the kitchen to shed her scalding tears. Her big, powerful helpless man was standing hand in hand with the girl in the window listening together, seeing with their ears.

"And now your wife is about to make a pot of tea, Mr Cleeve."

He tensed for a moment.

"How do you know?"

"She has lifted down the teapot and taken off the lid. She keeps her tea in a tin and has a spoon inside it. Listen now . . . and one for the pot. She'll close the lid in a second. There. And place it back."

He heard the lid close and a soft tap as the tin was replaced.

He raised his voice.

"And a cup for the young lady, Mother. And she doesn't take sugar."

Mrs Cleeve had poked her head round the kitchen door.

"How did you know I was making tea?"

Buller and the girl had chuckled in unison. Then the girl asked: "And how did you know I didn't take sugar, Mr Cleeve?"

Proudly Buller had said: "The last time you took tea with us I didn't hear you stirring with a spoon."

"Splendid."

It was Sam who had the brainwave after talking to the girl. She had said: "You must remember every detail of your trips to talk over with him. Every small point so that he can see you doing it. He does see you in his mind's eye, you know."

Sam had slammed a bunched fist into a cupped palm.

"I'll do better. You know trawlers talk to one another on the trawler radio band, don't you? We'll get him a set, the best there is, and he can listen to us every night we're at sea."

And it came to pass that although Buller Cleeve's life was dark there was also light.

CHAPTER TWO

BULLER CLEEVE's finger-tips caressed the radio knob. Voices came in, thinly at first, then stronger as he adjusted the tuning. Voices of men he knew, some of them he had trained, had watched them progress from decky learners to bos'n, to Mate, and finally to skipper. Some of the voices were those of men who had been his rivals. Men against whom he had pitted his wits and his experience.

Scottie Fraser came in, in his thick voice matching his dour, unsmiling disposition. If Scottie had shot his trawl outside the harbour, and by some miracle had filled his fish-hold at once, he would have found something with which to find fault. Scottie never accepted perfection and Buller smiled as he heard the thick, grumbling tones.

The tall, lath-thin "Monty" Banks, fishing from Charlie Bates's sister ship the *North Star*. "Monty" had spent two years of his sea-time, while steaming to and from the fishing ground, battling his way through Tolstoy's *War and Peace*, with a dictionary at his elbow. And confessed he was completely baffled when he finally completed it.

"Monty" had grown up under Buller's tuition. Buller listened for a moment to "Monty's" chatter, picked up a clue from the apparently innocuous conversation, and knew to within ten miles where "Monty" was trawling—and what he was catching. "Monty" had once sailed north with the other trawlers, their plumes of smoke like pillars in the sky, then he had disappeared into the grey murk and there had been silence for nearly three weeks. Nobody saw him or heard a whisper from him until he arrived back to meet a starved market with his fish-holds filled with prime fish. And a story of Russian trawlers fishing in teams off the Labrador coast and packing it into a factory ship. Their fleet was complete with parent ship.

"Monty" had related the story in the chromium and contemporary-furnished lounge of his favourite pub and had thought no more of it.

Three days later he had been called to the office to describe it all again with a quiet man, with grey-flecked hair, sitting alongside the director.

"Monty" had sailed again for Labrador with the grey-haired man as passenger. They were ten days at sea before "Monty"

learned that his guest was a naval officer who spent hours with
binoculars and a highly technical and expensive camera taking
pictures of the Russians' parent ship, which even to "Monty's"
eye seemed to have an abundance of radar and radio aerials
cluttering up its masts.

Buller listened to "Monty's" voice contrasting with Scottie's.
He knew that both were making a good living.

"Earning a crust or two," was Scottie's dour way of putting it.

Buller lingered for a few minutes among the German trawlers,
listening to their harsh, guttural talking. Good fishermen, he had
liked them, but no imagination. They fished like soldiers, by
numbers. They had had good ships, too, before the war.

The grandfather clock growled a warning. Buller fingered the
knob and came back to his sons.

"It's been down long enough. I'm going to haul." It was Ben
speaking.

"I'm moving out a bit before I shoot it again," Sam answered.
"Good night."

"Good night," Ben echoed.

Buller and his wife knew the boys were speaking to them.

"Good night," she whispered.

The clock delivered its eight-note message and Buller shifted
his finger to the switch and clicked it.

"They're making a living," he said. "Ben's doing a bit the
better, but it's early days. Sam'll come along."

Even in that simple sentence she recognized the slight degree of
favouritism. Buller's wife had always held the opinion that Ben's
startling likeness to his father, the same squat frame, the same
huge shoulders, the same bull-at-a-gate disposition, had erected
a slight barrier between her husband and his older son. When Ben
had transgressed, as a boy, Buller's punishment of him had been
more severe than that meted out to Sam, even though Sam's
offence had been equally heinous in their father's eyes.

Often had she puzzled over it, but lacking the analytical mind
she had assessed it as an oblique form of jealousy and had been
nearer the truth than she had imagined.

Buller had seen in Ben a picture of himself growing up again,
with all the faults, the dogmatic, almost ruthless disregard for
other people's feelings or points of view. In his way he had tried
to alter Ben for the better without realizing that it would have
been easier to prevent the ebb and flow of the tide.

She watched Buller now as he clicked off the radio set. He sat bolt upright in his chair, his unseeing eyes staring straight ahead. He was silently going over the past hour. Charlie Bates, Scottie Fraser, "Monty" Banks, Ben, Sam. He knew what all of them were doing as well as if he were on the trawlers with them. The picture was so vivid in his mind that he could almost feel the chill of the northern air, could feel the pitch and roll of the ship and could hear the deep clatter of the huge winch as the trawl was recovered.

He was *seeing* it, seeing it as the young woman had said he would see it. His face softened slightly, the hard lines became diffused and she smiled with him. No longer would she wake up in the middle of the night, heart pounding, to find that he was no longer at her side. Sometimes she had gone searching for him and had found him, head in his hands, rocking to and fro like a child in pain. It had been a secret terror of hers that one night she would not find him. That he had gone out into the darkness to end it.

No longer did she feel like that.

The wind soughed against the window, rattling it briefly.

"It's got a bit of north in it, Mother. Be some rain before morning. A following wind, p'raps put a knot or two on. Help somebody to catch a tide."

Everything was related to the sea, to fishing, to catching tides, to catching a market.

That was his life.

Ben Cleeve opened the lee-side wheelhouse door and jerked the dregs of his mug of tea over the side.

"I always forget to stir it and the last drop's like treacle," he said.

Geegee Porter, his next in command, grinned. "Scoop it out with your finger. Sugar gives you strength I've heard tell."

"Give me strength?" Ben said coldly. "You should eat a couple of pound before you tie the next cod end."

Geegee squirmed. Early in the trip, almost the first shooting of the trawl they had hauled after three hours to find that the cod end, the stouter bag-like end of the trawl, which required a special type of knot, had at some time become loosened. For three hours any fish that had got into the long trawl had as swiftly gone out the other end.

There was an art in tying a knot in a cod end, a jealously guarded, carefully taught art. It had to be tied so that it held against the buffeting and dragging along the bottom and against the building pressure of fish in the trawl end, yet could be undone in a flash when the dripping cod end swung high inboard. It was the bos'n or Second Hand who invariably ducked in under the bulging bag, jerked at the knot and released a shining silvery cascade of fish.

And on that haul the knot had been undone, the trawl had been empty.

There were no excuses and Ben had sworn fluently and descriptively while Geegee had squirmed.

Ben knew that Geegee would extend his giant strength to the utmost a dozen times before the trip was finished, but the stigma would remain, would be hilariously related, in shouting laughs, in half a dozen pubs until Geegee would take the last tormentor in hand. And the hilarity would die while the publican reached frantically to salvage his glasses—and anything else breakable—before Geegee and his victim were ejected to the wider spaces of the street outside.

Geegee's odd nickname had embroiled him in a dozen fights before common usage defeated him and he accepted it. It had come about in a curious way.

He had been bos'n on a trawler which had gone to the rescue of another in difficulties. Passing the tow in bad weather had been no small task and George Porter had performed the work of three men, his muscles cracking and bulging.

The story had got back to the port and a woman reporter, seeking colour for her story, had described him as a "Gentle Giant", drawing on skilful phrases to etch in her description of the huge, tongue-tied man she was interviewing and the man who had laboured in passing the tow.

"Gentle Giant" had been abbreviated, in the passing of time and over several homeric fights, to "G G". So "Geegee" he remained.

He shipped only with the Cleeve brothers. There was, in fact, a mild rivalry between the brothers to have him as their Mate. Between them they had shepherded him through the theoretical, painful studying he had had to do. He learned more of that from Sam than from Ben. When Ben explained a problem he bulldozed at it impatiently, almost forcing the slow-thinking Geegee to absorb it. It was the physical side he acquired from Ben.

"If that cod-end knot is slipped this time I'll go down with the trawl myself and hold it tight," Geegee said firmly.

"You'll go over, all right," Ben repeated. "You would tie a soldier's knot and us ten fathom thick in hake. Wonder what the Old Man would have said if I'd told him?"

"You didn't?" Geegee sounded almost piteous.

Ben covered a grin with a huge hand. "Slipped my mind. I meant to."

"And that Charlie Bates and his skimped-up scrawny Second Hand would have been listening with ears like bat's wings," Geegee snarled. "One peep out of him when we get back and I'll toss him through the window."

Ben grinned. He knew that Geegee invariably became embroiled in a fight of some sort each time they were home. There was no venom in the tussles, and not a great deal of deep-rooted damage.

Ben glanced at the brass wheelhouse clock.

"How long's it been down?"

"Long enough. Bit more'n a couple of hours. Shall I get 'em up?"

Ben nodded.

Geegee rolled down from the wheelhouse, swaying to the tilt and swing of the deck. He poked his head inside the mess-deck door and bellowed:

"C'mon. Up she comes, me lucky lads. Quit scratching and snoring."

Grumbling and groaning the men tumbled up, and soon the powerful winch was recovering the dripping wires. Ben, standing in the wing of the bridge, watched narrowly as the two heavy iron-shod wooden doors, which kept the mouth of the 120-foot trawl open, came clashing up to the steel gallows set into the deck on the foredeck and on the quarter.

Almost immediately, the bulging end of the trawl, the cod end, came surging to the surface a few feet astern. Packed as it was with fish, their distended lungs gave it considerable buoyancy and it broke surface like a shining whale.

Geegee looked up at Ben and grinned and Ben replied in kind.

Hanging over the rail, the men recovered the trawl, their clutching hands grabbing a handful of the icy-cold mesh and heaving in unison. A line from the stumpy derrick was led to the cod end. It swung high and inboard and Geegee ducked under it. He pulled at the complicated knot and disappeared in a mass of lashing, wriggling fish. As the men clambered into the deep fish pound, the partitioned-off part of the deck, Geegee stood up, thigh deep in fish. He had his fingers hooked in the gills of one half as long as his body. He lifted it for Ben to see.

"No dog stuff this," he yelled.

Ben nodded briefly. "That's what we put it over for. Shoot it again. It'll only get fish on the bottom."

Geegee knotted the twin lines at the cod end and signalled to the man at the winch. The trawl slid over the side, slowly at first, sinking reluctantly as it streamed away on the quarter. Then the trawldoors disappeared under the surface and the wires twanged as the winchman released his brake. He lifted his arm as the first marker came off, watched the wire until the second whirled around.

"That'll do," Ben said. The winchman screwed the brake wheel hard down. Ben set his telegraph to "slow ahead", studied the lead of the wires and turned to his chart. He studied it for a while, clean bottom, little rock, mainly sand and shingle. As he lit a cigarette he watched the oilskin-aproned men on the foredeck as their flashing knives ripped once, flicked valuable livers into a pound and then tossed the big fish through the fish-hold hatch where men below stowed them away with a liberal covering of ice.

This was making a living—"earning a crust", as Scottie Fraser called it. Many hauls would have to be made and between three and four thousand boxes or kits of fish would have to be stowed away in that hold before Ben could say: "Let's go home. That's the lot."

The squirming pile of fish disappeared into the hold and the men straightened their backs.

"G'wan, son, fetch it," one prompted a young smooth-faced decky learner. The youth struggled along the heaving deck, soon to return with a huge enamelled teapot. They would drink tea, talk for a while, then sleep an hour or two until Geegee's voice once more roused them to their labours, to reach over the side to grasp an ice-cold trawl, to heave, to stand waist deep in silvery fish, to gut and toss below, to stow. And it would go on day and night until Ben would shout: "That's it."

Ben tapped the barometer with a finger-nail, pursed his lips at the message it conveyed to him, looked out of the wheelhouse window at the grey, wind-lashed sky above him. He studied the seas, at the moment with just an occasional lacing of white foam which the wind whisked away in spray.

"It would," he snarled.

The legend the glass told him was, as yet, indecisive. It could mean a short, savage gale, or it could mean screaming wind and raging seas for days on end, possibly a week, when all the trawler could do was to put her nose into it and dodge slowly ahead. This used up time and fuel and could only be written off as lost.

In an ordinary gale, one such as those which would lash up short, frothing seas around the coast to send happily screaming holiday-makers scurrying for shelter from driving spray, Ben, and any other trawlerman worth his salt, would fish. The foredeck would be a streaming, whirling welter of water, sometimes the rail would dip deeply under and the men would have to hang on doggedly to what trawl they had recovered while their seabooted feet struggled to get a foothold. In such a gale fishing merely became arduous.

But in those wide-open wastes east of Iceland, past Bear Island and into the White Sea, a real gale was a screaming, destructive hell when all the trawler could do was survive—by the grace of God and the skill of her skipper.

"It would," Ben repeated.

He stared out of the window of the wheelhouse watching the last of the catch disappear.

"Geegee. Send one of the boys to the wheel, and you take the bridge for a bit."

Geegee settled himself comfortably in one corner of the wheelhouse and nursed his huge mug of steaming tea.

"A few more hauls like that and we'll be putting her nose south," he said complacently.

Ben touched the barometer with his finger again. "Maybe," he answered briefly. "See how this lot builds up. We'll give it a couple of hours down. I'm going to try to raise *Lodestar*."

He wrinkled his nose as he entered the radio room at the rear of the wheelhouse.

"Why is it you sparkers always work up a fug you could cut with a knife?" he asked of the young man sitting in a swivel chair reading a paper-backed novel. "You're all the same. You come aboard, bung up every hole you can find with paper, get out a thing like that and spend all your time reading tripe. 'Her sweeping eyelashes swept the gravel path,'" he mimicked. "Don't you ever come up for air?"

"Sailing day and arrival day," grinned the radio operator. "And that's plenty. There's the Met report if you want it."

He swivelled a clipped board round for Ben to read. Ben digested it swiftly and handed it back. "Nothing I don't know in that, and I'm wrong less times than they are. See if you can raise *Lodestar* for me."

The operator laid his book on the desk, cover upwards. Ben sneered at the highly coloured voluptuous cover as the operator switched over, started his generator humming and began a monotonous monologue, occasionally switching over to listen. Finally he handed the microphone to Ben and picked up his book.

"*Lodestar*," he said briefly.

"Pity to wake him, wasn't it?" Ben growled. "Hullo, *Lodestar*. Skipper got his head down?" He listened for a few moments. "Good, put him on."

After an interval Ben continued:

"What do you think of it, Sam?"

"I've just been reading it. Could blow itself out by the morning before it reaches us," Sam answered. "How are you making out?"

"Like I expected. A bit better than some. Why don't you shove along this way for three or four hours and have another try."

Both knew sharp ears were listening, both knew where the other was and could rendezvous quite easily.

"Crowded at all?" Sam asked.

"Haven't seen a soul all day."

"I'll push her along until midnight and have a go then."

"Mind my toes," Ben cautioned.

"Keep your big feet out of the way, then," Sam chuckled, "Well out of the way. Charlie Bates will be around there by daylight."

Ben grunted. "He would."

"Be seeing you, Ben."

"Huh, huh. Lost the Bogey Man, yet?"

"He followed me for a couple of hours, then packed it in when he saw I was really steaming away."

"He'll try hanging on to my stern one day, then—then I'll stem him," Ben said forcibly. "That twelve-mile limit is the flaming outside edge. They'll want all the ocean soon."

"I was around nine or ten miles out when he showed up. About where that Fleetwood trawler was last week when he knocked him off. Well outside the four miles."

"Something'll have to be done. Just as well the Old Man isn't around these days. He never did like those Icelandic blokes."

They were discussing a sore point with trawlermen. From time immemorial the international three-mile limit from the shore had been accepted as a line of demarcation.

There had been adventurous skippers who had raided the

breeding grounds inside the three miles, had got away with it several times, only to be caught in the end with the inevitable heavy fine and confiscation of gear.

They received scant sympathy from the majority of skippers, who frowned on these raids on the breeding grounds and who considered it beneath their skill to do so.

But the imposition of first a four-mile limit, then twelve miles —rigorously imposed twelve-miles limit, without international legal backing—infuriated them.

It cut into profitable fishing grounds and when a trawler was arrested by the Icelandic Fishery Patrol and was fined heavily and catch and gear confiscated when she was trawling ten or eleven miles out tempers became frayed.

Owners paid the fines under protest and extensive lobbying began in political circles.

Trawlers had for generations used Iceland as a place offering refuge when the bitter northern gales smote those wild wastes, and also a place into which they could race in an emergency. There was a growing little cemetery in two or three of the Icelandic towns where lay trawlermen who had been injured, raced to hospital and had died.

Now, under the friction caused by the new limit, that shelter was denied them.

"Soon they'll be waiting for us off the Humber light to pinch us for going to sea," Ben snarled. "It'll end up with the Navy having to do patrols around us while we fish."

"Could be," Sam answered. "Well, I'm going to get my head down for a couple of hours. What was your last haul like."

"Good enough. Even Geegee was pleased. Oh, Sam, if you get talking to him sometime ask him if he's tied any good cod-end knots recently."

"Not Geegee?" Sam sounded disbelieving. "Not Geegee?"

"He did indeed."

"He'll never live it down."

"I figure it'll be good enough for half a dozen fights before he is allowed to forget it. I'll be looking for you around daylight."

He handed the hand microphone to the radio operator.

"Will it be letting too much fresh air into here if I open the door for a moment?" he asked with heavy sarcasm.

The operator grinned. "I'll be opening it myself in a few minutes. I'm just going to have a quick run around the distress band then me for some sleep."

Ben grinned. "Always hoping for a spot of salvage, aren't you? We're up here to fish, my son, not play lifeboats."

"You never know. Bit of extra bunce comes in useful."

Ben tapped him on the chest. "We'd spend half a trip towing some broken-down crate in and wait eight months to a year for the money and fish hold only half full. Don't call me if you hear anybody squawking."

"You're telling me. I'd only have to whisper it and you'd be off like a scalded cat," the operator said scornfully.

"Try me."

"I've heard the story of the *Myrtle*," the operator said, airily looking at the deckhead above him. "If I've got it right somebody I could mention hauled his trawl and slammed all night to reach her and spent four days towing her. From what I've heard even Geegee prayed she'd hold together until *Myrtle* was reached."

Ben smiled. "Geegee doesn't know how to pray."

"He learned that night."

"You can pray next time." He picked up the paper-backed book, glanced at the lurid cover. "Where's he got her now. In the rose garden with her shoulder straps down around her waist?"

"He's past that."

"You won't sleep tonight. And if you do you'll dream."

"Yes, please."

Ben tossed the book back. "I could think of another use for it."

The heavy gale passed north of Ben's trawling area. His ship, the *Morning Star*, felt some of the weight and rolled heavily but the trawl was hauled and shot regularly through the night with satisfactory results.

Geegee, with his large wooden needle filled with tarred line, was executing some necessary repairs before allowing the trawl over the side again when Ben leaned over the front of the bridge wing.

"Looks like *Lodestar* poking herself up to the west'ard, Geegee."

Geegee stared over the side and nodded.

"He's been taking his time. Probably tried a shoot or two."

Lodestar seemed to creep towards them over the sullen, leaden sea until they were less than a hundred yards apart.

Ben heard the tannoy rasp hoarsely then Sam's voice came booming across.

"Not bad, Ben. Not bad at all. We had it down a couple of hours and it's prime stuff." There was a pause then almost silkily Sam went on: "Of course, we tied our cod end. That helped."

Geegee squirmed as a yell of laughter came from *Lodestar*. The group of men around him echoed the laugh and Geegee spun around.

"If any of you yelping bastards want to go over the side, just laugh. Go on, laugh."

He stood with legs astride, elbows outwards, head thrust forward truculently. His big fists hung down moving slightly.

Ben recognized the danger signs.

"All right, Geegee. Get her darned up and over the side," he said coldly. He turned to the switch at his elbow and turned on his loud hailer.

"The weather held off, Sam. Looks as if we're going to miss it. What have you got?"

"Around two and a half thousand kit."

"Fair enough. I'm around that figure, too. Seen anything of Charlie?"

"No. Saw some smoke an hour back at first daylight. Could be him. And there's one of the Lord's up to the norrard."

"*Lord Lloyd*, most likely. I saw him around yesterday."

They gossiped for a while, then moved apart and trawled steadily. So they fished day and night, each night talking so that Buller at home could visualize what they were doing.

Then came the morning when Sam closed *Lodestar* up to *Morning Star*.

"Four thousand near enough, Ben. What about it?"

And one night, Buller, listening at his set, called to his wife in her kitchen:

"They'll catch the morning tide, Mother. They'll be home by midday."

And almost on the first stroke of the coughing grandfather clock's booming note Ben thrust open the door.

"Mother. Your wandering boys are home."

Their greeting of their father was typical of each. Ben wrapped a huge arm round the old man's shoulders.

"Good enough, Pop. Near four thousand kit and not many trawlers in." He squeezed with his arm and Buller bunched his muscles to meet the power of it.

Sam just slid an arm around his father.

"Good trip, Dad. Charlie made the tide. Said he'd be up later." In the kitchen he stood by his mother.

"You look more beautiful every time I get back." He held her at arm's length affectionately. "Indeed you do."

"Get out of my kitchen," she scolded. "Where is it?"

He lifted a burlap bag containing a prime fish cleaned and ready for cooking. "Let me cut it up for you."

"When fish come into my kitchen it's my job," she said tartly. "You can catch them, I'll cook them."

CHAPTER THREE

THE taxi-driver glanced at the clock.

"Five and a kick will do it, guv'nor," he said.

Ben put his hand in his pocket. He glanced at Sam.

"Call it."

"Heads."

The coin spun briefly.

"Don't you ever lose?" Ben grumbled handing over the fare and a generous tip.

"Sell you a double-headed penny for half a dollar, guv'nor. That way you'll always win."

"Not with that lad," Ben said; "it would come down on edge."

They settled themselves down in corner seats in a first-class compartment. Sam looked at his watch.

"First or second lunch?"

"Second. That way we can have a couple of drinks afterwards."

When the smiling dining-car attendant came by second lunch it was.

Sam spread his morning paper out for a thorough digest while Ben ran his eyes over a tabloid picture paper more devoted to a study of the form beautiful rather than the news.

"Hey, Ben. Somebody has been asking questions in Parliament about that Icelandic twelve-mile limit. Hear what he says. 'Our fishermen must be allowed to fish in their lawful waters without let or hindrance by any country which, without international legal backing, decides to extend its so-called limits to include some thousands of miles of profitable trawling grounds. If necessary the Government should dispatch naval ships to protect our trawlers.' "

"Quite a mouthful," Ben grunted. "If any Icelandic bogey man tries running me in he'll find my stem jammed hard into his midships. And I'm not joking."

Sam chuckled.

"Come the day when I'll see it."

"You will."

Sam folded his paper for a closer digest of the item.

"Of course, as Dad says, we needn't go within a couple of hundred miles of Iceland. He made top hauls nearer Bear Island, and into the White Sea."

"It's a question of principle. Give 'em the twelve miles and the next thing is they'll be drawing a line from them to Norway and saying: 'Beyond this line fishing is *Verboten*.' Look at the Norwegians. They got away with a deal like that. You can be twenty-five miles off shore, and still within their limit if you take a line from one cape to another. And they made it stick."

"They were allowed to make it stick because the fishing there isn't worth a damn except for a few of those Aberdeen off-shore grubbers. This is different."

"Not all that different. It could——"

Ben broke off.

A man's back and shoulders filled the opening in the corridor door. Beyond the man, partially trapped by his arms as he grasped the wooden rail running along the window, they could see a girl.

"Will you please let me pass," they heard her say.

The man in the doorway chuckled.

"Certainly. All I'm offering to do is to see you to a seat."

"I can find my own seat. Now, will you please let me pass."

Ben stood up.

"Easy, Ben," Sam cautioned.

Ben slid the corridor door back with a jerk and the man took a half-step backwards.

"Seems to be quite a jam in the corridor," Ben said pleasantly. "They ought to make them wider." After a moment's pause he went on: "Or make men smaller."

The man half turned and looked at Ben from under his eyelids. He still kept one hand grasping the rail.

Ben put his shoulder against the man and applied a steady pressure until he was forced away from the doorway.

Sam reached round Ben and took the girl's suitcase.

"Room to spare in here," he said. "May I put this in the rack for you?"

The girl looked from Sam to Ben, onwards to the man who had been barring her way and back to Sam. The briefest of smiles crossed her face.

"This is a first-class compartment. I'm afraid I ..."

"That's soon fixed," Ben grinned, enjoying the quiet thrusting match he was having with the man in the corridor. "After all, it's our railway. We like to keep it pleasant for the passengers." The grin disappeared as he turned to the man. "Don't we?" he added softly.

Sam lifted the suitcase to the rack. "We'll meet that when it arises. In the meantime, which do you prefer, corner seat facing the engine or back to it?"

She stepped into the compartment, a smile twitching the corners of her mouth. "Whichever is available," she said.

"Take a choice." Sam spread his hands and she sat down.

Ben leaned forward until his face was only inches away from the man's. Suddenly his eyes had taken on a frosty glint. "Can I help you to find a seat? We might have to dust it off a bit. Say a coach or two farther along."

The man sized Ben up. He glanced at the broad shoulders, the obvious set of the muscles, and at Ben's long arms hanging down loosely at his sides.

"I was merely trying to be helpful," he said coldly. "And I'm not looking for trouble."

"Tck, tck." Ben clicked his lips. "It finds you without looking for it, doesn't it? And I'm trying to be helpful, too. I'm offering to help you find a seat."

The man strove to find a way out without losing any dignity.

"If the young lady is annoyed, or wishes to . . ."

Ben glanced over his shoulder at the girl sitting opposite Sam. He grinned at her.

"No complaints. She's not annoyed—now."

"Very well." The man turned sideways to push past Ben along the corridor. Ben did not give way an inch and the man had to draw his stomach in to get by.

"Have a nice journey," Ben said softly. He watched the man roll along the corridor.

"I'm glad there wasn't any trouble," the girl said to Sam. "I wasn't frightened, not really. I think I could have coped with him."

Sam smiled. "There wouldn't have been much trouble. Ben might have wrecked the coach, but otherwise . . ." He shrugged. Ben slid the compartment door closed and sat down alongside the girl.

"He's gone," he said solemnly. "I hope he finds a seat."

"It's coming to something when a passenger can't walk along the corridor of a train without being molested and pushed around," Sam said severely.

Ben nodded.

Sam went on. "I'm not so certain that I shouldn't report it when the ticket inspector comes along."

"Oh, please, it was nothing," the girl protested. "He wasn't harming me at all."

Sam shook his head. "I was thinking of that poor man being shoved and squeezed by that big baboon there." He frowned heavily at the grinning Ben.

"You do that. Tell the ticket inspector about it and I'll swear you egged me on."

Sam suddenly slapped his thigh. "We'll have to get another lunch ticket. Toss you for it."

Ben squinted at him for a moment, looked at the girl and back to Sam.

"Not this time. Let's have an honest toss for once." He pulled a coin from his pocket, handed it to the girl. "You do it."

As she lightly tossed the coin, Ben called: "Tails."

She looked at the coin in her palm.

"Heads."

"And I said 'honest toss'," Ben growled, climbing to his feet. Then he smiled. "Perhaps our friends will be farther along the train."

"Please," the girl pleaded.

Sam laughed. "If he showed up Ben would run the length of the train away from him."

"But not very fast," Ben chuckled, climbing to his feet. "I'd better chase that dining-car flunkey."

He slid open the door and rolled along the corridor.

Sam offered his open cigarette-case to the girl and when she had accepted one tendered the flame of his lighter.

"How far are you travelling?" he asked.

She told him.

"So are we. That well-dressed gorilla is my brother. We've been up to London for a long week-end. My name is Sam—Sam Cleeve —and the other one is my brother Ben. We live in Scoresby. Do you know it?"

She accepted it as an invitation to exchange names.

"I'm Eve Benson and I'm going to live in . . . in . . . your home town. I've been working as secretary at a girls' boarding school in Sussex, now I'm going to live with my uncle and work for him. As secretary."

"Now we've met formally, how do you do?"

"I'm very well, thank you," she said primly, then her face dissolved into a smile. "You were a bit late with that, weren't you?"

Sam leaned back and looked at the girl through a thin cloud of smoke. For the few moments that she was looking out of the window at the swiftly fleeting scene Sam could study her without embarrassment. From beneath a saucy little hat her black hair escaped in artless small curls. Her face was oval with a suggestion of an up turn at the outer corners of her eyes. The nose was straight cut, mouth perhaps a shade too large for real beauty but was redeemed by its readiness to break into a smile.

Sam also took in the slim but shapely legs.

"What sort of business are you going into?" he asked. "Not another school?"

She shook her head. "Nothing like it. My uncle runs a fishing concern—owns some trawlers. He was my father's brother. My father died in the war and Mother died two years ago. My aunt and uncle have been urging me to go and live with them ever since. But I'd trained for secretarial work so I preferred to go my own way. I spent a holiday with them last summer and Uncle Job said why not work for him and live with them. So, Uncle Job, here I come."

Sam rubbed his chin speculatively with finger and thumb.

"Job. Uncle Job. And your name is . . ." He craned forward and peered at her left hand. ". . . No, you're not married . . . so your name is Benson." He held an upright finger against his nose and slowly pointed it towards her. "You're going to work for Job Benson's Stellar Trawling Company. Yes?"

Her eyebrows arched.

"Yes. That's right. Do you know of it?"

He held out a hand. "Shake. We'll be working for the same boss, Ben, you and I."

"But . . ." She swiftly studied Sam. "You're not in the office. You don't look like . . ."

"We're skippers of Job's trawlers, Ben and I."

"Skippers? You sail the . . . the . . . fishing boats?"

"God save us," Sam threw his head back and laughed. "Ben will love that one. "Fishing boats." I'm sorry, I shouldn't laugh at you. But haven't you ever seen a trawler?"

"No. But you say you and your brother are skippers?"

"Yes and our father before us. He sailed in the first deep-sea trawler Job Benson ever owned."

She looked solemnly at Sam then she laughed.

"Oh dear. All my friends told me that fishermen wore seaboots all the time, and blue jerseys and chewed tobacco and would breathe beer down my neck."

"Don't forget the gold ear-rings," Sam chuckled. "I'm afraid you are due to have some ideas rudely shaken."

Before they could pursue the conversation Ben slid back the door.

"I've searched the train from end to end and couldn't find him," he growled.

"Why you just had to go to the dining-car," Sam said. "He's bound to be there."

"I got the extra ticket, all right. I'm talking of the fellow who wanted to own the train. He must be hiding under a seat."

"Chump," Sam snapped. "Leave things well alone. Ben, meet Miss Eve Benson."

Ben lifted a broad hand.

"Hi."

Sam said: "He gets those bad habits from seeing too many American films. Miss Benson is going to work for Job Benson's trawling company as a secretary. She's going to see a lot of the fishing boats and their skippers," Sam said solemnly.

"A lot of the *what*?" Ben's head came forward with a jerk.

"That wasn't fair," Eve said with a smile. "After all, I could puzzle you with things about a girls' school."

"I wonder," Sam chuckled.

Ben took a deep breath. "Now just tell me what this is all about. Use little words and where I don't understand make motions."

Eve and Sam between them explained.

"Well . . . whaddya know," Ben said, leaning back in his seat.

"You see, a steady diet of American films does that for him."

Ben ignored the mild insult. "After that I feel like buying him a drink rather than dusting the seat with him. But who sprung that one about 'fishing boats'?"

Eve shrugged. "I'm afraid I did."

"Has muggsie here been pulling your leg . . . I mean teasing you?"

"No, no, of course not. But the only fishing . . ." she paused and sought for a word ". . . fishing craft I have ever seen are those around the south coast. You know, two or three men in them who go out early in the morning and in the afternoon hawk the fish around on a barrow."

A strangled sound escaped from Ben, then he clenched a big ham-like fist and held it under Sam's nose.

"Gwan. Laugh. Just one little snigger. Laugh."

Sam fought it for a time then exploded.

"I would love to see you pushing a barrow around yelling 'Fine 'ake, 'a lemon sole, all alive, o'.' I'd give three trips' money just to see it."

The fist hovered around Sam's chin. "Shall I? Just once. Say the word," Ben threatened.

She shook her head.

Ben allowed the fist to drop until his arm rested on his brother's shoulder. "I've been looking for an excuse to land one on that chin of his for about twenty years," Ben grinned. "But, because he's the baby of the family I've had to hold my hand."

"Are there any other brothers—or sisters?" she asked.

"No. Just the two of us and Mother has been heard to say that was plenty."

Ben leaned back in his seat. "So you're going to work for Job Benson." He scowled. "A slave-driver of the worst type. He'll make you work from early mornings until late at night and pay you in wooden farthings. Down with the capitalists. Up the un-employed. Let's have the gutters running with the blood of the wealthy."

Eve stared at him wide-eyed for a moment or two. Then she switched her glance to Sam. His twitching lips helped her.

"Yes and I'll sit at the scaffold knitting."

Ben thumbed his thigh. "A girl after my own heart. And that one . . ." A finger stabbed towards Sam. "And that one will be first up the steps. Do you know what he did?"

She shook her head.

"He and the porter at the hotel got their heads together and backed a horse. It was named North Cape." He waited a moment. "That doesn't mean anything to you? Never mind. They shovelled five quid on to the nose of that skin and it walked it on three legs and paid eights. Forty smackers he raked in and didn't even tell me that he was backing it. Brotherly love," Ben finished with a heavy sneer.

Eve looked slightly bewildered. "If somebody will explain I'll try to look suitably indignant. But . . ."

Sam chuckled.

"Well, North Cape is the northern tip of Norway. Usually the last bit of land we see before we head for the fishing grounds.

This horse, running at Lingfield, had no form, but . . . well . . . it was a busman's bet, betting on coincidence of name. See. It ran at eight to one against, and won. So the benevolent book-maker paid me out forty pound, plus my five pounds stake money."

"Now go on and tell how you never even whispered it to me that you were backing it," Ben growled.

Sam stared blandly at him. "All of it? All the details?"

Ben looked slightly confused. "There's no need to."

"I feel I should hear both sides," Eve said solemnly. "That is if I'm to be really indignant."

Sam leaned back, lit a cigarette, blew a thin cloud of smoke upwards. "Ben met a ravishing blonde the previous night. We were at a night-club. She was dancing with some other fellow and Ben——"

"Cut the cackle and trimmings," Ben warned.

"I can imagine," Eve said primly.

"Well, the other fellow decided to let her dance with Ben. And——"

A strangled sound came from Eve.

"Did you say something?" Sam asked. "*No*. When the other fellow went he forgot to pay the bill, so Ben, being well brought up, took it over. She promised to meet him for lunch next day. While I was pursuing a winner in the sport of kings he was pounding the pavement outside the hotel looking for her. My guess is that she seldom, if ever, gets out of bed before four in the afternoon."

"The least she could have done was telephone you," Eve said.

Sam laughed. "My other guess is that around five o'clock she and her dancing partner would meet and go to the club to collect their share of the boodle—and keep the same little bill for some other client. If we'd have gone there tonight——"

Ben interrupted softly: "That would have been fun. Such fun."

She looked from one to the other. "And you come down from Scoresby for that?"

"Not only that, as you call it." Ben said. "I saw a show and had some dinner, first. A cracking show. At the Prince of Wales."

Her eyes rested on Sam. He could almost tell to within a word or two how her thoughts ran. He nodded. "We had dinner together and I saw a show, too." He laid the slightest of emphasis on the end of the sentence. "I saw *Sin with a Halo*."

Ben exploded. "He's seen it twice. Dragged me there the first time. Never again."

Her lips moved in the smallest of smiles. She had them neatly docketed.

"I saw *Sin with a Halo*. It opened at Brighton before coming to London. I'm afraid it was slightly beyond me."

"It's beyond me, too. But, I'll see it again sometime and I'll get it."

The dining-car attendant slid the door open.

"Seats for second lunch, please." He rattled and closed the door.

As they proceeded with lunch she did little of the talking, but with a few artless questions gained confirmation of her earlier docketing. If she glanced at Ben it was to feel a slight stir at his obvious virility. When she looked at Sam it was in a more enigmatic way.

They were docketed in such a fashion that only another woman would understand.

The train slid into Scoresby's smoky, begrimed station and emptied itself.

"Will anybody be meeting you?" Sam asked.

"I didn't say what time train I would be coming on. Just that I would arrive today."

Ben waved to a couple of taxis. The drivers obviously knew the brothers.

"Take this young lady to Job Benson's house. That will cover it," Ben said handing the driver some coins.

They watched the taxi pull away.

Their own driver asked: "Who'd you see. Arsenal?"

Sam nodded, his eyes on the disappearing taxi.

"Lousy game up here," the driver went on. "Sooner we get a couple of good backs the better. Our cripples are killing the forward line. Straight home?"

Ben nodded and they climbed in.

After a few minutes Sam chuckled.

"What's funny?" Ben asked.

"'Fine 'ake, 'a lemon sole, all alive, o,'" he said softly. "I must get you a truck."

"I'll get you a thick ear," Ben threatened. Then he, too, smiled. "Nice, isn't she? Fancy old Job having a niece like that. Really nice."

"Really nice," Sam echoed.

Ben leaned forward and looked into his brother's face.

"Well, blow me down," he said softly. "Blow me down. Just wait until Ma hears about this."

Sam snorted. "About what?"

"About this," Ben said. "Just wait until I tell her. I'll bet you even pay for this taxi without wanting to toss."

And he was right.

Their greeting of their mother when they arrived home was typical and had Eve Benson been present it would have added strong confirmation to her docketing of the two sons of Buller Cleeve and his wife.

Ben dropped his soft canvas bag with a thud, grabbed his mother by the shoulders and held her at arm's length.

"Have you missed me? Have you been true to me while I've been away? There's another man in your life. I can tell by the gleam in your eye," he accused outrageously. "Where is he?"

Ben's mother was used to these flamboyant outbursts by Ben. Oddly enough they never occurred after he had been away for three weeks or so on his trawler, but only after a week-end in London or away racing for a day.

"Stop mauling me, Ben Cleeve," she said severely. "And pick your bag up or you'll have your father sprawling over it."

She looked over Ben's broad shoulder at smiling Sam, and Eve Benson could have isolated a tiny fragment to add to the docketing. Her eyes wrinkled even a little more at the corners as she looked at Sam.

"Have a nice time?"

Sam nodded. He was slipping back the zip fastening of his bag. "Fair enough. I—er—got a present for my best girl." He pulled a neatly packed parcel from his bag.

"From Woolworth's," Ben jeered. "And him winning forty quid on a three-legged skin."

"What did you bring?" his mother asked, with just a breath of asperity.

"Couldn't see anything nice. I'll buy you the biggest bunch of flowers in Scoresby this very evening. Where's Dad?"

"Having a snooze, but you can wake him. He's got some news for you."

"Huh, huh. Over the short wave?" Anything about trawlers was news.

"He'll tell you."

Ben strode from the room.

She stood like a demure little girl in front of Sam as he rezipped his bag. He stood up with the small parcel in his hand.

"Do you want to open it? Or shall I?" It was a dainty little comedy they always played out. He would no more have unwrapped the parcel than he would have cut off a finger.

"I . . . I . . . think I will."

Slowly, she undid the wrapping, making it last so that the climax would come slowly with the end of the packing.

It was a piece of porcelain—two figures, a boy and a girl. The girl was seated, her face framed in a little poke bonnet. The figure of the boy stood alongside her, one arm protectively over the girl's shoulder.

The whole was in white and delicate-tinting blue.

"It's lovely, Sam," she breathed. "Look, you can even see her finger-nails. And her eyes."

Sam smiled down at her.

"Like it?"

"It's lovely."

Caressingly, her hands smoothed over the piece of china, touching very lightly.

Sam's head came down to the level of hers. "I'm glad you like it."

She looked up and for a fragment of time their eyes met in complete understanding, a wedding of feelings which neither of them could have put into words. She laid her cheek against his and her fingers ran the length of his jaw. Then she stepped back.

"I must put it away in my case before it gets broken."

They heard the rumble of Ben's voice merging with that of his father's.

". . . A fiver he laid on that catsmeat, Dad, and it had the form of a cab-horse. And it comes up. Forty perishin' quid an' me down to tenpence."

Ben was still grieving. Sam chuckled.

"Get him to tell you why he wasn't around when I backed it, Dad. You'll understand."

Ben lifted a bunched fist. "One squawk. Just one," he threatened.

Their mother retreated to the doorway and stood for a few seconds watching. Ben was so like his father, so like Buller when he was that age. No subtleties, no hidden depths. As the three men talked she could see, and hear, that Ben and her husband were on the same plane, there was just a tinge more of enthusiasm, almost an echo of his inner self when talking to Ben.

She saw Sam looking at her over their shoulders. She clasped the little piece of china to her bosom and smiled momentarily at him.

Then she pointed to the wrappings on the floor.

"Now, don't leave that lying around. Tidy it up, there's a good boy."

Sam nodded and gathered up the fragments of wrapping paper.

She went into what she called her front room. A seldom-used room which smelled faintly of furniture polish and camphor balls. The furnishings were old fashioned, set primly around the room. In one corner was a glass-fronted bureau and on its shelves were pieces of china. Of the value of each individual piece she had no idea—and didn't want to. They were beautiful in her eyes, and that was enough. But for one piece. It was a hideous, overlarge, roughly made copy of a lustre vase. Even to her inexperienced eye it was a nightmare of china.

But when her husband's eyes were beginning to fail he had taken her and the two boys, then still at school, to a fairground. By dint of spending many shillings shooting at a target which misted over, Buller had scored sufficient points to win the monstrosity. They had carried it home carefully and it had been installed in the bureau.

She had planned to have an accident some time in the future, a little momentary carelessness in her dusting. But one day, when every hour had become dark for Buller, she found him in her front room fingering the vase. It was one of his last links with the days when there was, for him, light.

No delicate piece of Sèvres was ever handled more carefully after that.

She found a place for her latest acquisition, stood back to contemplate it, and was happy.

A roar of laughter came to her from the other room and she joined them.

Her husband was speaking.

"Perhaps he was hiding in the lavatory," he chuckled.

"I thought of that and bumped on a couple of doors," Ben said ruefully. "I collected a small boy and an old lady with a temper like Charlie Bates. You know. More acid than explosion."

Buller clicked his fingers. "Speaking of Charlie Bates. I got something to tell you boys. Come along."

They sat watching the slightly complicated but confident operation of filling and lighting his pipe while they waited for their father to start talking.

He gave it two or three vigorous puffs to get it well alight.

"Had a visitor last night. Job Benson." The pipe took a little attention. Ben and Sam exchanged glances. "Stayed a couple of hours. Spent some time listening to chat among the trawlers."

The pipe was finally disciplined and was glowing nicely.

"Charlie's doing very well. He's a couple of hundred miles east of Bear Island. Says the ice is well north this year. Ten fathom thick, the fish are."

He pointed the stem of his pipe towards them as if he could see them.

"Take my advice and stay out of this Iceland wrangle. The Navy might put a box for you to fish in, and guard you with ships, but one day, sooner or later, you'll want to slip into Reykjavik or Seydisfiord for shelter, or in trouble. Then they'll nab you. All the years I was fishing——"

"About Charlie Bates," Ben prodded gently.

"Oh, yes. Well, Job Benson is having a new trawler built. The latest type. Diesel-engined, around seven-hundred tons. She'll shoot the trawl from aft, no for'rad gallows. She's being built in Germany. She was for a German concern, but Job offered them a price and now she's his."

"And Charlie Bates?" Ben guided softly.

"Job wants Charlie to take her. She'll be easy to work and easy for the skipper."

Ben snorted. "Can you see Charlie taking her? You know how he feels about diesel jobs to start with, and trying to get him away from that rattle-trap he calls a trawler will be some job."

Buller's lips pursed. With some asperity he said: "I had that rattle-trap, as you call it, for five years. And made a good living out of her. She may be old, but she's a good trawler."

Sam's lips twitched and he grinned at Ben.

"I can't see Charlie taking her, Dad," he said. "He's too set in his ways."

"That's what I told Job." Buller leaned back and surrounded his head in a cloud of smoke. "That's exactly what I said. But Job feels that as senior skipper in the firm Charlie should have first refusal."

"Consider it refused," Ben said shortly.

Sam leaned forward. "And if he does, Dad? What then?"

Buller rasped a hand around his square jaw.

"That's what Job is coming about tonight. He'll be here around talking time." He added to the smoke cloud: "It'll be one of you two boys. You've the bets he has. You ought to be."

"What were you telling your father?" their mother interjected. "What was that about disturbing people in the lavatories?"

Between them they related the episode of the train. She pursed her lips and looked from one to the other.

"She was a nice girl, I hope. You weren't pestering her, were you?"

Sam grinned. "She is a nice girl, Mum. And it wasn't she who was pestered. And who do you think she is?"

Their mother shrugged.

"She's Job Benson's niece. She's coming to work for Job as his secretary." Sam slightly overplayed the casual air.

"She's been a school-teacher, now she's going to handle the men who take the fishing boats to sea——" Sam started. Ben picked it up.

"And then hawk the fish around the streets yelling: 'Fine 'ake, 'a lemon sole, all alive, o'. I'm going to get a truck."

Hilarious explanations followed and Buller chuckled deep and long, but his wife flew to the girl's defence.

"I hope you didn't tease her. She could probably teach you quite a lot."

"You're telling me?" Ben exploded.

"I believe she could," Sam said softly.

The clock rumbled its warning, struck the booming notes and Buller leaned back to switch on the radio set.

From the kitchen came the soft clatter of cups.

Buller twisted the knobs delicately. They listened intently to the fragments of conversation over the air.

"Charlie's a bit late tonight," Ben said.

"He's listening. He never misses," Buller said.

Almost as if in answer to their words, Charlie Bates's asthmatic, rasping voice came over the air.

They exchanged grins.

". . . I'm figuring on another day or two and that will be my lot," Charlie said. "I've managed to scratch a crust or two." There was silence then Charlie went on: "If certain young fellows I know was to be up here instead of gallavanting around in London town they'd make a good living instead of dragging three-four thousand kit of rubbish back to market. I've given up hope of teaching 'em. Easy come, easy go they wants it. Take a bit more sugar, Buller."

And nearly three thousand miles away Buller Cleeve located the bowl and dipped his spoon into the sugar basin and did just that.

"He's got second sight," Ben said.

"He's got a lot of plain hoss sense," the father said brusquely.
"He made a living when others starved."

The doorbell clanged loudly.

"That'll be Job," Buller said. "You let him in, Ben."

They heard the murmur of voices coming from the little front
hall.

Sam looked up from the radio set.

Standing, smiling in the doorway in front of Job Benson was
Eve.

CHAPTER FOUR

THE brief introductions were soon over.

"I gather that you young men made yourselves known to my
niece on the train," Job Benson said unsmilingly. "I'm grateful."

"So were we," Sam answered. "I hope she told you the bit where
Ben and the other were butting at each other like goats in the
corridor."

Job glanced briefly at Ben. "A young bull rather than a goat, I
fancy."

Mrs Cleeve took charge of the girl. "Let me make you a cup of
tea. Not from that pot," she indicated the large pot near Buller.
"That's much too strong for you."

"It's just like we drink on fishing boats," Ben said wickedly.
"We stir it with a stick dipped in tar."

"Ben!" Mrs Cleeve infused a degree of asperity into the one
word.

"I don't mind," Eve smiled. "They teased me on the train because I didn't know much about trawlers. But I'm learning. Uncle
Job has told me quite a lot, and I expect to learn more before
long."

"They've still a lot to learn, yet," Job said flatly. "Quite a lot."

Mrs Cleeve conveyed Eve to a corner away from the men and
poured her some tea into a much more delicate cup than those
being used by the men.

"So you're coming to live in Scoresby, are you?" Mrs Cleeve
started. "And you're going to live with Mr Benson." For the next
few minutes Eve found herself being subjected to a mild but progressive questioning from which Mrs Cleeve learned of the work
she had been doing and why she was coming to Scoresby.

At intervals Eve looked towards the four men who had their

heads over a set of blue prints. Occasionally Buller would ask a question and would listen intently to the answer, his eyes blinking.

Eve found it hard to believe that he was blind.

She mentioned it to Mrs Cleeve who smiled gently.

"He had to learn to see with his ears and his fingers." She twisted her fingers as she talked. "A young lady, just like you, taught him. She's blind, too."

Eve nodded slowly and looked towards the group once more. Suddenly she found that Sam was no longer peering at the blue print.

He was looking at her. As their glances interlocked he smiled, a twitching smile which lifted one corner of his mouth quizzically.

"Mother squeezing you dry?" he asked with a lift of the chin.

"I'm squeezing nobody. We're just having a little talk while you go on about ships and——"

". . . 'And sealing wax and cabbages and kings'." Ben wrinkled up his face into an impish grin.

Mrs Cleeve shook her head. "I don't know what they talk about half the time. Nobody mentioned cabbages, or anything about kings."

Buller leaned back in his chair.

"It's not entirely new, Job. The Germans tried a couple of them out before the war. They had a stern chute like a whaling factory ship and conveyor belts running to the fish-hold. How they did I don't know."

Job Benson rubbed his chin. "I know, I know. But they were designed for rapid conversion to minelaying."

"There's no reason why it shouldn't work," Ben said. "What was the first reason for using for'ard and aft gallows?"

"On the small trawlers of the old days it was the only way to work the width of the trawl," Job said.

Sam pursed his lips. "There's going to be a few fingers lost until the lads learn how to handle it."

"There are fingers lost now," Job answered tersely. "Even with the trawls we use."

Sam lit a cigarette with short, vigorous puffs.

"I can't see Charlie Bates handling that," he said, tapping the wide-spread blue print. "Even though it might be easier than the present system.

Job Benson nodded slowly and as if he could see him doing it. Buller Cleeve nodded in unison.

"Neither can I," Buller mused. "For that matter, if I was still fishing I wouldn't care to think of taking her over." He leaned back in his chair. "Five thousand kit she'll have to fill to make a good living. Five thousand and more. Not that Charlie couldn't find 'em if there are any fish about. But five thousand boxes. That's a lot of fish."

Job tapped him on the chest.

"Remember when I bought the *Blue Star* from Black's of Grimsby? You took her to sea and brought her back with two and a half thousand kit when trawlers were making a living with a thousand kit. Everybody said you would be in the red three trips out of five. You never had a loser did you, Buller?"

"No, I never had a loser," Buller said softly. "Not even when I had to spend five days towing the *Letitia*."

"It's not the five thousand kit that'll scare Charlie," Ben said. "He just doesn't like diesel-engined ships, and as for that stern-chute trawling. No, not for Chairle."

Job Benson held his chin in his hand and looked from Ben to Sam, then back again.

"Are you scared about the five thousand kit?"

"Who me? Not on your life," Ben exploded. "Nor diesel engines. But I'd want a dummy trip or so to train the crowd."

Job nodded slowly. His eyes met Sam's.

"And you?"

"Same goes for me, too. I'd like to have a shoot or two with the builder's men aboard to show us the know-how, then I'd try her in the best place for a trial. Where she'd catch fish."

"And end up with tuppence for the trip," Ben snorted.

"And a million pounds' worth of experience." Sam said it softly. "I'd prove whether it could be done or not."

"It can be done," Job said. "I'm not buying a pig in a poke you know. There's nigh on half a million quid tied up in that trawler."

Ben grinned at Sam. "And get a trawl warp and half your trawl around your screw first time over it would give you a million pounds worth of experience, wouldn't it?"

Sam nodded. "It would."

Job Benson placed his hand on Buller's knee and pressed it firmly. "Well, somebody'll have to take her to sea and fish with her. We'll have to see what Charlie Bates says—then go on from there."

"I'll tell you now what Charlie will say. I've heard him say it too often," Ben said.

Job Benson stood up, his hands thrust into his coat pockets, his elbows askew.

"I've been hearing Charlie Bates talk for nearly half a century," he said flatly. "I've known him a long time. A long, long time."

He turned to Eve. "Well, my dear, we'll have to be getting back to your aunt. When are you boys off again?"

"Tomorrow," Ben said and Sam nodded. "Evening."

"Well, then, we'll be seeing you in the office forenoon, eh?"

As they moved in a little group to the door, Sam suddenly opened a closet and took out his hat and a light coat.

"I'll walk a little way with you," he said. "I could do with some fresh air."

Job Benson tilted back his head.

"When did a trawlerman ever want fresh air?" he snorted. "You should be in the wheelhouse with them sometimes, Eve. You could cut the air with a knife."

"I'll still walk a way with you," Sam smiled.

Ben sat looking at his father and mother for a few moments after they had gone.

"Fresh air, he says. That boy is quick on the draw, I'll say."

"What was she like to look at, Mother?" Buller asked. "She had a nice cool touch, and I liked the sound of her voice."

"She seemed a very nice girl. I didn't know Job had a niece."

"Job's younger brother. I've heard him mention that he was a builder or something and lived on the south coast. What was she like to look at?"

"I can tell you that," Ben cut in. In a few sentences he described Eve to his father. "And she goes out and in in just the right places," he concluded.

Buller filled his pipe.

"Sounds like your mother when she was that age. She had 'em running after her by the dozen."

"Nonsense," Mrs Cleeve said sharply. "I never ran after any-body, ever."

"That wasn't what I said," Buller grinned. "There was one fellow, used to sing tenor love-songs at parties. If I was there he would burst out with 'The Fishermen of England'."

"He was just a nice boy, a nice-looking boy, too," Mrs Cleeve said. "And there was no call for you to do what you did."

"Oh, oh! Out come the skeletons." Ben's eyes opened wide. "Rattle dem bones, Pop. What happened."

"I caught him kissing her and——"

"You didn't catch anybody. It was a kissing game at a party. Everybody was kissing everybody else," Mrs Cleeve cut in. "It was all very innocent."

"Go on," Ben urged. His eyes widened when he saw that his mother was smiling.

"I wasn't kissing anybody," Buller said. He applied another match to his pipe which gave out a satisfactory cloud of smoke. "Neither did he, after I'd finished with him."

"Did you wreck the joint?" Ben asked.

"I wrecked him," Buller chuckled.

Ben threw up his arms in mock indignation. "Fighting over women. Tck tck. Those were the bad old days."

Mrs Cleeve shook her head slowly and a soft smile stole over her face. As she moved to her kitchen with her hands full of crockery she heard her husband say in his deep voice:

"Not women, son. A woman."

"That'll be the day when I fight over a woman. Hey, Mom, if there's a drop left in the pot don't waste it."

Job Benson, Eve and Sam turned out of a narrow street, crossed the road and stood against a waist-high wall which ran around the rim of the port like a rampart. At intervals the wall bellied out into a shallow bastion into which were set seats. Below them stretched the two long narrow docks, two oblongs of water glistening whitely in the dock lights. Ranged along the walls of the two docks were trawlers by the dozen.

"What time is tide, Sam?" Job asked.

"Ten o'clock, round about."

Job pointed downwards to the dock.

"You'll see half a dozen or more of them slipping out to the roads at that time," Job went on. "They'll go straight out to Clarion light. There it is, winking away, see?" She followed his pointing finger and saw a pin-point of light a long way out in the darkness of the sea. "Nine miles out that is. Then they turn north. The Clarion bank light is the beginning and end of a fishing trip."

"And how long is a trip?" Eve asked and her head was turned to Sam.

"Eighteen, twenty days, more or less. Depends how the fishing goes, and the weather, of course."

"But in winter, when it is so often bad weather, what then?"

Sam chuckled softly. "If the wind blows the funnel over-board we stop fishing. That's bad weather. Then the office starts asking if we're on a pleasure cruise, so we start again," he said wickedly.

"The day the office tells you to start fishing you let me know," Job growled. "That'll be history."

He leaned against the wall.

"All you can see in front of you is history. Men have been fishing from Scoresby for nigh on a thousand years." He swept an arm around. "Where we are standing now there used to be guns to protect the harbour.

"From whom?"

"From the Dutch—and in case the Spaniards or the French tried a raid. Big old muzzle-loaders they were, and I can remember when some of them were loaded with blank and were fired on special days, like the birth of a royal child or a coronation."

"I remember the guns," Sam said. "I was only a kid but we used to play around them."

"They were taken for scrap in the last war, all except one which is now kept at the Town Hall."

Job turned until his back was to the wall and he was facing the young people.

"I sailed out of here as a decky boy, a pound a trip and my keep. I was fifteen then. Six years later I sailed as skipper." He seemed to be looking over their heads into space. "And three years after that I stood on the quay wall and watched my own trawler sail. She was a rattle-trap, too. She was forty years old— an old Aberdeen hansom cab—and on her last legs. But she had a tip-top skipper on her, same age as me. I was up to my eyebrows in debt but he cleared it for me. The best in the port he was. There hasn't been one quite like him since. He fished off Iceland when most skippers were scared to go north of the Faroes. And when most men were afraid to go north and east of Iceland he sailed to Bear Island and east of that, too."

"Wonderful," Eve breathed.

"Aye, although he wouldn't thank you to say as much. In two years I was clear of debt and owning another trawler. Another hansom cab. And in ten years I owned eight. I wanted him to come ashore and handle them for me." Job chuckled. "Know what his answer was? 'You buy 'em or build 'em. I'll fill 'em with fish.' And he did. Boys sailed with him, grew to be men, and became Benson skippers."

"And that is an accolade?" Eve asked softly.

"It means that a man is a top skipper if he's a Benson man," Job said shortly.

Eve turned to Sam who had been listening, a smile on his face.

"You are a Benson skipper, aren't you?"

Sam nodded. "So is Ben."

Job Benson squared his shoulders. "And that grand old blind ruin you saw tonight was my first skipper. Buller Cleeve."

"It was he who sailed to . . . Iceland . . . and . . . Bear Island?" She turned again to Sam. "You must be proud of him. Indeed you must."

Sam nodded slowly. "We are, but we daren't tell him so."

"It's time we were getting on home," Job said. "Your aunt will have me on the mat for keeping you out late. I don't know why you insisted on coming with me when you heard I was calling on Buller Cleeve." He peered down at his niece. "You can't be interested in trawlers, diesel or steam. Not yet, anyway."

"No, Uncle," she answered demurely. "Not yet. But I'm learning. For instance, I want to know what a . . . hansom cab . . . is?"

"You tell her, Sam."

As they walked along the broad rampart Sam explained. "See those trawlers? The bridge is in front of the funnel, then comes the foredeck. The old-time hansom cab had the bridge behind the funnel. Gave them more deck room . . ."

"And kept them warmer," Job chuckled. "I don't suppose there is one afloat now."

"There is, you know," Sam said. "She's a boxer for an Icelandic outfit.

"There you go again. No, what is a boxer?" Eve asked.

"The Icelanders fish on their own doorstep. It would waste their time to make a run down to our markets so the old trawler takes the boxes on board and does the run while they carry on fishing. She goes back loaded with coal."

They walked along the grey rampart side by side.

"Iceland. You've mentioned it quite a lot of times," Eve said. "Is that where all the best fishing—trawling I mean—is done?"

Job's shoulders hunched up belligerently around his ears.

Sam provided the answer.

"Broadly, yes. At least in that part of the ocean. Iceland is really the top of a range of mountains which are under the sea. We fish the valleys and lower rides near Iceland."

"And Bear Island?"

"The same applies. Look," Sam went on. "On the wall in the office there's a large chart. I'll come down tomorrow and show you."

Job concealed a smile behind a large hand.

"What time are you sailing, Sam?" he asked.

"Around seven o'clock tomorrow evening."

The smile stayed concealed.

"And you're coming in to the office in the morning?"

The question was bland, guileless.

"Er . . . um . . . Well, I wanted to talk to Sooty Giles about . . . about the winch."

"Been giving trouble?"

"A bit, now and then."

"Did your chief engineer report it when you came in?"

Job wiped the smile away. "Well, Sooty Giles should have seen to it. Let me know if it isn't done."

Sam hastened to avert any criticism of the shore engineer Sooty Giles.

"Oh, it will be done all right."

"And you want to see it is?"

"Something like that."

Eve had detected that Sam was being gently led to the end of the plank and mercilessly joined in.

"There's no need for you to make a special journey in tomorrow morning just to show me the map."

"Chart," Job put in briefly.

"I was coming in, anyway," Sam said airily.

"I gathered that." Job kept it flat.

"I've heard a lot about Iceland. And read bits about it," Eve said. "Aren't they trying to stop you fishing . . . trawling?"

"Fishing . . . trawling . . . both the same," Job growled. "Just splitting hairs."

"They're not trying to stop us. They're trying to extend their limit from three miles from the shore to twelve miles," Sam explained. "There's something to be said for both sides. You see, they claim that the breeding grounds are close inshore and are being cleaned out. . . ."

Job snorted. "Whether that's so or not is beside the point. What *is* the point is that they are trying to impose a twelve-mile limit without international approval."

"But can they?"

"They are. And if they catch a trawler inside the twelve-mile

limit they arrest it and slap heavy fines on the skipper and con-
fiscate his catch and gear."

Eve looked at Sam. In the reflected light from the docks she
could see a glimmer of a smile on his face.

"Have you been . . . caught?"

He shook his head. "I usually fish well away from Iceland. I've
got my own pet places. But Iceland is useful. In bad weather we
could shelter there or run in with a sick or injured man. Now
that's ruled out."

"You mean that if you went in for shelter or with somebody
hurt they would . . . ?"

"The Bogey Man *could* claim that you had your trawl down
inside their limit. And possession being nine points of——"

"Oh, dear. Stop a moment, please. Who or what is the Bogey
Man?"

"Icelandic Fishery Protection ship."

"I see."

They turned off the rampart down some wide stone steps into
a road in which the houses were large and were set well back. As
they walked down the steps Sam placed a hand under Eve's elbow
to assist her. Ever so slightly she leaned upon it and Sam kept his
hand there after they had reached the bottom step and on to the
broad-paved walk.

"Thank you." She said it softly.

"Here we are." Job paused by a wide gate. "Well, thanks for
seeing us home safely, Sam. I don't know how we would have
managed without you."

"Indeed. Thank you. It was most interesting. I'm looking forward to tomorrow," Eve smiled.

They stood in a little group by the gate.

"It's about time that fly-blown grubby chart came down. First
thing I'll have it shifted," Job Benson said flatly.

Sam chuckled. "Do that. I'll bring one of my own. And there'll
be no flies on that."

Job joined in the chuckle. "I'll bet not. But lots of tea stains.
Eve, those boys use their charts for tablecloths—or to work out
their football coupons. Well, we'll say good night, Sam." He held
the gate open for Eve to pass through.

She turned and extended her hand. "Thank you, again . . .
Mr Cleeve.

Sam held her fingers rather longer than necessary.

"The name is Sam," he said softly. "See you tomorrow."

Sam walked back up the steps and along the ramparts treading on air. He could still hear a soft voice, feel soft fingers.

"Oy, oy," Ben shouted when Sam entered. "Did you catch pneumonia out in the cold fresh air?"

"P'raps he felt like a walk," Mrs Cleeve said severely, always ready to defend Sam.

"Yeah," laughed Ben. "As much as I want a ballet skirt." He looked at the clock. "I'll take a chance, Sam. What say we walk up to the club? I'll give you a black start in a game of snooker."

Sam nodded. "Suits me. Don't wait up, Mum."

An hour or two later they were breasting the bar in the lavishly furnished club.

"Chin chin," Sam said. "I was a bit off form tonight."

"Off form!" Ben barked. "I could have given you four blacks start and licked you. Mud in your eye. Same again?"

Mrs Cleeve switched off the light and snuggled down into the warm bed. She could hear Buller's heavy breathing.

After a few minutes she half turned.

"You asleep, Buller?"

Buller grunted.

"She's a very nice girl, isn't she?"

The grunt was echoed.

"There's not so many nice girls around these days."

"Never were, anyway. Why don't you go to sleep?"

"I was thinking about the boys. Sam . . . and Ben. . . . She's a very nice girl indeed."

Buller heaved himself up on one elbow. "What's running through your head now. What idea are you churning over?"

"Nothing. I was just saying that she's a very nice girl."

"And in the next breath you start talking about the boys. What's in your head?"

"Nothing. Nothing at all."

"So you wake me up to tell me that she's a nice girl."

"Yes. You weren't asleep anyway."

"Very nearly. Couldn't it have waited until tomorrow? She'd still be a nice girl then, wouldn't she?"

"Yes. Good night! Buller."

"Good night!" Buller snorted, and heaved at the bedclothes.

"A very nice girl indeed." He heard it, scarcely above a whisper. "Very nice."

CHAPTER FIVE

THE ritual at the breakfast table when the boys were home never varied. While their mother cleared away the debris of the breakfast Sam and Ben read out aloud or gave a potted version of what items they felt would interest their father.

The items they read were typical of them.

"Hey, Dad, that horse Torch is running again at Kempton Park," Ben said, folding his paper to a more convenient size. "With the weight he's carrying he'll win dragging a sledge behind him. Want me to put five bob each way on him for you?"

Buller snorted. "You said he would win last time . . ."

". . . 'Dragging a hearse behind him,' " Sam laughed. "Why don't you pick a horse that's carrying a jockey?"

"He was only having a breather the last time," Ben stoutly defended his choice.

"So you put a quid each way on him and help him breathe."

"Nothing venture nothing win," Ben grinned.

"I've heard that before somewhere," Buller said. "Anyway, I'll chance five bob each way."

"Get Job to stop it out of his earnings if it loses," laughed Sam. He glanced at his watch, checked it against the grandfather clock and stood up.

With studied carelessness he said: "I'm going to call into the office this morning. I want to check on one or two things. May have to have a new winch next trip if this one keeps going wrong on me."

Ben studied his brother from beneath lowered eyelids.

"Let's have another bet. You won't be back for lunch. You'll eat at the club."

"I may do."

Ben waited until he heard the click of the front door.

"I'm calling at the office, too. Like I always do on sailing day. Like he always does. But never . . . *never* . . . at the crack of dawn." He snorted. "Check on his winch. Huh."

"She's a very nice girl," his mother said severely, as she swept up a few errant crumbs. "She is very nice indeed."

"Who? The winch?"

"You know what I mean, Ben Cleeve."

"You bet I do." Ben laughed as he unfolded his paper. "It

looks as if we're heading for a show-down, Dad. The Navy is going to send ships to protect us off Iceland. I didn't think we would call their bluff. I wonder what will happen if the Bogey Man tries to pinch one of our trawlers and the Navy tries to stop him. Would it come to shooting, do you think, Dad."

"Some damn' fool could start anything. Take my advice and stay out of it. There's plenty of fish elsewhere."

Sam stood in front of the large-scale chart fastened to the office wall. It was full of pin-holes and still stuck into it were ten or a dozen coloured tags.

He explained to Eve. "That is roughly where our trawlers are fishing. Each skipper decides more or less where he will go and keeps the office informed. He may not be exactly in that spot, he might even be running a bluff for a day if he's being shadowed by other ships."

Eve leaned against the wall and looked at Sam.

"I'm sorry, but I'll have to stop you now and then to explain things. You've shown me how Iceland and Bear Island are mountain tops. You've shown me the depths—soundings you called it, didn't you?—which are the valleys. That is like geography. But what is running a bluff, and why? And if there are fish there why can't another man catch them without having to shadow a ship?"

Sam was suddenly aware of two wide eyes in disturbing proximity. Above them an errant strand of hair lay across a smooth white forehead. He badly wanted to stroke it back into position. The tip of his tongue went over lips which were suddenly dry and his heart increased its tempo with a distinct thud.

"You were saying . . . ? Well, fish are not always in the same spot. Lots of things affect them. Food moves, a current shifts and the plankton drifts away. A good skipper takes all those things —and others—into consideration. Things like the ice moving south from the Arctic. Fish don't like it too cold, you know. Then he tries a trawl or two, searching there and elsewhere until he gets a good haul. Then down goes a dan buoy and he starts fishing seriously."

"I see," she said slowly. "And he wants to keep it to himself. Although you said there were plenty of fish in the area."

"True. But he's had to work out by trial and error where. Then along comes a man who's not so hot and he wants to profit by the other fellow's brainwork."

"How do you stop him?" she asked. "Shoo him away?"

Sam grinned. "Trawler skippers don't shoo away easily. No. We drop a dan buoy some way off—where we know it is bare and pretend to start searching. He does the same, gets nowt and ends up by steaming away to fasten himself to some other skipper."

"More questions, Mr Cleeve. Or should I call you skipper or captain?"

"Sam will do. Fire away."

"I know how you find your way from, say, Clarion Light, isn't it? to Norway and to Iceland and Bear Island. By compass and speed. But how do you know when you are over a valley or a mountain top when they are under the water?"

"Soundings. Echometer."

He fumbled in his inner breast pocket and brought out an envelope.

"This will do," he said, laying the edge of it against the chart. "Now watch. The soundings are shown on my echometer. I can check them. See how they don't vary along a line? So I know I am on the top of a ridge or running over a depression. If it varies sharply I am cutting across a ridge or valley."

"Oh dear. There is so much to learn."

"I doubt if you'll ever have to learn it. I suppose I could say the same thing about teaching in a girls' school."

"I wasn't a teacher, I was a secretary."

"And have you started here yet?"

"Not until later in the week. Uncle Job said use the first few days for meeting people and finding my way around."

"Good. How would you like to see a trawler at close hand? I want to go aboard mine to see to one or two things."

"I'd love it."

In a few minutes they were walking side by side along the fish quay, now empty of salesmen and fisher humpers and glistening still from the attentions of a hosepipe.

"Two hours ago, or a bit more, this quay was full of boxes of fish with buyers and salesmen yelling their heads off," Sam explained. "I must confess that I've never fathomed what goes on. They speak a language of their own."

She looked around her with widening eyes. Alongside the quay, red with rust, and some still with the grey-white salt on their bridges and funnels, were ranged trawlers.

"Did all these come in last night?"

"Most of them. When they are empty they move away from this

quay to coal and store up ready for the next trip. The skippers don't do that. Harbour moves are done by the ship's husband and his crowd."

"By the what?"

Sam chuckled. "I thought that would get you. It always does. I said the 'ship's husband'. It's a good name too. He looks after everything, storing, coaling, sees that trawls are in good shape and she is ready to steam. Just everything is done by him."

"Like a good husband, in fact," she smiled. She waved a hand. "And how many of them belong to Uncle Job?"

"All those you see with a blue funnel, black top and a white star on it."

Silently she counted. "Nine."

Sam nodded. "And two more in dry dock for a semi-annual refit, five more coming home, three outward bound—it will be five tonight when Ben and I sail—and seven up north fishing."

She counted silently again.

"Twenty-eight. That's a lot of trawlers."

"There are bigger firms with three times that number of trawlers. But none better."

Her mind darted off at a tangent.

"You like Uncle Job, don't you?"

Sam paused before answering. "It goes deeper than that. He and Father sailed as boys together. Job Benson went ahead, and would have taken Father with him, but Dad preferred to stay as a skipper. You heard Job talk last night. Do you know, when Dad was losing his eyesight Job pestered specialists for the names of the best eye-men in the world. If they could have done any good Job would have brought them all over here. They couldn't, of course. But he would have done it."

"So Uncle Job knows the hard side of fishing . . . trawling?"

"Every skipper does. There is no easy back door to being a skipper. There is no *Conway* or *Worcester* for us. We sailed as decky learners, Ben and I, and had to work our way up. Bos'n, Second Hand—that's Mate—to skipper."

"And is that a good way?"

"I can't think of a better."

Again she went off at a tangent.

"Which is yours?"

He pointed ahead. "That one near the dock head. And that's Ben's astern of her. Nice and handy to drop out on the first of the tide."

They paused on the quay alongside Sam's trawler. Eve was struck by the sudden appearance of power and strength of the ship now she was close to it. Until then the trawlers had been merely ships.

Now she was impressed by the squat, half-round bridge, the short wide funnel with its decided rake, the long clear foredeck, its stained and disfigured decking rising in a sweeping curve to the forecastle.

And suddenly she became aware of a new tone in Sam's voice. It had a new crispness about it, an undertone of authority.

"Believe me, she's not as filthy as this once I get her to sea. That foredeck is as clean as a hound's tooth—and as white." He raised his voice. "How's it coming?"

A small group of men working around the large, powerful winch immediately in front of the bridge lifted their heads and stared when they saw Eve.

"All right now, Skipper. We've a new slide valve in, and re-packed her. She's been running O.K." The grease-covered man who spoke still had his eyes on Eve. "If you're coming aboard you'd better have a couple of pieces of this?"

He extended a handful of multi-coloured cotton waste.

"Things are a bit grimy just now," he explained.

Sam grinned. "If I was by myself they couldn't care less." He helped her to the boat deck and to the main deck.

"Is that the ship's husband?"

"No. Maintenance fitter."

Sam pulled a bunch of keys from his pocket and opened a door. "This is my berth."

Eve's heel clicked against the high breakwater below the door and she would have stumbled had not Sam shot out an arm and supported her.

"I'm sorry," he said a little breathlessly. "I should have warned you. That breakwater is to stop the sea getting into my berth."

His arm still half-encircled her and slowly she lifted her chin until it was almost on his shoulder.

"Thank you," she said softly. "And does it? The breakwater, I mean. Does it stop the water?"

"Small stuff. In bad weather I don't use this door. There is an inside ladder up to the bridge."

Eve looked around the berth. She took in the expensive-looking panelling, the plated portholes, the plated lights, the large electric fire, also plated, the rich curtains which hung in front of the bunk.

On the opposite side of the berth to the bunk was a low wide settee covered in the same material as the curtains.

"This is . . . is . . . opulent," she said with widening eyes. "I would never have dreamed that such a room—berth you called it, didn't you?—could be on . . . on . . ."

She paused.

Sam smiled and completed it for her. "On a trawler. Is that it?" He sat on a corner of the table and pointed to a door. "Behind that a bathroom, with shower, and that," he indicated another door, "is a wardrobe."

Eve pursed her lips for a few seconds.

"I heard you talking last night about kits of fish. Explain, please."

Sam took out his cigarette-case and offered her one. He lit hers and his own with a lighter. He caught her eyeing lighter and case. They were both silver and engraved.

Sam placed them in her hands. She traced out the monogram "SC" on both.

"Mother gave me the cigarette-case when I got my skipper's ticket. I still sailed as Mate for a few trips, then got a trawler of my own. On my first trip I made her pay handsomely. Then Dad gave me the lighter."

"To him you had to prove yourself?"

"Partly."

"And . . . your brother?"

"Ben? The same. In the old days, before wrist watches came in, skippers used to get a gold watch and chain. Job gave Dad both after his first trip. You were asking about kits," Sam continued, getting to his feet.

He crossed over to a porthole and peered out. "See here. See those flat boxes?"

She stood by him raising herself to tip-toes to look out. She saw the piled-up empty boxes with names stencilled on them.

"That's a kit. They hold about four stone of fish. We stow it in the fish-hold, on ice, and it's loaded into those boxes when we get in."

"And you have to fill five thousand of them to make a trip pay?"

"Not exactly. Three thousand would cover expenses and leave a bit over, but a skipper who manages to get only the 'bit' wouldn't last very long."

"What sort of fish do you catch . . . or . . . wait, I'll get it myself . . . what sort do you trawl up? Is that right."

Sam smiled. "It'll do. Oh, hake, haddock, turbot. A living can be made on cod, even on dog fish, which the fish-and-chip shops sell as 'rock salmon', but hake, turbot and haddock are the best." Sam laughed out loud. "There used to be an old skipper sailing out of here some years ago who used to wait for his first haul and if the Second Hand shouted out that they were into haddock he would scramble down from the bridge and would pick up armfuls of the fish and pour them over his head and shoulders. He was in the money."

Eve wrinkled her nose. "Gracious me." She half turned towards Sam. Her face was but inches from his. For no reason that she could define she suddenly found herself breathless.

She opened her lips to speak. Sam lowered his head until his lips were nearly touching hers. He slipped an arm round her back. The other he placed behind her head. He felt her brace against him for a few moments. Her head went back. Her eyes closed. Sam's lips met hers. His grip tightened. He could feel the slim length of her body pressed against his.

After what seemed ages to her Sam lifted his head.

"I'm sorry," he whispered.

"I'm sorry, too. Sorry you did that," she whispered. Then she smiled. "No I'm not. I'm not a bit sorry."

"Is that the truth?"

She nodded quickly.

"Not a bit."

Sam lowered his head again to her waiting lips. She lifted her mouth to meet his.

"Is there anybody aboard this rattle-trap?" Ben's voice came from outside and they heard his feet thump on the deck. "Don't try fixing that winch. Dump it and get another," they heard him jibe at the fitter. "It's like the rest of this hooker. Held together by rust."

They swiftly sprang apart. Sam stood looking out of the porthole, Eve leaned against the table. Ben cluttered into the berth.

"I heard you were sight-seeing. Why don't you come and look at a real ship?" He grinned at them.

Sam looked at him unsmilingly for a few seconds. Then he grinned. "Where's the real ship? You show me."

Eve deliberately drew on her cigarette and blew a thin stream of smoke towards the porthole.

"I've been learning all about fish," she said calmly, hoping that her face was not flushed. "I now know that haddock is the best catch . . . haul, isn't it? I know how many stone to a kit and how many kits it takes to make a trip pay."

"You'll be shipping as decky learner next," Ben grinned. He looked at his brother and one eyebrow lifted quizzically. "Anything he teaches you would be suspect. Now I've run you two to earth I've got an idea." He turned to his brother. "You were saying you were going to feed at the club. Let's all go there and have lunch. What say?"

Eve glanced at Sam then turned to Ben.

"I'd like that. But will somebody explain what is the club?"

Sam moved away from the porthole, stubbed out his cigarette, looked at Ben and nodded.

"Fine with me. The club is the Starboard Club. It may sound like swank, but it is the most exclusive club in the town. Skippers only . . . and that is an inflexible rule."

"Skippers only and guests," Ben amended. "Proposed by the chairman—and that's Sam. . . ."

"And seconded by the vice-chairman—and that's Ben," Sam laughed.

Eve felt more composed. Somehow she had had the feeling that she had been hovering on the edge of something tumultuous. Oddly, at one and the same time she was glad that Ben had come in when he did, yet she slightly resented it.

"Sounds like the Cleeve Club to me."

Sam laughed again. "It is, very nearly. Dad is a life vice-president."

"And who is president?"

"Your Uncle Job."

As they walked along the fish quay, between them they explained. Sam started the narrative.

"The club was an officers' club when the Navy was here during the war. A lot of our skippers were in command of minesweepers and patrol trawlers sailing from here. They liked the club atmosphere."

Ben took it up. "Some of us didn't like the pubs much so we took over the club at the end of the war and now it is a skippers' club. It's got everything a pub would have and a whole lot more. For instance, I beat the pants off Sam here at snooker in comfort . . ."

"And from the lounge window you can get the best view of the harbour and the sea," Sam added. "And we have quite a good library."

Ben chuckled. "I've only been in there once. There were no comics around so I leave it to the Brains Trust like Sam. I'll let you into a secret. Most of the skippers use the library to sleep."

"From what I've gathered that is not unusual in most clubs," Eve said primly.

Although she concealed it very successfully, Eve felt a strange mixture of exhilaration and heart-fluttering emotion walking between the two men. They were young, virile, powerfully alive, both with an almost arrogant way of looking and speaking.

Her life had been more or less circumscribed, first as an elder girl at a school where frivolity had been frowned upon, and to be caught looking at boys or talking to them was viewed as the first step towards expulsion.

Later, as secretary at a similar school, she had had no opportunity for meeting many young men and the men she had met had been the "proper" sort—devitalized, young men who in another age would have written sonnets for her and would have delivered them tied with pale-blue ribbon. There had been extremely mild episodes, stolen milk-and-water kisses in the concealment of an arbour and an easy avoiding of tentative approaches by hopeful, but disillusioned elderly would-be wolves.

The two young men now escorting her emanated an almost animal arrogance, but in different ways. At intervals, as they found their way across the inevitable clutter on the quay and around the dockside, either Sam or Ben would place a hand under her elbow to assist her.

It was sufficient to send a slight electrifying tingle through her. Ben, she assessed, would be ruggedly ruthless and satisfyingly brutal. Sam, on the other hand, would be as ruthless but it would be a polished, steel-smooth ruthlessness.

She only partly listened to their fragments of conversation as she walked with them. She wondered what was behind Sam's sudden kiss. Was it merely the prelude? Briefly she allowed herself to conjecture what might have happened if Ben had not come on board. With an effort she thrust it from her.

It was Sam speaking who drew her back.

"That rusty old job—the one over there under the crane. That was the first trawler I sailed on. She was a broken-down old rattle-trap then."

She followed his pointing finger and saw a dilapidated rusted trawler lying forlornly against the quay in a corner of the dock.

"I did a couple of trips in her, too," Ben laughed. "She leaked like a basket, below and above the water line. It was like turning in in a shower of rain when she started shipping any seas—which was as near to always as didn't matter."

"But she made money," Sam said. "Dad had her for several years when she first came here. She wasn't new then."

"And is it . . . she . . . being repaired now?"

Ben laughed again.

"Repairing her would be like building a new one. No. She's being cannibalized—spare parts for some of the older trawlers. When she's gutted she'll be run up on the hard and burned."

"Burned? But she's iron."

"Steel," Sam amended. "She'll be cut up with oxy-acetelyne blow-torches and sold for scrap."

"Doesn't it make you feel sad to see her—your first ship—going like that?"

Ben shook his head. "Not me. Every time I look at her I start feeling cold and wet."

"I think I feel a little . . . not sad . . . but a little regretful," Sam answered slowly. "She was my first trawler, and the first one I sailed in as skipper. She may not look it now, but she was a dandy to handle. Like a ballet dancer."

Ben snorted. "Some ballet dancer. Like a drunken pig."

"Drunken pig, nothing. I was glad she could be handled once," Sam retorted. "And I'll tell you again, I would think twice about trying it with the trawler I have now."

Eve looked puzzled.

"I'm afraid I'm out of touch with the conversation."

Sam said quietly: "It's nothing."

"I'll take you out to dinner one night when I get back," Ben cut in quickly. "It's a long story. And a good one. That's a promise. When I get back?"

He made the last sentence almost a query.

Eve nodded. "I'll be looking forward to it."

"That's settled." Ben grinned at Sam over her head. "I know of a good fish-and-chip shop. A couple of bob lots, four penn'orth of chips and a bit of cod and a couple of bottles of Guinness. Fit for a queen."

"Why not have them wrapped up and take them up to the ramparts to eat?" Sam said bleakly. He found the thought of Eve and Ben dining together suddenly distasteful.

Eve gurgled. "That will be an entirely new experience for me. Won't we drink the vinegar out of the paper or something?"

"You will," Ben laughed. "You learn a lot of things. Never a dull moment, that's me."

Sam looked at him unsmiling.

CHAPTER SIX

THEY climbed the steep incline from the docks and walked along a road of opulent houses until they reached a larger one set well back. In the forecourt were parked a number of cars.

"This house used to belong to a man who made a fortune from fishing," Sam said. "He died without family. It was empty for a while before the war, then the Navy took it over. Now it's our club."

They passed into the wide spacious hall which was panelled from floor to ceiling. A man came forward smiling.

"'Morning, Sam, Ben. You're away tonight, I hear." He looked inquiringly at Eve.

"Miss Benson . . . Mr Crawford. Our steward," Sam made the introductions.

"And the lousiest judge of a racehorse in the port," Ben laughed.

"Bar one, but no names," Mr Crawford smiled. "Miss Benson. Any relation to . . . ?" He left the sentence in mid-air.

"Yes. Job's niece," Sam said. "She's going to work in his office."

"Very nice, too. So Job Benson is your uncle. Welcome to the Starboard Club, Miss Benson. We must find somebody to bring you to one of our Ladies' Nights. Once a month we have a Ladies' Night and——"

"All fixed," Ben said briskly.

"You might be at sea."

"Then alter the date. What's the good of being chairman and vice-chairman if we can't pull wires."

"We'll see. But I'm certain Miss Benson would not be short of an escort." Mr Crawford rubbed his hands together. "Same table, Sam?"

Sam nodded. "For three, of course. In half an hour? In the meantime we'll have a drink."

Mr Crawford moved away to make his arrangements. The two brothers and Eve went into the bar. A number of deep easy chairs were disposed around tables. The bar itself was a model of subdued lighting and glistening glass.

"Grab a pew," Ben said. "I'll pass the order. You, Miss Benson?"

"A medium-dry sherry, please. And my name is Eve . . . Ben."

A little muscle twitched in the corner of Sam's jaw.

"The usual, Sam?" Sam nodded and Ben walked away to engage the white-coated barman in conversation.

"I think I'll powder my nose while I'm waiting," Eve said. Ben, at the bar, watched her walk across the room while the barman executed their order. Then he looked across at Sam, raised his eyebrows in approval and did a "thumbs-up" sign.

Sam frowned.

"Here we are, Ben. Two large Scotches and a sherry," the barman put the drinks on a tray and pushed the book of chits towards Ben for him to sign. He leaned on the bar.

"There's a horse running today. Torchlight. Been tried out against some hot stuff over the distance and it'll——"

Ben took the tray. "That means it'll come last by a street. Save your money for your old age," he grinned.

The barman stood upright in mild shock. The mention of a racehorse to Ben usually meant a long and analytical conversation of almost every horse running. This brusque dismissal of a most important topic was a real shock.

Ben carefully placed the tray on the table and looked quizzically at his brother. He took a seat and leaned back, drink in his hand. He lifted the glass until it was level with his eyes.

"Everything all right on board?"

"Yes. All O.K."

"Winch all right now?"

"Yes."

"Did you have a good look at it?"

"Of course I did."

Sam wondered where the conversation was leading to.

Ben tossed his head back in one swift move. Then he let his head go back again and laughed.

"Then that's where you got it on your face, was it?"

"Got what?"

"Lipstick. Suits you, too."

Sam stood up with a jerk, his face set into hard lines. He pulled a handkerchief from his pocket, held it for a moment, then without a word strode across the room towards the men's cloakroom. Behind him he could hear Ben's chuckle.

He was still chuckling when Sam returned.

"Couldn't you find it?"

Sam looked at him unsmiling.

"There wasn't . . . I wasn't looking for anything."

Ben's chuckle took on an extended lease.

"That why you went off scrubbing your kisser?" He leaned back in his chair and a look of admiration came into his eyes.

"Full ahead, eh? Quick worker, our Sam. Well, gimme time. Time and the chance and you'll have a run for your money."

Sam stood over his brother, the hard lines still engraved on his face.

"Listen to me, Ben." His voice was low, clipped and cold. "I want you to get this straight. So far as Eve—Miss Benson—is concerned there is nothing——"

"Easy, boy. Here she is."

Ben stood up as Eve rejoined them.

"We were just deciding what to eat," Ben said calmly. "Toss you who collects the menu from the bar." He put a hand in his pocket. "I'll lose, of course."

"Let me toss," Eve smiled.

"If I remember I lost then. I'll get it." He looked severely at Eve as he stood up. "We have a rule here, anyway. There is no gambling in the bar."

He collected the large framed menu from the bar and as he took it he said to the barman: "Is that straight about Torchlight?"

"Straight! It'll win dragging a dust-cart behind it."

"When you ring Dicey Cummings put a quid each way on for me. And it had better win or I'll have your curly locks for a cod end."

The barman grinned. He was as bald as a billiard ball.

"I'll do that. It'll pay off about fours."

As Ben handed the menu to Eve he said to Sam, with a jerk of the thumb towards the bar: "He was just telling me about a skin called Torchlight. It's due to win dragging a cannon behind it. I've had him put a couple of fins on for me. A fin on the nose and another to show."

Eve's eyebrows arched. She spread her hands hopelessly.

"Will somebody please explain?"

"I warned you. Ben sees all the American films going. A skin is a horse. Somebody has told the barman that it's going to win so Ben has put two pound on it. A pound to win and a pound that it comes home in the first three."

"And there's a rule about gambling in the bar?" She said it softly and wickedly.

Sam smiled. "That's not gambling. That's charity. It's providing for the bookmaker's old age."

"Anyway, I'm vice-chairman of the club," Ben said, seating himself. He lifted his empty glass significantly. "No bird can fly on one wing, Eve?"

She lifted her eyes from a scrutiny of the menu. "Not for me, thanks."

Sam signalled to the barman for two more drinks.

"I've quite a choice," she said, running a finger down the extensive list. "But I don't see a bob lot."

"We keep them for Ladies' Nights," Ben said.

They tossed the gambit of small talk around between them and covertly Eve studied the brothers. They were so different to what she had been led to expect of fishermen. They were clean-cut, virile, in their opposite ways each showing, without realizing it, a confident strength.

"See the man standing at the bar, the one with the round red face?"

It was Ben speaking. She looked and saw a young man who she guessed to be about twenty-three or -four.

"The young one?"

"Yes. That's Scottie McBayne. Last year he earned a bit more than twelve thousand pounds. Job, your uncle, found him pushing around an old Aberdeen open-bowed trawler, scratching hard off the Faroes for a thin living. Job persuaded him to come to Scoresby. It wasn't hard. Scottie sailed as Mate for two trips. One of them with Sam, then Job gave him a trawler and said: 'Make or break yourself in two trips'."

"And . . . ?" She left it on a rising note.

"Two record trips. Since then he hasn't looked back."

Eve looked around her. Gradually the bar had filled with men, different in appearance, colouring and age, but all with the stamp of quiet self-reliance.

"Are all the men skippers?"

"Most of them. Some of them from our company. Others are with different firms. See the man talking to Scottie?" Sam leaned forward. "He's a German. A first-class skipper. He's with the firm your uncle's buying that diesel trawler from."

"The one which shoots the trawl over the stern?"

"Oy, oy? We're learning," Ben said admiringly. "A few more lessons and you'll be sailing as decky learner." He grinned at Eve. "With me."

Eve's eyes levelled on his. Somehow she found Ben made her feel slightly breathless in a different way to how she felt with Sam.

"And I would learn?"

"A lot." Ben's grin took on a wicked slant. "The entire works."

A little pulse beat incessantly at the angle of Sam's jaw.

"Yes, I imagine so." Eve locked eyes with Ben for a few seconds and saw the glow of flame a long way back behind his eyes. Slowly she turned her head until she was looking at Sam. Very gradually the corners of her eyes wrinkled. "There is so much to learn," she said softly.

"So this is where you're gallivanting?" Job Benson said, coming to a stop at their table. Sam and Ben climbed to their feet. "They told me at the office that you had gone out to learn something about trawlers and I find you guzzling drinks." He frowned heavily at the two men.

"Guzzling is right," Ben laughed. "I found them tearing a winch to bits on Sam's trawler. Their faces were smothered in . . . grease," he concluded. He shot a wicked look at Sam. "Can I get you a drink?"

In a few moments Job was seated at the table nursing a large glass. He looked benevolently at his niece then at the two brothers.

"Anything you don't learn from me you'll learn from this pair," he said.

"That's just what I was saying," Ben started. "I was saying——"

"It's time we took up our table," Sam cut in sharply. "Join us, Guv'nor?"

"Delighted. You can pay for mine."

"That's how he makes his money," Ben chuckled. "We pay for his lunch and he puts his cash into an old sock. But I was saying . . ."

Sam put a hand under Eve's elbow and helped her to her feet.

"We'll lead. That way Ben can have the chair with the back to the window."

The little procession filed into the dining-room, Eve and Sam side by side, Job following and Ben bringing up the rear.

As they reached the table Job turned to Ben. "What's funny? You're snorting down my neck. Let me in on it."

"You're in. Ringside seat," Ben laughed. "Right where you can be splashed with the blood."

Job Benson looked intently at Ben, shifted his gaze to Sam and onwards to his niece.

"Might be I'll have to climb into the ring myself," he said in a flat voice. "She's a new experience for me. I hardly knew she existed a couple of weeks ago. Now she's important."

Ben grinned at him. "Yeah, I can see that."

Job went on as if there had been no interruption. "We, that is her aunt and me, intend to see that she has a good time. A good time, and . . ." he lightly tapped Ben on the chest with a rigid forefinger ". . . and that she doesn't get hurt. Let's feed."

They joined Eve and Sam at the table. As Sam had forecast, Ben got the chair backing on to the window. This left him facing Sam with Job on his right hand and Eve on his left.

They busied themselves for a few moments with their orders, then relaxed.

"The first one to talk shop—ships and fishing—pays for the lunch for four," said Ben. "But before that I will personally cut his throat."

"Oh, please," Eve protested. "I like to hear all about trawlers and fish and . . . and . . . trawlermen. It's all so new."

"In six months you'll be fed to the teeth with it all," Job said. "But fire away, what do you want to know?"

Eve rested her elbows on the table and placed the tips of her fingers together.

"We were looking at that poor little trawler which is being broken up. The one you said was a ballet dancer to handle, wasn't it?"

Job looked inquiringly at Sam. "That the *Esmeralda* she's talking about?"

Sam nodded.

"She paid her way twenty times over," Job said. "But to keep her running now would start to swallow it all up. You equalled your father's top take in her, didn't you, Sam?"

"Had some luck one or two trips."

"You did something with her which you said you wouldn't like to try with your present trawler. What was that?"

Sam bit his bottom lip briefly.

"Who started this topic?"

"I did. And I want to know."

Ben and Job exchanged swift glances.

"You, Ben. You were there."

"All right." Ben looked at his brother and Eve saw the spirit of raillery slip from his face and a warmth take its place.

"Me and Sam were racing home from Iceland. That trip the office had ordered us to go to Fleetwood."

He grinned briefly at Eve.

"If ever you ship with me as decky learner you'll sail some time around the west side of the Orkneys." The grin returned. "Great place for growing daffodils, the Orkneys. Black rocks sheering straight out of the sea. A grand place to be in a hard westerly gale and visibility down to feet."

The trace of raillery disappeared from his voice and his eyes half closed as he went on.

"About halfway round, on the west side, is the Sound of Hoy. And sticking up like a big black finger is a rock, the Old Man of Hoy. I was bound home, or for Fleetwood anyway. Sam was about three hours astern of me, in *Esmeralda*. About three hours ahead of me was a Fleetwood-owned trawler, the *Sunburst*. It was blowing a gale and a half. A real stinker, wasn't it, Sam?"

Sam nodded briefly.

"Then it added some more with snow for a bonus. *Sunburst* took a full-sized sea aboard, flooded her engine room and stoke-hold and her steering went for a burton. And she was only three or four miles off the Old Man."

He paused while the waiter served them with the first course and unconsciously heightened the drama of his story.

"*Sunburst* let out a yelp," he continued, wiping his lips with a serviette. "She was drifting as fast sideways as she had been steaming ahead. I had *Sirius* then—a nice little handy ship, easy to push around. I started looking for *Sunburst* in the thick stuff—and found her."

He turned his head until Eve could see his profile sharply cut against the window behind him. Again he paused for a few moments. Then he dismissed an epic in a few words.

"After a bit I got a tow to *Sunburst* and heaved her away from the Old Man. Might have got away with it, too, if the tow hadn't parted. Then I lost her again. By that time Sam had come up. I told him where I had lost *Sunburst* and he goes feeling his way in. We could hardly see our fo'c'sle heads. Sam goes sashaying in and finds her practically rubbing herself against the Old Man."

"This is developing into a serial story—and everything is getting cold," Sam protested. "To cut a long, long story short I got a tow to her and yanked her away. Now let's eat."

Job donated a second long glance at his niece, at Ben and at Sam and permitted himself a thin, fleeting smile.

"Yes, we'll give Ben's mouth a rest. It amounted to this, Eve. *Sunburst* and *Esmeralda* were being thrown about like corks.

There was a backwash off the Old Man of Hoy capable of smothering both ships. Remember, they couldn't see more than a couple of hundred feet. Pass the salt, Sam."

Eve waited for the story.

Ben took it up. "By the time Sam got a tow to her—and both of 'em were jumping about like corks—they were practically touching the rock."

He leaned back in his chair.

"I thought Sam had gone crazy. He was towing *Esmeralda* right at the rock. Smack-bang-dab at the Old Man of Hoy. We got one more flurry of snow. I lost sight of them and when the snow cleared I expected to see both of them piled up on the Old Man. Instead, I couldn't see anything. Not a glimpse of either of them. Then they came slamming round the rock, going like scalded cats to the west'ard."

Eve tried hard to get the significance of that.

Job finished the story.

"Sam had used the backwash to help him. He had got a tow aboard and had steamed right around the rock—something no sane skipper would do in fine weather. It only wanted one slip or misjudged move and both would have gone ashore where nobody could have got at them in the Sound of Hoy just inshore from the Old Man."

Eve nodded. "I see."

Ben looked steadily at her. "I doubt if you do. But Sam had to time *Esmeralda*'s moves to meet those of *Sunburst* rolling in the backwash. If he hadn't timed them to a second both of 'em would have bought it. I wouldn't have chanced it in *Sirius*. No, sir, not me."

Eve asked: "And what happened to . . . to . . . *Sunburst*?"

Ben threw back his head and laughed.

"The tow parted later on, I got one aboard and towed her into Stornoway. I was the hero."

Eve looked at Sam and her eyebrows lifted.

For the first time Sam smiled.

"Get him to show you his newspaper cuttings. They're pretty dog-eared by now, but he'll show them to you."

"There's a nice end to that," Job smiled. "While Ben was towing *Sunburst* into Stornoway Sam plugged on ahead and caught the cream of the market at Fleetwood."

"Poetic justice," Eve chuckled.

"I still think he chopped the damn' tow and left her to me,"

Ben complained. "And if you're in doubt I can recommend the apple pie and cream. Try some?"

Eve nodded. "I'm in your hands completely."

"Let's not rush things," Ben grinned. "Time enough." He included Sam in the grin.

Job leaned back in his chair. In a few seconds he gave each of the young men a shrewd glance.

"Speaking of time," he said. "That marches on. In a month or so one of you will have to take a couple of trips off and go over to Germany for me to collect the new trawler. I'll send a full crew over as well. We might as well start off from scratch."

Sam and Ben exchanged looks.

"I might go over myself and sail back in her," Job went on. "It will be a nice break for me."

"You'd have to take your secretary, of course," Eve said guilelessly.

Ben slapped his leg and laughed.

"I said you would end up as decky learner with me."

Eve looked from her uncle to Ben and on to Sam. "Why? Are you taking over the new trawler?"

Job settled it. "I haven't made up my mind yet. I'll have to offer her to Charlie Bates, of course, but we all know what he'll say."

"I can almost hear him saying it." Ben dropped his voice to an asthmatic growl. "'Stinkin' oil-boxes. Gimme coal and three good firemen.'"

Sam said: "What about Fraser or one of the others? Don't they come into it?"

Job began climbing to his feet. "When the time comes I'll settle who takes her. Come on, young lady, it's time we got back to the office. I don't usually spend nearly two hours over lunch. I leave that to my skippers. They have more time to spare."

"Unless somebody else is paying for it," Ben said wickedly.

While Job, assisted by Ben, manoeuvred his car from the car park, Eve and Sam stood together.

"What time do you sail tonight?" she asked.

"Around seven o'clock. Ben and I will be first out of the lock. Why do you ask?"

She shrugged slightly. "I might persuade Uncle Job to take me out on the ramparts to watch the ships—trawlers—sail. Out to Clarion Light, isn't it? And then north."

Sam laughed. "You're filing things away, aren't you?"

Her lips twitched slightly. "Decky learners must learn."

She half turned in her seat in the car as it pulled out of the forecourt and waved her hand to the two brothers. As it slipped easily down the hill, she said: "Who is going to have the new trawler, Uncle Job?"

Job changed gears to go round the corner.

"I'm not certain yet. At least not quite certain."

Job gave her one of his rare smiles. "Now, Miss Secretary. Which one would you pick? The one with the blue eyes?"

Eve remained silent for a few minutes until the car was being turned into a side opening alongside Job's office.

"I don't know which one has the blue eyes," she said finally.

Job cut the engine and leaned back.

"Neither do I," he chuckled. "But you're beginning to see the problem. Right, now let's get down to some work. Do you speak or write German?"

"I'm afraid not."

"Well, that's no difficulty. I'll dictate some letters in English and you can take them to the German consulate and get them translated." He climbed from the car and stalked through the outer office, half turning as he did so.

"Bring your book along," he said crisply.

Later he dictated: " 'We will be a small party of four, myself, the skipper who will take her,' leave a long blank there, Eve, for me to fill in the name, 'my secretary and the chief engineer. Will you please arrange hotel accommodation . . .'"

Eve's head, bowed over her book, hid her smile.

CHAPTER SEVEN

GEEGEE PORTER had elected to sail once more with Ben. His reason had been crisp and short. As the trawler lay in the lock waiting for the tide out he had clambered up to the wheelhouse where Ben was leaning against the small chart table.

Ben looked critically at him.

"How's the head?"

"I've had worse," Geegee growled.

Ben peered critically at Geegee's face. One side was puffed and a magnificent black eye defied concealment.

"What happened? Did you walk into a door?"

"I did not. Me and that skinny-gutted Second Hand off

Lodestar had a few words." He glanced obliquely at Ben. "One word led to another and . . ."

"And he gave you a hammering," Ben prompted mercilessly.

Geegee grinned, then grimaced painfully. He lifted his fist towards *Lodestar* which was just astern. "He's crawling the fo'c'sle of her. Ask him."

"Maybe I will." Ben reached for his megaphone. "Did he offer to teach you how to tie a cod end?"

Geegee blocked the megaphone with a fist.

"Don't you . . ." he warned in a growl.

Ben grinned and wrenched the megaphone away.

"*Lodestar* ahoy," he hailed.

Sam was standing outside his wheelhouse door. He had in his hands a pair of binoculars which, ostensibly, he was focusing but most of the operation directed them to the grey walls of the ramparts which stood out clearly in the reflected lights from the docks. He concentrated on one of the empty gun emplacements and was almost certain that he could see a figure standing there.

Impatiently he adjusted the focus. The figure remained dim.

"*Lodestar* ahoy," came Ben's voice.

Sam frowned impatiently and reached for his megaphone.

"Yeah. Go ahead, Ben."

"Like to have a little bet, Sam? A fiver on the run from Clarion to North Channel light. I'll wait for you."

Geegee whispered urgently in Ben's ear although there was no need for silence.

"You're on," Sam's voice came back.

It meant a race of fifty miles.

Ben's voice took on a chuckle. "Geegee wants to say something to Lofty." He paused and grinned at Geegee. "He'd like to have a quid bet with him."

After a pause Sam replied. "Lofty says it's on. Hey, Ben. What shape is Geegee in? Lofty looks as if he has been trying to bite barbed wire."

Geegee chuckled grimly alongside Ben.

"I told you, didn't I?"

Ben grinned. "Geegee's full of beans, might almost say fighting fit."

"Fighting is the word. There she opens, Ben."

Ben glanced at the dark lock gates. A widening glisten of water came through them. He rang the telegraph, heard it jangle stridently below and heard the lighter tinkle of the reply.

"I'll wait for you. Same rules."

The trawlers slid out through the lock gates and once clear Sam tried once more to focus his binoculars on the dim figure on the ramparts. He was not certain, but the figure was still there.

Lofty climbed to the wheelhouse juggling with two mugs of hot tea. He sucked at his noisily then blew painfully as the hot tea punished his massacred lips.

"Try pouring it down your ear," Sam said unfeelingly. "Why do you do it? Every trip you get tangled up with Geegee and he eats you."

Lofty gingerly helped himself to some more tea.

"A fella's got to have some fun ashore, ain't he? Life ain't all work."

A little more than four hours later only a few hundred yards separated the trawlers with *Lodestar* astern by half that much.

Ben reached for the whistle lanyard as North Channel light came abeam. He yanked at it and a hoarse bellow came from the whistle.

Thinly from Sam's tannoy came the words:

"Sheath your sword. Victory is yours."

Geegee rubbed his hands.

"I'm a quid up and the trip only four hours old."

"Right. Spend the next four hours working out how much beer that will bring you. I'm going to get my head down. Call me when Franken light is abeam. I'll turn her out at that."

Geegee settled down to a four-hour watch. Astern he could see the side-lights and masthead lights of *Lodestar*. Gradually she was drawing away at a widening angle. They might meet again in Arctic waters, they might not.

Geegee grinned into the darkness.

"Fourteen pints at one-an'-six a pint is . . ." he murmured. "Maybe I'll manage a Scotch or two just to send 'em on the way. Say ten pints at one an' four . . ."

In the next few days the pewter-coloured fiords of Norway slipped past. North Cape hung like a black cloud in the sky and they were in the Arctic seas.

Ben bored *Morning Star*'s bow steadily north-east until one grey morning, after a prolonged study of the chart and frequent scanning of the echometer, he said crisply: "Right, we'll try it here."

A score of miles to his north lay the lonely bleak sentinel of Bear Island with a fringe of receding ice-field skirting it.

For two or three days *Morning Star* trawled without breaking records but steadily stowing away a satisfactory haul of fish.

Ben and Geegee stood on the wing of the bridge idly talking, but subconsciously both of them taking in several matters as they talked. They watched the grey scudding clouds streaming overhead critically; they watched the lead-coloured seas breaking into a white foam-topped crest as the wind whipped them. They studied the thrumming wires leading from the winch through the gallows and into the water. Both of them could almost see what the trawl was doing below. It was clean ground under them, but there were wrecks, some charted from bitter experience, some unknown from the days when convoy after convoy had been fought through to Murmansk. There were wrecks, plenty of them, but that was something upon which they had to gamble.

The door of the radio room behind the bridge opened a mere crack and the operator peered through.

"Got some good news for you," he grinned. "There's a gale warning. Iceland, Faroes and all places north."

He clutched the door as *Morning Star* butted into an ambitious sea, arrogantly scattered it in a shower of spray, lurched over it and slammed her twisting way down into the grey-green valley beyond.

"It looks as if it's arrived, doesn't it?" Sparks looked at the sea.

Geegee's eyebrows lifted.

"A gale? this a gale? This is a mill pond." He looked up at a brief, diffused circle of yellow light in the grey sky. "I'm practically down with sun stroke."

The radio operator gave him a scornful look.

"News will be on in a few minutes, Skipper."

Ben glanced at the brass clock screwed to the wheelhouse bulkhead.

"Another hour and we'll look at it. If it's no better I may haul off to the west'ard."

Ben went into the radio room, sniffed distastefully and sat on the edge of the table.

They heard the three pips of the time signal then came the suave, disembodied tones of the BBC announcer. He read through some parliamentary news, the brief details of an air crash, then embarked on something which made Sam sit bolt upright.

After a potted review of the Icelandic Government's aggressive attitude towards British trawlers fishing near Iceland, he went on:

"The Government has decided to afford British trawlers fishing in the vicinity of Iceland naval protection. The Admiralty has dispatched two frigates to the area with orders to see that British trawlers are permitted to fish inside the twelve-mile limit at present imposed by the Icelandic Government. In order to facilitate these fishing operations the Admiralty on instructions from the Government, and in collaboration with the Trawler Owners' Federation, have created two areas or boxes on the fishing grounds which will be patrolled by the frigates so long as British trawlers fish therein. The Admiralty announced this morning that in addition to the two frigates two destroyers are also being dispatched to the area."

Ben whistled. "Strewth! That's getting tough."

The radio operator looked at him. "What happens if the Icelandic Bogey Man tries to pinch one of ours? Would it come to shooting?"

Ben whistled soundlessly and shook his head. "That's anybody's guess. I would say not. Don't forget, the Navy's an old hand at this display of power and protection. They've been sending midshipmen ashore with half a dozen marines and a gun for generations."

The radio operator said: "The old mailed fist in the velvet glove, eh?"

"Something like that. But those Icelandic boys are not easily bluffed." He clicked his fingers. "See if you can raise anybody in the area. P'raps they can tell us if the frigates have arrived."

The operator twiddled his knobs until he cut in to the trawler band, adjusted it and cut into a voice laden with excitement to a point where it occasionally cracked.

". . . There are I, ten miles off an' me trawl down when up breezes the Bogey all set to pinch me," the voice went on. "'You can't touch me,' I says, 'I'm more'n ten miles out.'

"'I can,' says the Bogey, 'and I will. You are under arrest. Haul your trawl and follow me into port.'

"'Like hell I will,' I says. And lets out a yowl for the Navy." The voice paused for dramatic effect. "And got it. Out of nowhere comes this frigate. Right out of nowhere. Hitting the high spots, she was, pushing half the ocean in front of her. Slam-bang between me and the Bogey Man she shoves then I heard a voice say: 'Morning, Skipper. Anything wrong?' 'Not a thing, now,' says I. 'And if you come a bit closer I'll give you a good fry of fish.' 'Splendid,' says the Navy bloke. 'But first I must talk to the gentlemen on your port beam.'"

A deeper voice cut into the wavelength.

"What happened? Did they have an up-and-downer?"

The first voice was almost tinged with disappointment.

"No, they just went waltzing off talking to one another on their loud hailers, and by 'n' bye back comes the frigate. 'I'll have that fry now, Skipper,' he says, and he drops alongside me as neat as a whistle. Quite a young fella he was on the bridge. All smiles, too."

Youthful Lieutenant-Commander Walton, D.S.C., R.N., listened in to the conversation on the frigate *Gadfly*, which was his first command. He grinned at his First Lieutenant.

"Quite a début, Number One. Must be that new toothpaste I'm using. You might pass the word to the petty-officer cook that I like my chips nicely browned with my fish."

"So do I, sir," Number One grinned back. "I thought the Icelandic gent was rather tame, sir. He took it all very quietly."

"Just the first call, Number One. We called one club and he passed. Should be fun when we get to shouting three no trumps doubled. By the same token with luck—your luck—we might take a couple of bob off Pilot and the doctor tonight if all is peaceful."

Commander Walton smiled reflectively.

Number One asked: "Do you think they'll get tough and start a hot war up here? Guns is rather uppity about his shooting."

"Scandalous thoughts. Diplomacy is our chief weapon, Number One. That and the soft answer. In the meantime concentrate on getting Pilot and Doc to the block with their heads nicely shaved for the axe."

There came a knock at the door and a bridge messenger stood there.

"Excuse me, sir, officer of the watch says there is another trawler asking for help. 'Bout eight miles away."

Lieutenant-Commander Walton sighed. "Here we go again. Diplomacy and the soft word." He moved towards the door.

The First Lieutenant grinned. "Diplomacy, up eight hundred, right four. Soft words 'Shoot'."

"Much too aggressive, Number One. Much too much." He climbed the ladder to the bridge. The sub-lieutenant on watch smiled at him.

"Trawler called the *Lodestar*, sir. Says he was steaming towards Seydisfiord with an injured man when the Icelandic Fishery cruiser tried to arrest him for being inside the limit."

Lieutenant-Commander Walton's eyes took on a frosty glint and his jaw hardened.

"This might be different. In the meantime tell the doctor I might want his services. Where is she, sub?"

"Seven miles away, sir. We've got them on the screen, sir. They seem to be very close to one another."

"Right. Let's turn the wick up a little. Twenty minutes should do it."

Gadfly drummed as the turbines increased their hum and sent her slicing through the seas.

When Sam parted company with *Morning Star* he steered west of the course followed by Ben until he was approximately fifty miles east of Iceland. The place he wanted to assay for fish was a tricky one. It was not a long ridge but was a broken underwater valley with a double fault, but Sam was convinced that it was heavy with fish and his first hauls confirmed it for him.

They shot and hauled steadily and Lofty's healing face was twisted into a perpetual grin.

"If the weather holds off we'll break the back of this trip inside another five days," he said as he dealt faithfully with a large mug of tea. "Six days at the most."

"If the weather holds off," Sam said. "You heard the weather report."

The excited voice of the radio operator came from the radio room.

"Hey, Skipper. One of our warships is tangling up with the Bogey Man. The Bogey tried to pinch one of the Fleetwood trawlers and the frigate stopped 'em. Come and listen."

Sam, Lofty and the operator listened in to the trawler's recital. When it was complete Lofty slapped his hands together.

"That's the bloody order. Treat 'em rough."

Sam looked thoughtful. "I don't like it. I don't like it one bit."

Lofty's brows arched. "Wad'yer mean? Would you let the Bogey get away with it? The Gov'ment isn't going to, anyway. And the Bogey has been getting right out of hand this last few weeks. They've been knocking off trawlers which didn't even have a trawl down just because they were inside their limit."

"I still don't like it. It will come to this. No matter what you are doing, dodging bad weather or going into an Iceland port, if the Bogey comes up on you you'll be pinched."

Lofty shook his scarred head disbelievingly.

"All right, shake your big block head. You'll see," Sam said. "Now how about getting it up."

Lodestar shot and hauled with satisfactory results through the remaining daylight and into the night when the cluster-lights flooded the long foredeck and fish pounds with light.

Sam was leaning over the wing of the bridge watching the stooping, oilskin-clad men working swiftly. No time-and-motion-study man could have improved on their economy of movement for the given task. They seized a huge fish, slid a gleaming knife into it, gutted it, flicked the liver into a special pound and with one swing sent it to join an ever-growing pile.

Sam heard a high-pitched yelp of pain, saw the smooth movements of the men come to a stop as they crowded around one youngster.

"What's up?" he called.

Lofty looked up at the bridge.

"Grimmy's gashed himself in the guts. He's bleeding bad," Lofty called.

Sam slipped swiftly down the short steel ladder from the bridge to the foredeck. The men were grouped around a crouching figure who was groaning and clutching his stomach.

"Lost his foothold and jabbed hisself," one man volunteered.

"Christ, he ain't half bleeding."

Sam examined the wound as best he could. Through the gashed oilskin and thick clothing beneath he could see a wound which was bleeding profusely.

"Get him to my berth," he said.

Lofty and two seamen struggled across the slippery deck and through the doorway leading to Sam's berth. In a few moments they had removed his oilskin and some of the clothes so that the whole wound was visible.

A few moments' examination was enough to convince Sam.

"This is a job for a doctor," he said. "I figure I can make Seydisfiord in about four hours. Lofty, get that trawl in snappy now."

The men stumbled out of the berth and Sam used the full resources of his limited first-aid chest. He drew the gaping edges of the wound together, placed a thick pad on it and strapped it. He used the simple, but effective capsule for an injection of morphine and made the man as comfortable as he could on his long settee.

In a few minutes Lofty put his head round the door.

"She's in." He looked at the prone man. "How is he?"

"Looks bad. A slash from the groin half across the stomach. It's a hospital job."

Lofty rasped a hand across his stubbled chin.

"Skipper. Do you think the Bogey Man will get fussy and pinch us?"

Sam's face wrinkled into a snarl. He pointed to the heavily breathing man. "Does he look as if I'm going sneaking inside their damned limit for a few fish? Talk sense, man."

Sam climbed to the bridge, studied the chart for a few seconds then rang for "full ahead". He amplified it with a shout down the engine-room tube. "Give her all you've got, Chief. Everything."

For a little more than three hours *Lodestar* pitched and cork-screwed over a rising sea, each one climbing up out of the darkness white-crested to recoil from the trawler's sharp bow.

A searchlight stabbed out of the night and bathed *Lodestar* in white radiance.

"Trawler ahoy. Stop your engines," came a thick voice. "I will come close alongside you."

Sam pressed a switch and lifted the microphone of his tannoy loud hailer.

"*Lodestar,* of Scoresby. I've got an injured man aboard, badly injured. I'm taking him in for medical attention."

The thick voice carried a chuckle. "I can see your registration letters and number. You are now under arrest. You are inside the twelve-mile limit."

Sam exploded. "Damn you. Of course I'm inside your limit. Well inside, but I didn't have a trawl down."

"That we shall see when I get you in."

"Stem him," Lofty snarled alongside Sam. "He's timber-built and we'd cut right through him."

Sam turned to the man at the wheel.

"Hard a'port. Hard over."

"You wants to go to starboard if you're going to crack him one," Lofty said.

Sam disregarded Lofty's bloodthirsty advice.

Lodestar swung away in a broad curve plunging into successive seas which climbed up around her bow then parted to curl aboard over the long foredeck.

"*Lodestar,* ahoy. Stop or I'll shoot," came thinly from the fishery boat.

"Shoot and be damned," Sam snarled. "Sparks." He ham-

mered on the small trap leading from the wheelhouse to the radio
room. "Sparks, see if you can contact that frigate. Tell her I am
trying to get into port with a badly injured man and the Bogey
Man is trying to arrest me."

A spurt of flame came from the shadowy fishery boat now
astern of *Lodestar*.

"Missed," Lofty snapped.

"Blanks," Sam snapped. "But he might use a loaded shell at
that next time."

The Icelandic ship still kept Lodestar in her searchlight beam
as Sam kept Lodestar wriggling around.

A voice came thinly from the pursuing ship.

"*Lodestar* ahoy. You are at liberty to take your injured man
into port. I will order an ambulance for you."

"Sez you," Lofty grunted.

Sam switched on his tannoy.

"And then what?" he asked.

"I will charge you with being inside the twelve-mile limit
imposed by the Icelandic Government. It will be up to you to
establish that you were not fishing when you come up in court."

Sam thumped the trap to the radio room.

"Any answer from that frigate, Sparks?"

"Yes. She's on her way."

Before Sam could say anything more another and more powerful searchlight cut across the water illuminating both *Lodestar*
and the Fishery boat. A metallic voice came over a loud hailer.

"*Lodestar* ahoy. What's the trouble?"

"Now start shooting, you bastard," Lofty said.

The Fishery ship cut in.

"I am arresting this trawler for fishing within the twelve-mile
legal limit and am ordering her to follow me."

The frigate came plunging past, throwing showers of spray
away from her bow, spun sharply round almost in her own
length until she was between *Lodestar* and the Icelandic ship.

"*Lodestar* ahoy," came a cool voice. "Drop down to four knots,
maintain your present course—you are making me giddy at the
moment. Protection ship ahoy. I would point out two things. One,
your twelve-mile limit is not recognized, and secondly this trawler
is trying to get a sick man to port for treatment."

The metallic dialogue passed to the Icelandic ship.

"I am aware of that, Captain, but my orders are to arrest and
board trawlers inside the twelve-mile limit . . ."

Lieutenant-Commander Walton turned to his First Lieutenant. "This could be the test case. Have your seaboat's crew at the stand-by. I'm going to put Doc aboard the trawler to see what's wrong with that man. The Icelandic gent might—I say might, Number One—try to board."

"Aye, aye, sir." He grinned youthfully at his commanding officer. "Can I have first chop at 'repel boarders', sir? We've got Leading Seaman Cleverly on board, sir, and he's light heavyweight champion of the Rosyth command. It could be——"

"You came out a generation too late, Number One. The general scheme now is peace at any price. You know, turn the other cheek."

"Of course, sir. But what happens when the other cheek is slapped?"

"Then I'll put you and Leading Seaman Cleverly aboard the protection ship and steam off into the darkness leaving it to you both to exercise diplomacy. Now is Doc ready?"

The flat voice came over the light-flooded waters.

"*Lodestar*. Stop your engines. I am sending a doctor over to look at your injured man."

Sam turned and stared at the dark bulk of the protection ship which was slightly astern of the frigate.

"And if he tries to board me?" he called.

The disembodied voice from the frigate was heavily laden with a chuckle.

"I don't think that will happen, somehow."

Leading Seaman Cleverly, bow oar in the pitching whaler, gave a grunting laugh.

"And I hope he does."

"Way enough," the sub-lieutenant snapped as the whaler pitched and tossed alongside the trawler. "Stand by, Doc, to jump. And watch your step. That foredeck will be like an ice-rink."

There came a few brief moments when trawler and whaler lifted to the same sea and rose to it together. The young doctor made a scrambling jump, straddled the rail and a trawlerman grabbed his case.

"Give way together," the sub-lieutenant ordered.

As much by design as accident, the whaler dropped slightly astern of *Lodestar* so that it lay directly in the path the protection ship would have to take to creep up to *Lodestar*.

Lieutenant-Commander Walton studied his pitching whaler

as it lifted and disappeared in the troughs of succeeding seas. Then he switched his glasses to the Icelandic ship which was dropping astern. He reached for his microphone.

"Fishery protection ship ahoy. I would point out that I have a whaler in the water just ahead of you." His voice took on an almost glistening suavity. "We wouldn't want anything to happen to it, would we?"

Thinly from the protection ship came the answer.

"I can see it."

"Splendid. I propose to drop astern a little to pick it up." Then, almost apologetically: "You won't stand on my tail, will you?"

Lieutenant-Commander Walton turned to his navigating officer. "Where am I? Exactly. Not just thereabouts."

The young lieutenant pored over his charts, made a little cross. "Thirteen point two miles out, sir," he said.

"Good," Lieutenant-Commander Walton almost whispered. "I thought the wind and tide would be on the side of the just."

The young doctor straightened himself and looked at Sam. "I'm afraid this is too big a job for me on board you. Either you get him into hospital in Iceland or we get him aboard the frigate."

"If I go inside I'll be charged with poaching, fined and my catch and gear will be confiscated," Sam said. "Anything up to ten thousand pounds."

"On the other hand this man's life is at stake."

"Would he have a chance on the frigate?"

"A better chance, certainly. On board you very slim, I would say."

"Let's see what your skipper has to say."

They climbed to the bridge and Sam took the microphone. "Frigate ahoy. Your doctor wants to talk to you."

"Go ahead, *Lodestar*."

Briefly, the doctor explained the problem.

Lieutenant-Commander Walton made an instant decision. "Get him aboard here. Do you have a Neils Anderson stretcher?"

The doctor glanced briefly at Sam, who nodded.

In less than an hour the wounded man was strapped into the cane-and-canvas stretcher which kept him rigid, was transferred to the pitching whaler and from that to the frigate where he was taken to the sick bay.

"I'll run your man down to Lerwick," Walton called to *Lodestar*. "I'll keep you posted." He paused a moment or two then went on. "You are now fourteen miles out. That is the high seas and you are free to trawl without let or hindrance."

"Thanks," Sam answered. "Thanks for everything. But I'll be forty miles away by daylight."

"Right, goodbye."

Lodestar's bow swung east, the frigate turned south. The searchlights were switched off.

Sam was resting, but not sleeping, on the long settee in his berth when the radio operator tapped the door.

"Skipper. Are you asleep?"

"No. What is it?"

The radio operator stepped into the berth.

"Just got a call from the frigate." He paused a few moments. "Grimmy's dead. He died half an hour ago."

Sam stood up. "Go on."

"There's isn't much more. They're going to land his body in Lerwick."

Sam chewed at his bottom lip for a few seconds. "All right. Don't spread it around until daylight."

CHAPTER EIGHT

BEN was leaning on the wing of the bridge. *Morning Star* had her trawl down. The men had cleared the last haul from the pounds into the ice-packed fish-hold. Ben was feeling satisfied. Although he was not breaking records, he was making good catches. He lit a cigarette and flicked the match into the wind, watched it curve away.

The door behind him opened and his radio operator poked his head out.

"Skipper. *Lodestar*'s in some sort of trouble. She's just let out a yelp for the frigate. The Bogey Man is trying to arrest him."

"What!" Ben made it explosive. "Arrest him? Sam isn't within forty miles of Iceland!" He pushed past the operator and went into the small fug-laden room. He and the operator listened intently to the radio conversation between *Lodestar* and the frigate.

Then there was silence.

"Shall I contact *Lodestar*?" the radio operator asked.

Ben shook his head. "No. Sam will be busy. Bye and bye." He stayed in the radio room for a while, then said: "Give me a call if anything pipes up. There's something wrong somewhere. Sam must have a badly injured man to risk going inside the twelve-mile limit. What did he say, again?"

The radio operator repeated it like a lesson.

"*Lodestar* said she was taking an injured man into port and said the Bogey Man was trying to arrest him for being inside the twelve-mile limit. Then the frigate said she was coming along fast and told *Lodestar* to keep moving. Since then, nothing."

Ben's jaw stuck out pugnaciously.

"I ought to be there. If he tried any lark like that on me I'd jam my bow against him."

The radio operator hid a smile behind his hand.

Ben paused at the door.

"Let me know the minute they pipe up again."

After a while he called: "Geegee. Get it in."

The trawl was hauled, the catch was sorted and trawl was shot again when the radio operator called to Ben.

"The frigate's calling *Lodestar,* Skipper."

Ben hurriedly ducked into the radio room.

In silence he and the operator listened as the frigate reported the death of Sam's seaman.

He clicked his fingers as the message ended.

"All right. Raise *Lodestar* for me. I want to know what this is all about."

In a few minutes he heard Sam's voice coming thinly from the loudspeaker.

"Go ahead, Ben. I knew you'd be listening."

"What happened?" Ben asked.

Sam told him in a few sentences. And twenty or thirty skippers of other trawlers listening in growled and swore deeply.

"So it amounts to this, Sam. Whether you're fishing or not inside the twelve mile they're going to knock us off and try to arrest us. It'll be our word against theirs. And what a chance we'll stand in their courts."

"That's about the weight of it. I was forty miles away when Grimmy gashed himself. My decks were cleared and I went all out for hospital for him."

There was silence for a few moments then Ben said: "Hard luck on Grimmy. He was a good fella. You'll be reporting it to Job, of course."

"I'll wait till daylight."

"O.K., Sam." Ben slipped into business. After a few innocuous sentences which told Sam where he was working Ben went on: "Why not move out here, Sam. The going is good."

"I might do that. I might see you tomorrow sometime."

A wide-awake local correspondent for the London newspapers stood on the windy quay at Lerwick in the Shetlands and watched the grey-painted frigate slip smoothly alongside the quay. The White Ensign at half-mast intrigued him. So did the ambulance waiting on the quay.

He judiciously waited until the blanket-wrapped figure had been carried down the gangway and had been placed in the ambulance before he approached an officer and introduced himself.

"You'd better see the captain," the sub-lieutenant said. "Slip into it, though. We're sailing in fifteen minutes."

Lieutenant-Commander Walton rubbed a hand round his chin for a few seconds.

"I'm not certain how much of this I can tell you," he said. "Briefly, we took an injured man off the trawler *Lodestar*— badly injured—and brought him here. Unfortunately he died on the way."

The newspaperman was a shrewd individual.

"Where did you take him off the trawler, sir?"

Lieutenant-Commander Walton cocked an eye at him. "I wondered if you'd ask that. It was roughly eleven miles off Seydisfiord. Maybe a shade more," he added flatly.

"Couldn't the trawler have landed him in Iceland, sir? There is a good hospital there."

There was a tap at the door and the sub-lieutenant poked his head round.

"All ready to slip, sir."

"Very well." Walton stood up and smiled. "Maybe you would learn some more if you made contact with the trawler *Lodestar*. She can tell you more."

The newspaperman was nothing if not persistent.

"You are on a sort of protection patrol, aren't you, sir?"

"We are."

The next question came flatly.

"Did the Icelandic authorities refuse to allow the injured man to be put ashore?"

Walton stood up and held out a hand.

"Young man," he said gravely, although a twinkle in his eyes belied the gravity, "you are cross-examining me and incidentally you are holding up the Queen's Navy. Get hold of the trawler."

The newspaperman stood by the bow as men on the quay waited to cast off. Casually he lit a cigarette and talked to the seamen.

"The Icelandic ship was tough, eh?"

A teenage seaman snorted. "Tough? Tough hell. He wanted to pinch the trawler and we said 'no'. All the trawler wanted was to put the hurt man ashore."

"Stop gossiping and stand by those lines," the sub-lieutenant snapped.

The newspaperman moved away. He was satisfied. One more thing remained. He would have to get his friend at the radio station to contact the trawler *Lodestar* and he would have a story to spread over the country.

He did and he got his story from Sam.

The London news agencies spread it abroad, the national newspapers gave it half a column, the Scoresby local newspapers splashed it, and Grimmy, the obscure, inarticulate trawlerman who died following a common-enough accident on trawlers, became a martyr who died, in the eyes of an indignant country, because of the inflexible attitude of an Icelandic patrol ship.

Job Benson frowned heavily as he digested the newspapers at his breakfast table.

"I'll wait until I get to the office," he scowled at his breakfast. "This is all . . . all cockeyed. Sam Cleeve wouldn't be inside the twelve-mile limit fishing. The last we heard of him was . . . was . . ." He left the sentence incomplete and looked at Eve across the table.

"He was about fifty miles east of Iceland and was working north of that," Eve said crisply. "And Ben was east of him again, almost off Bear Island."

The corners of Job's mouth twitched momentarily. "Ben . . . Sam . . ." he almost whispered. "I'll bet you can't tell me where *Southern Star* is. Not right now."

Eve recognized the trap and looked confused. "N . . . no. I can when we get to the office," she added hastily.

"Well, let's get there," Job said, standing up.

Half an hour later he leaned back in his chair.

"As I thought. Sam was just going in with the injured man

when the patrol boat came along. Get your book. I want to send something to *Lodestar*."

Mrs Cleeve stumbled through the newspaper reports as Buller listened grimly.

"Some of that is lies," he said. "Sam wouldn't be fishing anywhere near Iceland. Ben might, just for the sheer cussedness of it. But not Sam. Don't worry about it, Mother. We'll hear all about it when the boys come up tonight."

"That poor man, dying, and them refusing to let him go ashore to hospital," she said with quivering lips.

"They didn't refuse," Buller grunted. "Sam could have gone in, but he would have been charged with fishing inside the twelve-mile and that would have cost him his catch, gear and a big fine."

"And so the poor man had to die."

"He might have died anyway."

The day passed slowly until the grandfather clock solemnly cleared its throat and slowly embarked on recording the passage of time.

Buller felt around for the heat of the teapot, fingered his way to the bowl of the pipe and put out a hand to the switch of the radio set.

And there was a knock at the door.

Buller frowned heavily.

Mrs Cleeve came back into the room fussing in front of Eve. Buller's frown disappeared.

"Good evening, Mr Cleeve. I remembered that you listened to the . . . to your sons at this time, so I thought I might be allowed to listen with you."

"Surely, surely. Mother, get another cup for Miss Benson." Mrs Cleeve was already preparing a pot of milder mixture than was in Buller's pot.

"Any minute now," Buller said. "Me and Mother always have a little bet which one will pipe up first. Sometimes it's Ben, sometimes Sam."

"Wasn't it dreadful about that poor man dying," Mrs Cleeve said, placing her best teapot alongside Eve.

"Uncle has been getting messages from Sam . . . from your son during the day. The papers have got some of it wrong. He wasn't fishing inside the limit. He was just taking the man in for treatment."

"Just what I said," Buller agreed. "Sh . . ."

A thin metallic voice came from the loudspeaker.

"Sam," Mrs Cleeve whispered.

Buller delicately touched a knob and the voice came in louder.

The oblique dialogue followed.

"I suppose everybody knows about Grimmy now," Sam said. "I've been sending messages all day."

Ben knew as much about the messages as did Sam but he also knew who was listening home in Scoresby.

Ben said: "You explained you were forty miles out when Grimmy gashed himself?"

"Yes, and how the patrol boat came up on me about eleven miles out and accused me of fishing."

Buller snorted and Eve was almost certain that his blind eyes flashed.

"That leaves you in the clear, anyway. If it had been me I would have bounced my stem off him."

Buller chuckled and Mrs Cleeve made disapproving noises. "He was always the wild one," she whispered.

"Would Grimmy have stood a chance if you could have got him ashore to hospital."

"I don't know. The frigate's doctor said he had only a slim chance from the minute he chopped himself."

"How did it happen?" Ben was asking on behalf of the blind man nearly two thousand miles away.

"Slipped when he was gutting, put out his hand and fell against the knife."

Buller leaned forward towards Eve and said softly, as if not wishing to interrupt a conversation going on in the room: "I always preached at 'em, if you slip drop your knife. You can always pick it up again." He shook his head. "More gashes than you can count because they will hang on to their knives."

As if echoing his words, Ben said: "They never learn, do they. They'll never drop a knife."

A husky croak cut across the disembodied conversation.

"That sounds like that Bates fella." Ben chuckled. "Bet he's got some good advice to offer."

"It'd be a waste of time offering advice," Charlie Bates rasped asthmatically. "Some folk will never learn. Bit of hard luck on you, Sam and Grimmy." He paused a moment, then went on:

"I suppose you wasn't fishing inside the limit, was you, Sam?"
Buller chuckled deeply.

Sam's voice was almost explosive. "What do you think?"

"If you had you'd have seen Charlie in there somewhere scratching around for a crust or two," Ben laughed.

"I'll have a little bet with you that there won't be twenty stone of fish difference between us," Charlie Bates said complacently.

"Hey, Sam," Ben went on wickedly. "This business is going to complicate things for you now you can't land anywhere in Iceland, particularly Seydisfiord."

"Why?" Sam asked.

Ben's voice was heavily laden with laughter.

"You won't be able to see that dizzy blonde you meet ashore there."

Sam failed to see the trap yawning open. His voice climbed up on a query.

"What blonde are you talking about?"

"What blonde," Ben said scathingly. "The one that's always hanging around the quay when you slip ashore." His voice became a thin falsetto. "Oh, Sammy, I am glad to see you. You are staying ashore for few hours?"

Sam gagged explosively.

"What in hell are you talking about, Ben? I haven't been ashore there for months. What's got into you?"

"How about the trip before last? You told me yourself . . ."

"Oh, that. That was business. I had condenser trouble and I was ashore only about two hours."

Ben slammed the trap.

"Long enough." He chuckled.

Charlie Bates, recognizing that Ben was ribbing Sam, helped to bolt the trap.

"Too long, knowing Sam," he wheezed.

Sam decided to abandon what to him was a pointless joke.

"How are things with you, Charlie?"

"Couple more days and I'll be happy. Not a record, but I'll earn a crust or two. How about you, Ben?"

"I'll give it two or three days. That'll keep the wolf from chewing up the doorstep. And you, Sam?"

"I've lost a bit of time over Grimmy. I'll see how the next couple of hauls shape. I don't like the weather much, it's got some snow in it."

Buller Cleeve nodded his grizzled blind head. As if he were

there off Bear Island on a trawler he knew what each of them was doing and how rewarding were their hauls.

"I'll be seeing you, Sam." Ben's voice came clearly out of the radio set as loudly as if he were in the room with them.

Buller reached out and delicately fingered the knobs, bringing in voice after voice, some in the deep-toned broad-vowelled accents of Hull, the more nasal of Grimsby and the even broader Lancashire of Fleetwood. Once or twice there was the guttural accents of a German.

Finally Buller switched it off. He had been around his little world, had listened and had a complete picture in his mind of the weather, the catches and the disappointments of a dozen or more skippers.

"Isn't it wonderful," Eve said. "It's just as if they were talking in the room to you, yet they're nearly two thousand miles away. Do they always talk like that to each other?"

"Skippers gossip and pass information to each other," Buller said. "When I was young and we were just breaking into those waters we didn't have wireless. Then we were fitted with the old spark set, everything had to be sent in morse to Wick."

He paused and chuckled.

"When these talking sets first started some of the boys used to talk to one another forgetting that the rest of the world was listening and they used to use real ripe words. Some even started sending bets by radio. But the authorities soon stopped that. They have a Bogey Man listening and he jumps good and hard on bad language. Mostly they keep to talking about fishing now."

Mrs Cleeve stood with some empty cups in her hand.

"What was Ben talking about? A giddy blonde in that place? Sam never said anything to me about a blonde."

Buller chuckled. "That's Ben, he's always ribbing Sam. Sam takes it all in good part." He leaned back with his hands clasped in front of him. "I figure Charlie Bates will be home middle of next week with three and a half thousand kit and Ben will be a tide or two after him with about the same. I'll know how Sam's doing tomorrow night."

Eve's eyebrows raised.

"However did you find out that? I listened carefully and didn't pick up anything like that."

A laugh rumbled deep down in Buller's chest.

"Charlie Bates said he'd earn a crust or two." Buller Cleeve paused for a moment then repeated it with slight emphasis.

"A crust or two. That means that Charlie has topped his three thousand kit, he wants to more than pay his way—what he calls earning a crust—and has two or three hundred kit of prime fish over that."

"And Ben?"

"About the same."

Eve smiled and rested her hand on Buller. "Thank you, Mr Cleeve. It has been fascinating. May I come again?"

"Certainly, Miss Benson. Come as often as you like."

"Thank you," she said softly. "And, please, my name is Eve."

The frigate *Gadfly* butted into a rising sea as she headed north back to her patrol area. The whining wind brought with it flurries of snow with a promise of more.

Lieutenant-Commander Walton switched off the repeater loudspeaker in the chart room, stubbed out a cigarette into a tin serving as ashtray and grinned at his navigating officer.

The young officer grinned back.

"They do gossip, these fishin' fellas, don't they, sir?"

Walton nodded as he headed towards the door.

"Just like women over a garden wall. We must get into the act. I'll be able to tell them all about my operation."

The youthful lieutenant chuckled. "I must learn more of that dizzy blonde ashore, sir. She sounds just the job for Sub."

Lieutenant-Commander Walton lifted his chin in query.

"How come?"

"His name is Sam, sir. I liked the lingering throaty way that skipper said, 'Oh, Sammy!'"

"I'm afraid I can't oblige with any shore leave, much as I would like to play Cupid. See I get a call in two hours' time or if the weather gets worse."

"Yes, sir."

Shortly after dawn the next day *Gadfly* made radio contact with *Lodestar*.

"Sorry about your man, *Lodestar*," Lieutenant-Commander Walton said. "My doctor says he had only a thin chance, anyway. The knife had gone in deeply."

"Thanks just the same," Sam answered. "It's just one of those things."

"Whereabouts are you now?" Walton queried. "Out of trouble? I mean with the patrol ship."

Sam chuckled briefly. "I'm far enough away from him."

A rasping growl cut in. "Tell the truth and shame the devil. Tell the gentleman that you're scratching around picking up dogs' stuff fit only for fish meal."

"Who in the world is that?" Walton asked.

"Oh, he's just an old dead-beat who hauls a floating scrapyard around hoping to strike lucky. Used to be good years ago, but he's past it now."

Walton waited for an abusive contribution from the growling voice. None came, only a throaty chuckle.

Sam asked: "Anything else to say, Charlie?"

"A five-pun note says there won't be twenty stone difference between us," the rasping voice went on. "Scrap-yard or not."

"It's a bet."

"Right, I hope to meet you some time," Walton cut in. "Call on us any time you like. It's your Navy, you know."

"Thanks, we will."

Walton handed the microphone to the signalman.

"I'd like to hear those blokes really start insulting one another. It should be good." He glanced at his youthful watch-keeping sub-lieutenant and his face took on severe lines. "But I'd have to clear the bridge of children. Heaven knows what words they would pick up. Let me know when we reach the box, Sub."

"Aye, aye, sir." The sub grinned.

Three days later, on the dot at seven o'clock, Ben made contact with Sam.

"Sam, I'm heading for home. Enough is as good as a feast. Even Geegee can't grumble what with the quid Lofty owes him."

"Righto, Ben, I'll give it another day or so."

CHAPTER NINE

JOB BENSON paused in his dictation and glanced at Eve.

"Read back that last bit," he said.

Eve turned back her page in the shorthand book and glanced at it. A flush climbed up her face to the roots of her hair.

"Go on, read it back."

"I'm sorry, Uncle. You'll have to give it to me again. I rather lost the trend of your dictation."

The corners of Job's mouth twitched slightly. "If you had read it back it would have sounded funny, I'll bet half a crown."

With exaggerated politeness he went on: "Can we try once more, Miss Benson?"

For the next fifteen minutes Eve concentrated and got the dictation correct. Finally she stood up.

"That all, Uncle?"

"That's all. Let's hope it comes out all right in the wash." He glanced at the clock. With artless guile he went on: "Ben Cleeve is quite a thruster. He'll be first in through the gates. Give him fifteen minutes to get tied up, another ten to get here. If I were a betting man, which I'm not, he'll be crashing in here in a minute or so under the half-hour."

He lifted his head and stared bleakly at Eve but he underestimated his niece.

She glanced at a clipped folder.

"Skipper Banks and Skipper Bates are also due to dock and *Polaris* might make the end of the tide."

"You'll be glad to see them, won't you?"

Her face was as composed as his.

"I like Skipper Bates very much."

Job gave up.

She turned towards the door, then paused.

"We received confirmation of the accommodation in Germany—for three—this morning on the dates arranged. There is no alteration, I presume?"

Job contemplated renewing the battle for a moment. He thought he might possibly turn her flank by an oblique reference to *Lodestar* being a few days late. But he had learned to respect his niece's ability to counter-attack. He leaned back in his chair and rubbed his chin.

"Let me see now. Refresh my memory. Both *Lodestar* and *Morning Star* are due for a boiler clean and touching up here and there. Has Parker got those defects and repairs lists ready?"

"Went to the dockyard yesterday."

"Good. That'll give the Cleeve boys a few extra days at home. Unless I miss my guess they'll go tearing off to London sowing some wild oats here and there."

"And we're going to Germany on Friday—today is Tuesday —so they can sow for quite a harvest, can't they?"

"One of them. The other I'll want around for a briefing before we fly over." Job stroked his nose with a long forefinger. "Let me see, we had more or less decided that it was the boy with the blue eyes, wasn't it?"

He should have known better.

She flashed back, almost primly: "I don't know how you select your skippers, Uncle. Whether they have blue eyes, green eyes or . . . or . . ."

"Red hair." He chuckled.

"Or red hair," he repeated with a chuckle. "Red hair helps."

As she turned again towards the door Job clicked his fingers. "Remind me that tomorrow I am meeting our M.P. I want to brief him, as far as possible, on this Icelandic trouble. And on Thursday I have a meeting of the Trawler Owners' Association at eleven o'clock.

Eve scribbled briefly on her pad.

"That all?"

"That's the lot." He glanced at the clock. "Eighteen minutes to go and when he gets here show him straight in."

Eve closed the door with the nearest thing to a snort a cultured young woman can manage.

Almost as if he knew the timetable the door of Eve's outer office flew open with a bang and Ben Cleeve came in. Before Eve could stand up he was towering over her. She could feel the animal magnetism of the man as he stood, tips of both hands resting on her desk, leaning slightly forward looking down on her.

"Here I am, fish scales to the eyes, my fishing boat all loaded down and waiting for the little hand-truck. 'All alive O' and I hope you've put some lead in the pan of the scales. Must earn an honest copper somehow. What sort of mood is the great Job in? Fair to bloody as usual?"

Eve leaned back as if she would disengage herself from him but merely succeeded in fanning what she sought to diminish. Her action tightened the rather prim white blouse she wore, accentuating the curves of her bosom.

Ben took it all in in a one-second glance and momentarily his eyes widened.

"Not bad," Eve said. "At least he isn't biting the carpet yet, which is a good sign. We were so sorry to hear about Sam's man."

Ben straightened up. "It happens. Just as well it wasn't me. I would have given that Bogey Man something to worry about. See if his Highness will see one of his humble skippers."

Eve pressed a switch on the internal phone in front of her.

"He will, he's waiting for you. He prophesied what time you

would come through the door." She glanced at the clock. "He was right to the minute."

"Did he, indeed!"

The little loudspeaker embodied in the phone clicked and a thin, hollow voice came from it.

"Send him in, you can gossip later."

Ben wrinkled his nose. "Maybe squalls in the offing. Be seeing you, Babe."

Job waved towards a chair. As Ben sat down he ruffled a clip of papers in front of him, pursed his lips and nodded slowly.

"How are you, Ben?" he started conversationally. "If that bet you made still stands with Charlie Bates you'll owe him a fiver. You're not twenty kit different."

"I've been forking out to that old rascal for years. I ought to know better. I'm certain he buys his catch from the German trawlers. He came behind me on the tide."

Job leaned back. "Bad business about Sam's man, Ben. You were miles away, of course."

Ben stood up and moved over to the large-scale chart of northern waters hanging on Job's office wall.

He put his hand over an area about sixty miles east of Iceland.

"I was around here," he said. He moved his hand slightly. "And Sam was here. At least forty miles from the box. We knew the Bogey Man was around. We'd been listening to some chinwag by *Connaught*. The Iceland protection boat had been chivvying him around—he was in the box, about ten miles off shore and according to what the skipper of *Connaught* said the Navy craft just shooshed him away."

Ben walked back to his chair.

"So I understand, Ben. Things are going to get rough up there after this. And it will take a fleet of naval ships to maintain that box."

"The first time a Bogey Man starts pushing me around he's going to buy himself some trouble," Ben said pugnaciously. "A trawler is tougher than those wooden ships."

"That is exactly what I don't want," Job said firmly. "As the Government has taken an official standpoint and is sending the Navy up there we'll have to conform. The way I see it one or two bloody-minded skippers could deliberately provoke an incident which would complicate things."

He leaned back and steepled his fingers in front of his nose.

"Ben. When did you last shoot a trawl off Iceland? I mean within, say, ten or twelve miles off?"

"There's always a good living there," Ben hedged.

"That wasn't what I asked."

"Oh, once or twice last winter maybe when the weather stayed bad. You see, Guv'nor, in a bad spell we could shelter and when it eased up a bit nip out and make a few hauls. Or we could lay up in one of the fiords until the weather improved." He smiled at Job. "As if you didn't know, anyway."

Job nodded slowly. He knew as well as if he had taken a trawler up there as indeed he had years ago.

Ben gently pounded his knee with a clenched fist as he went on. "I could be fishing sixty miles away, like Sam was, and something could happen, or the weather could break down and if I ducked in shelter instead of dodging outside they could knock me off, like they threatened to do to Sam."

Job studied the man opposite him from beneath lowered eyelids. He made no comment.

Ben went on: "Look, Guv'nor. It's all very well people ashore saying 'don't start anything, don't provoke the Icelander into anything', but they're not up there." He paused a moment and grinned. "I don't mean you. It's all an open book to you, but I mean those ginks in Parliament and so on. From what Sam told me the Navy bloke gave him his exact position when the Bogey Man started chivvying him. It was nearly twelve miles off shore give or take a couple of cables. Sam could have been twenty miles off and it would have been his word against Sam's had it got to court. You know how much good that would have been, and about ten thousand quid would have gone down the drain."

"Maybe, but there are enough hotheads around without a Benson skipper starting anything. If I had my way I would say to any of my skippers: 'Fish within forty miles of Iceland and you're for it.' But I must conform to the trawler owners' decision. The Navy has been ordered to hold that box off Iceland and protect any skipper fishing there. If a right is established we must uphold it."

Job drummed on the top of his desk with his finger-tips for a few moments, then went on: "You know as well as I do that you can get all the fish you want miles away from Iceland, hundreds of miles. But . . ."

He left it in mid-air.

Ben went off at a tangent.

"It will take a flotilla of destroyers to hold it. One or two Navy ships won't do it. They can't. They could be at two points in the box arguing the toss with the Bogey Man and another Bogey could board a trawler the far end of the box. And you say we mustn't provoke anything." He grinned, a thin-lipped grin, and almost silkily he continued. "All right. I'll fish in the box and perhaps they'll try to board me."

"And if they do then you follow orders and enter harbour." Ben's eyebrows shot up.

"And make 'em a present of the best part of ten thousand quid by the time you count the fine. A skipper would starve to death at that rate."

"Did you ever know me not to stand behind a skipper when he was in the right?" Job said bleakly.

"No, but you'd starve to death, or nearly anyway. They could climb aboard me thirteen or fourteen miles out, swear that they had seen me inshore with a trawl down, and where would I go from there?"

At that moment Job made up his mind.

"So far as you are concerned it won't arise. You are coming to Germany with me on Friday to look over that new stern-trawling trawler I've bought." He rested both hands flat on the desk and spread his elbows in preparation to levering himself upright. "And I don't propose to use her anywhere in those waters. Now, let's look at the plans of her again."

Ben stood up with Job. "I don't know that I'm all that fond of the idea. It will mean breaking in a crew to handle her and——"

"You have time and enough to spare on that. I've been thinking. We might try her for a couple of trips in the close waters, say off Rockall or the Faroes. You won't have far to slip back if anything goes wrong."

Job unrolled the blue prints of the new trawler and spread them on the desk. He picked up a bound folder of closely typewritten sheets.

"The Germans have been using these ships for a couple of years. This is a translation of notes made by some of their skippers. By the time you've digested that lot you'll know as much as they do."

Ben held the thick folder in his hands as if to weigh it. His face twisted into a mixture of amusement and dismay.

"Well, blow me down. I never thought the day would come when I'd have to start going to school again to learn how to fish."

He ruffled through the pages until they made a whispering noise.

"Do you know, Sam isn't going to like this. I have an idea he thought he might get her. He got the workings all set in his mind."

Job looked at him from the corner of his eyes but made no audible comment. To himself he said: "And Sam isn't likely to go off half cock and cause trouble off Iceland. You might."

He spread the blue print on the desk, pinned the curve down with a book and leaned over it.

"Sam will have his chance. I'll be in the market for others. And I'm selling four of the stars to a Polish concern."

"Not *Morning Star?*"

"No."

"Nor *Lodestar?*"

"Not yet. But they'll go ultimately. You see, Ben, the time will come when shipping ice and stacking fish on it will be as out of date as the old sailing ketch trawler. In a couple of years trawlers will be combined trawlers and refrigerator ships. Your catch will be stowed and will arrive in the shops in the same condition as it was within an hour of being caught. You will, on that sort of ship, be able to stay out five or six weeks, fish off Greenland, or Nova Scotia. Those Grand Banks men have only scratched at the fish off there."

Ben rubbed his chin. "Charlie Bates isn't going to like that, either, nor 'Monty' Banks. They're sort of set in their ways."

Joe smiled thinly. "That's a minor problem. I remember when Charlie Bates thought that any trawler-owner sending his ships to Bear Island was mad. But he went. Now he thinks that is his own private backyard." He smoothed the blue print with the edge of his hand. "Incidentally, Charlie Bates is taking over *Morning Star,* so shift your junk out of it."

Ben leaned back and his eyebrows arched. "Charlie taking over *Morning Star?* What about his pet piece of scrap iron?"

"She's hardly that, Ben. But she's seen her best days. I've no doubt the Poles will make her pay her way for a few years to come."

Ben grinned. "Let me be around when you tell Charlie. Aw, shucks. Ah, never gits much fun."

"You won't be around. But I have a way with stubborn skippers," Job said artlessly.

Ben looked from the blue print to Job and back to the blue print. "Do you know, I believe you have."

Job dropped each word like a bit of ice dropping on a sheet of glass.

"Indeed I have."

For a few minutes they studied the blue print and referred to the folder on technical points.

The desk phone clicked and Eve's voice came faintly and hollowly from it.

"Skipper Bates is here, Uncle. Are you free?"

Ben said softly: "Here we go. Now, come out of your corners fighting, and let's have some blood around the ring."

Job said flatly: "Send him in, Eve."

Charlie Bates's greeting was typical.

"Hullo, Job. We did fair to middling without a lot of crowing about it. We didn't tell the world every time we got something in the cod end. But we got by." He turned to Ben who was leaning against the large chart. "And you owe me a fiver, young man."

"Toss you, double or quits."

"Do your gambling elsewhere. In the club if you want. This is a business office," Job said severely, although the twinkle in his eyes belied the severity. He liked to get his skippers wrangling good-humouredly. It gave him the feeling that he was still in touch, was still a trawler skipper who could hold his own in either fishing or in the cut-and-thrust of an argument.

Job picked up the thick folder and handed it to Ben. "Take that with you and look at it once or twice before the weekend," he said.

Ben grinned. "All right. But I was hoping to stay here to pick up some pearls of wisdom."

Job inclined his head towards the door and Ben lounged towards it.

"Nice ship, the *Morning Star*, Charlie. A real nice trawler."

Charlie Bates squinted at him for a moment. "Nuts. I could catch more fish in a rowboat than that floating boudoir."

"Sez you. But she's still a nice ship, Charlie."

Charlie wheezed ominously and Job said crisply: "Out."

When the door closed behind Ben Charlie Bates looked directly at Job.

"I thought it might have been *Lodestar* I was getting." Charlie Bates paused for a while. Then he went off at a tangent. "I know old Buller doesn't agree with me, but I think Sam is the better man. You think the same as Buller, do you?"

The old man's faded eyes came up almost with a jerk and bored into Job's.

"Not necessarily. Of the two Sam is a thinker, uses his head, Ben is a . . . a . . ." He hesitated for a moment and Charlie Bates provided the word.

"Ben is a basher."

"I wanted a different word, but that will do. Sooner or later Ben would get tangled up with the Icelandic protection people, and as like as not be in the wrong when he did it. There would come a time when, instead of appealing to the Navy for protection, like Sam did, he'd go hard over on his helm and all hell would break loose."

"Just like his Old Man. That would be Buller all the world over. I remember him once chasing a Frenchman around for the whole of one forenoon trying to stem him because the Frog had fouled his trawl."

Job chuckled. "And where were you when all that was happening?"

Charlie's asthmatic wheeze joined Job's chuckle.

"I was chasing Buller."

Job returned to business briskly.

"You've got a few days lay-off, Charlie. *Morning Star* is going in for a few details to be put right. About the middle of next week she'll be ready."

Charlie looked out of the window down over the dock. His eyes fastened on a red-rusted trawler lying snugly against the quay.

"When do the Russians take her over?" he asked.

"Poles, Charlie, not Russians."

"They're all the same to me. Frogs are Frogs, Scandawegians, Danes, Dutch, Germans, they're all square-heads, and all them others from the Baltic is Russians. When do they collect her?"

"They're putting her in dock here for an overhaul. About a fortnight, I should say."

Charlie turned his eyes from the window. "She's good enough now. There's nowt wrong with her."

"Maybe, but it's part of the contract." Job joined Charlie at the window and together they looked out over the dock. It was Job who broke the silence.

"It's been a long time, Charlie, since I had just the one broken-down old hansom cab and was in debt to my eyes. Then I got another one . . ."

Charlie picked it up. "And Buller Cleeve was skipper and I was Mate—and we made a go of it."

He turned from the window. "They was hard days, Job. Work like horses and play like donkeys."

"Earn it like horses and spend it like asses is what you're trying to remember, Charlie."

"Something like that. It's a young-man's game. Even with electric fires, and bathrooms and closed-in bridges, it's still a young-man's game. I reckon a few more trips and I'll join old Buller and sit and listen to 'em jabbering on the wireless."

"Nonsense, Charlie. They'll freeze you stiff and set you on Bear Island with a light in your hand like that Statue of Liberty outside the Hudson River."

"Maybe."

In the outer office Ben teased Eve. "If I rob the gas meter I'll have enough to buy you a dinner at the club tonight. Right? Seven o'clock. I'll pick you up."

Eve demurred, for no reason at all that she could articulate.

"I don't know. I've a lot to do."

"Wash your smalls tomorrow. All right? I'll make it seven-fifteen, then."

"But I'm going to Germany with Uncle on Friday and——"

"So am I. Hasn't he told you? Right. Seven-fifteen it is then. Be seeing you."

Eve felt a vague, undefined regret.

With the Norwegian fiords a vague shadow astern. Sam turned *Lodestar's* cleaving bow slicing diagonally across the North Sea. For the tenth time he looked astern at the creaming wake behind him. He blew down the voice-pipe to the engine room:

"What are we loitering for?" he rasped. "We're crawling along."

An indignant voice came back up the pipe.

"She's doing all of twelve. What do you think she is—the *Queen Mary*?"

"And with a two-and-a-half-knot tide under our stern. I could swim it faster."

Sam tried a little self-analysis to isolate his feeling of irritation without success. It became jumbled up and involved the death of Grimmy, the delay and through it all was a fine thread involving a pair of soft eyes, a rather deep throaty, gurgling laugh, the feel of soft lips and an indistinct figure standing in the dusk in a gun emplacement.

One more experienced than Sam might have hazarded an opinion that he was perilously near falling in love. And might have been right.

CHAPTER TEN

BULLER CLEEVE stirred restlessly in his chair. His gently moving but accurate fingers reached for his tobacco. He filled his pipe and completed the ceremony of tamping down the glowing pile in the bowl.

Without moving from that chair he had known, with pin-point accuracy, exactly what had taken place in the roadstead. Half a dozen trawlers had weighed their anchors and by skilful touches ahead or astern had just held themselves against the tide until the large blue flag had fluttered to the top of the flagstaff. Then the rat race had started with the little group of trawlers going hell for leather for the dock gates.

To a layman on the end of the jetty it would have looked almost inevitable that at least three of them would collide as they reached the gates. But Buller, interpreting the hoarse squawk of steam whistle, knew which trawler skipper had found something wanting in his nerve and had dropped to slow ahead, even going astern.

There had been an asthmatic hooom, three short blasts and Buller knew that *Hyacinth* was taking way off by going astern. Then had followed two shrill notes and another trawler was swinging away to port to eventually turn again into the end of the procession.

He knew that ultimately all would be orderly with perhaps an admonitory wag of a hand from the dockmaster as the winner slipped into the gates with a shade too much speed.

He waited until he heard the deep bass notes of a whistle which told him that *Morning Star* was swinging hard to port in the harbour and Buller visualized what was happening as if he had been on her bridge. Ben would keep her moving at slow ahead until she pointed for her berth. Round would come the stem until she was parallel with the quay wall with its watching audience of humpers standing near the pile of boxes and the casks of ice, their yellow oilskin aprons a touch of colour. Two or three feet of dirty grey water would be between the ship's side and the quay, lines would flick over, a touch astern on the engines. Then "stop", and *Morning Star* would be berthed and almost before Ben could climb down from the bridge the wicker baskets would be swinging aboard and down into the ice-and-fish-packed hold.

Morning Star had completed yet another trip.

Buller cleared his throat.

"Ben's home, Mother. Give him time to look in at the office and he'll be here. 'Bout an hour, I'd say."

The formula never altered.

Neither did her reply.

"Yes, dear. I'll have a nice pot of tea ready for you while he tells you all about the trip."

Buller had sometimes wondered, in the days when both his sons were new skippers, what would happen if their respective trawlers were in the van of the rat-race to the dock gates.

"Would Ben give way or would Sam?"

Not Ben, was Buller's verdict. Not Ben any more than Buller had given way in his day. But Sam had nerve.

It was Sam who had given him the answer.

"For the sake of a few minutes, Dad, risk damaging the trawler? It isn't worth it. If I'm on tide I get in with plenty of time to spare."

But Buller had still wondered.

He went on listening, detecting and tabulating all the noises of the port which to him made up a complicated but accurate picture in his mind. He isolated the strident sound of a lorry horn as it swung on to the fish-quay ready to take its quota of fish-boxes.

The dismal descending toot of the little shunting engine as it pushed railway fish-vans into the sidings at the rear of the quay; soon they would be part of an express train racing south and west with their loads of fish.

There was the harsh, blatant, steam whistle which Buller knew came from a Fleetwood trawler diverted while still at sea from her home port to Scoresby to meet a demand. That whistle always started with a powerful burst of sound which dwindled away as if there was not sufficient steam to maintain the first urgent demand.

The one which made him wrinkle his nose was the almost motor-car-like sound from a compressed-air siren on a Belgian diesel-engined trawler. It was no noise for a self-respecting ship to make, it sounded more like a foghorn.

It had taken a couple of weeks before Buller had been able to identify it. Sam's picture had eventually drawn it for him.

"They're flush-deck ships, Dad. Around two hundred tons, a little squat bridge with a stump of a funnel. They fish mostly off the south end of the Dogger. And they're painted up like a Dutch barge. One of 'em even has little curtains on the wheelhouse windows."

Buller's snort had showered glowing sparks from his pipe which Sam had laughingly extinguished with a wet forefinger.

"Just what I thought from the sound of her."

Charlie Bates's whistle always wrinkled his face into a smile. It started as a moan and continued in a descending plaintive note almost as if she were saying: "Look, I'm tired, just don't bother me, just let me get into my berth and you can have the rest of the world for yourself."

Finally came the concerto of whistles from the tail enders; those who had swung away from the first rat-race and were now belatedly telling the world that they were bent on getting in regardless of anybody else's stern.

Buller listened. One hoot for starboard, two for port, three going astern until eventually, after much whistling and engine telegraph, they finally managed to squeeze into a berth.

Then through the locks poured those which were outward bound, red rust from the previous trip hidden under new coats of paint. Jaunty little ships, bows cocked up arrogantly, steaming north to gamble, to gamble on weather, on finding fish to return in two or three weeks either jubilant, or with a story of hard times and the trip in debt.

And it was all there for sightless Buller, every move, every telegraph order, every heavy hammer-rap, or ripping sound of a riveting gun. The complete picture.

She stood by the kitchen door, wiping her hands on her apron. "Won't be long now, dear. The kettle's singing."

"Aye, Charlie Bates is in, too. He'll be up tonight."

Buller made his second pipeful last as long as he could until eventually he was drawing just hot ash. Sam had upset the timetable and Buller felt aggrieved.

Then he heard the click of the gate and a few seconds later Ben's tumultuous clamour in the small hall.

"Hiya, Dad. Where is she? Hiding away some place, for a bet."

Buller's face wrinkled into a smile.

"Just wetting the tea, lad. Fair trip?" He chuckled deeply. "Old Charlie came near to wiping your eye, didn't he?"

Ben met his mother in the doorway of the kitchen. "Good and strong, Mum. None of your pale stuff."

She twisted her tiny body away from him.

"Mind, mind. You'll have the teapot out of my hand in a moment."

Carefully she placed it down close to Buller's hand where he could find it, and put two substantial cups alongside.

"Now, tell me all about yourself? Was the weather bad? And poor Sam's man."

Ben watched his father locate the teapot and the cups and marvelled again, as he had a hundred times, at the uncanny accuracy with which the old man poured out two cups.

Once, and once only, had he offered to help. That was in the early days of his father's affliction. The angry snarl had made his eyes widen. It had been the young blind teacher who had tried to make it clear to him.

"Many little things, ordinary trifles to you, will have to be big achievements for your father from now onwards. To accept help in doing them would only emphasize his helplessness to him. He will burn himself, even scald himself slightly a few times but he will conquer them and will feel independent. Interfere, and I mean interfere, and you will spoil things."

Ben had only dimly grasped what she was saying.

"But I only wanted to help."

"It wouldn't be help. Don't do it."

Ben had posed the problem to Sam.

"Do you get it?" he had asked. "He's burning himself, burning holes in the furniture, and pouring tea over his fingers."

Sam had not answered for a few seconds. Then he had said: "Let him. He'll learn."

He watched his father touch the teapot with a thumbnail, then the cups, watched him tilt the teapot until the cups were filled to within half an inch of the top, then the milk, and finally the sugar.

Ben took up his cup and sat on the corner of the table.

Almost carelessly he said: "Old Job Benson has wished that new German trawler on to me. I'm going over to Germany with him this week-end."

Buller leaned back and pursed his lips.

"He couldn't have given it to a better man, Ben."

"I dunno. Sam was more keen on the idea than I was. I reckon I'll want a couple of short trips to get the hang of her before I really start working her. Those dumb oxen we ship for deckies now could tangle up a plain straight hand-line off the end of the pier."

"Get a good Second Hand and you'll be all right. Got anybody in mind?"

"I hadn't got as far round as that. I suppose Job would let me have Geegee or Lofty as bos'n."

Ben signified that he had emptied his cup by ostentatiously sucking at the dregs. He slid his cup along the table until it barely touched his father's hand and watched it being refilled with unerring accuracy.

"Not quite so much sugar this time, Dad. It's for me, not for Charlie Bates. Charlie is having *Morning Star,* by the way. His old rattle-trap is being sold to the Poles."

Buller shook his head slowly.

"That's Job all over. Always changing things. 'Progress', he calls it." Buller rested his elbow on the arm of his chair and prepared for retrospective reflection.

"He hasn't altered in all the years I've known him. When he started he had one old trawler. No sooner is he out of debt and me and Charlie earning a few pounds with her than he mortgages her to buy another one."

Buller shook his head once more.

"I can't see what's wrong with most of his trawlers now. Maybe Charlie's is a bit shaky, but you mark my words, Job will be selling more trawlers, and some of them only a few years old."

"I gathered that from what he told me this morning in the office. He has ideas about trawlers nearly a couple of thousand tons and fitted as refrigeration ships. You know, catch it, freeze it right away and stay at sea for weeks until you got about eight or nine thousand kit aboard."

Buller sat up. "And what are you going to do with your catch? Ship it home in a carrier? That's going back to the old days when I was a boy. We used to trawl in a fleet under an Admiral off the Dogger and shift it over to a carrier in our small boat, collect some grub while she went tearing off to Billingsgate. There's nowt new in that."

"It's not going to be that way, according to Job. He says that he'll send 'em over to Nova Scotia and off the Grand Banks where it's only been scratched and——"

Buller snorted.

"Grand Banks! Newfoundland! Nova Scotia! 'Monty' Banks tried that years back. Took him ten days to get there, and ten to get back. And what did he have when he got back? A hold full of cod which he could have caught off Rockall or the Faroes."

Ben sampled his tea thoughtfully.

"And he got that catch in four days' fishing. And don't forget, Dad, 'Monty' was fishing in strange waters. He just took a chance. Give us a couple of years to learn the waters and the bottom and we'd make history."

"You go to sea in trawlers to catch fish, not make history."

"And steam at eleven and half knots to do it, if your boiler doesn't salt up. And that's only a knot and a bit faster than the old hansom cab you took to sea for Job more'n forty years back, nearer fifty."

Buller's sightless eyes seemed to peer into the past. Deep in his mind he could see those days as clearly as if he were living them now.

"Aye, and six or seven hundred kit for a trip meant a few bob in the pocket. I remember my first thousand kit. Off the Faroes, it was. I took on coal at Aberdeen, loaded it on deck 'cos my bunkers were half full of ice, and me praying twenty-three hours a day that the good weather would hold otherwise that coal would have been over the side and me as helpless as a new-born babe."

Buller chuckled. "Old Job sweated blood until he got my telegram—no wireless in those days, we used to close the pilot cutter at Aberdeen and give 'em a fry of fish and pass a telegram. I got married on that thousand kit, my boy. And old Job was waiting on the pier-head dancing like a Dervish. The weather had been bad and only three trawlers made the tide. Got their price, top price in golden sovereigns, did those three trawlers."

He thumbed a new load into his pipe, started it glowing and waited until he had got it drawing in slow, measured strokes.

"A lot depended on that trip. There was your mother waiting to get married and Job waiting for the catch to put something down on another trawler. We got married, Job got his trawler and Charlie Bates, who had been Second Hand with me, got his bridge."

Ben chuckled.

"A half a gale off the Shetlands and you would have lost your coal, Mum would have escaped and Charlie Bates might still have been a Second Hand."

Buller's wife had stood in the background listening.

"He might have lost his coal, Ben, and Job might not have got his trawler. But we would have been married." She looked at the blind old ruin in the chair. "What your father didn't know was that I had got a bit put away in the toe of a stocking. We'd have got married all right."

"And me shipping away for the next two or three trips flogging the dead horse," Buller growled.

"It was a biggish toe in that stocking. It would have seen us through."

Ben slid his arm over his mother's shoulder.

"A born schemer, isn't she, Dad?" He smiled down at her. "Half the time we think we are having our own way when really it's she who is slipping one over on us."

"Sounds as if you're learning sense at last," Buller growled. He blew a thin stream of smoke towards the ceiling and lifted his head almost as if he could see the thinning smoke.

"How long are you going to stay in Germany?"

"Couple of weeks, I gather. Job is fixing for me to have a short trip in a similar sort of trawler. Look, feel that." He dropped the thick folder into father's lap. "That's all about them, translated from German. It would take me a week to read it. . . ."

"And six months to learn anything from it. Good fishermen those Germans. Very thorough. You'll get more from a couple of trips than you will from all this."

He lifted the folder and Ben took it from him.

"Bit of bad luck on Sam, wasn't it?"

"Bad luck on Sam getting tangled up with the Bogey Man," Buller growled. "They'll file his number and watch their chance. He'll never be able to put into anywhere in Iceland now."

"Never is a long time. It'll be settled sooner or later."

"Who by? Those fellers in the House of Commons? If they get to wrangling about it we'll end up allowing the Icelanders to put on their twelve-mile limit. And that'll be that."

"And by then we'll be fishing off Newfoundland and they can keep their limit."

"They'll never learn, deckies, will they? I've seen 'em gash themselves. I've swabbed 'em with iodine, bound 'em up and seen 'em hang on to their knives when they'd go sprawling. Never learn."

" 'Grimmy' won't anyway," Ben said softly. "Perhaps it's just as well it wasn't me. I'd have given the Bogey Man something to think about."

"Then your number would have gone on the file, and if one of her crew had been injured or killed you'd have been for it even when you got back here. You keep your stem away from 'em and let the Navy do its job."

"Listen to Saint Buller Cleeve talking," said Ben scornfully.

"I never risked my trawler in some damn' fool crashbang argument," Buller rasped. "It's all very well you talking about stemming somebody, but you could cut one of them wooden ships clean in half, and you couldn't talk your way out of that one, not in any court in the world."

Ben looked reflectively at the ceiling.

"I seem to remember Charlie Bates telling a story or two about you chasing some trawler or other breathing fire and blood because he had cut across your trawl. What would you have done had you bashed into him?"

Buller concealed a grin with a large hand.

"Chasing 'em and catching 'em were two different things. If we had got alongside him I might have nipped aboard and clouted him a bit, but mostly we slung lumps of coal at 'em. Anyway, I was young and daft then."

"And what do you think I am?"

"Young and daft. Now read some bits from that bundle of paper. Let me get it how they work those stern trawls."

"And before you start where did you put the fry of fish?" his mother asked.

Ben touched it with his toe and his mother disappeared into the kitchen with the little canvas bag of fish.

As she worked on preparing it she could hear the drone of Ben's voice as he read extracts from the papers with an occasional interruption from his father. She was struck, not for the first time, at the similarity in their voices. They sounded more like twin brothers. There was a far greater difference between Sam and Ben than there was between Ben and his father.

And as she allowed her thoughts to drift towards Sam her face softened into a gentle smile.

She would have liked a daughter. A daughter to whom she could have shown some tenderness, a girl who would have turned to her with all her problems, a girl she could have moulded into something near her heart's desire. With Ben, even from his earliest days, she found a barrier between them. When he would fall and hurt himself any attempt to help him would be met with flashing, burning eyes. Ben would be convulsed with tiny rage and would fight his way to his feet, stand swaying unsteadily then the rage would disappear and his face would light up with triumph.

Sam had been softer. He would come to her for his little hurts to be mended, but only if they were alone. From his earliest days Ben had modelled himself on his father, there had been the same hunched-up shoulders, the same arrogant poise of the head, Buller in replica. He was still doing it, perhaps unconsciously.

Possibly she was the only person in the world who, in her simple way, had uncovered the fact that while Ben did things—and said things—without being aware or caring of the ultimate result, Sam introduced an element of rivalry into what he did. He was younger than Ben, he lacked Ben's bull-like build, but anything Ben did, Sam, too, did likewise, not even content to equal it. If it was humanly possible he would better it.

A girl, a daughter, would have been so different.

CHAPTER ELEVEN

CHARLIE BATES preserved an impeccable timetable. The old clock was beginning its first rumbling warning that it was about to audibly mark the passing of time when Charlie knocked at the door.

Buller could hear his brief greeting to Mrs Cleeve in the little hall and his sightless eyes warmed.

"'Ullo, Old 'Un," wheezed Charlie.

"Sit down and help yourself to a cup," Buller said dourly. "You youngsters always want to be wandering around a room instead of sitting down."

As they were both hovering on the three-score-years-and-ten, with not more than eight or nine months between them, it was an opening gambit which neither was afraid to follow.

"Anything on that noise box tonight?" Charlie asked. "I've lost the run of old Bill Fraser this last few days. He's a deep one is Scottie."

"Haven't heard him myself for a day or two," Buller answered. His fingers played delicately with the knobs on the set as the clock drummed out its measured strokes. "I'll tell you where he isn't. And that's fooling around in that damn' box they've measured up off Iceland."

Buller appeared to be staring at something over Charlie's shoulder.

"Were you there?" he continued, after a few moments' pause.

"Talk sense, man. When did I have to have anybody to tell me where to fish. I was about twenty miles from Sam and around thirty to forty from Ben." He drew heavily on his pipe. "In a way I was glad it was Sam and not Ben. That big boy of yours would have started something."

"Maybe."

"You know damn' well he would have. And I can put my hand on somebody who would have done just the same if he had been there."

Buller stirred in his chair.

"And we both know that would have been daft. I was telling Ben that a while back. Sam did the right thing."

"Anyway, Ben is going to be away from trouble for quite a while. Did he tell you that Job is giving him the new trawler he's bought in Germany?"

"He did. And Job couldn't have picked a better man."

"I know one as good."

"Sam?"

"Yes."

Buller moved the knobs gently through a cacophony of appearing and disappearing sound. Voices came in, were held for a second or two then merged into the background.

Buller held on to a voice for a while and Charlie cocked an ear to absorb what it was saying.

"Getting some bad weather up there, eh?"

"Aye. It's blowing a bit."

"And there'll be no ducking into a fiord for a bit of shelter until it eases up."

"When do you figure Sam will make it?"

"Friday morning tide, with luck."

"Was that Grimmy boy married?"

"He was, and had two kids."

"Um, um. Job will look after 'em. He always has done."

"They won't learn sense, will they, Charlie? How many times have you told 'em, 'If you slip, drop your knife'?"

"Hundreds, p'raps thousands, but it's like talking to a brick wall."

With a clatter of feet down the stairs Ben burst in on them.

"Hullo, Charlie. Told Dad you're going to have a real trawler at last?"

Charlie growled.

"I could give you twenty kit start and a beating with me in an old open-bow wreck, and don't you forget it, young fella-me-lad." Charlie peered at Ben. "You going to a wedding or something? And smell what he's got on his hair, Buller. What is it? Cod-liver oil?"

"I'm taking a lady out to dinner." Ben smiled. "Up to the club."

"If I hadn't made a shrewd guess who it was I would say that anybody that goes out with you is no lady. But in this case I hope she'll learn better. She seems to have her head screwed on the right way."

Ben rested his hand on his father's shoulder. "Anything doing on the old chatterbox, Dad?"

"Nothing much. There's a bit of a blow on up there."

"Anything from Sam?"

"Not a squeak. He's on his way so we won't until Friday morning. I figure he should make the tide."

"I hope he does. I'd like to have a chinwag with him before I go to Germany. Hey, Charlie. Like to see the homework Job has set me?"

He tossed the heavy folder over to Charlie who caught it clumsily.

"How to catch fish in twenty-five easy lessons." Ben grinned. "It's all translated from the German."

"The only way to learn how to catch fish is to go to sea and do it," Charlie retorted, weighing the folder in his hands. "The old way is good enough for me. Why Job wants this new-fangled trawler I can't for the life of me understand."

"You should hear Job on the topic of a trawler fitted for refrigeration and catching eight or ten thousand off the Grand Banks."

"I've heard him. He's had that bee in his bonnet for some time. Didn't he send 'Monty' Banks out there on a gamble?"

"He did. And 'Monty' filled up in four or five days' fishing. Cod ends filled to burst every haul."

"With nearly a three weeks' steaming time to get there and back."

"Job figures opening up a market in Canada and America." Ben rubbed his chin reflectively. "I'd like to see something of America."

"You youngsters. Always chasing something out of sight. The grass is greener in the next field."

Ben surveyed his reflection in a small mirror over the mantelpiece and stroked an errant strand or two back into place. "I wouldn't have to stretch out far to touch a couple of men who tried that next field once or twice. Anyway, I'm off."

They heard the door slam and for a few moments neither of the two old men spoke.

Charlie broke the silence.

"He's right, too, damn him. Me and you was always chasing the greener grass. First the Faroes, then Iceland. Then we went up to Bear Island."

Buller chuckled deeply.

"And it was greener, too. Wasn't it?"

Charlie performed the delicate ceremony of getting his pipe going and watched Buller doing the same. Until their pipes were satisfactorily alight neither of them spoke.

"It's in the cupboard, same place, Charlie."

Charlie Bates reached into the cupboard and extracted a bottle more than half full of a glowing amber liquid.

"Can we have some water, Ma?" Buller called.

Mrs Cleeve, completing her tasks in the kitchen, filled a small jug and placed it close to Charlie Bates's elbow. It was the only thing Buller would allow having done for him and only three people were allowed to do it; his two sons and Charlie Bates.

"When," said Charlie, carefully measuring out a generous portion. "When," he said again as the water followed. "She's about half and half, Buller, by your right elbow."

Buller's finger-tip moved slowly until it touched the glass.

Charlie's glass was raised to eye level and uncannily, as if he could see, Buller raised his.

"A couple of nice boys, Buller. So long as Ben is around you'll always be going to sea. He's the dead spit of you."

Mrs Cleeve settled a wicker basket in her lap and sorted out some socks.

"Sam's a nice boy, too," she said softly.

Charlie allowed a thin spiral of smoke to climb from his lips towards the ceiling.

"They're both good lads," Charlie repeated. "The best in the port. After all, didn't I have something to do with shaping 'em?"

"A whole lot," Buller said. "Especially in the last few years."

Mrs Cleeve found a sock which required extensive repairs.

"I just don't know what Ben does to his socks," she said. "There's more hole than there is sock." She pushed her fingers through a gaping hole.

"Use 'em for cod ends, probably," Charlie chuckled.

Out of nothing Mrs Cleeve said: "She's a nice girl, too."

Charlie looked shrewdly at her. His mind travelled swiftly over their assessment of Ben and Sam, over the state of Ben's socks to her oblique and brief mention of a nice girl. Slowly his face wrinkled into a smile.

"Ever since Job brought that niece of his into the office you can't move for young skippers cluttering up the place. I wouldn't be surprised if one or two of them didn't take a shine to her and start hanging up their hats there."

He stared blandly at Mrs Cleeve who was busy nipping off a piece of wool with her teeth.

"I wouldn't be surprised," she said critically, inspecting another sock. She went off at another oblique angle. "I wonder why Job gave the new trawler to Ben. He didn't sound as if he was very pleased about it."

"Because he's the best man for the job," Buller rasped. "Far and away the best man."

"Maybe," Charlie mused. "Anyway, only one of them could have her, until the next one comes along," He peered into the bowl of his pipe, blew sharply down the stem and loaded it once again. Then he finished the last drop in his glass and reached for the bottle. "By your elbow, Buller, 'bout half and half. By the time Job has finished with his fancy schemes it will be a job to find a Benson skipper fishing the old way."

Buller snorted and attacked his drink. "Then he'll want to start trawling with aeroplanes or something new-fangled. They even have to have some fancy asdic to help 'em to find fish these days. I could find 'em without any of that business."

"So could I," Charlie said softly. "I can now, but I use it and it cuts down the haul on the gamble."

Buller achieved another masterly snort.

Ben looked at his watch as he pushed open the gate of the Benson home. It said one minute to seven. Ben grinned as he pressed the bell-push.

"Come on in," Job growled. "So you're the reason she's been titivating herself since about half past six." He led the way into the lounge. "It's young Ben, Ma. Now we know why Eve has been rampaging all over the house for the past hour."

Mrs Benson smiled up at Ben. "Don't take any notice of him. She'll be down in a moment. Is there a dance on at the club tonight?"

"No, we'll just have some dinner, p'raps do a bit of hoofing, then we might take a run down to the Head."

"And watch the moon over the sea," Job sneered. "As if you don't see enough of it. Have you looked through that folder yet?"

"A few glances. I read bits of it to Dad."

"I'll wager there were some comments made."

"You'd win. There were. I still think Sam would be the better man for her. And I mean that."

"He'll have his chance and before long. She's only the first."

The door opened and Eve came in. Ben looked at her and his grin of greeting softened into a smile. Momentarily she made him catch his breath in a slight hiss.

Only Eve detected it and somehow she felt pleased: she felt a sense of mild triumph.

"I wasn't certain whether you said 'seven' or 'seven-fifteen'. I played for safety and came at seven."

"I believe I said nothing, except perhaps maybe."

"And that's why you are dressed up to kill," Ben grinned.

He helped Eve on with her coat and allowed his hands to linger for just a few seconds longer than was necessary as he adjusted it over her shoulders. Eve felt a curious electrifying tingle as he did so and was momentarily furious with herself for permitting it.

"Don't be late, will you, darling?" her aunt said.

"What do you call late?" Ben smiled. "Around two o'clock or thereabouts?"

"You arrive here at two o'clock and you'll find the door bolted and barred and your things on the doorstep," Job growled, but belied it with a twinkle. "You've got a key, haven't you?"

"Yes, Uncle. But it will be long before two o'clock, I promise you."

As Ben closed the gate behind them he said: "I could have got a taxi, but it's such a fine night I thought you would prefer to walk. Do you?"

"Much prefer it. Can we go along past the bastions?"

"Sure."

He found it necessary to cup his hand under her elbow as they descended the stone steps to the old gun emplacements.

Once again Eve felt the faint tremor which had disturbed her.

She stopped by an empty emplacement and looked down over the flood-lit harbour.

"This always fascinates me. I come here quite often in the evening and just stand here to look at it. I think it is wonderful."

"Smoke?" Ben offered her his cigarette-case.

"No, thanks, not here. But you smoke, please."

"What is there to see except trawlers and quays?"

"But doesn't it grip you when you look down at it and think of all that it means?"

"I can't say it does. To me it is a bunch of trawlers lying alongside the quay and tomorrow some of them will be plugging north bent on making a trip pay."

"Strictly practical, aren't you?"

"So far as trawlers are concerned. I've been running *Morning Star*. She's a good trawler, but she's just a trawler to me. I could take *Sirius*, or *Lodestar* or *Orion* out next trip and she would be just a machine, designed to catch fish, and I would catch fish with her."

"If you have a good crew."

He half turned to face her and she could see the gleam of his teeth as he smiled.

"Any crew I have is good, otherwise I don't have them. Do you know, you ought to get Sam talking about trawlers being something beside machines. He's got some cockeyed ideas that some ships are bad from the day their keel is laid until they go to sea. And some, by the same token, are good."

"Do you mean that they have a personality, a character, or something like that?"

"Yes, something like that. Shall we walk along, or do you want to stand here and absorb some more romance?"

"You're making fun of me."

"I'm not. But if you catch cold Job and Mrs Benson will take it out of me, and you'll be confined to bed instead of going to Germany on Friday. See?"

As they walked he found it necessary to take her arm again.

"Sam can build you up a good case for his argument. See that trawler right up in the corner?" He flicked the glowing end of his cigarette out into the darkness and pointed to a trawler which seemed to lie apart, forlorn. "Now, she's a well-built trawler, about three or four years old, but she's run into more bad luck in those three or four years than all Job Benson's trawlers put together. She's broken two skippers, she's always having accidents and it's a job to get her a crew or a skipper. But you can't convince me that it is anything but just bad luck, which will end sometime. Sam thinks different. He says she was born bad and will stay bad."

"What's the name of her?"

"*Carpathia*. And that isn't the name she was launched with. As a matter of fact, Job meant to add her to his fleet. He went aboard her when she was up for sale after a collision. The price was right, she is well built, belonged to Fleetwood then. Job went aboard her and in ten minutes said 'No'. Flat, just like that. Ask him why and I'll bet you a pound he won't tell you why."

"Had Uncle bought her would you have taken her out?"

"For a trip or two, yes. Just to show that it was bad luck and no more. Sam said he wouldn't take her beyond the Head for a thousand pounds. Now she belongs to a couple of brothers who have two other trawlers and she spends half her time in harbour either being repaired or trying to get a crew."

"Then she is a challenge, or as you would call it—a gamble?"

Ben's grip on her arm tightened. "I don't gamble on trawling, only with a side bet with Sam or Charlie. To me she is just a machine which would have to run properly. And she would, believe you me."

"Somehow, I do believe you."

"Go on believing it. Anything I want to do, I do. Anything I want, I get."

His voice dropped down into a deep bass and Eve found the tremor hard to control. It even showed in her voice.

"One day . . ." she started. Then she paused, fought to contain the tremor, then went on. "One day you will lose and . . . and . . ." She allowed the sentence to trail off.

"And it will be good for my soul. Is that what you were going to say?"

"Something like that."

They walked along in silence for a few moments, a silence which Eve broke.

"You are very much like your father, in speech and in appearance, aren't you?"

"So folk say."

"I went to your home one night to hear all the trawlers talking. It was fascinating. It was just as if you and your brother were talking in the room to us."

"It gives the old man something to do. He never misses a night. It is just as well for us that he can't answer."

"Who is the blonde in Iceland?"

Ben tilted his hat over his eyes and rubbed his head in puzzlement.

"Blonde? You've gone right over my head."

"Oh, I heard you teasing your brother Sam about him not being able to see his blonde friend now he was in trouble with the Icelandic people. And I wondered . . ."

Ben roared with laughter. "Oh, that. It was just a leg pull. Anyway, they are all blonde in Iceland. I wish I had known you were listening. I would have ribbed him some more. Sam takes easily to ribbing."

"You are so different, you two brothers, different in appearance, different attitudes, yet in many ways you are alive. . . ."

"Well, we're not twins, you know."

Eve gained another sidelight on Ben's severely practical outlook when he handed her the menu at the club. They both chose soup, then Eve settled for duck, orange sauce and green peas with new potatoes.

Ben ran his forefinger down the list and ordered plaice, chips and peas.

"Red or white wine, or will you settle for a sherry?" Ben asked.

"Red wine, I think. I would have thought that having been catching fish for a couple of weeks or so that you would have been pleased to select something else."

Ben caught the waiter's eye and ordered a bottle of wine.

"Why should I be fed up with fish? Does the farmer who breeds bullocks swear off steaks, or off potatoes just because he grows them?"

"I asked for that one, didn't I?"

"No. But it makes my point, that to me a trawler is a machine which helps me to earn a living, just like our farmer's tractor. No more, no less." He grinned at her and she found his grin both stimulating and disturbing.

Ben pursued his point. "Even you or Sam would be hard pressed to give a tractor a personality, good or bad, because it does a good full day's work, or else runs over somebody's toes, or runs a big end."

"Yet I know people who endow, is that the right word, I wonder? Endow will do, who endow motor cars with . . . shall we say personality. I used to own a little runabout car, it was pretty ancient. It was full of personality. Sometimes it was stubborn and just wouldn't go properly. Another time it would run like a sewing machine. Then it was a joy to be out in it."

"Dirty plugs or grit in the petrol," Ben said scornfully.

"You don't own a car?"

"Not now. I have done. You know, big flashy American cars. I like 'em. But what's the point in me owning a car. Seventy-five per cent of my time I'm at sea. When I want one I either hire one or borrow one. I've borrowed one for tonight. I thought we might take a run into the country later on."

He finished the sentence on an over-casual note.

Ben suddenly dropped his eyes to hers and once again Eve felt the tingle of the tremor.

"We'll settle that later," she said softly.

"Just as you wish," Ben said carelessly. "It's up to you."

Later. "Black or white coffee?" The club waiter hovered over her shoulder, cream jug and coffee jug poised ready.

"Black, please."

"And a brandy?"

Eve pondered for a moment.

"I think I will."

Ben relaxed back in his chair, opened his cigarette-case and offered her one.

She leaned forward to take a light from his lighter and was disturbed to find that the cigarette in her lips trembled slightly. Even when she tried to steady it with her fingers it still trembled.

"You're drunk," Ben said solemnly. "Plastered to the gills. That's what comes of going on the skite with men from fishing boats. Before we know it you'll be doing a 'Knees up, Mother Brown' on the table and trying to kick the chandelier."

Eve gurgled. "Will you catch me if I fall?"

"Not on your life. You're a big girl now. Do your own falling." He leaned forward slightly and looked down at her crossed legs. They were slim, nylon-clad. "Nice knees, too." Ben looked artlessly around the room as Eve quickly twisted her legs out of view under the table.

For no reason that she could isolate she badly wanted to get the topic away from anything physical.

Ben completed his quick survey of the room and looked at her. It was a level, steady gaze which held her despite her efforts to break away from it.

She licked her lips delicately, then with finger and thumb appeared to capture an errant shred of tobacco.

"There was nothing there," Ben said. "Every woman does that when she has been momentarily knocked off her balance. Is the chandelier too high for you?"

Once more her tongue momentarily moved over her top lip and her fingers strayed up towards her mouth.

"Still nothing there," Ben said.

Eve breathed in deeply, held her breath for a few seconds and slowly exhaled.

She took the offensive.

"You ask me out to dinner, then spend all your time teasing me and trying to make me feel uncomfortable. Why?"

She expected a contrite Ben to dissolve into apologies. Instead he grinned at her.

"I take the first round on points, do I?"

"If you choose to see it as a contest."

Ben stubbed his cigarette out and turned his head to look through the wide double doors of the dining room to the dance floor beyond.

"That's the best dance floor in the north of England," he said. "We'll have to make do with a radiogram. But it's a good one and we have all the latest and best records."

"Is that an invitation to dance?"

"What else?"

Eve made a little moue.

"It would make me feel as if we were doing an exhibition. Just we two on that floor."

Ben stood up.

"Twenty seconds after we hit the deck half a dozen other couples will be dancing. You'll see. The thundering herd just wants a leader."

Eve came perilously near a giggle as she stood up.

"I'm no world beater and . . ." She paused and grinned wickedly as she looked at Ben. "Thundering herd might be the right phrase."

Together they walked towards the radiogram where Ben selected a waltz played by a famous orchestra whose music was full of haunting, descending violin passages.

As the music pulsed out Ben put his arm round her.

"Stand by, chandelier," he said softly.

Eve expected to be moved around the floor vigorously, almost explosively. Instead she could scarcely feel the pressure of his arm round her. She seemed to float away on a wave of sound. They circled the room alone for one circuit then two or three other couples took the floor.

"You were right," Eve whispered.

"Ssh," Ben said softly. And they danced the rest in silence.

When the record finished Ben stepped away from her and looked down at her.

"Apart from three crushed toes and a skinned shin you don't dance at all badly," he grinned. He dropped his voice until it was a low, deep, vibrating bass. "That was wonderful, Eve. Again?"

She nodded. Foxtrots, quicksteps and more waltzes followed in quick succession until Eve, her eyes sparkling and her lips slightly parted, said: "I must sit down or I will float out of the window."

As they resumed their seats Ben said: "That floor and the ballroom came out of a liner complete. When she was broken up the club bought it lock, stock and barrel. Heaven knows how many millionaires and their women have danced on it crossing the Atlantic."

Eve leaned back and let her arms hang down at the sides of her chair.

"None of them could have enjoyed it more than I did."

Ben clicked his fingers. "I know just the thing for this mood." He held a finger up to attract the attention of the club waiter. He took the wine list, scrutinized it for a few seconds, then jabbed with his finger.

"That. And mind it is iced."

Eve sat back barely taking in what Ben was doing. Her chin was tilted so that her neck rose up from her frock in a long, slim white column. Ben breathed in deeply and it came out almost as explosively as if he were blowing a flame out.

Expertly the waiter polished two wide shallow glasses and placed them down, then took a bottle of champagne from an ice-bucket and removed the cork with a loud "plop".

Eve sat up.

"Good gracious. You will have me drunk. I don't know that I . . ."

Ben held up a hand, sipped the champagne and nodded to the waiter.

"Never on your life, not on this. Anyway, if you like I'll drink two to your one. It's just the thing for the mood and the music. If you feel slightly high we'll hit the deck again."

Eve shook her head.

"I can't explain it, but I don't want to dance any more tonight. I feel it would spoil it. Do you mind?"

"Not a bit. I know what you mean."

Eve moved her chair so that she was facing the window. She leaned forward to look out.

"When we were dancing I wondered about your sense of rhythm and balance. I . . . I . . ."

Ben's lips twisted into a grin.

"What did you expect? That I would stomp on the floor and slap my hands. Balance? Try a trawler deck in hard weather and without a sense of balance you'd soon break your neck. Rhythm? Well, you just have it or not."

Eve spent the next few minutes looking around the room and into the ballroom where by now a dozen couples were dancing smoothly.

Ben shifted his chair so that he was sitting alongside her.

"The past few weeks have altered quite a lot of your ideas, haven't they?" he asked.

"They have. Especially about . . . about fishing boats and fishermen." Her nose wrinkled up as she smiled.

"Schoolmarms aren't what I expected, either," Ben chuckled.

"I never was a schoolmarm."

Ben offered his cigarette-case and she shook her head. Carefully he applied a match to his, examined the bottle and partly filled their glasses.

"Like another?"

"Please no. My head is swimming slightly now." Eve gazed at the moon riding high, pale gold, in the sky.

"Isn't it wonderful? The moon I mean."

Ben looked at it briefly. "I suppose it is. To me it just means good visibility.

"Moon, lunar. A period in which people do mad things. Lunatic."

"Yes, ma'am," Ben grinned. "Look, would you like to see it over the sea, the open sea, and not just over the docks?"

Deep down, Eve wanted to say "No".

"I think I would," she said softly.

"Good, let's go," Ben said briskly. "I'll get the car keys from the bar. It's Gus Wolmer's car, but when he's at sea we borrow it."

As Eve settled in the seat alongside him Ben studied the array of shining knobs and switches.

"Gus has a new car every year. I never know what will happen when I pull all these knobs. Music, gin or eggs-and-bacon."

Despite his gloomy comment he drove swiftly but expertly until they stopped at the top of a cliff. The by-road to the top of the cliff ended in a short "T" section. Behind the cross-road close-cropped grassland ran back in a rolling slope to a fringe of bushes.

"If you want to know the name of this bit, it's called Lovers' Leap," Ben said. "Seventy-five per cent of the courting done in Scoresby is done around here." He waved an arm expansively. "And heartbroken lovers are supposed to jump off here to the rocks below."

He stepped near to the edge.

"It's around two hundred feet or more. Take a look."

Eve crept forward, clutched his arm and peered down to where the sea was rolling to the cliff bottom and breaking into yellow-tinged foam over the rocks.

"It makes my head swim. Come back from the edge, please. You might slip."

Ben chuckled.

"Sam and I have climbed down and up it after seagulls' eggs when we were youngsters. It's no spot for a weak head, I admit."

Eve turned from him and walked slowly to the top of the rolling grass verge. She stood with her head up, arms stretched out from her sides and let the light breeze ruffle her hair.

Ben followed her and stood looking at her.

Eve looked at the almost unbroken path of gold which ran from the horizon until it disappeared into the cliff bottom.

"Wonderful," she breathed. "That moon gives me a lump in the throat it is so beautiful."

Ben followed the line of her neck from the chin until it disappeared and merged into the curve of her bosom.

"A moon for madness. Lunar, lunatic, I think you said."

Slowly she turned towards him. Almost imperceptibly she swayed.

Ben put his arm round her and pulled her close to him. He tilted her face with his free hand and slowly dropped his head until his lips were only an inch or two from hers.

He could feel her tremble as he kissed her. His arm tightened round her and he felt her return the pressure of his body.

Suddenly he picked her up and strode over the grass to the fringe of bushes.

"No . . . no, Ben, please." It came in a gasp.

Ben lay beside her. He grasped her hair and bent her head back. As he kissed her again one inarticulate sound escaped from her.

"A night for madness, moon madness," he said thickly.

Ben rolled over to a sitting position then climbed to his feet and walked towards the edge of the cliff.

Eve brought her outstretched arms to her side and found that in her hands she was clutching handfuls of grass and dried leaves. Slowly she opened her fingers and let the debris fall.

She turned on her face and laid her cheeks on the cool grass. Ben returned and sat beside her.

"Cigarette?" he said softly.

She shook her head.

Ben leaned over her.

"You're not crying, are you?"

Suddenly she sat up, resting her weight on her two hands beside her. Her chin was lifted.

"It's the . . . the . . . conventional thing to do . . . on these occasions, isn't it."

Ben stroked her hair.

"Shall I say I'm sorry?" he said in a whisper.

She turned and looked directly at him.

"Are you?"

Ben kissed her gently.

"No."

He shot his glowing cigarette over the cliff in a red arc.

"It isn't the end of the world, is it?"

"P'raps not." She stood up. "I want to go, please."

As he stood up beside her he put his arm round her shoulders.

"Don't, please. Don't touch me."

Ben drove swiftly until they were outside Job's house.

"Don't come in, please."

"All right, but won't your aunt and uncle think it odd."

"Don't come in, please."

"As you wish. I'll see you tomorrow?"

"If you come to the office you are bound to see me."

Ben found her detached attitude slightly irritating. "Look, Eve . . ." He moved closely to her and she retreated.

She rummaged in her small handbag and produced her key. She opened the door and stood with it half-opened.

"Good night, Ben."

Again he tried to get close to her and she put the half-open door between them.

"Good night, Ben," she repeated flatly.

"Very well." Suddenly he smiled until his teeth gleamed.

"You'd better get used to me, Eve. We'll be seeing a lot of one another in Germany. Two whole weeks."

Eve shut the door in his face.

Her aunt had gone to bed. Job sat reading some papers.

"Oh, you're home," he said, looking at her over his glasses. "Have a good time?"

"Yes, thanks, dinner at the club and some dancing. And some champagne."

Job snorted.

"Champagne. I've seen the time when skippers would be glad to have two pints of beer."

"I've a little headache, Uncle. I think I'll go to bed."

She kissed him softly on the cheek and went up to her bedroom. Slowly she undressed and donned a filmy nightgown. For a few moments she stood studying herself in the long glass. Somehow the events of the night seemed so unreal, part of a dream.

She climbed into bed, switched off the light and lay on her back.

Then she rolled over face down. And did the conventional thing.

She cried until sleep came.

CHAPTER TWELVE

THE moon laid a wide bar of gold from the horizon almost unbroken until it reached the widening "V" as the waters parted from *Lodestar*'s bows.

It was like a gigantic snake held by the head and wriggling slowly as the slight, oily swell lifted it. Beneath his feet Sam could feel the vibrations as the triple expansion engines thudded around at a hundred and twenty revolutions a minute.

Lofty, leaning against the open side-window of the bridge, turned his head.

"The old Chief is bumping her along, Sam. With the tide under us we're doing better than thirteen."

Sam pressed his chest against the front of the wheelhouse as if he would add extra speed by the pressure.

"I think I'll get a mug of tea," Lofty said, heaving himself upright. He paused by the open door for a moment.

"This is the sort of night people pay good money for, just to go to sea. You know, a shilling spew around the lightship, and the girls kidding the blokes that nobody has ever cuddled 'em before. D'you know, there are folk who do daft things when the moon is full like this. Real daft things."

Sam turned coldly towards him.

"You don't want a moon for that. Any time suits you to do daft things."

Lofty clattered away down the bridge ladders and in a few minutes returned with two mugs of strong tea. He placed one at Sam's elbow and nursed the other between his cupped hands.

He stared down the moon's path for a few minutes, then turned to Sam.

"We'll make it tomorrow morning's tide with a bit of luck." He took a generous and noisy mouthful of tea from the mug. "I can feel the first pint going down now."

Without moving his head Sam swivelled his eyes towards Lofty.

"And that's what it will be until we sail again. Pints, pints and a couple of fights thrown in. It's time you got married and settled down. Had somebody to grab your pay when you land and begin to look after you."

Lofty snorted.

"I'm not that daft! I see 'em doing it. Work like horses for three weeks and then some dame is waiting outside the office suffering from the grabskies. Some of the blokes are lucky if they end up with a quid to spare for a drink. I'm not that daft."

"There's more to being married than that."

"I know it. A string of kids all wanting boots and clothes and half the house on the never-never. I've got a landlady where I lodges who looks after me. And cheap, too. If I want a night on the skite with the boys she doesn't screech about it when I get home. And if I want a night out with a judy, still no screeching. She gets my things cleaned for me ready for when I sail. What do I want getting married? I've got it all."

Noisily, more of the tea disappeared. Lofty propped his elbow on the window-sill and prepared his next broadside.

"Come to that, why aren't you married?"

Sam clicked his lips.

Lofty pressed his advantage.

"Why don't you try a plateful of what you're feeding me?"

Sam turned on him.

"One day I'm going to ship a bos'n who can do something else besides chatter all the time. It'll be a change."

Lofty grinned. "You got one who can tie a cod end, anyway." The grin developed into a chuckle. "Me and Geegee had quite a shindig over that. I walks into the Chain Locker and there was Geegee all lined up and four pints ahead of me. I ties a knot in my handkerchief and drops it on the bar. 'There's a knot what'll hold, come hell or fine weather,' I says. Geegee didn't wait for any more. He clears the bar with one arm and makes a swing at me with the other." Lofty threw back his head and laughed out loud.

"We nearly wrecked the joint, then me and Geegee grabs a taxi and does the rounds." He became serious for a moment. ' That new landlord of the Chain Locker wants to watch his step. Do you know what he did? The bloody fool sent for the police." Lofty repeated it in a louder tone as if he was deprecating sacrilege. "Blew a whistle and sent for the cops. Real interfering, he was."

"The police should have locked you up for disturbing the peace."

"We didn't disturb no peace. We bust a few glasses, that was all. And the cops, they hides their helmets behind their backs and grabs a front-row place to see the scrap."

Lofty drained the last of the tea.

"Maybe if Morning Star hasn't sailed me and Geegee can have another night out. I owe him a quid, anyway."

Sam suddenly peered ahead, lifted his binoculars from a box and studied the dark bulk of a ship approaching. Her masthead light and port light shone brightly despite the moonlit flooded night. As she drew abeam Lofty glanced carelessly at her.

"Bayleaf or Oakleaf," he said, dogmatically. "Nice little trawlers. Short trip up to the Faroes, five or six days' fishing and back home inside the two weeks."

He had identified a ship which to a landsman would be just a shapeless dark bulk passing a mile away. As she slid into the path of the moon and was clearly cut against the yellow, Lofty said: "Bayleaf. She's the one with the stumpy derrick. Nice boy, the skipper. Took Carpathia out for his first trip as skipper and did a bit better than break even. It was enough. The 'Trees' offered him a job and now he's made."

Sam pointed a moral.

"And three years ago he was a deckhand. He didn't waste his time ashore."

Lofty stood upright.

"Cor. If we're going to have any more sermons tell 'em to the seagulls. I'm going to get my nut down. I'll give the Mate a call."

Sam had the bridge to himself and apart from an occasional glance at the compass to see that the deckhand wasn't wandering he gave his thoughts full rein.

And they were mainly around a pair of slumbrous eyes and a smile which made a nose wrinkle slightly. Which Sam found disturbing.

Sam allowed his thoughts to wander. The new German trawler Job was ordering. There would be problems, trials and errors, but he felt that it was a challenge. He recalled as much as he could the layout of the trawler as he remembered it from the drawings Job had shown him. He even visualized one or two alterations from the system tried by the Germans.

She would be quite a trawler to take to sea.

Then he fell to thinking about Grimmy. Was there something he could have done immediately to give him a chance of living? The young naval doctor had seemed so deft, ignoring Grimmy's groans as he explored the wound with expert fingers where he had blundered along with clumsy hands.

Other trains of thought travelled through his mind but almost inevitably he came back to the smiling eyes and the wrinkling nose.

Perhaps she had a man friend down in Sussex. He had never raised the point. After all, apart from a train journey and a lunch, and short conversations in the office, there had been nothing between them.

Sam heard the door rattle behind him and the Mate arrived for his four-hour watch on the bridge.

He listened morosely as Sam gave him short instructions, courses to steer and a time to give him a call.

As Sam talked, the Mate rolled a cigarette of a coarse rank tobacco, struck a match and lit it.

Sam wrinkled his nose in distaste.

"Why do you smoke that marline?" he asked. "It's bad enough to turn all the fish."

The Mate blew a lungful of smoke towards the window.

"Can't stand them pansy ready-mades. This is a real smoke. Three of these in a watch and you've had something."

"Given time and enough tobacco you could stay ashore and hire yourself out as a smoke house, though what effect it would have on haddocks I wouldn't like to say." Sam turned to the door. "Give me a shout around four. We should be at Angle Light by then. If there's no fog around then—and there might be with this moon and no wind—I'll shove her through the inside passage."

The Mate looked up in surprise.

"We'll make the morning tide with time to spare going outside, Skipper. What's the point in——"

"Call me at four or when we reach the Angle, whichever comes first," Sam said brusquely.

The Mate shrugged and concentrated on his watch for a few minutes. Then he turned to the deckhand at the wheel.

"I'll take her for a few minutes. Get a couple of teas. And see that there's some sugar in mine."

The deckhand was back in a few minutes.

"Skipper's a bit grumpy, isn't he?" he said conversationally.

"A bit. He seems to have something on his mind."

"Maybe it's because of Grimmy. And that shindig with the Bogey Man. They'll have our number up now, of course."

"Grimmy would have been all right if he'd dropped his knife when he fell. But you never learn, you deckies. Never learn." The Mate went on with a sneer: "Not that you would come to any harm with that bit of hoop iron you call a knife. You couldn't gut a jellyfish with it."

The deckhand laughed and changed the topic.

"How do you figure we've done this trip? Bit of all right?"

The Mate snorted. "Did you ever make a trip with a Cleeve as skipper and not do well. This one, or Ben."

"Ben Cleeve. Now he would have been the boy to have handled the Bogey Man. I've heard tell of once when he——"

"Stick to your steering and not so much jigging on the wheel or you'll have the skipper up here."

The Mate concentrated on another poisonous cigarette at which the deckhand sniffed with exaggerated distaste.

A slight mist turned the climbing sun red as *Lodestar* headed into the outer harbour at the head of a small procession of trawlers. Sam timed it exquisitely so that he was one of three heading slowly towards the lock gates as the blue flag climbed to the head of the tall flagstaff.

Sam motioned to Lofty at the wheel.

"Port a bit, Lofty."

Lofty juggled the wheel slightly and *Lodestar*'s head began to swing. From the corners of his eyes Lofty could see the stem of another trawler edging in towards the gates on *Lodestar*'s beam.

Sam reached up for the whistle toggle and yanked it twice.

The other trawler began to drop back.

"That'll larn him," Lofty growled.

He steadied *Lodestar*'s bow on the open lock gates as Sam rang down "slow ahead".

Once he was inside the inner harbour and swinging towards the quays Sam blew a short blast to signify that he was turning to starboard, then three short ones to indicate that he was going astern. *Lodestar* slid into an empty berth and Sam rang: "Finished with engines."

In a few minutes he was thrusting his way through a crowd of lumpers already whipping baskets and boxes of fish ashore where a group of salesmen, working for Job Benson, were talking to their hereditary enemies, the buyers for the big combines.

Soon they would be talking in a jargon intelligible only to themselves.

Some of them smiled and spoke to Sam.

"What's aboard, Sam?" called one.

Sam smiled at him. "What do you expect. Only the best, and don't give it away. I've got to live."

"Hard luck on your decky, Sam. And the trouble with the Bogey Man. Lucky it wasn't Ben. He'd have stemmed him."

The smile slipped from Sam's face. Why did people infer that Ben would have handled the situation differently. Had they expected something different from him?

"Maybe, but Ben's no fool," he said brusquely, and strode up the quay.

Buller Cleeve settled back in his chair, his pipe drawing to his satisfaction.

"Sam's all tied up, Mother. Give him an hour and he'll be home."

She put her head round the kitchen door.

"I'll have it ready for you. I'm glad he made the tide before Ben goes away. Where's Ben gone this morning?"

"Down on *Morning Star* handing over a few things to Charlie and collecting his own things."

Sam found himself lengthening his strides as he approached the office and he could feel an elation which made him rather annoyed with himself.

He pushed open the door.

"Good morning."

It was not at all as he had visualized it. He intended to saunter in casually with something like: "Hullo, Eve. Nice to see you."

"Sam." Eve stood up and walked round her desk with a hand outstretched. "How nice to see you. We knew you were in."

Sam stood there for a moment just looking at her until Eve, slightly confused, retreated behind her desk.

"Well, yes. I got in all right."

Eve took charge of the conversation.

"Uncle has two other trawler owners in with him at present. But I don't think they will be long."

Sam offered her a cigarette which she declined. "But you smoke, please do."

Sam stood in front of the desk looking down at her. He had collected himself and smiled easily at her. When she answered with a smile the eyes warmed, and the nose wrinkled just as he had imagined it a hundred times during the trip.

"I'm in no hurry to see Job. I've got all the morning."

"I was so sorry to hear about your man who died. Your father was explaining that when a man slips and falls he should drop his knife, but they seldom do. And then there's an accident."

"Have you been home then?"

"Oh, yes. I went one night and your father let me listen to all the trawlers talking. He explained a tremendous lot to me. I heard you and Ben talking."

"Did you?"

Her lips twitched. "That was the night when Ben said you would miss going into anywhere in Iceland." Her eyebrows arched innocently and she pretended to tidy up some papers. "I'm sorry you won't be able to visit your blonde friend any more."

Blank astonishment registered on Sam's face.

"Blonde! I don't know any particular blonde anywhere in Iceland. Anyway, they're all blonde up there."

"I was only teasing. Ben explained that he was ribbing you, as he called it. He said they were all blondes."

"That will cost him something. I always have the last word. Now, before I get in to see the High Nabob himself. You'll have lunch with me at the club today?"

The smile disappeared from her face.

"I'm sorry. But I promised Ben. We . . ." She recaptured the smile. "Why not join us? We'd——"

"No, thanks." Sam clipped it out. He choked back his rising resentment. "He hasn't by any chance booked you for dinner tonight, has he?"

She shook her head.

"N-n-no."

"Good. Then I'll pick you up at seven o'clock."

"I'm sorry, Sam. That'll be impossible. You see, I'm flying to Germany at three o'clock this afternoon with Uncle Job."

"The new trawler, I take it."

"Yes."

"I've been giving her quite a lot of thought and I've got a few suggestions to make to Job. And Ben will have to buy my dinner tonight if I can chisel him on the toss."

She straightened her papers, drew the point of her forefinger down the edge of her desk. Her voice sounded small and faint.

"That won't be possible, Sam."

"I know, you're flying to Germany. But it's Ben I'm going to catch. I owe him a fiver, anyway."

She looked up at him directly.

"P'raps I'd better tell you now. Ben is going to Germany with us. Uncle Job is giving him the new trawler."

Sam's eyebrows knitted down into a dark frown. He stared at Eve as if he didn't quite believe her. Finally he drew it out in almost a whisper.

"I see."

He looked down at a large envelope in his hand, looked up at Eve who was staring at him with the corners of her mouth slightly downturned.

"Sam . . . I . . ."

He tossed the envelope on to her desk.

"Those are official extracts from the log about my deck-hand's accident and death. And my report on the incident with the patrol ship. It's all there."

"But you can give them to Uncle Job yourself, Sam. He'll be through in a minute or two."

"Just give them to him. It's all there, plus an extract of costs and the catch."

"But you must . . ."

Sam turned to the door.

"I may call back later."

She dropped her head as the door clicked shut behind Sam. She smoothed her forehead with a palm.

"Oh dear," she whispered. "Oh dear."

Job's inner-office door opened and he came through with two men.

"Well, that seems to be the answer," Job said. "You get it put into the agenda for the next meeting. I'll support it. We should get it through."

As Job talked he looked around the outer office.

"That's fine, Job. I think that's the answer," one of the men replied and the other nodded agreement.

"See you in two or three weeks, then," Job said.

When they had gone Job looked at the clock on the wall, then at Eve.

"Usually takes about fifteen minutes, but I rather fancied that something makes my skippers clip it to around thirteen minutes. Did I hear a voice out here?"

Eve nodded. She held up the envelope.

"Sam . . . Skipper Sam Cleeve left this. It's something out of the log and his reports."

Job took the envelope and stood tapping it into the palm of his other hand. He studied Eve's face as he did so.

Softly he said: "He left this. His log extracts and his reports. Just like that?"

Eve nodded.

"I see. All right." Job turned and walked back into his office. He sat in his chair for a few moments then slit the envelope open.

He read the contents swiftly then leaned back.

"That's Sam Cleeve." He pinched his lower lip between finger and thumb. "I wonder. Maybe I should have picked him." Job looked at the door leading to the outer office. "Could be, too."

Buller Cleeve lifted his head in surprise as the front gate clicked and a moment later he heard Sam in the little hall.

"Mother. Sam's here." He lifted his sightless eyes as Sam's arm went round his shoulder. "I didn't expect you for a while yet."

"Got through the office quickly," Sam said. "Job had some owners confabbing with him."

He embraced his mother as she came in with the large teapot. "One day I'm going to sneak in quietly just to catch you without that teapot."

A few minutes later he asked with emphasized carelessness: "Where's Ben?"

Buller answered it obliquely. "You've heard he's getting Job's new trawler?"

"Yes. Eve Benson told me."

"Well, Ben's down on board *Morning Star* clearing up some odds and ends. Charlie Bates is taking her." Buller sampled his tea and leaned back. "You was first in this tide, Sam. You don't often make a dash for it. What was the hurry?"

"Oh, just wanted to get things cleared up."

Buller's head poised slightly sideways.

"Here's Ben coming now."

Ben's greeting was boisterous. He slapped Sam heavily on the shoulder.

"Hiya, Big Boy. Saw you come in on the tide. Me and Charlie were watching. I thought you were going to ram a hole in the quay. Andy Corcoran was cussing a bit the way you made him swing away. He generally gets that treatment from me."

Sam smiled briefly. "I just wanted to get in." He went on carefully and distinctly: "Are you going to the club for lunch?"

Ben grinned. "Sure am. I'm entertaining."

Sam's lips thinned. "So I've heard."

Ben looked at him curiously. "Why did you ask? Eve tell you?"

Sam nodded.

"I understand I have something else to congratulate you about. You've got the new trawler, too."

"Job pushed me into it. You can have her if you say so. I'm happy enough with *Morning Star.*"

"You've not been wasting time, have you?" Sam said coldly.

Ben laughed as he walked to the kitchen and returned with his tea mug. He poured himself out a mugful.

"Chin chin, Pop. I'll have to get my cook to take some lessons from Mother in making tea." He grinned at Sam. "I've been getting about. Took Eve to the club the other night, had some dinner, a bottle of bubbly, too. Then we had a dance and I drove her out to the Head." He chuckled. "She nearly swooned when I let her look down. Then we stayed there a while and I drove her home."

Sam stifled his growing resentment.

"Missed anything out?"

"Not a thing."

Sam lit a cigarette and puffed at it vigorously in short puffs.

Ben watched him with a glimmer of a grin on his lips.

"You got the needle, Big Boy?"

Buller sat slightly puzzled. He could sense the growing atmosphere. This was not good-humoured raillery, the hard-hitting but laughing combat in which the two boys usually engaged.

Ben, too, was conscious that Sam's words tinkled with ice. He sought to turn the conversation into another and more general channel.

"How did you make out with your catch?" he asked. "You were doing all right the last time I spoke to you."

Sam brought back the topic which was uppermost in his mind.

"I did all right," he answered briefly. Then softly he continued as if reviewing the points already mentioned: "You've got the new trawler. You've taken Eve—Miss Benson—out to dinner, you had champagne, you drove out to the Head."

"Sure I did. What of it? I didn't want the damn thing. You can have it. *Morning Star* is good enough for me and I've told Job that half a dozen times."

"So you say."

Ben wiped the smile from his face. His lips tightened.

"At least half a dozen times, and I mean it. You can have her."

"You mean the trawler?"

"I mean the trawler."

Sam lifted the large teapot and filled his father's mug.

"By your hand, Dad."

"I can pour my own tea," Buller growled. "What's biting you, Sam? If Job thinks Ben is the best man, then he's the best man and that's all there is to it."

Ben watched Sam with a curious gleam deep back in his eyes.

"By God, you're jealous. And what about? Because I get your fancy trawler and your fancy girl."

"What in hell's up with you two boys? Now stop it, the pair of you. You're squabbling over nothing. Stop it, do you hear?"

Buller's voice rose almost to a rasping roar. Mrs Cleeve stood framed in the doorway, twisting her hands into her apron until it was bunched into a knot.

"Don't quarrel, there's good boys. She's a nice girl and wouldn't like it if she knew. She's such a nice girl."

Ben sat on the edge of the table, a grin on his face.

"You're dead right there, Mum. I don't know what's eating him. She's no more his girl than she is mine, or anybody else's."

"Well, don't quarrel about it any more. I'm sure Job will let you have the new trawler if Ben and your father explain to him."

"Job's picked the best man and that's that," Buller growled. "Put some more boiling water on this tea. It's gone cold."

Ben looked at Sam and his nose wrinkled up slightly as he showed his teeth in a grin.

"Well, well," he said softly. "Little Sam gets hurt because he can't have everything his own way."

Sam turned on him passionately.

"It's you who've grabbed everything." His face twisted into a sneer. "Including the owner's niece. Follows the pattern, doesn't it? Get around Job by making up to Eve. Marry her and you'll be a director in a couple of years."

"Marry her?" Ben chuckled. "Not me. Not this chicken. Fun, yes." He poked Sam in the chest with his forefinger. "Lots of fun. We're going to be together in Germany for best part of three weeks. Figure that one out."

Sam grasped Ben by the lapels of his coat with one hand and swung a punch at him with the other.

"Stop it, you bloody fool," Ben said, warding off the punch. He thrust Sam from him.

Buller struggled to his feet and groped to get between his two sons. Sam drove in again, swinging punches with both hands. Ben ducked under one and swayed away. Before Sam could stop it the blow landed on sightless Buller's head. He staggered back reaching blindly for support. He clutched the table on which rested the radio set and his weight sent it crashing.

"Goddam' you!" Ben raged. He smashed his fist into Sam's face and sent him staggering against the wall. Mrs Cleeve came running from the kitchen and crouched down by her husband. Buller was bleeding slightly from a cut above his eyebrow.

Ben stooped down and got his arms round his father. With scarcely an effort he lifted the old man up and placed him in his chair. As Mrs Cleeve wiped the trace of blood away, Ben righted the table and restored the radio set to its place.

Then he turned towards the room, his face set, his lips in a tight slit.

Sam was gone.

Ben heard the front door close with a bang and started to stride towards it.

Mrs Cleeve caught him by the sleeve.

"No. No, Ben, no," she pleaded. "Help me with your father."

Buller groaned and touched his head.

"What happened?" he asked. "What happened?"

Ben looked at his mother and his lips twitched. He nodded to her.

"Me and Sam was scuffling and you got in the way," he said. "Nothing much."

"Who hit me?" Buller rasped.

"Now take it easy, Dad. It wasn't meant. It was an unlucky one which came your way."

"Who hit me?" Buller reiterated.

"Sam did, but it was accidental," Mrs Cleeve said. "I'll get some water and wash it off."

"Sam hit me. Sam did it," Buller whispered as if to himself.

CHAPTER THIRTEEN

SAM walked unseeing out of the house and went on walking. It seemed to him that he had walked for hours with that one moment when his blow had hit his father frozen in his mind. Nothing else registered. He could feel all the time the impact of his fist landing on his father's head. Why hadn't he checked his blow? Why had he struck at all?

Finally he found himself standing on the edge of the sheer drop at the Head. He was staring down at the seas breaking over the foot of the cliff.

What had it all been about?

Sam began to go over it word by word but could find no sense in it.

Ben had taken her out to dinner, they had danced. And that was all. She was a free agent to go and do as she wished.

And if Job chose to appoint Ben to the new trawler, then that was Job's decision.

Slowly he turned from the cliff top and started walking.

He pushed open the front door quietly and entered the room. His father sat immobile, his sightless eyes seemed to stare into space.

Sam crossed over to him.

Softly he said: "Dad, I'm sorry." He rested his hand on his father's shoulder.

Buller shrugged it off, but made no other move.

"Dad, I wouldn't have had it happen for worlds. You know that."

Mrs Cleeve came into the room from the kitchen.

"There, Father. Sam's come back and he says he's sorry. It was all an accident, wasn't it?"

Sam nodded. Once again he placed his hand on his father's shoulder.

"Listen, Dad. I was angry and Ben was ribbing me and . . . and . . ."

Buller shrugged his shoulder again so that Sam's hand slipped off it.

Quietly, so softly that it was almost a whisper, Buller said: "Get out."

"But, Dad——"

"Get out."

Slowly Sam moved to the foot of the stairs. He paused as his mother crossed over to him.

"He'll be all right by and by. Come back later."

Sam looked at his father, patted his mother on the cheek and climbed the stairs.

He looked at Ben's cases packed beside his bed and slowly started to fill his own case.

At the foot of the stairs he paused for a moment. He could see his father sitting immobile at the table. He stared at him for a moment then quietly strode to the front door which he softly closed behind him.

Mrs Cleeve, in the kitchen, heard the door close.

"Who was that?" she asked through the doorway. "Was it Sam?"

Buller slowly filled his pipe and lit it. He made no answer.

Mrs Cleeve shook her head gently.

"Sam didn't mean it, Father. He'd sooner chop off an arm than hit you. You know that. The boys were scuffling . . . and . . ." She allowed it to trail off. She had meant to say that it was partly his own fault for trying to push between them. Instead she said: "When he comes back tonight he'll say he was sorry and . . . and . . . then everything will be all right. Won't it?"

"Job picked the best man for her. That's all there is to it. The other one didn't like it."

She sighed. "No, dear."

The old clock started its warning rumble then sonorously chimed out its seven reverberating notes.

Mrs Cleeve watched him, waited for him to reach out to switch on the set.

Buller didn't move.

"It's seven o'clock, dear. Aren't you going to switch on?"

Buller shook his head slowly, ponderously, like a weary bull irritated by flies.

She stood in front of him twisting her hands until her fingers were knotted tightly together.

She heard the front door click and her face brightened.

"Perhaps that is Sam. P'raps he's come back," she said eagerly. It was Charlie Bates.

He looked at the clock, looked at Buller, then wrinkled his face into a frown as he turned to Mrs Cleeve. She shook her head.

"What's up, Old 'Un?" Charlie Bates asked huskily. "It's turned seven a piece." He inclined his head towards the radio set as if Buller could see the gesture.

"We've had a bit of trouble," Mrs Cleeve said tremulously. "The boys were . . . struggling . . . and the set got knocked over."

Charlie Bates looked from Mrs Cleeve to Buller then reached out and turned the knob. In a few seconds the set started to hum and a jumbled cacophony of voices came thinly from it.

"Sounds all right," Charlie said.

Buller moved one hand and switched the set off.

"What in hell's up? Begging your pardon, Mrs Cleeve."

Mrs Cleeve shook her head from side to side. Tears began to roll down her cheeks.

"He'd better tell you," she whispered. "I'm going into the kitchen."

Charlie stepped over to the cupboard and produced the bottle. Without speaking he filled two glasses and pushed one towards Buller.

"There's no water in that. Now start telling me."

Buller reached for his glass and took a generous sip. Gradually, slowly at first, with long pauses, he started to tell Charlie Bates what had happened.

Charlie waited until he finished without making any comment.

"'Twas your own bloody fault. Shoving your big blind head in between two boys having an up and a downer. Why, their mother might have got in the way and got hit. Why in hell didn't you leave 'em alone. They've been scrapping since they were no bigger than my seaboots. What's new about them having a scuffle?"

"This was different."

"Squabbles are always different. Where's Sam now?"

"Don't know."

"But I damn' well do, and I'm going to find him. Then I'll give him a clip alongside the earhole and march him home by the scruff of his neck. If he wasn't so big I'd shove him over my knee, and not the first time."

Charlies Bates stood up.

"Switch that on and listen. I want to know what's going on up there if you don't. I'll be back with Sam in a couple of jiffies. G'wan. Switch it on."

He winked at Mrs Cleeve standing in the doorway then went on pugnaciously: "What I like to do is to get you in a room and me with a bag over my head then we'd both be blind and let the best man walk out of the room."

Buller's mouth twitched. "I wouldn't even bother about salt to take you, you shrivelled-up herring."

"I'll be back."

Charlie shut the door forcibly.

Mrs Cleeve walked slowly over to her husband. "I'll make a little pot just for you and me and I'll sit in here and have it with you. In my best pot," she said softly. Her hand strayed out and stroked his head.

"Do that, Mother," Buller whispered.

He reached out and turned the switch, adjusted it delicately and leaned back.

Charlie Bates strode into the club and up to the ornate bar.

"Seen Sam Cleeve?" he asked abruptly.

"If you're not blind you can see him, too," the barman answered. politely. He lifted his chin to point towards a far corner of the lounge. "And I'd give a week's wages to know what's hit him."

Charlie turned his head. Sam was sitting alone in a corner. His head was down on his chest.

"Do you know?" the barman pursued.

"Yes."

Charlie turned from the bar.

"Hey, wait a bit," the barman said. "Tell me this. Sam Cleeve never drinks more than three Scotches all night. Not ever. To-night he's had six." He glanced at the clock. "And the night is young. Six." He leaned forward impressively. "Six doubles."

Charlie strode over to Sam. He stood in front of him without speaking. Slowly Sam lifted his head. As he did so his eyelids drooped slowly and hooded his eyes.

"I'sh you, ish it?" he slurred.

Charlie waited until with an effort Sam opened his eyes. Charlie sat down by him.

Gently, softly, he said: "Yes, it's me. Now, son. Let's get this straight, shall we."

"Nothin' t' straighten. Lesh have a drink." He waved an arm expansively towards the bar.

Charlie Bates cancelled it with a brief, economical gesture of the palm.

"No more for you. You're going home."

"Home!" Sam lifted his head and sneered ponderously.

"Yes, to my home, until I can straighten you up. I'd hate for your mother to see you like this. Come on, Sam."

Despite a show of reluctance he got Sam to his feet.

Sam swayed towards the bar. "Le'sh have another drink," he said.

"Not on your life. If that barman served you I'd have him up before the committee."

With exaggerated balance and picking his feet up unnecessarily high, with Charlie's steadying arm under his elbow Sam rolled towards the door.

"Keep his chin up and he won't spill a drop," the barman grinned as they passed him.

Charlie turned and looked at him through narrowed eyes. "I'll come back to deal with you later," he said venomously. "You've got too much lip for my liking."

The walk through the cool night steadied Sam up slightly, and Charlie Bates had no difficulty in getting him undressed and into bed. He stood looking down at the heavily breathing young man.

"A clip in the earhole, or bending you over my knee wouldn't do you much good right now. But, you'll feel it in the morning. Now I've got to square your old man off, and your mother."

"Sam got a bit hot under the collar and had a drink or two too many," he explained later to Buller. "You know how it is. He'll be around in the morning. And," he infused a warning note into his voice, "so will I. And you'll both mind your tempers."

Charlie Bates awoke in the morning from an uncomfortable sleep on a couch to find the bed empty and short note lying against the clock on the mantelpiece.

I remember some of last night. Thanks, it read. *I have a room at the Queen's Hotel. Again, thanks. Sam.*

Charlie snorted. "I'll give you Queen's Hotel, my young fella-me-lad. Your place is home."

Sam Cleeve walked into the dingy office of the Melhuish Brothers and said to the shrivelled clerk behind the small counter: "I want to see the boss. Andrew Melhuish."

"Name?"

"Sam Cleeve. Ever heard of it?"

The clerk had heard of it. He slipped from his stool.

"Just a moment, Mr Cleeve. I'll see if he's available."

Andrew Melhuish rose from his desk. His cadaverous, lined face, dismally creased, partly due to the problem of running badly manned trawlers and partly to the ulcers from which he suffered, wrinkled into something approaching a smile.

"Good morning, Skipper Cleeve. I know you, of course, by name. I know your father, too. What can I do for you?"

Sam told him.

Andrew Melhuish's thick eyebrows climbed upwards until they threatened to disappear into his hair.

"You mean . . . you are asking me . . .?"

He sat down heavily and leaned back.

"I'm afraid I don't understand."

To Melhuish it was as if a prima donna were asking for a place on the programme of a fourth-rate music hall.

He went on: "Are you thinking of buying a trawler?"

"No. Just a job as skipper."

Melhuish looked at Sam in complete puzzlement. "But you are with Job Benson. You and your brother are top skippers with him. Would you like to explain?"

Sam clipped it out. "It's quite simple. I no longer sail with Benson's. I want a job with you. Is that clear? If not you, then another company. But not Benson's."

"Sit down, Mr Cleeve. This has taken me by surprise. I have no wish to probe into your private affairs, but this . . this desire of yours to leave Benson's has nothing to do with the . . . the—er —recent trouble you had off Iceland?"

"Nothing. I want a change, and that is all."

"I see. And when would you want to make this change?"

"Now. Today. You have a trawler waiting for half a crew and a skipper, I believe. I'll take her."

"You mean the *Carpathia*?"

"Yes."

Melhuish rubbed his hand over his chin and Sam could hear the faint rasp.

"Well, Mr Cleeve. She is ready now. She has just undergone

extensive . . . she has just been given a refit and we were thinking of manning her in a day or so."

Sam smiled thinly. He knew that the trawler had returned from a trip full of trouble, had made a loss and had been damaged by a drunken skipper.

"I'll pick one or two men and will sail her when you are ready. When do we sign?"

"This afternoon. Suit you?"

"Very well, this afternoon."

Sam had scarcely left Melhuish's office before the news started to circulate. Andrew Melhuish had a feverish, almost breathless telephone conversation with his brother into which the clerk in the outer office eavesdropped.

Andrew called the clerk in.

"Complete that crew for the *Carpathia* this afternoon. See that she is iced-up and coaled. She sails forenoon tide tomorrow."

"About a skipper?" the clerk asked. He knew, but did not want to show it.

"That's all fixed. Skipper Sam Cleeve is coming in with us. Get everything all ready."

Over his modest beer and sandwich the clerk retailed it to several cronies. They spread it. It became the much-discussed topic at the club, and eventually the pubs.

Lofty and Geegee, drinking some friendly pints, were explaining the sterner facts of hectic life to the new landlord of the Chain Locker when it reached them.

Lofty gagged and nearly spilled his pint.

"Are you gone completely daft?" he asked his informant. "Gone right off your rocker? Sam Cleeve wouldn't use a Melhuish trawler for ballast."

"It's true, I tell you. She's signing today and sailing tomorrow, and Sam Cleeve is taking her. I'm signing. I should get a living out of her with him on the bridge."

"You!" Geegee snarled. "Sam Cleeve wouldn't use you for a fireman's sweat-rag."

"All right. You'll see."

Geegee and Lofty ponderously turned it over for two or three pints. It was Lofty who had the brainwave.

"Ring up Melhuish's on the phone. They'll know."

The landlord graciously found the number for them and let them use his telephone.

Geegee replaced the phone and turned to Lofty. Complete bewilderment registered on his face.

"It's true. S'welp me, it's true."

Lofty looked at the clock. "One pint more and we'll take a look. Where's she lying?"

They stood silently together on the quay and watched coal slipping down into *Carpathia*'s bunkers. They knew the next move. She would slide under the endless belt and the ice would slip into her.

Geegee looked at the sky, then once more at *Carpathia*.

"I was figurin' on going with Charlie Bates on *Morning Star*. She suits me."

"Me and Sam got on all right on *Lodestar*," Lofty said dully. "But this . . ." He completed it with a shrug.

Silently they crossed the railway lines and climbed the hill to Melhuish's office. A group of men stood outside. Geegee looked at them critically.

"Gawd's strewth. Is this the shower that's signing on?"

Both he and Lofty knew every deadbeat trouble-maker and lazy-bones deckhand in the port and there was a fair selection in front of them.

"This ain't a crew, it's a dog's mess," Lofty snarled quietly. "There's three or four in that lot I'd use for fish manure, no more."

The shrivelled little clerk came importantly to the door.

"Signing in fifteen minutes," he said. "Any of you fellas ever shipped as bos'n?"

Geegee looked at Lofty for a few seconds. Then he pulled a coin from his pocket.

"Call it," he said softly. He spun the coin.

"Heads."

"Tails it is." He replaced the coin in his pocket. "That means me."

"I lost the toss," Lofty protested. "I ships in her."

"Who said anything about 'losing'?" Geegee said coldly. "I won and I has the pick."

"C'mon. Is there a bos'n among you?" the clerk repeated impatiently.

Geegee stepped forward until he towered over the under-sized clerk.

"Yes," he snapped. "I'm a bos'n."

The clerk looked up at him. "What trawlers?"

"Last one with Skipper Cleeve in *Morning Star*. Ben Cleeve. And before that in *Lodestar* with Sam Cleeve. That enough?"

It was more than enough. The clerk seemed to shrink.

"Yes, sir," he answered. "Come inside. Skipper's waiting." Lofty spluttered.

Geegee turned at the door and stared coldly at Lofty.

"You be at the Chain Locker around seven o'clock. And be sober. Me and you's got one or two things to settle."

"Yes, *sir*." Lofty grinned.

Sam sat at a table with the papers spread before him. The clerk fluttered around and occupied a chair. "This man says he has been bos'n before, Skipper. Do you know him?"

Sam's eyes and Geegee's met with something almost approaching a clang. No word was spoken for a few moments.

"Is it all right?" the clerk flustered.

"Quite all right. Sign him," Sam said softly. "And bring the rest of them in."

The deckhands and firemen trooped in and stood shuffling their feet. In the mixture of men who sailed from the port in trawlers they were the dregs. They were the men who would be drunk joining and would quarrel and fight, and scrimshank and skulk throughout the trip, narrowly avoiding being logged for misdemeanours because the skippers who accepted them were but little better.

Now they were standing in front of an aristocrat of their trawler world.

Sam watched each man scrawl his signature.

"Be on board at ten o'clock tomorrow morning. If you're late you've lost her."

Geegee stood to one side, surveying them critically, and although one or two tried a pugnacious engagement of eyes with him they failed dismally.

Soon the office was empty but for Sam, Geegee and the clerk. The clerk shuffled into the inner office leaving Sam and Geegee alone.

"How come?" Sam said softly.

"We heard, me and Lofty. We tossed who'd ship with you."

Sam grinned thinly, without mirth.

"And you lost."

"I won."

Sam's eyes warmed slightly. Briefly he rested his arm on Geegee's powerful shoulder.

"Thanks, Geegee," he said quietly. "One day I'll tell you all about it."

Geegee's elemental mind only dimly grasped what Sam meant.

"I know some fellas that are going to know all about it by tomorrow. I'll make deckies of 'em or strew 'em from North Cape to Bear Island." He grinned.

A bosom friend of Charlie Bates broke the news to Charlie. And stood back out of range of the expected explosion. It never came.

Charlie pinched his lower lip between thumb and finger for a couple of seconds.

"Good for him," he said quietly. "I didn't think he had it in him. He's a Cleeve all right."

"What will his old man say?" his relieved informant asked. "Old Buller will hit the ceiling."

"Maybe. Maybe. We'll see."

Buller sat immobile for a few moments when Charlie told him bluntly what Sam had done.

"What do you think, Charlie Boy?"

"Same as you, Old 'Un."

They sat in silence for a couple of minutes.

"In the cupboard, Charlie. And I'll take mine neat."

Charlie Bates set them up. "By your elbow, Buller. It's a big 'un."

Charlie smacked his lips as the neat whisky warmed his throat.

"I always said he was a Cleeve, didn't I? A Cleeve through and through."

Buller Cleeve nodded.

"He didn't really hurt me, Charlie. I . . . I sort of over-balanced."

"He'd have had to use a sledge-hammer to hurt you, Old 'Un."

Mrs Cleeve said tremulously: "Oh dear, what will Mr Benson say now. And Miss Benson. She's such a nice girl, too."

Charlie grinned. "I'd like to hear that."

"Top 'em up, Charlie Boy."

Charlie recharged the glasses. Buller raised his.

"He'll lick her into shape in a trip or two. You'll see."

Charlie Bates raised his glass in salute.

"No doubt about it. And do you know, Buller, you ain't called me Charlie Boy since I don't know when."

"Back when we was young. Young and daft."

"Daft was right. A lot dafter than these young 'uns."

Buller's bottom lip was thrust out.

"He'll lick her, Charlie . . . Charlie Boy."

CHAPTER FOURTEEN

JOB BENSON and Eve sat in the wide window of the lounge of their hotel. Around them eddied the harsh, guttural sounds of conversation in German.

Job carefully applied a light to a cigar, inspected the glowing end critically then leaned back, one elbow propping upright his forearm.

He studied his niece through the thin skein of smoke rising from his cigar.

"Penny or a pound for them, Eve," he said softly.

Eve turned to him with a smile.

"They're certainly not worth a pound, Uncle."

Job waited for her to elaborate but Eve returned to her staring out of the window.

Job shrugged.

Suddenly Eve leaned forward and peered down at the front of the hotel.

"Ben's just arrived with two other men."

"Now we'll hear all about Benson's Folly," her uncle said with a smile. "If not today then soon, as soon as Ben has made a short trip in her."

"I liked her, Uncle Job. I thought she looked beautiful. And she looked much bigger than the trawlers in Scoresby."

"She is. The largest I have, and that's the largest in England, are *Morning Star* and *Lodestar*. They're around six hundred tons. This new job is seven hundred tons and she's more complicated with her freezing plant as well.

Job blew a thin spiral of smoke towards the lofty ceiling, then went on reflectively: "We'll have to find a name for her, Eve. After a star like the rest of my fleet."

Eve chuckled briefly. "You've got thousands to pick from, Uncle. How about *Orion*?"

Job rubbed his chin.

"I had an *Orion*. A nice little trawler she was, too. She was sunk as a minesweeper during the war. *Orion* might do." He turned his head as Ben and the two Germans crossed the lounge. "Ah, there you are." He stood up. "I was just saying to Eve that we'll now be hearing all about Benson's Folly."

"Good name for her, too." Ben grinned.

The two Germans bowed over Eve's hand.

"No, Mr Benson," one said, taking Job's banter in literal-minded seriousness. "There is nothing foolish about this ship. We Germans do not build until we have—what is the saying?—until we have ironed out the bugs."

"That's good American." Ben grinned. "But there'll be more, I've no doubt. We sail on a trawling test tomorrow, and try her out for three days." His grin widened. "It would be funny if we caught enough to make a small profit, wouldn't it?"

The literal-minded one took this up, too.

"I don't think it possible, Mr Cleeve. We just try her out where we know there are no wrecks. It will be just a test. Yes?"

Ben nodded solemnly. "Just a test."

Job said: "Can I offer you gentlemen a drink?"

They accepted and Job caught a hovering-waiter's eye and he soon produced a tray of drinks.

"*Prosit.*" The Germans clicked their heels and bowed slightly. "To the test tomorrow."

Ben lifted his glass. "And may the trip show a profit." He caught the Germans' eye and hastily added: "I'm only joking, mister."

The Germans smiled uncertainly.

Ben winked at Eve who had difficulty in keeping her face straight.

Over dinner later Job said: "Why don't you two young people go out and see a show tonight?" He peered from one to the other. "I've got a pile of paper-work in front of me."

"Can I help, Uncle? After all, I am here as your secretary."

"Not with this stuff, Eve. You go out."

"And you can't dodge that. It's practically an order," Ben said.

"How would you like to see a beer garden? Or there's an opera on. In German, of course."

"I'd love that," Eve said solemnly.

"Then a night on the town it is. And no opera."

They tried two beer gardens, with their heavy ornate furnishings and buxom girls carrying incredibly loaded trays of foaming beer. Around them sat heavily built Germans, some with their women with them, getting more red in the face as the night progressed and the successive lidded steins of beer disappeared.

"I think I've had enough of this," Eve said. "The smoke is making my eyes smart and the noise is dreadful."

They walked in the cool of the evening, neither speaking, both conscious that there was between them a flimsy barrier which either could have demolished in one sentence. They passed a quiet, subdued little place and suddenly Ben spun her round and turned back.

"Listen," he said. They paused at the door and haunting, plaintive music came through it.

"Remember that?"

Firmly he propelled Eve through the door. It was the complete opposite to the noisy, garishly lit beer gardens and beer cellars they had visited. The softly lighted tables were in little alcoves and the centre of the room was a small dance floor on which half a dozen couples slowly, dreamingly revolved. On a minute platform an orchestra of four dispensed music. They were dressed in almost musical comedy Hungarian gypsy costumes. Voluminous sleeves with a wealth of gold-wire embroidery on dark waistcoats.

A little dark-faced man came to meet them.

"A table? Yes? Just for two."

He conducted them to a discreet alcove and stood waiting.

"What would you like?" Ben asked. "Wine or champagne?"

"We have Heidsieck, Moet, Dry Monopole. Anything," the waiter urged.

"A wine, I think," Eve said.

Ben ordered hock.

"Shall we dance?"

Eve felt the tremors return as Ben put his arm round her on the floor. Neither of them spoke during the dancing until they returned to the table.

"Smoke?"

Ben lit the cigarettes. "This is the first time we have been alone together since we left Scoresby. Design? or accident?"

"Not design. After all, we've been here only two days and they've been full. I might add that you've been extremely quiet except when talking trawlers with Uncle Job."

"Have I?"

"You have. And even now you are not . . . not . . ."

"Myself. Is that what you were going to say?"

Ben sipped his drink and leaned back.

"Perhaps I had better tell you. You'll hear it from somebody, I suppose. And Job will, too."

He leaned forward and looked fixedly over Eve's shoulder.

"Just before we left Scoresby Sam and I had a . . . a . . . quarrel. Quite a row. There's nothing much in that. We've always squabbled with no real depth in it. But this time . . . well, we started swapping punches. I don't know what happened, quite, but Dad tried to come between us."

He stopped speaking and Eve could see his lips tighten up.

"Go on," she said softly.

"Sam swung a punch and knocked him over."

"No!" She said it explosively. "By accident, of course."

Ben shook his head. "I don't know. I was trying to shove Sam off, Dad was hauling at him and it happened."

"Was he seriously hurt?"

"No. A little cut. I lifted Dad up and set him in a chair and Mother started to attend to him. I . . . Sam had gone . . . it was just as well . . . I wanted to kill him. I haven't seen him since. Well, there it is, all of it."

"It must have been an accident. The last thing Sam would do would be to strike your father."

She leaned forward and stared at Ben.

"What were you fighting about?" she questioned softly.

"Oh, just things. I ribbed him a bit and he was touchy and exploded."

Eve persisted. "I'm scarcely what you would describe as a 'thing', am I?"

"Well, that was part of it." Ben turned his head sharply towards her. "How did you guess?"

Eve told him of Sam's visit to the office and his attitude when she told him that she was going to lunch with Ben and that Ben was getting the new trawler.

"That could explain it. And believe me, Eve. I mean this. I don't want the damn' thing. I don't like her. And for me Sam can have her. He was enthusiastic about this new way of trawling. I'm not."

"Why not tell all this to Uncle? He'd understand."

"He might. He knew Sam was keen on her."

"Has it occurred to you that he has given her to you to keep you out of trouble off Iceland?"

"Well, I'll be damned," Ben said softly. "But I fish well away from Iceland. Seldom trawl off there as close as the box they've made."

"But the owners have decided that to back up the Government they will send trawlers to fish in the box. And you might be one of them sent there."

"And that would be fun. If one of their patrol boats tried boarding me he'd get a thick ear in quick time."

"Exactly. And that is what Uncle Job wants to avoid."

Ben stood up.

"Let's dance. I feel the better for telling you about it. Maybe when we get back it will have cleared up and Sam will have made peace with Dad."

As they walked towards the dance floor Ben paused to speak to the waiter, who nodded.

They danced to the heart-searching descending passages of the violin music until Eve stood back.

"Enough. But I could go on all night."

The waiter was twirling a bottle of champagne in an ice-bucket when they reached their table.

Eve set her lips. "No, thanks," she said firmly.

"Just to celebrate peace breaking out," Ben pleaded.

Eve fought back the tremor which threatened her lips and wished that her heart wouldn't pound so much and that she didn't react to the sheer animalism of Ben. In trying to establish a point she provoked what she sought to prevent.

"Let me make it clear," she said as firmly as she could. "I am not in love with you. Nor likely to be."

She waited.

Ben leaned forward and she could see the immense power in his shoulder muscles as he hunched them up.

"Do you believe me?" she pressed.

"I think I do. Yes, I do."

"Ben, I don't want you to get hurt by thinking you are in love with me. You are not, are you?"

He slowly revolved the glass with the stem between finger and thumb. Without lifting his head he slowly raised his eyes.

"Truthfully . . . no."

Eve drew in her breath slowly and tremulously.

Ben went on.

"Ask me if I want you and you'll get another sort of answer . . . truthfully."

Eve stood up.

"Shall we go? I feel tired and the wine has gone to my head slightly."

In almost complete silence they walked back to the hotel. Ben took the keys from the night clerk at the counter. In silence they climbed the stairs. Ben inserted the key in her door and opened it. She stood framed in the doorway for a moment, then impulsively reached up and kissed him full on the mouth.

"Good night, Ben. And thank you."

The door closed with a click.

Ben ruefully rubbed the short hair at the back of his head.

"You can write that off as a dead loss, Ben, my boy," he murmured. "Maybe I ought to unship the door and storm in." He turned towards his own room swinging the heavy key and brass tab on one finger. Removing only his coat and tie he lay down on the bed with his hands behind his head. Fragments of disconnected thought raced through his mind.

Of course he wanted her. Wanted her with all the passion he could muster. But was that being in love with her? No, truthfully he had answered and truthfully it was. But people he knew had married on that basis. Then what? Had Sam gone back home and made peace with their father? Why was Sam so touchy about Eve? If she asked Sam how he felt towards her, what would be his reply? Was Sam in love with her, or was it just the same for him. Did he just want her physically? Why didn't he want the new trawler? She was a challenge, and he revelled in challenges. He didn't like her and that was that. He would tell Job so in the morning. He would ask him to let him go back to *Morning Star* or one of the others.

Ben found his eyes drooping and he undressed and got into bed.

Eve lay in bed one palm under her face, the other arm downstretched.

Why had she so resolutely shut the door in Ben's face? Was she disappointed at his truthful reply that he wasn't in love with her? Couldn't he see that she was balanced on an emotional pin-point? What would she have done if he had twisted his face into one of his devastating grins and had thrust open the door to enter her room? Could she have . . . ?

She twisted around in bed seeking for a more comfortable position.

Why had Sam exploded? Was he in love with her? Or was it just as it was with Ben. Pure animalism. They were both hard men, living hard lives, so vastly different from the men who circulated in the life she had lived at the school.

Was Sam in love with her? Was she in love with Sam? The question kept recurring. *Was* she in love with Sam? Eve was still trying to answer this when she dropped off to sleep.

Ben was a little late coming down to breakfast. Instead of the well-cut tweed suit he had worn on the previous day he now wore a double-breasted blue serge, equally well cut. It emphasized the breadth of his shoulders and the depth of his chest as he swayed past other tables to reach the one where Job and Eve sat.

More than one woman, toying irresolutely with a meagre breakfast, looked at him speculatively then turned disillusioned eyes on their escorts.

"Good afternoon," Job said pointedly.

Ben refused the bait. He smiled at Eve as he took his seat.

"Good morning. You look a million dollars. Wiggle your eyes a bit and we should get a bit off the price of this floating fish factory we're going to try out."

Job's lips twitched slightly but he, too, rejected the gambit.

"What time are they picking you up?" Job asked.

"Around half past ten. We sail at eleven."

"And Uncle Job said I can come down to the quay to watch you go." Eve smiled. "I'll stand there waving my little hanky until you disappear."

Job snorted.

Eve stood up. "I've one or two things to do before we go out. You'll forgive me."

Ben came straight to the point. He poured himself another cup of coffee, tested it and leaned forward with his crossed forearms on the table.

"I don't want it, Mr Benson. Not one little bit."

Job carefully rearranged a salt-cellar, a knife and fork and his coffee-cup until they made an intricate but orderly pattern.

"The new trawler, you mean?"

Ben shook his head impatiently.

"The new trawler," he repeated. "I spent a lot of time thinking about her last night. She's not for me."

"Afraid you won't be able to make a living in her?"

The pattern was dissolved and a new one started.

"I'd make a living in any trawler built, and you know that.

It's just that I'm not . . ." Ben left it in mid-air and gestured with one hand.

"'Enthusiastic', is that the word?"

"Look, Job. I was almost born on a trawler, grew up with them, listened to Father and to Charlie Bates and so far as trawlers are concerned I'm conservative. What was good enough for Dad is good enough for me."

Job swept the pattern away completely.

"Ben. Your father, Charlie Bates and I all started as deckhands together. For them a paying trip was enough unto the day. They were conservative. They were stubborn. They fought me when I went out for larger trawlers, when I said three or four thousand kit was the target. Now I am an owner and they . . ."

He spread his palms and shrugged.

"Well, you know."

Ben stuck doggedly to his point. "I don't want her. Give her to Sam. He's your best man. He's really enthusiastic about her and the new-fangled way."

Job leaned back.

"You really mean that?"

"Indeed I do."

"Give me one of those cigarettes you're always smoking."

Ben extended his flaming lighter and Job puffed steadily at the slim cylinder for a few moments.

"If it will help you," Ben said, "I'll promise you that if you order me to fish in the Iceland box under the eyes of the Navy, then I'll fish there." He leaned forward and tapped the table with a finger-tip. "And I'll keep my nose clean. If a Bogey Man shows up I'll just call for the Navy and sit back and do nothing. That's a promise."

"Confidential secretaries are supposed to keep confidences," Job said suavely.

"I don't know what you're talking about. Dad and Charlie Bates saw through it that you were worried in case I got into trouble. But I've given you my promise."

Ben leaned back. "Now, get Sam over here. I'll take her out on tests and put him wise to what goes on."

Job stubbed the cigarette out and stood up.

"Right. Have it your own way and for your benefit I always thought that Sam was the better man. For this trawler, I mean."

"And you're right."

"I'll put a call through. *Lodestar* isn't due to sail until tomorrow. Young Mayne can have her. He's been doing well in *Shooting Star*."

"That bundle of scrap iron. It's a wonder you didn't break his heart in her. You nearly did mine, anyway."

"I've broken a few hearts in her, Ben," Job said, resting his hand briefly on Ben's shoulder as he passed. "But I've found some good skippers in her, too."

Eve came to the table and sat down.

"You look—what's the word I want?—pensive. Have you been arguing with Uncle? He passed me in the vestibule without even seeing me."

"We talked. Now he's on his way to phone for Sam to join us. He's going to have the new job. Me for the *Morning Star* or one of the others."

"And that is what you really want? Truthfully?"

Ben looked at her steadily.

"Truthfully."

Eve studied her lacquered finger-nails for a few moments.

"You're given to speaking the truth, aren't you, Ben?"

"On occasions."

The finger-nails suffered another scrutiny.

"'The moment of truth'," she murmured.

"What's that?"

"When the bull-fighter has the bull poised for the kill that is 'the moment of truth'."

Ben smiled at her. "You're likening me to a bull, are you?"

"In some respects, yes. Rugged, ruthless to a point, but no finesse, no seeking deeper."

"You've gone right over my head, I'm afraid."

Eve spread her hands flat on the table, knuckles up. She looked at Ben who was momentarily surveying the room. His eyes came back to the table and eventually met Eve's.

Breathlessly, almost passionately, she said: "You damn' fool, why didn't you push the door open last night? Didn't you know? Couldn't you see?"

She stood up, looking down at him. She captured her bottom lip and gnawed at it. "You big stupid animal."

She turned and walked away from the table. Ben watched her go. His eyes blinked slowly.

"'The moment of truth'," he whispered to himself.

Job Benson met Eve in the doorway of the breakfast room.

"I want you, Eve."

"I'm going to my room, Uncle. I won't come down to the new trawler. I've got a headache."

"Damn the new trawler. And your headache. Come, I want you."

She followed Job back to the table. She avoided Ben's eyes.

"Sam has sailed," Job said abruptly. "He sailed yesterday."

"But *Lodestar* isn't due to go until tomorrow or even the next day," Ben protested. "At the earliest tomorrow morning's tide."

"He's sailed all right. He's taken Melhuish's wreck *Carpathia*."

The table jolted and the cups and saucers rattled as Ben jumped up.

"Hell's bloody bells," he exploded. "I'll knock his goddam' block off for this. Who told you?"

"The office. I phoned to get Sam over here. They told me about *Carpathia*." Job stared at Ben, his eyes narrowed down to cold slits. "Charlie Bates was in the office. He told me a few more things, too."

Ben sat down slowly.

The tears welled up into Eve's eyes. She searched in her bag for a handkerchief. Job handed her his.

"If you're going to bellow, do it into something substantial," he snarled.

"I'm not bellowing, as you call it."

"Well, snivelling, then."

Eve sniffed then stood up and walked from the room.

"And she'll be a lot of good to me this morning. Just when I want her," Job snapped.

"What are you going to do?" Ben asked.

"I could contact Andrew Melhuish, get him to appoint another skipper and intercept Sam at Aberdeen, or the Orkneys, and have him flown to here."

Ben grinned.

"Two things. Melhuish's are not going to release a top skipper like Sam so easily, and Sam might say 'No'."

Job twisted his face into a snarl. "Melhuish will do as I say or I'll break them. And I'd fly to Aberdeen myself to talk to him."

"Take Eve with you," Ben said softly.

Job opened his mouth to speak but no words came. He rested his elbow on the table and wrapped his fist around his chin.

"So that was it? That's what the fight was about. That was why Sam struck your father."

"It was a sheer accident. It could have been me."

"True. It would have been more in character, and your father would have cussed you plenty and would have accepted your apology."

Ben scratched the back of his head.

"What are you going to do? Sam will say 'no'. You know that, of course."

"I do."

Job Benson stood up.

"Let's get going. You take her out on the tests. We'll decide who sails her when we get her back to Scoresby."

"We'll decide that right now," Ben said softly and distinctly. "I test her, I take her out and I fish with her until Sam is ready."

"I own her, Skipper Cleeve. I decide who sails as her skipper."

"And you find a better man than me or Sam and he can have her. Until then she's mine. I'll take her where you wish, I'll fish with her my way, and I'll make her pay, Mr Job Benson."

Slowly Job's face lost its hard lines. His eyes twinkled and he rested his hand on Ben's hunched-up shoulders.

"I remember a Skipper Cleeve talking to me like that forty years ago and more. You're your father's son all right, Ben. I never did find a better man. Until now."

"My father has two sons," Ben said softly. "Two sons. Me and my brother Sam. I'll get my hat and coat."

Job watched him stride across the room, then more slowly followed him.

"God help you if you're appointing yourself your brother's keeper. You'll want all the help He'll give." He shook his head slightly. "*Carpathia.* Glory be!"

CHAPTER FIFTEEN

GEEGEE climbed the short ladder. *Carpathia* was punching into a short, steep sea which was a modest legacy donated by a heavier gale farther north. He timed his thrust to the pitching roll of the trawler and pushed open the wheelhouse door.

Sam stood leaning against the for'ard bulkhead peering out through the spray-washed glass.

"I've just took the log," Geegee said carefully. "She's doing a shade under nine." He waited for a few moments, then continued artlessly: "Mind, she's got a bit of sea against her."

Sam made no reply.

"Two whole days and she's still steaming," Geegee went on. "Bloody marvellous."

"What are you doing up, now?" Sam asked coldly. "You've got the middle watch."

Geegee carefully rolled a cigarette, which ended up as a cone-shaped wreck from which errant strands hung in festoons.

"I've been speaking to one or two of the deckies," he said flatly. "One or two of them were not feeling well the first day out. I made allowances for that. Then they said they didn't feel very well today and wasn't going to go on watch."

Sam stood immobile.

"Then the Chief said one of his firemen wasn't feeling well either. The Chief spoke to him." Geegee let it hang in mid-air for a moment. "He had words with the Chief. So I spoke to him. And to the other invalids."

He turned his head towards Sam and blew his knuckles.

"Well?"

Sam turned his head.

Geegee caressed his knuckles tenderly.

"They're not feeling well now. But they'll come on watch. And Chief is getting his steam."

Sam's mouth twitched at the corners.

For a couple of minutes they stood in silence swaying to the rolling and pitching of *Carpathia*.

Sam broke the silence.

"That could be serious, Geegee. They could complain, and have you logged."

Geegee spit a few wandering shreds of tobacco from his lips and wiped them with the back of his hand.

"Would you like me to bring 'em up so that they can complain? They can still walk," he urged.

"If they have a complaint they'll make it to me in time."

"A quid gets you three they don't," Geegee said flatly. "I knows the pub they uses when they're ashore. Which is nearly always."

"Here, try one of these," Sam said, offering Geegee a cigarette.

Geegee got it glowing before he spoke again.

"Did you see Lofty on the quay when we sailed?" he asked.

"Yes. I saw him. Couldn't he bear to see you go?"

Geegee shored his hat up the back of his head until the broken peak was over his eyes.

"Lofty was there in case any of this dog's spew didn't turn up.

He figured there'd be a chance of a good man shipping as decky with us."

Sam glowed inwardly but said: "Two of you in one trawler. No, thanks."

"Let me tell you, mister," Geegee went on pugnaciously. "If I could have got ashore at the pier-head one or two of them late comers wouldn't have made it. They'd have been feeling *very* unwell. Then we'd have had to take Lofty on a pier-head jump."

"They'll lick into shape. They'll have to. I've got a living to make. So have you."

Geegee traced an intricate pattern in the misted condensation on the glass. He contemplated it for a few moments, then demolished it with the side of his hand. He opened his mouth to speak. Sam checked him.

"I know what you're going to ask." Sam paused, then went on. "Don't ask it."

Geegee turned on him indignantly.

"You got one of them glass balls like a fortune-teller had at Blackpool?" He grinned at Sam. "She ogled into it for a few minutes then told me I was going to suffer sorrow and pain. A dollar she charged. And she was right. Dead right." Geegee's grin developed into a chuckle.

"I'd got a head on me like a bucket after a skinful. And that was sorrow enough. Then I meets up with a couple of Fleetwood deckies who was having a week-end there. One word led to another and we has an up-and-downer. They wasn't bad, wasn't bad at all. Not for Fleetwood, anyway. And that was where the pain came in."

For the first time since he had walked in a daze from his father's house Sam laughed out loud. Had anybody mentioned psychology to Geegee he would have squared off and sparred for the first crack to avenge the insult, but vaguely he knew that if he could interest Sam in his simple little pleasures it would reduce the obvious tension under which Sam was labouring.

"You can laugh. The train back to Scoresby had square wheels and I was sitting right over one of 'em."

Then with startling abruptness he turned and towered over Sam.

"Why are we on this bloody rattle-trap?"

Sam locked eyes with Geegee for long seconds. Slowly he rested his forearms on the ledge in front of him and stared out of the window. Slowly at first he related to Geegee what had happened. He completed his narrative breathing heavily.

"Is that all it was about?" Geegee scoffed. He got straight down to elementals. "It would take more than a clip in the lug from you to hurt your Old Man. Why in hell didn't you and Ben go outside and slam it out? You could have let me and Lofty know and we could have got a grandstand seat." He drove his bunched fist into a palm with a sharp slap. "A couple of trips in this rack-and-ruin and you'll be back with Benson's."

Sam shook his head.

"No."

"We'll see."

Geegee rolled another travesty of a cigarette which he lit carefully.

"I've seen this Second Hand we've got somewhere. He doesn't say a lot, but he seems to know his way around. Do you know him?"

"I know of him. Andrew Melhuish asked me to take him." Sam turned from the window. "He was skipper of her a couple of trips ago. He put her ashore at the top end of the Sound of Islay and had his ticket suspended."

Geegee blew hard and his wreck of a cigarette showered sparks.

"That's fine and dandy," he exploded. "How come?"

Sam tilted his hand as if drinking.

"Huh huh," Geegee contributed.

"From what Melhuish told me he'd had a hell of a trip. He'd been working the Faroes and was on his way to Fleetwood with just enough to cover expenses. He'd had trouble. Lost a complete trawl. Trouble with the deckhands and he hit the bottle. He didn't get to the bridge in time when it came on thick and the Mate had let her go too far to the east'ard. She ran up on the beach. And that was that."

"Damage her much?"

"Not a lot, but the trip was a dead loss. They had to get tugs from Greenock."

"Them bleedin' pirates."

Geegee rolled towards the door of the wheelhouse.

"I'll take a squint at the log just to see that she isn't goin' astern then I'll take her for the next watch. O.K.?"

Sam nodded.

Carpathia plugged her laborious way until the dark, craggy fiords of Iceland were visible through the occasional lashing showers of rain.

Sam sighted a trawler slowly jogging along with trawl down. He studied his chart for a couple of minutes then clicked the switch of his loud-hailer.

"*Lynn Head* ahoy!" His metallic voice bounced over the spume-flecked rolling sea.

"Go ahead, *Carpathia*."

"I make it about eleven miles out. What do you make it?"

"'Bout the same."

"Any trouble with the patrol boats?"

"Not this end. They've been a bit fussy the other end. But the Navy's there. Two of 'em. One is a destroyer. Who are you, Skipper?"

Sam paused for a moment or two. "Skipper Cleeve. Sam Cleeve."

There was a pregnant silence.

"Did you say Sam Cleeve?"

"Yes."

"Sam Cleeve of Scoresby? Weren't you with Benson's?"

"I was."

Lynn Head was a Hull aristocrat with an equally aristocratic skipper.

The interval of silence was so long that Sam thought *Lynn Head* had finished speaking.

Then: "Good luck, Cleeve," came thinly over the sea.

Sam waved his arm.

He turned to his Mate. "I'll work east of here. Put it over about three-quarters of an hour."

Sam switched on his echo-sounder and closely studied the flickering green line which raced across the grey-black screen. It showed him he was running along a ledge. When it deepened he could see that his soundings were showing him a valley. It was that valley he intended to search.

He stepped out on to the bridge wing and lifted his arm. Geegee had the tall-poled dan buoy with its string of football-sized pellets hanging over the side on a slip hook.

Sam waved. Geegee swung a hammer and the buoy dropped and was soon bobbing and swaying in the water.

The heavy wooden trawl doors, which would tend to swing outwards and keep the hundred-foot trawl's mouth open, hung from the gallows on the quarter and on the fore-deck.

"Over with it."

The long conical trawl slipped over the side snaking out astern, then the doors dropped into the water as Geegee released the powerful brake on the big winch. Geegee watched the markers on the wires slipping off the drum and kept his eyes on Sam leaning on the bridge.

Geegee yelled the amount of wire out.

Sam twisted his arms as if screwing the brake down and Geegee wrestled with the big brake-wheel.

"All fast," he signalled.

Aft the Mate secured the two snaking wires close to the ship's side with a huge block. He rested his finger-tips on the wires and could feel the thrum of them as the heavy trawl rolled along the bottom. His finger-tips told him the trawl was running fair. He held his hand up with thumb erect.

Sam turned to find Geegee at his elbow.

"I wouldn't fly kites with them trawl warps," Geegee said. "And they've been end for ended once already."

"They'll do. I'll give her around two and a half hours just to see how it shapes."

Nearly three hours had elapsed when Sam signalled, "Bring it in."

Slowly the twin wires rolled dripping wet around the drum of the winch shedding silver drops as it did so. When there was only a couple of hundred fathom out Geegee eased back the steam on the winch.

"Up she comes," a deckhand yelled, pointing. The tightly packed cod end in the toe of the trawl suddenly broke surface astern, filled to bursting point with fish, their distended lungs giving it tremendous buoyancy.

As *Carpathia* rolled so the men leaned over the side and slowly won in the trawl foot by foot. Then a wire from the derrick was made fast to the cod end and it swung aloft.

Geegee ducked under it, pulled the complicated knot and ducked away again from the silver cascade of fish.

"Luvverly stuff," he yelled up to Sam. "There's not a dog in a ton of it."

"Get it over again," Sam replied coldly. "It will only get fish if it's on the bottom."

And over it went.

Straddle-legged against the roll of the trawler the men worked swiftly gutting, flicking the livers to one side and tossing them below where men packed them in the ice.

"This bleedin' skipper can catch fish," one decky panted, straightening his back momentarily. "At this rate we'll soon pack her full."

"Less jabber and get 'em below," Geegee snarled. "Then we can have a mug of tea."

On the bridge Sam suddenly picked up his binoculars.

"Huh huh," he grunted. The Mate looked in the same direction.

"The Bogey Man. I wondered when he'd show up."

The patrol ship slowly circled *Carpathia* with two officers on her bridge studying the trawler.

"Taking our number," the Mate said. "Do you think he'll come alongside?"

"Here's his playmate," Sam said.

The Mate followed his pointing arm. As if materializing out of the grey shadows there came the long, lean length of a destroyer. The naval ship spun around and at slow speed steamed alongside *Carpathia*.

"'Morning, Skipper. Any trouble?"

"Not a speck," Sam answered. "Can you get close enough for me to give you a fry?"

The answering voice held a chuckle.

"Watch me."

The gap narrowed until the destroyer was only a few feet from *Carpathia*. They heard a faint "plop" and a line snaked over. In a few minutes a large bag of fish was transferred to the destroyer.

"Is that your black-and-white buoy on your port quarter?" the officer on the destroyer asked.

"Yes."

"Well, for your information, it's eleven miles six cables out. Near enough. You're quite in order fishing here."

"And the Bogey Man?" Sam asked.

"If he touches you, scream for Mamma." The chuckle became more obvious. "I'm Mamma." The chuckle disappeared. "Don't try anything yourself, will you?"

"If we stemmed him with this rattle-trap we'd shove the bow back into the engine room," Geegee growled.

"I won't," promised Sam.

"We'll never be far away from you. Scream good and hearty. 'Bye now."

The patrol boat had moved away. There was a sudden gout of

smoke from the destroyer's funnel, she seemed to shoot forward, then adjusted her speed so that she was not far astern of the patrol boat. And so they disappeared into the murk.

The weather was kindly to Sam for the next week or so, and although his hauls were not phenomenal they were good. Even the deckhands seemed to feel that they were working under a master of his craft and not merely with a man who scratched a living.

If there was one man of the crew who was puzzled by Sam it was the radio operator. Each evening at seven o'clock Sam would step into the office, switch on to the trawler band and listen.

The radio operator in one of his rare excursions into the open air joined Geegee on the bridge.

"Skipper says two more days and we're bound for the Rio Grand," he started conversationally. "He's in the office now listening to the jabber. But he never joins in. Not a squeak."

"Just as well," Geegee growled. "There's too much chinwag going on."

Sam stood in the office leaning against the small desk. He gently thumbed a knurled knob round until the thin voices became plainer. Eventually came the voice he was listening for.

Charlie Bates's asthmatic wheeze was as clear as if he were in the room with him.

"I was wondering," said Charlie to the world at large, "how some of them sheep in that box was making out. Just like sheep, they are. Fishing by numbers. Lining up to take their chance. How some of the scrap-heaps I know about has the nerve to come this far north beats me."

Sam smiled. Charlie Bates was dangling his bait skilfully.

"Filling the fish-hold with dogs and other rubbish," Charlie went on remorselessly. "Ashamed to tell how they're doing. I've met 'em." Charlie slipped an innocuous sentence into his monologue which told Sam where he was fishing. Charlie Bates was nearer to Bear Island than he was to Iceland.

Sam listened for a few minutes more to the general chatter then flicked the knob.

Buller Cleeve, too, sat listening. Night after night he had switched on his set as the old clock started its ruminative rumble.

The low rumble brought Mrs Cleeve to the door of the room and she watched Buller Cleeve switch on and delicately turn the knobs.

The voice he waited to hear did not come from the set.

"Perhaps he's busy," Mrs Cleeve said. "That old trawler may be making him work hard. I do wish he hadn't gone on her," she said, repeating what had become almost a litany with her.

"He's listening all right. Charlie will get him on sooner or later."

And eventually Sam called: "Right. That's the lot. Home we go."

Carpathia was but a few hours out from Scoresby when the Chief Engineer came clattering up to the wheelhouse.

"You'll have to slow her down. I've got a cross head running hot. It's almost glowing."

"I was wondering when her luck would give out," Geegee snarled. "This is it."

"Knock her back, Chief. Let me know how things go," Sam said coldly. "If you want her stopped do it now, not later when I'm in the channel." He turned to Geegee. "And less talk about luck—in or out."

Two hours later the Chief called up the voice-pipe: "I've fixed it best I can. There's less tools in this thing than in a kid's Meccano set. She'll clout, but she'll make it if we don't drive."

Andrew Melhuish rubbed his hands when he saw Sam's report of the catch.

"Very good, Skipper Cleeve, very good." He looked at Sam from beneath lowered eyelids. "You'll—er—you'll be taking her next trip?"

"Why not?"

"I—er—I wondered if—er—perhaps you'd make peace with Benson's. . . ."

"I haven't quarrelled with Benson's. Here is a list of defects and some replacements. Sail Tuesday?"

Andrew Melhuish pulled a long face when he saw the list. "This will take some of the cream off," he said mournfully. "Quite a lot of it."

"Without them attended to there'll be no cream," Sam said levelly. "A man is just as good as the tools in his hand. Those trawl warps have been end for ended anyway."

Sam had his way.

He stayed away from the club and avoided haunts where he might have met friends until *Carpathia* was ready to sail again.

A red-eyed, morose Geegee was leaning against the rail as Sam boarded her.

"Lost the toss again?"

"I didn't lose it. I won it last time. Lofty is with Charlie Bates in *Morning Star*. Lucky son of a bitch."

"You did all right last trip, didn't you? As much as you would have got on *Lodestar*."

"I ain't moaning." Geegee brightened a little. "I see we got a couple of new warps. That's something anyway. And most of the invalids are coming again. A couple of 'em even bought me a drink or two."

Carpathia slipped from the quay and lifted her bow to the gentle swell outside. Then she swung north.

Sam was in his berth lying on the settee reading when Geegee called down the voice-pipe.

"Hey, Skipper. Come an' take a look at this lot."

Geegee extended an arm as Sam joined him.

"She looks like a perishin' battle-cruiser. She's in Benson's colours and she's got 'SY' on her bow."

Sam followed Geegee's pointing arm. A mile away, pushing a rolling wave in front of her, was Job Benson's new trawler bound for Scoresby.

Sam lifted his binoculars and three figures on the bridge jerked into view. There were two men and a woman. Job, Ben and Eve.

The mile was reduced to less than half as the two trawlers converged. The woman waved, a resonant booming note came from her siren.

Geegee reached up to the whistle lanyard to give an answering whistle.

"Leave it," Sam snapped.

"I was just going to give her a toot."

"Leave it."

Sam stood with his hands in his coat pockets staring ahead as the new trawler, *Orion*, passed within two or three hundred yards. He heard the hollow zonk as the loud-hailer was switched on.

"Hey, Sam. Sam," came booming over the water. "How are you, boy?"

Sam remained motionless.

Then a thinner, higher voice came from the loud-hailer.

"Sam. This is Eve. How are you?"

Sam turned abruptly and walked into the wheelhouse.

Soon *Orion* was astern and eventually disappeared into the autumn haze.

"Well, I'll be goddamed!" Geegee said softly. "I'll be goddamed twice."

As *Carpathia* slipped astern, Eve walked across the wide bridge and stood gazing out at the sea. Ben moved as if he would join her. Job checked him with a hand on his arm. He shook his head.

Eve did comforting things with a minute fragment of handkerchief.

"He could have answered, couldn't he?" Ben said. "Especially when Eve spoke to him. Well, couldn't he?"

"If he had I would have been surprised," Job said softly. "Very surprised." He looked at his watch. "We should catch the tail-end of the tide with luck. We'll try to get old Buller down on board tomorrow. His comments on this ship would be worth hearing."

"A pound gets you two you won't get him aboard," Ben grinned. "That's a bet."

And Ben lost. Buller Cleeve, guided by Job Benson and Ben, stepped gingerly on board *Orion*, listened carefully to a detailed description of her workings and shook his head.

"Job," he said, when they were sitting in Ben's capacious berth, "I could still find my way around on a real trawler. But this factory . . ." He finished with a shake of his head. "She's not a trawler, not a trawler at all."

Job laughed and held out his hand to Ben. "Two pound, please."

CHAPTER SIXTEEN

BEN had taken *Orion* through her steaming and trawling without developing any further enthusiasm for the ship.

"Don't misunderstand me," he had explained to Job. "If Sam had been available I would have stepped down. As he isn't, then I'll run her for you. Unless, that is, you can find a better man."

Finally the day came when Job and the German directors sat around a table studying in detail some long foolscap sheets which eventually were signed by all parties.

"Now she's ours." Job smiled at Eve.

"I nearly said 'ours to sink or swim'. It would have been an unfortunate remark," Eve said to Ben. "I'm afraid our literal-minded German friends would have taken me seriously."

"She won't sink, never fear."

Eve held just a glimmering of a smile.

"Not only our German friends, I see."

Eve waved away a replenishment of her glass but Ben had his filled.

"Eve. You've been avoiding me on the few days I have had ashore. Not exactly dodging me, but taking care that I would not be alone with you. Why?" He almost snapped the last: "Are you afraid of me?"

"Truthfully?"

"Nothing else but."

Eve slowly traced the outline of her cheekbone with her forefinger. Suddenly, decisively the finger went up over her temple and through the cluster of hair about her ear.

"Yes and no."

Ben jeered. "That's truth if you like. I pays my penny and I takes my choice." He laid his hand on her forearm. "I'll tell you what. Your uncle will be quite happy with these builders. Let's cut dinner. We'll go to that little club again, feed and dance. It's our last night here. Let's do the town, shall we?"

Eve's first instinct was to say "No". Instead she nodded. "If Uncle approves."

"He will." Ben grinned at her wickedly. "I'll tell him that you don't want to sit through dinner with half a dozen old fogies."

"Don't you dare." She watched Ben walk over to the group of older men and saw her uncle nod his head after a quick glance in her direction. Suddenly she felt a tremulous shiver and could feel her heart pound some extra-heavy beats.

"That's that," Ben said with satisfaction. "Let's go."

Ben went into earnest conclave with the waiter who nodded repeatedly and wrote rapidly on a pad. Two icy-cold glasses containing pale-green cocktails started the evening. They danced between courses with a couple of bottles of hock. Eve shook her head against a brandy and they were on the dance floor when the waiter produced the champagne and had it open as they returned to the table.

"To *Orion*," Ben said, lifting his glass.

Eve sipped at hers and held the glass level with her eyes. After two or three glasses she found she had shed some of the reserve she had erected. Somehow her steps seemed to be lighter. Somehow Ben's arm seemed to be round her just a little firmer. She could feel the muscles of his shoulder ripple slightly as he turned her. Gradually her arm crept a little farther round his neck. Ben fancied that she clung just a little tighter to him, her body seemed more supple. He looked down and found her head was tilted up to him, her lips were parted slightly. There was a liquid glow about her eyes.

Ben stumbled slightly, quickly recovered his poise and stopped in the middle of the floor. They stood as they were for a few moments, he with his arm round her waist and she with her arm round his neck.

"Let's sit down," Ben said thickly.

Eve nodded. As she walked back to the table she wished with all her heart that she could control the weakness of her legs. They felt watery and from them little darting tremors ran up her back like tiny electric shocks.

She sought refuge in raillery.

"You're drunk, Ben."

She expected a determined denial. Ben lit a cigarette and drew heavily on it two or three times before he answered.

"Blind drunk. Really pickled." He leaned forward and covered her hand with his. "Completely intoxicated. But not on brandy or champagne."

"On what?" Eve could have bitten off the end of her tongue a second after she asked the question.

Ben stood up. He looked down at her. Two little muscles in his cheeks twitched rapidly. His voice was so low it was almost a hoarse whisper.

"You."

He held out a hand and helped her upright.

Outside the club Ben called a taxi. As they sat down in it he put his arm round Eve and she prepared to resist an attempt to kiss her. He made no such attempt. His fingers closed on her shoulder and the pressure came near to hurting her, but she made no protest.

"Has my uncle gone to bed?" Eve asked as Ben collected their keys.

"More than an hour ago," the night receptionist answered.

Ben opened the door of her room and stood to one side for her to enter. She switched on the lights and stood looking at him. He took one step into the room and she retreated one step from him. Without turning he reached behind him and closed the door. Swiftly he put a finger on the light switch and switched the main light off, leaving only the restricted light coming from a bedside lamp.

Eve stood erect, lips slightly parted, breathing quickly, almost in tiny panting breaths.

Ben suddenly swooped and picked her up in his arms, meeting

no resistance. He strode over to the bed and laid her on it. Then he bent over and kissed her brutally on the mouth. He lifted his head.

"Ben," she whispered in a small trembling voice.

"Eve."

"We won't want this either," she whispered, and she switched off the bedside lamp.

"Ben, oh, Ben."

"Eve." He began searching for the unfamiliar fastenings.

Ben stood looking out of the window. The only light was diffused from the city lights outside.

"Eve. Will you marry me?"

She didn't answer. He repeated it.

"Eve, will you marry me?"

"I can't answer that now, Ben."

He turned. In the diffused glow he could see the slim white column of her body lying on the bed. He crossed over to her.

"I want you to."

"But . . . but I'm not in love with you, Ben. Not *really* in love with you. At least I don't think so. Please don't press me to answer that now. Give me a little time to think it out."

"You'd be happy, Eve. I promise you that."

"Not now, Ben, please."

He slipped one arm behind her head and lifted it up. His lips met hers and her arms crept round his neck.

"But I love you, Eve. And that's the truth."

"Ben. Oh, Ben," she whispered. And once again it was complete and sweet surrender.

At breakfast the next morning Job tossed a buff telegram over to Ben.

"Your crew arrives this morning. Ten of them. The builders are sending some engine-room staff over with you so you have some firemen and deckhands."

"Fair enough. I'll meet 'em later."

Job pinched his lower lip between finger and thumb.

"I've been thinking, Ben. Eve can fly back this afternoon and I can sail over with you. It's been a long time since I was on a bridge in the open sea."

"Why can't I come, too?" Eve sat bolt upright.

Ben and Job exchanged glances.

"One moment," Ben said, standing up. "There's something I want to know first of all."

He strode from the room and returned in a few minutes carrying a flimsy sheet of paper.

"A mill pond all the way." He smiled. "I've been getting the weather forecast. 'Winds light, visibility ten to fifteen miles.' The North Sea is no place for a greenhorn in even a moderate summer blow." He grinned at Eve wickedly. "But if you feel squeamish I'll pat your hand and hold your head."

"I'll look forward to that. How long will it take?"

"Twenty-four to thirty hours. We won't drive her hard. I've asked the desk to cancel your air bookings. That all right?"

Job nodded.

"Then all passengers aboard by twelve o'clock," Ben intoned. "Deck quoits, deck-chairs and tickets in the sweepstake may be obtained from the Chief Steward."

Eve gained a new insight into Ben's character as the new, large trawler was skilfully manoeuvred from the quay wall. She and Job remained discreetly in the background on the bridge as the pilot and Ben took her seawards through a maze of buoys and an almost endless stream of incoming shipping.

Orders came swiftly and crisply as *Orion* swung away from a fat-bellied freighter pushing a yellow foaming bow wave in front of her. It appeared as if the ocean-going ship was bent on driving her stem into *Orion* but the trawler passed her with two or three hundred yards to spare. On the freighter's bridge some officers studied *Orion* through binoculars. Then they waved and Eve waved back.

The yellow-funnelled pilot cutter came alongside and took off their pilot and Ben headed her for the open sea.

Eve was fascinated, not only by the scene around her but by the crisp, brief orders with which Ben controlled the ship. Only once did he spare a few moments from his task. He looked at Eve and found her wide-open eyes gazing at him.

Ben smiled.

"Enjoying it?"

"Immensely."

"I won't be quite so busy when we get into the open sea."

The sun hung a hairsbreadth above the knife-edged horizon later that afternoon and Eve, who had spent some time below with her uncle, climbed once more to the bridge.

"Now I can talk," Ben said. "Fire away with your questions."

"I haven't any. At least I've a million, but they can wait. I want to enjoy this moment. Look at that sun."

"I'm thinking of the fog it might bring with it tomorrow. Sometimes it does follow a sun like that."

Half-darkness laid a tentative claim as the sun swiftly slipped out of sight and Eve suddenly found that what had appeared to be open sea was filled with a bewildering array of lights.

"A lightship. Shows the south edge of a shallow bank," Ben explained, pointing to a flashing white light a few miles away. "That one ahead is a buoy. It flashes three times every ten seconds so I know what it is. It's marked on the chart. Look, I'll show you."

They went into the chart room and Ben showed her the light-ships and the buoys marked clearly on the chart with their characteristics printed alongside them."

"But when it's thick fog, or raining, and you can't see, how do you get along then?"

"Steam and pray." Ben chuckled.

On the bridge again Eve shivered.

"I feel cold, Ben. I think I'll go below to my room. I feel tired, too. It's been an exciting day."

"Tomorrow will be another when we steam into Scoresby with this giant."

"When will you get some rest?"

"The Mate will take her over at midnight. I'll get a few hours' sleep."

Eve found the subdued drone of the diesel engines soothing. She could feel the faint tremor of them, and although *Orion* was on an even keel in an almost flat calm sea the curtains moved slightly as the torque of the propeller caused her to roll slightly. She started to think over immediate past events. Of Ben, of his masterful, ruthless domination of her. She had watched him through the day with increasing realization that while he had his gay streak he could be chilled cold steel demanding instant obedience. She had, too, realized that he knew what he wanted, knew where he was going and interference would be brushed aside. She snuggled into her pillow and started an analysis. Was she in love with him? Was it love? Was there something missing?

And she awoke to find daylight streaming through her porthole and a youngster standing alongside her bunk with a cup of tea precariously balanced in one hand.

"Skipper said to give you a shout and to bring you a cup of

tea, miss. And he said we'd be in Scoresby Roads in about two hours. We've made good time."

Eve knelt on the settee and gazed out the porthole. The deep-green sea, fractured into a million flecks of white as *Orion* drove her clean bow into it, seemed to be rushing past in a smother of foam.

In the distance she could see a cloud of black smoke dwindling down to a small, tall-funnelled ship.

"Sleep all right?" Ben smiled later on the bridge. "Did you have a nice breakfast?"

"I slept like a top and they offered me about four times as much as I wanted for breakfast. Where are we?"

Ben pointed to a dark-grey mass which hung low in the sky ahead like a solid cloud.

"That's the Head. Scoresby sits just under it."

He offered her his binoculars and she peered through them. It still looked like a cloud to her.

Job Benson climbed slowly to the bridge.

"You won't catch this tide, Ben. What will you do? Anchor her in the roadstead?"

"We might catch the end of it, with luck."

Ben lifted his glasses and studied two or three trawlers steaming past.

"None of them ours," he said briefly. He lifted the binoculars to look at another trawler.

"Well, well," he said softly, still staring through his glasses. "Could be." He handed them to Job. "You know the numbers better than I do. Who is she?"

Job looked steadily at the approaching trawler, adjusted the focus then looked at Ben.

"It's *Carpathia*."

Ben paused and spoke briefly into the wheelhouse and *Orion*'s bow swung slowly to take her closer to the other trawler. Soon they were within half a mile of her and closing rapidly.

Ben reached up for the whistle lanyard and the deep note boomed out and rolled across the sea.

Through the binoculars they could see two men standing on the bridge wing. The powerful glasses brought them to within a few yards.

"That's Sam and Geegee," Ben said. "That damned traitor Geegee."

He turned to find Eve standing at his elbow.

"Please," she said softly. Ben handed her the glasses. She lifted them to her eyes.

No answering whistle came from *Carpathia.*

Ben switched on the loud-hailer.

To Eve it was so close that she felt she could reach out and touch Sam. She handed back the binoculars to Ben and walked to the edge of the bridge. She waved and waited for the answering wave.

There was none.

Ben lifted the microphone to his mouth.

"Hey, Sam. Sam," he called. "How are you, boy?"

They waited.

Eve held out her hand.

"Please," she said, taking the microphone from Ben.

"Sam. This is Eve. How are you?"

One of the two figures turned and walked into the wheelhouse. The other remained outside. As the two ships passed he lifted one arm briefly and waved.

"Geegee, the damned traitor," Ben gritted softly. "A couple of damned traitors."

Job's mouth twitched slightly.

"D'you think so?" he said in a low voice.

Ben stood with his chest pressed against the front of the bridge, a scowl on his face. His hands were thrust deeply into coat pockets.

Job caught Eve's eyes and his face dissolved into a gentle smile.

"I think I'll go below and help myself to a coffee," he said. "Join me, Eve?"

She shook her head.

She stepped up close to Ben and stood beside him.

"Hurt?" she asked.

"I'll hurt him. I'll hurt both of them when I get a chance," Ben growled.

"That wasn't what I asked you."

Ben stared ahead without answering.

"I asked you if you were hurt?"

"Not hurt. Bloody furious. It's not like Sam to carry a grudge this far. After all, he's my brother. And blood is thicker than water." He turned sharply to Eve. "Is it my fancy or do you lean over backwards to find excuses for him every time we mention his name?"

"No. But I think I understand more than you do."

"Tell me, Eve. Are you in love with Sam?"

Eve took her bottom lip between her teeth and gnawed at it slightly.

"Apart from the meeting on the train and lunch at the club I've seen nothing of Sam. And you know it. The question of being in love hasn't arisen."

"Is that supposed to be an answer?"

"It is an answer." She laid her hand on Ben's sleeve. "You asked me once if I was in love with you. You asked me to marry you." She turned away to the broad ladder at the top of the bridge. "The answer to that is 'Yes'. I will marry you, Ben."

Before Ben could assimilate her last sentence she was gone down the ladder.

He stood there breathing deeply for a moment, took a half step towards the top of the ladder, turned back again and shouted into the wheelhouse:

"Keep her steady now. Don't do any wandering." He put his hand on the telegraph and jammed it down to "Full speed".

Eve took a chair opposite her uncle.

"I've changed my mind. I will have coffee, Uncle."

She stirred it slowly.

"Uncle Job. I'm going to marry Ben Cleeve."

She waited for her uncle to show surprise.

"Is that what you want, Eve."

She nodded slowly. She dropped her head and her eyes filled with tears.

"I've accepted him."

"Your aunt will be pleased, Eve. He's a good boy." Her uncle climbed to his feet and walked round the table. "They are both good boys."

She was alone with her thoughts.

As Job climbed the ladder he said softly to himself: "And there are three traitors at sea this good day. Three traitors to themselves only."

CHAPTER SEVENTEEN

A BOISTEROUS autumn wore itself into a prolonged and savage winter, gale followed gale with scarcely an interval between them.

Sam drove *Carpathia* and her crew remorselessly until the men reeled down to their bunks with a weariness in their bodies and their souls. But they sailed with him trip after trip. Melhuish agreed to a bonus scheme for the deckhands and some of them ended up each trip with more in their pockets than they had earned in six months before joining *Carpathia*.

The ship, too, complained almost continuously, complaints which articulated themselves in doleful prophecies by the Chief Engineer and more lurid criticisms by Geegee.

The weary giant draped himself over the steering-engine casing in the wheelhouse and rested his chin on his forearm.

"You're riding your luck, Sam Cleeve. Riding it hard. This rattle-trap won't stand up to it. One day that winch is going to rip itself out of the deck and take half a dozen deckies with it. The trawl boards . . . well . . . I don't know how they're keeping together."

"We fill her up, don't we?" Sam said coldly.

"Yes, we fill her up," Geegee answered wearily. "But this luck won't hold. Sooner or later she'll pay us out."

"When that happens I'll meet it. Until then, stop moaning."

Geegee remembered the day that Sam learned his brother was to marry Eve. They had sailed late in the evening and *Carpathia*'s head was pointed north. Geegee had the bridge as Sam changed into his sea-going gear in his berth.

The deckhand at the wheel yearned for conversation.

"I was swapping yarns with some of *Orion*'s crowd in a pub," he started off. "They're still having trouble with that stern-trawl lark."

"They can keep it for me," Geegee growled.

"The lads on her are looking forward to a booze-up when they get back."

"How come? They going to set up a new record with her?"

"No. Ben Cleeve is going to marry that bint of Job Benson's next trip home. He's——"

The startled deckhand felt himself wrenched from the wheel and brutally jammed against the bulkhead. Sam had quietly climbed to the wheelhouse in time to hear the remark.

"What did you say? Say it again." With each phrase Sam slammed the deckhand against the bulkhead, his hands grasping the man's thick woollen jersey.

"Easy, Sam, boy," Geegee yelled. He exerted all his strength to wrench Sam away from the youngster.

"He's lying. I'll break his damned neck," Sam panted.

Geegee turned to the young deckhand. "You hang on to the wheel, son." With his gigantic arms wrapped around Sam he

wrestled with him until he had him pinned against the door.
"Now take it easy, Sam. The kid's only repeating what he's
heard."

Gradually Sam fought his rage until he had control of himself.

"All right, Geegee. Let go." He turned to the deckhand. "Now
tell me what you heard."

The deckhand shuffled his feet, afraid to retail his news in case
it started another violent attack on him.

"Go on, son. It's all right," Geegee urged.

"The Mate of the *Orion* and some of the lads was in the Rose
and Crown. In the saloon bar," he added, as if it were to give it
extra authority. "They was saying that next trip home they was in
for a booze-up because . . . because Ben Cleeve was going to marry
that girl of Job Benson's. They'd been promised a slap-up do."

Sam spun sharply and left the wheelhouse.

After a few minutes' silence Geegee said silkily: "You wasn't
thinking of making anything official about that bit of a push the
skipper gave you?" He put his face close to the deckhand's. "You
wasn't, was you?"

The decky shook his head.

Sam hazed and drove the trawler and her crew until they were
on the verge of mutiny that trip and arrived back with a catch
which made even seasoned trawler skippers raise their eyebrows.
One of them summarized it.

"Anybody who can land a catch like that in the weather we've
been having is either a genius . . . or he's stark raving mad."

The next trip was a repetition of it.

The day his brother married Eve Sam slammed *Carpathia* alongside the quay wall, reported to his owner and disappeared until
it was time to sail, then he arrived on board red-eyed and explosive.

For the rest of the trip, through foul, vicious weather, the faithful giant Geegee acted as a buffer between Sam and the crew.
But when they steamed into Scoresby, battered and weary, the
ship red with rust, Geegee felt he had had enough.

"I'm not coming next trip," he said shortly to Sam as they stood
on the deck. "I feel like a rest."

"As you wish. There are plenty of bos'ns around." Sam turned
on his heel and entered his berth.

But Geegee sailed nevertheless.

Partly because of Eve.

Her wedding day had dawned sun-kissed by a pale winter sun

which flooded into her bedroom as her bridesmaids helped her to
dress.

Her aunt had entered the room and had stood back to admire
her.

"Eve, you look wonderful. And you're going to be so happy. Ben
Cleeve will be a good husband for you."

Ben had turned as he heard her and her bridesmaids coming
up the aisle and had caught his breath at her sheer beauty.

His glance travelled to the pew in which stood his father and
mother and he could see his mother, mouth close to Buller's ear,
giving him a word picture of Eve. He smiled briefly at his mother.

And he and Eve were joined together in holy matrimony.

Ben had one unspoken regret. His best man should have been
his brother.

Although *Carpathia* and *Orion* were but a few miles apart in
succeeding trips they never made contact. Sam never joined in
the multiple conversations going on over the radio.

Ben had listened, so had Charlie Bates, and Buller Cleeve's
sensitive fingers had twirled the knob in vain.

Then one night, walking along, head down against a driving
rain Sam had bumped into somebody.

"Sam Cleeve, as blind as a bat as usual," a voice had wheezed.

"Hullo, Charlie."

Charlie Bates took a firm grasp of Sam's arm.

"Now, either you buy me a drink at the club or I twist this
arm off. Which is it to be?"

"I'll buy you one."

The first drink was restrained. Sam refused to come out from
behind his barrier. He nodded briefly to skippers he knew and
answered Charlie Bates in short, clipped sentences.

Finally in exasperation Charlie said: "I ought to knock your
block off—or shove you across my knee. You're making your
mother and father unhappy. You're making me unhappy and . . ."
He paused.

"Go on."

"All right. Ben and Eve are unhappy, too. Just because you are
a pig-headed obstinate boy who hates the thought of being second
best. Now you've got it."

Charlie climbed to his feet, lifted his glass, surveyed the
remnants of a drink in it and tossed it back.

"Bah. You make me tired," he snorted, and strode from the
room.

As he stood in the vestibule, struggling into his heavy raincoat, he glanced through the curtains at Sam still seated at the table. He was leaning back, head on his chest, slowly twirling the empty glass. The club waiter approached him and Charlie saw Sam shake his head.

Charlie went out into the rain with a half-smile playing about his mouth.

A little later, as he carefully poured out two drinks for Buller Cleeve and himself, he said softly: "Met Sam tonight. Wouldn't be surprised if he showed up or joined in the talk on his next trip. We'll see."

Sam walked from the club. The rain had stopped and wind-racked clouds raced across the face of the moon. Without conscious guidance he walked up to the bastions and stood against the wall, looking down at the docks with its wriggling maze of reflections lacing the water.

He became aware of somebody standing alongside him.

"Sam," she said softly.

He jerked around.

"Eve." It escaped from him almost in a gasp.

"It's been a long time, Sam. Too long."

Suddenly he felt calm and collected. Almost cold.

"So Charlie Bates was saying a little earlier."

She laid a hand on his arm.

"Sam. I'm going to take a lot of short cuts. We want you back. All of us. Your parents, Uncle Job, me. . . ."

"And Ben? Your husband."

"And Ben, my husband?"

"Quite an array of people wanting me. I'm here. I'm living a life I want."

She moved closer to him.

"I've been puzzled, Sam. That . . . that brawl you had with Ben, when your father was struck . . . well, it was all over in a few hours. Yes, it was." She sensed he was going to speak. "Your father told me so himself. And Ben was ready to laugh it off. Why did you, Sam? Why have you cut yourself off from everything that was yours?"

She waited. Then she went on.

"Was it because Ben got *Orion*? Well, listen to me. Ben wanted to give her up in Germany for you. He didn't want her. He doesn't now. You can have her. Was there anything else in the world you wanted? Anything?"

Sam turned swiftly. He put his arm round her and before she could avoid him by twisting away he kissed her full on the mouth.

"Yes. There was. Good night, Mrs Ben Cleeve."

And he was gone into the darkness.

But Geegee found him more amenable, not so steel hard and, not without some half-formed misgivings, he decided to sail with Sam yet again.

"You're riding your luck, Sam Cleeve. Riding it hard. This rattle-trap won't stand up to it. . . ."

Carpathia slammed steadily north through foul weather, lurching up to the crest of white-topped seas, descending into the troughs in a vicious twisting roll before plunging her whale-backed bow into another sea with a jolt which shook her as if she had hit solid rock.

"There'll be no Bogey Man around this weather," Geegee hazarded. "We could fish two miles off and get away with it, never mind twelve."

Sam tapped the compass. "See the course? That's not for Iceland. I'm going to try off Bear Island."

Geegee sighed.

"Why do we ship ice at Scoresby? There's enough up there for us."

"You'll love it." Sam grinned.

Five days later they were dodging slowly, almost hove-to, when the full fury of a gale remorselessly started collecting its victims.

Sam was lying down on his settee when the radio operator entered his berth.

"Trouble," he said succinctly. "Somebody's met it."

Sam struggled wearily over to the chart and checked the position.

"A hundred and seventy miles away. Anybody answering him close to?"

"A couple."

"Let me know what goes on. What's the weather forecast? As if I can't guess."

"Then you'd guess wrong. Gales are going to die away and it's going to be cold. Bloody cold."

"That'll be a change."

Then came a phenomenon which old trawlermen could only vaguely remember as having happened once before. The gale died away to a mere whisper in a few hours and the thermometer dropped steadily through zero to more than twenty degrees below. More than fifty degrees of frost. There was no wind to ruffle the oily slow swell and a thin grey mist rose from the sea in a writhing curtain little higher than mast high.

"It looks like steam, doesn't it?" a deckhand said.

"Draw a bucket of water and put your hand in it," Geegee scorned. "And you'd lose your fingers."

"Ever seen it like this before?" Geegee asked Sam later.

"Never. I've seen ice build itself up on a trawler, but never this."

"Look at her! She looks as if she has been sprayed with grey paint. Only it's thicker."

The thin, tenuous mist settled softly on *Carpathia* until it was a couple of feet thick.

"I've heard Father talk about something like this. The Germans call it the 'Black Frost'." Sam tapped the thermometer with a finger-nail and it jerked down a few more degrees until the quicksilver was out of sight. "Nearly sixty degrees of frost, Geegee."

Geegee rubbed his hand over his short stubbled hair. "I've seen trawlers iced up before this. Remember that trip on *Lodestar* when we had to have the hands chopping ice off her? Some of that was two or three feet thick, but you could give the bulkhead a bit of a belt and fetch the ice down in a shower. This stuff . . ."

He thumped the wheelhouse window with his knuckles.

"Look at it!" he exploded. "It's like . . . like frozen treacle. You can't shift it."

"Skipper. Can you come in here a moment?" The radio operator's voice carried a note of urgency.

"What's up?" Sam asked.

"Listen." The radio operator adjusted his set.

". . . I've never seen anything like this," a tenuous voice gained strength as the radio operator touched a knob. "I've just hauled and my trawl and fish are frozen into a solid mass. I've got the lads trying to chop it free. But it's not much good." The thin thread of fear began to show through the weave. "And she's as sluggish as hell. She's top-heavy with this ice. A bit of a blow and I'm in trouble."

"You're in trouble!" a deeper voice cut in. "I'm still half full of water after that last gale. I can't get her head up. She is nose down like a pig."

A high-pitched voice with a Lancashire accent said: "What

are you fellas talking about? It's cold where I am, but the sky is clear. Brilliant sun. But really cold."

Sam listened carefully for the next hour or so and made notes. Then he checked on the chart and drew two pencil marks.

The dour Second Hand and Geegee were in the wheelhouse where Sam joined them.

"This is something beyond me," he started. "Look."

He spread the chart and Geegee and the other man craned over his shoulder to study it.

"*Saracen's Head* and *Lynn Head* are fishing here." Sam stabbed at the chart with a finger. "That's about ninety to a hundred miles to the west'ard. Now, they are in flat calm, cold but clear. We are here." Again the finger stabbed down to a spot a few miles south-west of Bear Island. "So far as I can find out there is nobody east of us. Get it?"

Geegee and the Mate exchanged glances.

"No. What are you driving at?"

"This . . ." Sam waved a hand expansively. "This black frost is not more than a hundred miles wide, if that. It's drifting down slowly from the north. I can turn and steam west and get out of it in eight or nine hours, or wait and see if it drifts away."

"It's got me scared. Watch." Geegee opened the wheelhouse door a trifle and they could feel the biting cold hit them. Geegee spit copiously to the wing of the bridge. The spittle hit the mass of grey-black ice clinging to the inner side of the wing, spread slightly then froze.

"Three seconds," Geegee said. "That's *real* cold out there."

The Mate looked unseeingly at the chart. "It seems a pity to lose this calm. We could make a couple of good hauls to offset the ones we missed when we was dodging."

Geegee snorted. "Hopeless."

Sam shook his head. "Everything would be frozen hard together in a solid mass. *Duncansby Head* is having that trouble now."

His finger strayed towards the chart to a small ring inside which was marked a cross.

Geegee leaned over him.

"Who's that?"

"*Orion*," Sam said shortly. "*Duncansby Head* saw her close to just before this stuff closed down."

Sam stared out of the small window and looked aft. Every stay and rope, instead of being three inches or so in circumference carried a thick grey-black beard of lace-like ice curtain. Astern of him a thin black channel of water showed where *Carpathia* had steamed through the sea. On either side of the water was grey-black ice.

He turned.

"Bring her round to west. I'm going to steam out of it."

Geegee said dourly: "Gimme a gale any time. Blow high, blow low, I'll fish in it."

"Easy to please, aren't you?" The Mate's face twisted into a sneer.

"Skipper! There's been a collision." The radio operator's voice soared upwards and threatened to crack. "A bad one by the sound of it."

Sam clattered into the radio office.

"I was taking a quick peep around the distress band and up she comes. Listen."

". . . May Day . . . May Day. . . . This is *Duncansby Head*. Have been in collision with unknown trawler. Starboard side badly holed amidships. Taking water fast."

"What of the other one. Anything?"

The air was cleared of chatter and a thousand ears listened intently. In The Hague, in L'Orient, in the Admiralty, at Wick and on the naval ships off Iceland ears were strained.

The voice, deeply laden with fear, came up again.

". . . *Duncansby Head*. My bow is stove in, too. She's making water fast. She's going. We're taking to the boat. Water is up to the boilers."

Sam closed his eyes and visualized the chart.

"Eight hours' steaming away," he whispered.

Three trawlers cut in briefly to give their positions and to advise the stricken victim that they were racing to her aid.

". . . Can't stay much longer. Only me and Sparks aboard now. The rest are in the boat and in the raft. She is going over on her beam ends."

"Why doesn't the other one come up?" The radio operator looked up at Sam. "He couldn't have gone so quickly as all that."

"Keep listening."

Ben pulled his woollen scarf tighter around his neck and opened the wheelhouse door.

"This lot's got me beat," he said to Lofty. "No wind. Not enough to blow this out." He lit a cigarette and held the match up. The flame burned brilliantly.

Lofty took his mug off a shelf and stepped to Ben's side. "Watch this." He tipped the dregs from his mug and almost at the instant it touched the deck it froze. "And that wasn't cold when I dumped it," he concluded significantly. He peered round the edge of the wheelhouse. "It looks like fog, but . . ." He held out his hand for a moment, let the grey-black film settle. And on the cuff of his coat and the hairs of the back of his hand a thin film of ice formed.

"I've been listening to the gabble," Ben said. "I'm going to steam west a couple of hours. We should run out of it."

"Well, *what* is it?" Lofty asked. "I've never seen anything like it. It's just frozen fog and we can't shift it off the deck or the bridge. An axe won't look at it."

Lofty screwed up his eyes and peered ahead.

"If it's fifty yards' visibility that's about all," he growled. "More like half that." Suddenly he stiffened and thrust his head forward.

"Summat on the starboard bow, Skipper. It's a trawler. *Trawler on the starboard bow.*" His voice rose to a high-pitched yell.

The vague shadow, scarcely more than a thickening of the fog-ice, suddenly took on the outlines of a trawler. Her bow wave flashed white as she drove at *Orion*.

"Hard a'starboard," Ben shouted. The wheel spun and the converging trawler, approaching *Orion* at a wide angle, seemed to swing across her bow. But the rudder failed to swing her enough in time. The trawler's knife-edged bow drove deeply into *Orion's* side amidships and partly rolled her over on her starboard side. As she slowly recovered the trawler ground along *Orion's* side wrenching a scream of tortured metal from her twisted plates. They swung together with a shattering bang, then the trawler reeled off into the grey-black frozen fog.

Ben picked himself up from his hands and knees and started a scrambling rush for the door. He had scarcely reached it when *Orion* shook to a deep, booming explosion somewhere aft. A cloud of thick black smoke rose from the engine-room skylights. The explosion continued in a diminishing roar and the smoke slowly cleared.

"What the hell's that?" Lofty asked, shaking his head.

"Find out," Ben snapped. "See where she's making water."

In a moment or two he realized that the engines were no longer running. He could not feel the vibrations.

"Skipper. My set's dead." The radio operator's voice came up the pipe. "I was going to send out a message. I'll have to switch to emergency power."

"Right. But get it out."

Lofty returned, helping the Chief Engineer.

"She's a bloody shambles down below," the Chief said dully. "When it happened the engines seemed to stop for a couple of seconds . . . then they was jolted off their bed . . . and then there was the bang . . . I dunno what it was . . . the engine room filled with smoke . . ."

"Get him below," Ben snapped. "What's she like?"

"Taking plenty of water aft, engine room is up to the bed plates, but all the lights are out. There's one of the blokes trapped down there somewhere. Who you reckon it was hit us?"

"That doesn't matter now. Get the Chief below, then see if she's making any water in the fish-hold."

"Skipper, *Duncansby Head* is sending out a message. She's in a bad way." The radio operator's voice was shrill. "I'm getting one away. But only on the emergency set."

"Keep at it. Let me know if anybody answers."

The Mate joined Ben on the bridge.

"She's in a bad way, Skipper. It's flooding in down in the engine room and Lofty says he can hear it coming in somewhere 'midships. Coming in real fast." He looked at Ben with almost an appeal in his eyes. "D'you think she'll go, Skipper?"

"Get the boat swung out and the raft over the side. Tell the lads to stand by them and to get as many clothes on as they can."

The Mate listened apathetically.

"God help us if we have to go over the side in this." He waved his hand vaguely at the window. "We won't last an hour."

"You won't last a few minutes if you don't get cracking. Now, jump around. Get that boat swung out," Ben snarled.

Orion gave a slow lurch which lifted her bow as her stern settled. It was a laborious lurch and Ben held his breath until the ship checked it, then recovered slightly.

"Anybody answering, Sparks?" he called down the pipe.

"*Saracen's Head* and *Lynn Head*. They say they are a couple of hours away. The Navy is calling up everybody. And . . ." The operator paused. ". . . And *Carpathia*'s come up. She says she is about seven or eight hours off." He paused again. "He said: 'Hold her up, Ben. I'm coming.' Do you want me to keep at it, Skipper?"

"Keep listening. I'll let you know in plenty of time." Ben

stared aft with unseeing eyes. "'Hold her up, Ben.' It's not going to be all that easy, Sam boy," he whispered. "But you keep coming. I'll be waiting."

Sam jammed the telegraph over to "Full ahead", then amplified it with a call down the voice-pipe.

"Chief, I want every ounce of steam you can give me. I'm going flat out."

"She won't stand up to it, Skipper. She'll fall to bits."

"Then I'll drive the bits. Open her up."

The inevitable happened.

"Skipper." Sam turned in the wheelhouse. "I'll have to stop her for a while. I've got a cross-head you can toast bread on. It's red hot."

"If I don't stop her how long will it last?"

"I could keep her going with a hose on it at half speed. But full out it could go any time."

"I'll give you one hour. Get cracking."

The hour lengthened into two and at the end of the second hour Sam's ice-cold hold on himself snapped. He stood on the bridge wing and raved at the sea, at God, at the Chief Engineer and temporary insanity, almost homicidal, flared from his eyes.

"If I'm too late I'll hold that Chief over the side and drown him," he raved. Geegee pinned Sam to the rail.

"He's doing his best, Skipper. Now you stay where you are. I'll see how things are going below."

He was back in a few minutes.

"Quarter of an hour. No more," he said. "But the Chief says he'll not be responsible if she goes more than three-quarter speed."

Sam stood immobile for the fifteen minutes. Then a thin, reedy voice came up the pipe.

"She's all slacked back, Skipper."

Sam slammed the telegraph over. "Full ahead." *Carpathia* gradually built up a grey-white bow wave as she thrust through the turgid film of ice on the sea.

"This time, God, help her to hold out," Sam whispered. "Hang on, Ben. Just hang on."

The Mate and Lofty clambered up to the bridge.

"Boat's out and the crowd are standing by," the Mate said. "She's going fast. You'd better come now, Skipper."

"All right. You take the boat, and you go too, Lofty. Keep a line to the raft. On your way."

"I'm staying with you," Lofty growled obstinately. "There'll be room in the raft." He grinned briefly. "And a bottle of Scotch. I put it there a few minutes ago. And if you want to know where I found it go look in your berth," he concluded defiantly.

Ben turned to the radio office voice-pipe.

"Right. Pack it in, Sparks. You're for the boat. Put as many jerseys on as you can find."

Once more *Orion* lurched.

"Skipper . . . Ben . . . come on. You can't do any good up here," Lofty pleaded with acute urgency.

Ben took one last look around and followed Lofty to the raft. Both the boat and the raft were held fast to *Orion* by lines. In a few minutes the crew were in the boat and crouched in the inflatable yellow raft.

"Cut away," Ben ordered. "And pull like hell. When she goes she'll go quickly."

But neither boat's crew nor the men on the raft saw the last moments of *Orion*. They pulled away from her, the boat towing the raft until they were lost in the grey-black frozen fog.

They heard a low, prolonged rumble, a sound almost like a deep sigh and towards them through the fog came a lifting, darkening swell followed by a series of diminishing little waves.

Orion had slipped under quietly with scarcely a sound.

"Christ, it's cold!" A deckhand said it suddenly and loudly and it emphasized the silence. So quiet was it that they could hear the chuckles of the water as it ran alongside the boat.

"Take turns rowing. It will keep you warm. We'll soon be picked up. In less than an hour, I reckon." Ben urged. "And keep listening."

The cold gripped them until lethargy reigned and they sat crouched together. And so it was as the fog turned black as daylight, diffused and scant as it was, disappeared.

Sometime in the night Ben heard a whimper coming from the deckhand crouched at his feet. He wrapped his arms around the youngster and held him to his chest like a mother holding a baby. He felt Lofty's arm steal over his shoulder and could feel his head resting against him.

The fierce cold bit into their arms, their legs, and soon their bodies began to surrender. Only their brains, as if taking over briefly in a disturbed sleep, functioned briefly.

Ben sighed once, a long-drawn-out sigh which trembled on his lips. His arm tightened around the deckhand and Lofty lifted his head. Ben had a smile, a strangely soft smile on his face. Lofty's head drooped for a few moments then once again he lifted it. Ben was still smiling, his eyes almost completely closed.

Lofty smiled too. If Ben Cleeve could smile then everything was going to be all right. Lofty tried to tell Ben that, tried to tell him how he felt. The effort was too great. Once more his head dropped down to Ben's shoulder.

They were still smiling when Sam found them ten hours later.

They saw the boat first, its pitiful little crew were huddled together like tired children. So they had died. Then they saw the raft alongside the boat.

As *Carpathia* touched the boat, Sam leapt from the low rail into the boat, which set the huddled mass of men swaying slightly, as if protesting at being disturbed. Then into the raft, which rocked perilously.

"Ben . . . Ben . . . It's Sam. Come on . . . wake up, man. . . ."

Sam tried to lift Ben up but the four men were frozen together and frozen to the side of the raft.

"It's no good, Sam. They're gone. They're gone, Skipper."

Sam looked at him dully then looked down at his brother. He shook his head as if trying to clear it.

"Ben . . . you've got to . . ."

Geegee firmly but quietly guided Sam back on board his trawler.

"I'll see to . . . to . . . things, Sam. Leave it to me."

Sam had no knowledge of passing time until Geegee joined him on the bridge.

"They're all right now, Sam. . . . I . . . we didn't have any sail-cloth aboard. . . . Some of the boys gave a few blankets . . . and I've wrapped 'em in some old trawl."

He peered at Sam as if seeking approval.

"They're all right now, Skipper."

Sam rubbed his forehead with the flat palm of his hand, squared his shoulders and blew sharply.

"All right, Geegee . . . and thanks."

Geegee shuffled his feet. "Will you put 'em over the side here or . . . ?"

"In half an hour, Geegee."

The silence was eerie as *Carpathia* lay stopped, reflected in the dark-green water. The silence was so profound that a gentle hiss of steam from the whistle valve sounded inordinately loud.

"I commit these bodies to the deep and to your care," Sam said softly, and one after another the dark bundles slipped into the water with a sullen splash, sinking from sight, leaving only a momentary trail of white bubbles in the water.

Sam stood watching them until the last trace disappeared, then turned to the bridge ladder.

"Stand by to shoot the trawl in half an hour," he said shortly.

"Well, the hard-hearted bastard. He sees his brother go over the side and 'Stand by to trawl', he says."

Geegee spun on the deckhand and pushed his face close to the other man's.

"What you want him to do? Cry?" he snarled.

The deckhand slouched away muttering.

"He will, but you won't hear him," Geegee said to himself. "So will I."

CHAPTER EIGHTEEN

ALL Scoresby grieved with Buller and his wife, with Eve and with those who had lost their men. It was an undemonstrative grief, almost soundless.

Job Benson and his wife and Eve went to the memorial service in the severe, brown-stone church and gained some comfort from the understanding and sympathetic words with which the gentle-eyed rector explained that death was but a momentary parting, that those who had gone had merely gone on before.

"Take comfort from this. They suffered no pain. They merely went to sleep, a sleep from which we will all arouse at the first sound of the trumpet."

Mrs Cleeve did her crying in the privacy of her kitchen and kept the secret of when Buller did his grieving as he lay in bed at night.

Eve called on them one night, arriving just as the old clock musically marked the passage of time.

Gently she kissed Buller on his cheek and allowed his fingers to stray over her face.

"Are you . . . switching on tonight, Mr Cleeve?" she asked softly.

Buller stretched out his hand and twisted the knob. He sat immobile as if he could stare ahead at something out of the window.

The jumble of voices came thinly from the loudspeaker, then louder as Buller touched a knob.

Mrs Cleeve looked at her daughter-in-law and shook her head. "I'll make some tea, Father," she said.

"Let me help," Eve said, and followed Mrs Cleeve into her kitchen.

"He turns it on every night, listens for a couple of minutes, then switches off," Mrs Cleeve whispered. "It's been nearly a week now since . . . since . . . we heard. I wish . . ."

"Mother . . ." Buller bellowed it. "Sam's up. It's Sam."

They raced into the small room and stood near him, listening intently. Buller's head was inclined sideways towards the radio set as if he were afraid he would miss even a syllable.

"Charlie Bates," he whispered as a growling, asthmatic voice went on.

"I was wondering where you were. You're a bit late, Sam. How are you doing?"

"I'm in time, Charlie. That big old clanger has only just finished striking seven."

Mrs Cleeve and Eve clutched each other's hands. Buller swallowed heavily. The tears welled out and ran down his cheek.

There was a pause, then Charlie Bates took up the talk.

"Sorry to hear about it, Sam. But so it goes. Folks will want to know a bit more when you get home, lad."

"They'll hear . . . everything. Charlie, if you want to know where . . . where they are they're about twenty miles sou'-sou'-west of Bear Island."

"Thanks, Sam. Thanks for telling me." Something of the old irascible Charlie Bates came back into his voice.

"Are you still scratching around for fish manure in that rattle-box? When will you learn sense? After all we've taught you, me and your dad."

Quite clearly they heard Sam's short chuckle.

"Takes some of us a long time to learn, Charlie." There was a pause. "But we learn in the end."

"Not before time," growled Charlie.

"I'm on my way, Charlie. See you sometime."

"Huh huh."

Then Sam's voice came low and clear.

"Good night. I'll be seeing you."

And Charlie Bates didn't answer. He knew it wasn't for him.

Buller Cleeve blew his nose vigorously.

"How about that tea, Mother," he complained. "It's away past time. Sam'll be home Tuesday, with luck."

Eve rested her hand on Buller's gnarled fist.

"Thank you, Mr Cleeve," she said softly.

Mrs Cleeve walked to the front door with her and Buller heard their low voices in conversation. When his wife returned he said brusquely: "She didn't wait for a cup of tea, Mother."

"Gracious me, I forgot to make it," she cried. "That's the first time in I don't know how many years."

She paused at the kitchen door.

"She's a nice girl, isn't she?"

"Eh. What's that you say?"

"I said she's a nice girl."

"Yes. Now make that tea."

Carpathia slipped through the lock gates and into a berth at the beginning of the tide.

"See you Friday?" Geegee leaned against the rail as Sam stepped ashore.

"I don't know yet." Sam rubbed his chin. "Depends which one is going."

He turned and walked up the quay wall and turned his steps towards Benson's office.

Eve was busy with some papers and was not aware that he was in the room until he said softly: "Eve."

She dropped the files. "Sam."

She rounded the desk and took his hand.

"Eve," he whispered again. Then he smiled. "Job still keeping your nose to the grindstone?"

She managed a wan smile.

"Still the old slave-driver." She looked up at Sam. "I . . . was with your father and mother last week when you . . . when you talked to Charlie Bates. It was wonderful to see your father's face."

"Was it?"

The door to the inner office opened and Job Benson stood framed in the doorway.

"Sam," he said unsmilingly, "you've been a long time getting to the office. Too long. Come in."

Eve fussed with papers, not quite realizing what she was doing. Finally, with a display of impatience, she threw them down.

"I've done that three times already. Now pull yourself together, girl," she snapped at herself.

Finally the inner door opened.

Job went right to the point.

"Skipper Cleeve is taking over *Lodestar*. She sails on Friday night's tide," he said flatly. "She should be out of dry dock by Friday morning, shouldn't she?"

Eve nodded. Then her smile expanded into a trill of laughter. "She'd better be."

Job turned to Sam.

"Now I've a shrewd idea that there's a pot of real trawlerman's tea brewing somewhere not far away. You'd better get lined up there for your cup, Sam."

The office door clicked behind him.

Suddenly Eve felt desperately shy. She wanted to say something, anything to break the silence between them.

It was Sam who finally broke it.

"Come up home tonight, please."

"I will."

"I . . . I'll be seeing you . . ." He trailed off lamely.

When he had gone Eve sat with a half-smile on her face for a few moments. Then she entered her uncle's office.

"Uncle Job. What's Melhuish's reaction going to be to you stealing his best skipper?"

"I'm not stealing him. I'm merely recovering a loan," Job said. "Anyway, I've talked to Melhuish and that's that."

Geegee leaned against the bar in his favourite pub, but somehow it had lost its flavour. Around him stood trawlermen and their talk failed to register with Geegee. Without Lofty his life seemed empty.

Some of the men tried to engage Geegee in conversation, tried to extract even more details of the slam through the night, of the black frost, of the finding of *Orion*'s crew.

Geegee wearily shook his head and refused to be drawn.

One of the men grinned behind a hand and winked at his companions.

"You tied 'em up in an old cod end, didn't you, Geegee?"

Geegee nodded.

The grin expanded.

"Let's hope you tied the cod end properly," the man made his point and applauded himself with a guffaw.

Geegee looked at him dully, lifted his pint glass and disposed of the remnants in it.

He turned and walked from the bar, his shoulders slouched, his feet dragging. He stood irresolute on the pavement for a few moments cogitating where he might find a pub with a greater degree of comfort.

"Hiya, Geegee," a tanned and gnarled trawlerman said. "'Ave a drink."

Geegee shook his head.

"I just got it from Benson's ship's husband that young Sam Cleeve it taking over *Lodestar* on Friday."

Geegee jerked upright.

"You've got *what*?" He thrust his face close to the old man's."

"Straight up now, Geegee. He had it in writing. Coal-and-ice-up Friday, sail on the night's tide. Young Sam Cleeve is taking her."

Geegee breathed in deeply.

"We'll have that drink on me. C'mon," he said. He and his informant turned into the bar.

"Two pints," Geegee said, leaning against the bar.

"Now two more," he ordered a few moments later, wiping his lips with an expansive hand. He half-turned, surveyed the bar, disposed of half his drink then stood upright. Slowly he walked over to the man who had made the gibe about cod ends.

"You was saying a few minutes ago something about tying cod ends," he started silkily.

"Grab the glasses, for Chris' sake!" the landlord yelled, scurrying around the bar. "Get 'em outside. They'll wreck the place."

The massacre was described in lurid detail in many a bar for a week afterwards, and slipping cod-end knots went out of fashion as a vehicle for humour when Geegee was in the neighbourhood.

Sam let the gate click behind him. He paused outside the front door, resolutely turned the knob and strode in.

"Dad," he said in a low voice.

"Sam." Then Buller lifted his voice. "He's here, Mother. Dead on time. Bring it in."

His mother came flying in from the kitchen carrying the huge teapot.

"Sam . . . Sam, my son." She slammed the teapot down on the table. "There, there. You don't have to cry," she said.

"Who's crying?" Sam said.

"Just a bit of a sniff," Buller bellowed. "And where's the dam' pot. I can't find it."

Sam stretched out a hand and pushed it into position.

"Same amount of sugar for me, Dad. Not too sweet."

For the next hour Sam talked. His father listened intently, only occasionally interjecting a word or two. When Sam came to tell of finding Ben and his crew his mother dropped her face into her hands. Sam rested his hand on her head.

"And he looked as if he were smiling, Mother. Smiling like he used to do when he'd pulled a fast one on me."

"He knew you'd be along," Buller said softly.

"He knew you wouldn't let him down. He knew that, Sam. Blood's thicker than water. He knew you'd get to him."

The next few days slipped by easily and Sam felt as if the past months were all part of a dream. The details became blurred as he once more entered into the rhythm of preparing a trawler for sea under the Benson flag.

He never saw Eve alone and only occasionally when he shot glances in her direction did he find her looking at him enigmatically.

Friday night's tide was at ten o'clock and Sam sat at home with his father and mother. The old clock started its sonorous legend and in silence they listened to the sound drumming away.

Sam looked at his mother and raised his eyebrows. She placed a finger across her lips and gently shook her head.

Buller stretched out a hand and switched the set on. Almost immediately an asthmatic voice croaked out of the loudspeaker.

"'Bout time somebody did something about that clock. And one or two other things around it." The croaking voice paused. "And here am I, only a day or so out of port and coming home fast and I break my rule by yapping on this thing. I've heard. *Red Star* told me this morning. Showed some sense at last. He didn't learn it from his Old Man, anyway. I'll be seeing you." And there was silence.

"That's Charlie all over," Buller said. "Says a lot and means little . . . sometimes."

The front-door bell jangled lightly and Sam answered it.

Outside stood Job Benson and Eve.

"Thought we'd call on you to . . . well, sort of celebrate," Job said.

"Just had old Charlie on. He'll make it Sunday, p'raps," Buller said. "Pity you missed him."

"I see too much of him and hear too much from him as it is," Job said flatly.

And the talk flowed on for another hour before Job and Eve rose to go.

"I'll walk along with you," Sam said.

They paused at one of the bastions and stood looking down over the harbour.

"Remember how you stood here your first night in Scoresby?" Job said softly. "I told you it was history, didn't I, Eve?"

"You did. Now I know what you meant. History with its little triumphs, its little failures . . ." His voice dropped. "And its tragedies. I know what you mean."

Job squared his shoulders.

"Don't think I'm going to stand here in the cold looking at something I helped to make. Goodbye, Sam. Have a good trip."

Sam and Eve stood in silence for some minutes looking down over the harbour.

Suddenly she started to talk. In a low voice, almost a whisper, she went on:

"I ought to be prostrate with grief. I'm not. I'm deeply sorry, deeper than I can describe it. But . . ." Her voice became stronger. "I'm trying to be honest with myself . . . and with Ben. His death hasn't torn anything out of my heart. I wouldn't want to die with him. Am I sounding disloyal, Sam?"

Sam shook his head.

"Ben knew I wasn't in love with him. He hoped . . . and I hoped that it would come. I'll never know now." She half-turned and looked up into Sam's face. "Do you know when . . . and why I accepted him? He had asked me two or three times before we left Germany. I said 'No'. At least I implied 'No'. Then . . ." She paused a moment before going on. "Then the day we passed you at sea you refused to answer us. And . . ."

"I know," Sam said softly. "I know."

Eve's face was lifted to his. In the reflected light from the harbour it seemed to glow with a soft radiance.

Slowly Sam lowered his head until they were almost touching.

"Eve," he said in a hoarse whisper.

"Sam," she breathed.

Very gently, it was almost a caress, he kissed her on the lips.

"Sam."

"Eve."

In a moment he said: "Shall I take you home now?"

"All right . . . but . . . I'll be standing here when you sail." Her head came up almost defiantly. "I've stood here many times when you sailed . . . in that other ship . . . trawler. Many times."

"Come." Sam took her elbow.

Geegee fingered a lacerated lip and blew on his knuckles.

". . . So he pulls a crack about tying cod ends and we gets stuck into it. Quite a time we had. I wanted him to ship on here with us. 'Nothin' doin',' he says. Pity."

He realized Sam wasn't listening. Sam stood on the wing bridge with his binoculars trained on the bastion. A shadowy figure stood there. Sam almost persuaded himself that he could see an arm wave.

He reached up for the whistle lanyard and gave it a brief tug.

"Gates are opening, Skipper," Geegee said.

Lodestar glided out into the dark open water of the roadstead. Once more Sam trained his glasses on the bastion. The figure was still there.

Sam raised his arm once in salute.

"Good night . . . good night, Eve," he whispered.

He turned to Geegee.

"Full ahead. Let's get up there. Then let's get home again."

Geegee blew on his knuckles.

"Yah. Let's."

He jammed the telegraph to full ahead.

PHYLLIS

E. V. Cunningham

"Phyllis" is published by André Deutsch Ltd.

PART ONE

PHYLLIS GOLDMARK

PHYLLIS became the matrix of a number of things, but she was not cast for melodrama, and too much of it was melodrama. She would not agree; she holds that the sum and substance of our lives—not just Phyllis and myself but you as well—is a tinny, jazzed-up melodrama, not fit for any audience of civilized people. But the measure of civilization is thin and delicate, believe me.

Let me say that she was not cast for romance either, which is the pervasive fiction of the lives of all young ladies. At that time when I was instructed—"This is an order, Clancy, and duty by God and your country"—to win her love and trust and affection, she was not as young as romance and young ladies. She was twenty-nine years old. They commiserated with me over the fact that she was no beauty—as they put it—for even the great captains of mankind, the directors of destinies, are meat for the Hollywood and Madison Avenue grinder; and when their romance is extracurricular, they see it only in terms of long legs, enormous mammary glands, and a face as standard as and less varied than our native automobiles.

Phyllis was not that, but slender, unaggressive, with brown hair that she cut short, and a pleasant face. She looked younger and acted older than her age. She was an assistant professor of physics at Knickerbocker University. She was shy but not painfully so, and introspective and burdened with the difficulties of an only child. Her father was dead. She lived with her mother in a four-room apartment on Washington Heights, and out of her wages she paid the rent and provided for both. She had been educated at Julia Richmond High School and Hunter College and had taken her doctorate at Columbia. When her father died, he left behind five thousand dollars of insurance money, the largest portion of all his worldly goods, and this had seen them through her post-graduate studies and kept body and soul together for herself and her mother. When she could get the work, Phyllis's mother did odds and ends of dressmaking, shortened hems and adjusted sleeves. Phyllis had worked in department stores. She had all the guilts and profound survival-sadness of poverty—to which I, Thomas Clancy, was no stranger.

She also had large, steady brown eyes that looked at you directly and inquiringly. Her sex life, so far as I knew, was Professor Alex Horton, forty-one years old, the same department at Knickerbocker as Phyllis. They had gone together, more or less, for two years. They were as intimate as two such people might be presumed to be. They sometimes went to the movies and sometimes to the theater. They had appeared together at four faculty affairs. As far as marriage went, it was never concretized. Horton was a Methodist; Phyllis was Jewish. A friend of Horton's had remarked on the difficulties presented in this situation by Phyllis's mother. Professor Edward Gorland, the chief of the physics department at Knickerbocker, also commented on this.

Professor Gorland was a careful man for success. On every level and in every nook and cranny of what constitutes success in our world, there are careful men with proper techniques. They are versed in the language and delicacy of their movements. Granting that a department head in so great a university as Knickerbocker was of considerable importance, as such things go in the academic world, Professor Gorland made more of much, a great deal more. He was careful and pompous, in his late fifties, and filled with the idiocies of "top-level". The fact that his field and department was physics nurtured this. "Having changed the world, Mr. Clancy," he once remarked to me, "we must never lose touch with that change, must we?" He had a long, dignified head, and like most actors I know, he had mastered the trick of raising one eyebrow. "A pilot who changes the course, a new course, you don't drop him?"

I had no opinion on pilots or courses or ships, and the substance of his manner was in fact that he was prying. Inside, he was filled with envy and annoyance because he did not know exactly what I was doing in his department or why I was there. He would have given anything to know, and he kept hinting that the dean over him did know. I didn't know who knew, nor did I care; but the fact of such men as Gorland is that within their practised delicacy, they are indelicate as hell. About Phyllis, he referred three times in a single conversation to the fact that she was Jewish.

The first time, he made it plain that there were no distinctions drawn in his department. "I mean," he said, "it would hardly be cricket to have a whole department of Jews. Here in New York, that can happen. It would become reverse discrimination, so to speak. And you can't really separate physics and security any more, can you? I mean you people in security are inclined to look twice where a Jew is concerned, aren't you?"

"I wouldn't know," I said. "As I told you, Professor Gorland, I am not in security of any kind and I don't work for the federal government. I'm just a New York City cop."

The second time, he mentioned that Phyllis was a lady, and you wouldn't think just to know her or talk to her that she was Jewish. "Why not?" I asked him, and he said, well, there it was—you just wouldn't think so. I told him that I would, and that came of a gutter education and growing up on the city streets with all kinds of elements, and that anyway I was never sure of what a lady was except a female.

The third time, he said that since I was an Irish Catholic, that would make it worse.

"Worse for what?"

"Well," he said, "I mentioned Alex Horton."

"Yes, you did."

"Of course, when a man's a bachelor as long as Horton, marriage is difficult."

"I suppose so," I agreed. "What has that got to do with me being an Irish Catholic?"

"I mean that Miss Goldmark's mother is one of the old-fashioned religious kind. So I gather, at least. The fact that Horton was a Methodist made a difficult thing more difficult. Would it be presumptuous for me to suppose that as a Catholic, the difficulty will be accented?"

"I can't say what is presumptuous, Professor. I don't intend to marry Phyllis Goldmark. And does it follow because my name is Clancy that I'm a Catholic?"

"Believe me, I have no prejudice against Catholics. And I think I am justified, Mr. Clancy, in feeling that your manner towards me is antagonistic. I am only trying to co-operate in what is at best a most delicate and troublesome matter."

"I understand that and I appreciate it. If I appeared antagonistic, I am ready to apologize."

"Not at all, not at all!" he said. "No need for apologies at all. I feel better. I feel that we're squared away, Mr. Clancy. I was simply concerned——"

"I'm sure," I agreed. "As a fact, I am not a Catholic, if it makes any difference. My grandfather came from Belfast. My father and mother were Presbyterians. I'm not sure that I'm anything very much, and I'd just as soon be taken for a Catholic as not. But there's no use making it more difficult, and if Miss Goldmark inquires, you could tell her that—or get it around. I don't care."

"You understand my position?"

"I understand your position," I said.

"I mean, I am in the dark, entirely in the dark. If I only had some inkling of what all this adds up to. Mind you, I am not asking —I am not prying——"

I shrugged.

"—We're all soldiers in a vast army now, aren't we? I mean as a little more than a figure of speech."

"I'm not a soldier," I said. "I'm just a cop, Professor Gorland."

I took two lecture classes a week, which was all I could possibly prepare for, even with the help I got; and that meant ten days of preparation, living with the subject and breathing it and reading until my eyes blurred and refused to see. I don't suppose I did too badly.

Phyllis came to the class the first time I took Horton's students. The subject of my paper for that day was the meaning and origin of high-energy cosmic radiation, and I faced eighty-three young men who knew more of physics and more about the mathematics of high-energy radiation than I would know if I had taken ten months instead of ten days to prepare. On my side, I had the empty dignity and overbearance of my age—thirty-seven—expert help, and a recent survey of things that Enrico Fermi, Bruno Rossi, Pierre Auger, Robert Millikan and Carl D. Anderson had written upon the subject. Phyllis came in just before I began, stood at the rear of the room for a few minutes, a slight, almost wistful figure, and then found a seat in the last row as I explained that the most imposing difficulty, when dealing with the origins of cosmic radiation, lay in the fact that the various points or directions from which they bombard our planet seem to have no actual connection with what we have determined as plausible points of beginning or origin.

She listened intently, chin resting on the back of one hand, as I developed the lecture I had somehow put together; and in spite of myself, I found that I watched her for reactions and assurance. I wanted the lecture to be a good one, and that was apart from the fact that I had to stand up here and deliver it. I wanted the students to respect me, and I even wanted to believe for a little while that I was a part of a university faculty, and that my own life had some direction, sense, and purpose. Maybe, as I continue with this, I will be able to make clear why I wanted all this.

When I had finished and dealt passably well with the questions and not made an ass of myself and the students were on their way out, Phyllis came up to the podium and introduced herself and told me that Professor Gorland had suggested that she sit in on my first lecture. I had seen her before on several occasions, but this was our first actual meeting.

"Not to spy or observe you, you must understand," she said, "but our work is complementary. It would be good if you could find the time to sit in on one or two of my classes."

"I'd like that," I nodded, "Miss——?"

"Goldmark," she said. "Phyllis Goldmark. You're Thomas Clancy. I hear that you were in research. Do you enjoy coming back to teaching?"

"I'm not coming back, Miss Goldmark. It's my first time."

"Oh?"

"I'm sure my nervousness was apparent."

"As a matter of fact, it was not," she said. "I thought you were quite poised and self-assured. I can't believe that you have never done any teaching. I have been teaching for seven years, and I must say that I would give a great deal for your self-assurance."

"That's a great compliment. You're very kind, Miss Goldmark."

Until now, she had been formal and correct and uninhibited in the small talk of one faculty member to another. Now that broke; she became uneasy, and said that she thought she must be going. I made a point of being a stranger in a very large university, alone and bewildered and even a little frightened, and begged her to join me for a cup of coffee and a sandwich. She admitted that she had not yet lunched, and I admitted that I did not even know where the faculty cafeteria was.

It pleased her to be knowledgeable, even about the geography of an eating place, and it was less her timidity that made her shy than her difficulties with men. There are women in whom this difficulty intensifies with age, and I remember thinking to myself that soon, all too soon, she would become professionally a spinster, just as she was already professionally a teacher. She would dry up, turn inward upon herself, and suck the remnants of her own juices until they were gone and wasted. She did not lack beauty or femininity, but she lacked the ability to comfort herself with either quality or to make other people aware of them.

As we went into the cafeteria, she nodded to several people but did not introduce me. We each took coffee, a sandwich, and a piece of pie, and we found an empty table. She was explaining that the food was adequate here but not very good. But at least it was on campus, and since the pseudo-Gothic vault of the place was half buried in the basement, it was always cool during the hot months.

"If you expect to stay that long?" she asked me.

"Perhaps. My future is still uncertain. I was brought in to plug up a hole, I suppose, a sort of odd man. Professor Gorland mentioned a discussion of my future, as soon as he gets around to it."

"Now you don't seem very much like a teacher," she smiled. "I don't know why."

"Perhaps because I am not really a teacher. Not yet."

"Yes, I suppose so." She would drop her eyes as she ate.

"I read your essay on refraction," I said.

"Where ever did you find it?"

"Here in the library. It's very good."

"No—well, I mean there's so little that's original in it. But I am delighted when anyone mentions that he has read it. I sometimes wonder what it is like to be a popular magazine writer and have a million people read what you write—instead of twenty."

"It depends on what you write, I would say."

"I guess so."

At this point, a stout, red-faced man in his forties, carrying a heavily loaded tray, paused by our table and said, "Hello, Phyllis. Is that our new man? Won't you introduce me?"

"Professor Vanpelt," she said. I stood up and shook hands with him. "This is Mr. Clancy—the new assistant."

"Glad to meet you, Clancy," Vanpelt said, chopping with his head, a jovial man and full of smiles. "Mind if I join you?"

"Please."

He had the chair out already. Unless he had not eaten for weeks, he was a glutton, his tray loaded with beef stew, potato pancakes, mashed potatoes as a side dish, apple sauce, a double portion of bread, four pats of butter, and an enormous piece of chocolate layer cake. He began to eat immediately and talked through a full mouth. "I hear you're a research man, Clancy. Hell if I had one of those twenty-five thousand a year jobs with a big outfit, I'm damned if I'd come here. Not for teaching. Take it from me what you can do with teaching. I come into class filled with the joy and glory of knowledge, and then I face that rippling field of snotnose youth, and it goes, it goes. Anyway, don't let them bug you, the way they did Horton."

"Horton?"

"Your predecessor, Professor Alex Horton—may he rest in peace."

"What a cruel thing to say!" Phyllis burst out. "He's not dead."

"He's not dead, he's not alive—and he's neither here nor there," Vanpelt mumbled, his mouth full of beef stew. "What did they tell you, Clancy? That he resigned?"

"I just took it for granted that he left for reasons of his own. It's not my problem."

"No. Oh, no. No one can spend twenty-four hours at Knickerbocker and remain that innocent. Do you mean to tell me that no one let you into the mysteries and delights of the Horton affair?"

I was watching Phyllis, whose face was pale, controlled, and angry. There is a chain of command and an order of precedence and protocol in a university as precise and numbing as in the Army. I had already realized that Vanpelt was major to Phyllis Goldmark. She said quietly and carefully,

"I don't think it's our business to go into that. If Mr. Clancy should be told whatever we don't know—and we know nothing—let those who are supposed to do it."

"Bosh," said Vanpelt. "He's over twenty-one, isn't he. The fact is, Clancy, that Professor Alexander Horton walked out of here one day and vanished from the sight of honest men. Poof! Like that. Whereupon a veritable horde of G men, T men, S men, cops and so forth descended upon these drowsy academic halls and picked them as clean of information as a turkey's bones of flesh on December first. All very quiet, very genteel, and not one blessed word of it in the press. Fourteen, fifteen days ago. Still no word in the press, no sign of Alex—nothing. Not even the G men."

"I'm afraid I don't understand," I said.

"Neither do we," Phyllis said. "Neither does anyone here. I don't see any sense talking about it."

I saw Phyllis again in the cafeteria the following day, and I was able to join her for lunch. Whether I could have pushed our acquaintance so quickly under other circumstances, I don't know, but she was lonely and afraid—not so afraid that she was ready to pour out her heart to me, but still possessed of fear she could not conceal. On the other hand, I had not established myself as anyone importantly receptive to the outpouring of a woman's heart.

"I wanted to ask you about Vanpelt," I began at one point, but she shook her head.

"I don't want to talk about him."

"He's a full professor?"

"Yes."

"A glutton? Always that way?"

"Mr. Clancy," she said, smiling for the first time since we had met today—her smile was warm and uncertain at once and transformed her whole face—"to a new teacher from an old hand at it, just let me say that personal observations have a way of getting around. There are neither secrets nor privacies in a place like this. You appear to be a very nice person and very open."

"Thank you."

Again the dropping of her glance, the retreat.

"What were you getting at?" I asked her.

"The way you called Professor Vanpelt a glutton just now. Do you always say whatever is on your mind?"

"Not always. But Vanpelt is a pig with food. Some people are. I wouldn't make such an observation if I thought you cared a fig about him, but it was plain enough that you don't like him——"

"I don't want to talk about Professor Vanpelt, if you don't mind," she interrupted me, and then I steered away from that and we talked about our work and she asked me about my research at Consolidated Dynamics, where a card in a file said that I had done research, and I made answers that I was prepared to make. I cut that off as quickly as possible, suggesting that since I was free for the rest of the day, I might sit in on a class of hers, if she had one?

"I don't. It's my free afternoon too."

"Would I be pushing too hard if I asked what you intend to do with it?"

Again the smile. "Nothing very important, Mr. Clancy. They're showing *The Great Dictator* at the Museum of Modern Art. I never saw it, and I thought that this would be a good time, and anyway I want to get away from the ivy walls for a while. Do you like Chaplin?"

"At times—yes. At times, no. This afternoon, yes, if you would let me come along, Miss Goldmark?"

She hesitated a moment, her eyes flickering across the gold band

on my left hand. "I know you're alone in the city, Mr. Clancy——"
she began slowly.

"My wife died two years ago," I said. "I'm very much alone in
this city, Miss Goldmark."

"Oh?"

We sat in silence for a little while then, until she said, "Please
come with me. I would enjoy that."

I nodded, and she saw what must have been in my face and
asked me whether something was wrong. "No—no." I shook my
head.

"Is it because——?"

"I'm fine," I said. "Shall we go now?"

She got up, and we left the place and went out into the cool
sunshine of the campus and then walked over to Broadway and
the subway. It was a fine, brisk day, with a clean wind blowing in
from the west, the best kind of a day in New York; and since we
had plenty of time before the showing, Phyllis suggested that we
walk to the next stop before we take the subway. We walked south
on Broadway, and when I looked behind me twice, I tried to do
so casually. But I imagine she noticed. When we got into the
subway train at 103rd Street, only one man entered our car with
us. The car was almost empty, and the man who had entered with
us went to the other end of the car and seated himself facing us.
He was middle-size, ordinary in appearance, neatly dressed in gray
sharkskin and gray worsted topcoat, and involved in the *New York
Times*. His paper was opened to the financial section, and he was
studying the stock listings intently.

"I saw you looking behind you," Phyllis said to me.

"Yes?"

"Did you feel we were being followed, Mr. Clancy?"

I smiled and shook my head. Phyllis shivered, and for a while
she was silent, and then she said,

"Please look at the man across the car—the one with the newspaper and the gray topcoat."

"What about him, Miss Goldmark?"

"I must sound like a fool. I saw him yesterday. I think he is
following us, Mr. Clancy. I'm sorry. Do I sound like a hysterical
fool?"

"You don't sound hysterical."

"Could he be following us, Mr. Clancy?"

"I don't know," I said.

At the museum, Phyllis went to the powder room, and I had an opportunity to call Centre Street. I asked for my exchange and asked them whether I or Miss Goldmark was being tailed.

"Not today. Where are you?"

"The auditorium of the Museum of Modern Art. In twenty minutes, they are showing *The Great Dictator*. I am seeing it with Miss Goldmark. When it breaks, we will stand in front of the museum for at least five minutes. I will try to persuade her to have dinner with me. If she agrees, we will go to the Blue Ribbon, a small German restaurant on Forty-fourth, between Sixth and Seventh. I think we'll walk."

"Did you see the tail?"

"Possibly."

"Description?"

"Caucasian, fifty, small blue eyes, brachycephalic, five-eight, dimple in left cheek, white-collar type, gray sharkskin suit, black shoes, gray worsted coat, white shirt, blue pin-stripe, dark blue tie with diagonal sky-blue stripe, black gloves."

"After dinner?"

"I imagine she'll want to go home. I'll take her home, if possible."

"Are you sure you were tailed?"

"I told you what I know. I'm not sure of anything."

But I was more certain when the man in the subway car took a seat at one side of the museum theater. Phyllis did not notice him, which was just as well. She enjoyed the film; if she had noticed him, she would have been too nervous to relax and have a good time. I found that I wanted very much for her to relax and enjoy herself, which was rather strange, for I would have said that my interest in her was controlled, narrow, and limited. I had seen the film before. I like Chaplin, but I am not one of those who turn him into a cult or the be-all and end-all of films. Anyway, I had too many things to think about, and I found myself thinking about my wife. I didn't want to think about that.

The man in the gray sharkskin suit left before we did, so Phyllis did not see him again; and when the picture was over, we stood in front of the museum for a little while. I suggested dinner together, and as I had suspected she would, Phyllis protested and said that she ought to go home, and that her mother was expecting her, that she had work to do; but her demurrer was without conviction. As with so many women who have no assurance in their femininity, she had to be doubly assured that she was wanted. She was full of anxiety, and I suggested that she call her mother. It was my own need, I pointed out. I ate all my dinners alone. Then she agreed and went inside to call. I smoked a cigarette. Across the street, in the parking garage facing the museum, I noticed a man; not the one in the gray sharkskin; this one stood like a pro, and downtown was written all over him. They are good men but obvious.

Phyllis returned, and we walked over to Sixth Avenue and then downtown. The evening sky was gray-blue, wild and turbulent, as it sometimes is in March, with small clouds in passage like demented geese and with long slanting spears of sunset coming from the side streets. Phyllis responded to the weather; she shed the anxiety. She had a small but trim body, and she walked well with long, sure strides, and her face was alive and comely. She was unselfconscious until she caught me looking sideways at her, and then she blushed, something she did easily.

"Don't feel sorry for me, Mr. Clancy," she said suddenly. "I couldn't bear that."

"Of all the damn things to say!" I burst out. "Good God, how do you fall into saying something like that, Miss Goldmark?"

"I didn't mean to make you angry."

"Angry? Angry hell! I just don't make any sense of what you said. I had a good time this afternoon. Didn't you?"

"Of course I did. I loved the picture. And it was very pleasant to be with you."

"Then why all this about feeling sorry for you?"

"I don't know. It was just something I said."

"Don't ever say it again when I'm with you."

"No——"

"Remember that!"

"I'll try to remember." Her small, hesitant smile flickered on her lips.

We ordered dinner. The restaurant was not expensive, not beyond the means of an assistant professor, and the food was good. We were both of us hungry after our walk and the cold evening air, and I found myself feeling alive. It was a particular and simple feeling—but strange to me for a considerable time. It didn't change when she talked about me and about my wife.

"You said you eat alone so much," Phyllis remembered. "Don't you have any family, Mr. Clancy? Or perhaps you don't want to talk about personal matters?"

"I would be delighted to talk about anything you want to talk about, Miss Goldmark. Or do I know you well enough to call you Phyllis? Do you know that in any other part of these United States, or if we were in any other occupation, I guess I mean, I would be calling you Phyllis and you would be calling me Tom. Still, I imagine that on the faculty of Knickerbocker, we could go on with Miss Goldmark and Mr. Clancy for another year or two?"

"We could." She smiled.

"Would you call me Tom? I'll call you Phyllis, if that's all right."

"Yes, it's all right."

"Very good then. Phyllis. I don't mind talking about personal matters. I have a brother who is an army colonel, stationed in Korea. He has a wife and two children, whom I have never seen. I haven't seen him for seven years. He considers me an impractical person, an egghead and a fool. My feelings toward him are neutral. I have a sister who is married and lives in Philadelphia. Her husband has the largest Buick agency there, and he's well-fixed, and they have no children. I see her about once a year. My father and mother are dead. I was born in Brooklyn Heights, raised there, went to New Utrecht High School, discovered I had considerable mathematical aptitude, won a scholarship to N.Y.U. Engineering, majored in physics, got my degree in 1941, and enlisted in the Army——" It trailed off there. She was watching me intently and thoughtfully.

"You are a strange man, Mr. Clancy. Tom."

"We all of us are, Phyllis. Strange men, strange women. Two-bit philosophers, saints and idiots——"

"There were never any children? In your marriage, I mean?"

"I was married only a few months before my wife got sick. She died of leukemia."

"How terrible!"

"Yes——" What does one say? Death is terrible; the death wrapped in the mystery of ignorance, fear, and perhaps our own human viciousness, is a little worse.

I took Phyllis home at about nine—she lived on 174th Street, between Broadway and Fort Washington Avenue—and then I rode back downtown to my two rooms in a brownstone, converted, on West Sixty-eighth Street. It was a good enough place, as such places went, a high-ceilinged room about twenty by sixteen, a kitchen, a bathroom, and a bedroom about eight by ten, but it was filled with the taste and thought and dreams of a woman who had been dead two years and would dream no more. It was also inhabited by my memories of her, and it fed my aloneness and frustration. I had thought of leaving it, but it was not just an apartment that was sick; it was myself, and I would take my own cud of bitterness with me wherever I went.

Tonight, I made coffee, smoked a cigarette, read an article on fusion, read a chapter of Fermi, showered, and went to bed. I lay with my thoughts for company, and I know it was past two in the morning before I slept.

The following day, I sat in on Phyllis's lecture—"Concerning Light as a Particle"—and afterwards we had our sandwich and coffee together again. She seemed to look forward to this and to gain a degree of her own restrained pleasure out of it. After lunch, I had a meeting with Professor Gorland, who said that for appearances' sake, and considering that I could handle it, he would like to give me a seminar of twelve students. I asked him for a day or so to think it over. Then I worked in the library for about an hour, and as I left, I ran into Professor Vanpelt.

"The top of the afternoon to you, Clancy," he said.

"How do you do, sir," I nodded.

"A fat flower in the acres of ivy—I do well, Clancy. Are you a drinking man? Surely, with that name, you will join me for a drop of the stuff?"

"It's my pleasure," I agreed, and we walked over to Broadway to a bar where Vanpelt was no stranger. He ordered gin and bitters, and I took scotch on ice. He asked me how I liked Knickerbocker, and I said it was too soon to decide. Then I asked him about Alexander Horton, since he had brought up the subject the day before.

"Horton, huh? He had a Victorian romance—for want of a better word—with your Miss Goldmark. She's Jewish, you know."

"I had guessed it," I said soberly. I was Clancy, without feelings or sensibilities. "You say he disappeared?"

"Whisked away," Vanpelt grinned, watching me carefully. He was a glutton and fat, but under the fat, hard and shrewd.

"Well—I mean you're making a mystery out of it."

"Great mystery. It's all there."

"What did you mean yesterday?"

"Just needling, Clancy. I meant nothing at all. You don't intend to disappear the way Horton did, do you?"

"Not yet."

"Oh? Tell me, Clancy, what kind of work did you do up there in Rochester?"

"Rochester?"

"Weren't you telling me that you were on the research staff at Consolidated Dynamics?"

"Was I?"

"Well, word gets around. I suppose it was on this top-secret kick."

"Not at all," I smiled. "I worked with heavy water."

"Heavy water. That's enlightening."

"We'll talk about it some time," I nodded. "I'm afraid I must get back to my work now."

"Chew some mints. Gorland is bugged on hard water. Hard water—heavy water. Very good, yes? Have a mint."

I took a mint and tried to pay for the drinks, but he wouldn't hear about it. Then I went back to the science building, to the tiny office that had belonged to Alexander Horton, and called my exchange at Centre Street.

"Are we on tape?" I asked.

"You're being recorded, Clancy. Go ahead."

"I want a full run down on John Vanpelt, full professor at Knickerbocker, science department, age about fifty, weight about two-twenty, possible slight foreign accent—his Gs seem to click with a K sound, blue eyes, bald on top, gray sides and back, one gold cap, upper left, a glutton over food, which might indicate a habit. I'll have a picture of him tomorrow."

"That's all?"

"For the time being," I said.

Then I went to Gorland's office and asked whether he had a picture of Professor Vanpelt that I might borrow.

"Really, Mr. Clancy," he said, "we're operating a school, you know. We don't keep dossiers with photos attached."

"Yes, of course," I agreed. "Possibly in a yearbook—or something of the sort." Gorland sighed and hunted on his shelves and came up with a small picture of Vanpelt in Knickerbocker's scientific quarterly.

That evening, I let myself into my apartment on Sixty-eighth Street and flicked on the lights in the living room, and two men were sitting there. One of them sat in the captain's chair that Helen and I bought during our honeymoon on Cape Cod. He was the hard-boned kind; they prefer chairs that are not upholstered. He sat erect and stiff and alert, a small, thin, narrow-faced man, neatly dressed, and holding a big Luger on me. The other sat on the couch. He was two hundred pounds of broad shoulders and muscle gone to middle age, the whole meaty slab of neck and shoulders overbuilt and sagging, the size seventeen neck holding up the head of the all-American boy athlete, crew cut graying, cheeks flushed with alcohol instead of buoyant health, and one big ham hand holding a .45 service model that he didn't need. He was over my weight. But he held the revolver carefully as he grinned and made me welcome in my own home.

"Surprise," he said. "Just like in the movies."

"Just like in the movies," I nodded.

"Stop clowning and see if he has a gun," said the one in the captain's chair. "Around and behind him, Jackie." The accent was Spanish or Portuguese.

"Yes, sir, Mr. Brown," a reply of respect mixed with the need on Jackie's part to deny that he was a muscle-bound dolt. He moved around behind me, lightly and gracefully, and ran his hand under my arms and across my pockets. "No gun," he said.

"I thought so. What would they say at Knickerbocker, a professor who carried a gun? We have searched your place. Where is your gun, Mr. Clancy?"

I shrugged.

"Sit down there, Mr. Clancy," he said, pointing to a Hitchcock chair that had been a wedding present to Helen from her grandmother. I sat down and waited. Mr. Brown did the speaking. He asked me why they were there.

"I have no idea," I said.

"Can't you guess, Mr. Clancy?"

"I suppose I could guess. I could go on guessing all night. Is that what you want me to do?" I noticed now a bulging accountant's brief case next to Mr. Brown's chair.

"No, we don't have all night," he replied, putting the Luger into a shoulder holster. Then he said to his helper, "Put your gun away, Jackie. This is not an ape we are dealing with. This is a cultured man, a civilized man. I have been looking at your books," he explained to me. "Culture is not synonymous with a knowledge of physics, as we both have reason to know. But look at a man's books and you are looking into that man's soul and mind. Know a man by what he reads. The word makes the man."

"Most of the books belonged to my wife," I said.

"I admire Americans. Faced with a personal compliment, they become cynical and vulgar. They are obligated to a certain image of themselves. But we are not here to talk about books, Mr. Clancy.

We are here to bribe you. After all, we are not diplomats. Why go through a diplomatic exchange of nonsense? I believe in coming to the point. My employers feel that every man has his price. In this brief case beside me are seven thousand five hundred twenty-dollar bills. It is clean money, not stolen and not recorded, and it can be spent with impunity. One hundred and fifty thousand dollars—they have decided that is your price."

"I'm flattered."

"Naturally. Who would not be? When your federal taxes are considered, this is a fortune—believe me. Men have done terrible things for such an amount of money."

"And what am I supposed to do for it? What am I being bribed for?"

He shook his head. "There is no need to discuss that. I do not propose to be led into any tiresome discussion of ethics. I do not ask, will you take a bribe? The bribe is given to you. You have no choice in the matter—none. I ask you no questions—because we know all that it is necessary for us to know. We know where you go and what you do. And when we pay for something, we get value in return for our money. Is that plain, Mr. Clancy?"

"No," I said. "It's not plain."

"It is plain to us, Mr. Clancy. Now just remain where you are for a little while. The money is in the brief case."

With that, they both rose, walked to the door, went through and closed the door behind them. Just as simple as that. I locked the door behind them, bolted it and went to the brief case. It was stuffed full of packages of twenty-dollar bills. I did not doubt that there were exactly seven thousand, five hundred bills.

It was nine o'clock. I called my exchange at Centre Street and told them what I wanted. I told them that I would wait thirty minutes, then leave my apartment, walk to Columbus Avenue and two blocks north to Seventieth Street. I would be on the southeast corner, and I would like a cab cruising east across Seventieth to pick me up. I would also like a good man in the cab. I also asked them to reach Commissioner Comaday and said that I would see him in his office when I got to Centre Street.

They told me that the Commissioner was in his office and would wait for me, but they asked for an hour, which would give them time to set up the cab and driver and get them to Seventieth Street. They told me that the cab would be a Green Checker and that it would cross Columbus Avenue during the sixty seconds after ten o'clock. I got a time check on my watch and reminded myself to remind them to run a test on my telephone and make certain it was not tapped.

Then I put on a pot of coffee, strong and black, drank a cup, smoked a cigarette and did some thinking. It was not pleasant thinking or productive thinking, and like most of my thoughts recently, it was evocative of no profound conclusions. I then went to the brief case, emptied it, and stuffed seventy-five packages of twenty-dollar bills into my shirt, one hundred and fifty thousand dollars close to my heart and skin. It bagged out my shirt, but my suit jacket pressed the money into shape and my loose raglan top-coat covered the bulge. I walked downstairs, hands in my pockets, over to Columbus and north. Now I made no effort to see whether I was being followed. It was just ten o'clock when I reached the corner of Seventieth Street, and as I paused on the corner, the light changed and a Green Checker moved across Columbus. I signaled the cab; it stopped; and as I got in the driver asked me,

"Are you Clancy?"

"That's right." My heart was hammering as I closed the door and sat back. The cab moved along Seventieth. As we reached Central Park West, two more cars had come into the street.

"What do I do?" the driver asked.

"Right turn and then go into the transverse. I want to see if we're followed."

One of the two cars turned right, a Buick convertible. When we made our left turn into the transverse, the Buick continued south on the avenue.

"We're clean," I said. "Take me downtown now." Then I leaned back and lit a cigarette and smoked it slowly and with pleasure.

It was an interesting revelation to me that I could become as afraid as I had just been and that I could follow that feeling with the sense of security I now had. Riding downtown, I made up my mind that I wanted a gun. I had never liked guns or put much faith in them, but I realized that my being afraid was beginning, not ending. The gun is a symbol, just as the crisp money against my skin was a symbol.

At Centre Street, a uniformed officer was waiting for me and he took me directly to the Commissioner's office. Commissioner Comaday was waiting there, and with him was Sidney Fredericks from the Justice Department.

"Sit down, Clancy," the Commissioner said, nodding at one of the brown leather chairs. " I suppose you had to come?"

"I thought it best, sir," I said, but before I sat down, I removed my coat, opened my jacket, and put the money from my suit on the commissioner's desk. Then I sat down. Comaday and Fredericks examined the money.

"A lot of money," Fredericks said.

"Suppose you tell us about it," the Commissioner nodded.

I told them what had happened and gave a full description of the two men. They listened thoughtfully, and when I finished they were silent for a little while. Then Comaday cut in his inter-office and asked for Jacobs, the currency man. While we waited for Jacobs, Fredericks asked me about the Spanish accent of Mr. Brown.

"I could almost swear that it was Spanish," I said, "but almost —you understand. It could have been Portuguese. It just could have been Italian or Rumanian or French. I don't know why I decided that it was Spanish. That was just a reaction. He began to talk and I pegged it. I don't mean that he was Spanish, necessarily. Only the accent."

"A thick accent?"

"No, sir. Very slight."

"Did he talk like a foreigner—I mean, grammatically, did he formulate his sentences as a foreigner would?"

"No. His English was excellent. A trifle pompous, but excellent."

"You left the brief case there?" Comaday asked.

"Yes, in case I was being watched. Also, I would appreciate it, sir, if you had my telephone checked out for a tap."

Comaday made a note of that. Fredericks shook his head and said, "We won't learn anything from the brief case. These are careful men. What do you think of fingerprints, Clancy?"

"The same thing, sir. Careful men."

Jacobs came in then. He was a thin, nearsighted man in his fifties, steel-rimmed glasses and a wisp of gray hair combed back over his bald head. Against the squat, bulldog bulk of Comaday, he was wraithlike, but he drew a look of intense interest from Fredericks. In a limited circle, Jacobs was not without fame.

"Take a look at that money, Joe," Comaday said to him.

Jacobs went to the desk, spread out the packages, riffled several of them, and then drew a bill from each of five packages. He examined the bills carefully and knowingly.

"Well?" Comaday demanded.

"Seventy-five packages," Jacobs nodded. "One hundred bills in each. I'm going by bulk, so that's not an exact count. One hundred and fifty thousand dollars. Just an opinion."

Fredericks nodded and smiled slightly.

"Clean money?" Comaday asked.

"I wish it was mine, Commissioner. Made in Washington by the United States Government—pretty as a picture."

"Is it hot?" Fredericks asked. "Or couldn't you tell us that?"

"I might at that," Jacobs grinned. "Just a guess, you understand." He riffled through a dozen more packages. "No—it's not stolen. That can be checked out. But if you want a snap opinion, it's not stolen money."

"How do you know?"

"This year's money. I keep abreast of the movement of stolen funds. There's been nothing in twenty-dollar bills over the past twelve months that adds up to one hundred and fifty thousand. That doesn't mean that part of it couldn't be hot. I just doubt it. I got a feeling it's nice money."

"Not nice money," Comaday said.

"Well—in a manner of speaking."

"Thank you, Jacobs," Comaday nodded. "I'll get it down to you tonight. I want a full report."

Jacobs left, and we sat in silence again. We sat in silence until Comaday said, "A lot of money. A bribe. Just like that?"

"Just like that," I agreed.

"A lousy, stinking situation this is!" Comaday burst out suddenly. He was Police Commissioner of New York City. I was a little surprised.

"Difficult." Fredericks agreed.

Silence again. Then Comaday asked me, "How are you making out, Clancy?"

"I don't know."

"Progress?"

"I don't know. This isn't anything I enjoy doing or anything I've done before."

"Right now, none of us enjoy what we're doing."

"I know, sir, that it's none of my business. But I can't help being curious about other efforts. You can just tell me to mind my own business."

"We've drawn a blank, Clancy. Nothing has changed."

"I see. And is that the case in Moscow, too, sir?"

"As far as we know. Incidentally, Clancy, one of their top

security people is here, and he would like to meet with you. His name is Dmitri Grischov, and he suggested that you come around to their place on Park Avenue."

"What can come of that?"

"I don't know," Comaday said with a shade of annoyance. "I can't see that any harm will come of it."

"And if I'm being tailed."

"You're a cop. Just make sure you're not being tailed!"

"Yes, sir. And about the bribe?"

"What about it? "

"That's just it. I would like to know something more. I feel like someone in a thick fog at midnight."

"It's a feeling we share." Fredericks smiled.

On my way out, I stopped at the door and said, "One other thing, if I may, Commissioner?"

"What is it, Clancy?"

"I would like to wear my gun."

"Why?"

"I'm still a cop."

"A gun can wreck the whole thing."

"I know."

"You feel strongly about that?"

"Very strongly," I said.

"All right then. Pick it up on your way out."

PART TWO

THOMAS CLANCY

This was the second time I had been in the Commissioner's office. Fifteen days before, I had been Detective Sergeant Thomas Clancy of the New York City Police, attached to Homicide, with the reputation, beneficial and otherwise, of being an intelligent cop on his way up. Five feet eleven inches, one hundred and seventy pounds, blue eyes, brown hair, and a college education. I was frequently reminded that I had a considerable future. For myself, I felt less optimistic. My past outweighed my future. I had been in a war that did something to me; I trained for a profession and a career, and I threw it away because it was no good and spoiled for me; and I married a woman I loved as much as I had ever loved anyone, and I watched her die. I was thirty-seven years old, and I was not waiting for anything, yearning for anything, or hoping for anything. I lived alone, and sometimes I read a book and sometimes I went to the movies. I welcomed twenty-four-hour duty, and if I did not go home for three days and lived by an electric razor and ham-on-toast. I had no complaints. That helped to make me a good cop.

Briefly, that was my condition a few weeks past when I was instructed to report to the Commissioner's office at Centre Street. I was there at two o'clock in the afternoon, and the Commissioner's secretary sent in the information that Detective Clancy had arrived. I was told to wait. For thirty-five minutes I gave my attention to a printed copy of the budget of the City of New York, and then I was asked to go in.

In the Commissioner's office, there is a mahogany table that is used for high-level meetings and, I suppose, for some of the endless discussions as to why a police department can't make the largest and least homogeneous city in the world the crimeless equivalent of Pretty Valley, Vermont. Around this mahogany table, six men were seated. Going from my left to my right, I believe that they were seated in this order—first Joseph Maggio, a police stenographer, then John Comaday, Police Commissioner of the city, then Arthur Jackson, a plump, gold-eyeglass banker type, who was attached to Central Intelligence, then Sidney Fredericks of the Justice Department, that is, the Federal Bureau of Investigation, whom I spoke of before, then Jerome Greene, Mayor of the City of New York, and finally Senator Hiram U. Dawes, who was the senior member of the Senate Internal Security Committee.

As I came in, they all turned to look at me, but only John Comaday rose and offered me an empty chair. There were things about the Commissioner that I liked. There were other things that I would learn to hate. "Sit down, Clancy," he said to me, and then he went around the table introducing me to the people present. They nodded. Only Fredericks, who was seated beside me, bothered to shake hands; but the others were troubled, and sometimes when you are troubled, you can forget the small niceties.

"We called you in here, Clancy," the Commissioner said, "because we need a city cop with certain qualifications. Maybe a couple of other men on the force have those qualifications, but we are pressed for time, and a quick rundown sorted you out. Now, the point is that we are engaged in a matter that must remain very confidential. From the people present here, you can presume that this is a matter which affects the federal government and the welfare of the entire nation—as well as specifically and pointedly, the welfare of this city and its people. Maybe it's the nastiest thing we ever had to deal with and maybe it isn't. That remains to be determined. The point is that it's a large thing, yet up until now knowledge of the circumstances has been restricted to no more than thirty-five people. This had to be and this is important—for reasons you will soon be given. No word of this has leaked to the press and no word must. What is told to you here today is told to you in the utmost confidence. Do you understand?"

I nodded.

"I would make it stronger than that," Senator Dawes put in.

"No use making it stronger," Comaday shrugged. "A man gives his word. That's it."

"Tell us something about yourself," Jackson, the intelligence man, said. He made it sound ominous, but that was a trick of speech he had with everything he said.

"What sort of thing?"

"They have your official biography," Comaday said. "Just fill in."

"I was born in Brooklyn, grew up there. Local high school, then New York University——"

"We know that," Jackson nodded. "No radical organizations in your youth—Young Socialist League, Young Communist League?"

"I held a job through high school and college. I had no time," I said.

"Just time? Not a matter of conviction?"

"I worked eight hours a day through college. I was too tired for convictions."

"This point interests me," Senator Dawes said. "According to your record, you were an honor student. Your mathematical aptitude is noted as extraordinary. You majored in physics. We are told that you did a remarkable piece of work on cosmic radiation——"

"It was not original work," I noted. "I collated the work of other men and drew some long-shot conclusions."

"Yet your record shows talent, even brilliance. You had your degree. Yet when the war was over, you chose to join the New York City police force—at a time when this nation pleaded for support from every scientist?"

"Yes, sir. That was my own personal decision."

"At a moment like this," Jackson said sharply, "nothing is personal, Detective Clancy."

"That was eleven years ago, sir. I did not want to be a scientist."

"You were at Hiroshima after the bombing," Fredericks put in quietly. "Did that influence you?"

"Yes," I replied.

"Did you think we were wrong in using the atom bomb?" Senator Dawes asked me, but before I could reply, Commissioner Comaday said,

"Please, gentlemen—you knew as well as I do how pressed we are for time. With all due respect, I can't see how this line of questioning can profit us. We need a policeman who is a physicist. We can't have one, unless we begin with the premise that he had good and sufficient personal reasons for changing his profession."

"There is also a question of loyalty!" Jackson snapped.

"The fact that he is here as a member of my department speaks for his loyalty," Comaday replied with growing irritation.

Mayor Greene spread his hands. "Just a moment, gentlemen— let me say that my point of view takes another direction. So far, you have kept this a closed thing. But unless we come up with some answers in short order, it can't be kept that way. I am not trying to impugn the motives or necessities of intelligence or counterintelligence; let me only point out that very soon this may become the concern of ten million people in the metropolitan area. This is not a question of loyalty in any narrow sense; it's a question of survival."

Fredericks nodded and said, "I go along with that, Mr. Mayor. I think the department would. We are more concerned with intelligence in the old-fashioned sense—Detective Clancy's intelligence. Because unless we use our brains, our common sense, and our intelligence, we are in a very great pickle indeed."

"Agreed!" Senator Dawes said. "Tell me, Mr. Clancy, you're a physicist?"

"I'm a policeman, sir. I studied physics a long time ago."

"Have you kept up with your reading?"

"Somewhat."

"What do you know about the atom bomb?"

"What anyone else does."

"Surely a little more. You are a physicist."

"A little more," I admitted. "I can follow the mathematics as well as the theory."

"More to the point," Commissioner Comaday put in, "could you make an atom bomb, Clancy?"

"What?"

"I said, could you make an atom bomb? I address you, Clancy, in the framework of what you are. You are a policeman with a grounding in physics. I am asking you whether you could make an atom bomb?"

"You can't be serious," I said.

"I am deadly serious. We all are. Now see whether you can give us a serious answer."

"All right." I took a deep breath and nodded. "If you mean, could I produce plutonium 239 or uranium 234, the two fissionable elements from which the simplest types of bombs are constructed, the answer is no. No individual could. No nation could unless it could assemble a very large investment in plant and power and undertake some sort of diffusion process with the uranium ore."

"We understand that," the senator said impatiently. "The question Mr. Comaday asks is whether you think you could make a bomb given the finished products—plutonium or uranium 235?"

"Alone?" I asked bewilderedly.

"Yes, alone."

"Well, that depends. I mean, that depends on whether you were going to say to me, here and now, make a bomb. I have only a cursory knowledge of what goes into the bomb. I would want to do some reading."

"We grant that," Comaday said grimly.

"Well—I don't know. It would be a very dangerous business. For me, I mean. But I might."

"Just a moment," Jackson, the C.I. man, said. "Do you mean to tell me that you would have all the information at your fingertips? That this classified information would be available to you?"

"It's not classified, sir," I said. "It's not secret either. It's been published a thousand times in a thousand different places. Any competent physicist knows how to make an atom bomb."

"We've been through all that, Mr. Jackson," Commissioner Comaday said tiredly, "and we've had the same answer from half a dozen people. All we wish to do here is to establish certain facts about Detective Clancy to the satisfaction of what we represent. You asked to be here. Would you permit us to continue?"

"I can't say that I appreciate your attitude," Jackson replied.

Almost harshly, the Justice Department man put in, "Whether you appreciate an attitude is beside the point. Are you forcing me to point out that my department, not yours, is concerned with internal security? What are we to do, quibble like children? The question was put to Detective Clancy. I, for one, would like to hear his answer."

"Go ahead, Clancy," the Commissioner said.

"Well, sir," I said hopelessly, "I don't want to presume on what you already know—undoubtedly as well as I do——"

"Take it that we know nothing, damn it!" Comaday snapped. "That's not far from the truth. Just talk about the bomb you are going to make and how you would go about it."

"Very well." I looked from face to face. The Senator was smoking, so I lit a cigarette. Heaven knows I needed one. I also needed a stiff drink, but that was not available. "I'll try not to be too lengthy," I said, "and to talk simply." The senator smiled, as if to say, "This I would like to see." I went on.

"We're talking about a process of fission—that is a chain reaction within the structure of the atoms of fissionable material. The result is an explosion of enormous heat, speed, and force. Thereby the bomb. I mentioned the first step, a large industrial process to produce the two fissionable materials we work with, uranium 235 and plutonium 239. Considering that we have these two elements—either one of them—what now? Well, the explosion itself, which we cause by inserting an extra neutron into the atomic structure of the fissionable material. I'm trying to be brief and clear——"

They nodded, watching me intently.

"Now what happens in the explosion is this: we'll think of the fissionable atom as a sort of motor, running at very high speed. If we can cause a neutron to enter that motor and remain within it, we overcharge it, so as to speak. It becomes unstable and tears itself to pieces with tremendous force and immediately transmits the instability to the atoms around it. This is a chain reaction and an atomic explosion. The fact that this happens makes it plain why these two fissionable elements are found unconcentrated in nature. They are too unstable. The air around us is full of stray neutrons——"

"I'm not clear on the origin of these stray neutrons you talk about," the senator said.

"Yes, sir. Cosmic radiation for one thing. Radioactive substances in soil, stone, water for another. Bricks emit neutrons. I would guess that this room contains thousands right now. That is central to the problem. If we had on this table in front of us a piece of uranium 235 the size of a lump of sugar, we would be in no danger. That is because the mass of such a piece is too small to block a stray neutron, to capture it, and to set it in what they call 'resonance' with the fissionable atomic structure. In other words, the neutrons plunge right through this small piece of uranium 235 without triggering it. Then such a small piece of fissionable material would be called a non-critical mass.

"To be critical—that is to be large enough to insure the trapping of a neutron and the subsequent explosion—a piece of uranium 235 would have to have a diameter of at least ten centimeters, or about two inches. But of course a two-inch cube or ball of uranium 235 can exist only theoretically, since at the instant of its existence, it ceases to exist and becomes an atomic explosion."

"Yet they do exist," the Mayor said.

"Yes—if you can think of existence in terms of one ten-thousandth of a second. As a matter of fact, there is the problem of the bomb. I have read that when plutonium or uranium 235 are produced at the plant, they are manufactured in thin sheets of less than critical mass, and that these sheets are separated by insulation of cadmium or boron, both of which have the property of trapping stray neutrons. If these packages were immersed in heavy water, I imagine that the danger factor would be reduced to zero, since heavy water also traps neutrons. But you give me the problem of making the bomb. Well, let us suppose that I have sixteen cubes of uranium 235, each cube one half inch square. I could lay them out around this table, four cubes to a side, but I would not have an explosion. I would have to push them all together before I could have an explosion."

"It sounds simple enough," the senator said.

"No, sir—not at all, if I may say so. It's not simple. In the first place, this is highly radioactive material, and if I played with it carelessly, I would be injured beyond recovery. Secondly, if I just spread my arms and pushed the lumps together, I would get a partial explosion, enough to kill me and wreck this building—but no more than that. You see, once the fission begins, the released neutrons involved in the chain reaction move at a speed of about eight thousand miles a second. Since these neutrons have to cover only the few inches where the uranium is, the process is to all purposes instantaneous. It starts and finishes quicker than we can measure time, and it will start the moment any part of the mass becomes critical. In other words, if I pushed the lumps together, I would achieve only a partial explosion and a small one in atomic terms—no matter how quickly I moved. Not to mention the fact that I would kill myself."

"Why wouldn't the chain reaction leap to the other cubes of uranium?" the Mayor asked.

"Because the blast blows them away even quicker. The point is that the non-critical masses must be united in the same fraction of a second. That is why I couldn't make the kind of a bomb you could drop from an airplane. I would want a machine shop and a staff of expert technicians for that. But while I've been talking here, I have been trying to think of what kind of a bomb I could make. I'm not sure. I would want a lot more time to think about it. But just off the top of my head, suppose one took twenty non-critical masses and loaded them into shotgun shells. Then suppose one mounted the shotguns so that they were fixed on a single short-range target, say inside a room like this. Then it would only be a question of a technical problem—how to fire the twenty shotguns simultaneously. I think that might be a bomb —I'm not absolutely certain because I have been talking about this only in the vague general terms I remember. It's not a comfortable thought."

"No, it's not a comfortable thought," the Mayor agreed.

They asked a few more questions before Commissioner Comaday said,

"Then it wouldn't surprise you, Clancy, if I told you that some-one claims to have made a bomb?"

"It would surprise me, yes. But I've thought of it."

"What do you mean, you've thought of it?"

"That someone might make that bomb," I replied, thinking that of all the things on God's earth, I hated that bomb most and feared it most.

"You make it sound too simple," Fredericks said, and I told the F.B.I. man,

"It's almost as simple as I make it sound." Then I added, "Pro-viding you have the fissionable material." There was a little while of silence then, and after that, Comaday said,

"What I am going to tell you now, Clancy, is a particular kind of secret. It may stop being a secret tomorrow or the next day or next month; but until it stops it's a rotten, miserable secret, and you will regard it as such. Do you understand?"

I nodded.

"All right," he continued. "We begin with a man named Alexander Horton, a physicist—not a terribly brilliant man, not over-talented in terms of his discipline. But a man of education, competence, and conscience."

"I would hardly call it conscience," Jackson interrupted. "Treason, disloyalty——"

"I am not indoctrinating Detective Clancy," Comaday said angrily. "I am attempting to give him a necessary picture of a man, and we'll all be better off if I give him that picture and get it over with. I'll thank you not to interrupt me again. If you want to tell the tale your way, you can have your turn."

Jackson waved a hand and said, "Go on, go on—as was pointed out to me, I am here only by sufferance."

"I said conscience," Comaday turned back to me. "Other things as well—a touch of paranoia, perhaps, emotional instability, a depressed person. Consider all of these things. Alexander Horton, forty-one years old, five feet ten inches, blue eyes, slim, almost emaciated, physically in poor health if not worse, graduate of M.I.T., doctorate at Cornell, post-graduate work at Princeton, two years in the service—and then detached to work on the Manhattan Project. Then, after the war, five years at Oak Ridge —during which time he contracted a form of radiation sickness. He was hospitalized and convalescent for two years. When he had recovered his health sufficiently to work again, he did not return to government service but found a place on the science faculty at Knickerbocker University, here in the city——"

I had my notebook out, but he shook his head fiercely.

"No notes. Just remember what I am telling you. It will stay with you. If you have any questions, throw them at me."

"Please go on, sir," I said.

"Any questions. Don't worry about notes."

"Yes, sir."

"Now we come to last summer. Last summer Horton spent four weeks in Great Britain. During those same four weeks, a delegation of Soviet physicists were being entertained in England as guests of the Royal Nuclear Society. You know the organization?"

"I know of it," I nodded. "Sir Julian Bell."

"That's right. Bell is the chairman. Now understand that Horton is not without reputation in scientific circles. He was invited as a guest to a banquet of the Royal Society given in honor of the Russians, and he was seated next to a Russian physicist, Academician Peter Simonovsky. Evidently, they developed an immediate rapport. Simonovsky's English is excellent, and they were able to talk without the intervention of a translator. When the banquet had finished, Simonovsky left with Horton. They went to Horton's hotel room, where they spent most of that night talking. During the subsequent two weeks, Horton and Simonovsky met on six different occasions, and at least once they spent an entire day together.

"Now about Simonovsky. He is fifty-three years old, a tank commander during World War II, decorated for gallantry and with a record of impeccable loyalty to the Soviet State. He was one of the key figures in the development of Soviet atomic weapons. Like Horton, he has no close relations. His parents died in a Nazi concentration camp. His wife and three children were killed by a bomb in Kiev during the war. He is described as a thoughtful, quiet, and deeply unhappy man.

"Very briefly. Clancy—but you now have the background to our problem. The problem itself came to light a week ago, when three identical letters were delivered by mail. One was addressed to the President of the United States. The second was addressed to the Secretary of State. The third was addressed to the Mayor of New York City. Later on, a copy of this letter will be furnished for your careful inspection. Since it is a long letter, I have summed up the first part in what I have just told you. The letter was written by Alexander Horton."

"And mailed where?" I asked him.

"In New York City. Morningside Station. I am now going to read a part of that letter. I quote:

"'The result of all my discussions with Mr. Simonovsky was a decision to go ahead seriously with what we had first considered as an improbable mental game. I think the factor that decided us was our ability to lay hands on the fissionable material. A careful check through the files at Oak Ridge will reveal the discrepancy between inventory and manufacture—a super-critical quantity of uranium 235. I have managed to obtain this critical mass, through circumstances I naturally cannot reveal. Mr. Simonovsky has been equally successful. When you receive this communication, both mechanisms will be in existence, mine in the heart of New York City, Mr. Simonovsky's in the heart of Moscow. A short discussion with any competent physicist will remove any doubts concerning our ability to construct these explosive mechanisms. And I assure you that in each case, the explosive mechanism is powerful enough to wipe out the entire heart of the city.

"'So at this point, gentlemen, the fate of the two largest cities in the two most powerful countries on earth, lies not with ambitious, querulous, and irresponsible politicians, but with two men of science. You may reasonably doubt that this improves the existing impasse. We feel that it does.

"'We feel that the situation previous to our intervention was intolerable and ultimately dangerous to all life on earth. We also feel that since we were at least in part responsible for creating that situation, our responsibility for dealing with it continues. We make no choice or preference between two sets of intractable rulers. We make no resort to ethics, for the only ethics we see at work are the ethics of power. Therefore, we have resorted to power on our behalf.

"'We are now possessed of the power to destroy New York and Moscow. Forty days from the date of this communication we shall exercise that power and destroy both cities—unless before the expiration of those forty days the United States and the Soviet Union come to some agreements for the banning of all atomic weapons.

"'You will obviously doubt our abilities and our determination. But we believe that where the test of our sincerity is so costly, you will choose to accept our declaration. We devoutly hope you will.

"'A letter similar to this one is now being read in Moscow.'"

The Police Commissioner paused and laid the letter aside. "Signed Alexander Horton. There it is, Clancy. The day it was posted, Mr. Horton disappeared. Mr. Simonovsky also disappeared."

So that was how it began, and from that time to the time I brought one hundred and fifty thousand dollars down to the Commissioner's office, fifteen days had passed. Before that, between the time they received the letter from Horton up to the time they had me into the Commissioner's office to convince me that I ought to give my all to save mankind—or at least two cities to which mankind was somewhat attached—seven days had passed. Fifteen and seven add up to twenty-two. Eighteen days were left.

I am telling the story as best I can. If it moves backwards and forwards, it is because that's the way Clancy moved. It makes sense to me to go back to the beginning at that time when I had returned to my apartment one hundred and fifty thousand dollars poorer than when I had left it. I made fresh coffee, lit a cigarette, and reflected upon the way it began. Now, telling the story, it seems to me to be the appropriate moment to go into the beginnings. There is also another factor, however; we live generally and at ease with the smaller and larger lunacies of mankind. We are devoted to the proposition that we are sane and that most of our actions are the actions of sanity; this is because we forbear to look at ourselves or our world objectively. I had withheld that objective point of view until the night of the bribe. Then I was forced into it, and found myself sitting in an empty room and laughing. If I were a woman, I would have been weeping; and inside it felt the same.

And peculiarly, I had no regrets for the money, even though I sensed that the money might be the price of my life as well as other things. I was not yet in possession of what they were paying me for, and I might never be in possession of it; but let them find out what I had done with the money, and the life and future of Tom Clancy would hit a new low.

As to why I had acted the way I did, that too rested in the depths of Clancy. John Comaday, a wise man, had not embraced me for my honesty. Honesty is a loosely descriptive term. So is conscience, which Comaday had used descriptively concerning Alexander Horton. At the root of the matter was the fact that I did not want the money. I never joined hands with it. It stayed aloof from me, as so many things have remained aloof since Helen's death. I didn't want to sleep under the same roof as that money, and I brought it downtown.

Now even though I had never met Comaday, the Police Commissioner, before that day of the gathering in his office, Comaday probably knew something about me. A man in his position can ask and will get answers, and here and there were people who worked with me and knew me, at least a little. They might have told him that Clancy was less brave than careful; possibly, he wanted that. They might also have told him that I never waved a flag of platitude if I could help it, and possibly that too was something he wanted. In any case, he trusted me enough to tell me what he told me; and then he sat back and looked at me for a while before he said,

"No questions, Clancy?"

"Questions. I don't know where to begin, sir."

"You heard it. You were pretty damn sure that you could make a bomb when we put it to you. Do you believe Horton?"

"Well, sir," I said, "it's not a question of believing him. That puts it on me, which is meaningless. One would have to know a great deal about Horton and how his mind works. One would also set them to taking inventory at Oak Ridge or wherever they keep that damn stuff and see what's missing."

"It's missing."

"How much?"

"The equipment for one large fission bomb—that is, the uranium."

"How?" I began, but he interrupted and almost snarled,

"Don't ask me how, Clancy! You were in the Army, weren't you? You know how they run things? They're not even sure it's missing! They're also not sure it's not missing! They just seem to be short the arming of a bomb!"

"I hardly think that's called for," the Senator said mildly.

"No, sir? I think it is, by God!"

"And in Russia? You've been speaking to them?"

"Speaking to them? Indeed, Clancy. We share a mutual sense of idiocy and a mutual case of jitters. Possibly it's cheering to know that they are as irresponsible as we are. They will not admit that uranium or plutonium is missing; they also refuse to state that it is not missing. They love their secrets, so they prefer to keep their secrets but confess their very bad case of nerves."

"They have not found Simonovsky?"

"No, indeed. They have not found Simonovsky. We have not found Horton. For seven days we have been using every shred of experience we possess in the art of finding a missing person. We have not found him. That's not hard to understand. If we were to publicize this business, we would have a major panic on our hands. Major is a small word. We would have a first-class disaster. Try to imagine the consequences of depopulating the metropolitan area!—granting that it can be done. Where do you house ten million people? How do you feed them? No, it's not even that— it's the breakdown of everything that goes with it! That's what we have to contend with in our search for Horton. It has to be a quiet search, a silent search—yes, a secret search."

"Still, it could be a hoax," I said.

"You answered that, Clancy. When we find Horton, we'll know whether it's a hoax or not. And we have to find him and quickly. He is a sick man, and he may be a dying man. He underwent a remission of his illness, but he isn't cured."

"What do you want me to do?" I asked.

"In a moment. First, understand what we are up against, because you will be up against the same thing. When we question people, we can go so far—no farther. The cat stays in the bag."

"Yes, sir. I think I understand that."

"We are putting a lot of our hopes on you. On you, Clancy.

You are going into Knickerbocker University as a replacement for Alexander Horton. You are going to teach physics."

"What? It's fifteen years since I left physics."

"You never left. It's all there, somewhere. Bone up."

"In forty days?"

"In one week, Clancy. One week. For one week, you will eat, sleep, and dream physics. Then you report to Dean Edward Gorland at Knickerbocker. He's not in on this, but he is prepared in terms of top-secret necessity. That is all he knows, and it's enough. We have prepared a suitable background for you, which accounts for the years since the war."

"I can't move into a college physics department with five days of preparation."

"You can and you will. Gorland will work with you. Don't sleep for seven days. Men have done that and survived. But you're going in there on time and you're going to pass as the real thing! Because if you don't, so help me God, Clancy, I'll make you wish you were never born!"

"I wish it," I said.

"You're going in there, Clancy, and you're going to find some lead to Horton. We trained you as a cop, and you're supposed to be a smart cop."

"Thank you, sir," I said.

"The hell with that, and the hell with the clever talk! You just do what you're supposed to do, Clancy! There's a woman teaching in the same department. Her name is Phyllis Goldmark, and on and off during the past two years, she has spent some time with Horton. There was no romance, as I understand it, but she was the only real friend he had. You will receive a complete dossier on Miss Goldmark, and you are going to know her, and you are going to win her affection, her respect, and her trust——"

"No," I said. "No, sir. I will not."

Then there was silence—a long painful silence, while they all watched me. Jackson, the intelligence man, started to say something, but Comaday told him to shut up. Then there was silence again. Then Jerome Greene, the Mayor, said to me in a surprisingly gentle voice,

"I don't sleep any more, Clancy. I'm very tired. I'm as afraid of dying as the next man, but I think I would die without much protest if I could find the answers to this. I can't find them. God help me, I can't find them."

"Don't think we haven't tried," said Fredericks. "We've questioned the woman. We know what she knows. She's not consciously holding back. We want to know what she doesn't even realize she knows."

"We have to know," Greene whispered.

"I'm a small figure," I whispered. "I'm nobody in a room full of brass. I'm just a cop from Homicide who can say his piece because you want more from me than I'll ever want from you. So I can talk to the Police Commissioner and the Mayor and a U.S. senator and a G man and a cloak-and-dagger man—and I don't give two damns about being pushed out to Staten Island in a uniform. But why don't you ask me how I feel? I was lucky enough to love one woman the way a man can and she died of leukemia! Leukemia! I saw Hiroshima with my own eyes and I married a woman who died of leukemia! That's why I became a cop! I hate physics! I hate your rotten, stinking bomb! I hate it as much as Horton does!"

Fredericks waited. No one else spoke. Then Fredericks said, almost lazily, "I don't think Horton hates the bomb at all. Commissioner Comaday referred to him as a man of conscience. All right. I didn't argue the point, because I think it helps in a sort of descriptive manner. I reserved my opinion. You want it, Clancy? All right. Man of conscience hell! You hate the bomb, Clancy? Are you sure you hate it more than I do, more than Mayor Greene does, more than the Commissioner does? I don't see you building any fancy bedroom bombs. But Horton is drooling over a big fat bomb, somewhere here in New York. Oh yes, he's going to save mankind! He's willing to send ten million of us to kingdom come—just to save mankind. To hell with that kind of savior, Clancy!"

"Only there's one thing you've forgotten," I said.

"Yes?" Comaday asked, watching me narrowly.

"We could have a pact and outlaw the bomb."

"I'm just a cop," Comaday nodded. "Just a cop, Clancy. I rank you, but I'm a cop. I don't make treaties. Let Washington and Moscow worry about a damned treaty. I'm all for that. But I also know this—whether or not they make a treaty, nothing is changed. Horton still sits in his room with his bomb, and my job remains—to find him! Maybe he is a man of conscience and maybe he isn't; whatever else he is, he's sick, mentally and physically. Even if he dies wherever he is, this city will be untenable until we find that cursed bomb."

I had no more arguments left then. I said I would do it.

Now, sitting alone in my apartment fifteen days later, smoking a cigarette, drinking my black coffee, I accepted the fact that secrets are for girls' schools and cloak-and-dagger boys. Our secret was no longer a secret by at least two, Jackie, the all-American boy, and Mr. Brown, with the Anglo-Saxon name and the Latin accent. They knew all about our secret, and they were willing to pay in advance, one hundred and fifty thousand dollars—or their backers were—and never even ask for a receipt. All they wanted was a bomb, conveniently placed in New York City—when I knew the proper address. They were even willing to wait. But they would not wait forever; and I very much doubted that they would wait out the eighteen days that remained.

I did my thinking, but it was the kind of thinking that goes around in circles and then settles like a sickness in the pit of your stomach. Then I tried to sleep, but I was late sleeping and early waking, and I dressed as the sun rose—full dress, so to speak, with a little snub-nosed gun strapped under my arm, a pathetic reassurance for a man who hated guns and what guns did. I held out one hand to see whether it trembled noticeably, but a steady hand is a poor indication of what goes on inside.

I had my coffee at home and then went up to the University; and when I got there, I was ravenously hungry suddenly and I went into the cafeteria for some bacon and eggs and more coffee. Phyllis was there, alone at a table, and I brought my pile of food to join her orange juice and toast.

"Good morning," she smiled at me. "Do you always eat such a nourishing breakfast?"

"As a matter of fact, I don't. I guess I was up too early, and that gave me an appetite."

"I was thinking about yesterday afternoon," she said. "I think it was one of the nicest afternoons I ever spent."

"I'm glad."

"I think you are," she nodded. "You really enjoy making other people feel good, don't you, Mr. Clancy?"

"I don't know. I never looked at it that way."

"Your eggs are going to get cold if you don't eat, Mr.———" She took a deep breath, then finished her orange juice and put sugar into her coffee. "Why is it so hard for me to call you Tom? You asked me to, didn't you?"

"I asked you to."

"I had such a nice time yesterday—and afterwards I argued with myself that you wouldn't be so nice to me unless you enjoyed being with me and wanted to be with me."

"That figures, doesn't it?"

"You're just amused at me. About the eggs—I mean my mother gives me no peace when I let food get cold on my plate, and I suppose I got the habit from her. Won't you please eat. You said you were hungry."

"Then I'll eat," I smiled. "If it makes you feel good."

"You're a very nice person, Tom."

"Yes? Well, as such things go—maybe. I don't know. I try. We're both lonely. Would you have dinner with me again tonight?"

"Oh——"

"I know it's two nights in a row."

"Why are you asking me?"

"I think because I would enjoy having dinner with you again. That's probably the whole reason. Do you have a date?"

She nodded.

"Well, then——"

"Not a real date," she said. "I'm invited to my cousin's house for dinner. They live in Great Neck."

"Do you have a car?"

"No. No, I can't afford a car, Tom. I don't even drive."

"I have a car. I'll drive you out and drive you back—if you will bring me."

"That would be so nice," she sighed. "I hate the railroad. That would be nice. But I couldn't—I couldn't impose on you that way. It wouldn't be right."

"What would not be right? My driving you there or you inviting me there?"

"I don't mean that. I mean you wouldn't like these people."

"If you do, why shouldn't I?"

"I'm not sure that I do, Tom," she said. "It's someplace to go. You're asked someplace instead of sitting at home. I'm a teacher, twenty-nine years old, and not married and not terribly attractive. I'm not giving away secrets. You must realize this."

"Do I sound that way when I feel sorry for myself?" I asked softly.

It was like striking her. She turned white and stared at the table. She must have remained that way for a minute or two, and then, not looking up, she whispered,

"You don't feel sorry for yourself."

"Then neither do you," I said.

"Do you really want to go with me tonight?"

"Yes."

"All right, then. But I'll have to call her. She won't say no, because I'm bringing a date. Sometimes they make me miserable because I don't have dates. I'll call her and I'll meet you at your office at five o'clock."

"Thank you, Phyllis."

"You're welcome," she said, and began to stir her coffee again, still not looking up at me.

PART THREE

DMITRI GRISCHOV

IT was not until I was at the door of the house on Park Avenue that I spotted the tail, and by then it was too late. I saw him quickly out of the corner of my eye, standing across the side street and downtown from me, still wearing the gray worsted coat, the black shoes, and the black gloves. I felt like a damn fool and a bad cop; but I had felt like a fool sufficient times before not to be too thrown by the feeling, and it had never occurred to me that I was a model policeman in any category. I went into the house, which was the only thing I could do.

Maybe you have seen the house on Park Avenue, which is the diplomatic stronghold of the Soviet Union in New York City. It is a very fine and elegant house, a corner affair, built out of red brick in the Georgian style or in some sort of turn-of-the-century rearrangement of the Georgian style. I have heard it told that the man who sold it to the Russians needled them about their desire to have one of the best houses in New York in the best neighbourhood in New York; but I think that's a short view. If you run a country, no matter what kind of country, you put your best foot forward or you borrow a best foot to put forward.

I went inside through a door that was opened for me by a sombre, square-cut gentleman in a dark suit. His face was square, his body was square, and he was in no mood for smiles or cordial welcomes. He raised his brows at me but said nothing aloud, and I said to him that I was there to see Dmitri Grischov.

"Who is Dmitri Grischov?" he wanted to know.

He had an accent which I will not attempt to reproduce. He was my first Russian, in terms of the Soviet Union type of Russian, and the marble floor of the mansion's foyer was my first excursion onto Russian soil. It was cold and aloof and unencouraging; and when I informed him that he should know better than I who Dmitri Grischov was, his face relapsed into its original square, blank expression. I stood there and he stood there, and the seconds ticked by until a young lady at the far back of the entrance-way, sitting behind a desk and doing whatever she was supposed to do, realized that an impasse had been reached and came forward to help. She was a very presentable young lady, not over-weight, nicely dressed; and after looking me over carefully, she essayed a sort of half smile.

I had already gathered that while this place might be jovial on other occasions, its tendency toward mirth would be suppressed in my presence. The young lady asked me what she could do for me, and I repeated to her my desire to see Dmitri Grischov. She considered my request thoughtfully and then she said something in Russian to the large, square man who had originally intercepted me. He answered in Russian but carefully did not permit any expression upon his face. Then she turned to me and, with the other half of her original smile, informed me that there was no Dmitri Grischov at this address.

A broad flight of handsome marble stairs led up to the second floor of the building. Now a third party came down the stairs and joined us. He was slim, dressed in a suit of dark clothes, and un-smiling. With the other two, he shared an expression of wary emptiness that I had already come to associate with the diplomatic front of the Soviet delegation. His accent was barely noticeable as he asked me what he could do for me.

"I made an appointment with Mr. Grischov," I replied to him. "One hour ago I took my telephone, dialed the number of this building, spoke to Mr. Grischov, and agreed to meet him here. After that I attended to one or two matters and then put on my hat and coat, got a taxicab and came over here. Upon my arrival here, both this gentleman on my right and this lady on my left assure me that there is no Dmitri Grischov."

The thin man smiled—he gave me a full smile without reserving any part of it. "Dmitri Grischov," he said, after his smile had completed itself.

"Dmitri Grischov," I repeated.

He spoke in Russian to the young lady, she spoke in Russian to the square-set gentleman. He replied to both of them in Russian. The slim man then said something—also in Russian—and next a reply to that from the young lady. Then the Russian language was laid aside for the time being and the slim man asked me who I was.

"My name is Thomas Clancy," I told him. "I'm a professor of physics at Knickerbocker University. I'm thirty-seven years old, and I live in New York."

The slim man nodded and looked at me thoughtfully. Then he said in a thoughtful and reserved manner, as if he were contemplating carefully each word he spoke,

"You may be all that, Mr. Clancy. There is another fact of some importance that you failed to mention. You are carrying a gun."

His observation was not a question but a matter of fact. I asked him how he knew.

"My friend here," nodding at the square gentleman, "has been trained to observe such matters."

"I didn't think it showed."

"Not perhaps to anyone who isn't trained to look for such things. I myself, you must understand, am not trained in that direction. Perhaps it's in the way you stand, the way you hold your arm, I'm sure I don't know. But if he says you're carrying a gun, I have no doubt but that you are carrying a gun. You must understand, Mr. Clancy, that this is not any building, this is a special sort of building. This is the house of the Soviet Delegation to the United Nations. We have an understandable reason to be cautious and even somewhat suspicious of anyone who comes in here carrying a gun and informs us that he is a college professor. This being the case, I think it would be better for you if you left."

I shook my head. "Not until I see Mr. Grischov."

"You have been told that there is no Grischov here."

"I have an appointment with Mr. Grischov. I intend to see Mr. Grischov."

The slim man was now more thoughtful than ever. Then he smiled and asked whether I would object to leaving my gun where it would be taken care of.

"I have no objections," I said.

"Then please don't move, Mr. Clancy. Just stand as you are with your hands at your side. My friend here will remove the gun."

I stood as I was and the large square man reached inside my coat, removed my gun, glanced at it quickly, and then dropped it into his jacket pocket. Then there was a brief exchange in Russian, after which the slim man suggested that I sit down and wait a few minutes. After that, he and the girl both disappeared. I sat on a straight-backed chair and the man whose business it was to know who carried a gun and who did not stood across the hallway from me and observed me with professional curiosity. A few minutes passed and then the girl reappeared, smiled a full smile at me and told me that she would take me to Mr. Grischov. I followed her up the stairs, through a large square reception room that was marble-floored and hung with heavy red plush drapes, into a sitting-room library—a large, handsome room with oak paneled walls, oak floors, and the massive, proto-Renaissance furniture that must have been added to the mansion at the time it was built.

The young lady left me at the door of this room and Grischov came forward to greet me. He shook hands with a strong and brisk grip, said he was delighted to see me—this with only a suggestion of a Russian accent—and asked me what I would have to drink.

"Nothing," I assured him.

"But surely some refreshment—a brandy, an apéritif, a glass of fruit juice."

"Nothing, thank you," I said.

He was a tightly knit, well-dressed man of about forty-two. His gray flannel suit might have come from Brooks Brothers. He wore a white shirt and a black knit tie. His cuffs showed good gold cuff links. He was blond, blue-eyed, alert, and moved with ease and decision. He offered me a chair and then sat down facing me, his hands on his knees, and an expression of pleased surprise upon his face—as if he had measured me and weighed me and decided that I was precisely the type to do the work I had to do.

I mentioned to him the difficulties that I had encountered on the floor below. He shrugged and smiled and explained that they had their ways and we had ours. "Like yourself," Grischov said, "I am, in a manner of speaking, a visitor here. I represent a branch of the service that they don't take too kindly to. No one likes to think that a professional investigator is eating and sleeping under the same roof that he is. That's human nature and human nature is still very much evident in the Soviet Union, Mr. Clancy, in spite of certain opinions in your country to the contrary."

"I have no opinions about the Soviet Union," I said.

"That is an accommodation, Mr. Clancy, but hardly true. Whatever else any American has or has not, we can both be assured he has opinions on the Soviet Union. I might even make it a little broader—there is no Russian who hasn't opinions on the United States. But that is all beside the point. We face each other in a professional sense and only in a professional sense. We are, both of us, deeply concerned with the actions of two irresponsible men. I know who you are. I wonder what you know about me."

I was beginning to like Grischov. Consciously or unconsciously, he repudiated stereotypes. Downstairs I had felt like someone who steps on to the stage of a revue and finds himself in the middle of a badly written script about the Soviet Union. Grischov was straightforward, matter-of-fact, and practical.

"I know your name," I said to him, "and I know that you are attached to this case. I'm afraid that's all I know."

"We have a little more in common," Grischov smiled. "For one thing, like yourself, I studied physics. Before the war, I taught physics for two years at a small college in the Ukraine. After the war, I joined the Foreign Service. I spent two years in England and learned to talk the language passably well. It's a very difficult language—perhaps the most difficult, apart from Russian, that exists. But I listen and I try. Then I was detached from the Foreign Service and brought into our equivalent of your Department of Justice. That has its positive and its negative aspects. As a professional, I don't sit in judgment. I try to do my job. I was sent here on this case because I speak the language and because I have a background in physics. I would like to work with you if I can help you. On the other hand, I do not wish to be a nuisance. I do not wish to force myself upon you. As I understand it, you have a delicate and difficult job. For my part, I would not like to be in your shoes. On the other hand, in a manner of speaking, I am in your shoes."

"You are? I wonder, Mr. Grischov."

"At least in this sense. I am here in the city and I'm the only one of my people who knows why I'm here and for what reason. Let us say, that makes me uneasy. Knowing what I know, I would prefer to be in Moscow."

"You mean that, don't you?" I said.

"It's not heroics, Mr. Clancy, I mean it. I haven't taken the time to think through just why I mean it. There are too many things that need thinking through, and I don't have the time for it now. The fact remains that I am here. I want to be of some service to you. I could say to you that all of the resources of our country in this, your country, are at your disposal. That would be meaningless. The only resources that will do you any good are the resources in your own head. Am I right?"

"More or less."

"Still and all, I could be of some service—possibly."

"Possibly," I agreed.

"Then we'll bypass enthusiasm and the formalities. What can I do for you?"

I took a long moment to look at Grischov before answering him. It had occurred to me that in our own way, whatever the limitations and pressures, he and I were unique. We were engaged in a most peculiar pursuit—perhaps the most peculiar that had involved a Soviet citizen and an American citizen since the end of World War II. There was a thousand things that we could profitably say to each other, a thousand discussions we could profitably engage in, but in all likelihood none of them would come about. We had a professional relationship in terms of a rather dubious profession, yet it occurred to me that perhaps, at the same time, we were opening a unique path in the simple—or complex, as some would have it—practice of civilization.

"You could begin by telling me something about Simonovsky," I said.

"Very well. Peter Simonovsky, Academician, aged fifty-three. Lived in Kiev. Born in a small Ukrainian village where both his parents lived. His parents were alive when the Nazis occupied the territory. Both of them were taken to a concentration camp. They died in the camp. He was married to a beautiful and talented woman, Alexandrova Charnoff. If you were a Russian of my age, you would know the name. Miss Charnoff was a ballet dancer—perhaps as fine a dancer as Ulanova. I saw her once before the war. She was something to see—something to watch. She moved like music, not like flesh and blood, and she was as beautiful as she was graceful. Why she chose to marry Simonovsky I leave to the novelists. I am no authority on why one man prefers one woman or one woman a certain man. Nevertheless, they were married and, from all I can find out, it was a good marriage. Not without difficulties. Personally, I don't believe that there is any marriage without difficulties, and the ballet dancer with the physicist, that's in a class by itself. But it was a marriage that worked. In 1942, while Simonovsky was in the Army—he had a commission as a major—his wife and children were killed by a bomb explosion. One child was four years old, and there were twins who were six years old. That was something Simonovsky never recovered from. It put him into a condition of very deep depression. Like many men who did not desire to live, he took large chances during the war. He was wounded twice and each time he recovered and went back into action. He was decorated with the Order of Stalin and my sources tell me that the decoration was meaningless to him and that he regarded it with contempt. That is understandable under the circumstances. In 1946 he underwent drug therapy in Moscow for the condition of depression. It appeared to help him and he was able to do useful and profitable work upon our atomic energy project. So far as we know, he had neither correspondence nor communication of any sort with Alex Horton before meeting him in London last summer. His attitude toward war was negative. He hated war and he hated the bomb, but you must understand, Mr. Clancy, that both of these attitudes are not unusual in our country."

"Curiously enough, they are not unusual here," I said.

"So there you have him," Grischov nodded. "All in all, I think he was a very different man from your Horton. It was time, circumstances and a moment in history that brought them together, that provided for a concurrence, so as to speak, of insanity and desperation."

"Then I take it that you haven't found him."

Grischov looked at me keenly and then he nodded.

"Why?"

"For the same reason that you haven't found Horton, Mr. Clancy. From what I know about you, your experience has been with criminals—to some extent, mine has also—if criminals of somewhat different background and persuasion. The criminal is a psychopathic mind. He is also, in most instances, ignorant. The legend of the master criminal is a romance. The reason why crime is pursued with so little intelligence is that intelligent people do not pursue crime."

"Not a petty crime, I agree."

"Precisely, and in the world we live in, Mr. Clancy, it is the petty crime that is punishable. When a criminal goes to earth, you can find him. He has his associates, his habits, his neighbourhoods. He has behind him a whole history of uninspired criminal activity. With an intelligent man it is something else entirely. An intelligent man who goes to earth in a large city need not ever be found."

"Do you believe that?"

"Unfortunately, I do," Grischov nodded. "Don't you?"

"It's meaningless, as far as I'm concerned," I said. "I have to find Horton; even granting that he can't be found, I have to find him. I was only thinking that it might help if you found Simonovsky."

"It might help," Grischov agreed, smiling slowly. "But Simonovsky is in Moscow and you and I are here."

"We are here," I agreed. "In any case, we are here for two weeks more."

"Where we'll be after that is a theological problem and I don't intend to argue theology with Americans. The point in question is, What can I do to help you? You understand that I am limited. This is not my country. This is not my city. I have certain resources at my disposal, but I can't use them. I may appear to be critical of some of your methods—that doesn't help me. I can only help you—if I can in any way."

I took out a reproduction of Vanpelt's picture and handed it to him. He studied it for a minute or two and then raised his eyes inquiringly.

"Do you know him? Have you ever seen him?"

Grischov shook his head.

"His name is John Vanpelt," I told Grischov. "Fifty years old, professor of physics at Knickerbocker University. That's a poor picture but, at the moment, it's the only one we have. Could you check it through your records? I don't mean only here; I mean could you send it to Moscow? Have it checked out thoroughly? Give me some clue, some lead, to what this man might have been?"

"I can try. What are you looking for?"

"I have no idea."

Grischov nodded and put the picture in his pocket. We talked a little more about this and that and then I rose to go. As he shook hands with me, Grischov said,

"One thing, Clancy, before you go . . . do you believe they made the bombs?"

"What I believe is beside the point. We're dealing with a question of presumption—not of belief."

"I would still like to know, if you don't mind."

"Why?"

"Because," Grischov said slowly, "and you will forgive me for speaking about it—but because you have the look of a man who lost something that he can never find again."

"Would that make me a personality like Simonovsky or Horton?" I said, with some irritation.

"Perhaps."

"When I find Horton, I'll answer your question."

"If I have offended you with this," Grischov began.

"Nothing offends me," I said shortly. "If I was not offended by your reception committee downstairs, I don't think anything you said here can offend me."

"I'll see you again—I hope," Grischov said, almost sadly.

"I'm afraid you will," I replied.

He walked downstairs with me and waited while the over-large, square-faced man returned my gun and helped me on with my coat. Then I left.

PART FOUR

HANS KEMPTER

IT was twelve o'clock when I left the building of the Russian Delegation on Park Avenue. The sun was shining and out of the west there blew that kind of sweet-scented wind that comes not so often in New York City but only now and again, like the perfume of the whole broad continent westward of us. It's a wind that washes the city clean and sharpens the sunlight and the shadows until everything is radiant and polished and gleaming—and parts of the city respond to all man's dreams and hopes and pretty notions of what a city should be. At such times, if you know the city and love the city, it becomes almost an individual possession of yours; you fill up with the dogged and peculiar pride which is the unspoken armorial asset of New Yorkers and so little understood by anyone who is not a New Yorker.

It was this feeling that made me wonder whether or not there were Russians who felt the same way about Moscow. It took the threat of an almost senseless destruction of two cities to enable Grischov and myself to talk together without a sense of two worlds and two cultures and two types of arrogance building a wall between us. If, at this moment, I were in Moscow, I might be able to see more precisely how Dmitri Grischov felt about New York. In any case I had the feeling that he felt a little differently about it than any other Russian ever had.

For myself, I was full of an unusual and not unpleasant sense of being alive. You have to know what depression is and have lived with it and taken it to you through night after night of empty loneliness to be able to appreciate the feeling of that same depression lifting. You have to carry a thousand years and a thousand tons on your shoulders in the dreary, heart-crushing march of minutes and hours and days and months and years to appreciate the full measure of a desire to live and an appreciation of life. That was how I felt. For the first time in months I wanted to live. Instead of breathing as a part of my body's function, I took in the air consciously, tasted it, and offered my thanks for it. I felt my body as I walked. I felt the spring in my steps, the tension of my muscles. I felt the wind on my face and I smelled the wind and, instead of the people around me being faceless and nameless, they became personalities—the old and the young, the large and the small, the happy and the unhappy. It happened to me without my being fully aware of what was happening, yet it registered inside of me. I was losing my neutrality. I had an opinion about Grischov. I had an opinion about Alex Horton. I had an opinion about Peter Simonovsky. I had an opinion about Arthur Jackson of Central Intelligence and about Phyllis Goldmark I had more than an opinion—a feeling, a relationship, a need that had been present and now was beginning to grow, to expand, to creep into me as a physical part of me. It had been a long time since I felt a need for any woman except one, who was dead.

I was hungry. When I crossed Park Avenue I picked up the tail out of the corner of my eye. I walked eastward, turned downtown on Lexington Avenue and stopped in a drugstore for a sandwich and a cup of coffee. The tail waited five minutes before he entered the drugstore and then he sat down at the other end of the counter.

He kept his eyes away from me and I was able to look at him in the long mirror behind the counter. His face was small and pinched. He had no eyebrows, only a blond fuzz, and the bones of his head made smooth loops into his eye sockets. His face was unhappy and determined and afraid.

I finished my sandwich and went into the phone booth and dialed Centre Street. When I reached my exchange, I told them that I was going to pick up the tail. They asked whether I thought it was wise, and I replied that I thought it was wise. They asked whether I didn't want to wait until Commissioner Comaday had been consulted. I told them that this was something I had decided and that I did not want to wait until Commissioner Comaday had been consulted. I told them that I would pick him up on Second Avenue between Sixty-second and Sixty-third Street. They were to have two cars there and at least two men on foot. I didn't look for any trouble, but I wanted the two cars there anyway.

Then I went back to the counter and ordered another cup of coffee and thought about it a little more. The action I was proposing was probably foolish, impulsive, and ill-advised, but there was not enough time left to stretch this thing out; it could not go on without a break. It had to break somewhere and this was probably as good a place as any. Having adjusted the situation to that extent, and having come to several meaningless conclusions, I left the drugstore and walked south on Lexington Avenue. When I crossed Lexington, moving east, the tail was leaving the drugstore.

Slowly, apparently immersed in my own thoughts, I walked from Lexington to Third and from Third to Second. He remained forty or fifty feet behind me. He was not a good tail, and I decided that tailing people was not his business. He was clumsy and awkward and he knew nothing about what is essentially an art —the ability of a man to blend into a crowd, a building, a street, or even a landscape. For my part, I had begun to be afraid. You will hear it said that cops are not afraid and that they do whatever is called their duty as calmly and as deliberately as a bus conductor collects his fares. From what I know and what I have experienced, that's hogwash. Of all people who know fear, cops, I would say, in our modern city, have the deepest and the most profound knowledge. They work against it and they eat themselves up with ulcers and coronaries and diabetes.

When we reached Second Avenue, I had a feeling that I had moved too quickly, but there was no way to slow it up. I walked down Second Avenue and when I came to the corner of Sixty-third Street, I waited. At the same time I turned around and watched the tail. My abrupt stop and the fact that I was watching him made him keep on walking. I had expected that this would be the result. If I had not been looking at him, he would have stopped. Since I was looking at him, he decided to go on walking and to pass by me. He passed me without looking at me and, as he walked past, I dropped into step behind him, closed up to him, took my gun out of my shoulder holster, put my hand into my coat pocket, and let him feel the gun in his side through my topcoat. I spoke to him quietly and reasonably.

"I have a gun in your side, so don't move and don't try anything foolish. Just go on walking as you were."

He continued to walk. A prowl car moved south along the avenue. A tall man in a brown topcoat appeared from behind us and fell into position at the other side of the tail.

The tall man said to me, "All right, now, I'll take him downtown."

I increased my pace and walked ahead of them. The prowl

car edged over to the sidewalk. I deliberately went on walking without looking behind me. When I reached the corner, the prowl car passed me, with the tail sitting inside between the two officers. Then I stopped a cab and took it down to Centre Street.

The prowl car made better time than I did in the cab. When I reached Centre Street, they were waiting for me and told me to go straight up to Comaday's office. The Commissioner was in his office with Sidney Fredericks, the man from the Justice Department. They nodded as I came in and Comaday motioned for me to sit down.

"What about it?" Comaday said to me.

"He was tailing Miss Goldmark. He switched to me yesterday."

"Then he switched to you. You know where he is. What's the point in picking him up?"

"I'm on my own, Commissioner. You put a man on his own and you've got to let him act on his own."

"You didn't act on your own," Comaday said. "You involved the Department. You had cops pick him up. How does that make sense? How clean are you at this moment? How do you know one man was tailing you? or two? or three? or five?"

"It was one man."

"How do you know?"

"I know. Nobody knows anything for sure. I think I know. Maybe I'm wrong. That's a chance you have to let me take. I don't have six months or a year. You counted out the days for me. This thing has to break. It has to break somewhere. If I get a chance to make it break, I have to take the chance."

Comaday looked at Fredericks and raised a brow. Fredericks nodded. "I think Clancy has a point," Fredericks said. "It's beginning to build up around him. He has to prick it somewhere."

"How do you want it now?" Comaday asked me.

"I want to question him. I want to talk to him."

"You alone?"

"Not alone. I want you to be there. I want Mr. Fredericks to be there and I want you to get Grischov down from the Soviet building."

"Grischov?" Fredericks said. "When did you see him?"

"I saw him this morning."

"How does he connect with the tail?" Fredericks wanted to know.

"Grischov has a broad acquaintance. Maybe this is someone he knew. Maybe it isn't."

Then there was a moment or two of silence. Frederick's face became impassive again. Comaday watched me thoughtfully. Then he nodded. "All right, Clancy, we'll play it your way. I'll send for Grischov and meanwhile we'll all of us have a conversation with your tail." The Commissioner picked up the telephone and gave his instructions. Then the three of us left his office and went to a quiet room.

It was a plain, bare room about fifteen feet square and the walls were painted cream color. In one corner there was a sink and running water. In the middle of the room there was a table, a plain wooden table, and four chairs, plain wooden chairs like kitchen chairs. There was a light bulb over the wash basin and another light bulb under a green shade hung from the ceiling. There were no windows in the room. The air came through a grille, and the heat came from a radiator. It was a quiet room because no matter what went on in there you couldn't listen outside. The walls weren't soundproofed; they were just heavy stone and plaster walls, and the door was a heavy wooden door.

When we entered this room, my tail was sitting at the table. A uniformed officer stood behind him and a second uniformed officer faced him across the table. The tail's topcoat, his suit jacket, and his tie had been removed; his pockets had been emptied and the contents of his pockets were spread out on the table. When we entered the room, the officers nodded to us. No one said anything. We grouped around the table and went through the contents of his pockets. He had a billfold, which contained $411. His change was not loose, but in a small suede purse—a European habit that was as good as a European label. Aside from the money, there were no papers in his wallet, no cards, no identification. There was also among his possessions a key chain with two keys attached, one a car key, and a small card, folded and dirty. However, there was no licence to go along with the car key. On the card was written "Thomas Clancy" and then my address. A small penknife of mother-of-pearl completed his worldly possessions. The three of us went through his things. Comaday was interested in the money. Among the $411 there were eight twenty-dollar bills. Comaday separated these, took one of the officers aside, whispered to him, and gave him the money. I suspected he was sending it down to Jacobs to see if it could connect in any way with the twenty-dollar bills that had been left with me. Then Comaday motioned for the other officer to go. The three of us were left in the room with the tail. We pulled chairs up to the table, sat down, and looked

at him. He was afraid now. Fear was stamped into him, written
all over him, and coming out of his skin in tiny droplets of sweat.
He sat facing us, both his hands gripping the edge of the
table.

Minutes passed and none of us said anything. Fredericks was a
guest. I was taking my cue from Comaday. At least at the beginning of this thing, I would say nothing until Comaday said something. If Comaday wanted to wait, I was willing to wait. As a
matter of fact, the waiting and the silence could be more profound
and more efficient than any questions.

So we sat there and we waited, and the minutes ticked by, and
the tail looked at each of us, from face to face, and then at the
table, and then at his hands, and then at us again. In such circumstances, three or four minutes can be an eternity, and it could not
have been more than that before someone knocked at the door. I
rose and let Jacobs in and he nodded at Comaday, who came over
to join us.

"No connection, Commissioner," Jacobs said. "The money is
plain clean money."

"Clean money, hell!" Comaday muttered.

Then he dismissed Jacobs and we went back to the table and sat
down again. A minute more was all that the tail could stand. He
burst out at us,

"What do you want with me? Why do you bring me here? I
have committed no crime."

His voice was high-pitched and strident with a fairly clearly
defined German accent. He made his plea and there was no answer.
We continued to sit in silence. For myself, I thought Comaday was
overdoing it. It was a little old-fashioned and it had reached a
point where it ceased to make much sense—at least to me. Then
the tail broke the silence again,

"I have committed no crime. Why do you bring me here?"

After that a few more seconds of silence.

"You can't hold me here. I am not a criminal. I know what the
law is. I want to call a lawyer. That is my right. I have the right to
call a lawyer. I have the right to know why you have brought me
here."

Comaday sighed. He looked at me and nodded, and I asked the
tail what his name was.

"I don't have to answer that. I don't have to answer any
questions."

"What's your name?" I repeated.

This time he answered briefly and to the point. "Hans Kempter."

"Why were you following me?" I said to him.

"I was not following you."

"I say you were following me. Why were you following me?" He shook his head.

"Why were you following Miss Goldmark yesterday?" He shook his head again.

"Who do you work for?"

He pursed his lips and tightened them. Then there was another knock on the door and this time Comaday answered it. He stood at the door, talking to a uniformed officer, and then motioned for me and for Fredericks to join them. We went over to the door and Comaday told us about the fingerprints. They had done a local check and there were no prints. The check from Washington would be back to us in about thirty minutes. Then Comaday told the officer to take the material on the table. The officer scooped it up into a brown envelope and left us. We sat down at the table again facing Kempter. Comaday glanced at me and said,

"Go ahead, Clancy. Do it any way you want to do it. This bastard is here and that's it."

Kempter had been gathering up his courage. "I have rights!" he burst out.

"You haven't any rights," Comaday said tiredly.

"I want to make a telephone call!"

"There's no telephone here," Comaday said just as tiredly. "No telephone, no lawyer, nothing. You're here with the three of us, Kempter. All the law and the rights and the privileges that you've memorized about this country are suspended. There's no law in here, there's no rights, there's no privileges. You know why."

As wildly as an animal, Kempter stared from face to face. He pushed back his chair and stood up.

"Sit down!" I said to him. It wasn't my kind of work. It wasn't work I enjoyed. There are those who enjoy this kind of thing. You'll find them on a police force as well as in other places, and some of them have a talent for it, and some of them even elevate it into an art. I had no talent for it.

"Sit down, Kempter!" I repeated. Kempter sat down slowly, warily.

"Why were you following me?"

"I was not following you."

"Who do you work for, Kempter?"

He shook his head.

"Who do you work for?" I repeated.

He shook his head again.

"Who gave you that card you had in your pocket?"

When he didn't answer, Comaday rose and walked around the table and stood behind him. "You can make it easy for yourself, Kempter," I said softly. "You will have to put away everything you learned about our law, our police methods, and your rights. You haven't any more rights. You know as well as we do how big this thing is. You can die here. It doesn't make a damn bit of difference—not to any of us—not to anyone in this building. Nobody asks any questions. The size of this thing is that ten like you could die here and it still wouldn't make a damn bit of difference. Do you understand me?"

He stared at me out of his pale blue eyes, licked his lips, and tightened himself to the presence of Comaday behind him. I had never realized before how brutally wide and powerful Comaday's body was. When you are a Police Commissioner, you get away from the dirty things that are done in quiet rooms. But Comaday hadn't forgotten. He hit Kempter with an open hand that was like a ham, and the force of the blow flung Kempter out of his chair and sent him sprawling on the floor. Then Comaday walked back around the table and sat down again.

Kempter picked himself up and crouched on the floor on his hands and knees. "Get up and sit down," I told him.

He was an interesting type—an interesting man—an interesting personality. He crawled over to his chair and then worked his way up and into it, and I began again.

"Who are you working for?"

It went on like that for the next fifteen minutes. The mythology of courage is as phony and as formalized as most other things in our society. I have sometimes thought that when you come down to it no one is brave in the meaning of the word that we accept. It adds up to a question of fear. There are men who are either dull or sick or insensitive and their bodies and their minds don't experience fear; but for the run of men, it's a question of what fear predominates, and as often as not, the fear of being a coward will make a hero out of a man. Kempter was a coward because his life was mean and dirty and without virtue; but he had a large fear of something else—of a place or a man or a time. It was a large enough fear to make him very hard to break.

So fifteen minutes passed and there was a knock on the door

and this time it was Grischov. I answered the knock and when I saw who it was, I took him out into the corridor and explained. He asked only one question,

"Have you tried him in German?"

I mentioned the fact that we were not linguists and that Kempter's English was passable.

"Do you mind if I try him?" Grischov asked.

"Whatever you wish," I shrugged.

He was watching me with a trace of a smile on his face. "Soviet methods?" he asked.

"I have read this and that," I said. "I don't pass any judgments. My whole philosophy has improved. Live and let live."

"I don't think philosophies improve," Grischov said, almost sadly, "they grow tired. The hell with it, as you put it. Let's go in there."

We went into the room. I stood to one side, leaving my chair for Grischov in case he wanted to sit down. But he walked around the table, his eyes fixed on Hans Kempter. Then suddenly and sharply Grischov broke into German, barking his words savagely. Kempter was taken unawares. He stiffened, cringed, began to stand up, and then relaxed back into his chair. Grischov hammered at him in German again. Kempter shook his head. Grischov walked over to him, dragged him out of his chair, held him by his shirt, roaring at him in German. Comaday looked at Fredericks and then both of them at me. None of us said anything. Grischov flung Kempter across the room and into the wall, and Kempter hit the wall and slid down to a sitting position. Grischov closed in on him, moving like a prowling beast, and roared at him in English,

"Get up! Get on your feet, you lousy bastard!"

Kempter did not move except to cringe and to try to force himself into the angle where the wall met the floor. Grischov kicked him savagely in the buttocks and sent him sprawling on his face. As Kempter tried to rise, Grischov kicked him in the ribs and shouted at him again in German. Kempter was weeping. Again Grischov in German and this time Kempter answered him.

I looked at my watch. It was half past one and at three o'clock I had a class at the university. I wanted to get out of here. I felt a sick disgust that was almost evenly divided into several parts. It included Comaday and Fredericks, who had watched Grischov with aloof and professional curiosity. It included Kempter, who quivered on the floor, more like an animal than anything that resembled a man. It included Grischov, who was a product of our same exalted twentieth-century civilization that had produced a method which would enable a man, no better or worse than any of us, to eliminate in a moment a city of eight million human beings. It also included me.

Grischov walked back to the table and sat in the chair Kempter had occupied. He was not excited, not disturbed, not even angry.

"Do you know him?" Fredericks asked.

"Him? I don't know him. I know his kind. He is a small leftover from the Third Reich. A small, cheap, unimportant remnant, who found that the work he could do was done with and then maybe he did this and that until he could find more work that was like the work he used to do."

"What did he tell you, Grischov?" I asked him.

"He works for someone and he doesn't know who he works for —that's what he said."

"That's a tired one," Comaday said. " 'I don't know who I work for'—that's the most tired one of all."

"I have to go," I told them. "It's a long way uptown."

"You bring this and dump it in our laps and then you have to go," Comaday said flatly. "I don't understand you, Clancy. So help me God, I wonder what I picked in you."

"Maybe you picked a turkey," I said. "It's too late to make any changes. What do you want from me? You've got a whole god-damned police force here and you've got Grischov. I'm a teacher with a class to teach. You can't do that off the cuff. You can't do it the way you beat up a man. It takes a little peculiar thought."

Grischov was watching me out of his small pale eyes. I think he was amused by me, and I, in turn, was glad that I amused him. "I think Clancy is right," Grischov said.

"I didn't ask you what you thought," Comaday observed with annoyance.

Out of the corner of my eye I was watching Kempter. He crawled along the floor like an animal and, when he reached the sink, he pulled himself up and turned on the faucet. Grischov hadn't been watching him, but when Grischov heard the water run he barked in German at Kempter. Kempter turned the water off and stood next to the sink.

"I know you didn't ask what I think, Commissioner Comaday," Grischov said gently, "but perhaps I have a more objective view of this whole matter. I think we can spend a few hours very profitably with Hans Kempter."

Fredericks's face was hard and calm, his eyes distant. He nodded and said, "I agree with Mr. Grischov."

"You break the habits of a lifetime more easily than I do," Comaday muttered. Then he stared at me thoughtfully. Then he said, "All right, Clancy, go ahead. Get the hell out of here."

"Thank you, Commissioner," I nodded, and then I left.

PART FIVE

MAXIMILIAN GOMEZ

THE seminar that afternoon was a nightmare. Again and again I lost the thread of the discussion and blundered and wallowed and covered up and backtracked in a manner that must have put my students to wondering whether I was drunk or an imbecile. There is an old theory that it is sufficient unto a teacher to keep a paragraph ahead of the one he teaches, but that breaks down where physics is concerned. There is simply too much to know and no possible way of getting around the fact of knowledge. In any case, I finished it, apologized as best I could, explained to my patient students that I was not feeling too well, and went to meet Phyllis. But at least I went to meet her with a need for her and not as the next step in my job. My nerves on edge, my whole body rasped and ragged, I felt, for the first time in a long while, that what I wanted most was to be with someone who would extend to me a little sympathy and perhaps even a little affection.

Phyllis was waiting for me at my office. She wore a black dress and she had gone to a hairdresser who had cut and shaped her brown hair into a mold that combined well and naturally with the shape of her head. She was pleased to see me, and excited, and her parted lips and the sparkle in her eyes made her quite attractive—almost beautiful. This did not change her; no miracles had been worked; but at one time or another every woman touches the edge of beauty. She offered me her hand and hoped that the seminar had gone well. When I told her that it had not gone well at all but very badly and that I was pretty much of a washout as a teacher, she disagreed and held that I was a good teacher and would be a better teacher. I watched her face, so much younger today, so much more alive and alert, as I asked her how she could possibly know.

"It's not a hard thing to know," she said. "After you're with a person for an hour or two and you've watched him and you've listened to him, you'll know what kind of a teacher he'll make."

"You like being a teacher."

"I like it. I don't think I ever spoke to anyone about how I like it and why I like it, but I do like it. I don't know of anything that can make you more tired. Sometimes I'm so tired when I've finished that I can't think or talk or even relate myself to anything in the world or anyone—if you know what I mean——?"

I nodded.

"And then there are other times," she went on, searching for the words, "when I feel that there is nothing better in the whole world—I can't explain that—do you know what I'm trying to say, you want so desperately for some justification, just for being alive, just for existing. Have you ever felt that way?"

"I've felt that way, Phyllis," I said. "I've often felt that way."

"You're a strange man."

"More or less, we all are, aren't we?"

"I don't mean that way. I mean for me. You know what's happening to me, don't you? I feel awkward and foolish and frightened of myself and then I'm so afraid——"

"What are you afraid of, Phyllis?"

"This is the wrong way, isn't it? The worst possible way, isn't it?"

"Why do you worry about a right way or a wrong way?" I asked her gently.

"Because it's not mine to say that I think I'm falling in love with you. That's the worst thing in the world for me to say, isn't it? At least I should have enough sense to keep my mouth shut and then I become so afraid because I'm convinced it's going to stop."

I didn't say anything to that—only sat and looked at her and after a while we both stood up and I put my arms around her and kissed her. That was all right. I had done something for myself and not for Comaday or for Fredericks or for New York or for Moscow, but having done it I didn't care to think about it or probe into it or examine it and weigh the pros and cons and the circumstances and the morality.

We were still early for the evening in Great Neck. So on our way out we stopped at the cafeteria and had coffee and smoked a cigarette. During the few minutes we were there Professor Vanpelt stopped by, leaned over the table, and observed that we made a consistent twosome. Either Professor Vanpelt haunted the cafeteria or his hours coincided exactly with ours or else he kept his benevolent eye upon us with remarkable obstinacy.

We were in the car and driving across town toward the Triborough Bridge when I asked Phyllis what had been her cousin's reaction to her bringing me to dinner tonight. She gasped and discovered that she had forgotten to call. "I meant to call," she said. "I started to call during lunch and then something happened and I was going to call just now. I think we'd better stop now."

I thought not. I pointed out to Phyllis that since we were on our way, we might as well continue, admitting to myself that there was more than one reason why I didn't want anything to break up this evening. By this time we were on the approach to the bridge and calling would have meant turning back; and Phyllis began to enjoy the notion of doing something unexpected and very likely irritating to her cousin. As we crossed the bridge and came on to the Grand Central Parkway, she told me about her cousin, whose name was Rita Golden and who had married Jack Golden, who had $3,000,000 or $4,000,000 or $5,000,000 that he had made in the business of importing sugar. She told me about their house, their pretensions, their aspirations, their three-car garage and their Bentley; and I was glad that she recounted it matter-of-factly with neither envy nor annoyance. I can tolerate poor people who don't like rich people, but when the dislike is ninety per cent envy, I tend to move the other way. Phyllis wasn't envious; if anything, she was indifferent to the fact and substance of their wealth; however, she was uncertain as to whether or not I would be indifferent. She explained to me, and it came as a sort of apology, that she went out there because she had very few relatives. She didn't want me to think that she went out there because they were rich or because she envied them their riches or because she enjoyed having some of it rub off on her. She was nervous and uncertain and becoming aware of the fact that she had flung herself at a man and exposed herself to a man about whom she knew very little indeed. She was not a simple person or an obvious person—except in relationship to a man with whom she had found herself falling in love. She knew a great deal about a great many things, but very little about men; and I found myself saying things to myself about myself and about Comaday and about the whole rotten, lurid, distorted turn my life had taken.

Then, after that, Phyllis was silent for a long while and we drove on together in silence, the road darkening as night came, the inside of the car becoming a cave in which we sat, each of us alone with our thoughts. When she finally spoke, she said that she had been making a fool of herself.

I didn't argue with her about that; I only pointed out that this was not easy for either of us and that the best thing we could do would be to let it happen in whatever way it would happen.

"You won't like these people tonight," she said. "They're cheap and they're vulgar and you won't like them and then you'll have to turn it into something about me."

"It has nothing to do with you," I said to her. "No matter what they are, the best thing to remember is that it has nothing to do with you. You are yourself. That's what I am. That's all that any of us are. I like you a great deal, Phyllis. I want to be with you tonight. If I wasn't with you tonight, I'd be home reading a book or sitting and staring at a blank wall or in a movie house without seeing what goes on on the screen. I don't have anything to give or at least very little and very little joy to give it with, but we should neither of us ever apologize to the other again—never again. Do you understand?"

"I think I do," she said.

It was quite dark when we reached the Goldens' house. But two bright lamp posts lit a sweeping half circle of driveway into which I pulled, parking my Ford behind a Chrysler Imperial that nudged the rear fender of a Cadillac convertible. The house was a huge sprawling single-story affair of graystone, white clapboard, picture windows, and split levels. When we sounded the chimes at an enormous front door, which hung on brass hinges and had enormous brass decorations splattered all over it, a brass door knob and a brass knocker, it was opened for us by a butler or a converted chauffeur or a houseman or whatever he might be, in a black coat, who took our coats and then led us into the living room that was large enough to be impressive, carpeted from wall to wall with dusty blue carpet, filled with French antiques or with what looked like French antiques to my untutored eye, a grand piano, a big ornate bar, and five people. The one of the five who was Rita Golden swept toward us. She was a tall, brittlely groomed woman, good-looking, self-possessed, with a flashing patchwork quilt of brown and blonde hair. The other woman in the room, whom we were later introduced to as Jane Carlton, had the same patchwork head of hair, sprigs of pale yellow alternating with sprigs of brown, and as much like Rita Golden's as if they were twins. They were twins in other ways—they moved alike and spoke alike and reacted alike and through the evening they said, for the most part, the same things.

Only Rita Golden was not delighted to see us—at least she was not delighted to see us together—and as Phyllis introduced her to me she had a difficult time covering her surprise and her indignation. She said that she was delighted to see me and in the same breath she was unable to understand why Phyllis had not called her or informed her that she would not be coming alone. In fact, at this very minute, her car was at the station and her chauffeur was looking for Phyllis; and Phyllis was no match for this; she was no match for any of them there. She was stricken with guilt and unhappiness as she tried to explain a series of circumstances that had brought me with her. I let her explain and smiled and stood there with the foolish smile printed on my face and presently her cousin gave it up and accepted both of us and introduced us to the other people in the room.

Jack Golden, Rita's husband, was a solidly built, overweight man in his middle forties. Even with his weight, he was good-looking and comfortable among his French antiques. He was less disturbed than his wife and he made me feel that, even if my coming there was a blunder, I was welcome. Fred Carlton, the husband of the other woman present, was a skinny wisp of a man who, I later learned, was an important figure on the Sugar Exchange. Jane Carlton was a woman whose pleasure increased with martinis and with men. She had a martini in her hand when we were introduced and from the manner in which she clung to my hand, I guessed that it was not the first drink. She was delighted to see me, she said pointedly, and she looked at Phyllis defiantly.

The cause of our hostess's discomfiture was the extra man in the party. His name was Maximilian Gomez. He was about thirty-five years old, six feet two inches tall, almost cadaverously thin, with honey-colored skin, a charming smile that was by no means inhibited by my presence, and a flashing set of teeth, white enough and perfect enough to make me wonder whether they were dentures. He, at least, won my vote for making Phyllis welcome. He appeared as delighted to see her and meet her as if she were Marilyn Monroe. He took her hand and bowed and kissed her hand without self-consciousness; with just a trace of a Spanish accent, he informed us that he was charmed to meet both of us, but let it be known plainly that he was much more charmed to meet Phyllis.

Unfortunately, at the moment, this meant little to Phyllis. She excused herself and, as I learned later, went to the powder room to weep over the abysmal disaster that her evening had turned into. I also learned later that Rita Golden had followed her there and had demanded to know what she possibly could have been thinking to bring a dull clod like myself with her when she, Rita, had gone to such trouble and to such pains to have Gomez here on this evening to meet Phyllis. Phyllis pleaded that she didn't know what she had been thinking and had certainly had no idea that Rita had planned anything of this sort. As a matter of fact, as we eventually learned, Rita was a liar and had not planned it. Gomez had begged his own presence, but that was something for later.

When Phyllis and Rita returned to the living room, I was half through a martini and flattered by a general interest in physics. I had learned that physics was not an abstruse and rarefied area of science, but a matter of intense concern to anyone who had ever set foot on Wall Street or any extension of Wall Street. I had also learned that the path to riches and happiness was no longer smoothed by oil or steel or aluminum but by transistors, diodes, and vibrating crystals; that atomics was not simply a source of power, but the fastest growing source of profit in the United States, and that a simple-minded professor at Knickerbocker University was a source of wonder and gratification to three men whose involvement with sugar did not preclude them from a much broader and more catholic interest in the microcosmos of the electron. Even in that short time I had come to envy them, for a meticulous dollar-and-cents appraisal had taken the edge of horror off the atom bomb. In their world there was nothing to worry about except the problem of backing the right atom.

At least it cheered Phyllis. Evidently it did not occur to her, as it did to me, and certainly not to her relatives or to the other guests, that she knew more about atomics and physics in general and particles in particular than I had ever known or would ever know if I had a lifetime to live instead of an uncertain two weeks. She was not only a woman, she was a poor relation, and she was unmarried, which made her a failure on every level which would entitle her to their respect.

In all truth, however, she didn't mind. She listened to their curiosity and observed their attention with increasing pleasure and bit by bit the muted misery which she had returned with from the powder room began to disappear. Gomez confined his attentions to her. By the time we were ready to go to the dinner table, she was able to smile.

They seated Phyllis between Gomez and Carlton; on my side of the table I had Jane Carlton on my left and Rita Golden on my right. Jack Golden sat at the head of the table, alone, and free to cope with the food, which was rich and plentiful. He received the eating honors. He was at least fifty pounds overweight, to begin with, and I could see that he treated each meal as a challenge. Jane Carlton ignored the food, finished another martini, and then gave her attention to the wine. Rita Golden attempted to recollect that she was the hostess and to talk to me. Perhaps it was not as hard as talking to her husband—something she avoided completely—but it was not too successful. She attempted one or two questions about my relationship with Phyllis and then more or less gave it up and resorted to pressures under the table.

Phyllis, on the other hand, had the consuming attention of Maximilian Gomez—and it was consuming. Gomez talked to her, whispered to her, bent toward her, filled her wine glass, and almost hovered over her—if such a thing can be accomplished sitting down. He claimed her entirely and never gave Fred Carlton an inch. Carlton talked to Jack Golden about business, which was mostly sugar and very much on the brink of some kind of disaster—so much I was able to gather from fragments of phrases that I was able to pick up. Now and again Phyllis looked at me hopelessly. When she did, I smiled back encouragingly. I neither liked nor disliked Gomez, but I was pleased at the picture of a man giving all of his attention and all of his charm to Phyllis, particularly since he was, at the same time, almost indifferent to the two other women present.

At the same time I was trying to sort out of my memory file of names the name of Maximilian Gomez. Even a bad cop learns to file names, to remember them, and to recall them; and the name "Maximilian Gomez" was certainly not a common name. I watched him; he was very handsome—much too handsome—much too obvious and much too glib to be enchanted by Phyllis. Either his face, his manner and his clothes were a whole lie or else his enchantment with Phyllis was. Unless I was a fool and a failure as even a primitive psychologist, his taste in women would run in very different directions. Then I placed him. He had been married to and divorced from a second-rate Hollywood star. He had made a small sensation in Havana, pre-Castro, by dropping $900,000 in one night in a single casino. He had been photographed with a yacht, with race horses and high-powered cars, and he was connected with an unsavory dictator in Latin America. Additional facts emerged from my memory and filled in the picture. He had made the headlines of the newspapers some years ago when a political opponent of the dictator had disappeared in Miami, under very suspicious circumstances, from the hotel where Gomez had an apartment. I worked my memory on the details surrounding the disappearance of the dictator's political enemy —and I realized with the kind of uneasy wonder that a seemingly far-fetched coincidence provokes, that this man, the political opponent who disappeared, had been a physicist; and of course, to frame it nicely and to put each thing into its proper place, the major crop and sustenance of the Latin American dictatorship was sugar.

My face must have been dreamy-eyed, benevolent, even wistful as I watched him now, considering the fact that here he was in a house in Great Neck, paying court to Phyllis Goldmark, a guest of an overstuffed man who had become a power as a sugar importer. It worked gently and nicely and precisely, and I sympathized now with Rita Golden's anger and consternation when she had discovered that Phyllis was not alone. The utter grotesqueness of the concept added a smile to my benevolence—that and the thought of Phyllis Goldmark as an object of matrimony for Maximilian Gomez.

He looked at me at that moment and tore his attentions away from Phyllis for long enough to observe that I appeared unusually contented.

"Oh?" I said.

"As if you had some remarkable and pleasant fancy, Mr. Clancy."

"The food is very good," I said.

Jane Carlton said, "I never met anyone before who was actually named Clancy; in fact, I thought the name was an invention. You are the first Mr. Clancy I ever knew—only you don't look like a Mr. Clancy. Do you know what you look like——"

"For Christ's sake," Fred Carlton said.

Mrs. Carlton's voice faltered and ceased. She spoke no more.

"I was putting together the pieces of a puzzle." I smiled at Gomez.

"I am intrigued by that." Gomez spoke soberly and thoughtfully. "I would imagine that much of a physicist's life consists of that kind of activity. All of existence is a puzzle to you, and you must eternally try to put it together—or am I being romantic, Mr. Clancy?"

"A little romantic, I think."

"All of existence is so much," Phyllis said softly.

"I would leave that to the philosophers," I agreed. "You must understand, Mr. Gomez, that a scientist will spend a lifetime trying to understand a part of the structure of a single atom."

"Yet we live in times when a single atom becomes all of existence. Or do I speak in riddles, Mr. Clancy?"

"Not at all," I smiled.

"I mean that there was a time," Gomez went on, "when all of existence was an endless thing. Now it can be compressed into the small space that a single atom bomb occupies. So the very large and the very small come together, so to speak. Wouldn't you agree to that, Mr. Clancy?"

I decided that in composing my mental file I had been ready to misjudge Maximilian Gomez. He was something in addition to the sum of the racing cars and the polo ponies and the West Coast wives. "I think I would agree with that in a manner of speaking," I nodded. "But you see, Mr. Gomez, a physicist can't afford to be a philosopher."

Gomez smiled and wondered whether a physicist could afford not to be a philosopher.

After dinner we went back into the living room. Jane Carlton complained of feeling ill and Mrs. Golden took her upstairs to rest for a while. Gomez continued to pay his attentions to Phyllis, and for a half hour I sat and listened to Jack Golden and Fred Carlton discuss the various intricacies of the sugar market. I gathered that the hopes and the dreams and the aspirations of a good many people rested on fractional changes in the price of sugar and that a deep and pervading interest in these fractional changes could become the basis of a man's existence. At ten o'clock Rita Golden joined us again and informed Fred Carlton that his wife was asleep. He received the news with the same indifference he had displayed to her all evening. Phyllis joined me, Gomez trailing after her, and for a few minutes more there was small talk about the weather and life in the suburbs and the local school situation. I gathered that there were children somewhere in this large household, but throughout the evening I had neither seen them nor heard them. Then Jane Carlton, shoeless, came stumbling down the stairs and became very sick in a corner of the living room. Rita Golden's face tightened with anger;

Gomez and Jack Golden pretended not to notice; and Fred Carlton, swearing under his breath, went to the aid of his wife. Phyllis excused herself, pleading the long drive and an early class in the morning. The only proper good-by when we left came from Maximilian Gomez, who said with devotion that he hoped he would see Phyllis again.

Back in my car and driving toward New York, Phyllis asked me whether I knew the story about the little boy who hit his head against the wall and, when asked why, replied that it felt so good when he stopped.

"I know what you mean," I said.

"When I came in there," Phyllis said, "it was like a nightmare, and then it went on and on, it never stopped. Tom, have you ever been caught in something that felt like a nightmare and refused to stop?"

I nodded, but pointed out that Gomez had been more than attentive.

"He's a horrible man," Phyllis said.

"Really? You don't mean that. He seemed to be a very charming man and very devoted to you."

"I don't like him," Phyllis said. "There's something wrong with him. In every part of him and in everything he does, there's something wrong with him. Why was he that way with me, Tom? You know who he is."

"I know who he is."

"Then why did he treat me as if I were charming and beautiful?"

"Because it's very possible that you are charming and beautiful and maybe he's not quite what the newspapers say he is."

"I don't like him. I'll never go there again. I'm sorry I took you there. I'm sorry I got you into this whole thing."

"I thought it was an interesting evening. I'm not sorry you took me there. What did Gomez talk to you about?"

"Everything. My work, my home, my interests, and he asked questions—ridiculous, stupid questions."

"What kind of questions, Phyllis?"

"He has something about the bomb. I don't like to talk about it, but he kept coming back to it."

"Did he ask you whether you could make an atom bomb?" I said casually.

"How do you know?"

"I must have overheard," I said.

PART SIX

JOHN VANPELT

THE next day I had no class until midafternoon and I slept late. At 11 : 30 I brushed my teeth and, after that, began to shave. In the middle of my shaving the phone rang. It was Police Commissioner Comaday and he said that I could expect him in half an hour. When I wondered about the advisability of his coming to my apartment, he said something in no uncertain terms about the advisability of my going down to Centre Street. Then I didn't argue with him, but only mentioned that I would be delighted to see him in half an hour.

I finished shaving, dressed, put coffee on the stove—and tried to accompany all of these actions with some sort of constructive thought. The thought processes, however, were limited. I moved in circles, reached no destinations and returned always to the starting point—that the essence of the matter was to find Horton and not to be led astray by the problems and fancies posed by others who were perhaps equally interested in Alex Horton.

I was smoking a cigarette and drinking my first cup of coffee when the doorbell rang. It was Comaday. I took his coat but, when I offered him a cup of coffee, he snorted and shook his head with annoyance. Instead he took out a cigar, bit off the end of it, lit it, and settled himself in an armchair facing me. He took several deep puffs of the cigar, meanwhile examining the room, moving his hard professional gaze over my books and my furniture. Years of training and practice had turned every movement Comaday made into a police action. He could not just look at a man; he had to look at him accusingly. He could not simply glance at something; he had to examine it, consider it and put it into its appropriate file. He had spent his life in a world of crime and hostility and this world had exacted from him an appropriate payment. As I watched him, I thought to myself that any man with a little strength, a little character, a little determination, and more than average brains could become like Comaday. It was no ambition of mine. I had reached a point where it was no longer easy for me to remember and determine precisely why I had ever become a cop, but I think I had also reached the point of deciding that I no longer wanted to be a cop.

I continued to smoke and drink my coffee. Comaday smoked and finished his examination of my worldly goods, and said to me, "So, this is where you live, Clancy."

"I call it home," I nodded.

"You read a lot?" Comaday wanted to know, glancing at the books.

"More than a cop should," I replied.

"Don't get down on cops, Clancy. I can't stand a cop who makes a philosophy out of hating other cops and what he does for a living."

"You didn't come here to talk about philosophy," I said.

Comaday stood up, took a few paces, and then whirled on me, pointing at me with his cigar. "No, I damn well didn't! I came here because I'm sick and tired of having you run down to Centre Street. I'm also sick and tired of the way you're going off at loose ends. You had one simple assignment, Clancy—to find out where Horton is, providing that someone up at Knickerbocker University knows where Horton is; that's all—just that—not to play cops and robbers and not to decide that you're some kingpin who can brush aside any law or right that the citizens of this county have."

For whatever it was worth, it was my house, my own small miserable castle, and not Comaday's office. He was in my house and I pointed that out to him. I also said that I was sick and tired of this whole lunatic business and that I would be delighted to resign—to resign from this and to resign from being a cop. Comaday circled back to the chair, dropped into it, and puffed his cigar. Then he shook his head.

"You can't resign, Clancy. Let's stop that kind of talk. All I'm saying is that we're getting nowhere."

"You're also saying that I should get the hell out of here and find Horton. You've got maybe twenty thousand men in the Department; you've got squads that specialize in everything under the sun; and you've got the Department of Justice and the Army and the Navy, too, and you can't find Horton; but I'm supposed to find him. You give me a lousy two weeks and tell me that the fate of this city depends on my paying court to an old-maid schoolteacher and raising up some subliminal clue to where Horton is. That doesn't make any sense; it doesn't make any more sense than this whole damn thing or the lives we live or what this lousy world has come to. You want to know how I feel about it?"

"I might as well," Comaday said. "I asked for it."

"This is how I feel about it. I feel that maybe the Neanderthal mentalities that are running this earth should sit up and pay attention to Horton and throw away that goddamned bomb!"

"Nerves," said Comaday, taking the cigar out of his mouth and spreading his hamlike hands in a pacifying gesture. "My nerves, Clancy, your nerves, we all got a set of nerves and they don't get any better. I'm sorry, but you know that it wouldn't make a damned bit of difference whether they outlawed the bomb or not and we'd still have to find Horton and over in Moscow they'd still have to find Simonovsky. I'll tell you something else, Clancy—we can't go the limit; in ten days we'll have to make this public. You don't evacuate a city like this overnight. It takes some time."

I studied him thoughtfully for a while and then I got up, found another cup and saucer, and poured coffee for him. "I apologize, Commissioner," I said evenly. "I'd like you to join me in a cup of coffee. I make good coffee."

He put his cigar in an ash tray and joined me at the table and became almost human. He asked me about living alone.

"I get along," I said, "I suppose there are worse ways to live."

"I have six kids," Comaday smiled. "That makes living alone a little strange to me." He tasted the coffee and agreed that it was good.

"What about Kempter?" I asked him.

He nodded and took another mouthful of the coffee. "What about Kempter?" he repeated. "You got to understand, Clancy, that I've been a policeman for a long time. It's not easy to break the rules. We pulled Kempter in because you asked us to and we worked him over for twelve hours. Now we got him locked away out of sight. That's just as well. He's not pretty to look at now. But how long do we keep him out of sight? What do we do with him? What happens when, sooner or later, as has got to happen, he gets to a lawyer?"

"The hell with that," I said tiredly. "I don't care what happens to Kempter. Neither do you. I once read in some snotty newspaper editorial that it actually makes no difference whether one man dies or whether a million men die; but I'm at a point where I know it makes a difference. The difference is 999,999 lives. So I haven't any tears for Kempter."

"I envy you," Comaday muttered.

"Did Kempter talk?"

"He talked—not much—apparently he didn't have much to talk about. But he talked. The Russian got him to talk. He told us who he was working for."

That stopped me. I guess I just sat there at the table and stared at Comaday, and then after a moment or two I was able to ask him who Kempter had been working for.

"For a man called Maximilian Gomez," Comaday said flatly. Then he got his cigar, lit it, and waited—all the while watching me out of his shrewd, accusing cop's eyes.

I thought about it before I said anything. Then I observed that it was something, possibly something important.

Comaday shrugged and puffed on his cigar. "The hell it is. It's not important. Not one goddamned bit important, Clancy. I tried to get you last night and to talk to you about it last night. Where were you last night?"

"I was with Maximilian Gomez," I replied.

It was Comaday's turn to be thoughtful—not to be surprised; it would not have been fitting for him to exhibit surprise or amazement in front of me—but he was thoughtful. He remained thoughtful while I told him about the evening before, and then he shook his head again.

"It doesn't mean a goddamned thing."

"All right," I agreed. "So it doesn't mean a damned thing. Suppose you tell me why it doesn't mean a damned thing."

"Because we haven't found Horton!" Comaday exploded. "Can't I get that into your head, Clancy? We haven't found Horton and we're no closer to finding him."

"A man tails Phyllis Goldmark," I said, keeping hold of my temper. "Then he switches to me. He tails me. We pick him up. He informs us that he works for Maximilian Gomez; but to you it doesn't mean a damned thing."

Comaday got up and began to pace the floor. "Look, Clancy," he said to me, "I've got nerves. I keep blowing off. That doesn't mean anything. The only thing that has any meaning is what we're after. Now what about Gomez and this little louse Kempter? We don't have to lecture each other on who Gomez is or what he is. He's connected with the filthiest image of a country in this hemisphere. I know and you know what it would mean to a gang like that to have an atom bomb solidly placed in the centre of New York and another in Moscow. It's the answer to all their dirty, benighted dreams. Maybe they hired those two creeps who gave you the money. Maybe they didn't. Right now, I don't know.

But do you think that if they knew where Horton is they'd come near you?"

"They know who I am," I said. "They know that I'm looking for Horton."

"Sure they know that. What are you trying to tell me? That something leaked out of the Department? Maybe it did. Maybe someone downtown saw that letter and blabbed about it, but we don't know that. Maybe it was someone in Washington. Maybe there was a payoff somewhere. You can buy an awful goddamned lot in a country with an income tax law like ours. But that's speculation, Clancy, and it's philosophy, and I don't give a damn about speculation or philosophy. I'm not interested in that. I'm interested in only one thing—the whereabouts of Alex Horton."

"We could pick up Gomez," I suggested, because I had nothing else to suggest.

"Doesn't anything I say register with you, Clancy? We could pick up Gomez! The hell we could pick up Gomez! For what? With what charges? Are you losing your mind, Clancy? And suppose we did pick up Gomez—where are we then?"

I shook my head. Comaday stopped pacing and turned to me. His voice became soft and cajoling. "Help me, Clancy, that's all I'm asking—help me. There's only one lead—one direction to Horton and you're on it. It's up there at Knickerbocker University —up there. That's all that matters. That's all we can put any money on."

I said nothing. I sat there and looked at him.

"All right, Clancy," he sighed, "all right." I nodded. He put on his coat and his hat and then he left. The room was full of cigar smoke. I opened the windows, thinking of how a conditioned bachelor begins more and more to resemble a crotchety old maid. Then I closed the windows and washed the dishes and the coffee pot. Then the phone rang.

It was my exchange at Centre Street. The nameless, faceless voice at the other end of the wire assured itself that I was Clancy and then asked me whether I wanted to hear their rundown on Vanpelt.

"That's why I asked," I said. "If I didn't want to hear it, I wouldn't have asked."

"You are touchy," the voice said. "Well, here it is. He has no criminal record. He's been at Knickerbocker as a teacher for twelve years. Before that he taught for two years in a high school at Paterson, New Jersey. Before that he did three years in the Army.

He served in the infantry without distinction. He saw no battle service but did six months of occupation duty in Germany. He was married in 1938 and his wife died in 1940. She died of food poisoning. There are no suspicious circumstances unless you want to think that food poisoning is always suspicious. Vanpelt was born in Allentown, Pennsylvania, in 1910. He went to grade school and secondary school in Allentown. His college training was at the University of Pennsylvania. In 1934 he made a trip to Europe. We have no information yet as to what he did in Europe or where he went, but we expect to come up with it. More or less, that's it.'

"Is that the best you can do?" I wanted to know.

"We'll do better, but give us time. What the hell, Clancy, it's not the end of the world. Give us a little time."

"Sure," I said, "you can have all the time in the world."

I had a lecture class that afternoon and I had taken as my subject "The Van Allen Belts". I expected little difficulty since my topic was fairly well formalized and involved almost no mathematics. As a matter of fact, most of what I said could have been pieced together by any intelligent newspaper reader. I was on the subject of the outer belt and elaborating the theory that it consisted of electrons ejected from the corona of the sun, when Vanpelt entered the room and took a seat in the last row. This, in itself, was not out of line and it was a not infrequent occurrence for one professor to wander into the lecture room of another—the more so in the physics department. On the other hand, I was being dogged by Vanpelt. He was becoming an inhabitant of all my waking dreams. I slipped in the middle of a sentence, reformulated my thoughts, stumbled on, and then had recourse to the notes I had prepared. My lectures were not becoming easier but increasingly difficult, and the presence of Vanpelt took all the joy out of this one.

When I finished at last, a handful of students gathered around my desk with their questions and their doubts. Vanpelt remained seated in the last row. I dealt with the students as best I could and, when the last of them left, Vanpelt rose and sauntered up to where I was putting my papers into my brief case. As always, his smile was knowledgeable and distasteful. It implied intimacy and suggested that we shared a secret.

"I enjoyed your lecture, Clancy," he remarked to me.

"The hell you did! It was a lousy lecture."

"Short-tempered, aren't you?" Vanpelt smiled.

"What is it, Vanpelt?" I said to him.

"The pleasure of your company, Clancy," he replied easily. "Come and have a drink with me. Rest your nerves."

"My nerves don't need resting."

"Have a drink with me anyway."

I met his eyes and we looked at each other appraisingly. His smile was perfectly natural; the sneer it contained was in my mind. I put my brief case together and accepted his invitation as we walked out of the University and down Broadway to the same bar. Vanpelt ordered gin and bitters. I had some whisky on ice. We sat in a booth and drank and looked at each other, and finally Vanpelt came around to the fact that we could be friends.

"I don't think so," I replied politely. "I don't think we could be friends, Professor Vanpelt. I don't think I want to."

"Why not?"

"I don't particularly like you."

"That's a snap judgment, Clancy," Vanpelt said. "You don't know me well enough to like me or dislike me."

"I know you well enough to dislike you," I said. "For whatever reasons you have, you've been seeking my company. But I don't enjoy your company—not at all."

"Still you permit me to buy you drinks." He allowed himself to be hurt, but only slightly.

"That's a question of curiosity. Let's say that I'm curious to know why I should be the object of your affection, Vanpelt. I haven't been kind to you. I've tried to be rude to you. What is it that you want?"

"In the broad sense or in the narrow sense, Clancy?" Vanpelt smiled. "If you mean what do I want in general, that could be simply answered. I think I want what every American boy wants—I want money and I want the things that go with money, and I want the power necessary to have both. That's a normal, healthy desire, isn't it, Clancy?"

"Is it?"

"I think so. On the other hand, if you're interested in what I want from you, that's a horse of another colour. You're curious; let's say that I am also curious. I'm curious about a man who steps into Alex Horton's job but knows nothing about Mr. Horton or what he was or who he was or what happened to him. I am also curious about a college professor who carries a gun."

"Do I carry a gun, Professor Vanpelt?" I asked carefully.

"I think you do. Of course, I could be mistaken. Am I mistaken, Mr. Clancy?"

I shrugged.

"If I were mistaken, this whole conversation would be ridiculous and you would let me know that it is ridiculous. As a matter of fact, Mr. Clancy, you are only moderately successful as a teacher. I have spent a good many years of my life around teachers and you are not only exceptional, but you have all the work habits of something else entirely. Why should I beat around the bush? I think I know what you want here, Clancy, and since you obviously know what you want here, there is no question of a secret, is there?"

"Suppose you tell me."

Vanpelt shrugged. "If you wish me to. Since you already know, it makes no difference. I think you're here to find Alex Horton."

"And why do you think that, Professor Vanpelt?"

"Because I can put two and two together and came up with four, as any mathematician should. I think you are looking for Mr. Horton and that you have chosen Knickerbocker University as your starting place. That's a matter of guesswork, but it's logical, sensible guesswork. I also think that the knowledge of Mr. Horton's whereabouts is a matter of great value. That's an independent conclusion on my part, if you follow me. Let us say that I also am curious about Mr. Horton's whereabouts because I believe such knowledge would constitute a not inconsiderable financial asset. Suppose that I had some connections, Brother Clancy, with people who might feel that Alex Horton's secret was to their advantage. Does such a supposition interest you?"

"I told you before, in a general sense, that I'm interested in your curiosity."

"Fine—fine." Vanpelt finished his drink and called the waiter for another. I refused a second drink and Vanpelt smiled understandingly. "I will presume upon your interest," he said. His drink came and he took a long sip of it, all the while stuffing himself with handfuls of peanuts from a bowl upon the table.

"I said I will presume that you are interested. Now let us suppose, Mr. Clancy, that someone were willing to pay a great deal of money for knowing Horton's secret."

"Suppose he has no secret," I said. "Suppose he's dead."

"We could go on all day with suppositions. However, I make a premise. I make a premise that Professor Horton has a secret and that he is not dead, and I say to you, 'Suppose that a great deal of money were to be offered for his secret.' "

"How much money?" I said.

"An interesting and pointed question. How much money? It would have to be a great deal of money even to interest you. You have all the earmarks of an honest man and it is always far more expensive to appeal to an honest man than to a dishonest man. Do you agree, Mr. Clancy?"

"It sounds reasonable," I said.

"Then suppose we say a round sum—half a million dollars."

This time I smiled at Vanpelt and, when he asked me what I was thinking, I told him. "I think you're a fat, unpleasant fool, who drinks too much. I think, if you had a lot of money, you'd be a drunk. You'd be an unpleasant, overbearing drunk."

Vanpelt's face tightened and his eyes narrowed. "I said half a million dollars," he whispered.

"You make me tired, Vanpelt," I told him. "You've been reading too many bad books. You're also a fool. You also like to play in games that aren't good for you. I think you also make me sick. I don't want you to buy me any drinks." I took five dollars out of my pocket and threw it on the table. "You have a bad effect on me. I'd feel happier if you left me alone. I want to repeat what I said before; you make me sick."

Then I got up and left, but it was a little less than the truth. Vanpelt didn't make me sick, he made me afraid—and I was afraid enough without his assistance.

It was raining when I returned to the University plaza. A cold, wet March rain that turned to sleet and then back to rain again, cold and wet and uncomfortable, the sky dark and dreary—as if to assure me that its brief promise of spring was over and forgotten. Within myself it was also over. I felt pinched and tired and filled up with dreariness. The sneering face of Vanpelt danced in front of me like a fat mask. I put my head down and ran for shelter. I was cold and soaking wet when I came to my office, my clothes wrinkled and shapeless. I had intended to stay there for awhile and work, but now all I could think of was to go home, get out of my wet clothes and lie in a hot bath.

I was sitting there in my office shivering, unable to warm myself, when someone knocked on the door. It was Phyllis. She came in, glanced at me and asked me whether I was ill.

"No, I'm all right," I said, "a little tired, but all right."

Her face was full of solicitude—the kind of solicitude and anxiety that I had not seen on any woman's face for a long time.

"You have to rest," she said to me. "I know how hard all this is for you."

"You do?" I smiled.

"You're very nice when you smile," Phyllis said. "Your whole face changes; you know that."

"Nobody knows that. You can't smile at yourself in the mirror; it doesn't work."

"It works," she said. "I smiled at myself in the mirror today. Do you know I told my mother about you. Does that sound silly— for a woman of my age to say that I told my mother about you?"

"It doesn't sound silly," I said. "What did you tell her?"

"I told her that you were very nice and kind and gentle and thoughtful."

"All of those things?"

"More. I told her you were good-looking, too. And now she's worried about me and she told me to ask you to come home with me tomorrow night to dinner."

"Because she's worried about you?"

"That's right," Phyllis said. "Can you come?"

"Of course I can come," I said. "I'll be happy to come."

So I arranged to meet her the following afternoon and to drive her home. Then I went downtown. I didn't have my car at school that day and it was still raining. I walked through the rain to the subway and through more rain from the subway to my apartment. I was too wet for the rain to matter now, soaked to the skin when I opened my door.

The place had no welcome or warmth for me. It was not the place I had left. Someone had been there, looking for one hundred and fifty thousand dollars. They had looked well. The furniture was ripped open, the cushions on the couch were slashed, their insides torn out. Every drawer in the apartment had been removed and the contents dumped on the floor. The book cases were emptied, the books flung around as if they in themselves constituted an object and reason for savage hatred. In my bedroom the same thing—every drawer empty, the bed stripped, the mattress slashed and ripped. The pictures on the wall were down, smashed, plucked out of their frames. Here and there a knife blade had plowed through the wallpaper and pieces of wallpaper were hanging crazily. The drapes were ripped down, the shades pulled off their rollers.

In stunned silence I walked among the ruins of what had once been my own small world. Here and there I made an effort to pick something up—to put this or that to rights. But the motion was more symbolic than practical. My whole body and mind hurt as I assessed what had happened, thinking to myself how much easier it would have been if a fire had consumed whatever I owned and destroyed it. That way it's clean and easy and simple and it's done with and you start over; but this way nothing was done with—only torn and broken.

I got out of my clothes, filled the tub with hot water and sank into it gratefully. I suppose I lay in the tub for better than an hour, adding hot water whenever it showed signs of cooling. I lay there and I tried to think. I tried to think about an oversized, overweight hoodlum called Jackie and his partner, Mr. Brown, who had one hundred and fifty thousand dollars as a retainer for future efforts, and I tried to think about a professor named John Vanpelt, who talked even larger figures of half a million dollars. I tried to put this and that together and to make it come out reasonable and logical, but none of my thinking was too successful, and nothing was reasonable or logical.

I was very tired. After the bath I took fresh sheets and patched up and covered the mattress on my bed as well as I could. Then I lay down and pulled the blankets up around my chin. It was only nine o'clock but I fell asleep almost immediately, and slept through for almost twelve hours without stirring or waking.

In the morning I was able to face the wreckage and set about putting it to rights.

PART SEVEN

ANNA GOLDMARK

DRIVING uptown with me from the University to West 174th Street, Phyllis talked about her mother and about herself. These were not easy things for her to talk about. She was fighting her own battle just as I was fighting mine and we both of us lived in our separate shadow worlds. I don't know exactly what connected us then at that time but it was stronger than either of us dreamed; and if our coming together was not made out of the romantic love that a man and a woman should find in each other—according to all the books and the way they tell it—it was understandable, for we were not young and we were not bright with all the pleasure of being young. Perhaps we clung to each other because it was a moment of desperation for each of us. At least we needed each other and slowly, bit by bit, we were coming to value each other.

Phyllis told me about her mother. Often enough when she spoke she would clasp her hands in her lap and look down. The words would begin slowly and then the intensity would increase. She told me of a woman who had come to this country from Europe and had made little of it. There was no pot of honey, only work that went on and on, and never lessened and never ended.

"I look at her," Phyllis said, "and then I try to understand her, and then I'm filled with doubt as to whether I understand myself. I mean that I begin by thinking of how much I love her and how, more than anything else in the world, I would want her to have some peace and happiness; and then it always ends with the love turning to pity and with my asking myself whether there is any more in it than guilt. Do you know what I mean? Do you know what I'm trying to say?"

"I think I know," I nodded. "I think I can understand what you're trying to say. My own mother came from somewhere else, but it wasn't so different."

"I know what it's done to me," Phyllis went on. "I know how my life has shaped itself to her life."

"It's only natural," I said. "It's not anything to brood about."

"I didn't brood about it until I met you, Clancy. I keep calling you Clancy instead of Tom—do you mind that?"

"I don't mind it," I said.

"But when I met you—would you believe what was the first thing I said to myself when I met you? I shouldn't tell you, but then it seems to me that it won't make any difference and I'll feel better if I tell you. The first thing I said to myself was, 'Oh my God, Phyllis, don't spoil it this time.' Do you understand, Clancy? I wanted so desperately for you to like me. I just looked at you and then all I knew was how desperately I wanted for you to like me. And then after that I came home and I looked at my mother and I found myself telling myself that I hated her. Can you imagine what a terrible thing that was, Clancy? She's not someone you can hate. She's a sweet, good, kind, and self-sacrificing woman. Everything in her life added up to me. She would try to tell me sometimes that without me nothing in her life made any sense or reason. She once said to me that without me she would have lost her faith, she would have cursed God, she would have thrown her whole life back into God's face. I mean that sounds very dramatic and strange when you say it in English, but the way she said it, it wasn't dramatic or strange. It was just her way of trying to make me understand what I meant to her."

"We all live by what we mean to someone else," I said. "You're not any different, your mother's not any different either."

"But my God, Clancy, suddenly I looked at her and hated her."

"You didn't go on hating her," I said.

"No, no, that's true. It went away, but it didn't leave me the same. I was all mixed up then, and the next day I could only think of one thing."

"I suppose the next day you decided to resign from the University."

"How did you know?" she whispered.

"I know you a little," I said to her. "It didn't start exactly the same way for me. I had a job to do at the University. Then I began to know you."

"So quickly. It's all too quick, isn't it?"

"I don't know. I don't know whether its being quick has anything to do with it—whether it makes it any better or any worse."

"But then I talked to her about it, Clancy, I stopped hating her and I talked to her about it. I told her about you—as much as I knew about you—and I told her what I thought about you, that it would be all right, that everything would be all right, and then she wanted to know you and to see you. So that's why I'm bringing you home with me. I want you to understand her because I think that if you understand her, you'll like her."

"I'll like her," I said. "Don't worry about that, Phyllis."

"I worry about it, Clancy. I guess I'm too old to be in love with a man for the first time in my life—really in love—and because of that I'm full of all kinds of fears and worries. There's no certainty and there's no security, but I don't want to ask you to give me any of that. I have to find it my own way, don't I?"

"I think so, Phyllis," I agreed. "That's not something I can give you. You have to find it your own way."

"I mean this is something that I'm doing—not you. You didn't ask me to marry you—I have no right to even expect you to ask me to marry you. I've created all this myself. I've built it up the way a silly little girl builds up a fairy tale and now I'm living on it. Don't you see how bad that can be?"

"I don't think it's bad. People work out that kind of thing and, if you don't dream about it, what validity has it? Anyway, I'm hungry. Is your mother a good cook?"

"She's a good cook," Phyllis smiled. "A wonderful cook, Clancy, and tonight she'll cook everything that she's best at."

We were almost there by then. Following Phyllis's directions, I turned left off Broadway to Fort Washington Avenue and then drove slowly, looking for a place to park. I didn't find one until 176th Street. We left the car there and walked back. The house itself was a gray, shapeless, characterless apartment building. Once, perhaps twenty-five or thirty years ago, it might have had touches of elegance about it. Now the building was run down, dirty, and poorly kept. The hallway was full of a rank odor, the self-service elevator was a cheap contraption of thin metal, and inside it was scratched and mutilated with the senselessness of frustrated kids who have no other way of throwing their defiance at the world than to chip at whatever part of the world is closest to them at the moment. We went up to the third floor and then down a hall.

Phyllis was in front of me. She rang the bell but not before she had her key out and then she didn't wait for her mother to answer it, but opened the door with her key and called out, her voice suddenly bright and youthful,

"Mom, I'm home!"

She shouldered the door open and said, "Come in, Tom. Come on in." She had remembered not to call me Clancy. I stepped into a small, rather stuffy hallway, waited there a moment while Phyllis, unbuttoning her coat, walked past me into what I subsequently learned was the kitchen. She was saying something as she stepped into that room and then the words broke off and died. A part of her world died with them. She screamed—not a loud or shrill scream—but a scream low-pitched like a moan of unbearable pain, and when I rushed in after her I saw what she had seen— the body of her mother lying on the kitchen floor.

I pulled her out of the room into the living room of the apartment and held her while she trembled and whimpered and begged me to let her go and help her mother.

"You can't help her, Phyllis, your mother is dead. Try to understand me. Your mother is dead. I don't want you to go in there again."

"How do you know she's dead? I can't leave her like that, lying on the floor. How do you know she's dead?"

I knew. The thought came to me then and there and suddenly that many years of my life had been devoted to occupations in which people died and the proof of their death was written on them. I convinced Phyllis that she should stay there and I went back into the kitchen and looked at what had been her mother. I have seen a lot of death in a variety of shapes and forms, and the horror of it and the pity of it and the waste of it; but I had never before seen a woman in her middle fifties beaten to death in a manner like this—senselessly and insanely beaten; her neck broken; her body covered with lacerations and bruises; her skin ripped by brass knuckles. It was a brutal and inhuman definition of the horror that lived inside of someone who walked as a man among other men. I looked at her, touched her, felt her pulse when there was no need to feel her pulse, and then went out and closed the door behind me.

Phyllis sat where I had left her, and as I entered she turned her white face to me and asked all the questions wordlessly. I nodded.

"Phyllis, your mother is dead," I said. "You have to accept that. There's no use in going inside and looking at her. Just believe me; your mother is dead; someone killed her."

"Why would anyone kill my mother?"

Then I lied to her and said I didn't know—when I knew it as surely as I had ever known anything.

"Tell me, Clancy, why would anyone kill my mother? Please tell me."

"I don't know, Phyllis. It happened. You have to accept the fact that it happened. Can you do that?"

"No one would want to kill her, Clancy. No one in the whole world. I hated her for a little while, but then I stopped. Clancy, no one else ever hated her—no one!"

Then she began to cry. I walked through a doorway into a bedroom. It was Phyllis's bedroom. A small room, but bright and cheerful, the windows hung with organdy curtains, a colorful patterned spread upon the bed. Without analysing what I was seeing, I saw her life beginning and ending in that room—a few dolls and stuffed animals that she had treasured through all the years, her books, her things of value which had no other value than their relationship to her and their meaning to her. I saw it only briefly and in passing as I picked up the phone and called Centre Street. This time I asked for Comaday, got through to him, and told him what had happened. He said to wait for him there—not to touch anything but to wait for him. Then I went back to Phyllis. Until Comaday came I sat with Phyllis and talked to her sometimes—but most of the time only sat with her while she let grief sink into her and tried to understand why someone would kill her mother. My own grief was of a different sort and I held a longer conversation with myself than I did with Phyllis. Whether the necessity would forgive me or not, I had managed the murder. The murder was presented not as a deed of hatred or malignancy, but as an object lesson. It was brought home to me that I was not playing ball, that I was not producing what I was supposed to produce, that I was not moving in directions I was supposed to move in and, after all, what was the life of an old woman when the game was played for millions of dollars and millions of lives? So I talked to myself and debated with myself and tried to comfort Phyllis until at last Comaday came and with him Fredericks of the Justice Department and with them the whole paraphernalia of Homicide—the uniformed officers and the officers in plain clothes, the fingerprint men and the photographers and all the other specialists in the world of murder—including the neighbors, who said they wanted help and fell over each other in their desire to see the body.

My respect for Comaday went up in that he had brought with him a policewoman who was also a registered nurse and who was able to take care of Phyllis and give her a sedative and make those few hours a little easier for her. The only small thing I could do was to make sure that no questions were directed at her. I convinced Comaday that there were no questions she could answer, and whatever questions he had were best directed at me.

His own world was better ordered than mine and he accepted less easily than I did the fact that a brutal, senseless murder like this could be merely an object lesson and a warning. We sat in the living room and talked and Comaday kept coming back to the fact that it could have been a coincidence—a thief, a prowler. After all, it was a large city and no week went by when some woman alone was not attacked or even murdered.

"Like this?" I said to Comaday. "Prowlers attack and murder a woman like this?"

"It happens," he said.

"It happens," I agreed, "but when it happens to Phyllis Goldmark's mother and when it happens the night I'm on my way up here and when it happens the way it happened, coincidence has been pulled too thin. It didn't happen that way, Comaday, and you know it."

"I don't know a damned thing," he said.

We were alone in the room then—just Comaday, Fredericks, and myself—and I said to him, "Then maybe it's time you knew something. Maybe it's time you learned something. Maybe it's time you learned what that goddamned home-made bomb of yours is worth! I was offered half a million dollars for it yesterday."

"The hell you were!" Comaday cried.

"That's peanuts," I said. "The large offers are still to come."

"You should have told us," Fredericks said. "You get nowhere keeping stuff like that to yourself, Clancy; you should have told us."

"The Commissioner here is tired of hearing my stories," I said.

"Why didn't you tell me?" Comaday snapped.

"You told me to find Horton," I said. "This didn't change anything. Anyone can say to me, 'There's a million dollars in this for you, Clancy.' It's just talk and talk is cheap."

"Not anyone," Fredericks said.

I looked at him.

"Not anyone, Clancy, only someone who knows about the bomb. I don't want to begin to think that you keep things to yourself. Only trouble can come from keeping things to yourself."

Comaday looked at me strangely and asked quietly, "Are you going to find Horton, Clancy?"

"I'll find him," I said.

I went in to Phyllis after that. She had been given a sedative and she lay on her bed on the brightly colored quilt with a robe spread over her. The policewoman sat next to her. I bent over Phyllis and kissed her on the cheek. Then she clung to me.

"Don't leave me, Clancy," she begged me.

"I won't leave you," I said, "believe me, I won't leave you, Phyllis. Not any more. But now we have to get in touch with someone—some relative of yours. Can you think of someone I should get in touch with?"

She gave me the numbers and I called an aunt and also the cousin in Great Neck. I didn't go into any explanations over the telephone except to say that Mrs. Goldmark had died suddenly, that I was a friend of Phyllis, and that arrangements would have to be made. I liked Golden better when he agreed to drive in immediately and take care of whatever had to be taken care of. The aunt said she would come to the apartment and stay with Phyllis tonight.

Then I went back to the living room and asked Comaday to put a man on at the apartment for the rest of the night. He agreed to that. I also told him that I wanted five hundred dollars of expense money in cash. Comaday thought it was a good deal. His world might be coming to an end, but that alone was not sufficient reason to shell out five hundred dollars of expense money to a plainclothesman. However, I managed to convince him. I told Phyllis that I would see her later and then I rode downtown with Comaday to pick up the money.

PART EIGHT

VANPELT REVISITED

COMMISSIONER COMADAY pushed the five hundred dollars across his desk toward me, his cold eyes contemplating me judiciously. I knew what the action did to him—five hundred dollars was probably more money than he had ever before given to a cop on the job. He was probably thinking that it undermined the basic concepts of his Department and instituted a new era of senseless waste. His eyes followed me as I tucked it into my wallet, and he couldn't help saying,

"That's a damn lot of money, Clancy. I don't know what the hell you're going to do with all that money."

"Whatever is left over, I'll return."

"That much money is a temptation to a cop," Comaday said, "to any cop."

"Look," I told him, tiredly, "I brought one hundred and fifty thousand dollars down here to you, didn't I?"

"That's different."

"Sure, that was different," I agreed. I got up to go. Comaday said,

"Wait a minute, Clancy. What goes on with you? Are you in love with that girl?"

"Does that also come under the call of duty?"

"What the hell, Clancy, take the chip off your shoulder. Nothing's under the call of duty. You've got no duties to me—I've got no duties to you. We're just doing the best we can."

"That's what I'm doing—the best I can," I agreed. And then I left.

Outside in the street I turned up my collar, put my hands in my pockets, and began to walk uptown. It was a cold, raw night and my bones were full of death and all the fatigue of sorrow. I felt nothing or else I felt so many things that it added up to nothing.

I felt that it was none of Commissioner John Comaday's god-damned business how I felt about Phyllis Goldmark or any other woman, alive or dead. I also tried to tell myself and persuade myself that it was none of my own business, but that didn't work too well. I was full of a death sickness, a horror sickness; I was filled up to surfeit and to overflowing with the whole mood and temper of our time, with its civilized cruelty and its barbaric brutality, its senseless fears and its dismal uncertainties. I could only reply to myself that I was playing an idiot's game with a cast of idiots surrounding me and I was sufficiently well read—or poorly read, if you would have it so—to know that it had never been very much different and that now, as a thousand years ago, there were no sane answers to what we were doing, where we were coming from or where we were going. I had five hundred dollars in my pocket; I could take a taxicab to the airport and buy a ticket for somewhere —for anywhere. I was lost already, so it made sense for me to ask myself why I should not be lost entirely, completely and forever.

I accepted my own prerogative and asked myself whether I was in love, and then I was able to explain to myself that I did not intend to be in love, that I did not want to be in love, and that this was necessary to my own defense and my own existence. I could survive almost anything and everything in this world I had never made and had never wanted; the fragment of doubt lay in a woman. I had survived the death of one woman I loved, but not easily, and now I was filled with a monstrous anxiety concerning Phyllis. I felt it in my head and my heart and in the pit of my stomach, and I had to persuade myself not to go to the nearest telephone and call her and get my own proof that she was alive and unharmed.

I thought of all this as I walked on through the night, turning east on Canal Street, and then I did it anyway. I went into a drugstore and used a telephone. The policewoman was still there and she said that Phyllis was sleeping. Golden was expected, Phyllis's aunt was there, and the policeman was posted outside the door.

"Tell her when she wakes up," I said, "that I called."

"I think she'll sleep through until morning," the policewoman answered.

After that, I was ravenously hungry and I turned into Mott Street, where there was a place I knew and where the food was good. The owner, Ling Chun, joined me at my table and kept me polite and respectful company while I stuffed myself with sea bass, fried Chinese style, and bean curd. Finally he observed that I appeared to be eating more out of anger and frustration than out of reasonable appetite.

"And that, Clancy," he said to me, "is not a civilized approach to food. We serve very good food here and only now and then do we have customers whose discrimination matches it. I have always considered you such a customer, and it grieves me to find you so disturbed."

I said to him, "Tell me, Chun, you live here in an island in the world. How do you live with it? Doesn't the world ever disturb you?"

"No one is ever as much disturbed as a cop," Chun replied thoughtfully. "You know, Clancy, that in the olden times there were no police. I believe that the first police force, as we know it, was set up in London in the nineteenth century. A policeman is something very new, and he has never been worked out properly."

"He has been worked out properly, believe me."

"No, I mean it a little differently. You asked me about the island here, which we people call Chinatown. The world touches us, but we build our own walls. This is because we are a very old people who never actually became modernized. I think that everyone has to build some kind of a wall, except a cop. He has no walls—not even to carry around with him—so the practice of living comes very difficult for him and he is not prepared for it the way a physician is or the way a priest is."

"I will tell you what I think," I said. "I think that every god-damned one of you Chinese carries around the burden of proving that he's a philosopher. I hate two-bit philosophy warmed over for the occasion."

"You have a point there," Chun nodded. "A modest point but, nevertheless, an element of truth."

I finished my fish and then I said to him, "Tell me, Chun, how would your philosophy respond to the fact that the world was going to end in about two weeks?"

Chun shrugged. "You and I are alive tonight, Clancy. No one has guaranteed us two weeks more. The world will probably come to an end tomorrow. I took a course in statistics and probabilities which brought home to me the fact that we live arithmetically; it's the law of averages that maintains us and the universe."

"That's cold-blooded and pessimistic. How the devil did you come to take a course in statistics?"

"At one time I had seriously intended to become an insurance salesman. I even dreamed of being the oriental tycoon of the insurance business. I ended up running a Chinese restaurant."

"I ended up as a cop," I said. Then I finished eating and used his telephone directory. I found the address I wanted, said goodnight to Chun and then considered going all the way uptown to pick up my car. I decided that tomorrow would be time enough for that, and I took a taxicab to the address I had found in the telephone book. It was almost midnight when I rang Vanpelt's doorbell.

It was a brownstone house on 112th Street near Riverside Drive. Vanpelt lived on the third floor and, as with so many of the converted brownstones, his place consisted of one large, square room, a tiny kitchen, and a tiny dressing room. He was still dressed when he opened the door for me and certainly surprised to see me—sufficiently surprised to have no words to greet me with. He ushered me into the room and closed the door. He was in shirt sleeves and a sleeveless sweater and he had been watching his television and helping himself out of a bottle. He was a little drunk but not very much so. He walked straight enough, as he went to turn off the television, but when he faced me after that, his eyes had trouble focusing, his speech was a little thick. He told me that he was surprised but pleased. He tried to smile and he apologized for the condition of his place, which could have been cleaner and neater. I took off my hat and coat and threw them on an old, spotted overstuffed couch. Vanpelt wanted to know whether I wouldn't join him in a drink. I shook my head.

"Well," he said, "it seems a little late for a social call, Clancy, but I must say I'm delighted—I am—I'm delighted. I'm not a good sleeper. I never really get to bed before two in the morning. Are you sure you wouldn't like a drink?"

"I'm sure," I said.

"The way the place looks," Vanpelt said, "I mean a woman comes in in the morning and cleans the place up but she doesn't do a very thorough job. It gets to looking seedy about this hour."

"Do you know what happened today, Vanpelt?"

He stared at me and then shook his head. He went over to the easy chair where he had been sitting, fell into it and picked up his drink. "Should I know?" he asked. "Is it something important?"

"Miss Goldmark's mother was murdered."

He put down his drink and stared at me without any particular comprehension. "Do you mean Phyllis?" he said.

"That's right, Vanpelt, her mother was murdered today."

"That's a terrible thing," he said slowly, "that's a shocking thing."

He picked up his drink again, but I walked over to him and knocked it out of his hand. I grabbed him by his shirt and sweater, pulled him out of his chair, and flung him onto the couch. The shirt ripped. He lay sprawled on the couch for a moment and then rolled onto the floor. He picked himself up from the floor and faced me, trembling.

"What's wrong with you, Clancy? What are you doing? You're my friend."

"The hell with that! I'm no friend of yours, Vanpelt. You turn my stomach."

"I didn't ask you here," he cried, "for Christ's sake, Clancy, I didn't ask you here."

"Then I asked myself here. You talked big yesterday, Vanpelt. You talked very clever and very big and you talked about half a million dollars—half a million dollars for what?"

Vanpelt shook his head slowly. I walked over to him and twisted his shirt and sweater in my fist. I felt sick and ashamed of myself and his hot alcoholic breath in my face made me feel sicker; but I had started this and I had to finish it. I had to finish the whole thing. It had waited too long and it wouldn't wait any more.

"You were buying something for half a million dollars, Vanpelt. What were you buying? And what were you using for play money? Who's behind you and who's in this with you?"

He began to blubber. "It was bluff; it was all a bluff; I tell you it was just a bluff, Clancy. I was poking around in the dark. I was looking for something. Didn't you ever look for something?"

"I've looked for something," I nodded.

"Then you can understand."

"I don't understand a goddamned thing."

He was afraid of me—terribly afraid of me—and totally unaware of the fact that I had ever been afraid of him. He blubbered and squirmed in my grasp and tried to explain to me how a man sits and waits and watches and hopes that something will come along that can be turned into money.

"You offered me the money!" I shouted at him. "You miserable, fat son of a bitch—you offered me the money—whose money?"

"I tell you it was bluff, Clancy, believe me."

I held him with my left hand and slapped him hard with my right hand. I slapped him twice and he crumpled to the floor, tears rolling down his cheeks.

"Get out of here," he whimpered, "get out of here and leave me alone. Goddamn you, you've got no right to come in here and beat me up. Who in hell do you think you are? Leave me alone!"

I bent down, grabbed his foot, and dragged him around in a circle. He rolled over on his face and I kicked his buttocks and told him to get up. He sat up then, the tears still flowing, and stared at me with a mixture of hate and hopelessness.

"Who hired you?" I shouted at him.

"No one hired me," he whimpered. "I swear to God, Clancy, no one hired me. I guessed that you were a cop or an agent or a G man or something, and I knew it was big. How smart do you have to be to know that the way Horton disappeared was something big? Then I said to myself that they put you in to find out where he was, and where he was or whatever you could find out could be worth a lot of money."

"You're not that stupid," I said disgustedly. "No one is that stupid, Vanpelt."

"I am," he replied. Then he put his face in his hands and began to cry. Then he dropped his hands and looked up at me through the tears. "What are you going to do to me, Clancy?"

"Nothing," I said. I put on my hat and coat. When I walked out, he was still sitting there on the floor, tears rolling down his face.

I felt that I should not have been born. I no longer hated Vanpelt—only myself. I walked for a long time and when I looked at a street sign, I was at Eighty-sixth Street and Broadway. I went into a bar there and had four drinks. It was a beginning. I wanted to get drunk—more drunk than I had ever been before. The four drinks left me sober and cold with not even the thinnest edge of happiness. So I paid for them and went home, and walked through the wreckage and the debris of my own apartment, and crawled into my own patched-up bed.

PART NINE

RABBI FREEMAN

I was awakened the following morning at six forty-five by my telephone, and when I picked it up and mumbled into it, there was Dmitri Grischov, as bright as a beacon and telling me that he had to see me.

"Not today, Grischov," I said. "For heaven's sake, whatever you want to see me about can wait."

"It has to be today," he insisted.

"I have a funeral today. Can't you understand that? I have things to do, Grischov. For God's sake, it's a quarter to seven in the morning."

"I know where you live," Grischov said. "I'll be over in half an hour."

I was shaving when he came in. I came out of the bathroom with the lather on my face to open the door for him and then I went back to finish shaving, leaving the bathroom door open and able to observe him in the mirror.

After he took off his hat and coat, he paced slowly around the room, looking at the chaos and at the debris. I had made some attempts at straightening up the place, at restocking the drawers and clearing away a little of the general confusion; but all this hardly made more than a dent in the general disorder. In the mirror I saw Grischov pause, pick up a smashed picture, examine it. I saw him give his attention to the big armchair that was torn and shredded. When I came out of the bathroom finally, through shaving and ready to face the world, Grischov was standing in the middle of my living room, hands in pockets, brooding over its condition.

"I don't always live like this," I explained to him as I set about making coffee and opening a can of frozen orange juice. "Only now and then."

"I didn't think you did," Grischov said somberly. "Who visited you?"

"I don't know. Probably the same madman who murdered Anna Goldmark."

"What was he looking for?"

"One hundred and fifty thousand dollars."

"Oh? Did he find it?"

There were moments when I found Grischov almost bearable; I mean there were moments when I overcame my conditioned dislike of what he was and what he stood for and was able to credit him with a sense of humour of sorts—not that I was ever actually certain. Apparently Grischov had been trained not to laugh. There were times when he smiled, but such an action was always accompanied by a certain amount of reluctance, and I would think of him as saying to himself, "This is precisely the correct time for me, Dmitri Grischov, to smile." Of course that implies prejudice on my part, and prejudice is a hard thing to overcome. The fact that I could always recognize when Grischov was going out of his way and making a difficult effort to be pleasant to me should not have lessened the virtue of his gestures. Now I told him that they had not found the one hundred fifty thousand dollars, and he allowed himself a fleeting trace of a smile as he asked me whether I always kept that much money on hand.

"Not always," I admitted.

"It is a rich country," Grischov said, "but even in our country, which, if given ten peaceful years to build its economic structure, will be a good deal richer than yours, policemen are not that well-paid."

"I was bribed, Grischov," I said. "Two unbelievable men came here and gave me one hundred fifty thousand dollars as a bribe."

Grischov raised his brows. "That's a large bribe. What did they want?"

"They wanted Horton and his atom bomb."

"But you don't have either Horton or his atom bomb."

"The bribe was payment in advance. You see they trusted me. They figured that one hundred fifty thousand dollars buys a certain amount of trust—no matter what. Then from somewhere they got the idea that I had turned the money in and that I was no longer trustworthy. That's when they came here looking for the money. I haven't had a chance to clean up yet. You can observe it and put it down to capitalist degeneracy. When they didn't find the money, they killed Anna Goldmark to make a point."

I put the orange juice on the table, two glasses of it, and put toast in the toaster. Grischov needed no urging to join me. He drained his glass of orange juice and observed that our frozen orange juice was very good.

"I don't think so," I said. "I think it's a pale imitation of the real thing."

"You can afford real oranges, Clancy. This country overflows with real oranges. There are more oranges here," he said bitterly, "than in all the rest of the world put together."

"For God's sake, Grischov, I don't control the orange crop and neither do you. If it helps any, I can assure you that if I was an orange magnate, I'd make a deal with you. The trouble about real oranges is that I'm too lazy to squeeze them."

"Typically American. Do you know who the murderers are?"

I brought toast and butter and coffee to the table. Grischov liked my coffee and liked my toast. He ate heartily.

"I think I do," I said.

He watched me thoughtfully for a moment before he asked me. "Or are these things top secret?"

"The hell with that, Grischov; I don't know what's top secret or what isn't. I don't work for U.S. Intelligence or for the Department of State. I'm a second-rate cop pretending I'm a physics teacher and all I have is guesses. I'm guessing that this crowd comes from a dirty little island in the Caribbean."

It was at that moment, at exactly ten minutes to eight, that my telephone rang again. It was my morning for early phone calls. I picked up the phone and a voice told me that it was Maximilian Gomez—nor did I question the information. I knew the voice. It was a very polite voice. It apologized for calling at such an hour. According to the voice, Maximilian Gomez had read in the morning papers of the murder of Anna Goldmark. He was calling me as a friend of the family. Did I know when the funeral would be and where the funeral would be?

As a matter of fact, I did not know; and I reminded him that he could find out as easily as I could. He remained polite and he thanked me.

"This is a terrible thing, Professor Clancy," he said.

I had no desire to talk to him and there was nothing I could think of that I wanted to say to him. I finished the conversation as quickly as I could, brought another order of toast to the table and asked Grischov whether he had ever heard of Maximilian Gomez.

Grischov considered the name for a little while before he nodded. "Your Caribbean island," he said.

"It could be."

Grischov finished his coffee, finished his toast, and leaned back comfortably in his chair. He lit a cigarette and puffed thoughtfully. Then he said, "What will you do when you lead them to Horton, Clancy?"

"You think I'll lead them to Horton?"

Grischov nodded.

"When?" I asked.

Grischov shrugged. "Today—tomorrow—the next day—I have a great deal of respect for you, Clancy."

"I don't share that."

"Ah well—that's for you to say. You are very close to this. On the other hand, I have a notion—I want to talk to your Phyllis Goldmark."

I shook my head. I got up, went to the kitchen, and returned with the coffee pot, pouring a second cup for each of us. Grischov didn't object; he liked American orange juice and American coffee. "No," I told him. "It won't do any good for you to talk to her, Grischov, not today. She's been through too much."

"What she has been through," Grischov said slowly, "is exactly what we needed. Don't look at me like that, Clancy. I know what you're thinking. Your ideas of Russians coincide with our ideas of Americans. You were wondering whether I was heartless enough and cold and calculating enough to have her mother murdered. Am I right? Tell me now, am I right?"

"A cop suspects everyone," I said tiredly.

"Oh no, Clancy, not at all. Let me put you at rest. I did not have her mother murdered. I am just trying to make you understand that a shock like this will change all her thoughts. It will shake up her brains. She will forget things that two days ago she remembered quite clearly; she will remember other things that maybe she had forgotten. I want to talk to her. I'm not saying that you shouldn't be there. All I'm saying is that I want to talk to her. You can arrange that, can't you?"

"I can arrange it," I said. "I just don't know whether I want to arrange it."

"Well, think about it." Grischov rose and put on his hat and coat. "Think about it, Clancy, and if you change your mind, I will be where you can reach me. I'll take a place at the Biltmore Hotel. I'll be there all afternoon. Thank you for the breakfast. You make good coffee and good orange juice."

"Good toast," I said.

"Good toast," Grischov nodded, allowing himself a thin smile. "About your Maximilian Gomez, I will see what we have that may be pertinent. The way I think, Clancy, it doesn't make any difference. Gomez and anyone else—they're only waiting for you to find Horton. It will not change anything whatever we discover about Gomez. The only thing that will change something is Alex Horton himself. Do you see?"

"I see," I nodded.

Then Grischov left. I cleaned up the dishes and finished dressing and it was nine o'clock. I called the Goldmark apartment and Phyllis's aunt answered the phone. I told her that I was an associate of Phyllis from the University, Professor Clancy. She said that she had heard about me and that Phyllis was all right and that the funeral services would take place at half past ten at the Uptown Memorial Chapel. I thanked her and said that I would be there.

I went uptown to get my car first and then I drove the short distance from there to the Uptown Memorial Chapel. The chapel itself was a small, well-kept building of yellow brick on a street that was rapidly turning into a slum. All the other houses on the street were shabby, poorly kept, and run-down; only the Memorial Chapel preserved its glittering exterior, its neat sense of middle-class respectability, its precise paint, and its clean sidewalk. Already in front of it a hearse and a single black funeral car were waiting.

I went inside and a somber man in a frock coat and mourning trousers inquired as to whether I was a member of the family. I answered that I was a friend of Miss Goldmark and he said that, if I desired to, I could join the family in the sitting room or else I could take a seat in the chapel. I decided that I would join the family. It would not be pleasant, but I have never found anything about a funeral to be pleasant and, if possible, I wanted to be with Phyllis. The sitting room was a dimly lit room about twenty by thirty feet. At one end of it, the coffin sat on its trestles with some candles burning behind it. Phyllis sat on a couch with her aunt on one side of her and with Rita Golden on the other side of her; with Jack Golden, that comprised the family—a tiny family, almost as tiny as my own, pathetically small and pathetic in its loneliness here in the big room. There was one other man present—a tall thin man who wore glasses and whom Jack Golden introduced to me as Rabbi Freeman. The policewoman of the night before was also present. She was in plain clothes and she sat quietly by herself in a corner of the room. A little later two elderly women appeared, who were friends of Anna Goldmark. But that was all, and that was the whole of those who mourned for the senseless passing of a single and elderly woman who had died without apparent cause or meaning.

Phyllis did not see me when I came in. Jack Golden came over to me and shook hands with me and introduced me to Rabbi Freeman.

No one talks in such a place. Everyone whispers. "I am glad you could come, Clancy," Golden whispered to me. "It was very decent of you to come."

Rabbi Freeman looked at me thoughtfully and shook hands with me. Then Phyllis saw me and I went over to her. She had been dry-eyed until then, but when I put my arms around her, she began to cry. The two women drew her back to the couch. They regarded me with hostility, their expressions demanding to know what right I had there and by what right did I introduce embraces into a situation like this one. I walked across the room toward the coffin and observed, with some relief, that it was closed. Then Rabbi Freeman caught my eye and I walked over to him and he asked me to step outside with him.

As we came into the foyer or lobby of the funeral parlor, the attendant was arguing with two newspapermen and a cameraman. They broke away from him and came over to us and wanted to know who I was and who Rabbi Freeman was. He told them. The camerman took his picture, the flash explosion bizarre in the darkened hallway. A reporter said to the rabbi, "Look, Rabbi, we don't want to make any trouble for anyone, but we got to get some pictures of the family. We got to talk to someone in the family."

"What are they going to say to you now?" the rabbi asked softly. "This is a small family. There are four people in there who belong to the family. A poor old woman was murdered by a thief—that's not a story; that's no different from a hundred other stories. What are you going to do with it?"

"Still, it's a story."

"Leave them alone for a while now," the rabbi said. Then he took me by the arm and led me into the chapel.

The chapel was empty. It was a small hall with pews for about sixty people, hung about with curtains, lighted as dimly as the sitting room, and with a modest organ at the front.

"Is it enviable being a rabbi, Mr. Clancy?" Freeman said to me. "I was called in last night to a family I don't know and had never met before to bury one of them. She is mourned by a tiny handful. I don't know if I've ever run into anything just like this before. It's hard to believe that people could be so much alone in the world."

"A great many people are alone in the world. It's not so hard to believe, Rabbi."

"Perhaps yes, perhaps no. The point is that last night I sat and talked for a long time to the girl. What do you think of the girl, Mr. Clancy?"

"That's an odd question."

"I expect it is. It's an odd question for me to ask. This girl talked about her mother and she talked about you. She thinks that you know why her mother was murdered. Murder is a terrible thing. It's become something we read about every day in our books and our newspapers and, if we are so disposed, we can watch it every night on the television. But I've been a rabbi for thirty years, Mr. Clancy, and I've never officiated at a murder before. Do you know why this woman was murdered?" He was watching me and I was tired of lying. I had lied too much already and about too many things, so I nodded and told him that I knew.

"You can't tell me, of course."

"No," I said, "I'm sorry, Rabbi, I can't tell you."

"Phyllis said that you're an associate of hers at the University —professor of physics—is that what you are, Mr. Clancy?"

"No," I said, "not really."

"Whatever you are," Freeman murmured, "I doubt whether it is any more difficult or thankless than being a rabbi. That, I am sure, is something you never gave much consideration to, Mr. Clancy. I suppose there never was any good reason why you should have given any consideration to it. On the other hand, it is something I have lived with and tried to understand—that's not so strange—I wonder how many of us understand what we are and why we do the things we do. I can tell you that we have fewer gratifications than you might imagine and, in the end, it comes down to comforting a person who needs you. I don't suppose that there is much more than that that any priest can offer, and we are priests of a sort—if of a most peculiar sort. I mean that I was struck very strangely by that girl—by that woman, Phyllis. I have seen all kinds of agony, Mr. Clancy. I was a chaplain during the war and anyone who moves among Jews becomes used to the varieties of agony, but I don't know that I have ever seen just the kind of agony that this woman suffered last night. Did you know that?"

"No," I said slowly, "I didn't know it."

"I walk where angels fear to tread, Mr. Clancy. That's a poor prerogative of my business. You know that she loves you?"

I nodded. "Yes, I know that she loves me."

"She is on the edge of a precipice, Mr. Clancy; if she falls off it, her world will come to an end. All of this is none of my business, but when I am called in by strangers to say prayers over the dead, I feel an understandable sense of futility. The living are something else. Wouldn't you agree?"

"Yes," I said tightly, "the living are something else."

"When I began this, Mr. Clancy, I expected you to be angry."

"I am not angry," I said. "I just can't see what all this has to do with yourself and me. I have a relationship to Phyllis Goldmark, but that's something that only I can work out."

"Only you can work it out," the rabbi agreed.

"Then exactly what are you getting at?" I wanted to know.

"Have you ever lived in a nightmare, Mr. Clancy?"

I nodded.

"Then you know the habitation. I don't have to offer any arguments or persuasion. She is living in a nightmare, Mr. Clancy. Let me say that in walking where angels fear to tread, I put two and two together and it does not add up to four. That gives me the right to ask you whether you led her into the nightmare."

I was silent for a while after he said that. The organist came into the chapel, nodded at us and walked up to the organ. He sounded a few notes, as if he were tuning it. Then he began to play one of the Bach funeral pieces. The rabbi walked over to him and said a few words to him, and the music stopped. When the rabbi came back, he explained to me that there was a considerable division of opinion among Jews as to the desirability of music at a funeral. It seemed to me that I heard him from a long distance away. I was absorbed in my own thoughts, of which I had only too many.

"I presumed a great deal," the rabbi said. "Now it seems to me that perhaps I presumed too much."

"I don't think so. What else were you going to say to me?"

"I was only going to ask whether you could lead her out?"

"Like the blind leading the blind?"

"Yes, if it has to be that way."

Then we returned to the other room and, when I entered it, Phyllis came over to me. "I thought you had left," she said. I shook my head; and she said to me, "Stay next to me, Clancy, please don't leave."

In the dim light I looked at her—perhaps more strangely than I imagined. Her eyes opened wider in a sort of fear and then I kissed her gently on the cheek. Her face was drawn and pale and tired, but I realized that she remained beautiful for me and would remain that way, and I told her that I would not leave her again, not ever again.

PART TEN

THE BEACH

THE cemetery was far out on Long Island. There were only three cars in the funeral procession after the hearse—the hired limousine in which Phyllis rode with her aunt and Rabbi Freeman, then a

Bentley which belonged to the Goldens, and then my car. The policewoman had wondered whether she should go along, but I told her that she didn't have to and that I would remain with Phyllis for the time being and let them know downtown if I left her.

It was a dismal and overcast day, the sky heavy hung with gray clouds, and by the time we reached the cemetery a soft misty rain was falling. The grave was ready and waiting and we stood around in the rain under umbrellas that the cemetery provided while Rabbi Freeman said the few words that he had to say. The coffin was lowered, the grave filled, and then it was over and we walked away back toward the cars. The Goldens wanted Phyllis and her aunt to return with them to their home, but Phyllis said no, she was going to remain with me. Rita Golden did not like this. She almost made a point of the fact that she had gone to some trouble to be there and if it was not thoughtless, it was at least ungracious for Phyllis to decline to return with her. Jack Golden kept looking at his watch. It was past lunch time now and he said that the best thing might be for all of us to go somewhere and have lunch. I felt a little sorry for him because the occasion was very awkward and the mere handful of people present robbed the burying of any meaning or ceremonial dignity that he perhaps considered it should have.

Phyllis, however, was firm. She would not go with anyone. She kissed her aunt, who was sobbing violently, and sent her back in the limousine which was returning to New York with Rabbi Freeman. The Goldens stood around, awkward and ill at ease and uncertain about what to do now. Jack Golden repeated his lunch invitation. Rita Golden mentioned that she had an appointment with her hairdresser and her husband looked at her bitterly and told her, without words, to shut up and to hell with her hairdresser or anything else that might concern her. It was all in a look but she read it and understood it and retreated into the Bentley. "Gomez is having dinner with us again tomorrow night," Jack Golden said uncertainly, "it might take your mind off things." Phyllis stared at him vacantly. He tried once again to persuade her to return with him and then his feelings began to be hurt. He had taken a day away from his business and he was missing his lunch. The whole thing made no sense and he said so. I had kept silent but now I said to him that it would be better if he went and I would take care of Phyllis; and that, after all, it was what she wanted.

"All right, Clancy," he shrugged, "you're the doctor. If that's what she wants, she wants it." His feelings were injured and, without another word, he got into the Bentley and drove away. We stood there in the rain-soaked cemetery watching his car as he drove down the road. In our whole world there was no sound except the wind and the rain and no life or movement except the four cemetery workers trudging away through the rain with their spades and rakes over their shoulders.

I took Phyllis's arm and led her to my car. She was dry-eyed now, her face remote and dull with almost profound inwardness. "Don't go back to New York, Clancy," she said to me. "Drive somewhere."

"Where, Phyllis?"

"Anywhere, but not back to New York."

I turned toward the South Shore and we drove on, both of us sitting in silence behind the even swish of my windshield wipers. There were few cars on the road; the Island was as gray and lonely as the day, and I had the strange feeling that, coming from nowhere, we were bound for nowhere—only driving through time without place or destination. Then Phyllis said to me,

"The worst part of it, Clancy, is that no one really cares."

"That isn't so," I said. "You care, I care. I think, in their own way, the Goldens care."

"You're just saying that, Clancy, because you can't admit that death can come and produce indifference, but it isn't true. Nobody really cares. I tried so hard to care and I find that I can't. I'm full of the horror of it, but horror isn't grief. All my life I'll live with the horror of it, but the little bit of grief is gone already. That's the terrible thing, isn't it, Clancy?"

"It's not terrible," I said. "Grief isn't anything you can measure. It's no virtue. It's nothing to be proud of. It doesn't define you or your mother either, or whatever was between you. I know. I have become a sort of minor specialist in the field of grief. It's nothing to be proud of. When you come down to it, it's a sort of divorcement—it's a reason to remove yourself from the whole world of life and people and hope and beauty."

"Did you do that, Clancy, remove yourself?"

"I did it," I said.

She was silent for a while after that and then she said to me, "The way I was before, Clancy, I tried to tie strings to you—that's no good. I can't tie any strings to you. I want you to be with me now, but in the end, when you take me home, Clancy, you go your own way."

"What is my own way, Phyllis?"

"That's up to you, Clancy."

"Then leave it up to me."

She nodded without replying. We drove through a town and then through meadows of high dead grass. The rain had stopped but the sky remained gray and leaden. Now the road paralleled a long, empty beach separated from us by an endless row of tiny, shabby summer houses—empty and deserted at this time.

"Can we stop here?" Phyllis asked me. "I want to walk. If you don't mind?"

I turned the car into one of the driveways and parked there. We got out of the car and walked down to the beach and then walked through the sand along the beach. I took Phyllis's hand. It was cold and wet, but the strong east wind was sweet and refreshing. The surf thundered on the beach and broke in great combs of white spume. A few gulls circled above the water. Otherwise the beach was deserted as far as we could see in either direction. In silence we walked about half a mile and then turned back. I looked at Phyllis. Her hair blew in the wind and her face was flushed and alive. I stopped suddenly and took her in my arms and she said to me, "Only if you want to, Clancy, not if you don't want to."

I kissed her and felt the salt taste; the smell of salt and the damp of spray was all over us. A gull sailed crazily on the wind and came swooping down almost at our feet. With my arm around Phyllis, we walked back to the car, chilled now and glad for its shelter and its warmth. Seated in the car, we lit cigarettes and smoked.

"Do you know what I was thinking?" Phyllis finally said. "I was thinking about a story I once heard."

"I was thinking about you," I said. "I was thinking about you and me. If we can begin with some truth between us today, Phyllis, then it's the first time I ever really thought about you and me—in this way, I mean."

"I know, and I was thinking about this story I once heard. It's an old, old story—I don't know how old it is, Clancy, and I don't suppose anyone really knows who wrote it in the beginning. It's a story about a man and a woman who loved each other. Their love was supposed to have been a very remarkable and true love. It was the kind of love that poems are written about and songs are made from. I guess there was never a bad word between them—only this love which was like no other love that the world had ever seen."

"It's a story," I said. "That kind of love is worthless—that kind of love is a fairy tale."

"I know it's just a story, Clancy, but, according to the story, that's how they loved each other. And then the man died. When the man died, the woman had no more desire to live. I mean that, according to the story, she had loved him so much that life without him was impossible and all she wanted was to die. In those days they didn't bury people the way we do today. They took his body and they put it in a big crypt and his wife went along with the body and remained beside it. She told everyone that she was going to remain there until she was also dead. She would not eat or drink, only stay there in the crypt by her husband's body and die beside him. That's what she did. She sat beside him, moaning and weeping, and because everyone knew how great their love was they understood and they sympathized with her and they left her there and went away, closing the door of the crypt behind them."

She paused and looked at me. I watched her curiously. Did I want to hear the rest of it, she asked me? I told her to go ahead.

"Well, outside the crypt, Clancy, was a place of execution. There was a gallows outside the crypt and a thief was hanging from the gallows. He had been executed that same day. A young soldier stood at the foot of the gallows, leaning on a spear. The soldier was guarding the thief. In those days the bodies of thieves were cast into lime pits and I suppose the authorities felt that the thief's relatives would try to steal the body from the gallows and give it a decent burial. That's why the soldier had to stand there all night, guarding the body. Well, while he stood there, he heard a sound. The sound was the weeping and the mourning of the woman who had decided to remain in the crypt and die with her husband. The soldier followed the sound and it led him to the crypt and he went inside the crypt and discovered this beautiful woman, who had condemned herself to death.

"When he saw how young and beautiful she was, he was horrified at the thought that she had decided to die there beside her husband. The young soldier spoke to her. He comforted her, Clancy. He dried her tears and he whispered to her about life and living. He must have been very persuasive, that young soldier, because presently from comforting her he turned to embracing her and then to making love to her and so they lay there together in the crypt on the bier, making love to each other, the poor woman in all her grief and the soldier in all his youth and health, and then suddenly the first light of morning lightened the crypt. The soldier stood up and went to the door of the crypt and looked out and, when he saw what he saw, he let out such a moan of sorrow and despair that the woman came running to his side to see what the trouble was. He pointed to the gallows. The body was gone. It had been stolen by the relatives of the thief. 'Do you see what that means?' he said to her. 'I was assigned to guard the body of the thief. Now it has been stolen. Therefore, my own life is forfeit and they will hang me on the gallows for my failure to do my duty.'

"The young wife was horror-stricken at this—to be parted by death again from someone she had come to love as she did this young soldier was beyond her power to bear; so she assured him that he would not die, that everything would be all right; that she would make it all right."

Phyllis's voice trailed away. I waited for a moment or two and when she didn't continue I said to her, "And did she make it all right?"

"She made it all right," Phyllis said. "You see, she and the soldier took the body of her husband and hung it from the gallows instead of the thief."

I thought about it for awhile and then I backed the car out of the driveway and started toward New York. "The trouble with a story like that," I said, "is that it tells too much and too little. Our own story is much simpler and yet much more complex. Yet we do what we have to do and they did what they had to do. The worst part of it, in any case, is to be called upon to sit in judgment. I can't sit in judgment, Phyllis. I'm not a judge. I'm a cop —a policeman—and that's the beginning of it and the end of it." I didn't look at her but kept my eyes on the road, and I think I would have known if she had been surprised or terribly disturbed, but it was none of these—only a long silence until she answered me and said that she had known.

"Since when?"

"I think from the beginning, Clancy, or almost from the beginning. Anyway, I knew the other day. I knew when you took me in your arms. I felt the gun. A teacher doesn't carry a gun."

"You have to be afraid to carry a gun or ambitious—very ambitious."

"And do you know who killed my mother, Clancy?"

"I think so."

"And why she was killed?"

Then I told her the whole story. I told it to her while we were driving back to New York—all of it—leaving nothing out; and when I finished, I asked her whether she believed me.

She gave it some thought and then she said that she believed me. "I think you always tell the truth, Clancy, or you try to unless you gave your word to someone that you were going to lie. But now I think you're telling me the truth. I'm glad you told me. It's easier to stop loving someone when you know that you're not loved."

"I didn't tell you that."

"I think you did, Clancy."

"You said that this time I was telling you the truth. You said that you believed me. Can't you believe me if I say that I love you, Phyllis?"

"No," she said simply. Her voice was very tired.

"You begin something one way," I said desperately, "and then it finishes another way. Don't you understand, Phyllis?"

"I understand," she said. "It always finishes another way."

PART ELEVEN

THE HOTEL

WE were back in Manhattan when I told Phyllis about Grischov. It was not a simple thing to tell. In my own small way I had discovered that nothing that existed between the United States and the Soviet Union was either simple or reasonable; it was only by considering two smoking gaps in the tissue of what passed for civilization—one where Moscow had been and the other where New York had been—that I could make a matter of fact thing out of my association with Dmitri Grischov, and now he wanted to see Phyllis and to talk with her. I explained that to her; then I tried to explain that, while in some ways Grischov might appear to be very like myself, in other ways he was very different from myself. No one lives apart from politics, but I had almost succeeded in keeping politics hidden deep in whatever passed for my personality. I suppose I was afraid of politics, which is a not too uncommon attitude in the United States.

"But why should he want to see me?" Phyllis wondered.

"I tried to explain, Phyllis. All of us—we know things and we don't know that we know them."

"I don't know where Alex Horton is," she said slowly.

"If you don't you don't. You haven't any obligations to me and certainly you haven't any to Dmitri Grischov. I told him that I would ask you and that, if you wanted to come, I'd bring you. I didn't promise anything."

"What will he do to me?" Phyllis asked almost abstractly. Her interest had withered away. Her voice was flat and listless.

"Only talk to you. I'll talk to you, he'll talk to you."

"And pick my brain and find something that isn't there, Clancy? I've been picking my own brain. I've been trying to find my mother and to discover why she isn't there, and there aren't any answers, Clancy. I don't have a brain that can be picked at. It's all locked in and today it's all gray and shapeless—formless. I try to think through the gray and to remember things about my mother that will allow me to bring back a time when she was happy. But the trouble is I don't know whether she was ever happy, Clancy. I took her to the theater once I remember, but she didn't seem to know what was happening on the stage or to understand any of it. She was like a locked box that I could never open and now, after what happened, I think that the thing that saddens me the most is knowing that I'll never open that box now—never at all. Or are we all like that, Clancy, locked up and separated from each other—eternally?"

"It's only natural for you to be depressed now," I said.

"What does a man mean when he says that something is only natural, Clancy? Have you ever tried to put yourself in the place of a woman and think the way she thinks?"

"I have tried," I agreed.

"Did it work for you, Clancy? I keep asking myself how you felt when they told you to go up to Knickerbocker and teach a class in physics and make love to a dowdy little teacher called Phyllis Goldmark. That would be a way to save the world. So I wonder whether you felt like a savior, Clancy, or at least it would save a lot of effort and panic, wouldn't it? I mean that if these bombs ever existed. You see I'm not sure they exist; all the thinking is the way a man thinks and, when you come right down to it, Clancy, it's the way a little boy thinks, isn't it? All of you playing at some kind of foolish game of cops and robbers and bombs and threats, you and this Commissioner Comaday and that FBI man you brought up to the house, and poor Alex Horton. You never met him, did you, Clancy?"

"No, I never met him."

"That's a pity—I mean it's a pity that you and your Mr. Comaday and the Mayor and all the other important people you told me about—it's a pity that none of them ever met Alex Horton because, you see, Alex Horton couldn't make a bomb. He's too frightened. That was our bond, Clancy, that was what existed between Alex Horton and myself—a community of fear; when we discovered that it existed in each other, we became very close for awhile. Not close the way I thought that you and I were close, Clancy; it was something else. It had nothing to do with his being a man and my being a woman. He wasn't a man in that sense, but we both knew how to be afraid. We had both of us lived lives that were threaded through with fear—not with danger, Clancy, but with fear. Do you understand what I'm trying to tell you?"

"I think I do."

"But he couldn't make an atom bomb and so I'm not sure that I believe in these bombs of yours at all. I don't know about this Professor Simonovsky in Moscow, but if he was anything like Horton, he couldn't make an atom bomb either. But then if you were to believe that, Clancy, what would become of your mission and the heroics and the fact that Phyllis Goldmark is expendable?"

"I never implied that you were expendable," I said desperately. "That was not any part of it, Phyllis; you know that it wasn't."

"Oh, what do I know, Clancy? I know very little. But still I think I know more than you do. If a person's love is expendable, is that any less important? Or a person's one hope of paradise? When I was a kid, Clancy, my mother and I spent two weeks at a little boarding house in the Catskills. I climbed a mountain and I climbed it all alone. I don't suppose it was much of a mountain, but it was a big adventure for me to climb it all alone. Then when I got to the top and stood there with all the world underneath me, feeling myself just as tall as God, I felt close to paradise. Do you know what I mean, Clancy? I felt the way I felt when I told myself that you loved me."

There was nothing I could say, and I said nothing. I drove downtown, concentrating on the changing lights, on the flow of traffic, on the rain-glistening streets, and trying to absorb myself and all that I was and thought and had ever been into the necessities of a job that had suddenly become aimless and pointless. It is passingly difficult to be a hero, but to be a deflated hero is certainly one of the most difficult things in the world. I was able to be brash and defiant with Comaday, to sneer at a United States senator, to put myself on the same level as the mayor of New York City. I was even able to walk around, knowing that two cretins called Jackie and Mr. Brown were out gunning for me, and tell myself that I didn't care and that I was not going to be intimidated by them. I was a very brave and depressed and desperate man, Thomas Clancy by name, and through all my depression and self-pity I had at least built up a picture of myself that conformed with all the desirable stereotypes that fill the mind of any fourteen-year-old American boy. I wasn't quite certain how Phyllis had managed to deflate it and remove it so simply and gently and without being angry at me and without saying anything that was calculated to hurt me; but she had done this and done it most successfully. Now I would drive downtown to the Biltmore Hotel where Dmitri Grischov had engaged a suite of rooms and he and I would set about extracting from Phyllis's mind information she didn't know she had. That was to be our great coup and through it somehow we would save mankind from Peter Simonovsky and Alex Horton. Only the whole thing had become childish and meaningless and I had reached the point where I thought as little of Grischov as I did of myself.

Phyllis was silent until after we had parked the car and were going into the hotel; and then, curiously and quietly, as if we had been speaking to each other all along, she asked me whether I believed in God.

"Isn't that the kind of question you never ask a person?"

"Not even when you love him, Clancy? And what about your friend, Dmitri Grischov? It would be un-Russian or something of the sort for him, wouldn't it?"

"Do you believe in God, Phyllis?" I said.

"Only if I was convinced that she was a woman," Phyllis replied, smiling slightly. She took my arm as we went into the elevator; her fingers tightened and she looked up at me, still smiling. It was good to see her smile. Something happened to her face when she smiled and it became strange and rare and beautiful. "Clancy," she said to me, "you're a very nice man. You're a brave man, too. I don't want to hurt you."

I shook my head without replying. Inside of me, I had given up and for me it was all over. I was not a cop any more—I was not anything any more. It would take some time before I was able to resign from my profession and get out of it. There was still the job to be done and to be finished with, but that was a

matter of time, not of perception. The changes inside of me had
already taken place.

We walked to the suite that Grischov had engaged. It had been
his idea to take a place in a hotel. My own apartment was not fit
to bring anyone into and he felt that the building the Soviet had
on Park Avenue would intrude with too many factors not to the
point and not to the problem. A hotel suite was impersonal. The
three of us would enter it on an equal basis—or at least that's
what he thought and I saw no reason to disagree with him.

He was not insensitive, Mr. Grischov. When he opened the
door for us he examined both of us quickly and penetratingly
and he drew his conclusions just as quickly. He went out of his
way to be warm and gentle to Phyllis and as I watched him I
wondered that anyone brought up in the place where he had been
brought up and in the way he had been brought up could be
so charming and thoughtful—and even courtly. I made up my
mind that I would ask him about it some day—in fact, I had
decided that when the time and the place were appropriate,
Grischov and I would sit down and have a long talk.

Right now there were other things and I let Grischov play it as
he had planned it. He had ordered a tray of sandwiches and a pot
of hot coffee. The table was set, the chairs drawn up to it, and
he insisted that we must all have something to eat before we
went into the serious part of our discussion. Phyllis barely
touched the food, but I found that I was hungry and that I was
bolting enough food to fill my stomach. I was nervous and tired
and I had lost my last shred of pride, which was the worst thing
of all. I ate too much and too quickly and then I felt heavy and
sick. Like Phyllis, Grischov hardly touched the food. He was
telling Phyllis about his wife, who lived in Moscow. He had
never told me about his wife or about his children, and it had
never occurred to me that a man like Grischov had such appen-
dages, but at least it forced me to contemplate what my own feelings would have been had the circumstances been reversed, considering that I were in Moscow and I had left a wife and children
in New York. The normal reaction was to comfort myself with
the proposition that Russians really had no feelings compatible
with mine or comparable to mine, and I suppose that to some
extent I did this. I left them sitting at the table, talking about
Moscow and Leningrad and Soviet physics, a new telescope they
were building in the Soviet Union, and I walked over to the window and looked down. Far, far below me the traffic scurried

north and south with distant and senseless abandon. God was a man, after all, whatever Phyllis proposed, and I could easily enough picture myself as God looking down at the random anthill of human existence; and I tried to know honestly and truly whether the fate, real or unreal, hanging over this city, moved me in any profound manner. Phyllis had given me a burden of truth to carry and the truth was that I did not really know what I felt or feared or dreamed or hoped. I had been in a war where bombs were dropped on the cities and the habitations of men; but somehow or other I could not associate my memories of war and bombing and death and mass mayhem and mass murder with the effect of an atom bomb melting this city and these streets and all they contained into hot and formless insanity. The atom bomb was an abstraction; and for the first time with the help of this abstraction, man's existence had departed from all the strictures of reality.

I turned back to Phyllis and Grischov. They had left the table. Phyllis was sitting in an armchair, her legs stretched out, her hands folded in her lap, her head back and her eyes closed. Howsoever he had done it, somehow Grischov had won her confidence, had enabled her to relax. Now he sat on the couch, his feet drawn up and his arms clasped around his knees, nodding at Phyllis and telling her,

"Just go on, Miss Goldmark, because you see there's nothing you can say about Alex Horton that isn't important."

"The trouble is I know nothing that is important."

"Or you know everything that is important. For example, you've eaten lunch with him—perhaps you've eaten dinner with him. What did he like to eat?"

"He couldn't eat rich foods," Phyllis remembered. "There was something wrong with his stomach. He always felt it was a part of the radiation sickness. I remember that in the cafeteria he would order poached eggs on toast. That always annoyed the women behind the counter. It wasn't that they minded short-order things, it was the poached eggs."

"No rich foods at all?" Grischov smiled. "No stew, not even a piece of roast meat?"

Phyllis shook her head. "Very often it would be just tea and dry toast."

"Such an existence I don't envy," Grischov sighed. "I don't know what is worse, to have to eat the food they cook in this country or not to be able to eat it. What do you think, Clancy?"

"I ate in a Russian restaurant once," I said. "It was no bargain."

"The worldliness of Americans," Grischov shrugged. "Everything withers under capitalism, including the taste buds."

He had managed to make Phyllis smile. She opened her eyes and sat forward, watching Grischov curiously.

"Did he like the theater?" Grischov asked.

"We went twice. No, I don't think he liked it. I think he was bored."

"Movies?"

"He didn't like moving pictures—moving pictures frightened him. You must understand what I mean. I tried to explain it to Mr. Clancy. He was filled with fear. I tried to tell Mr. Clancy how that was something that brought us together. It was an odd kind of relationship."

She looked at Grischov tentatively and he shrugged and observed that most relationships were odd relationships. "Here I am," he said, "a policeman, a kind of Soviet G man, or secret service man or brain washer." He looked at me. "That's the way you think of me, isn't it, Clancy? I'm a brain washer. I may be even more sinister than that. And I marry a nurse in a hospital, a gentle sweet little woman very much like yourself, Miss Goldmark, who has nothing but disdain for the work of a policeman. Yet our marriage manages to exist, even if I am away from home so much. But what did he wish for, Miss Goldmark?"

"I don't understand."

"I mean Horton. We all wish for something. I wish for a beautiful dacha in a suburb of Moscow. Clancy here—I don't know. Maybe Clancy wishes to be a police commissioner, like Mr. Comaday. You, Miss Goldmark, well I wouldn't dare even speculate about what you wish for, but a man like Alex Horton, what did he wish for? What did he want?"

Phyllis thought about it a long time before she answered. Grischov got up and poured himself another cup of coffee. He drank his coffee sweet. He put four teaspoons of sugar into it and stirred it and couldn't resist the temptation to make some observation about the United States having a corner on all the best coffee in the world.

"But you will grow better coffee in Russia than they do in Brazil," I assured him.

"Give us time, Mr. Clancy, give us time." He drank his coffee, watching Phyllis, who had still not answered his question.

"Consider Hitler," Grischov said, "he wished to rule the world.

On the other hand, you had a President in your own country. Now
he is retired and wishes no more than to play golf."

"What does Khrushchev wish for?" I asked caustically.

"Easy, Mr. Clancy. I will not allow you to trap me into a
position that could have such dire consequences for me. On the
other hand, at the risk of being quoted, I can say that I have a
little daughter of six years, who wished nothing in the world
more than for me to bring her back from America a very large and
beautiful doll with hair that you can wash and eyes that open and
close. She claims that our Russian dolls are inferior, but of course
she's only a child. All this is silly, is it not, Miss Goldmark? But
the fact remains that everyone wishes for something. It defines
us as human beings. If we are angry at someone, we say that he is
greedy. If we respect him, we say that he is ambitious. But even a
saint cannot be accused of wanting nothing. The saint is very
ambitious for his sainthood, isn't he, Clancy?"

"I wouldn't know."

"But Horton, Miss Goldmark, what did he wish for? What was
he ambitious for? What did he want—wealth, power, notoriety?
Did he want a great laboratory in which he could make all sorts
of wonderful contraptions? Or did he want women? What did he
want, Miss Goldmark? Try to think."

Phyllis looked at us strangely and shook her head again.
"Nothing," she said, "there was really nothing he wanted."

Grischov put down his cup and walked back and forth across
the room. "That is impossible, isn't it?"

"He wanted nothing," Phyllis repeated. And I said,

"It's not impossible, Grischov. He was sick. You don't admit in
your country that a man's soul can be sick and dying inside him.
That presupposes a soul. But she answered your question. Horton
wanted nothing."

"It makes no sense," Grischov muttered.

"It makes more sense than you think," I told him. "He wanted
nothing. That's a curious ambition, but don't throw it away."

We continued. An hour passed and then an hour and a half.
We were all becoming tense and ragged and I think that Phyllis
was at the point of tears. If it had been me, I would have stopped.
But Grischov would not stop. He kept picking at her, clawing at
her, pulling bits and pieces of Alex Horton out of her mind. I
will admit that I would not have thought such an evocation to be
possible. Bit by bit, Alex Horton came into focus for us—as if
Grischov, like an untalented but dogged and persistent sculptor,

were shaping a formless mass of clay there in the room in front of us. He picked through emotions, habits, phrases, clothes, odors, fancies, and finally he had come to happiness.

Again Phyllis shook her head and again Grischov fought it through, insisting that there must have been moments of happiness for Horton. He said to her, "Think, Miss Goldmark, I know this has been a hard day for you; I know that this has been a terrible day for you. Just a little more. Soon we'll stop. But now think; he must have been happy. There must be a moment in the life of every human being when he's happy."

"Even in your country, Grischov?" I put in.

"Even in my country, Clancy, people are happy. It defines them; it distinguishes them. An animal is content or he is discontent; an animal is not happy. We go through our lives being unhappy, but the unhappiness must be based on some flicker of revelation, of joy."

"I don't see where this can lead to," Phyllis said. "I want to help you, but I don't see where it is going. What possible difference could it make? What will you do with it? Alex Horton was a sad man. He was filled with sadness. I know what you want, but how are we going to find it? If I remember that he was happy?"

I went over to her and sat on the arm of her chair and touched her hair, and suddenly she looked up at me and smiled. That was better. Grischov walked over to the window and looked down. I whispered to Phyllis,

"I'm jealous of Horton. That's the truth, Phyllis."

She took my hand and said, "Oh no, no, Clancy. No, believe me, in all the times I was with him, there was only one moment when I felt close to him—when I felt anything from him. We were walking across town and we came to that big place, that big section near the park where they are tearing the buildings down—where it looks like a whole part of the city had been bombed out and only wasteland left—you know where that is, don't you, Clancy?"

I nodded.

"We walked there and it was evening and somehow I had the feeling that Horton was alive, as if that terrible sense of a wasteland had reacted upon him in terms of its opposite and he was alive and he said something to me and I felt this warmth for him, closeness to him—only that time, Clancy——"

Grischov had leaped away from the window and stalked over to us and now he bent over Phyllis and snapped at her, "He was alive and he was happy, wasn't he? You walked in something that looked like a wasteland and he became alive and was happy. You said that, didn't you?"

"I suppose so," Phyllis whispered hesitantly.

"Why there? Why there?" Grischov insisted.

"I don't know," Phyllis said.

"Think—think!" Grischov insisted. "I'm only asking you to think!"

It was the last straw and too much. Her face quivered and the tears began to flow and I said to Grischov, "It's enough, Grischov. For God's sake, it's enough. Leave her alone. Leave her alone."

I let her cry then. It had been building up all day and she wept loosely and easily like a little girl. Then I gave her my handkerchief and she dried her eyes and told us that now she would be all right.

PART TWELVE

THE TENEMENT

WE left the hotel and took my car and drove uptown. The three of us together in the front; the three of us strangely quiet and tense and perhaps a little somber too. The rain had stopped and the wild March wind tore the gray sky into ribbons of clouds. It was late afternoon now.

"I'm glad the rain stopped," Phyllis said.

I knew what she meant. "I like the weather in March. It changes in the course of the day—it can rain and snow and then the sun can shine and then it can rain again—all in one day."

"Like ourselves?" Phyllis said.

I shrugged and asked Grischov what was March in the Soviet Union and he replied sourly that he supposed March was March. We spoke a few more words about the weather but not about anything else until we were at the University. Then we agreed on a place for us to meet fifteen minutes later. Phyllis went to her office to freshen up. I took Grischov with me to the little hole in the wall that had served me as an office.

As we walked through the corridors of the old building, Grischov glanced around him curiously and reflected upon the incongruity of a policeman who could teach physics. I observed that nothing was as simple as we like to make it out to be, and Grischov looked at me shrewdly and said,

"There are times when I could almost bring myself to like you, Clancy."

"I have felt something of the sort about you, I must admit," I nodded.

We met Vanpelt in the hallway there. He was coming from his office and I suppose he would have evaded me if he could, but we were caught in the same corridor and so he strode past me with a defiant stare. It made no difference. Phyllis had left too little of my pride for any of the remnant to be affected by Vanpelt.

In my office I went through the messages that had been left for me and found a note to call Comaday. I dialed Centre Street and asked for him, and when he was on the phone he said to me, with that harsh annoyance that was part of his nature,

"Where the hell are you, Clancy, and where is Phyllis Goldmark? I don't like this. You go off on your own in whatever half-baked direction takes your fancy and, as far as you're concerned, we don't exist."

"You exist," I said.

"Thank you," Comaday spluttered, "I am charmed and delighted. What about Miss Goldmark?"

"She's with me."

"I don't want her uncovered, Clancy, not for one moment. I want to put a man on you as well. Do you understand? Where can we meet?"

"I don't know," I said. "Give me a little time, Commissioner. I don't want to take her home and I don't know yet where she'll spend the evening. Let me call you back."

"In how long?"

"In about an hour," I said, "it shouldn't be much more than an hour."

Grischov regarded me with a raised brow as I put down the phone. He was checking a gun—a small, efficient-looking automatic of a type I had not seen before. Now, as he replaced the clip, he said,

"That was the Commissioner?"

"Put the gun away. Suppose someone walks in here. What the devil are you thinking about, Grischov? What does this add up to for you?"

He shrugged and shook his head.

"If I was in Moscow," I said, "would they let me walk around with a gun?"

Grischov put the automatic into the side pocket of his jacket and replied impatiently, "Sometimes, Clancy, you make me sick."

"This is no time for either of us to make the other sick. Or if we do, let's keep it to ourselves."

Grischov nodded, rose, and put on his hat and coat. I was wearing an old raincoat which I threw over my shoulder. We went out of the building and walked over to Amsterdam Avenue and stood on the corner and had time, each of us, for a single cigarette before Phyllis joined us. Grischov managed to conceal his irritation and when Phyllis came he greeted her with a smile and we arranged ourselves on either side of her. She took our arms as we walked downtown bearing eastward, and she said,

"I like both of you, but liking you has a bad reaction on me. It makes me a little sad and I want to cry and then I want to laugh. Where are we going now? What do you expect to find?"

"Horton," I told her foolishly. Grischov shrugged and said,

"Whatever we find, Miss Goldmark, maybe we can take your mind away a little from all the troubles you have and all that you've been through today. So we'll pretend that we're just walking in the early evening with a beautiful young lady."

I silently thanked Grischov for that. Phyllis squeezed my arm and we walked on. Below 110th Street we turned east to Columbus Avenue and walked south and then there it was—what we were looking for; the wilderness and wasteland of buildings going up, buildings being wrecked, buildings half torn down and skeletons of buildings, block after block of piled rubble, the whole gigantic housing development dwarfing one's imagination—a city within a city being destroyed and reconstituted.

I looked at Grischov and he was responding to the sight. His eyes gleamed strangely as they wandered over that tangle of broken houses and new beginnings. He said to Phyllis, "Was this the way you walked that day with Horton?"

"We were across the street," Phyllis said.

"Take us the way you went then."

We crossed the street. Phyllis clung to my arm a little more tightly. We walked south again and then we turned into a side street. Here, among the litter of half-destroyed buildings, three old tenements still stood side by side, boarded up and isolated.

"Like so many other people in my country," Grischov said, "my first feeling for America is jealousy. I admit that we've done things. We've put rockets up where you've never dreamed of putting them but in all the world there's no one who ever built the way you do. My God, how you can build! You tear down a city and build it up again. With us a war destroys a city and it's a tragedy. But you take a mile of city and do to it what only a war could do and, while you're wrecking it, you're building it again."

"I often wonder," I said, "what you mean, Grischov, when you say 'my God'. Is it just an expression?"

"I learned your language, Clancy. It's full of God. That's the way you shaped it."

"Why do you two keep tearing at each other?" Phyllis demanded. "Have they succeeded in making both of you so sick that you must perpetually fight your little war?"

It was the last thing in the world that I had expected her to say, and we stopped there and both Grischov and I looked at her and then at each other. Then I looked at Phyllis again and I realized that I was meeting her newly, the way you meet a stranger. I was being introduced to her. Her eyes met mine, as if they were saying to me, "Your job is over, Clancy. You can look at me now—no more duties and no more obligations."

"What you said about Horton before," Grischov wanted to know, "it was here, Miss Goldmark?"

Phyllis nodded. "It was here."

His voice soft and different and wary, Grischov said to me, "What do you think, Clancy?"

"It's a long shot, but why not?"

"Do you think that Miss Goldmark should leave us now?"

I looked at Phyllis again and then I shook my head. "No," I said, "I think that she stays with us unless——"

"I want to stay with you," Phyllis said.

"Then suppose we try the center one first," I suggested, nodding at the three lonely boarded-up tenements across the street from where we were. "I suppose the power's turned off. You wouldn't have a flashlight with you, would you, Grischov?"

He shook his head and I made some observation on what kind of cops we both were. Then we went across the street. In front of the tenement Phyllis squeezed my arm and whispered to me,

"Thank you, Clancy."

Grischov had gone on ahead a few paces. He was on the little stoop, trying the front door.

"For what, Phyllis?" I asked her. "Only tell me for what."

"For the whole day, Clancy. I couldn't have lived through today without you. I don't care how it began, Clancy, no matter how it began, I love you very much."

"I love you," I said. "I had to resign from the police force and stop being a cop before I could say that and have it make any sense. That's what happened today. So far it only happened in my own mind. But I talked to myself about it and I made my decision. Even if there was more time than there is now—even if there was all the time in the world, I wouldn't know how to make it clear to you, Phyllis."

"You have made it clear, Clancy."

"I love you. Do you believe me?"

"I believe you."

Then we went up the stairs to join Grischov, who explained that the door was locked. We were all of us talking in whispers now. I don't know why. It was after five o'clock and the workmen had gone and there was no one in sight in that whole broken world of destruction and construction except the three of us; yet we talked in whispers, oppressed by the conclusions we had drawn and somehow forgetful of the fact that we had spun this whole involved fancy out of thin air. It did not matter that we had spun it out of thin air. We had taken a line, a path, and followed it to a conclusion.

The upper part of the door was glass. I took out my gun, used it to break one of the panes, and then reached inside and unlocked the door. And then we went in. It was an old-law tenement, the kind of building in which the apartments long, long ago took on the name of railroad flats, and through all my youth and growing years had been called that and nothing else. Still speaking in whispers, I explained about that to Grischov, that there were two apartments on a floor, each apartment stretching through the length of the building from the street in front to the courtyard in the rear, a string of tiny rooms linked together in darkness and squalor.

"That means," said Grischov, "that there are no windows in the center rooms."

"No, there are windows—on either side of the building there is a narrow courtyard. If my memory serves me, there might just be a room without a window, but the front windows are boarded up anyway. Perhaps not the real windows. We're acting like damned fools, Grischov. We should have brought flashlights."

"I guess so, but we're here."

I nodded and led the way forward into the dark hallway. It was filled with the stink of wet plaster and ruin and abandonment and all the lingering, fetid smells of the poverty and the airlessness of half a century.

"Take the left hand apartment," I said to Grischov. "I'll take the one on the right." I whispered to Phyllis to stay close to me. "Close enough so that I can feel you," I said. I tried a doorway and it moved under my hand. A ground floor apartment. It was almost pitch black. I stumbled over a piece of broken furniture and heard rats scurrying in the darkness. Phyllis's hand clenched on my arm and her whisper came in my ear,

"It's all right, Clancy, I'm all right."

Toward the rear of the apartment there was a flicker of gray light from the air shaft windows and from the rear windows which, as I expected, were not boarded over. The rear of the apartment was empty of anything except filth and abandoned rags and broken furniture. Back in the hall, Grischov was waiting for me, a shapeless figure in the semidarkness.

"Nothing," I said. And he said, "Nothing, Clancy." I led the way upstairs to the second floor and once again we each of us examined an apartment. When we rejoined each other in the almost pitch blackness of the hallway, Phyllis whispered,

"It makes no sense, Clancy. It's evening now and it's getting dark outside. You can't do anything here without light."

We went up to the third floor, feeling our way, step by step. Again Grischov took the apartment on the left, Phyllis and I the one on the right. But this time the door of the apartment was locked. I moved the handle and tried to force it, but it would not give. "There's another door in the rear," I whispered to Phyllis. I held her hand as I felt my way through the black hallway to the rear door. It was also locked. Guided by the wall, we felt our way to the front door and waited for Grischov. After a moment or two, I heard the shuffle of his feet as he made his way toward us in the darkness.

"Grischov?" I said softly.

"Nothing in there, Clancy."

"This one's locked."

"What kind of locks are they, Clancy?" he wanted to know.

"I can't say. These buildings have been standing for sixty, seventy years. They keep changing the locks."

"Let me feel it," Grischov said. I guided his hands toward the door and then heard the soft rustle of his fingers caressing the lock. It was very still in that hallway. We could hear the creaking, the contracting and the expanding that is a part of any very old house. We heard rats moving. I heard the hoarse breathing of Phyllis as she pressed close to me there. Grischov whispered into my ear,

"I think I can open it, Clancy. I'll try, anyway." I heard the jangle of his keys as he removed them from his pocket. "Skeleton keys and all. You never miss a trick, do you, Grischov?" His soft laugh was reassuring. We were all three of us very tense, and the scraping of his keys as he tried one after another in the lock sounded loud enough to arouse anyone in that old stinking ruin of a house. "This does it," he whispered. He turned the knob and the door opened. I led the way into the blackness, striking a match. It was the first match that any of us had struck and it flared with a brilliance that hurt my eyes. The room was empty except for a rat that shot past us out of the door we had just opened. The match burned out. I struck a second match and led the way toward the first connecting room. The door to this room was closed. When I opened it, a different smell touched my nostrils. The tenement had been full of cold dead smells but this smell was alive and threaded through with decay.

Phyllis must have sensed it too because she pressed closer to me. I took my gun out of my shoulder holster and dropped it into the side pocket of my jacket. My match burned out. Grischov lit another match. His matches were better than mine for illumination—the long wooden safety matches that are called torches. In one corner of this room on the floor there was a little pile of books. They had been eaten and chewed by rats. Grischov pointed to them. Phyllis stepped over and picked up one of the books, and I lit another match. It was a copy of Tolstoy's *War and Peace*, dirty, damp, and in part eaten by the rats. She opened it and there, on the inside of the cover, by the light of our matches, we read the name "Alex Horton". We looked at each other, all three of us, stared silently at each other until the heat of the burning matches caused us to drop them and plunged the room into darkness again.

I led the way into the next room, which was filled with a vague twilight that filtered in through the air shaft window. This had once been the kitchen of the apartment. There was no need for matches here. Paper that had once enclosed loaves of bread was scattered in fragments across the floor. Rats had eaten the bread. On one of the kitchen cupboards two cans of beans stood. There were two aluminium pots, one with some beans at the bottom of it and the other with a sour trace of canned soup in it. For some reason, the rats had not gotten to them. In the cupboard, behind the doors of the cupboard, we found four boxes of salted crackers. On the stove there was a large pot with about an inch of water in the bottom of it. Also in the cupboard were some cans of fruit juice and some bottles of ginger ale.

Now we went through to the rear of the flat. Here again there was enough light from the rear windows to enable us to make out what the room held. That we found Horton there did not surprise us; at this point it would have only surprised us if we had not found him there. He lay in one corner of the room, his back against the wall, a dirty and torn quilt pulled over him. His eyes were closed and he had a bad cut on one cheek, where, as we learned, a rat had bitten him. But there was no atom bomb in the room—no contraption of shotguns or gadgets or pellets of Uranium 235—nothing but filth, dirt, disorder, and, in one corner, what was left of Alex Horton under a ragged quilt.

PART THIRTEEN

ALEX HORTON

OF all the things that happened in that dark and rotten tenement building, the most amazing was not the discovery of Alex Horton, but the process that took place in Phyllis—a process I hardly know how to describe. It was a process of change, of growth, of saturation, of decision, of equanimity—and, I suppose, of other things too. Perhaps it was something that had been happening to her for many years. It builds up and it saturates and then suddenly it appears. It may also be that some such change was taking place in myself—I don't know; or at least I think I knew better from watching it and from watching her, what went on with Phyllis.

Now, while Grischov and I stood transfixed where we were, it was Phyllis who calmly and confidently went forward to Horton. She knelt beside him and raised his head. He was filthy and emaciated and his face was covered with a growth of whiskers and be-grimed with dried blood. He was full of the wretched smell of sickness and of his own decay; but this in no way deterred Phyllis or indeed appeared to affect her in any manner.

She called over her shoulder to us, "Find something for him to drink."

Grischov went back into the kitchen. I struck more matches. The faint light in the room was fading now, but here and there, perched on the wide ancient molding where the rats could not get at them, were stumps of candles. I lit four of these stumps, and since the room was a very small room, the candlelight gave enough illumination for us to do what we had to do.

Grischov returned with a can of fruit juice that he had opened and a glass that he was wiping clean with his handkerchief. He poured some of the fruit juice into the glass and handed it to Phyllis, who very gently and carefully fed it, sip by sip, to Horton. I would have moved in to help her—perhaps to raise Horton to a sitting position—but when Grischov saw me start, he motioned me back and shook his head. Horton's eyes were open, but they were glazed and without focus. He was very thirsty. God knows how long it had been since he had anything to eat or drink, and, though he could only sip, there was a ravenous need in the way he finished the juice. Grischov filled the glass again.

Phyllis raised Horton's head and said to him very gently, "It's all right, Alex. I am Phyllis Goldmark. It's all right now, Alex, everything is going to be all right."

His eyes found her and fixed on her and stared for a while in perplexity at the wavering candlelit image of her face.

"Phyllis Goldmark," she repeated slowly, "your good friend, Alex. You remember me."

"Yes, I remember you," he said suddenly and very clearly.

"You're going to be all right now. I'm here with good friends. They're good friends of mine and they're good friends of yours, Alex. Do you understand me?"

"I understand you," he said, his voice acquiescent and compliant, like the voice of a little child.

"How do you feel?"

"I feel very bad, Phyllis. I think I'm dying."

She handed the glass back to Grischov and touched Horton's forehead. I looked at her inquiringly, and she nodded as if to indicate that he was hot and feverish. "You're not dying, Alex; you're going to be all right. We'll take you to a hospital where they'll take care of you and then everything will be all right."

"No, I'm dying; I've been dying here for days. The rats were eating me. I felt them eating my face."

With my lips but silently I framed the words for Phyllis, "Ask him—ask him now." She shook her head. "Ask him," I insisted again, "you must. Ask him now."

Phyllis sighed and nodded. Horton never took his clouded, bloodshoot eyes from her face. "Alex," she said, "you must tell me now—where is the bomb?"

"The bomb?" he whispered.

"The atom bomb, Alex. The bomb that you made. You made an atom bomb here in New York. Professor Simonovsky made an atom bomb in Moscow. Do you remember? Do you understand me?"

He shook his head slightly.

"Do you know who Professor Simonovsky is?" Her voice was soft and with no note of alarm or anxiety—with no implication of any threat.

"I know Simonovsky," he answered weakly.

"Do you remember the letters you wrote? You said that you were going to make a bomb. Do you remember those letters, Alex?"

"I remember the letters." His lips trembled, whether in a smile or out of nervous hysteria I don't know, and he repeated, "I remember, Phyllis, but there was no bomb."

"You said you were going to make a bomb," she insisted. "Simonovsky said he was going to make a bomb."

"That is how we planned it," Horton whispered, "but not ever to make the bomb. We didn't have to make the bomb. All we had to do was to disappear. It was the threat that counted, Phyllis, don't you see, not the bomb."

"But the uranium was missing."

He was silent for awhile. He closed his eyes, and then lay there for a little while in silence. Neither Grischov nor I moved nor did we utter a sound. Phyllis crouched over him, holding up his head, waiting patiently, sitting with his head nestled in her arms as gently as if he were a little child and she was his mother. Then Horton opened his eyes and asked her, "The uranium was missing?"

"It was missing here," Phyllis said. "It was missing in Russia."

Horton smiled a real smile. It was the only time I ever saw him smile. "We counted on that," he said. "The way they do things— some would have to be missing. They do things loosely. You tell them that something is missing and then they'll find that it's missing. But there isn't any bomb, Phyllis. There never was a bomb— not here—not in Moscow."

Now she pleaded with him and again in her tone was the quality of a mother who pleads with a child. "Alex, tell me the truth.

Please, you must tell me the truth. It's very important for you to tell me the truth—the most important thing in the world. Where is the bomb?"

"No bomb. I've been here all the time, Phyllis, here in this apartment, day and night. I never left it. How could I make a bomb? Where would I put it? I never left this apartment and now I'm never going to leave it. I'm dying, Phyllis. Can't you see that I'm dying? I'm all eaten away, inside and outside. I'm glad you're here."

Phyllis nodded at him. There was no change in her face, but even in that dim candlelight I could see the tears form and well out of her eyes and run down across her cheeks.

"I didn't want to die alone."

"You're not going to die, Alex."

His eyes closed again and, after a moment or two, Phyllis lowered his head gently, rose, and came over to us. "He's very sick, I think," she said softly, "he's very hot."

"We have to get him out of here and get him to the hospital. That's the main thing now," I told them, "to get him to the hospital. We don't know how sick he is or whether he's going to live or die."

"Do you believe him?" Grischov asked me strangely.

"About his dying?"

"About the bomb," Grischov said.

"Yes, I believe him—or maybe I was ready to believe him. I have felt it from the beginning, that it would be this way."

Grischov shrugged. "Whatever the truth is, the main thing now is to get him out of here." And then a sharp, flat voice from the entrance into the kitchen snapped at us,

"I agree with you. That's the main thing to get him out of here."

We turned to face the voice. It was Maximilian Gomez. He stood in the door of the room, a heavy Luger in his hand and leveled at us. He was no longer the smiling, urbane, and soft-voiced sugar diplomat whom we had met in Great Neck. He was hard now, cold as ice and full of the triumph of the moment. As he must have seen it, the whole world was just almost—actually almost in the palm of his hand, and, as with Sodom and Gomorrah, here were two great cities that were his to wrap in columns of flame. He felt like God and spoke as he felt. He was tall and handsome and virile and triumphant—and filled with hatred and malevolence and concern for the great property of power that was about to be his. He was also honourable. He had no obligations, for the one hundred fifty thousand dollars he had paid to make me his leader into darkness had been declared forfeit. I had betrayed him, he had not betrayed me. And so his appearance was in summation and in action. But the realization of this was not nearly so long as it takes to put it down. When you make a story or a film out of such a thing it is full of conversation and dickering over the point of a gun, but when life becomes a little more of a nightmare than anyone can concoct, the gun finishes the decision, it does not begin it. I knew that and Grischov knew it; and when we turned around, we did what we had to do and there was no thought and no hesitancy and no more time lost than the fractions of seconds that disappear into the smoke of motion.

I flung Phyllis aside and dived for the wall. Grischov threw himself onto the floor, firing through the jacket of his coat, then rolling over and crimped against the wall and burning shot after shot through his clothes at Gomez. Gomez lost because he had two targets and it took him that fraction of a second that is life or death to choose. I shot first through my jacket and then, rolling on the floor, clawed my gun out. But Gomez was already staggering when my gun came up. Gomez fired twice. Grischov must have shot at him four times. I fired once through my pocket—the second time a wild shot and the third and the fourth time into Gomez's falling body. Gomez fell on his face and, when we got up and went to him and turned his body over, we saw that he had been hit five times, twice in the head and three times in the body.

Horton had fainted. He lay motionless where we had left him, his eyes closed. Phyllis stood pressed against the wall where I had flung her, breathing hoarsely and staring with wide open eyes and horror and disbelief at Gomez's body.

I went into the kitchen and locked the kitchen door on the inside. Then I felt my way through to the front of the house and turned the bolt on the front door. On the lower floors the windows had been boarded over, but when I felt for the boards here in the front room of the apartment, I discovered that the windows were covered only with drawn shades. I raised one of these shades and looked down into the street. It was nighttime now—a night of moonlight and starlight in this little wasteland in the heart of Manhattan, and on the street in front of the house I saw three of them standing. I recognized Jackie, the all-American forty-year-old boy. He stood in front of the house, heavy-set, large, thick, and ugly. One of the others might have been his companion,

Mr. Brown, but they were all of a piece—thugs, gunmen, hood-lums, hired guns and paid to kill and waiting there to kill. I made my way back to the rear of the apartment. Phyllis hadn't moved. Grischov stood at a rear window and motioned for me to join him. I went over to him and he pointed. In the rubble behind the house were two more of them, standing and looking up at us. I don't think they could have seen us—they just stood there and watched the building and waited to know what the gunshots portended.

There was a noise at the door of the apartment which led into the hallway from the back room. Someone tried the handle of the door and then, from the outside, a body pressed its weight against the door. Grischov took his gun from his scorched and burned pocket, leveled it thoughtfully at the door, seeking a place, and then just as thoughtfully and carefully pulled the trigger. Phyllis cried out as the sound of the shot thundered in the little room and outside, but not less clear for the closed door; we heard the man scream and heard the sound of his body as it fell.

Hard as ice and cold as ice, Grischov turned to me, looked at his gun, pulled out the clip, and thrust it back. "I have no cartridges, Clancy," he said, "do you?" I shook my head and spun the cylinder of my revolver. "Two shots left," I replied.

"Mine holds seven," Grischov said. "Two shots left to match yours. We are a couple of fine cops, Clancy, you and me. No lights, no cartridges, no telephone, and no way out. What do we deserve, Clancy?"

"They'll fire me," I said. My hand which held the revolver was trembling. "I suppose you'll be sent to Siberia or shot or something of the sort."

"Something of the sort," Grischov shrugged, and went over to Gomez and took his automatic. Quickly and expertly he went through Gomez's pockets. There were no cartridges there. Grischov removed the clip from the big automatic.

"How many?" I asked him.

"Five," he said. "Two in my gun—that makes seven—two in your revolver, nine all together."

"What are you?" Phyllis whispered. "Tell me what are you and what are you made of to stand there and count bullets like that? Alex is dying; you've killed two men. What kind of terrible games do you play, Clancy?"

Grischov shook his head. "The games of the world we live in,

Miss Goldmark. All the pretty games of the twentieth century. What should we do, Miss Goldmark? They're waiting out there. They're in the hall and they're outside in the street and they're waiting in back of the house. What should we do? Can you tell us what we should do?"

Phyllis stared at him without replying. I walked over to Grischov and said to him, "Give me Gomez's gun, Grischov. One of us has to get out of here and get through them."

Grischov pushed me away. "Not you, Clancy."

"I can do it better, Grischov."

"Like hell you can. This is my game, Clancy. I was trained for it."

"You weren't trained for it, Grischov," I said evenly. "You know damned well what is the case with you."

"You tell me," Grischov growled at me.

"Sure, I'll tell you. You'll go back to that goddamned house of yours on Park Avenue and you'll tell them what Horton said and you'll tell them that there's no bomb—not here and not in Moscow—and then they'll sweat you because they won't believe you."

"Will they believe you?" Grischov cried.

"They won't believe you and they'll sweat you and they'll twist and tear every nerve and muscle in your body. And you'll say that there was no bomb and still they won't believe you. And they'll give you a dose of all the ways that man ever devised to make men say what they don't want to say."

"You're a fool," Grischov snarled, "a stupid fool. You're filled up with your own lies and your own crazy thoughts. Now listen to me, Clancy, don't argue with me. Listen to me. I'll go out the front door of the apartment. I'll make it downstairs. You got two shots in your gun. You cover me from the window. Don't argue— I tell you there's no time to argue. Only don't let Horton die. You hear me, Miss Goldmark?" he said, turning to Phyllis, "Don't let him die. We can't have political discussions now. This is a trap we never made. Now cover me, Clancy."

Phyllis was watching both of us, weeping silently and silently shaking her head. Grischov put his automatic in his pocket, hefted Gomez's big Luger in his right hand, and then led the way through to the front of the apartment. At the door there he whispered to me,

"Bolt the door behind me. Now give me your hand, Clancy."

He passed the Luger into his other hand and we clasped hands there in the darkness, in the pit of black in which we neither of us existed or had being except in the sound of our breathing and in the flesh of our hands clasped together. His face close to mine, he whispered to me, "The hell with them, Clancy. The hell with all of them. The hell with their lousy world and their bombs and their politics. You and me, Clancy, we had a little bit of something else, didn't we?"

"We did," I replied chokingly.

"A little bit of what used to be and what maybe will be again, Clancy." He was proud of his Americanisms, that man Grischov. "Be good," he said to me.

"Easy," I said.

Then he was out of the apartment and I closed and bolted the door behind him.

I went to the front window and forced it open, raising it as high as I could. I was doing that when the Luger thundered on the stairs outside. And then I leveled my revolver through the window and prayed for my arm to stop shaking.

Grischov leaped out of the front of the house. I hadn't expected him that way. I hadn't dreamed that he would be so fast, that he would move with the wild agility of an animal. He came out of the front of the house in long, leaping strides. And as Jackie, who was dead ahead of him, raced toward him, Grischov dropped to the pavement, rolled over, came to a stop, and shot Jackie. The other two men were firing as they converged on Grischov, but you can't move or run and hit anything at the same time if you're using a pistol. I used my left hand to steady my right hand against the side of the window jamb and I aimed carefully and fired carefully. My first shot missed. My second shot brought down the small, thin man, who might have been Mr. Brown. Grischov got the third one, but now they were shooting at him from the hallway down below. Grischov staggered to his feet, fell, crawled on. Two men came out of the house down below and a third man came around the end of the group of three houses and ran down the middle of the deserted street toward Grischov. I flung my empty revolver at them and then they converged on Grischov and they kept shooting at him until he was dead—dead and filled with death. There were three at first, and then four and then five —all of them in a circle around Grischov and shooting at him. And I stood in the room upstairs with my face against the dirty window jamb, weeping and praying and feeling myself fill up with the sickness of waste and death.

It was then that the police cars came with their lights and their howling sirens to scatter what remained of Gomez's hoodlums and to pursue them across the broken wasteland of the project—first a single squad car, then a second, and then Comaday's big black limousine.

But it was too late.

I walked back through the apartment. Phyllis had been kneeling beside Horton, and now she rose to face me and told me that Horton was dead.

"Grischov too," I said.

Everything began to drain out of me now. I was becoming emptier and emptier. I walked over to Horton and lifted the quilt. One of the two shots that Gomez fired had found him and he lay there in peace now and at long last, a Luger bullet in his chest. I drew the dirty quilt up over his face and then I went over to Phyllis. There was nothing to say and nothing that I could say. I looked at her and, after a moment, she took my hand. Now the two of us stood together, waiting.

PART FOURTEEN

CENTRE STREET

THREE days passed before they sent for me, and I was taken up out of where I was and back to Comaday's office. Those three days were not in a cell but in a room in the main building. They put a cot in the room so I could sleep there. It was a quiet room, but during those three days it was not intended to be anything else. They were being kind and reasonable with me. They kept me well supplied with cigarettes, chocolate, Pepsi-cola and once a half-bottle of mixed martinis, hoping that I would take enough of it to make me amiable. I was amiable at the beginning, but it didn't last. The meals were good. They had the food sent in from outside. On the first day it was steak; the second day lamb chops; and the third day beef stew.

At first it was Comaday but only for a few hours, and then he turned me over to two men, whose names were Stark and Bingham. They were good men with years of experience in making people talk about what they wanted discussed. They were not muscle men or plug-uglies, but psychological types. They set out to win con-

fidence and friendship and they put a man at his ease. They turned
up on each of the two days at ten o'clock in the morning. They
sat down and suggested that I try some of their cigarettes; they
also had cigars in case my taste went to cigars. They were full of
smiles and they knew all sorts of ways in which to quiet anxiety.
Stark always began it. Stark would say,

"Bingham and I, we are reasonable, Clancy, we are essentially reasonable men. All we're asking of you is that you be
reasonable."

I would nod and demonstrate my reasonableness.

Then Bingham would say, "Let's take it from the top, Clancy."

Maybe one of the reasons Comaday made me a teacher was
because now and then I had demonstrated an exactitude of
language. There were expressions I avoided. I don't know whether
I would have stood by it but, now and again, it occurred to me
that I would let myself be strangled before I used an expression
like "take it from the top". So I would ask Bingham, "How do
you mean, 'take it from the top'?"

"The top, Clancy."

And Stark would say, "Work easy, Clancy, easy."

"We'll take it from the top, that's all I'm saying, Clancy, we'll
take it from the top."

Then I would say, "There's no bomb—that's the long and short
of it, beginning and end. There never was a bomb—not here and
not in Moscow."

"Did I ask you if there was a bomb, Clancy? All I said to you
was. 'Let's take it from the top.' We start at the beginning. We
start back the first time you ever heard of Alex Horton; then we
take it from there——"

And so it would go, hour after hour, back and forth and around
again in circles. They had patience if they had nothing else, but
then, when you think about it, they were drawing their weekly
pay check no matter what they did, and they might just as well
have spent their time in a little room with me as anywhere else.
As I said, the first day it was Comaday. The second day they
questioned me from ten o'clock in the morning until midnight.
They gave me no time off and in that room there was nowhere to
go and nowhere to hide. They questioned me while I used the
open toilet in the corner. They questioned me while I brushed
my teeth and washed my hands and undressed. They questioned
me while I lay on the cot that had been provided for me, trying to
sleep. They were soft, uninspired, and persistent. On the third

day they began all over again, but this time they continued only until four o'clock. At four o'clock a couple of officers in uniform came for me and took me up to Comaday's office.

There were three of them in Comaday's office—the Commissioner, Sidney Fredericks, the man from the Justice Department, and Jackson of Central Intelligence. I had not seen Jackson since this all began. He wasn't pleasant with me then and he was no more pleasant with me now. The three of them sat in leather upholstered armchairs in Comaday's office and smoked cigars and looked at me when I came in. Comaday waved the officers out. Then they went on puffing their cigars and observing me. No one asked me to sit down, no one smiled, no one made any gesture to indicate that I was roughly of the same species of human being that they were. They only sat there and smoked their cigars and looked at me. I didn't find the performance too impressive. I thought it was calculated and a little childish and, after waiting a few minutes, I said to Comaday,

"Where is Miss Goldmark?"

"She's here in this building," Comaday replied flatly.

"You haven't any reason to hold her here. Why don't you let her go?"

"We haven't any reason to hold you here, Clancy." Fredericks shrugged.

I ignored him and repeated to Comaday, "Let her go. You gave me a job and I did the job. You told me to find Horton and I found Horton. She wasn't in it. Let her go."

Quietly Comaday said, "Like hell you did a job, Clancy. Like hell you did."

I thought about that remark for awhile before I answered him. Then I asked, "Would you like to know what I think, Commissioner?"

"What do you think?"

"I think you're a louse, Commissioner. I think you're a cheap dirty louse—that's what I think, Commissioner."

His neck swelled and blood gorged his face until it was bloated and red. He started out of his chair and then controlled himself and sat down again. He took another puff on his cigar and then he said to me, "That will cost you, Clancy."

"What will it cost me, Commissioner?" I demanded, my voice so hoarse and muted that even to me the sound was like that of another person. "What will it cost me? What are you going to do, Commissioner? Are you going to have me murdered and put away? Rip up slabs in the basement and set me down under them?"

Comaday didn't answer, but Fredericks said, "Don't be so goddamned proud of yourself, Clancy."

"What then? I know what they would have done to Grischov. Grischov knew it too. Do you think he liked to die? You're three smart men. Do you think Grischov plunged out there into those guns because he was a hero? Like hell he did. He added it all up and he decided that six of one was half a dozen of another. So maybe he took the easy way—or maybe he just thought he was taking the easy way. But he was a Russian—we're not Russians, are we?"

Arthur Jackson spoke for the first time and told me, "You got a loud mouth, Clancy. You got a loud mouth and a big head."

Comaday said, "Make it easy, Clancy, make it easy for yourself, make it easy for us, make it easy for everyone."

I walked over close to the three of them and I said to them, almost in a whisper, "I told you before and for two days I told it to your psychologists downstairs—there isn't any bomb. There never was a bomb."

Fredericks jabbed a finger at me. "Even if we swallow your story, Clancy, hook, line, and sinker—even if we swallow it, how do you know Horton wasn't lying?"

"I know."

"You know a hell of a lot!" Comaday roared.

"I know he didn't make a bomb," I said, keeping my voice soft and somehow or other controlling it.

"You could make a bomb. Why not Horton?"

"Because I'm not Horton and Horton was not me."

"That's what we're afraid of," Jackson smiled. "You're not Horton."

I didn't like any of them, but I liked Arthur Jackson least. They were working on a theory and a presumption and, as a cop or a former cop, I could give professional credence to their theory and presumption and respect it and go along with it, at least to a certain point. But as far as Jackson went, it was neither a theory nor a presumption—it was a certainty. In either case, there was no more for me to say and no point in saying it, and when they began to talk, they simply asked the same questions over and over again.

I either kept my mouth shut or said "Yes" or said "No" until they got on to the subject of Grischov and then I asked them

whether they seriously believed that if there had been a bomb,
Grischov would have gone downstairs and out into the street the
way he did. I tried to make a point. I told them that Grischov
had a wife and children in Moscow.

"What does that prove?" Comaday wanted to know.

"That if there was a bomb, Grischov wouldn't have committed suicide."

"He didn't commit suicide," Jackson insisted. "He tried to
blast his way out of there. He had Gomez's Luger and his own
gun. He tried to blast his way out of there and leave you and the
girl and Horton like sitting ducks. Suppose there was a bomb—
in New York—that would mean a hell of a lot to Grischov. He'd
weep tears for New York, wouldn't he?"

"You turn my stomach." I said this directly to Jackson. "You
turn my stomach when you talk like that, I swear to God you do.
Grischov had as much chance of blasting his way out of there as I
have of blasting my way out of here, and you know it."

"We don't know a goddamned thing," Fredericks sighed.

"You're a snotnose," Comaday said with disgust. "You don't
learn, Clancy. You're sitting on the roof of the barn and you
don't climb off—not one bit."

Then they called back the two officers and they took me out of
there and back to my room. But now they had taken away the
cigarettes and the candy bars and the Pepsi-cola, and there wasn't
a book or a newspaper or a word of writing to read. They
took away my belt and my necktie and my jacket and my socks and
they left me like that until just before dawn. They had taken
my watch, too, so I don't know what time that was—maybe five
in the morning, maybe six in the morning. There was a tiny
window in the room, high up and sealed with a heavy plate of
frosted glass, but it seemed to be glimmering with a little less than
total darkness and that made me think that it was either the beginning of the morning or close to it.

This time three of them came in and they weren't psychologists.
They were old fashioned, old time, bullet-headed muscle boys
and they began to work on me. They used short lengths of rubber
hose and sometimes their hands, but they worked on me carefully
and professionally and did most of it so that it didn't show too
much. I don't know how long they worked on me; it might have
been three hours or four hours or five hours or maybe only an
hour; time ceases to have any meaning when you're living in that
kind of condition.

They worked on me and they asked me questions. They sat me in a chair and knocked me off the chair. They turned on a hanging light and put it into my face. They questioned me and worked me with their rubber hose. They let me lie on the floor and dream that it was over or that I would lose consciousness and then they worked me across the room with the toes of their boots. They stood me up against the wall and worked me expertly down to the floor and then they dragged me up again and repeated the process over and over until I lost count.

At first I tried to remember Hans Kempter and my own reactions when he sat in a quiet room. I tried to remember a homemade atom bomb and give them the due that while it did not exist for me, they had to establish the presumption that it existed for them. I said to myself that if I am reasonable and charitable and objective, I can maintain my sanity.

But the trouble with such a state of mind lies in its very artificiality. It is not rooted in the conditions that accompany it; and after a while I had to let go of my objectivity and begin to hate. Hatred is a sickness, but under certain conditions it becomes a medicine for survival and by the time they finished with me I hated them as I had never hated anyone before.

They picked me up and put me on the cot and then they went out. There was nothing personal in their coming, and nothing personal in their going. They had called me no names and they had used no obscenities. They did their work competently, professionally, and well.

After they had gone, I lay face down on the cot, whimpering and pleading to a God I only half believed in for unconsciousness. My prayers were answered—at least to the degree that a doctor's appearance occasioned. He examined me quickly but carefully and then gave me an injection of morphine and left me to float away into the peace and beauty of unconsciousness or sleep.

For two days after that they left me alone and in those two days I healed up and pulled myself together. When Fredericks came in to see me on the third day after the beating, I hurt only when I moved or when something touched the bruises. My eyes were opened and I could see through the swollen lids and a finger I had felt certain was broken proved to be only badly wrenched and sprained.

Fredericks sat down at the plain wooden table, which is always a part of the equipment of a quiet room, and nodded for me to join him. I seated myself across the table from him and accepted a cigarette he offered me. It tasted better than any cigarette I ever remember smoking, and when Fredericks saw the expression on my face, he tossed the whole pack on the table and said that I should keep them. I thanked him.

"How do you feel about me, Clancy?" he asked.

"The hell with that. I'm no good any more for personal observations. You're doing your job, Fredericks. Don't bring me any guilts."

"I haven't any guilts," Fredericks said thoughtfully. "We had to have a presumption, you know that, Clancy, as well as I do. Put yourself in my place and you would have the presumption too."

"I don't put myself in your place."

"All right, Clancy, the fact remains that we had to have the presumption."

"Where's Phyllis?" I asked him.

"She's here," he said. "She's all right. She's well cared for."

"Like I'm well cared for, Fredericks?"

"Look, Clancy," he sighed, "we can either talk like civilized human beings or we can sit here and throw recriminations at each other. Which is it going to be?"

"Civilized human beings," I smiled. It was the first time I had smiled in days and the smile hurt. The muscles of my mouth hurt and my broken lips hurt when I twisted them into the grimace, but still in all it was a smile. It expressed appreciation and amusement. It said to me, as well as to Fredericks, that I was still a human being; for the biological fact of the matter is that animals don't smile.

"What is this?" Fredericks wanted to know. "Are we playing for marbles or are we playing with the lives of eight million people here and maybe almost as many in the Soviet Union? Give us that break, Clancy, use your head. Use your brains. You're no fool."

"What do you want from me now, Fredericks?"

"Are you ready to talk sense?"

"I'll try," I nodded.

"All right, then," Fredericks began. "We had to state a presumption to ourselves, as wild as it might sound, we had to organize a premise on the fact that you and the girl knew where that bomb was. Now we've come to a point where our premise becomes inoperative. I'm not talking to the fact of whether or not there ever was a bomb, nor am I talking to the fact of my beliefs. My own beliefs don't count. John Comaday's beliefs don't count.

Beliefs are colored by experiences and emotion and by a philosophical point of view. You can hang your own life on a belief,
Clancy; you can hang your wife's life or your kids' life on a belief,
but you can't hang the lives of twelve or fifteen million people on
a personal prejudice. That's why we had to have a premise. Do you
understand me?"

"I understand you," I said tiredly.

"All right then. The premise becomes inoperative, not because
we have abandoned it, but because we have to face the fact that
we know of no way to make you or the girl tell us where that damn
bomb is."

I wasted enough breath to tell him that there was no bomb.

"Suppose there is no bomb, Clancy. For Christ's sake, think like
a cop for just two minutes—like an intelligent cop!"

"I'm not a cop any more, Fredericks."

"I'm saying 'Think like one!' Think like one, Clancy. Can
you ever abandon the premise? Could you ever go to sleep at
night without asking yourself whether Clancy and Goldmark
knew where that goddamned bomb was? Could you ever get up
on a witness stand and swear that they didn't know? Could you,
Clancy?"

I thought about it for awhile and then I shook my head. "No,
I couldn't," I said.

"All right," Fredericks nodded. "Now we have it established.
The premise exists. It's going to continue as long as you and Miss
Goldmark live and even afterwards. Maybe it will become com-
paratively unimportant, but it can never disappear, Clancy.
Horton is dead, Grischov is dead, and Simonovsky has not been
found. Maybe he never will be. Only you and Miss Goldmark
were with Horton and no one else on this earth knows or will ever
know what you said to him and what he said to you; so the premise exists. If we killed you now; if we followed your own crazy
romantic notions and did away with your bodies and destroyed
every evidence connected with you, that would still not change
the premise that Horton made a bomb and that the bomb exists."

"Don't argue the point, Fredericks," I said wearily. "Grischov
and I established the premise. I think we established it the moment
Horton said that there never was a bomb—the moment we knew
and understood that there never could have been any bomb. Do
you know, I never met anyone like Grischov. You're a Justice
Department man, Fredericks, so maybe it's a little hard for you to
swallow. He didn't come over to your side. He didn't chicken

out. He never turned his back on what he was or what he believed in. He just saw the premise all at once and clearly and he knew about it and that was the end of his road. He gave up. He had come so far and he could go no further. So he put a stop to it—to himself."

"But you didn't give up, Clancy."

"No," I said, "I didn't give up. I was in love, Fredericks, and the woman I loved was there in the room with me. Maybe Grischov was in love too—I don't know—but if he was, the woman he loved was five thousand miles away and his mind and his imagination couldn't bridge the gap to a point where he would ever see her again. The premise was there for both of us, but Phyllis was there with me. Grischov's wife wasn't."

"Have it your way," Fredericks shrugged. "My own advice, Clancy, would be to leave politics to the politicians. We're going to keep you here one week longer than the time limit in Horton's letter. That doesn't mean anything except that, if we're going to have the premise, we have to add an automatic device to it. When that extra week is up, you and Miss Goldmark can leave. We want you to remain in this city for the time being. You'll be watched, but not too carefully. Make it easy for us. Don't make it hard for us, and we'll stretch the premise as far as we can. Keep your mouth shut and let all this be a bad dream that never happened."

"It's been a bad dream, Fredericks," I said to him. "From the first hour when I walked into Comaday's office and saw you and Jackson and the rest of them, it became a bad dream; it was never anything else."

"There's no dream you can't forget," Fredericks said, standing up now and looking at me appraisingly. Then he stretched out his hand and I stood up and shook hands with him, and then he left. I never saw him again.

The remaining days went by slowly but they went by. They gave me things to read and they let me write letters to Phyllis and receive her replies. They brought back the chocolates and the soda water and the restaurant-cooked food. Then when the time was up they gave me a new suit and a clean shirt and took me up to Comaday's office.

I walked into the office and Phyllis was there, sitting in one of the leather-upholstered chairs and waiting for me. She was thinner than I remembered her as being, paler, smaller, but there was a light in her eyes that I had not seen there before and, when she stood against me with my arms around her, there was a wholeness about the two of us that I, at least, had never felt before.

I had only a few words with Comaday. We both accepted the fact that I was no longer on the force. The papers of resignation were prepared and I signed them, and then he took out of his desk a package of money.

"Here's five hundred dollars of expense money, Clancy," he said to me. "I don't know what you had in mind when you asked for it but you never touched it. It was in your wallet when we took your wallet. The money was written off and now I'm using it as severance pay."

"Keep it, Commissioner," I said shortly.

He lost his temper then and shouted at me, "Take it, you thick-headed Mick, and get the hell out of here."

I swallowed what I began to say and controlled myself and very softly, bending close to him, I let Comaday know what he could do with the money. Then we left. I didn't shake hands with Comaday and he didn't offer his hand to me. I think he disliked me as thoroughly and as conscientiously as I disliked him, and we were both of us content to leave it as it was. We walked out of there and out of the building into the spring sunshine. I took Phyllis's hand and we walked away from everything that had been. There was a great deal for each of us to think about and a great deal for each of us to say. But that could wait. Now, at this moment, our only purpose was to savor the taste of each other and the touch of each other, to breathe the clean morning air and to walk along with the knowledge that we were free—perhaps freer than either of us had ever been before.

DEATH OF A TOM

Douglas Warner

"Death of a Tom" is published by
Cassell & Co. Ltd.

The Author

Douglas Warner entered journalism with the *Derby Evening Telegraph* in 1932, became a wartime sub-editor of the *Daily Express* and peacetime Features Editor of the *Sunday Chronicle*. Since September, 1954, he has been writing and travelling, with occasional journalism, in many countries including Italy, Spain, Australia, South Africa and Ghana—where he was editorial assistant to *Drum* magazine. Back in England in 1959 he met ex-Detective Superintendent John Gosling and collaborated with him in a study of vice in London called *Shame of a City*. His previous experience as a journalist among crooks and prostitutes, allied with Gosling's knowledge of police procedure and criminal slang, helped him enormously when he came to write his highly successful thriller novels.

FOR

MY PARENTS

PART ONE

Seedtime of Murder

CHAPTER ONE

DETECTIVE-CHIEF INSPECTOR DAVID WYNDHAM, of D Division (Albany Street/St. John's Wood sub-division), Metropolitan Police, crumpled the sixth sheet of paper into a tight ball and flung it savagely into the wastepaper basket. He rubbed the back of his hand across his aching eyes. He said to himself: "Keep it simple, man. You're not composing deathless prose. You know what you want to say. Go ahead and say it."

He drew a fresh sheet of notepaper towards him. This time he wrote rapidly, sure of himself. The final sentence read: "For these reasons, therefore, I feel that I am not competent to discharge the duties which are required of me and I hereby tender my resignation from the Force, such resignation to take effect immediately."

He added the salutation, re-read the letter, folded it, and slipped it into an envelope. There was a knock on his office door. He yelled, irritably: "Come in!" He delayed addressing the letter until the intruder would have gone.

A uniformed constable entered, carrying a bulky brown foolscap envelope. He held it gingerly by the edges, as though a firmer grip would soil his fingers. "For you, sir," he said, unnecessarily, a note of suppressed excitement in his voice. "It arrived in the second post, a few minutes ago. The sergeant said he thought it might be the one you were expecting."

Wyndham said: "Thank you." The constable laid the envelope on his desk. "Ask Inspector Follitt to spare a moment."

Wyndham did not touch the envelope. When Follitt entered he said: "I think this is it, Jim, just when we'd almost given up hope. Get the boys to do all the usual tests, then I'll read it."

Follitt nodded without speaking. He took the envelope carefully and went out. Wyndham addressed his own letter to Sir Graham Dunstable, Assistant-Commissioner (Crime), at New Scotland Yard, and slipped it into the inside pocket of his jacket.

341

It was still there when the brown foolscap envelope was returned with the sheets of typing it had contained. He glanced at the accompanying report by the lab experts. He noted that the envelope was of a type which could be bought in quantity at any Woolworth's for a few pence, that the writing paper was sold by the thousands of reams by every branch of W. H. Smith & Son, and that the typewriter had been identified as an old Remington portable with a broken letter "t", the vowels "e" and "o" out of alignment, and sundry other identifying items, if it should ever be found. No fingerprints had been detected.

Wyndham put the report aside and picked up the typewritten sheets. The document was a diary, and presently he was engrossed in the story it told: the revelation of one man's megalomania.

Friday, June 16th. 11.30 p.m.: Bitch, bitch, bitch, bitch, *bitch*! (he read). The bitch has locked me out of our bedroom, and this time I know it's for good. And not a word to me about her intentions, the mean hag. All day she's been just the same as usual after a love-making: tight-faced, cold, deadly polite, and my meals chosen and cooked with extra care. In other words, bitchy, but not bitchier than normal. Nothing warned me. I wasn't even surprised when she went to bed early. I sat on a little longer than usual, thinking of love as it should be made, violent, inspiring, exhausting. Not with *her,* of course. I haven't thought of her like that for years. What man could? Sagging breasts, blotchy skin, the flesh thickening repulsively around belly and hips, ugly blue veins vivid in her legs. No. I was thinking about a girl I saw on the Tube this evening. About eighteen, nineteen. She looked cool and fresh in a tailored blouse, unbuttoned at the throat, and a neat, tight skirt. She wasn't wearing a bra, and when she leaned forward to pick up her suitcase her blouse fell open and I saw one perfect breast, firm and rounded. It was tanned, too, like her shoulders and arms, so she must have been a nudist. I couldn't get her out of my mind.

Then, when I was properly ready, I went upstairs. It wouldn't be with her like it would be with that girl, but I've got used to putting up with second best. Second best? Tenth best, twentieth best. It isn't true that all cats are grey in the dark.

When I reached the landing I saw all my things piled outside the bedroom: clothes, shoes, suitcases, everything of mine that was kept in the bedroom, outside. I stood for a moment, stunned. Then I turned livid with rage. I banged on the door, though not too hard in case the neighbours heard. I demanded to be let in. For a long time she wouldn't answer, but finally she did. I was locked out, she said. I could sleep in the spare room, tonight and every night. She told me where I would find sheets, blankets, etc. She wasn't going to be maltreated by me again. She had stood it long enough.

I couldn't get any more out of her. I thought of breaking down the door and taking what is mine by right, but it would have made too much noise. I'm not going to have the neighbours gossiping about us.

Maltreated, she said. By me. The liar. I've never maltreated her in our married life, not intentionally. I admit I was carried away last night. I was desperate. I hadn't touched her for a week. But I apologized, didn't I? A man can't do more. I apologized handsomely and she accepted it. Yes, she did. I remember her saying so.

Maltreated! Anyone would think I was a sexual maniac instead of a normal man who likes to enjoy his marital rights. The trouble with *her* has always been her upbringing. She was a virgin when we married. She knew nothing about sex. On our first night she was all tight, shivering, taut inside. It wasn't much fun for me, I can tell you. It hasn't been much fun since, either. She never learned. She simply "did her duty" as a wife, and not much duty at that. In her eyes there is only one way to make love and any other way is a perversion. Yet I've tried to teach her. I've explained, pleaded, cajoled. She took no notice. In the end I had to take what I wanted whether she liked it or not. Nobody can blame me for that. Sex the one way all through married life is like living on a perpetual diet of steak and onions, nice enough to begin with but tasteless at the hundredth repetition. You can't live like that. Nobody can. I bet nobody does. I'd like to peep in at a few bedrooms and prove it. An invisible man, capable of melting through locked doors and *watching,* gathering the true information about sex in the only way it can be gathered. It's a thought I've often had and I bet the book would be a sensation. It would sell a million copies, two million. Kinsey wouldn't get a look in. I wish I could write a best-seller. I bet I could, too, if only I had the time.

The clock has just chimed twelve-thirty. I suppose I must go upstairs to the spare room, make the bed and get some sleep. As usual, I've a heavy day at the office tomorrow—no, it's today, of course. I've half a mind not to go, say I'm sick. It would serve them right if I didn't turn up for a few days. They'd soon see that they couldn't get along without me. Teach a few of them a lesson, that would. Strutting around with their "do this", and "do that", and "do the other". With their "why isn't this finished"? and "I want that right away". Damn them! There's a limit to what one man can do. But I'll show them all yet. One day I shall be recognized. I'll get promoted right over their heads. The Boss has been giving me some appreciative glances lately. It's easy to see that he's weighing me up and not finding me wanting. Well, how could he? I'm doing a terrific job. And when *I'm* the top-dog I'll make a few of them jump. Oh yes, they'll jump all right, or they'll jump the bloody office.

I feel better just writing it all down. I've never kept a diary before but I think I'll keep one from now on. It releases tension. Makes you see things in perspective, including *her*. My initial reaction was too pessimistic. She'll come round in a day or two. I'll jolly her along. I'll tackle her about her wifely duty—that always gets her. Her and her duty! Damn her, damn them, damn everybody! I know how to handle them. I'm just biding my time.

Tuesday, June 27th: I can't understand it. She *won't* come round. She cooks my meals, does my laundry, looks after the house, speaks politely, and when friends drop in they'd swear there was nothing wrong between us. Yet she won't take my hints and unlock her room to me. She can't mean what she said that first night—is it only eleven days ago? She *can't*. It would be inhuman. What on earth would I do?

Tuesday, July 4th: Wonderful news! The Boss called me into his office today and talked to me for quite ten minutes. He never talks that long to anyone except his executives. Nothing promised, mind you, but from the way he spoke he is clearly considering me for the big post that is coming up. Naturally, I didn't let on that I knew what was behind his interest, but I flatter myself that I created a good impression. I was calm, decisive, respectful—but neither servile nor abrupt. He's a good judge of character, you can see that, and I'm confident that this means ME for the executive desk What other decision could any sane chief take? It's clear in my work—though I say it, who shouldn't—and in my whole manner and demeanour. I've always known that I am made of the stuff of authority. Oh, there's quality in me, no doubt about that. Only jealousy has kept me down so long. Now my chance is coming.

I told *her* about it when I reached home tonight (a little late because I stopped off to celebrate with a couple of drinks, small ones). You'd think she would be pleased at the prospect of being the wife of a top executive, but she only gave me a cold, calculating stare. And her room stays locked to me. Still, I shan't worry. I think—I'm almost sure—that I'm learning to live without sex— proper sex, that is.

Monday, July 10th: Only a few days more. It is an open secret that the appointment will be announced before the Boss leaves for his holidays on the 22nd. The strain in the office is almost unbearable. It is really quite amusing. I watch the other con- tenders, laughing secretly at their pathetic efforts to clinch their appointment at the eleventh hour. There are moments when I feel like telling them to stop worrying, that the decision has been made and that I am the chosen one. I would, too, if they were less despicable. When I think of the lengths they have gone to, individually and collectively, to swamp my talent, I could be sick. But no, I mustn't think disturbing thoughts. My hour is at hand and in the meantime I am serene. I feel strong and full of power. When Mr. X rebuked me—in front of the typist, as usual —for what he imagined was my fault, I kept calm. I straightened the matter out in a few well-chosen words, spoken without heat. He was quite nasty, but he can no longer hurt me. I really think he will have to go. He is incompetent as well as rude. Mr. Y's position, too, must be looked into, though on occasions he can be pleasant. Today he asked my opinion of England's chances in the remaining Tests against Australia and listened attentively while I explained my reasons for believing that England will win the series. I didn't convince him, though. He backed Australia. Not very patriotic.

Strange, the effect success has on a man; on me, at any rate. Nothing can touch me, nothing. Not the cheap vindictiveness of the men and women in the office. Not even *her*. She has not relented, but it no longer matters. Now I can take sex or leave it alone. I wonder: does frustration intensify sexual desire? I have noticed a marked drop in my own reactions to sex during these last few days. I still look at women as a man should, of course, but without the same intense desire to take them. It makes life much easier. I find myself able to talk to the women I meet as I have seldom been able to talk to them. They used to think me shy, but they were wrong. I have always wanted women so badly that I was afraid to approach them, and when I was forced to do so I could not act naturally with them. I felt that my desire would show in my eyes, and that I would act too soon, too violently. That was why I was so upset when *she* banned me from her room. Now I see that I was acting foolishly. All I need do is take a mistress. Lots of men do. I'm pretty sure that X keeps a woman. I don't think Y does, but from his sly dirty way of joking I suspect that he visits prostitutes. I know that this is a harsh thing to say of any man, but I will not recant. I will repeat it: I believe that Y consorts with prostitutes. I could never do that. I am a fastidious man. My very fastidiousness, together with my lack of ability to meet women naturally, blocked the outlets for my desire. To take a prostitute would be to defile myself. To take a mistress, or have a series of affairs with different women, would have been beyond my ability. Naturally, I have never cultivated such an ability—a man should stay faithful to his wife. But in my new mood—the mood that is the real me, the man of recognized power and strength—there is nothing to prevent me taking a mistress. Also, I shall be able to afford one. I shall not tell *her* what salary I shall be getting in my new job, and it will be simplicity itself to explain that the work will take me away from home several nights a week.

Oh, the future is wonderful, wonderful! I know the sort of woman I want. She will be young and trim, with small, firm breasts and flat belly. She will be pliant, obedient, responsive, adoring to be loved by a masterful man. I will insist that she wears a negligée whenever I am with her. I will sit back in a deep chair and watch her while she brings my slippers and pours my whiskies and lights my cigars—the best whisky and the finest Havana cigars. Afterwards we will play, deep into the night. She will be astounded at my youth, my vigour, and my knowledge of love. It is wonderful to be rich and successful and loved for one's own sake. I am already looking for the right woman.

Friday, July 14th: I think I've met her. My woman. For the day when I'm *somebody*. I went up West and lunched in one of those new-style restaurants where they print the menu in French. (I mustn't make stupid mistakes when I take people out to lunch and dinner. An executive is supposed to know these things.) The place was very full, of course, but it was very nice, most genteel, with paintings on the walls—murals, I think they call them—showing scenes of the French Riviera. The food was excellent, too. I had *bouillon Windsor*, followed by chicken *rôti* with *champignons et pommes frites* (it sounds so much tastier than **roast chicken**, mushroom and chips) and *glacé vanilla*. Instead of tea I drank a glass of *Bordeaux rouge* wine, only one and nine-pence. Of course, I shan't eat there when I'm an executive. I shall go to a real French restaurant, one of those places in Soho. I can't afford to go there yet. Besides, if I make a mistake over the menu at this place it won't matter so much.

I knew the moment she sat down that she was the sort for me. She asked me to pass the mustard and her voice was so low and sweet that it thrilled me. She is small and neat and has big blue eyes and wavy golden hair. She was wearing one of those transparent pink blouses and I could see her bra straps. She wasn't wearing a slip and, later, when she reached the door and stood against the light, I could see all her legs through the thin skirt. It was quite easy to get talking to her—nothing is difficult for me these days. She's a widow and lives in Bayswater. I didn't like to ask her name, not so soon, but she lunches in that place fairly regularly and so I'll see her again. I shall lunch there myself most days in future, though the food costs a bit more than I usually like to pay, and I'll have to spend more time travelling.

She is very helpless, poor thing. I think she misses her husband. She was carrying some parcels and she dropped them when she rose to go (she only took about ten minutes over her meal). I helped to pick them up and she was most grateful. When I jumped up I knocked over the remains of my Bordeaux wine and it spilled on her skirt, but she didn't mind a bit. She wouldn't even let me wipe it off with my handkerchief, though I offered to. The stain was high up on her left thigh. She gave me a lovely smile as she left. I shall certainly go there again.

Thursday, July 20th: I am nearly delirious with delight. Tomorrow is THE DAY! The Boss actually paused at my side today to compliment me on my work and say that tomorrow he will have good news for me. I went to lunch in a fever of excitement and *she* was there again. She wore a white cotton frock cut low at the neck (though not vulgarly low) so that I could see the swelling of her breasts, especially when she sat forward with her elbows on the table. She could see I was excited but I didn't tell her anything. I just dropped a hint or two about good luck coming. I was very bold, though. I asked her name and where she lived. She wagged her finger naughtily and told me I ought to know better, and me

a married man, too. I wondered how she guessed I was married
until she pointed at the signet ring on my left hand. I'd forgotten
it. It was a gift from *her* when we married. I've worn it ever since
but I'll get it off my finger before we meet again, which will be
at lunch tomorrow. My treat. I'll tell her my good news and get
really close to her. After . . . God, it'll be marvellous to have a
woman again. A real woman. Soft, clinging, pliant, intertwining
her limbs with mine, pressing close to me. To hell with *her*. *She*
can keep her key turned until the lock rusts.

CHAPTER TWO

Friday, July 21st. 10.30 p.m.: God! Oh, God! I've lost. My
enemies have triumphed. My life is in ruins. The job has been
given to Y. I was forced to congratulate him. I actually had to
shake him by the hand and wish him good luck. I'd liked to have
killed him. I suppose I didn't hide my feelings very well because
I heard him say to Miss A: "Do you know, I really think the chap
actually thought *he* was going to get the post. *Him!*" And they
both laughed. But why shouldn't I have got it? I'm as good a man
as Y any day of the week, *and* better. Why should they fob me off
with a meaningless title and an extra pound a week? It's an insult.
It's a shunt sideways into a dead-end. Are they all blind? Can't
they see that I'm the best man for the job? I am, I am, I am!
I know I am!

No, I'm not. I've been fooling myself. I'm no good. I'm tenth-
rate. I have no presence, no inner power, no gift for controlling
people and initiating work. I'm a cipher, a tiny O, whirling
round and round meaninglessly. They all laugh at me. They
despise me. They don't even have to plot to keep me down. I'm
down because I'm not good enough to rise. I make a mess of
everything I touch: my work, my marriage, my friendships. How
many friends have I got? Not one. A few acquaintances, neighbours, business people. We chat, we swop "shop", we talk horses
and cricket and party politics, but we aren't friends. Who would
want to be friends with a man like me? They're very kind to put
up with me as much as they do. I'm only a nuisance. I'd be better
dead. If I was dead they'd be sorry. They'd all be sorry.

No, they wouldn't. They wouldn't care. No one would care.
No one cares whether I live or die. I don't amount to a grain of
sand. Die, and I'll be an insurance policy for my bitch of a wife
to inherit. I'll leave a meagre job to be filled from any one of a

thousand applicants. A schoolchild could do the job. They'll probably give it to a schoolkid just to save a few pounds a week.

I didn't keep my date with *her* for lunch. How could I, after all my hints and promises? I couldn't afford to pay for her lunch, anyway. She probably didn't turn up. I don't blame her if she didn't. Why waste time on a creature like me? I'm surprised that she ever came back after the first time, when I spilled wine on her dress. I can't even perform a decent action decently. I always have to spoil it.

If I had gone, what could I have said to her? I can't afford a mistress. I can't even afford an affair. Flowers, chocolates, theatre-tickets, taxis, drinks, meals. A pound a week extra won't go far when tax has been paid and with National Health contributions going up and up. Free Health Service? It's a cheat, a sham, like all the world.

So I came straight home. I didn't eat at all. I'm not hungry. I had a bottle of beer at a pub. It's made my head ache, that and the emotion. *She* wasn't in when I got home. She isn't home yet. I wonder where she's gone? It's getting late. Nearly ten-thirty. What happened to the rest of the day? All the day since one o'clock I remember the beer—that must have been at three o'clock just before the pubs shut. Or was it six o'clock, just after they opened? Have I been walking around? Or did I come home and sleep? I don't remember going to my room.

Wait! I do remember. I didn't go into my room. Automatically I went into hers. It wasn't locked. I intended to stay there and wait for her and have it out with her, once and for all. She didn't come and I fell asleep. Then I woke up and came in here to write.

She's coming now. I can see her at the far end of the street. In the half light of the lamps she looks young and pretty. You can't see the blotchy skin and the blue veins, and her bra and roll-ons have lent her back her figure. She's pulled her breasts high and tight, and the thin cotton dress is moulded to her thighs by the evening breeze. My breath feels tight in my chest. It hurts when I inhale. I'm trembling as though I were scared to death. It's not fear, though. I recognize it. I know it only too well.

She's at the gate. I'll get into her room quick. I'll wait for her. I'll *make* her. I'll *make* her.

Later: I feel as though I'm wrapped in a big, black blanket and I can't escape. It fogs me. It trips me. I'm clumsy. I'm tied down.

They all hobble me. They bind me, muzzle me, make me fall down. And then they laugh. I have no rights. I am an outcast, a displaced person in the true sense. I have no home, no wife, no job, no place to go, though I have all these things. And the things I want, the things I need desperately, I have not got and shall never possess.

I failed with my wife. I waited for her. When she came in I stepped forward, intending to grab her. I stumbled on the edge of the carpet. She whirled round. She looked at me with her sour eyes and said: "Touch me and I'll scream until the neighbours come!" What could I do? We're respectable people. Besides, I'd have looked a fool struggling into my trousers. She said: "Get out and put some clothes on. You look disgusting." I tried to plead with her. She only turned her back. I felt like falling on her and strangling her where she stood, only I was afraid she might be stronger than me.

My head is still aching. I think there's a bottle of beer in the kitchen. I should eat, too, but I don't want to. She's left supper for me. I'll just drink the beer. No, I forgot. There isn't any beer. I drank it two nights ago.

What am I going to do? I must try to get my thoughts clear. I'm all confused. I only know that I can't go on like this, without a woman. Thank God tomorrow is Saturday. I have the whole week-end to consider my future.

Saturday, July 22nd. 10 p.m.: I have walked all day. The sun was hot. The city baked. The grass in the Royal Parks is yellowing under the heat. The flowers are wilting. The papers say it is the seventh day of a heat-wave. I hadn't noticed. Even today I hardly felt the heat, though I wasn't dressed for summer. I was conscious only of torment. Everything conspired to torture me, the bathers in the Serpentine with their naked limbs, the covers of the pornographic magazines on the pavements of Piccadilly Circus, the photographs in their frames outside the Windmill Theatre, the dirty books in the windows along Charing Cross Road. One of them showed a copy of Boccaccio's *Decameron* open at an illustration of a naked woman down on all fours like a dog. I looked at it for a long time. I wanted to buy the book but it was priced at thirty shillings the two volumes. There were other books I would have liked to buy: Hirschfeld's *Sexual Anomalies and Perversions*, the two Kinsey Reports, a history of sexual practices in England, etc., etc.

Sex has pursued me all day. A young blonde bathing in the Serpentine broke her swimsuit-strap as she emerged from the water and revealed one glorious breast, pink-tipped. She covered herself quickly but showed no shame. She and her friends—including men—just laughed. I found this slightly shocking. As I was passing a block of flats in Bayswater a woman came to a window and put a bottle of milk on the sill. She had nothing on—at least, she was naked to the waist, which was as far as I could see. I hung around for quite a time but she didn't reappear. In Maida Vale a gust of wind, hot and dry, swirled a woman's skirts over her head and I saw her panties. They were pink and transparent and edged with lace. Afterwards I remembered a piece of doggerel from my childhood:

> The wind, the wind, the wicked wind,
> That blows the skirts so high.
> But God is just, he sends the dust,
> To blind the bad man's eye.

Am I a bad man? I've tried not to be. I've been faithful to my wife. And God didn't blind my eye with dust, though there was plenty of it about. That means something. I *am* a normal man. I'm just deprived.

In the evening it was worse. Lovers were out in the Parks. I could hear them whispering and see them kissing each other. Once, I nearly stepped on a couple under a hedge. I turned and ran. The man swore at me and the girl giggled. In Regents Park I was accosted by a prostitute. I thought the Wolfenden Report—or do I mean the Act of Parliament which followed it?—had driven them off the streets. What are our police doing? Can't they enforce the law? If they can't, what are we paying them higher wages for? Wasting the taxpayers' money while these filthy creatures are allowed to accost respectable citizens in public. I brushed her off. I thought she would pursue me, but she didn't. She only shrugged and returned to the shadows of the trees. A dirty creature, and probably diseased. I stood and watched her from behind a hedge. A man came up and spoke to her. They talked together for a few moments and then the woman linked arms with him and they walked off. I caught a glimpse of his face. He was dressed neatly enough but his face was terrible. All lined and debauched. Well, it would have to be, to think of consorting with a woman of the streets. A man like Y. You can see the debauchery in Y's big bold face and insolent eyes. And the way he handles the typists. Always contriving to touch them. The odd thing is, the girls don't seem to mind. They'd mind if I touched them, though. Just as I'd mind if one of those creatures touched me. Loathsome! What makes even the worst of men go with them, I wonder?

She—the girl in the Park I mean—reminded me a little of the girl in the restaurant. Fair hair, slim figure. I think her eyes were blue, though I couldn't see properly.

I suppose prostitutes must be terribly over-sexed. Well, I mean, they must be, otherwise they couldn't go with so many men, and such types of men. Mind you, the one I saw wasn't badly dressed. He wore a blue suit. It looked like good material, nicely cut. It wasn't off-the-peg stuff. I know the look of *that*.

The heat is terrible. It reaches down deep into me, right to the thighs. Images return to my mind: the swimmer's bare breast, the naked woman at the window, the skirts flying over plump legs, the Windmill Girls, the photographs, the noises under the trees.

Do these girls charge much, I wonder? How can men afford them? Odd how she reminded me of the girl in the restaurant.

People are going to bed. Lights are going out, one by one. Nobody appears at the windows. Yes, there's one, a girl, way down the street. I can hardly see, though I'm straining my eyes. She's gone. The light has been switched off. I can imagine her with her lover, too hot even for sheets.

I have ten pounds saved up. *She* doesn't know about it. It's hidden where I keep this diary. Would ten pounds be enough?

If she resembles the girl in the restaurant perhaps she'll be like I imagined her to be, in bed. The man's suit was good, a lot better than mine. Perhaps she wouldn't have me. Perhaps I'm not good enough for her.

Yes, there's ten pounds. I was saving it up for something. I can't think what for. It's too hot to sleep. I'll go for a walk. Not to Regents Park, though. Why not to Regents Park? It may be cooler there. Nobody will be about at this hour, anyway. It's past eleven-thirty.

Later: How utterly revolting! How unspeakable! I feel as though I've been wallowing in muck. It was a cheat, too; an absolute swindle. Why, from the time we entered her room to the time I left it was only eight minutes, yet it cost me four pounds. It's monstrous! There ought to be a law against it.

She wasn't in the place where I first saw her, I wasn't really looking for her. She spoke to me out of the darkness, later. I paused. I wanted to have a closer look at her, that was all. I soon saw that her resemblance to that other girl was purely superficial. Her face was harder, tighter, more like my wife's. Only a facial resemblance, I mean. My wife's a good woman. She said: "Got a light, dearie?" I shook my head. She said: "It doesn't matter." She took out a box and struck a match. She bent to the flame and looked up at me over it. "Like to be naughty for half an hour?" she asked. Her voice held a Northern accent, Lancashire or Yorkshire, I don't know the difference. I said, as she shook the match out: "I don't think so." Her eyes darted from side to side as we stood talking. She noticed my curious glance and laughed. "The flatties," she said. "Coppers, policemen," she added, when she saw my bewilderment. "Next time they nick me I cop three months." She went on, without pausing for breath: "Nice and comfy, dearie, me own room and all mod. con." She laughed. Suddenly her face changed. She swung herself alongside me and slipped her hand through my arm. I flinched. She held tight. She said in a whisper: "Do me a favour, Johnny." (My name isn't John.) "Walk with me like we was pals. There's a flatty in the offing. My name's Rosie."

She forced me to walk. She talked gaily about the heat, about an ice-cream I was supposed to have brought her which she had spilled on her dress, about the pubs we were supposed to have been in together. Then, suddenly, she dropped my arm and said in her normal voice: "It's O.K. He's gone the other way." She squeezed my forearm. "Thanks, dearie," she said. "You're a real good 'un. For that, I'll let you have it for four quid. Usually I ask a fiver *and* get it."

I was thinking of the policeman. I said: "Would he have arrested you?" She shrugged. "Perhaps. Perhaps not. It was the Old Sardine—he's not a bad 'un. Doesn't chase you for the sake of his record of arrests like some of the young ones."

We were still walking and somehow we had got out of the Park on the east and were among narrow brick buildings. She said: "Well, look where we are! My gaff's only a step away. Coming?" She dug her hip into my thigh—and her eyes were bright. She tossed away the cigarette end with an impudent gesture. "I'll be good to you, Johnny," she said. "Real good." She leaned forward and looked up at me. I said, and my voice sounded funny: "Four quid?" She said: "Sure." I nodded. I don't know why I nodded.

The funny thing was that all my desire had fled. I felt detached, uninvolved, almost clinical. The feeling persisted upstairs, too, for quite a minute or two.

The room was shabby, with a wardrobe, two chairs and a bed. The bed was made up with a thick counterpane on top. She asked me for the money plus "half a crown for the maid". I didn't see or hear any maid. I counted the money out of my wallet. She went out. I undressed and started to pull back the sheets. She returned and laughed. She smoothed the bed. She said: "*On*, Johnny, not *in*." She laughed again. I felt a fool. I suppose she realized that I hadn't done that sort of thing before.

It was all over so soon that I felt cheated. I still do. She didn't even take off all her clothes. She seemed impatient to get me away. She said: "Time's money, dearie. Time's money." She practically hustled me out. I was home within the hour.

Sunday, July 23rd: She robbed me! I've just found out. I went to my wallet to put the six pounds back in its hiding place and it had gone. Thief! Bitch! Cow! She must have done it while she was helping me on with my jacket. No wonder she was in a hurry. She wanted to get rid of me before I discovered the loss. She's dishonest. I'll go to the police and complain. No, I can't go to the police, a man in my position, so I'll go back to her. I'll find out where she lives. I'll watch for her in the Park and follow her home. I'll make her give it back.

I can't. I can't. What *can* I do? Pound notes are unidentifiable unless you've kept a record of the numbers, and who does? She'll laugh in my face. If I kick up a fuss she might easily call the police and have me arrested for causing a disturbance.

Ten pounds it cost me. Ten pounds two and six, in fact. Well, I must try to look on it philosophically. I've learned my lesson. That is the first and last time I have any truck with creatures of that sort. Perhaps, in the long run, it was cheap at the price. Yet I was a fool. For ten pounds—even for four—I could have taken a girl out to dinner and seduced her afterwards. That way I'd have got value for money.

CHAPTER THREE

WYNDHAM put down the sheets, locked them in a drawer, and went out. He walked to the nearest pub and drank two double scotches in rapid succession. He needed them badly. He returned to his office, took out the diary, and resumed reading, his face grim. He noticed that the entries for the ensuing week were scrappy and cast in the form of grumbling. The diarist vented his muted spleen on Y who, in the absence of the Boss, was in charge of the office. Y was perpetually finding fault with his work, he was sarcastic in the hearing of junior members of the staff and smirked when he heard them snigger. When the diarist complained of feeling off-colour, Y told him bluntly that if he was ill he should stay at home instead of coming to the office to make mistakes. The grumbles were interspersed with dark hints about the diarist's real purpose. "Y is just trying to make himself look bigger by trying to make me look smaller," he wrote. "I won't stand for it. I'll show him. I'll show all of them. I'll make them realize that they're dealing with a Big man. I don't know, yet, but I'll think of a way." It was not until Wednesday, August 2nd, that the entries returned to the major key. Under this date Wyndham read:

Oh my God! I'm being blackmailed. She wants fifty pounds by Friday, otherwise she will send the photograph to my wife and the office. I shall be ruined. I haven't got fifty pounds. How can I possibly raise fifty pounds? She took all my spare money last week. I don't know what to do. I'm distraught with worry. I think I shall go mad.

The demand came in a letter by the first post today. It was a cheap envelope which smelled of cheaper scent. I stared at it, astonished. I had no idea who could have written to me. I opened the envelope and the photo dropped out, face upwards. If my wife had been in the room she'd have seen it and it would have been all up. I covered it quickly and ran into this room, horrified. It shows us together. It shows everything. I'm clearly recognizable. I tore it into little pieces and burned it but that's no good. I've got to get hold of the negative. The bitch! If I could lay my hands on her now I'd kill her. I would. I'd kill her. Oh God! What am I going to do? There must be *something*. I can't think.

Thursday, August 3rd: I feel better today. There's only one thing to do. I must go to the police. I've remembered that they keep the victim's name secret in blackmailing cases. I can't say I like the idea of telling *anyone* but I can see no alternative. Unless . . . yes, that's the idea. I'll keep the rendezvous with her tomorrow and I'll threaten her. Then, when she's properly scared, I'll relent. I'll tell her I won't prosecute if she hands over the negative. She won't stand up against *that*. She can't afford trouble with the police. She's only a common prostitute. I'll show her.

Friday, August 4th: I mustn't go to the police. I daren't. It would be nearly as bad as flaunting that photo in my wife's face or showing it round the office. She said it's not true that the police keep your name out of the case. Hundreds of people know: the local police, the people in court; you're seen going to the police station and the courtroom. The news gets around. There's always *someone* who'll tattle. Oh God, what am I going to do? I told her I hadn't brought the fifty pounds and she's given me till next Wednesday. When I said I couldn't raise it, she sneered. Oh, God, how I'd like to kill her!

Saturday, August 5th: She would be better dead. The country would be better off if she were dead. How many other decent people has she driven to misery with her demands? The man who killed her would perform a public service. Why must we live in agony because of her? Is it just? Is it right? Yet the law cannot touch her. I shall have to pay, as the others have paid, and when she has taken every penny she will explode my reputation in my face. I shall be an outcast, a laughing-stock. And what for? A momentary weakness. It is monstrous, foul. If only she would die, today, tonight, this week-end. In a road accident, perhaps. Thousands of decent people die every year in road accidents. Lots of them are killed at Bank Holiday week-ends.

But not her. No such luck. She'll live for years. Why is there no justice in the world? Why am I singled out for misfortune? The office, my wife, this woman—all are trampling on me, crushing my talent, tormenting me. Yet I know that this is not my destiny. I feel my destiny inside me, deep and solid. I am destined to make the world ring with my deeds. I can still do it, black though the future looks. I can. I will. I *must*. The obstacles must be cleared away. I must be resolute, bold, forceful. I have been too kind. None applaud me for it. They call it weakness. But I'll show them.

I'm a fool. How *can* I show them? I'm in the clutches of a blackmailer. I can see no way out except disgrace and ruin. It would be better if I killed myself.

Sunday, August 6th: I am calmer today. I have thought the problem out. It would *not* be better for me to kill myself. Why *should*

I die because of a cheap, thieving, dirty prostitute? I am an immeasurably better person than she could ever be. Besides, my death would solve nothing. She would circulate the photo just the same.

I carved the joint today, as I do every Sunday—every Sunday a joint—and I thought what an admirable weapon the knife would make. The blade is at least a foot long, extremely narrow with age and wear, but it is sharp at the point and the edge is like a razor. I must say that I do know how to sharpen a carving-knife. I wished I could have plunged it into that woman's heart. It would solve all my problems. But that would be murder. Besides, I don't know how to go about it.

Monday, August 7th: I am saved! My luck has turned! I have won the pools! In the worry about that woman I forget to check my coupon until today. And I've won! It won't be a fortune, according to the newspaper forecasts, but it should be at least £200. I can pay her. I'll get back the negative—and the episode will be ended. I feel quite weak with relief.

Wednesday, August 9th: I have won £247 18s. 6d. I cashed the cheque today. I've never had so much money in my hands all at once in my life. Yet I do not feel excited. In an hour I must hand over fifty pounds to that woman. What is worse, if I can't get the negative back, I shall have to give her more later, and more, and more, until it is all gone. Of course she won't give me the evidence. Blackmailers never do. It's like throwing money into the street. Whenever she's short of fifty or a hundred she'll return, and as long as I pay she'll continue to demand.

Nearly two hundred and fifty pounds! If only I could call it mine! I could take a holiday on my own. Or perhaps I could take that girl I met in the restaurant. We could go to Brighton. Why Brighton? Why not the Continent? I've always wanted to go to France. I've read about an island off the French coast somewhere where nudists live.

It's time to go and pay up. If only she will be content with fifty pounds. I'll plead with her. I *must* have the negative. I *must*.

Later: I have made up my mind. She must die. I have even decided how to do it. The plan flashed into my mind as I stood talking to her. I shall do it without remorse, without vengeance even; it is not for myself alone. I think of all the other men whom she is tormenting, and know that I must help them as well as myself.

I was pleading with her, grovelling. I am ashamed. She took the fifty and refused to give me the negative. She laughed at me. I went wild. I threatened. She turned nasty. She demanded another fifty, to be paid tomorrow. I pleaded. It did no good. I thought of all my money trickling into her hands and I hated her. That's when the plan came.

I shall go to the Park tomorrow with my knife. I shall wait for her. I shall kill her. There is only one difficulty: the recovery of the negative. No doubt she has a collection of them, which the police will find after her death, and every man will be suspect. They would be able to prove nothing against any one of us, but detectives would visit us, and we should all be under suspicion. So I must find the negatives and destroy them.

After she had left, therefore, I followed her discreetly and when she picked up her next customer I went after them to her place. I made a note of her address and the fact—which I had forgotten from my own encounter with her—that she carries her doorkey in her small purse. When I have disposed of her I shall take her key, let myself unobtrusively into her flat, search it until I find the negatives, destroy them, and leave. This is the only risky part of the business but the street in which she lives is narrow and dark.

I am convinced that no one else knows about the photo. I have questioned her, cunningly. I think I can believe her. After all, the less others know about blackmail the better.

I have just noticed that tomorrow is the night of the new moon.

Friday, August 11th: Really, it was too easy, so easy that it requires no description. I simply kept the rendezvous, stabbed her, found the negative in her purse (surely she was foolish to carry it?), threw the purse away and came home. I simply cannot understand why other murderers have made such heavy weather of their deeds. Mind you, my success was entirely due to careful planning and attention to detail. For instance, though my plan was clear in outline from the first, I realized this morning that some factors were vague. When I thought about it, I realized that I did not know positively where the heart is situated in the human body. Everyone knows roughly where it is, of course, but approximation was no good to me. So I consulted a medical dictionary in the local library and this evening I rigged up a rough dummy, marked the heart with chalk, and practised lunging at it. I became expert quite quickly, considering that I am new to the business and that the knife is balanced for carving, not stabbing.

I also bought some paper-back books on famous crimes. I thought that they might give me hints on things to avoid. Their chief impact was a feeling of disgusted amazement. The stupidity of these people is really astonishing. Take Neil Cream, for instance: he might just as well have stood up in Trafalgar Square and shouted his guilt from Nelson's Column. When I considered how superior my brain is to theirs, I had no qualms.

There was also the problem of the knife. My original intention was to carry it strapped to my forearm, but the blade was too long. It kept one arm stiff. Next I thought of doing it up in a parcel but discarded the idea as being clumsy and noisy. The solution, when it came, was simplicity itself. The handle is, of course much wider and thicker than the blade. I therefore cut a small slit in the seam of my right trouser pocket. It is just wide enough to take the blade, which swings by its haft against my leg.

My chief interest in the whole affair lies in my own reactions. I am extraordinarily calm. I astonish myself. Ever since I made up my mind to dispose of that creature my mind has moved better than ever in my life. The curious thing is that I don't *feel* as though I am thinking faster and clearer. That is the deception. At first I thought my brain was moving sluggishly. It worried me, until I saw the results. The *Daily Telegraph* crossword puzzle, for instance. I haven't attempted to solve it on more than a few mornings since my troubles began, but it used to be my regular pastime on the Tube to the office. I never managed to solve more than two-thirds or three-quarters of it and today, when I took it up, I was conscious that I was solving the clues in slow motion, as it were. Yet by the time I reached my destination the entire square was filled. I was amazed.

The same thing happened in the office. No problem was too difficult for me. There are always a number of complications in my routine tasks, and sometimes they occupy me for the better part of the morning. Today I took everything in my stride. A strange phenomenon. It fascinates me. Is it something to do with concentration? It would be interesting to discuss it with a psychologist, only I can't, of course. A pity. I feel magnificent. I have risked my life (or at least my liberty; I'm not sure that I could be hanged under the new law) to rid the world of a social pest. I shall get no thanks for it but at least I possess the knowledge of my deed and the superlative way in which I carried it out. Why, I believe I could remove as many of those creatures as I chose. Not that I shall, of course—though there are powerful arguments in favour of it as a final solution of an intractable problem.

I am tired. I must go to bed.

CHAPTER FOUR

THE entry for that day, August 11th, finished at the bottom of a page. Wyndham turned over, glanced at the date which headed the sheet, and paused, startled. It said: "Friday, September 8th." A gap of four weeks. Frowning, he riffled through the remaining pages (none were numbered) to see if any had become misplaced, but the later entries ran in correct sequence. He turned to the entry for September 8th, and began to read the text. He saw at once that the break had been deliberate.

It is four weeks since I killed that creature (he read). Twenty-eight days in which I have done nothing. I am ashamed. I have been selfish. I have been concerned only with my own problems and their solution. I solved those problems when I disposed of that creature. I forgot all those other men who are being destroyed by others like her. These men looked to me for their salvation and I failed them; I, who had the skill and courage to act in my own defence. I shudder to think of the torments they have endured owing to my negligence. I possess the ability to bring ease to hundreds—perhaps thousands—of tortured men, and I have not used it.

I have thought about this, guiltily, for a couple of weeks now. I have decided that God has called me to perform a special task. It is my destiny to rid the world of these pests. There can be no other explanation. How else can my own reactions be explained? The calm brilliance which burst on me after I had made up my mind to kill her, dominated me for several days. They recognized the new me in the office. A new respect was shown me from all levels of the staff. Y stopped being nasty. Once, he actually remarked that the quality of my work had "improved out of sight". He even asked my advice on a matter outside my department, and acted on it. But this state of mind did not last. Gradually I felt my powers slipping away. My intellect dulled. Physical discomfort assailed me when I thought that I was finished with sex. I made mistakes. The attitude of my colleagues changed. They sneer at me, they snigger, these little cowardly people who would not dare do what I have done. It has troubled me, this gradual going back to the past, to work-day worries, to the eternal problems of sex. Only in the last few days have I been able to see things clearly once again. Now I am resolved on my duty, however difficult or dangerous it may be. Only a very few men in any generation are strong enough to shoulder the burdens of the oppressed. I am one of those men and I must not shirk my destiny. I must rid the world of these creatures who prey on men.

Since I came to this decision I have been exploring the territory. There are numerous creatures ripe for destruction. They lurk in the Park, hiding in the shadows, but they shall not escape me. I will seek them out. I will make an example of them. I will drive their sisters from their abominable profession. If they attempt to skulk behind closed doors I shall root them out. I will put an end to this curse of man once and for all.

I have chosen September 10th—the night of the new moon— for my return to duty. It will be a spectacular return.

Wyndham turned over the sheet, but he did not read on immediately. He thought: This is where I came in, God help me. He shuddered. He pressed the heels of his hands to his aching temples. The movement caused the envelope in his pocket to crackle. His haggard face turned sour. The document had come too late to save him.

He sat back, weary, drained and sad. He laid his hands on the desk, palms upwards and stared at them. His fevered mind expressed surprise that there was no blood on them. There ought to be blood, he thought, a lot of blood.

PART TWO

Harvest

CHAPTER ONE

DETECTIVE-CHIEF-INSPECTOR DAVID WYNDHAM drove off the
night ferry from Dunkirk, out of the customs shed at Dover, and
surveyed his native land with a mental snarl. Everything about
England—the weather, the roads, the pubs, the food—conspired
to offend him, and by the time he reached his flat in West Hill,
Hampstead, he was in an evil temper. The day was exceptionally
warm for a second Sunday in September, but after seven weeks
combined sick and annual leave spent in Southern Spain and
Morocco, the air struck chill. The roads were not unduly crowded,
for it was early and he travelled against the main stream of traffic,
but after the fast roads of France and the emptiness of Spain his
old Hillman seemed to be crawling through glue. Cafés and pubs
depressed him, with their blank faces and secretive interiors. In
the sane countries of southern Europe at this hour, the gaily
decorated street cafés would be crowded with colourful people.
His flat was spotless and Mrs. Fuller, the woman who "did" for
him, had stacked the refrigerator with his favourite foods, but
the dull heavy brownness of the rented furniture stuck like stale
chocolate to a palate made sensitive by white-washed walls and
bright interiors.

Wyndham dumped his bags in the centre of the living-room
floor and refused to unpack, as though by delaying the operation
he might convince himself that his long holiday had not really
ended. He prepared lunch, not caring what he ate. At two o'clock,
restless and irritated, he tried to force himself to think about
tomorrow. I must pull myself together, he told himself; all
holidays come to an end. But he knew that his feelings went
deeper than peevish resentment at the ending of a leave. There
was a woman in it, too, and his new job.

Presently he told himself to go down to Albany Street and meet
a few of the chaps; get the feel of things; take the measure of the
Super, renew acquaintance with Jim Follitt, the only officer at the

station whom he knew personally. He went down to the Hillman and pointed its nose south. He drove automatically and presently found himself in New Bond Street, which was not on his route, looking for a shop window. He located it and pulled up on the other side of the almost deserted thoroughfare. He read the sign greedily: "Lindy Lou. Hats à la mode." The few models on display did not inspire him—he knew nothing of fashion—but in any case, though he looked, he did not see them. The window reflected a trim figure in a white linen dress, with pale hair, derisive blue eyes and a mocking mouth. His pleasure in the memory was clouded with pain. The verbal darts she had shot into his ego still dangled there like bandilleros in the hide of a fighting bull. She packed a wicked punch. She possessed none of the obviously endearing traits of the female, except her good looks, and yet. . . . And yet I come here and gawp like a gauche schoolboy at the shop she owns. Don't be an idiot, Wyndham! This sickening behaviour is caused by a woman who has given you no encouragement at all, who has mocked you, hurt you, offended your masculine pride, and finally left you standing foolishly in a street in the Casbah of Tangier while she drove off, laughing, to Spain.

Wyndham growled at himself: Let it go. You're a big boy now. It was holiday fever, and her treatment was a cold douche. Now the holiday's over. She made it quite clear, without actually saying so, that you haven't a snowball's chance in hell with her. So get going. You were on your way to Albany Street—remember?—to learn the worst about your new job.

He went to Albany Street, and what he saw and heard there underlined his fears. Detective-Inspector Follitt, whose calm friendliness might have soothed him, was not on duty. Detective-Superintendent Charles Bennett, Wyndham's new superior, was. They talked, briefly. Bennett was a large, thick-set man with a long and honourable career behind him, but his bulk was now a mere façade. The man was a ruin. Hard work, ill-health and family sorrows had destroyed him. He spoke brusquely and carried himself with an exaggerated military gait, but Wyndham divined, correctly, that these were camouflage to conceal the flaccidity of his mind and will.

His attitude towards Wyndham was at once grateful and resentful: the gratitude for young, strong shoulders and brains to ease the intolerable burden of office; the resentment of a once powerful man at the encroachment of one who would replace him, and might humiliate him in the doing of it. Wyndham walked back to his car with his sourness intensified. The situation was exactly as he had feared. He had been put in as Bennett's stooge. He would do all the work and Bennett would get the credit. He would carry the weight of the division, Bennett would possess the authority. His promotion was not a compliment, it was a dirty trick engineered by powerful men he had offended. They had taken him from a job he liked and did well and placed him in an invidious position. They wanted to cut him down to size. Wyndham, who was devoid of envy, malice or spite, raged in impotent fury, unable to comprehend why he had aroused these emotions in others.

Wyndham went home; there seemed to be nothing else to do. He unpacked. At the bottom of the last suitcase he came upon the gifts he had brought for Arthur Laidlaw and his daughter, Ruth: an enormous box of Havana cigars (not declared to the Customs) and a silk scarf which depicted the various phases of the bull-fight. He stared at the presents, astounded. How on earth could he have forgotten Arthur and Ruth?

He picked up the phone. He thought: They'll probably be at Brighton for the week-end. It would need only that to put the lid on a foul day. He listened morosely to the ringing tone. Just his bloody luck!

The ringing stopped. A man's voice answered. Wyndham said: "Arthur? It's David."

Laidlaw's delight emerged in a yelp.

"David! You old bastard! How are you? Had a good trip? The wound healed O.K.? Come right over. *Immediamento,* as the Italians say, if I remember rightly. Come for dinner. I'm on my lonesome—Ruth's away with friends for the week-end and Sunday is Lise's day off." Lise was Laidlaw's Austrian cook-house-keeper. "You'll see a change in Ruth when you meet, by the way. But why all this talking on the phone? I'll give you ten minutes. God! This has made my day. The soufflé at lunch was a disaster, an absolute catastrophe, by God." Laidlaw was an amateur chef. "Ten minutes, then, eh?"

Wyndham laughed for the first time for several days. "Nine and a half!" he said.

Laidlaw's flat in St. John's Wood was warm, luxurious and gay. It had been redecorated since his last visit, Wyndham noticed, in sharply contrasting colours. The motif was black, yellow, red and a dazzling white. Laidlaw saw Wyndham's glance and chuckled. "Ruth's idea," he said. "She's gone all modern. Must say I rather like it. All that antique brown makes a man feel old." His broad, fleshy face gleamed with pleasure. He handed Wyndham a drink. "God, it's good to see you again! We've missed you, Ruth and I. Not that we see much of you when you're in England, but it's different, knowing you're on the end of a phone."

Wyndham surrendered himself to the luxury of the cushions at his back. His bile subsided. It was good to have friends who were so patently glad to see you again. There weren't many in his life. It was the curse of the job. Few people chose to be on terms of genuine intimacy with a policeman, and the policeman had to be careful in his choice, too. But that wasn't the whole story. I'm a bit of a solitary, I suppose, Wyndham thought; sociable when I have to be, but not gregarious. It suddenly occurred to Wyndham, who was not an introspective man, that the real strength of the long friendship lay on Laidlaw's side. He felt a twinge of guilt. Without Laidlaw's quiet persistence their wartime friendship, formed during the long slog up the spine of Italy, would have foundered long ago in Wyndham's indifference.

Laidlaw bubbled on. "The Conquering Hero home again, healed of his wounds, heaped with fresh laurels! I should have congratulated you on your promotion. Read about it in the paper." He lifted his glass. "All the best, David!"

Wyndham acknowledged the toast, with a touch of gloom.

"I fear the worst," he said, moodily.

Laidlaw looked surprised. "But I thought it was a terrific bunk up for you—a chief-inspector and a division at the age of thirty-four. Isn't that somewhat unusual?"

Wyndham mentioned his suspicions and his interview with Bennett. Laidlaw listened intently. His boyish delight at the re-union was replaced by an expression of shrewd cynicism. Laidlaw, like many another man of business, could act the grown-up youth when he felt like it, but he remained a hard-headed stock-broker who had made good the years lost in war and prospered above the majority.

When Wyndham finished Laidlaw nodded sagely: "I get it. Promotion beyond the candidate's capacity in the hope that he falls down on the job, and can be sacked. In your case they can't sack you, but they could shift you into some backwater, I suppose, and keep you there?"

"But why?" demanded Wyndham. "It's not only nasty, it's

stupid. I only try to do my job, and I think I do it pretty well. I'm not an administrator and they know it; so why give me a job which demands an administrator? The Met. isn't so full of good officers that they can afford to waste any."

Laidlaw shrugged, cynically. "The way of the world, David. You're still a trifle naïve in some ways, despite your resounding success. You've aroused jealousy, anger, hatred—and they're taking it out on you."

"But *why*?" Wyndham repeated. "I've done nothing deliberately to offend anyone. I've simply tried to do my job the best way I can."

"And you've succeeded, brilliantly. That's why you're not popular in the Force. You're not, are you?"

"I've never courted popularity, if that's what you mean."

"I don't mean that. I mean what I say: that you're unpopular with the bulk of the officers, especially those you have outstripped and those who feel themselves threatened by your rise." He smiled with his mouth and his next words were light, but an undercurrent of seriousness flavoured the flippancy. "Good Heavens, David! You couldn't have done better if you'd tried. Just look at the list!" He ticked the items off on stubby, hairy, inelegant fingers. "From the beat to a division in twelve years —that's fast even for the jet age. In the process you've become a national hero." Wyndham wriggled uncomfortably. "Well, you have. Your last exploit clinched it. You risked your bally neck to arrest Vincie Brooks for a peculiarly atrocious murder, got a bullet in your chest for your pains, and finally, bleeding copiously, you lugged the blighter half a mile to a police station before collapsing. It wasn't even your case. You told me at the time that your superiors had their sights set on someone else."

"I was a bit tactless, I suppose," Wyndham admitted, "but what else could I do? I stumbled on the clue that proved my hunch and I had no time to notify anyone."

"But that's not all," said Laidlaw. "You're not an orthodox policeman; you're not even an orthodox Englishman. You don't plod painstakingly, you take inspired leaps in the dark. You don't tread delicately in debate, you charge in like a bull in a drawing-room when the Crown Derby is on display. You had the nerve to be born in Tangier and the effrontery to be brought up in France and Spain. You actually *like* frogs, wogs and dagoes. Then, too, your mother tongue isn't good enough for you. Oh no! You must also speak French and Spanish fluently. You don't keep a dog, smoke a pipe, wear tweeds, or don a bowler. And, having offended every susceptibility dear to the insular copper and the right-thinking Briton, you insist on remaining a bachelor into your thirty-fifth year. You're not a dyed-in-the-wool Englishman, David. You're a freak!"

"Note my four heads!" said Wyndham. He laughed, defensively. "I can't help my birth and upbringing, nor anything else, either. It's the way I'm made."

"You could get married," said Laidlaw, pouring more drinks. "Why don't you? A wife—the right wife—would be good for you."

The remark revived memories of Linda Ward. Wyndham said, sharply and unthinkingly: "Speak for yourself, Arthur." Laidlaw was not offended. "No thanks, David. I've had one. Mary was the best. In the twelve years since she was killed no woman has come within a mile of offering me the happiness she gave. And then, of course, there's been Ruth. We're pretty close; always have been. I couldn't ask her to accept a substitute mother unless I'd been absolutely sure the marriage would turn out all right. But you're different. There's a lot of nonsense talked about marriage, but it's still a good thing, with the right woman."

Wyndham said, gloomily: "I always pick the wrong ones. When I like them, they loathe the sight of me."

Laidlaw looked at Wyndham curiously. He sensed that Wyndham was on the verge of deeper confidences than usual and was human enough to be inquisitive. "Have there been so many?" he asked, seriously.

"No, only two. The first was a long time ago. She was an Israeli freedom fighter. Her name was Yael. Later, she was killed."

He paused. Laidlaw waited, intrigued. It was the first time that Wyndham had spoken of his serious love affairs. He hoped Wyndham would fill in the details, but he did not. Instead, he said, abruptly: "I met the other in Tangier, three weeks ago." Memories surged in a tide of frustration and loosened his tongue. He said, with unusual loquacity: "I met her four times. I took her to a café twice and to dinner once. I didn't even kiss her. She's an English businesswoman, lovely to look at, and as sharp as they come. She's got a disturbing knack of persuading you to talk about yourself and then, just when you're feeling good, she'll shoot a barb bang into your self-esteem. She has a natural gift for authority and uses it without a trace of patronage. She's fiercely independent and insists on paying her own way. She doesn't argue;

she simply takes up the bill, divides it in two, adds a tip, and that's that. She has a macabre talent for deflating the male ego. The first time I spoke to her, she was buying a wrist-watch in the Petite Socco. I'd glimpsed her once before and thought I'd like to see her again, so when I saw her outside the bazaar I jumped in with both feet, asked what price the dealer wanted, warned her to be careful of overpaying, took over the bargaining, and beat the blighter down from forty-five quid to thirty."

He paused, breathing deeply. Laidlaw said, puzzled: "What's wrong with that? She should have swooned in your arms with gratitude."

"That's what I thought. I didn't know that before I appeared she had already beaten the man down to twenty-eight."

Laidlaw whistled. "You mean she let you go through the whole rigmarole all over again, and fail to get as good a price? Oh dear!"

"Exactly. The last time I saw her I asked her to dinner at Hassan's. Hassan's, I told her, was the one genuine Arab eating-place in Tangier with absolutely no concessions to the West. She agreed. She let me build myself up as the one living soul who really knew Tangier, and especially Hassan's."

Laidlaw said, sympathetically: "And Hassan's had changed?"

"It's completely phoney now. All neon, new brass and American dishes. And as we walked in, while I'm still in a daze—I hadn't been to Tangier for five years, you see—Hassan greeted her like a long-lost friend."

Laidlaw shook his head sorrowfully. "Put her out of your mind, David," he said. "She's no good to man or beast."

"But that's not all. You know how I feel about prostitutes. You don't like them yourself, but they make me want to gag."

"I know," said Laidlaw, sympathetically. "Niggers and homos do the same thing to me."

"It's pathological, I suppose, but I can't help it. I loathe them. Anyway, outside Hassan's, a prostitute put her hand on my arm. I knocked it aside, a bit roughly, I suppose. And I got a real dressing-down! They were only doing their job, she said. Only trying to earn a living. If there weren't men who wanted them there'd be no prostitutes, and so on and so on."

"And that was the last time you saw her? I'm not surprised."

"Oh, but I didn't end the thing. She did. We left Hassan's and I suggested going on to a night-club. She shook her head. Deep regrets and all that but she was leaving for Málaga next day.

Must get back to her hotel to pack. And hey presto! a taxi appeared, she climbed in, said good-bye and was off, leaving me high and dry."

"Didn't you follow her?"

"I knew her name but not where she was staying. Naturally, I'd made inquiries at likely hotels but she must have rented a flat. I even followed her to Málaga and bought two tickets for the bull-fight—Sanmiguel was fighting; he nearly got killed that day, as a matter of fact—but I didn't catch up with her."

"A waste of a good ticket," said Laidlaw.

"Oh, the second ticket wasn't wasted," said Wyndham, absently. "Some Swedish matron whose husband spends the summer making money in Stockholm while she blues it for him in Spain. Charming woman. Beautiful, too. But after Linda she came nowhere. I felt as if I'd trained for a heavyweight championship and been forced to spar with a flyweight."

"Well," said Laidlaw, "it's pretty obvious that she's got under your skin, but I'd say you were well rid of her."

"I suppose so. The trouble is, I can't get her out of my mind." A sheepish half-grin drifted over his face. "I even drove down New Bond Street today to stare at the shop she owns."

Laidlaw looked up, interested, "Oh, you know that much about her?"

"Fortunately—or unfortunately, depending on the way you look at it. Lindy Lou's, a swank hat shop. Know it?"

Laidlaw shook his head. "Women's hats aren't much in my line and Ruth hasn't become addicted to the more *outré* models, yet. What's the charmer's name?"

"Linda Ward."

Laidlaw's whisky glass paused on the way to his mouth. He said, sharply: "What?"

Wyndham looked up. "Linda Ward. Do you know her?"

Laidlaw put down his glass and fumbled for his pipe. He said, "Oh, Linda *Ward*. No, I don't think so. I know a Belinda Warne. What does she look like?"

Wyndham described her. Laidlaw shook his head. "No, it doesn't ring a bell, though if she's a big fashion bug maybe I've read about her." He rose, abruptly. "I'd better fix some grub. Only cold collation, I'm afraid, but there's plenty of it."

He disappeared into the kitchen. Wyndham was glad of the interruption. He regretted saying so much about his private life. The topic was not referred to again until Wyndham was preparing to depart. As Wyndham reached the door of the flat, Laidlaw, who had been a trifle distrait all evening, said, quietly: "David, don't think I'm interfering, but I've been thinking over what you said about that woman. Frankly, old boy, you must admit that she gave you the brush-off. I'd accept it, if I were you. She obviously slings a nasty left hook. You'll only get hurt a lot worse if you pursue it. Put her out of your mind, David. Scrub the slate."

Wyndham felt annoyed, but concealed it.

"Thanks, Arthur. You're absolutely right, of course. Good night."

Scrub it? thought Wyndham, driving home through empty streets. Easier said than done. Arthur *was* right, of course; dignity, self-respect, common sense, all demanded an end to something that had never really begun. He hadn't a chance. He couldn't get through to her. She was impregnable. She was hard, perhaps selfish (or only self-centred? There was a difference). She was composed, always in command of herself, with a mind as cool and dangerous as a rapier in the hand of a skilled swordsman. If only there was a chink in her armour, as there had been in Yael's, through which he could get to the woman beneath.

He thought of Yael, raw, indignant, idealistic; Yael, who made him think of olives, blinding sunshine and a rough, wild honesty of purpose, a tumbling mass of molten emotion pouring out for the country which had not yet been born. Yael, so different from Linda.

Wyndham's thoughts jerked. So different? But no! They were alike, too, in their different ways. Yael would shoot barbs under your skin as soon as look at you. Shoot bullets, too, only he had caught her without her rifle. Yet what had Yael's antagonism really amounted to? Nothing but a box-hedge round her emotions. Once he'd broken through to the woman behind the idealist, the façade had collapsed like the walls of Jericho before the trumpet. Then, briefly, a little of the lava of her emotion had poured over him. For how long? A week, ten days? No more, and then she had slipped away in the night to return to the fighting and stopped a bullet in her throat. What a bloody waste. . . . Or, as she lay dying, had she thought that it was all worth while?

Wyndham garaged his car. Forget Yael! Concentrate on Linda. She *must* have a weakness; she couldn't be all ice. A scrap of their conversation returned to him. He had commented on her intransigence and she had admitted that perhaps it was a line of defence. A defence against her emotions, of course. Sometime, somehow, she had been hurt by a man, and she covered the wound with a bandage of verbal nettles. Well, he had been stung and stung badly, but so what? It would take worse than that to keep him away.

Whistling, his fighting spirit restored, he climbed the stairs to his flat. As he inserted the key in the lock, he yawned. It reminded him that he had slept poorly on the boat the night before and that it was midnight.

Wyndham closed the door. The phone began to ring.

Arthur Laidlaw knotted the cord of his pyjamas round his thickening waist, climbed into bed, and switched off the lamp. He did not immediately fall asleep. He thought: Linda Ward, for Christ's sake! I suppose I should have told him the truth, but how could I? He wouldn't have believed a bald statement of fact, and a full explanation is impossible. I did as much as I could. I warned him off. Surely he'll have the sense to take a piece of good advice?

Just before he dropped off to sleep he reflected, cynically, that good advice is the world's one free commodity which no one cares to accept.

The telephone said: "Chief-Inspector Wyndham, sir? Duty sergeant at Albany Street here. We've been trying to get you for half an hour. The Super asks would you get down to Regents Park right away and take over? A tom—prostitute, I mean, sir —found murdered."

Wyndham asked questions, made notes, put down the receiver. All his misgivings returned. He was in a rotten spot. Damn Bennett! The man couldn't even let him finish his leave in peace. He was to be plunged into a murder case before he'd had a chance to find his feet in the division, or even get to know his detectives. And what a murder! Some lousy cheap tom killed for the contents of her purse or in a sexual frenzy, the most difficult of crimes to solve and the least rewarding in terms of kudos.

Wyndham swore, and stumped wearily downstairs to his car.

CHAPTER TWO

THE area had been roped off and illuminated by the spotlights of police cars. Uniformed constables kept at bay a group of by-standers, mostly Pressmen. Inside the square stood a group of men in plain clothes, watching the official cameraman record the scene. Outside, hand torches probed the darkness as men searched for clues among the noisome litter of a park at night.

Detective-Inspector Jim Follitt, in soft hat, loose raincoat and black boots, stood slightly apart from the other men inside the square, watching the scene incuriously, mentally docketing and labelling the sparse quantity of information he had been able to collect. He had done all that could be done; the rest was up to Wyndham. Follitt felt a surge of pleasant anticipation at the prospect of working with him once again. He liked Wyndham; more, he admired him. Other men thought this strange, for they were opposites, and in a sense, rivals, as every career man must be the rival of his colleagues when the opportunities for advance-ment are limited. Follitt, who was on the edge of fifty, had been an inspector when Wyndham was a first-class sergeant. He was still an inspector and Wyndham would give the orders now. Follitt found nothing humiliating in the reversal. He had known for years that the best rank he could hope to attain was chief-inspector, and then only by a stroke of stupendous good luck. The luck had not come his way and now, most probably, never would. Follitt accepted the fact philosophically, as he had accepted many other unpalatable facts: the death of his wife from cancer, six months before; the loss of his only child during the war. Follitt, who was a non-smoker, a teetotaller, a vegetarian and a church-goer, did not know why these things should have happened to him. It was sufficient that they had happened. There was a time to grieve, and a time when grief must be put aside under the pressure of life. And now I plod, he thought a trifle ruefully, doing my work the best way I know how, trying to help others, trying to live up to my principles, such as they are. Oh well, this time comes to everyone, I suppose, and it is a time of peace.

A short, bulky figure with angry eyes and a long thin nose popped up beside him. It said: "For God's sake, Follitt, how much longer am I to be kept waiting around? Your boys have all finished. Wyndham can look at a hundred pictures of the body."

"I'm sorry, Doctor Lawrence. The body is not to be moved until the Chief-Inspector has seen it."

The doctor growled. "Anyone would think this new chap was an ogre. Are you scared to death of him?"

"I'm doing my job," said Follitt. "He is the officer in charge. I have never worked with him on a murder case so I do not know his methods. I do not know what he will see that I have missed. You can make a proper examination when he gives the word. Not before."

Lawrence, the police surgeon, who knew this as well as Follitt, blinked at the rebuke. He realized that he had trespassed beyond the limits of Follitt's tolerance. He said, to change the subject: "There's something odd about this murder."

Follitt, feeling unusually ruffled, thought of saying: "I can see that." He did not. He said: "What's odd, exactly?"

"How the devil do I know, *exactly?* All I can say for certain is that the girl's dead! But——" He paused. They heard a constable challenge an intruder, and the voice announcing identity. The constable said: "I beg your pardon, sir. Haven't had time to get to know you, sir." They heard Wyndham say, grumpily: "You will!" Follitt frowned slightly. The retort was not Wyndham's normal form. He turned as Wyndham strode across. The doctor decided to slide gently into the background.

Wyndham said: "Evening, Jim—or is it morning? You don't give a new boy much time to settle in, do you?"

Follitt smiled. " 'Evening, guv'nor. Nice to see you. Welcome to Albany Street."

"Thanks," said Wyndham. He felt a touch of pleasure at the genuine warmth in Follitt's voice. A flash sizzled. He looked at the body and the warmth chilled. He stepped forward. He was conscious of a surreptitious scrutiny from men who knew him only by his newspaper reputation, men whose careers he now controlled. The thought irked him but he said nothing.

He looked down at the dead woman. Dying, she had no doubt expiated her sins on earth, but he felt no lessening of his repugnance. He saw nothing pitiful in the dead face with its wide-open sightless eyes, and the heavy make-up which lay on the waxen skin like a crude mask. In life she had been a tom; in death she remained a nuisance.

She lay awkwardly on her right side on a park bench with her heels trailing on the ground. She wore a thick sweater of red angora wool and a tight, black skirt. Above the waist, apart from the inelegance of her posture, she might have been asleep, The legs, too, though limp and grotesque, were still shapely. One foot was bare and a spike-heeled shoe stood demurely by the bench, oddly precise against the imprecision of its owner's body. Between legs and torso. . . . Wyndham glanced briefly at the evidence of destruction.

"Has the body been moved?"

"Only accidentally, by the constable who found her. He thought she had fallen asleep and touched her shoulder. The body slid slightly sideways. He's here when you want to talk to him."

"In a moment. What does the doctor say?"

"She's dead!" said Lawrence. "If you've finished I'll have a real look at her."

Follitt introduced them. The two men eyed each other and were not sure that they liked what they saw. They shook hands, warily. Wyndham said: "You can have her now, doctor."

Men came with a stretcher and moved the body under the full strength of the spotlight. Wyndham and Follitt watched the doctor go to work. Wyndham said: "Weapon?"

"None in the body or anywhere nearby. I've got men looking for it." He shrugged. "It could be anywhere in the Park."

"Or back in the killer's pocket. . . . The time of death must wait on our peppery friend, I suppose."

"We can fix the outside limits without the medical evidence. Pilcher, the constable who found her, spoke to her less than an hour before."

"Good! Any belongings?"

"A purse of the type toms often carry. It had fallen to the ground, perhaps from her lap when she was attacked. It contained a ten-bob note, twelve and fourpence in change, a Yale key, lipstick, powder, a packet of ten Senior Service, and a box of matches. Nothing else."

"No means of identification?"

"None, but we know who she is. Pilcher's nicked her more than once."

Wyndham said: "I'd better have a word with the redoubtable Pilcher."

Pilcher was a stolid, heavy, flat-footed man with thirty-five years' service on the beat behind him. He saluted smartly. He said: "At approximately 10.17 p.m. on the 12th instant I was proceeding along my beat in the direction of——"

Wyndham said: "All right, all right! No need to be so bloody formal. You're not in the witness box now."

Pilcher reddened. Follitt's lips tightened slightly. Wyndham cursed himself. He need not be so damned impolite. He did not apologize.

Pilcher said: "I was walking along the main path about two hundred yards away, at about a quarter past ten, when I heard two pairs of footsteps approaching. Women's footsteps they were, going clack-clack. I shone my torch and recognized the girls as Connie Metcalfe and Ada Jopson." He indicated the body as it passed on a stretcher. "That's Connie, sir."

"Yes?"

"They were prostitutes, sir. Many's the time I've pinched 'em—arrested them, I mean. Well, Connie spoke to me——"

"What did she say?"

Pilcher shuffled. He said, gruffly: "She said, 'Evening, officer, how's the left big toe? Mine's killing me.'"

Follitt smothered a smile. Wyndham's face did not change.

Pilcher said, unhappily. "Once, when I pinched her, I happened to mention that I have a corn on my left big toe, sir. Seems she had one, too. That was the source of the remark, sir."

"I see. What then?"

"I told her to mind her manners and not to let me catch her up to any of her tricks or I'd get her the maximum. They both said good night and passed on, moving in this direction."

"Was there anything unusual in this?"

"No, sir. They both worked the Park, we all knew 'em." He looked uneasy. "We do our best to keep it down, sir, but you know how it is: we have our beats, and they're pretty fly birds."

"I know," said Wyndham, without sympathy.

Pilcher looked relieved. "Well, sir, they used to knock off around half-past nine, Connie and Ada, and go off for a drink together. They'd get back at about ten-fifteen and I'd usually see them."

"I understand. And then?"

"Well, sir. I walked one way and they walked the other. I completed my beat and on my way back, past here, I saw Connie on the bench."

"What time was that?"

"Five minutes past eleven, sir. She was sitting—lolling, rather —with her head back. I thought she was asleep. It was her face

I saw first, in the beam of my torch. I went over to her and touched her before I realized. . . . I'm sorry, sir."

"Can't be helped now. Can you describe exactly how she was sitting?"

"Not quite upright, sir. Sort of half sideways, if you see what I mean, leaning over, sort of, with her head back. I thought she must have been tired to have dropped off like that, because she didn't look comfortable. When I touched her she slid over. Then I saw as her eyes were open, and . . . and, what he'd done to her lower down. So then I blew my whistle, sir, and took notes until P.C. Long came and notified the station."

"I'll look at your notes later, Pilcher. In the meantime did you come to any conclusions as to how she was killed? You are the only person who actually saw her in the position in which she died."

Pilcher hesitated. "Well, sir, I did, sir, but I didn't intend to mention it, sir, because it couldn't have happened the way it looked as if it happened, if you understand me."

"Never mind the appearances, Pilcher. Just tell us what you thought."

"Very good, sir. Well, sir, I thought as she'd been stabbed in the back. I thought she'd been sitting there, leaning forward, and heard someone behind her, and tried to look, and been killed, sir." He paused. He added, gruffly: "I thought as how she'd been massaging her bad corn, sir."

Wyndham said, coldly: "You sound upset."

"Well, sir, Connie wasn't a bad sort of girl."

"She was a tom."

"Oh yes, sir, but there's toms and toms, sir. It's not easy to describe unless you know 'em as well as we do, sir. Around here, they're a big part of our job, and she was a good sort, was Connie. Not like the other one who dropped dead last month, Rosie Watkins."

"Other one?" Wyndham said, sharply.

Follitt said: "It wasn't my case, guv, but I remember it. She collapsed and died of heart failure. There was no reason to suspect foul play. She had a history of heart trouble going back to a bout of rheumatic fever as a child."

Wyndham's momentary interest died. He did not want to be burdened with the life and death histories of every tom who worked Regents Park. "Yes, yes. I see." He turned to the constable: "Thank you, Pilcher. Nice work." Pilcher flushed with pleasure. "I take it you've given Inspector Follitt all you can about Metcalfe and her friend—what's her name?—Jopson?"

"He has," said Follitt.

"Fine!" Wyndham nodded dismissal. He ground his heel into the turf. "Too hard for footprints," he said, gloomily.

Follitt nodded. "Yes. We've tested likely surfaces for fingerprints," he said. His voice announced that he expected nothing.

Wyndham sighed. "These cases are the very devil." He moved restlessly. "I'm afraid I'll have to leave the bulk of the donkey work to you, Jim. Right now I'm going to have my hands full with the division. Pick your own team. You know the ropes. Find the Jopson woman. See if she knew of anything in Metcalfe's life which might point to murder. Her pimp, if she had one. Contact all the toms who are known to use the Park. Better issue a public appeal to anyone who was in the Park at the relevant time to come forward if they heard, saw, or suspected anything unusual. The doctor's report and the post mortem might give us a lead when we get 'em. And keep up the search for the weapon and anything which the killer might have dropped. But I'd say that Jopson's your best bet. At least, she is if there's a personal as distinct from a sexual motive in the killing."

"Yes, *guv!*" said Follitt, delighted at Wyndham's confidence in him.

"It's commonplace enough," said Wyndham. "Alive or dead, toms are nothing but a bloody pest." He seemed about to say more but stopped as the doctor straightened up and walked towards them. He said: "What's the verdict, doctor?"

"Damned if I know!" said Lawrence, rubbing his chin, worried. "I've looked her over as well as I can under the conditions and I can't find anything to indicate cause of death."

"The wounds, man, the wounds!" said Wyndham, sharply.

Lawrence looked at him with a touch of contempt. Follitt felt uneasy. What was the matter with Wyndham that he hadn't seen it for himself?

"Oh yes," said the doctor, sourly, "she could have died from the mutilation—which consists of five or six slashes in the lower abdomen. But not in that position. She'd have had time to cry out, to move, even to crawl for help. She was slashed after she was killed." He turned away. "I'll get her to the mortuary and take another look. You'll want a post mortem, anyway. Good night."

A shout sounded faintly from their right. The three men turned. They heard the noise of pounding feet. A uniformed constable, helmetless, plunged heavily from among the trees and came up to them, panting.

"There's another of 'em, sir," he said. "Over there under a tree. We found her while we were looking for the weapon."

Follitt ran, shouting orders. Wyndham heard him say: "Get Pilcher." Wyndham followed at a more dignified pace.

Three minutes later he looked down at the crumpled body lying on its back. A cigarette, its tip scorched but not smoked, lay near the right hand. A box of matches lay by her feet, the contents scattered over the damp turf. The same look of peace lay on the painted face, the same evidence of savagery disfigured her body. He heard the voice of P.C. Pilcher.

"Yes, sir, I know her. It's Connie's friend. That's Ada Jopson, sir. That's Ada."

Wyndham thought: Oh for God's sake! It embraced his own self pity as well as his revulsion at Pilcher's sentimentality. He thought: A double murder. He thought: Routine, routine, routine, nothing but routine. Interview toms, interrogate pimps, interview more toms. Pry into every sleazy bedroom in the manor, talk to every hag and every ponce. And get nowhere. There'd be no leads; there never were, until the killer made a mistake, as he'd be sure to do.

He nodded to Follitt. "It's all yours. It'll have to be, I'm afraid —at any rate, just now. All the lines I mentioned, except that you won't get much out of Jopson. Keep me posted."

He turned and walked away. Follitt looked after him, scandalized. A double murder on his first day in a new division and he'd virtually turned it over to a subordinate! What had come over the man? And then censure was swept away in a tide of exultation. He should not carp. Wyndham had passed a vote of confidence in him. Clear this up and there'd be laurels for him. One thing you could say about Wyndham, he never pinched another man's thunder.

Follitt turned to his task. The faded hope of that last promotion glowing furiously amid ashes of ambition that he had thought were long since dead.

CHAPTER THREE

At four o'clock the following afternoon, Follitt gathered his notes together and headed for Wyndham's room. He was tired, his investigations had been fruitless, but he was not dismayed. He had a plan. He entered at Wyndham's call. Follitt's calm was dashed by the look of resentment in Wyndham's eyes. Follitt was offended.

Wyndham felt tired, angry and confused. He had snatched less than five hours' sleep during the night, and his first day as an administrator, even without the complication of a double murder, had been worse than he had feared. Bennett was more than a dead loss, he was an obstacle. The work of a division, with its teams of detectives in different sub-stations and its multiplicity of crime in an area which embraced every class of London's life, had revealed a mass of unsuspected detail which bothered Wyndham's tidy, straightforward mind. Crime was heavy and the division, like every other, was below strength. Every detective's case-load was overburdened. Problems, human as well as official, abounded. Policemen, like other mortals, have their problems, their jealousies, conceits, disappointments. They have sick wives or unhappy marriages, ailing children, hire-purchase debts and nagging mothers-in-law. Some of these problems, directly or indirectly, were now being inflicted on him. Wyndham did not fancy himself in the role of nursemaid or diplomat. He was a stranger in the division. He must learn to know his men, and especially those who worked well together and those who hated each other's guts. He would have to inquire into peccadilloes, watch expenses, organize manpower, get through a vast amount of paperwork, and (incidentally, it seemed to him now as he floundered in the welter of unaccustomed work) he must solve crimes, prepare evidence and secure convictions. Follitt's appearance reminded him of the double murders, and struck a deeper chord of uneasiness which he did not choose to probe.

He said: "Well, Jim, what have you got?"

"Nothing," said Follitt, coldly, still upset. "Not a sausage. None of the other girls in the Park saw or heard anything. Those who knew the dead women could think of no reason why they should have been killed. They give them good characters. Three people responded to the public appeal. They saw a dark form flitting among the trees and waving a knife which gleamed in the moonlight. Only there was no moonlight and none of them thought that this remarkable sight had any significance until they read their papers today."

Wyndham nodded. "The usual lunatics. What about the pimps?"

"Only one, the same man. He is heartbroken—God knows where his next penny is coming from. The girls got on well together and he didn't ill-treat them too much."

"Anything in Records?"

"Nothing. There are no unsolved murders anywhere which bear similar trademarks." Follitt paused. He said, seriously: "I'm afraid we've got a Ripper on our hands."

Wyndham looked at him without pleasure. "That's what the newspapers say. But why?"

"The medical evidence, guv. Both girls were killed by a stab wound through the back, to the heart. It was made by a thin blade at least five inches long, and not more than half an inch wide, which had been instantly withdrawn. It left a mark like a short scratch which had seeped only a little blood. That's why Lawrence couldn't find it at first."

"I don't see what that proves," said Wyndham.

"There's the rest of the evidence, guv. There are no signs that either woman was sexually attacked. In fact, as you saw yourself, all the appearances indicate that they were taken unawares. Someone crept up behind them, stabbed and mutilated them, and made off. It looks to me like someone with a vendetta against toms. In which case, he'll try again."

"What about the known sexual deviants?"

"We're checking their movements last night. Nothing in their records to indicate that they'd go in for this sort of thing."

"Well, you and the toms and the newspapers may be right, but I don't think you are," said Wyndham, who did not want to think so. The burden of the thought was intolerable. "I'm inclined to think in terms of a personal grudge."

Follitt said nothing, but felt rebuked.

"It isn't clear which tom was killed first, but the doctors are inclined to think that it was Metcalfe. It doesn't matter. Suppose one of them had been blackmailing someone, or had robbed him——"

"Both girls had good characters," objected Follitt. "Nothing against them except convictions for soliciting."

"You know how few of the victims complain in these cases," said Wyndham, impatiently. Follitt thought: Yes, but coppers like Pilcher generally know a good deal more about these girls than is shown in their criminal records. He did not say so. He was uneasy in the presence of this new Wyndham.

"He decides to murder her, and does so," Wyndham went on,

"but the other tom sees him and he has to kill her, too."

Follitt said: "But neither girl showed any sign of alarm. Surely, if——"

Wyndham interrupted: "She may not have known that whatever she had seen was dangerous to her. It could have been something which would enable her to connect the killer with the crime only when the murder was discovered."

Follitt thought, disrespectfully: You've been reading too many crime stories. He also wondered why Wyndham was taking so much trouble to play down the murders. It was one thing to hand over the investigation to a trusted subordinate; quite another to buck that officer's conclusions. Admittedly, it was not pleasant to think that a Ripper might be on the loose, but in the present state of the investigation the wise policeman looked at every angle. Was it because he loathed toms and could scarcely view them as human beings? Or was it the weight of his new office? Or a combination of the two? The first, though common in a certain type of person, meant a blind spot in a policeman; the second was weakness. Follitt felt disturbed.

Wyndham tapped his desk. "You've covered a lot of ground, Jim, very quickly. I'm grateful. I'd like to cut down your squad. Let me have Green and Martin back, will you? You, Harris and the aids should be able to cover the remaining inquiries."

Follitt looked up, mutinously. His scheme was in danger. "I was planning to put them on observation in the Park, together —if you'll permit it—with a few extra uniformed men. If the killer *is* a Ripper type—and I feel we must consider the possibility —he might try to strike again while the moon is new."

"Can't be done," said Wyndham, forcibly. "Pure waste of time and manpower. You can't possibly cover the entire Park—you'd need the army."

"I didn't want to!" said Follitt testily, disappointed. "Metcalfe and Jopson were killed within a small radius. We could cover that area pretty adequately. Besides, we can warn off the girls in other areas so that if he *is* after toms and only toms, he'll *have* to strike where we've got our men."

"Damn it!" said Wyndham, irritably, "even if you're right, he may not kill again for a month!"

"A few days is all I need," said Follitt, urgently. "I think the fact that he killed on the night of the new moon is significant. If he strikes again, he'll probably do it during this period."

Wyndham shook his head. "There are too many ifs and buts

about it. Frankly, I can't spare the men. If I had 'em, you could go ahead, but I haven't. It's much more important to stop this spate of thefts by the villain the Press is calling 'the TV peak-hour burglar'. The wealthy matrons of St. John's Wood are throwing a dozen fits."

Follitt said, coldly: "Murder is more serious than theft."

"And we'll have murder on our hands if we don't catch him. The man's armed! Our names will be mud if he blows some worthy housewife's brains out in the middle of a soap commercial."

Follitt felt deep anger.

"But nobody cares about two dead toms!"

Wyndham stared at him, surprised. "Of course we do!" he said, heartily. "But for Heaven's sake keep a sense of proportion! Toms are always getting bashed up or killed—they're occupational hazards. But how would you feel if your wife went out to make a cup of coffee in the middle of *Laramie* and was shot down in cold blood?"

Follitt's furious retort died, stillborn, in the ringing of the phone. Wyndham answered. His face brightened. "Ruth. . . ! I'm fine, thanks. Did you have a good week-end. . . ? Glad you liked it. I'll translate the Spanish under the pictures when I see you. . . . Thursday at seven-thirty? I'd love to, murder, theft and mayhem permitting. See you then. Give your father my regards."

He hung up. "Yes, Jim, we'll do that. Tell Green and Martin I'd like to see them."

"Yes, sir," said Follitt, formally. He went out. Wyndham stared after him, annoyed. The meaning behind the cold "sir" was clear. Follitt was deeply disturbed. But what the hell else can I do? Wyndham asked himself, irritably. I've a limited number of officers and an apparently unlimited amount of crime to police. The respectable citizen is entitled to protection. Toms put themselves beyond the law and in doing so forfeited a certain amount of regard. Of course the murderer must be brought to justice, and he would be. Of course he'd do everything, if that were possible. But there had to be priorities and Follitt's scheme rested on too thin a foundation. They'd get the killer another way. Meanwhile, he'd do his best to see that no decent people were killed.

Wyndham returned to his desk work, his conscience bludgeoned into insensibility.

Follitt could not remember a time when he had felt so much anger and contempt. It worried him so much that he endeavoured to argue himself out of it. Wyndham is right, he thought. The murder of two toms is a sensation but the murder of one housewife over her coffee cups is a horror. I know Wyndham can't do everything. I know we're overworked and under strength. I've no right to criticize. If I were in Wyndham's chair I'd probably make the same decision and for the same reasons. . . . No, I wouldn't! If I were in charge I'd say: Two women are dead. The man who killed them must be found. Such evidence as we possess points to a psychopath, who will kill and kill and kill again unless he is stopped. Against this fact the respectable must take their chance, and the risk is slender. The armed burglar has never used his weapon, not even when he was surprised in the act. He brandished it to effect his escape. We do not know whether the gun is loaded or even (positively) if it was a gun at all. We have only the evidence of a hysterical woman.

And I know why Wyndham looks the other way (Follitt's thoughts continued). It is because he loathes toms. How many times have I seen him shiver with disgust in their presence? How many times have I heard him say that he can spot a tom a quarter of a mile away by the rottenness that emanates from her? For Wyndham, toms are not human. That is the sole reason why he has shifted the bulk of the work on me and plays down the seriousness of the case. The responsibilities of his new job are only a convenient excuse. He is allowing prejudice to blind his judgment and his sense of justice, and that is unforgivable.

Follitt tightened his mouth and tried to close his mind to thoughts which were, he had believed, alien to his tolerant nature. But the anger slumbered through the passing hours until, at 11.30 p.m. on Wednesday, September 13th, he stood once more in Regents Park and stared down at the third body. Then the anger flared until he shook. When he had issued the necessary orders, he went to the phone himself. He answered Wyndham's sleepy voice in cold, precise words.

"He's killed again, sir. Number three, practically the same place, same time. But this time he's been seen." He paused. He added, furiously, "And if I'd had the men I asked for, that girl would be alive and *he'd* be in a cell."

CHAPTER FOUR

THE park again. The roped-off square, the blazing spots, a girl
dead on a park bench, the same dark figures moving in an aimless
pattern as though in a slow, mad dance. The same men—Follitt,
the doctor, Pilcher, a detective-sergeant. The same bystanders,
the flashing camera bulbs; Wyndham's nightmare thought, as he
strode towards the scene, that time had performed a back somer-
sault, was broken by the sight of two interlopers. A young couple
stood slightly apart from the main bunch of figures, the boy stiff
with screwed-up courage, the girl close to him, frightened.

Follitt noted the purposeful stride and thought, cynically:
He's on the ball now, all right. He's really stirred up—only
forty-eight hours and one murder too late. I suppose he will now
take charge, run the investigation with ruthless precision, make
one of his inspired leaps to the truth, and bring the murderer to
justice amid a blaze of publicity. Who will know or care, then,
that the same result could have been achieved with one death the
fewer and no heroics?

Wyndham nodded curtly at the men. If Follitt's rebuke had
touched him, his face revealed no trace of it. He said: "What's
the form, Jim?"

Follitt recovered himself. "Apparently she was killed in almost
identical circumstances to Metcalfe, as she sat on the bench.
Dr. Lawrence will confirm the medical details when he's had a
chance to examine the body properly. The chief difference this
time is that he was surprised as he was finishing the job." He took
Wyndham across to the waiting couple. "Miss Florence Browning
and Mr. Fred Anderson, sir," he said, and to them: "This is
Chief-Inspector Wyndham, who is in charge of the case."

"Oooh!" said Miss Browning, gathering courage. "I've read
about you in the papers."

Wyndham smiled. "I'm afraid you've had an unnerving experience, but I'd be grateful if you will tell me exactly what
happened."

The couple glanced at each other.

"Well," said Fred, "it was like this: Me and Florrie were standing under a tree over there"—he pointed to a spot about 200
yards away—"having a bit of a kiss and a cuddle, like——"

"Nothing wrong, sir," said Florrie, anxiously. "I don't believe
in letting boys go too far, even if we are engaged."

"Of course not. And then . . . ?"

"Well, all of a sudden this bloke ran up, shouting: 'There's another of 'em. Come quick! I just found her, down there.' He sort of waved and we both looked and Florrie said, 'Oh, no, Fred, I'm frightened.' Then the bloke said, 'Oh look! Someone else is there already. Come on, there's nothing to be afraid of!' I could see a torch flashing and I said, 'Come on, Florrie, it looks like a copper.' I started to run. Florrie didn't want to go but I held her hand and she had to run. The bloke started off with us, a bit behind, like, but when we got up to this place, well, he'd done a bunk. Nowhere to be seen. So I told the copper and he——"

"Thank you, Mr. Anderson. The constable will give us the rest of it. Now, Miss Browning, is that your recollection of the incident?"

Florrie nodded. "Just like that! I was really scared. I——"

"Naturally. What did this man look like?"

A pause. The couple looked at each other. Fred said, doubtfully: "Well, I don't rightly know. You see, it was dark, and I didn't look at him proper like, if you know what I mean."

"Let me see if I can help you," said Wyndham, gently. "Was he a big man, for instance. As big as me? Or . . . ?"

Florrie looked at Wyndham's six foot one inch and fifteen stone and said: "Oooh, much bigger than you! *Much* bigger. Wasn't he, Fred?"

Fred looked doubtful. "I dunno, Florrie. Seems to me he was smaller than that, not much above my height. Bit slimmer maybe."

Wyndham measured Anderson with his eyes. Height five feet eight or nine, weight eleven to eleven and a half stone."

Florrie said, indignantly: "He was not! He was *huge.*"

"Did he wear a hat?" asked Wyndham.

No, they were almost sure that he was bare-headed, but that was almost the whole of their recollection. Patiently Wyndham took them through detail after detail. Was he bald-headed, thinning on top, or have a good head of hair? Clean shaven, bearded or moustached? Colour of eyes? Nose straight, broad, crooked, thin? Lips? Chin? Ears prominent or flat?

Did he wear an overcoat? What colour and material? A suit, or jacket and trousers? Brown shoes or black, made of leather or suède? A string tie, a bow tie, a scarf or a muffler? Hands: good nails or bitten? Hirsute (hairy, I mean) or bare? Rings on the fingers? The voice: was it hard, soft, loud, grating? And so on and so on. It was a superb performance, delicate in approach, searching in its effect. Follitt thought, reluctantly: He can do the job when he wants to, few better.

Presently Wyndham said: "Well, thank you very much, both of you. You've been a great help. Inspector, provide a car to take them home. Oh! The driver had better back up their stories with their parents. They will be worried, it's so late." When they had gone he said to Follitt: "Useless! He is bigger than me and smaller. He wears and doesn't wear an overcoat; he is clean shaven with a moustache and one of those beatnik beards which clings apologetically to the line of the jawbone. He has wild staring eyes which couldn't be seen in the dark. He is partly bald with hair as thick as a lion's mane. We can also presume that he possesses two eyes, two ears, a nose, a mouth and a lust for killing. To put it bluntly, all they saw was a dark figure. Beyond the fact that it was a man, and that he was hatless, we've got nothing."

"He thinks on his feet," said Follitt, grimly. "He must have seen Pilcher's torch, bolted, realized as he saw the lovers that if he kept on running the hunt would be on, and used that trick to gain time to get away. I'm afraid he's going to give us a lot of trouble."

"Yes," said Wyndham, ignoring the implied censure. He turned and walked towards the doctor. Lawrence was exploring the girl's back under the light of a torch held by Detective-Sergeant Harry Harris. He looked up as Wyndham's bulk loomed over him.

"As usual," he said. "One stab wound straight through the heart." He poked a finger through the wool of the girl's sweater. "There's the slit it made in the fabric. Same weapon, I'd say . . . at any rate it's left the same mark. A cut that looks exactly like a scratch."

Sergeant Harris uttered a curious noise. They looked at him. His face revealed distress, wonder and chagrin. He said: "Oh, dear!"

Wyndham said: "What's the matter with you, Harris? Choking on a fish bone?"

"No, sir. I'm sorry, sir. What the doctor said just now. It's just clicked."

"What's clicked?" asked Wyndham, impatiently.

"The other one, sir. The girl who dropped dead in the Park last month. Now I think she might have been murdered, too, sir."

Wyndham felt guilty and frustrated; guilty because he had overridden Follitt's plea for more men; frustrated because witnesses failed to use their eyes. His feeling of inadequacy erupted in angry sarcasm.

"Don't tell me!" he said. "The girl was mutilated and you thought she'd cut herself climbing barbed wire."

Harris swallowed. "No, sir. The doctor said she'd died of heart failure. He knew her, sir—she had a history. Only I've just remembered—there were six or seven small scratches on her back, sir."

Wyndham stared at him. A faint hope stirred in his mind. He said: "Six or seven, Harris? These girls have only one."

"I know, sir."

"Doctor, let Harris take a good look at the wound."

A pause. Harris rose from the examination, his face pale. "There's only one this time, sir, but it looks exactly like those others. I remarked on them at the time but the doctor said they were only scratches."

"Doctor Lawrence said so?"

"Oh no, sir. A local doctor. The man who found the body."

The hope sprang to life. Wyndham felt the stinging sense of inadequacy leaving him. This was something to get his teeth into. This might be a lead. It might even be the break through.

He said: "Jim, take over here, will you? I'm going back to the station with Harris. We'll go through the papers on the case. Come with me, Harris."

Follitt watched them go. I guessed right, he thought. He's in full flight now. He'll have the case wrapped up in tissue paper in no time. All his own work. Positively no assistance.

Follitt wondered why the thought made him feel dejected and uneasy.

The file was labelled, "Rose May Watkins". Wyndham allowed it to lie on his desk. He looked carefully at Detective-Sergeant (second-class) Harry Harris, who stood with a finger marking a place in his notebook. By all accounts he was a conscientious chap, young and inexperienced but willing to learn. His face revealed anxiety at what might prove a black mark against his career, touched with chagrin at the thought that with a little more brilliance he might have detected a murder.

Wyndham said: "O.K., Harris, give it to me in your own words." He added, quietly: "You may have to give evidence in court."

"Yes, sir." Harris snatched a swift look at his notebook. "I was on duty in the detectives' room at 6.45 a.m. on Saturday,

August 12th, when I took a call from a Doctor Charles Barton. He said: 'I wish to notify a death. One of my patients collapsed and died of heart failure in Regents Park last night. There will be an inquest, of course, but there is no evidence of foul play. She had a history of heart trouble.'

"I took down the doctor's address, the name of the deceased—Rose May Watkins, known as Rosie—and the place where the body had been found. It had not been moved. I went to the place, which was on the north-east side of the Park towards Gloucester Gate, and there I saw the deceased and Doctor Barton."

"How did he come to find the body?"

"Apparently he frequently takes an early morning stroll in the Park. She was lying a few yards from a path, half hidden by a clump of bushes, but his eye was caught by a flash of yellow—the colour of her sweater, sir. On investigation he had found her dead. She lay on her left side, with her legs sprawled awkwardly under her.

"I took notes and sketched the position of the body. I searched the area for any untoward signs but found none. I questioned the doctor closely. Watkins had been his patient for eight years, since her arrival in London from Sheffield, where her parents lived. He knew her to be a prostitute. At the age of nine she suffered an attack of rheumatic fever which left her with a wonky heart. She had been warned repeatedly by Doctor Barton that she might die at any time. He had urged her to change her method of livelihood and live a quieter life, but her attitude had been that we all have to die sometime, so what the hell?

"There were no signs of violence on the body, sir, absolutely none; no blood, no contusions, and nothing in her posture or face to indicate alarm, fear or a struggle. I sent for an ambulance. Doctor Barton accompanied us to the mortuary where in my presence he conducted a more detailed examination."

"How did he explain the cuts on her back?"

"I drew the doctor's attention to them, sir. There were six or seven, in a small group. Each was about half an inch long and had bled slightly—very little, sir. The doctor replied 'Only scratches, sergeant. Could have been made by a cat, or a man.' I understood what he meant. The body was otherwise unmarked."

"No post mortem was made?"

"No, sir. I submitted my report and Doctor Barton expressed himself as willing to sign the death certificate. There was no reason to doubt his diagnosis. An inquest was held and the verdict was death from natural causes. Her parents claimed her body and it was taken to Sheffield for interment."

"Not cremation?"

"I don't think so, sir."

"Did Doctor Barton estimate the time of death?"

"He found her at 6.30 a.m. He reckoned she had been dead between seven and eight hours."

"Did he offer any explanation as to why Watkins had died at that particular time?"

"Yes, sir. He thought she might have subjected herself to unusual exertion—running, perhaps. Or the cold might have done it. There was a sudden cold snap that night, sir, at about eleven o'clock. Most unseasonable."

"Did you examine the girl's clothes, Harris?"

Harris flushed. "Not minutely, sir."

"How about her belongings? Handbag, purse?"

"Oh dear!" Harris was acutely unhappy. "I never thought of that, sir. There was nothing near the body."

"Did you go to her flat?"

"Yes, sir. It was the usual sort of place, a typical prostitute's room of the class: a bed-sitter with a small kitchen. No clothes in the wardrobe, no personal items at all. In the kitchen the remains of her evening meal and, in an old tin tea-caddy on a shelf, the sum of two hundred and eighteen pounds nine shillings in notes and silver."

Wyndham said: "How did you get in?"

"The owner of the house admitted me, a Mrs. Greaves. It's a largish Victorian place, sir, cut up into separate rooms, each with its own key." He paused: "Oh!" he said.

"Exactly. You don't imagine that Watkins asked the landlady to let her into her own room every time she brought home a client?"

Harris said, subdued: "I'm afraid I wasn't very clever, sir. I should have thought about the key."

"Which she would have carried in a purse or handbag, and its absence from the scene of her death would indicate something unusual."

"Yes, sir."

"Anything else? Anything at all?"

Harris thought. "A camera, set up behind a screen in the bed-sitter," he said.

"A camera!"

"Yes, sir." Harris looked uncomfortable. "Was it significant, sir? I thought perhaps she posed for obscene photographs."

"Did you find any?"

"No, sir. No film or anything."

Wyndham picked up the phone. "Get me Sheffield C.I.D.," he said. To Harris, as he waited: "Did Watkins have a pimp?"

"Yes, sir. A man called Joe Pope, known as Spider Joe. But he was in stir, sir, doing two years for living on her immoral earnings. He came out on the Monday after she died."

The phone muttered. Wyndham said: "Chief-Inspector Wyndham of the Metropolitan Police. Put me on to the officer in charge. . . . Hallo, Super. They work you all night, too, do they? What a life. . . ! Yes, we'll knock off a bank together and retire on the proceeds. Look, Super, I'd be grateful for your help. I'm handling these Ripper murders, for my sins. He's killed another tonight, and we think there might have been a fourth. Woman by the name of Rose May Watkins, of . . ." He turned over sheets in the file, found her Sheffield address, and gave it. "Death was certified as heart failure but we now think that she was stabbed. We'd like her exhumed for a post mortem. I'll get a Home Office pathologist and all the necessary papers up to you today but I thought I'd warn you in advance. Anything you can do to speed things up. . . . Much obliged! Thanks. Good-bye."

Harris said, unhappily: "I'm very sorry, sir. I hope you won't hold it against me."

"Never take anything for granted in police work," said Wyndham severely, and stopped, uncomfortably aware of the fact that his own handling of the case could be criticized. He went on, more gently: "You should not have overlooked the absence of the key. You can't be blamed for the rest." Harris looked relieved. Wyndham went on: "As soon as it's light, I want you to search the area in which Watkins was found in the hope of tracing her purse. I'll arrange for you to have assistance. The trail's a month old, now, and I don't expect much result, but it's worth a try. Now, grab a few hours' sleep."

Harris went out. Wyndham looked at the clock: 2 a.m. He ought to get some sleep but he did not feel tired. There was a lot to be done, much wasted time to be made good. He had blundered badly in his handling of the case so far, and Follitt had been right to be annoyed. Never mind, there would be no more errors of commission or omission. He had a grip on the problem now.

Wyndham picked up the Watkins file and began to read. From

time to time he made notes, and on occasion he used the telephone. He also spoke to the grey-faced Pilcher about the habits of
various toms, including Rosie Watkins. He was still at work at
eight o'clock when Harris returned to say that Watkins's purse had
been found, open and with its contents scattered, under a bush
about 100 yards from the place where her body had been
found. Wyndham examined the contents, which gave him no
clue, and rose.

"Let's go, Harris," he said. "We have a call to make."

CHAPTER FIVE

SPIDER JOE POPE opened the door a full six inches, saw Wyndham
and Harris, recognized them for what they were, and tried to close
it again. He was too slow. Wyndham's number ten boot was
wedged in the gap, and his bulk leaned heavily against the solid
panels. Spider Joe gave up the unequal struggle and retreated.
"You've got nothing on me," he said.

The pimp was a small-boned, swarthy man of Greek-Cypriot
origin whose real name was Popadopolis. He had the face of a
water-rat and the morals of a guttersnipe. He was still in his
pyjamas, which were striped in mauve and gold. At some date,
no doubt long distant, he had attempted to tone down the effect
with stains of coffee and beer. The room smelled of stale tobacco,
sweat and cheap scent. A hump in the middle of the bed moved
slightly. Mussed blonde hair and drowsy blue eyes appeared above
the grubby sheet. The eyes blinked at the detectives. The head
vanished under the sheets. The hump lay still. Harris felt
nauseated. From this room, less than five weeks before, Rosie
Watkins had walked to her death. Spider Joe did not waste time in
grief.

Wyndham walked across the room, pulled back a tall screen
of faded brown tapestry and surveyed the contraption behind it.
He said genially: "Setting up as Court photographer, Joe?"
Joe grinned weakly. "It's me hobby, guv'nor," he said.

"Pimping, you rat!" said Wyndham. "Pimping, filthy pictures
and a bit of blackmail on the side." He swung round. Spider
Joe cringed. "Who was Rosie putting the screw on, Joe?"

"I don't know what you're talking about!"

"Don't come the holier-than-thou with me, you swine! This
camera was here on the night Rosie died. Its lens is trained on

the bed. There's a hole in the screen and a device on the camera to delay the shutter action until Rosie and her client were in position. She didn't rig it up, Joe; she hadn't the know-how. You rigged it up, and she worked it. I want the victim's name."

"You can't prove nothing," said Joe. "I was in stir and Rosie's dead. Her heart conked out."

Wyndham shook his head. "Oh, no it didn't, Joe. Not naturally, anyhow. Rosie was murdered." This was mere assumption as yet but Wyndham was convinced of it.

"Murdered!" Joe sat down abruptly on the edge of the bed. "You can't pin it on me! I was doing time. I don't know nothing!"

"Rosie was blackmailing somebody. We know that. More than two hundred pounds was found in a tea-caddy in the kitchen——"

"Two hundred nicker!" Joe's eyes were full of horror. "Where is it? It's mine. We was married! We was, I tell you."

"Married but not churched. The money was claimed by her parents as her next of kin," said Wyndham, with satisfaction.

"The bleeding crooks! They ain't got no right to it!"

"We know that Rosie didn't save it over a long period—there are plenty of girls to confirm that she spent every penny she earned until a few weeks before you were due to be released. She got worried. She started to save. But she couldn't have saved two hundred pounds in those few weeks. Business was bad."

"Two hundred nicker!" said Joe, stunned. "I thought one of you lousy bogeys had nicked it, or that slut who owns the joint, poking about, no respect for the dead."

"So you knew she had the dough."

"She told me she'd got a bit saved up, but honest to God, mister, she didn't let on how much or how she'd got it. I'd asked her once or twice if she was using——" He stopped.

"If she was using the camera for blackmail," Wyndham prompted.

"All right, all right!" Joe gave up stalling. "So I rigged it up just before you bastards framed me, swearing on oath that you saw me taking money from her. You know I'd never let anybody *see* me. I told Rosie to use it while I was in stir, but she wouldn't. I nagged her about it, but she wouldn't. So I gave up. She told me I'd be all right when I came out. I swear to you, mister, she never blipped a peep about the black."

Wyndham contemplated him, thoughtfully.

"O.K., Joe. I'll believe you, though thousands wouldn't."

Spider Joe relaxed. Wyndham turned away.

"Sorry to have disturbed you." He glanced at the camera. "It's a nice job, Joe," he said, admiringly. "Where do you buy your film?"

"Old Perky in——" Joe stopped. Wyndham turned round, slowly. Joe's face moved agonizingly, as though he were biting off his tongue.

"And who would Old Perky be, Joe? The man you buy your films from, and who does your developing for you?"

Joe wetted his lips. He remained mute. Harris grinned suddenly and whispered to Wyndham. Wyndham nodded. He sat down. He said to Harris: "Ring the station. Ask them to send a man round here—a uniformed constable will do." He beamed at Spider Joe. "I wouldn't want you to waste your money on phone calls to people. Especially to Old Perky."

The lettering on the showcase said: "Mervin J. Perkins. High-class Photographer. Weddings a Speciality." The showcase displayed a variety of Mr. Perkins's high-class photography. Overweight brunettes simpered coyly over bare shoulders. A dancer in black rehearsal tights struck an attitude of agonizing stiffness. Wedding groups, the subjects scrubbed until they shone and posed in self-conscious attitudes like bad tailor's dummies, grinned in terrifying imitation of great joy. Harris, who was an amateur photographer of some skill, shuddered and followed his chief up the flight of narrow, uncarpeted stairs which led to the reception desk and studio.

The receptionist, blonde and bored, paused in the act of polishing a long crimson fingernail and said: "Yaiss?" Wyndham said: "Mr. Perkins." The blonde shrilled: "Perky! Two gents to see you." She returned to her fingernails.

Mervin J. Perkins, high-class photographer, was small, grey, rotund and benign. Pale eyes beamed hopefully through rimless spectacles. His hands and clothes were stained with chemicals. His fingernails were grubby. His smile changed from benevolent inquiry to mechanical fixity as he recognized them as police officers. The change made him look faintly nasty, like a clown in a filthy temper.

He said: "Come in, gentlemen, come in." He lifted the flap of the counter and ushered them into a small cluttered studio. He closed the door carefully behind them. He swept photographic prints from uncomfortable chairs. "Not much room, I'm afraid," he said. "Business is terrible." Wyndham said: "Don't bother, we'll stand. We are police officers. We are inquiring into the death of a woman named Rosie Watkins."

Perkins stood still. "Really?" he frowned. "Should I know her?"

"You tell us," suggested Wyndham.

"A client, perhaps?" Perkins blinked rapidly. Wyndham thought: Memory working overtime. Is it safe to deny knowing her? Were they ever seen together? How much do we know?

Perkins said: "Would you describe her, please?"

Wyndham said nothing. He produced a photograph. It came from police records.

Perkins licked his lips. He said: "Oh, yes! I remember her. So many girls come to have their photographs taken. It isn't easy to remember their names."

"Not even when business is bad?"

Perkins smirked uneasily, but said nothing.

Wyndham decided to try shock tactics. He was on weak ground. If he fired a broadside into Perkins, the man might lose his head.

"She died a month ago. She was murdered."

Perkins's pale eyes flickered, then became steady.

"She was a prostitute. She was killed by a man she was black-mailing, a respectable man who had been her client. You developed the negative she took of them together in bed."

Perkins's eyes widened. He said: "But what a monstrous suggestion! What evil creature dared suggest such a thing! Times are bad, officer, but I've always kept myself respectable."

Wyndham thought: It's no go. This guy won't crack, and we have nothing on him to use as a squeeze. He's a small timer, mostly straight, does a little crooked stuff on the side. Hasn't the nerve to go in for the big stuff. Nevertheless, he did not give up.

"You can describe that man. It is your duty to do so."

Perkins spread his hands. "Believe me, officer, I would help you if I could, but I can't."

"You're in the clear, Perkins. It's no concern to us what negatives you develop for your customers. We want a description of that man."

It was no good. Wyndham tried, hard and expertly, varying his verbal attack adroitly. He got nothing. Perkins had known the dead girl as a customer. He knew nothing about her private life. He had never developed a negative for her. There was nothing wrong in anything he had done. He was a law-abiding man.

"Then," said Wyndham, amicably, firing his last shot, "there will be no objection if we take a look round?"

He hoped for a refusal. There remained the slight chance that Perkins had kept a copy of the neg. to use for his own purpose—but Perkins merely said: "No objection at all."

They did the job thoroughly, though Wyndham knew it was hopeless. They found nothing suspicious beyond a collection of nude studies of the female, not retouched. The model was the blonde receptionist. "I do some work for the art magazines," said Perkins. "I have not yet had time to retouch these." Wyndham didn't believe him.

They were back at the reception desk on their way out when Wyndham suddenly swung back on Perkins and flashed a man's photograph at him.

"Do you recognize this man?"

Perkins looked. He shook his head. His denial sounded genuine. Wyndham walked out, frowning.

The photograph was of Dr. Charles Barton.

CHAPTER SIX

TEN days later, when the results of intensive inquiries, interviews, interrogations and observations had been collated and checked, Bennett, Wyndham and Follitt met in the Superintendent's office to discuss the progress of the case. The conference was held in an atmosphere of comparative calm. The first fine frenzy of Press and public, which had reached a peak with the announcement that Rosie Watkins had also been murdered, had subsided from a howl to a whimper. This was due to several factors. First, no more murders had been committed. Second, the period of the new moon had passed. The Press had been quick to point out that the killer had struck twice at the new moon and though this proved nothing, the public seemed to think that the murderer would play the game according to their rules. Third, Wyndham's statements on the progress of the inquiry had become increasingly confident. His words and demeanour, coupled with the glamour which surrounded his name, bred assurance. This factor had also helped to soften the attitude of their superiors at Scotland Yard, and, in particular, that of Sir Graham Dunstable, the Assistant-Commissioner (Crime), who had been directly responsible for Wyndham's promotion and transfer.

Of the three detectives, Bennett was uneasy because he might be called upon to make decisions, and decisions were now the

ugliest part of his job. Follitt was suspicious and antagonistic.
Wyndham was supremely confident, almost exuberant. He
admitted to himself that he had mishandled the job at the start
but that no longer mattered. He had found his feet; the old touch
had not deserted him; within fourteen days of being plunged into
the most difficult type of murder case known to the police, he
had solved it; not, it was true, without assistance from the murderer, but then the success of every investigation depended on the
criminal making mistakes. The fact that the solution he was about
to propound rested entirely on circumstantial evidence did not
worry him. Few criminals commit their crimes in Piccadilly Circus
during the evening peak hours. He glanced at the less confident
faces of Bennett and Follitt and thought: I've got my man. And
if I feel bucked about it, why not? It's bloody good work, though
I say it who shouldn't.

Wyndham laid two sheets of scribbled notes on the desk. He did
not refer to them as he talked. The facts, and the theory he had
built from them, were firm in his mind.

He said, confidently: "Barton's our man. We've got enough on
him to secure a conviction in the Watkins case, and if he killed
her he killed the others, no doubt about that. I think we could
convict on all four, but, of course, it isn't necessary.

"Here are the facts. Watkins was killed between 10.30 and
11.30 p.m. on August 11th. These are Barton's own times, but I
think we can rely on them because when he gave them he could
not be sure that another doctor would not be called in.

"We have witnesses to prove that at 10 p.m. on that evening
Barton went to a pub near his home, drank two double whiskies
rapidly, and left. He seemed upset. He had been worried for some
time previously.

"He was seen to walk in the direction of Regents Park. An hour
later he was seen to return. Two men spoke to him, he answered
and appeared more composed."

Follitt made a note. Wyndham glanced at him but went on with
his case.

"Early next morning, Barton returned to the Park and found
the body, 'accidentally'. This is suspicious. It had then been light
for the better part of an hour and there is a fair amount of early
traffic in the Park. I think we are entitled to ask why, if he had
no prior knowledge of the position of the body, he should have
found it when nobody else did."

Follitt's pencil moved again.

"We come now to his statement to Harris. Right from the start he was positive about the cause of death, though he also stated that he had not moved the body. But the girl was lying on her back when Harris saw her. How could Barton be so certain of his diagnosis until he'd had the chance to examine the body properly?"

Follitt opened his mouth, closed it, and made another note. Wyndham frowned.

"Later," he went on. "in fact, during all this time, Barton stressed the absence of violence and the naturalness of the death. He glossed over the nature of the cuts on her back. You might say that by describing them as scratches he deliberately misled Harris."

Follitt shook his head, dissatisfied, but he said nothing.

"Now to the other murders. We know that Barton's Park prowlings, which began some weeks before Watkins was killed, continued without interruption right up to the night when the fourth victim, Grace Eva Childs, was killed. They ceased thereafter partly because we then restricted traffic through the Park after dark and partly because all the toms who used it had fled elsewhere. More specifically, we can prove that Barton was in or near the Park at about the times when all the murders were committed. We can prove that, as a doctor, he had access to weapons similar to the one which must have been used to commit the crimes. And, finally, the skill with which the last three victims were killed points to a man with medical knowledge."

Follitt interrupted at last. "You can't have it both ways, surely," he said. "If the murderer knew so much that he needed only one stroke each to kill three victims, how can you reconcile it with the fact that he needed six or seven for the first?"

"I'm coming to that," said Wyndham, complacently, "when I deal with motive and state of mind."

He leaned back in his chair, lit a cigarette, and blew smoke at the ceiling.

"Barton is an unpleasant little man," said Wyndham, with distaste. "He used to have a fair practice, but in recent years it has declined, due almost entirely to suspicions regarding his relations with the prostitutes among his patients. There had always been a number of toms on his list, the practice being situated where it is, but recently he failed to segregate them from his respectable patients who, not unnaturally, were offended. It was also suspected that his attitude towards them was more than professional;

that he used them from time to time. Whether this was true or not, his practice declined."

"That's a dangerous line of attack," said Follitt, ominously. "Barton's a well-known man in his own circle. He used to be a keen social worker, a paid-up member of the Labour Party, and a contributor to the Party's literature on social reform. He offered to give evidence before the Wolfenden Committee on Prostitution; and when this was refused, he took the trouble to write a report based on his observations of prostitutes. His counsel will claim that his interest in toms, if it went beyond professional duty, was socially desirable, and that the rumours against him were founded in prejudice and spite."

"Granted," said Wyndham, coldly, "but that argument might weigh more heavily with a jury if our Doctor Barton was not known to be an abortionist."

"We've never proved it," said Follitt, swiftly.

"We're not far off it," retorted Wyndham. "We need only one of these women to come forward and give evidence and we've got a cast-iron case."

"But we haven't proved it," persisted Follitt, "so how are we going to get it admitted as evidence?"

"We'll find a way."

Follitt shrugged unkindly. Wyndham flushed. He went on, sharply: "As Barton's practice declined the proportion of toms among his patients rose. He took on more abortions because he needed the money. In the middle of July, following anonymous messages, we began to keep him under observation. He was seen to visit certain toms, including Watkins. At about this time he began to show signs of acute worry and a day or two later his Park visitations commenced.

"My theory is this: the Watkins woman was blackmailing him, either on the evidence of a photograph taken when they were together, or on evidence of an abortion. Exposure meant ruin. He might go to jail, he would certainly be struck off, it would mean the break-up of his marriage. His wife is an intensely respectable woman, a churchgoer, a social worker, a bit of a snob, and likes to play the Lady Bountiful. Not on a large scale, of course; she can't afford it. Vicar's garden party level, religious and other charities; very genteel. She knows of her husband's social 'investigations', which she calls (when she is forced to speak about them) as 'working for the under-privileged'. She knows nothing about his less praiseworthy activities. The knowledge would break her.

"So Barton makes up his mind to kill Watkins. On the night of August 11th he takes a surgical knife, intercepts her in the Park, kills her, and hurries home, vastly relieved. During the night, his mood changes. He suffers doubt. Has he covered all his traces? He rises early and goes to the Park. To his delight the body has not yet been found. He goes over to it——"

"Risky, surely?" asked Follitt.

"Why? He's a doctor. If he's surprised he need only say, 'I'm a doctor. I've found this woman dead. Please send for the police'."

Follitt nodded reluctantly, his face blank.

"He turns her over. He discovers to his surprise that there is no blood; not even an obvious sign of the cuts made in her clothing by the knife. A great thought comes to him. He can pass off her death as due to natural causes! It requires a little nerve, but not much. If the real cause of death is discovered he can plead that he was misled by his prior knowledge of her condition. Anyway, he takes the chance, and it comes off."

Follitt did not argue the point. He crumpled his notes, as if his objections had been answered. He asked: "What about the purse?"

"If the motive was blackmail by photograph, I'd say that Barton rifled it himself—looking for the negative, perhaps—threw it away, and later forgot it. If it was blackmail over abortion, then the most likely explanation is that the body was found first by a sneak-thief who saw the chance of a spot of loot."

Follitt shook his head. "It doesn't ring true," he said. "I still don't understand why he had to stab the girl so many times when he could have done the job with one."

Wyndham grinned, triumphantly. "He *did* do it in one. But he wasn't sure. He'd never committed murder before. He was overwrought. He stabbed again and again, to make sure."

Follitt said, doggedly: "It still doesn't fit. We're all agreed that one man killed all four girls. If, for the purpose of argument, we agree that Barton killed Rosie, why in hell's name should he kill the others? He has camouflaged the cause of Watkins's death. He has committed a perfect murder—a crime which no one suspects of being murder. Then tell me why he should go out a month later, killing toms right and left, and advertising their deaths as murder? No!" he went on in sudden passion, before Wyndham could speak. "I won't even accept your theory as a basis of argument. I think a clever defence counsel will tear it to shreds. You've made Barton out to be mean and dirty. But he

isn't like that at all—and he'll be in the dock for the jury to look
at. He's an amiable, well-meaning G.P. with a dwindling practice
and a snobbish wife. You can prove that Rosie had a blackmail
set-up in her room, but you *can't* prove that she ever used it because neither Spider Joe nor Perkins will talk. You can prove that
we suspected Barton of being an abortionist but we can't prove
that he was one. The defence will go for you bald-headed.
They'll say: 'If you were so sure of this man's guilt, why was he
not prosecuted? The truth of the matter is, officer, that you
couldn't prove it because it wasn't true. Your information came
from anonymous letters. You smear this man's good name and
accuse him of murder on a flimsy structure of circumstantial
evidence erected on a basis of poison-pen letters written in prejudice and hate!'" Follitt paused to draw breath, a little startled by
his own outburst, but he went on: "The defence will portray
Barton as a devoted social worker who defied disapproval and prejudice in order to investigate a social phenomenon. He gave of
his time, and risked his reputation, to offer knowledge to a Royal
Commission. And then, to his horror, he finds out that the police
are inquiring into his activities. He has done no wrong, but he
realizes that what he has done is open to misinterpretation. He
becomes worried. He can't sleep. He walks in the Park late at
nights and early in the morning. Why not? Thousands do. And
so on and so on and so on. I tell you, they'll tear you in strips and
toss you in the ash can."

Wyndham said, angrily: "But the swine *is* an abortionist. We
know it."

"We can't prove it."

"Because the murders came at . . . Wait a minute!" Wyndham
rose and paced the room. Follitt's attack had shaken him. The two
men watched in silence as he strode about, thinking. Suddenly
he halted. He swung on Follit triumphantly.

"Your argument doesn't invalidate my case! It strengthens it.
Look! When did Barton's habits and attitudes change? Almost
immediately after we started keeping observation on him in mid-
July. He got worried. You bet he got worried! At any moment we
might find the evidence that would put him behind bars. Then
Watkins starts blackmail, but not over a photograph. We'll scrub
that. We have no direct evidence, as you said, and it blurs the
issue. She blackmailed him with evidence that would send him to
jail as an abortionist. He pays. She asks for more. He hasn't got
it. He kills her, and gets away with it." Follitt opened his mouth

to speak. "No, wait a minute! But he still isn't safe. He's got away with murder but our investigation continues. He begins to see peril everywhere, in every tom who ever knew him. His mind wobbles. The weeks pass. The danger presses closer. He decides that he must destroy all the evidence against him. He strikes again and again and again. That's it! That *must* be it!"

"It doesn't explain the mutilations."

"Yes it does. They are the result of a ferocious outburst of anger against the object which threatens to drag him down to disgrace, ruin and jail."

"He's mad, then?"

"Not in the legal sense. Oh no! He knew what he was doing." Wyndham paced some more. "That clinches it. We'll be able to use all the evidence we collected while he was under surveillance; all his comings and goings, the visits to and by toms. They'll be admitted as evidence of state of mind. It seals the whole thing. No defence counsel in the world will be able to whitewash the bastard when we've finished with him."

Follitt looked at Wyndham for a long moment, then lifted his hands in a gesture of helplessness and defeat. Wyndham thumped him on the back. "You'd make a damned good defence counsel, Jim," he said.

Follitt said, sharply: "I'm overwhelmed, but unconvinced. I'm sorry, but I don't see it that way." He rose abruptly. "If you'll excuse me I have work to do." He went out. Wyndham watched him go, puzzled and slightly uneasy.

Bennett brightened. He would need to make no decisions. He knew what to do. The form was laid down in the book.

"Let me have your report, David. I'll submit it to the Director of Public Prosecutions. Let the legal blokes break their heads over it."

"Yes," said Wyndham, thoughtfully and without meaning. "Yes, I'll do that."

Later that evening, while Wyndham struggled with the composition of his report on the Ripper case, Follitt sat unobtrusively in a corner of the Emerald Grotto Club in Hampstead Road, keeping an eye on the third blonde from the left on the high stools at the crowded bar. The blonde was the playmate of Cat's-meat Brown, a screwsman; but since Cat's-meat had gone down for five years for his part in a bank robbery, the blonde had turned her bright eyes and hunger for diamonds on other men. Now

Cat's-meat, having heard the deplorable news along the prison grapevine, had broken out of stir and was on the loose, threatening awful consequences to the blonde or her men-friends or both. The call had come in as Follitt was going off-duty. He had taken it on because he had no one to go home to, and work was his anodyne. He sat, sipping a ginless gin and tonic, but his thoughts were not on the blonde or Cat's-meat Brown. He reviewed Wyndham's case against Barton, and his own outburst, and was ashamed. He tried to tell himself that his objections were soundly based but he suspected that they were dominated by emotions he thought he had outgrown. Was his antagonism to Wyndham's solution rooted in an inner certitude that some of the pieces in the jigsaw had been fitted in upside down? Or was he animated by disappointment, anger, envy, jealousy and spite. Follitt admitted the honesty of his rage at Wyndham's cavalier handling of the case at the beginning, but that was over. Wyndham had made amends. Was his non-acceptance due to a feeling that if Wyndham had listened to him, the Ripper would now be safe and that last hope of his career, the chief-inspectorship, might be a little closer?

Follitt shook his head at himself, miserably. He sipped his drink and tried to concentrate on the task in hand. He glanced at the blonde. He looked at the door. The door opened. Follitt shrank back into the thick shadows of the corner. He was known to Cat's-meat Brown.

A man and a woman entered. The man was huge, smiling and possessive. The woman was cool, slim and beautiful. Follitt stared at them, his mouth dry. He said to himself: I don't believe it. I can't believe it. I won't believe it. His eyes told him that he must believe it, and a terrible rage welled up in him from the depths of his honesty, his compassion and his tolerance. He sat watching them for a long time, his gorge rising with every second. He saw the man rise and go to the bar. Follitt could stand it no longer. He rose, his face set, and moved across the room.

Wyndham completed his report, sat back, and re-read the sheets. No doubt about it, he'd made out a tough case. Follitt's voice came back to him: "I'm overwhelmed but unconvinced. I don't see it that way." Wyndham felt annoyed. What other way *could* be seen? What had Follitt contributed except carping criticism? Had he offered an alternative suspect? Something had got into Follitt lately. He snapped. He grumbled. He quibbled. It was not necessary to listen to him.

And yet . . . Wyndham hesitated. Follitt's insistence had left a mark. If his theory were wrong it would be worse than no arrest at all. Should he hedge his bet?

He took up his pen, twiddled with it, then abruptly made up his mind. He would hedge. He wrote: "Nevertheless, despite the strength of the case, I would advocate a postponement of the arrest. I believe that he will make another attempt and that we can catch him redhanded. I recommend that the suspect be kept under constant surveillance at least until the next new-moon period (the two or three days before and after Sunday, October 8th), which is the most likely time for him to strike. The risk entailed by this delay is small. On the other hand, the evidence of a further attempt would strengthen the Crown's case beyond doubt."

Satisfied at last, Wyndham took the report through to the Superintendent's office and dropped it on the desk. He glanced at his watch, saw that it was 11 p.m., and decided that he might as well go home. Outside the station he changed his mind. It was Saturday night and he'd had precious little free time since the end of his leave. A little celebration would do him no harm. A visit to a night-club and then he would be ready to turn in. He thought for a moment of ringing Arthur Laidlaw. He might like a bit of a booze-up and it would make amends for the two dates which Wyndham had been forced to break owing to pressure of work. He had almost decided to go back to the station to call Laidlaw when a Ford Zephyr convertible, its hood up, slid to the kerb. A mocking voice said: "Good evening! How is the great detective?"

Wyndham's brian tingled. His spirits performed hand-springs. "Linda!" he said, delightedly. "Well, I'll be damned!"

"Undoubtedly," she said. "It is the fate of all policemen, as every criminal knows." She leaned across from the driver's seat but did not offer to open the door. She added: "I hope you enjoyed the bull-fight."

"You were there after all?" he asked, surprised and chagrined. "I didn't see you."

"Why should you? The arena was full to bursting."

"That reminds me," he said, severely. "You stood me up very neatly in Tangier. Tonight we'll finish what we began. I'm off duty and on my way to a night-club. How about making it a twosome?"

She hesitated. He said, politely: "Unless you have something else to do?"

"I had," she said, briefly, "but I guess it can wait." She opened the car door. She looked at him, slightly puzzled, but also with that hint of mockery which was never long absent from her eyes, as though she concealed a secret which he should also possess and was satirically amused that he had forgotten.

"Where to?" she asked. Wyndham shrugged. "I don't know. I haven't been up West since before my leave. Is the Emerald Grotto still any good?"

"It's changed," she said curtly, "like they all do. But it's not bad."

They drove the short distance to the Emerald Grotto in silence. The place was crowded. Heat, smoke, chatter, jazz and the smell of scent struck them as they entered. Linda made a *moue* of distaste but ignored Wyndham's suggestion that they might go elsewhere.

They found a table. Wyndham fought his way to the bar, procured drinks, and battled back. Linda was right. The place had changed for the worse. Three months before it had been the haunt of wealthy playboys, top crooks and first-class snouts. Tonight the clientele composed bookmakers, toms, pimps, a few show people and a sprinkling of out-of-towners wearing the bewildered, stupid, excited faces of people who think that any new experience is a thrill when in fact they are being bored. The Emerald Grotto, he reflected, wouldn't be much use to him now, even if he'd still been at the Yard.

He dismissed the mental dreariness induced by the clientele and concentrated on Linda. "You liked the bull-fight?" he asked. She shook her head. "I hate blood," she said, "but I like the ritual, the inevitability, like a Greek tragedy."

Wyndham chuckled. "I like a good fight."

"The two-fisted he-man," she said. "Well, I don't. I've had my fair share of violence." She sipped gin and lime. She said, maliciously: "Your girl-friend looked as if she found it upsetting."

Wyndham refused to be thrown. "She quickly recovered," he said, easily. Linda murmured: "I'll bet she did!" She finished her drink and rose. Wyndham did not try to insist on paying. When Linda returned she said, more amicably: "Caught the Ripper yet?"

"We will," he said, confidently.

"I hope so," she replied. "Though it's scarcely your type of case, is it? You're not a very good detective."

Wyndham laughed, invincible behind the armour of his police

record. "The Yard promotes the deadheads," he said. "It's a well-known fact. Ask any of the geniuses who are still pounding the beat."

"I meant," she replied, equably, "that you are scarcely a conventional detective. Too emotional, for one thing."

"Oh, I've been known to use my head while on a case," he said, indulgently.

"But not always. The Vincie Brooks case, for instance. You told me in Tangier that you acted on a hunch."

"The word 'hunch' is slang for inspiration," he said, lecturing her. "And 'inspiration' is the word for intuitive reasoning based on knowledge and experience but carried out at a pace too fast for the individual links in the chain of logic to be separated at the moment of vision."

"You don't say so!" she said. She was mocking him again, but now he was impervious.

"All the same," he conceded, "you're right about me being unconventional. I really shouldn't be a policeman at all. By nature I'm a bum. I'm the sort of chap who enjoys sticking his nose into other people's revolutions, or chasing after phantom gold-mines in the Amazonian jungle, or sailing dinghies across the Atlantic for the hell of it."

"Then why don't you?"

"Caution," he said. "Believe it or not, though I often act like an outsized bull in a small china shop, I possess one streak of prudence. I like my pay-cheque regularly. If I bummed around I'd never have a penny—I know me. As a policeman I get a fair amount of freedom, a ration of excitement with a spice of danger —plus a regular income."

"But it's not all you want?"

"It's about seventy per cent of it. I reckon that anyone who gets seventy per cent of what he wants out of life is doing pretty well. When someone offers me a job that gives me eighty or ninety per cent, I'll take it. Until then . . . the Met. will do me."

Her glass was empty. He picked it up and headed back to the bar. As he waited for the barman to attend to him, Jim Follitt said at his elbow: "'Evening, guv. Didn't know you frequented this dive." Wyndham said, surprised: "Or you either, Jim." He had forgotten his irritation at Follitt. He said: "Have a drink." Follitt said: "Gin and tonic without the gin." Wyndham laughed as he always did. He said: "By the way, Jim, I added a rider to my report. Recommended no arrest just now. We'll keep him under observation until he tries again." Follitt grunted non-committally. Wyndham shrugged mentally and nearly regretted offering to buy him a drink. Instead he said: "On a job?" Follitt nodded and told him about it. Wyndham listened without interest. He was trying to catch the barman's eye. As he did so, and gave the order, Follitt, whose eyes had not left the crowded bar, said, thoughtfully: "That's odd! I wonder what our Linda is doing here? It's not her usual type of joint."

Wyndham said, sharply: "Linda?"

"Linda Ward, the fair-haired tom at the table over there."

"Tom?" Wyndham felt shock travel through him from head to feet. He gripped the bar-counter convulsively.

Follitt said, not looking at him: "Don't you know her? No, perhaps not. You've always preferred to keep out of their way if you could. Linda's very high-class. One of the tops. You're bound to meet her eventually—her working flat is in our manor. Number fourteen, Harwell Mansions."

Wyndham muttered: "I didn't know." His voice sounded queer. The drinks came up. Wyndham did not move. Follitt sipped his tonic water.

"She's a fascinating character. Uses a car, mostly, in Mayfair, but since the Street Offences Act she's also used clubs. Not this type, though." He gazed at her meditatively. Clearly the subject of Linda Ward fascinated him. "One of the independents, girls from good-class homes, who took up the profession after the war. No pimps. Linda's got a little extra that the others haven't got, though. Matter of fact, Paul Charlton of the *Sunday World* wrote a piece about her a couple of months ago. Called her 'Queen of the Call-girls', though strictly speaking she isn't a call-girl."

"I didn't read it," said Wyndham, feeling that he should contribute to the monologue in case Follitt noticed anything. He wished that Follitt would go away so that he could smash something.

"It was never published. I saw it only because Paul asked me to check a few of his facts. His Editor killed it. Too hot for him. Apparently the Great British Public, bless their innocent hearts, must be allowed to keep the illusion that every tom is a moron from a bad home. In fact, Linda's a doctor's daughter. G.P. with a good practice in Kent. Mother died a couple of years ago, convinced that Linda owned a flourishing hat shop in the West End. She does, too: Lindy Lou's. Know it? Very snooty. But that's her cover."

Wyndham, his back to Linda, glowering at the bottles on the other side of the bar, wondered whether Follitt would ever stop talking.

"Making about six thousand a year, I'd say," Follitt went on, methodically, as though making a report on a case to his superior, "and probably saves about half of it. Banks with the Nat. Prov. Plays the Stock Market—her brokers are Elliot, Spencer and Thurston. Nothing cheap and nasty about our Linda. What else?"

He paused to marshal his thoughts in the manner of the conscientious workman who is determined to be nothing if not comprehensive. "Aged twenty-eight, went to school until she was sixteen, followed by two terms at a secretarial college. Fifteen convictions for soliciting, with the usual two quid fine, before the Street Offences Act. None since—she's too fly. Absolutely clean record otherwise. No stealing from clients or blackmail. Takes a month's holiday every year—recently got back from Tangier, as a matter of fact. Tangier!" said the disgusted Follitt. "The wages of vice are Tangier—and it takes me all my time to drum up a fortnight at Eastbourne."

"We're in the wrong racket," said Wyndham, mechanically.

Follitt chuckled, sardonically. "We're in the wrong sex. We'd look a bit out of place giving the come-hither look from a Ford Zephyr." A movement at the bar caught his eyes. "Must go," he said. "Our girl-friend's on her way. Better make sure that Cat's-meat doesn't cut her lovely throat." He glanced at Wyndham briefly, looked as though he would say something, changed his mind, drained his glass, and walked out.

Wyndham stood motionless, his glass untouched on the bar, shaking with the anger of abject humiliation and shame. He had been fooled. He had made a pass at a notorious tom and had not known her for what she was. No wonder she had mocked him. He had drunk with her, dined with her, visited this night club with her, thinking her a respectable, sophisticated woman when she was only a cheap whore. His face flamed. His fingers flexed convulsively. His skin crawled. He had touched her, wanted to kiss her, desired her. And she had led him on, taunting, mocking, enjoying every minute of the game as long as it lasted. God, he'd like to wring her filthy neck!

The barman spoke. Wyndham grunted. He tossed a note on the counter and did not wait for change. He picked up the two drinks and turned. He paused. Linda Ward's chair was empty.

Wyndham swigged his Scotch in one gulp, left Linda's gin and lime on the counter, and went out. Linda Ward was climbing into her car outside the club. His rage engulfed him. He stepped towards her, clenching his fists. She did not flinch or cringe. He tried to speak, and could not.

She said, coldly: "Go ahead. Blame me. Tell everyone how I egged you on, taunted you, flaunted my charms at you, lied, cajoled, pleaded with you. That way you can square the account."

He found his voice. He said: "Shut up! Shut up, you lousy, cheap tom. I don't talk to toms."

"No," she said, scathingly, "you prefer to seduce other men's wives."

She drove away, her face hard with contempt. Wyndham watched her go, his frame shaking with the intensity of his rage.

CHAPTER SEVEN

THE following eight days were the worst Wyndham could remember. The horror of Linda Ward scorched him. He hated her for not revealing herself to him. He sweated at the thought of the effect on his career if their association had become known. Men had been broken for less; nobody would believe that it had been completely innocent. He would have been branded as a hypocrite. He thanked God that Follitt had happened to come into the club at a moment when they were not together. Follitt, of all people! What would have happened if he had caught them sitting together, laughing, talking on terms of intimacy? Then another alarm bell rang: suppose someone in the club had seen them, recognized them, and talked in the wrong quarter? Thereafter he lived for several days in fear of a summons to Bennett's office, or even to the Yard.

The agony was so intense that Wyndham was incapable of rational thought on the matter for a full five days. On the following Thursday, for the first time, he began to take stock. At first, selfishly, it concerned his career. The dreaded summons did not come and when he thought back over the people in the club he could think of no one who might talk. This eased his mind. Next, he sought back over his association with Linda, and his essential honesty forced him to admit that he, and he alone, had been to blame. He had forced himself upon her and she had behaved as any woman in her position would have behaved: she had enjoyed her little private joke while at the same time doing nothing to encourage him. Nothing? On the contrary, she had gone out of her way to shake him off. Wyndham remembered Laidlaw's words: "She gave you the brush off. . . . Accept it. . . . You'll only get hurt a lot worse if you pursue it." For a moment he wondered whether Laidlaw had known more than he had revealed. It occurred to him to wonder what Laidlaw did for women; then he dismissed the thought as unworthy of a friend.

On the Friday his returning sanity received a check. He was sitting in his office, reading the reports on the latest series of thefts by the peak-hour burglar, when for no reason at all his mind leaped back to the scene at the bar which had begun with Follitt's appearance. He had assumed, then and since, that Follitt had entered the club at that moment. Now, with devastating clarity, he realized that Follitt must have been in the club all the time. Wyndham's own position had been such that while he would not have seen the door open, anyone entering must have come into his line of vision on his left. Follitt had come up from his right.

Wyndham's immediate reaction was one of fear. If Follitt had seen them together, and made a report. . . . The fear faded almost at once. If Follitt had intended to break him, he would not have taken the trouble to warn him. A surge of gratitude for Follitt swept over him. What a grand guy he was! He, Wyndham, had treated him badly over the Ripper case, yet Follitt had given him a warning, couched in terms which could not cause offence between them. And then doubt assailed him. Was generosity the only motive? Had something else lain behind it, and if so, what? The thought nagged at Wyndham intermittently all that day. On the Saturday, with characteristic straightforwardness, he sought an opportunity to get Follitt on his own and put the issue to him. The moment came at lunch-time. They met on the way out of the station. Wyndham said: "Come and have a pie and chips at the Green Dragon, Jim, and toast damnation to all villains." Follitt's agreement was reluctant, almost ashamed.

Wyndham ordered beer and a meat pie for himself; tonic water and a cheese sandwich for Follitt. They sat at a corner table. Wyndham said, conversationally: "You did it deliberately, Jim, didn't you? About Linda Ward, I mean. You saw us together. What I'd like to know is why."

Follitt stared at his cheese sandwich as though he expected little men to pop out from it and attack him with hammers. He said:

"I'm sorry, David. I've been sorry ever since. I felt cheap. I shouldn't have done it only . . ."

He paused. Wyndham waited. Follitt looked up.

"I was wild with rage. You've paraded your loathing for toms too much. You could spot a tom a mile away. You bungled the handling of the Ripper case because to you toms weren't really human. Your loathing cost a girl's life and—to put matters on a personal plane—perhaps ditched my last chance of promotion. And then I see you, in the company of the most notorious tom in London, talking and laughing as though you were old pals. At first I thought you were a hypocrite, and then I realized that you were only a fool. If you hadn't been so antagonistic to toms, you'd have known her in the way of business. You'd have interviewed her in connection with the Ripper case, as I did, because her knowledge of toms, pimps and the men who go with toms is unrivalled. You allowed prejudice to blind you, and the prejudice wasn't even founded in sound sense. If you'd been right about toms emanating a wave-length of disgust, you'd have picked it up from Linda." He stopped. He said, apologetically: "There I go again. I'm still mad, you see. But I'm sorry as well."

"Don't be," said Wyndham. "I won't pretend that I wasn't knocked silly; I was, and worse. But as a surgical operation it was a remarkably effective bit of work. Thanks."

They said no more until they were strolling back to Albany Street. Wyndham said, sincerely: "I'm sorry I muffed things so badly at the start of the case, Jim, and sorrier still that I messed up your chance of a bit of kudos. I'll try to make it up to you. But at least I'm glad that it wasn't any worse. We've got our man."

"I hope so," said Follitt, uneasily.

Wyndham's report on the Ripper had come back from the D.P.P.'s Dept., endorsed for action but without comment on his rider. Bennett, left to make the decision, vacillated. Now he agreed with Wyndham; next he wanted to make an immediate arrest, only to change his mind again. His indecision irritated Wyndham. Why didn't the man make up his mind one way or the other?

All through the weeks before the October new moon, uneasiness grew and spread. Newspaper and public speculation was resumed. The fear spread beyond the toms. With the deepening of autumn there now arose the threat of mist and fog, and under that cover the Ripper's knife might make a mistake. The uneasiness preyed heaviest on Bennett. His nerve cracked on the morning of Sunday, October 8th. In his heart he knew that Wyndham's advice was sound, if risky; but the fear associated with the approach of the new moon destroyed his defences. Accordingly, Dr. Barton was arrested at his home and taken to Albany Street. Wyndham read over the charge. The accused fumbled shakily with his straggling grey moustache. He said, weakly: "I didn't do it." The skin of his face was as grey as his moustache, except where mottled red and purple veins gleamed through the tissues. Wyndham said to a uniformed sergeant: "Take him away." He watched the accused shamble towards the cells, shoulders bowed, knees trembling, the portrait of a guilty man.

The sergeant returned, alone, Wyndham took up a telephone and spoke briefly to the Press Officer at Scotland Yard. He glanced at his watch as he spoke. It was nearly noon. The statement would catch the one o'clock B.B.C. and TV news. He put down the receiver, took up his hat, nodded cheerio to the sergeant, and walked out of the station. Well, it's done, he thought. Just like Bennett to hold off until the last moment and then let his uneasiness get the better of him. Still, it was no use worrying. The case was sound enough as it stood.

A clock chimed midday. Wyndham was due at the Laidlaw's for lunch at one-thirty, but he had plenty of time. He could do with a pint, and the Green Dragon kept the best beer in these parts.

The Green Dragon was one of Linda Ward's favourite pubs. She liked anything that was top-class, and the Green Dragon was top-class. It lay within easy reach of the squalor of Camden Town, the seedy, lower-middle-class gentility of Primrose Hill, the multi-racial hubbub of Swiss Cottage, and the wealth of St. John's Wood; and it attracted the denizens of all these areas. They mingled, stockbroker with teddy boy, artisan with clerk, because the skill and personality of Jimmy Leech, the tenant-landlord, welded the diverse elements into homogeneity at least during opening hours. It amused Linda to watch the mutually antagonistic classes of Britain jostling in harmony. She never entered the Green Dragon without metaphorically taking off her Lindy Lou hat to Jimmy Leech.

She made her mental genuflexion and glanced round the bar. It was already crowded but Linda succeeded in finding a seat. She always managed to find a seat. Nor did she need to fight her way to the bar. She caught Jimmy's eye over the heads of the customers and by the time she was seated her gin and lime was waiting. She surveyed the crowd and recognized a man, drinking with his wife and two other people, who had been a recent client. She noticed his uncontrollable start of horror and the unmistakable look of relief when she gave no sign of recognition. Such encounters were rare, but occasionally inevitable. Usually Linda did not think about them. Today, under the influence of the Ripper murders, they aroused sarcastic anger. She had marked the absence of any shrill note of fear in Press and public reaction. They wanted the Ripper caught because murderers are safest in jail, but there had been singularly little sympathy expressed for the victims. Behind this disregard lay the implied comment: "You know the sort of women they are. They deserve all they get." She noticed, with distaste, that the client had positioned himself so that he could watch her covertly without arousing his wife's suspicions. Linda read his thoughts in his face. He would be back in a day or two.

When Wyndham entered, Linda's eyes turned malicious. She did not hesitate. She caught Jimmy Leech's eye and made a small gesture. Leech said to Wyndham: "Brown and mild, sir? Right! Lovely weather we're having for the time of the year." He pushed Wyndham's money back to him. "It's on the lady, sir."

He bustled away. Wyndham stared at the mug, then across at Linda Ward, and his face tightened. Just like her damned nerve, he thought. And then the involuntary feeling of resentment evaporated. Follitt had cauterized the poison in him and he realized that he felt a touch of his initial admiration for her, mingled with a sense of shame. Tom or no tom, he had behaved childishly. His normal poise was not complete as he carried his beer over to her table and sat down beside her. He said: "Here's to crime!" Linda said, waspishly: "Not to cheap toms?" He flushed. "I withdraw the epithet," he muttered. "I'll give you credit for that—there's nothing cheap about you." She lifted her glass. "I've heard more gracious apologies," she said, "but it will do."

Wyndham looked at her, cool, elegant, poised. He said: "I don't understand! You've got looks, intelligence, and a superb dress-sense. You could get any man you chose!"

"Not me!" she said, emphatically. "Men are all right when they come and go. I'd hate to have one as a permanent fixture."

He laughed, despite himself. "We're not all that bad!"

"Oh, men are all right for women who like them. I don't."

He digested this in silence. Presently he said: "All right, then. But if you hate the idea of marriage you could still be a top-rank professional woman."

"I *am* a top-rank professional woman. You just don't like the profession."

"No!" he said, bluntly. "And I don't see why you should, either."

"Why not? I make money, lots of money. I like money. I like good clothes and stylish shoes and a little jewellery, an expensive car, a month's holiday a year in exotic places. And I positively adore receiving dividend warrants."

"Other professions pay well."

"But look at the work involved! I detest getting up at the crack of dawn and battling with crowds. And fancy spending five days a week in an office practising law, or being called out at all hours of the night to doctor sick people."

"You're utterly immoral," said Wyndham, flatly. "You have no values."

"Oh yes, I have," she said, sharply. "I'll admit that they aren't the majority's values, but so what? If the majority doesn't like my profession, the men can do to themselves what you are thinking I should do to myself: they should change. *I* can't change myself. I've tried it. It doesn't work. And the men who come to us can't change, either."

Wyndham said: "You're an exceptionally able apologist, Linda."

"I wasn't apologizing," she said. "I was explaining."

Jimmy Leech appeared with more drinks. Wyndham paid. He sat back and glanced out of the window thoughtfully. He caught sight of a drab, shuffling, shapeless figure at the far end of the street. It brought him back to reality. He said, abruptly: "Fine words are all very well, Linda, but *there's* your future." She followed his gaze.

"Lizzie the Bag?" she said. "Not me! I'm not a street-girl, and never will be. I can pick and choose my clients, up to a point. When that privilege is no longer available—which will be in two, or five or ten years, I shall retire. That's when I shall know I'm on Skid Slope, and once you're on that, you have to get off, quick." She grinned maliciously. "Unless, of course, the Ripper gets me first."

She intended the remark as a jab, because his words had touched a faint fear at the bottom of her thoughts, and she was surprised

when he did not flinch. He smiled. He said: "The Ripper won't
get you, Linda. At least, not our current one. We muzzled him
today." As he spoke the door of the pub burst open and a man
rushed in. He shouted above the babble: "They've nabbed the
Ripper! Just heard it on the radio. He was arrested an hour ago."

Linda asked: "Who is it?" Wyndham hesitated. The statement to the Press had said simply that a man had been charged
and would appear in court tomorrow. Still, what did it matter if
he told her? She'd get it soon enough through the underworld
grapevine. He lowered his voice, though there was little chance
of his normal tone being heard. "His name's Barton, Charles
Barton. A doctor," he said.

She stared at him. "You mean Charlie Barton, the G.P. who
made the wrong diagnosis on Rosie Watkins?"

"Yes. Do you know him?"

"Of course I know him! All the girls in the area know him."
She laughed suddenly, harshly, scornfully. "Charlie Barton never
killed anyone in his life—not deliberately. You've got the wrong
man."

Wyndham crushed down a collection of sharp phrases on the
lines of teaching grandmothers to suck eggs. Instead, he said, complacently: "The evidence is strong enough."

"I don't care what your evidence is!" she said. She was really
angry. It was the first time he had seen her lose her poise. It
eliminated the hardness in her eyes and mouth and made her look
more striking than ever. "I don't care if you caught him in the
act. Doctor Barton is a fool but he's not a murderer. He's a
bumbling, fumbling, ineffectual man with a failure complex, but
basically he's *kind*. His kindness has broken him. The girls
started going to him years ago when something went wrong.
He hadn't the heart to refuse or the nerve to make his fortune at
it. He's *kind*, I tell you, and the Ripper isn't kind. The Ripper is
mean and dirty."

Wyndham said, trying to sound light: "You talk as if you
know him."

"Of course I know him—his type, I mean. He's a moral coward
and something of a sadist. He's the sort I call hypocritical-
dangerous. Respectable, sanctimonious and *mean*." She swung on
him. "If you want to catch the Ripper why don't you ask the
people who know? Girls like me?"

"I hardly think you'd know——" he began.

"Oh, for Christ's sake!" she said, "give me credit for knowing my job!" It was the first expletive he had heard her utter. "I know men. Men are my business. I earn my living by knowing them. I keep my looks and my life because I can pick out the wrong 'uns. I had to learn the hard way, but once you've learned you never forget."

Her eyes went round the pub, rapidly, professionally. She said, flatly: "There are at least six men in this pub now who could be the Ripper."

Wyndham looked at her sceptically. He grinned. "O.K.," he said. "I'll try to pick 'em out." Amused, he ran his eyes over the drinkers. "As number one I'll choose that red-faced aggressive chap over there."

Linda examined the specimen. "No," she said, "though you're warm. He's a potential murderer, but not yet. In eight or ten years, yes, when he starts to grow old and gets scared about his manhood. But he'll kill once in a frenzy and be scared to death afterwards. You'd catch him easily—he'd give himself away." She shrugged at Wyndham's incredulous face. "You don't believe me. You don't have to, you know. The trouble with you men is, you think you're different, everyone of you a special apple set aside from the barrel. Don't you believe it. There isn't a man alive I can't categorize in a few seconds or a few sentences."

"And what category do I fall into?"

"Oh, no, you don't catch me like that. You'd be offended. Not because the description would be insulting, but because it wouldn't be insulting enough. Men are odd creatures. They love pretending to be respectable—and hate to know they are."

Wyndham said: "I don't consider myself as precisely a model of respectability."

"Exactly," she said. "I told you you'd be annoyed." She looked round the room again. "I wouldn't take the red-faced man as a client in a few years. He'd be all right now, rather jolly in a revolting sort of way. Terribly adolescent, of course. Tells dirty stories and shows filthy postcards to his friends. It makes him think he's a man of the world. No, I wouldn't be afraid of him, yet. But I would be afraid of . . ." She paused. She said: "You see the man leaning against that pillar? And the one over there, in spectacles? And the one by the door?" She looked some more, twisting her head to get a better view. "There are two more standing slightly apart by the fireplace. And . . ." she lowered her voice, "the fellow who's just moved away from the next table to buy another drink."

Wyndham looked them over. He said, dryly: "They look very much like quiet, respectable, lower-middle-class men. If I've got to look for the Ripper among that sort, I've got a few million to choose from."

"Yes," she said, "you have. But when you think you've got your man, look at him closely and listen carefully to what he has to say. In all those six men there is a meanness, a furtiveness, a secretiveness, and . . . and . . ." she groped for the right phrase, "a peculiar look in their eyes when they see a woman. It's a sort of glaze, or film. They can't look at you—if you're a woman, I mean —directly. They never make passes in public. They're afraid, you see. They're all bottled up inside, corked to bursting point by respectability and the fear that they'll go too far with a woman too quickly."

"All the same," objected Wyndham, half impressed, half repelled by her analysis, "they don't all go round killing people."

"One of them does," she said. "Your job is to find out which one. But Barton isn't in that category. You'll see."

"Well," said Wyndham, "there is one thing I needn't be afraid of. The Ripper—if he isn't Barton—won't get you."

"He won't go for me. For one thing, I'm above his price range. For another, I keep to the bright lights. The Ripper likes the dark places. He'll strike in parks, narrow streets, alleys, the railway arches near the main-line stations. He wouldn't even risk picking up a girl like me and driving with me for a few minutes. He might be seen and he mustn't be seen." She shook her head, sadly. "Poor old Charlie Barton," she said.

Wyndham rose abruptly. Suddenly he felt that he needed to get away from this woman who calmly classified men as potential murderers. She seemed to divine his motive in rising, as she divined so much—too much for comfort.

She said, reassuringly: "Oh, there are lots of nice people here, too. They'd never kill anyone, except in very exceptional circumstances."

He smiled with a pretence of amiability. "I'm afraid I must go," he said. "I have a date for lunch and I'm already late." She smiled disbelievingly but for once she was partly wrong. She had made him forget his date with the Laidlaws. But she was also partly right. He would have gone on forgetting if the urge to get away from her had not suddenly become overpowering.

Lizzie the Bag was hovering round the white Zephyr when

Linda Ward emerged from the Green Dragon. She ambled up to intercept her. "Hallo, dearie," she said, amiably. "Thought I reckernized the car."

Linda smiled briefly. Wyndham's words came back to her: "Your future." She looked at Lizzie the Bag with unusual sharpness. She thought: The image of what people call "a loose woman". Lizzie *was* loose. Everything about her was loose, from her morals to her shoe-laces. Her false teeth clicked when she spoke; her hair, dressed badly in a style thirty years too young for her, straggled about her head; her mouth, her breasts, the skin at cheeks and throat, sagged sadly; her stockings were wrinkled. The slackness was bred in her mind, which lacked tautness. It was doubtful whether she possessed a mind at all, in the technical sense; yet she was not simple in the sense of being lacking mentally, nor was she moronic. She was all emotion. Her friends—and she possessed a surprising number—remarked, in the clichés which composed the bulk of their conversations, that Lizzie had a heart of gold; that her heart was as big as her body; that she was generous to a fault; that she would do anything for anybody; that she would give away her last shilling to someone worse off than herself. They meant that Lizzie was congenitally incapable of saying "No".

Lizzie was sixty-two years old (she admitted to forty-seven) and had been a tom for forty-six years, since March, 1915. She had been unable to say "No" to the private of the original British Expeditionary Force who, having collected a blighty one at Mons, had seduced her at the age of fifteen. ("One of the perishing Angels of Mons," said Lizzie, who thought that the angels were synonymous with the heroes.) She had been unable to say "No" to the pimp who put her on the streets six months later. The pimp had seen a fortune in her and had enjoyed it until 1938, when he left her for a younger woman because Lizzie was then going downhill. Lizzie had been going downhill ever since. Now she was almost at the bottom, and she would never rise again.

Linda said aloud to herself, answering Wyndham again: "No!" Lizzie said, indignantly: "I ain't asked you for nothing yet." Linda laughed. "I didn't mean it for you," she said. "Come on, I'll give you a lift."

Lizzie squeezed her bulk thankfully into the front seat and Linda drove off. Lizzie looked at her affectionately. "You look tired, dearie," she said. "How many did you have last night?"

She meant customers, not drinks. Linda said: "Seven." Lizzie said: "Seven! And you with all those stairs to climb! Oh, your poor feet." Linda laughed dutifully at the joke. Tactfully, she did not return the question, but Lizzie told her.

"I had one last night," she said, sighing contentedly. "A lovely boy. Sailor. Thirty-five years in the navy. Said I reminded him of his dear old dead mother." She laughed suddenly, harshly, with a noise like a circular saw biting on lead. "'Jesus!' I told him. 'I hope not. If you had a mother like me I'm sorry for you.' Still it was nice of him to say so, wasn't it, dearie?"

She sank deeper into the seat, contentedly, and changed the subject. "Is that right, ducks, what I heard that feller shout? Have they muzzled the Ripper?" Linda said: "It seems so." Lizzie said: "About time, too. And when they hang him I hope they hang him by his——" Linda interrupted, savagely: "Shut up!" Lizzie blinked. She said, hurt: "Well, hanging's too good for a bloke as goes round sticking knives into girls what never did any harm." Linda said: "How do you know? We've got a few bitches among us."

Lizzie digested the comment in silence and, having nothing to say about it, said nothing. Presently the car drew up outside Lizzie's dingy lodging near Camden Town. Lizzie did not alight immediately. She said, apologetically: "Things ain't been too good this week, ducks. I'm a bit short on me rent. If you could help me out like—just for a few days. Business'll turn up soon."

Linda opened her bag, extracted a fiver from the bundle inside without exposing it to the vulgar light of day, folded it small, and dropped the pellet of paper in Lizzie's lap. Lizzie's eyes watered. She said: "You're the best of the whole lot, Linda dear, though there's some as says different. You've got a good heart to an old woman." Linda said: "Stow it, Lizzie. We can all have tough times. Take care of yourself."

As Linda drove away, her cash-register mind recorded the fact that Lizzie now owed her fifty pounds. She would never get it back. Fifty pounds invested at three and three-quarter per cent over ten years would amount to . . . Why the hell bother? Why not simply stop subsidizing the old hag? She couldn't imagine why she allowed the tearful, sentimental, foolish old woman to continue to tap her. Wyndham's words returned: "Your future." The bogey was wrong. She didn't keep Lizzie afloat out of an obscure feeling that by doing so she was securing her own future. A girl was entitled to one weakness, wasn't she? Lizzie the Bag was hers. An amiable weakness, that was all.

CHAPTER EIGHT

WYNDHAM rang the bell outside Laidlaw's flat and listened for Ruth's excited whoop and rush. It would end with the door flying open and the child running into his arms. He heard no sound. The door opened demurely. Wyndham stared. The young woman said, in mock censure: "You're horribly late! Daddy's furious. He said if you didn't turn up this time he'd never ask you again." She pecked him daintily on the cheek. "How are you, Uncle David?" She called: "Daddy! It's Uncle David at last." She took his wrist and pulled him inside. Wyndham followed her, dazed, unable to reconcile this girl in the sweater and matador pants with the image of round, felt, schoolgirl hats, gym tunics and thick stockings. My God! he thought, she's grown up. And it's only three months since I saw her. She's going to be a real beauty. She makes me feel old. We'll have to drop this honorary "uncle" nonsense now.

Laidlaw entered from the kitchen, a ladle in one hand, an apron tied round his thickening middle, his face flushed with the heat of cooking. He said, anguished: "The sauce is ruined! This morning I was inspired—positively inspired—and now it's ruined." Ruth said, callously: "Then let's have H.P." Her father winced. He switched the ladle to his left hand and the men shook. "The younger generation has no sensibilities," he said, pained. "Pure animal brutality." Ruth said: "Well, food's food, isn't it?"

Wyndham laughed contentedly. He felt the family atmosphere envelop him like a cloak and was the better for it. He said: "Did you hear the one o'clock news?" They shook their heads, their eyes questioning. "Then you can ruin the rest of the lunch while we drink a toast. We've muzzled the Ripper."

Laidlaw grabbed his hand again and pumped it. He said: "Congrats, old man." Ruth looked at him with wide-open eyes and said: "Ooooh! Aren't you clever?" She sat down cross-legged, her black matador pants and yellow sweater making vivid splashes of colour against the grey Indian carpet. She hugged her ankles and said: "Tell us all about it, Uncle David. Did you chase him in a fast car, with his guns blazing, like you did with that crook?"

Wyndham shook his head. "No," he said, "he came quietly, as a good crook should. As a matter of fact, he's rather a poor specimen."

He took the glass Laidlaw offered him. Ruth drank Coco Cola. Laidlaw said: "Here's to crime." Ruth said: "No, Daddy, here's to the cleverest detective in the world, Uncle David." She cocked her head on one side. She said, mischievously, quoting a magazine which had featured him after the arrest of Vincie Brooks: "'The Force's most eligible bachelor.' I really think I shall have to marry you, Uncle David. I couldn't bear to think of some other hussy getting her hooks into you."

Wyndham said: "If I were a few years younger, Ruth, and you were a few years older, I'd take you up on that."

Ruth said, with all the maturity of a sixteen-year-old: "Pooh! What does age matter? I think older men are much more interesting than boys." Her father, returning from a foray into the kitchen, said: "Well, you ought to know. You must be an expert on boys." He said to Wyndham: "I've lost count. She must have dozens."

Ruth said, wisely: "You'd be a lot more worried if I had only one and brought him home all the time."

Wyndham laughed. "Safety in numbers, eh?" Ruth said, petulantly: "Well, regular boys are so silly. They're always wanting to kiss you, and if you let them do it they're either clumsy and mess up your hair or they get excited and want you to go to bed with them."

Wyndham felt slightly shocked until he realized that, child-like, Ruth was trying to shock him. There was, he reflected, still a lot of the child in her. Her father said, ruefully: "The way kids talk these days! My parents would have had a fit if I'd talked like that at Ruth's age."

Ruth said: "Well, it's true. Some of the girls I know let the boys do it, too. Sillies! Who wants to be mauled about by some lout with his voice pitched on two levels? I'd rather have a Coke." She rolled over on her stomach and propped her chin on her palms, her interest in the arrest swamped by her interest in herself. "I think——" she began, but her father interrupted. "You think nothing, Ruth. Finish laying the table and we'll eat before the chicken is roasted dry."

Lunch was a quiet meal, punctuated by Laidlaw's comments on his cooking. He took his food seriously. Afterwards, Ruth washed the dishes while the men talked desultorily. Laidlaw gave Wyndham a market tip and criticized the Government's handling of the latest balance of payments crisis. Presently he extended an invitation for Wyndham, who had been asked to lunch, to make a day of it.

"We'd like it," he said. "We don't see you as often as we'd choose. We'll have the afternoon to ourselves because Ruth's going to the cinema. It will give us a chance to discuss men's business without interruptions from little Miss Know-All. But she'll be home for dinner."

Wyndham grinned. Ruth said: "Please do, Uncle David."

"On one condition," said Wyndham. "You drop this 'uncle' business. You're too old now and I'm too young."

Ruth said: "Very well, David."

Wyndham phoned Albany Street to give them his change of plan. Ruth disappeared to change her clothes. She returned in a brilliant red and black frock with wide skirts which twirled to show her lace-edged petticoat and splendid legs. Wyndham felt vaguely that the style was a trifle unbecoming; not exactly vulgar but a shade too cheap. He did not say so. When she had gone, moving with vivid lightness, the room seemed darker. She possesses an abundance of vitality, he thought, and she's a good sort. She was level-headed behind the vivacity, sensible under the forced sophistication. Considering that she had lost her mother at the age of four, Ruth hadn't turned out too badly. A lot of the credit, he supposed, went to Laidlaw. On an impulse he said: "You've done a good job with Ruth, Arthur. She's a credit to you."

Laidlaw flushed with embarrassed pleasure. He mumbled: "'Strordinarily good of you to say so, old boy. I don't deny that it hasn't always been easy. And now, well, I'm not looking forward to the future." He answered Wyndham's lifted eyebrows. "It's going to be devilishly lonely for me when Ruth gets married. She was right when she said I wouldn't like it if she stuck to one boy-friend. I'm dreading the day when it happens."

"It'll be a long time yet," said Wyndham, soothingly. "She's only sixteen."

"I don't know about that. Kids seem to marry hellishly young these days. Of course, I want her to go to University and keep off marriage until she's completed her education, but if she meets the right boy before that, I won't stand in her way." He stared into the fireplace. His eyes looked oddly haunted as though he were looking into a bleak future. "Yes," he said, half to himself, "she's a good girl. She's all Mary. Mary through and through."

He relapsed into silence. Wyndham did not break it. Presently the warm room, the good food he had eaten and the splendid wines he had drunk, induced drowsiness. A slight wheezing noise announced that Laidlaw had left his memories and fallen asleep. Wyndham stayed awake. He allowed thoughts, images, ideas, to drift around in his mind in a pleasant haze of physical well-being. He thought of Sanmiguel, bloody and torn, facing in the bull-ring at Málaga the beast which had almost killed him. He remembered the trouble in Palestine, which the Israelis called the War of Independence, and a doomed terrorist fighting with insane fury the men sent to destroy him. Wyndham had been one of the men and the killing had saddened him. He remembered Vincie Brooks, turning at bay with his gun raised and felt again the pain in his chest before he grappled with him and won. Then he wondered why violence should be dominant in a peaceful body and mind, and tried to think of more amiable thoughts: of Laker demoralizing the Australians during that unbelievable Test Match in which he had taken nineteen wickets; of Tottenham Hotspur completing the League-Cup double for the first time in the century. He remembered Tangier and, inevitably, thought of Linda Ward. A faint sense of uneasiness gripped him. "You've got the wrong man." "There are at least six men in this pub who could be the Ripper." Utter nonsense! Think about Ruth instead. "Here's to the cleverest detective in the world." That was better. His luck as a detective had been phenomenal. It would not let him down now.

The wheezing stopped. Laidlaw grunted, belched, yawned, and sat up, rubbing his eyes. "Must have dropped off," he said, as though he had committed a sensational departure from habit. He squinted at the clock. "Half-five," he said with satisfaction. "Time for a snifter, eh?"

When the drinks were poured and he was comfortable again, Laidlaw said: "You must feel pretty good, eh? This case—the Ripper—it's quite a feather in your cap."

Wyndham shrugged. "Won't do me any harm, of course. Still, in an odd sort of way, I don't feel terribly triumphant about it."

Laidlaw nodded as if he understood. "Don't suppose you can get worked up over a case like that," he said. "After all they were only toms."

Wyndham remembered all that had happened because of his own attitude and said, a trifle brusquely: "That's not a view I'm allowed to take."

Laidlaw laughed. "Don't go all frosty, man! I know what you're supposed to think, officially, and I know what you really think."

The detective said, slowly: "I'm not sure that I do, any more." Laidlaw looked up, his eyes sharp. He remembered their previous conversation and wondered if Linda Ward had anything to do with Wyndham's changed views. He decided not to ask. The subject was too delicate. Wyndham said: "But in any case, my private feelings don't come into it. The official view is that even toms are human beings."

"A doubtful premise," said Laidlaw, sourly. "As far as I'm concerned I'm sorry you bagged him. He could have killed a few more of the bitches, for me."

Wyndham felt angry, and recognized a little of Follitt's reactions. Laidlaw went on: "Those cows cost me the better part of fifteen hundred quid. Before the new Act we lived in Bayswater. Couldn't move for harlots. All over the bloody landscape. Respectable women and girls were being accosted by whores who thought their pitches were being queered. Ruth was growing up. Couldn't let her see that sort of thing, so I had to sell. Naturally I had to take a loss—property in that area was down in the cellar with no takers. Luckily I eventually found a West Indian to buy it, so I didn't lose as much as I might. All the same, I dropped at least fifteen hundred."

Wyndham knew the story—it was one of Arthur's favourites. Usually Wyndham said nothing. Today he remarked: "You didn't do too badly, Arthur. You've more than made up the difference in the appreciation on this place. The Bayswater area was going down, toms or no toms."

Laidlaw blinked, a little surprised to find that the detective knew enough to pull him up on the subject. Then he grinned. "You're getting smart, David." He looked at him with sudden sharpness, as though seeing him for the first time for many years. He said: "You know, David, this new job has done you good. There's something about you now, a sort of . . ." He groped for a word. He said, lamely: "Grown-upedness. Oh, I don't mean that you were a stupid kid, but there was *something*." He waved his hand, and gave up. "*You* know," he said.

He rose, a trifle embarrassed by his frankness, and mixed drinks. He said, to change the subject: "Six-thirty. Ruth will be home in an hour or so. Let's drink these and then I'll see about rustling up dinner."

Laidlaw put down Wyndham's glass. The telephone bell rang.

After the quiet of the day it sounded unnaturally shrill. It made
Laidlaw jump. He spilled drink on his shirt sleeve and swore.
He lifted the receiver and spoke his number. "For you, David," he
said. "Hope it isn't Albany Street trying to drag you away."

It could only be Albany Street because no one else knew he was
there. Wyndham took the receiver resentfully. Couldn't they
leave him alone even for a day?

The duty sergeant said. "Campion here, sir. The Super says
will you get down to the York Cinema right away."

"What is it?"

"Murder, sir."

Wyndham froze. The sergeant said: "And, sir, he says it looks
like another Ripper job."

"What!" Wyndham exploded. "For God's sake! Unless someone's let him out, the Ripper's in the cells." He was facing into
the room and he saw Laidlaw's eyebrows go up and his lips purse
in a silent "oh-ho!"

"Those were the Super's instructions, sir."

Wyndham collected himself. No use shouting at the sergeant.
The Super was doddering rather more than usual. He said: "Any
further details?"

"One moment, sir." He heard Campion's voice talking faintly
to someone else, or into another telephone. Then: "Are you
there, sir? Message from Inspector Follitt. He's down there now
with Sergeant Harris. Victim's a girl, sir, aged about sixteen.
Stabbed once through the back while sitting in her seat. Wound
resembles those on other victims of the Ripper's, but there's no
mutilation of the body." Wyndham and Laidlaw were staring at
each other. The stockbroker strained to hear the sergeant's faint
tinkling voice through the earpiece. "According to an envelope
in her handbag, her name's Ruth Laidlaw, number twenty-four
Ferncourt Mansions, St. John's Wood. That's all, sir."

Wyndham said something and put down the receiver. Laidlaw's
pudgy red face had turned a dirty white. His eyes glazed. He
swayed. Wyndham leaped for brandy and forced a glass to the
stockbroker's attention. Laidlaw looked at it stupidly. His eyes
cleared. His ashen face reddened again and then purpled. His
eyes raved. His lips twitched. He struck Wyndham's wrist and
the brandy glass smashed on the floor. He said, in a voice thick
with fury: "You bloody bungler! You said you'd got the Ripper.
You let him kill my girl. You let him kill my Ruth!" His voice
rose with every word until he was screaming so thinly that he

could hardly be heard. "Get out of my house," he said. "Get out of my house. Get out! Get out!"

Wyndham turned without a word. There was nothing he could do except send assistance—some other person whose presence would not be a monstrous affront to the stricken man. Laidlaw was still screaming "Get out! Get out! Get out!" while Wyndham was explaining the situation to horrified neighbours in the flat next door.

CHAPTER NINE

WYNDHAM looked down at the bright heap of death in its crimson seat and thought: "It can't be the Ripper. It mustn't be the Ripper. We've caught the Ripper. This is a terrible mistake. An imitative crime. Some foul teenage brutality. A boy she'd jilted. That was it. Revenge executed by some loutish kid because of a slight to his bloated ego. It mustn't be the Ripper. I've corrected my blunder. I've even exorcized my prejudice. I've been punished enough for my folly. Your errors don't pursue you once you have repented and made amends.

Follitt said something. Wyndham rubbed his forehead. He said: "Sorry, Jim, what were you saying?" He read the disapproval in Follitt's eyes and shook his head. "No, Jim, it's not that. I know her. She was my godchild, the daughter of my best friend. I was at their house, waiting for her to come home to dinner."

Follitt said: "Oh, my God!" Impulsively he laid a hand on Wyndham's arm. "Look, you shouldn't be on the case. The Super didn't know. Ask him to excuse you. He can get a man from the Yard."

Wyndham shook his head. "No, Jim, thanks. This case is mine. If it's the Ripper, or if it isn't." He braced himself. "I'm all right. Give me the form."

Follitt hesitated, and then nodded as though in approval.

"She entered the cinema at a minute or two to four o'clock, alone. She bought her ticket and some chocolates. She took this seat. No one saw anybody else in the row behind her. One witness, the youth who discovered the body, is prepared to swear that there was no one sitting anywhere near her at that time."

"Many people in the cinema?"

"Less than two hundred, and only sixty in the stalls here, spread well out."

"Yes."

"The house lights went down at four. The first feature, an old Hitchcock thriller *The Lady Vanishes,* came on at ten past. It's a real gripper and nobody noticed any movement in the auditorium. This means nothing. The staff admit that there's a surprising amount of traffic in and about the cinema while a film is on, new arrivals, people going to the toilet, or changing seats. No one takes any notice."

"Yes," said Wyndham, again.

"The lights went up again at 5.50 p.m. The body was discovered two minutes later. I've got the witness here——"

"I'll see him later. Give me the gist of it."

"He a youth named Ted Jackson. He said he noticed the girl as he came in. At the interval he looked across and thought he'd like to make her acquaintance. He bought two ice-creams first, and threaded his way along the row. He spoke to her and when she didn't answer he thought she must be asleep. He touched her shoulder and she slipped sideways in her seat. And then," said Follitt, grimly, "the young fool lost his head. Instead of going quietly to a member of the staff, he yelled out: 'Murder! Murder!' God knows why he thought of murder anyway—the effect of the picture, I suppose. He shouted, 'She's dead! She's dead!' Well, that really put the cat among the pigeons. A woman screamed. People got up. Some peered at the girl, some went out. Members of the staff came running, all flustered. By the time the manager had the sense to ring us and stop anyone else leaving, at least forty people had gone. And you can bet that our killer was one of them."

"Any worth-while descriptions from usherettes or box-office girl?"

"A few. Whether they'll give us a lead is doubtful. Most of them were regulars—and I don't think our man would risk murder in a place where he was known."

"Don't think wholly in terms of the Ripper, Jim," said Wyndham. He mentioned his thoughts. Follitt grunted non-committally. Wyndham said: "I know. Perhaps it's wishful thinking." He looked down at the vivid bundle and then quickly away. He said: "O.K., Jim. Let's get down to the routine grind."

They got down to the grind.

Shortly after nine-thirty that evening, in another part of the division, a man who was keeping a diary went out for the second time that day. His wife watched him go from behind the curtains of her bedroom. When his figure had disappeared into the misty gloom beyond the last street-lamp she left the window and went downstairs.

Her fingers trembled as she pulled at a drawer in the kitchen. She stared into it. She moved cutlery nervously. The clatter jarred her shaken nerves.

Presently, when she had failed to find what she was looking for, she closed the drawer and returned to her room. She said to herself: I don't believe it. It can't be true. I won't believe it. It isn't true. He couldn't do this to me. He *couldn't*. I must forget all about it. I must. I will. It's all a mistake. It isn't true. I won't believe it's true. I won't. I won't. I won't.

By ten o'clock that night the London air was chill with the first threat of winter. Mist drifted up from the river as the heat of the day cooled. It thickened by the hour. It swirled veil-like about the streets, blurring and distorting the outlines of everything it touched. The familiar turned fantastic. Lamp-posts stretched themselves grotesquely until they resembled monstrous fingers pointing at the sky. Human forms blurred into the shape of beasts, shambling through the murk. Car headlights glowed yellow like the eyes of fabulous monsters. It was a hideous trick of nature, an enormous optical illusion; but in the dark caverns of London's dirtier streets it shook the nerve of all but the most insensitive.

Lizzie the Bag was not sensitive. She saw no monsters when she emerged from the Queen's Arms at ten minutes past ten. Lizzie was in fine form. She was full of whisky. She overflowed with benevolence to all the world. She stood on the kerb, shouting good nights to all the splendid boys and girls who had helped her to ruin Linda's five-pound note. "'Night, Charlie. 'Night, Eva. 'Night, 'night, 'night. Be good. Don't do anything I wouldn't. 'Night. 'Night. 'Night."

The last conviviality faded. The bar lights dimmed in the pub. Lizzie, beaming amiably to herself, warm with liquor and good fellowship, ambled slowly down the street. She swayed slightly, like a tug in a swell. Her muddled mind tried to sort out impressions and make decisions.

She reached the corner of the street and stood irresolute. Gradually the cold reached through the threadbare thickness of her clothes and dowsed her good humour. Presently she realized that the fiver was almost spent, that the rent was still unpaid, that the landlord was turning real nasty and might even carry out his threat to put her into the street, and that she was cold and growing colder. Her face sagged with misery. It was a pity all the people in the world weren't as nice as that bunch of lovely boys and girls in the pub. Ooooh, what lovely people! Always good for a song and a joke. You got carried away, like, and forgot where you were.

Lizzie resumed her rolling walk. There might be a customer to be found in Regents Park. No, dear, not in the Park, on account of that Ripper bloke. Perhaps there'll be a nice man at Primrose Hill. Or perhaps anywhere. Almost certainly there'd be someone at the railway stations, with their convenient arches, secluded from the prying eyes of flatties. Not that she needed to worry. Nobody nicked Lizzie the Bag any more, not even the most zealous young officer with a poor record of arrests. There was no kudos to be gained by pinching Lizzie the Bag.

Lizzie sighed. The railway stations were her best bet. They were a fair walk away and her feet hurt, but a girl had to go where the money lay. She wouldn't meet nobody in these god-forsaken streets back of Prince Albert Road.

A footstep sounded behind her. Lizzie's mood brightened. Maybe she'd be lucky after all. Hadn't this been her lucky day? A lovely day it'd been, what with the sun, and Linda's five-pun note, and all the boys and girls in the pub.

She turned. She screwed her sagging face muscles into a come-on smile which no longer lured. It was a man. He came closer. Lizzie was surprised how close he came. She felt a sudden sharp pain in her chest and noticed that his hand was almost touching her breast. She said, "Ooooh," very low and surprised. Suddenly her legs no longer possessed the strength to hold her. It must be the drink.

Lizzie collapsed slowly to the dirty pavement and the man busied himself over her for a few moments before he returned, wraith-like, into the thickening mist.

Wyndham scribbled meaningless symbols on the paper before him. The first routine inquiries had been completed and now, back in his office, reaction had set in. His mind refused to work. Faces superimposed themselves on the white sheet. Voices shouted in his brain. Ruth lived again, garishly vivid against the carpet, saying: "The cleverest detective in the world." Ruth died and he looked at her, her plumage unruffled by the violence which had been done to her but now limp, no longer lit by the fire of her personality, the young eyes pools of death, the virgin body cold, a bright fledgling slain in flight. . . . Linda Ward mocked him, cold and brilliant as chromed steel: "They were only toms. . . ." Laidlaw bulged at him, bruise-purple, screaming: "You bloody bungler." Linda peered from behind the bloated image, fencing maliciously: "You're a bad detective. You've got the wrong man." The wrong man. Bungler. Fool. Smug, complacent fool. His own voice spoke to him: "You don't feel so involved when they're only toms." Laidlaw appeared again, smooth and waspish: "He could have killed a few more of the bitches, for me."

More faces appeared. They had crowded round him in the cinema, the eyes frightened, the minds wobbling, the voices shrill. Tomorrow the newspapers would echo them, television cameras would underline them, the radio would carry them. The storm would break. London would boil like a sulphur pot. He would be in the heart of the cauldron.

As I deserve to be, he thought. The sham is exposed. I'm a clumsy fool. I deserve to be posted to a manor where the gasometers and sewage farms outnumber the criminal population.

A tap sounded on his door. Follitt looked in. Wyndham said: "Come in, Jim." Follitt sat down. "It *is* a Ripper job," he said, gloomily. "The medical evidence proves it. There were no mutilations because even the Ripper wouldn't risk it in a place where he might be seen. He'd have had to stand over her to do it."

"Yes," said Wyndham. "I know. I knew at once. I didn't want to know. All the same, Jim, I think we'll keep it to ourselves. I think it would be the best from all points of view if we act on the assumption that we've got the Ripper and that the murder of Ruth Laidlaw is a solitary imitative crime committed by someone close to her—a jealous boy-friend, perhaps. We've had enough teenage killers lately to make it sound plausible."

Follitt stared back at him, unblinkingly. "Why the best?"

"Because we don't want to start a panic."

"A panic?" Follitt sat bolt upright.

"Panic, Jim," said Wyndham. "As this latest crime *is* the Ripper's work, it means that he has already claimed five victims with impunity—and that he is no longer restricting his attention to toms. To the public that means only one thing. It means that no woman or girl is safe at night wherever she goes and no matter how comfortable or familiar are her surroundings. They will think that he can kill when, where and how he chooses—and that we can't stop him."

Follitt said, unhappily: "I hate the idea of keeping an innocent man in the cells. And I can't see——"

"You know how we've been pestered by the TV Outside Broadcast units already. It's going to be worse now. There's something horribly normal about Ruth's murder. She's a sixteen-year-old kid. She goes to the pictures. She's stabbed in her seat. Most people go to the pictures. They can identify themselves with the victim. They won't even have to imagine it from what they read in the papers. The TV cameras will show them the whole humdrum scene: her home, her route to the cinema, the seat in which she sat—the lot."

Follitt said nothing. His face was pale.

"Our Ripper is the first mass-murderer of his kind in the TV age. Christie of Notting Hill is the only other multiple murderer in the past dozen years, and his crimes were all behind him when they were discovered. By this time, Jim, the murders have a horrible serial-story continuity about them." He said, suddenly, in a false voice charged with commercial bonhomie: "Keep watching your screens, folks, for the next instalment of this gripping, real-life drama. And don't forget: it *could* happen to *you!*"

Wyndham shivered at his own macabre illustration. Follitt's hand trembled. He said, in a low voice: "We'd better muzzle him, quick."

"We will," said Wyndham, with more confidence than he felt. "But in the meantime, I think we'll keep our Doctor Barton under lock and key."

"Yes," said Follitt. "I suppose you're right."

He looked at Wyndham with a new respect. Wyndham thought: "I'll qualify for a politician at this rate. Whatever's got into me? A week ago—a few hours, in fact—I'd never have thought of such a move."

He rose. He said: "There's not much more we can do tonight. Tomorrow we'll investigate Ruth's boy-friends."

"Yes," said Follitt. He turned towards the door. He paused, listening. Heavy feet pounded down the corridor. Wyndham frowned. The footsteps stopped at his door. The duty sergeant looked in, his face white.

"There's another of 'em, sir," he said, his control all gone. "Jackson found her—back of Prince Albert Road. Name of

Elizabeth Marshall, Lizzie the Bag, sir, an old tom, everyone knows her." He paused for breath. "And, sir, he says there's no doubt about it. It's another Ripper job. She's all cut up."

CHAPTER TEN

WYNDHAM returned to Albany Street at 4.30 a.m., feeling more exhausted than his exertions warranted. He had frequently gone thirty-six hours and more without rest, and felt less mentally and physically bedraggled. Emotional involvement, he reflected wearily, played hell with your stamina.

He sat down and pulled sheets of paper towards him. There was a lot to be done. He wrote at the head of the first sheet: "The Ripper, Latest Developments." He stared at the words for a long time, searching his mind for sentences. They would not come. Presently he felt his head lolling. It was no good. He must snatch some sleep.

He dossed down in the station. The duty officer woke him at seven-thirty. Wyndham rose, feeling like a trampled dish-rag, and went out in search of food, hot coffee and a shave. A cluster of idlers stood on the pavement opposite the station. They stared at him eagerly, consulted newspapers, and whispered after him.

The barber's hot towels refreshed him. On the way back to Albany Street, soon after eight-fifteen, he bought all the morning papers. The crowd outside the station had increased and it was no longer docile. The voices which commented on his appearance were hostile. He took no physical notice of them, but as he entered the station he thought: It's begun. They're frightened now, as they have every right to be, and it'll get worse before it gets better.

Wyndham read the newspapers carefully. There had been plenty of time to cover the new crimes thoroughly, and they were, of course, the front page leads in all the popular dailies. Even *The Times* had given them a double-column headline on its main news page. They told him nothing that he did not know and offered no sensible suggestions for coping with the murderer. That makes all of us, he thought, savagely; nothing to share among the lot of us. No clues, no footprints, no fingerprints, no weapon, no apparent connection between murderer and victims, no distinctive cigarette-ash dropped at the scene of the crimes, no pieces of torn material left hanging from a dead fingernail or a brooch pin, no convenient scraps of writing left lying about, not even a human hair except those of the victims. Wyndham had a momentary vision of the Ripper as a non-smoking, naked, bald-headed illiterate.

He fought down the fantasy. The trouble with this case, he told himself, is that psychologically it runs counter to every grain in your character. You like action; you like to get to grips with crooks and their confederates; you're not mentally equipped for fighting phantoms. And then he thought: Well, you'd better learn, and learn quick.

He returned to the newspapers. If they afforded him no help in detecting the murderer, they offered ample corroboration of the fear he had expressed to Follitt. The stories carried a shrill note of angry horror. The headlines screamed: "The Ripper Again—Twice"; "Moon-Mad Ripper Kills 5, 6." The sub-headings underlined the normality of the events leading up to the murders. A girl had gone to the pictures; an elderly woman had visited a pub. The crimes came home to them, entered their front doors, sat at their elbows, accompanied them on every trivial errand. The fear was worsened by the fact that none of the popular papers mentioned that Lizzie the Bag was an old tom with 115 convictions for soliciting. She was referred to as. "Mrs. Elizabeth Marshall, a widow, aged 62."

Speculation on the Ripper's identity was rife, and as he read them Wyndham's skin crawled.

All speculation centred on attempts to find a pattern which no longer existed. Ruth's murder (and Lizzie's for the readers) had broken the mould and there now seemed no logical choice behind the Ripper's victims. Yet a pattern there must be (so the Press argued) because it was unthinkable horror to imagine that the deaths were truely motiveless; that there existed a man, unknown and unseen, who was animated by nothing except blood lust; a man who would kill any woman whether she were young or old, respectable or disreputable, married or single, virgin or rake. But as he read Wyndham began to wonder whether the speculation was not a worse horror than the threat of a raving beast. Prejudice rose on the tide of fear. All the victims were Christians, said one newspaper. (For Christians read "Gentiles"; inference: the Ripper is a Jew.) Were they all non-Catholics? (Infer: the Ripper is a Catholic.) They were all members of the White Race. (Read: the Ripper is a Coloured.) It was nasty stuff and Wyndham felt dirty. He was about to toss the papers to the floor when his eye was caught by a cross-reference in heavy type at the foot of the *Daily Courier*'s front-page story. It read: "I Say: Sack This Man —Page 8."

Wyndham turned to Page 8. The layout was dominated by a large unflattering picture of himself. An enormous black arrow pointed from picture to headline, which repeated the wording of the cross-reference. Wyndham had an aversion to the presumption of headlines containing the first person singular, usually articles written by hacks who could turn out a shallow piece on any subject they were given. He glanced at the by-line and his face tightened. John Lewissen, the *Courier*'s crime man. Wyndham had fallen foul of him over the Brooks case. Perhaps he was now writing to order, but no doubt that little incident had added spice to his work.

The article contained nothing libellous. He was even given a fair dose of praise. But the barbs were there, sharp and spiteful, fashioned specially for the "Little Englanders" who made up a large portion of the *Courier*'s readership.

He read: ". . . ran away from home at the age of twelve. His mother made a public appeal for him to return. . . ." (Inference: ungrateful son who hated his mother.) ". . . saw action in Palestine and hit the headlines when he personally ambushed and killed a Freedom Fighter. . . ." (The man had been a Stern Gang terrorist and the *Courier* had praised him at the time. Today, the inference was: anti-Semitic.) ". . . prefers spending his holidays in the Latin countries, particularly France and Spain. He is fluent in both languages, and is a well-known bullfight fan. . . ." (Inference: un-English and brutal.)

The article concluded:

"Despite Wyndham's good record and exceptional luck, it was an error to promote him to Detective-Chief-Inspector at the age of thirty-four and give him virtual control of the St. John's Wood/ Albany Street sub-divisions.

"How can he be expected to handle successfully a baffling case which would tax the skill, brains and knowledge of the most experienced Superintendent on the Murder Squad?

"The Ripper case proves that he is not the right man for the job. Six women—one a mere girl—have died at this maniac's hand. With what result? The arrest of a man who is patently innocent and must now be released.

"How many more victims must die before the authorities see sense and place the conduct of this case in reliable hands?"

Wyndham crushed the newspaper violently. He thought: The oldest, most experienced Superintendent on the Murder Squad will be pleased. He tossed the newspaper on his desk. Well, the first shot had been fired and if he stayed on the job there'd be plenty more. He'd have to learn to take it.

The duty officer knocked and entered. He said: "The prisoner is ready, sir." Wyndham said: "Yes. In five minutes." The sergeant went out. Wyndham thought: Poor little man! Hope he doesn't take it too badly. It was a hideous blunder. I suppose he's got a claim for damages for wrongful arrest. And that reminds me: I must be careful not to say any more than I need. The Treasury doesn't like paying out. Yet I must be nice to the fellow. Tricky. Damned tricky. Damn and blast the bloody Ripper. Damn and blast him to bloody hell.

The crowd was larger still, and much noisier, as Wyndham emerged with Dr. Barton and walked towards the police car parked at the kerb. It had been joined, he noticed, by a number of Pressmen. Cameras focused on him. Reporters, held back by uniformed policemen, shouted questions at him. He said: "No comments." Barton preceded him into the car and they drove away. Somebody shouted abusive words. Wyndham reflected, sourly, a few months ago they had cheered him. He felt like an entertainer who could no longer grip his audience.

There were more idlers outside the court. They were even less docile than those in Albany Street. As he stood on the pavement waiting for Barton to alight a voice from the back of the crowd yelled: "Get back to your kid's school, copper." A woman's voice screamed: "You ought to be ashamed of yourself, letting all those lovely people be killed." A tomato, flung by an inexpert hand, splashed against the wall beside him. Wyndham took no notice. As he and Barton passed into the court, the constables on duty outside the building moved threateningly across the road.

The Magistrate took Barton's case first, at Wyndham's request. The doctor sat beside Wyndham—there was no point in the added cruelty of placing him in the dock—and the proceedings took only a few moments. Barton pleaded "Not Guilty" in a faint, guilt-stricken voice. Wyndham rose and offered no evidence. Barton was discharged. Wyndham turned to shake his hand. Barton blinked at him and ran out of court. Wyndham sighed, collected his papers, and went out. This time the crowd was silent.

Back at Albany Street—now empty of anyone except passers-by

—Wyndham went to his room and issued instructions that he was not to be disturbed for anything except developments in the Ripper case. Then he sat down and began to write, rapidly, the outline of his emergency plan to deal with the threat that would return at nightfall.

Linda Ward rose late in her modest flat in Hampstead—much less elaborate than her working flat in St. John's Wood—cooked bacon and eggs, took the meal to the kitchen table, and opened her *Daily Courier*. She read of the murder of Lizzie the Bag, and wept for the first time for many years. Poor old Lizzie! Lizzie had never harmed anyone except herself, and had brought comfort to many.

The moment of sentiment did not last. She repaired her face and ate her breakfast, now cold. She spared no sympathy for Ruth Laidlaw. Ruth came from the other side and the other side wasn't worth wasting sympathy on. She did, however, spare a thought for the girl's father, whom she recognized from a front-page picture.

She read the speculation and the attack on Wyndham and her lips turned cruel. She recognized the change in public reaction now that the respectable were suffering, and felt contempt. Let them suffer! she thought. It'll teach them that killers are dangerous. They start by killing toms and end by killing anyone they choose. I suppose the Laidlaw girl looked like a tom, with her bright clothes and many boy-friends, to anyone who didn't know toms. She felt no sympathy for Wyndham, who had blundered, and no sense of superiority at the accuracy of her forecast about Barton. She simply felt angry: anger at the Ripper and at the type of people she thought he represented.

She broke her journey to her working flat at a grocer's shop in St. John's Wood Village. She did little shopping there because the proprietor's wife epitomized the type of woman whom Linda most detested; but it was the only shop in the area where she could buy lychees. Linda was fond of lychees, and was not afraid of facing antagonism.

The shop was crowded. Linda took her place in the queue and waited patiently for her turn. Presently she saw that the wife had seen her. The woman's mouth tightened. She muttered something to the customer she was serving. The customer glanced round, met Linda's cool gaze, and glanced hastily away, flushing. She, in turn, spoke to her neighbour. Linda heard her say:

"She's one of *them*—*you* know." The phrase ran round the shop. Women close to Linda edged away. Linda smiled sarcastically but said nothing. She was used to it, as are all toms.

When it came Linda's turn to be served, the grocer's wife stared over her shoulder and addressed the woman behind her. Linda said, coolly: "I think not. I was in front of this lady." The wife, ignoring her husband's agitated signals, said: "Clear out! We don't want the custom of the likes of you."

Linda did not move. She said: "You serve me or you'll get no customers at all—my friends or yours. I'll see to that." The woman paled. She began to tremble. Her husband said: "Easy, Mary!" Linda leaned over the counter, picked up a can of lychees, and tossed down a pound note. The woman licked her lips, picked up the note by one corner, dropped it in the till, and flung down the change. Linda did not pick it up. She counted it carefully by gaze and said, quietly: "It was a pound I gave you. The change is for ten shillings." The woman said: "It was a ten-bob note. Are you calling me a thief?" Her husband said: "Mary!" Linda said: "Look, Mrs. What's-your-name, it's probably a mistake, but I've had these mistakes happen to me before."

The woman trembled violently. She began to scream: "You dirty, filthy whore, it was a ten-shilling note!"

Linda raised her voice slightly. "Give me my correct change or I shall call the police. I take the numbers of all my notes. The one I gave you is N 56 782318."

The woman turned white. Her husband said: "Go and sit down, Mary. It's only a mistake." His wife said: "Don't you dare apologize for me to the likes of her! It's dirty filthy creatures like her who are getting decent women and girls murdered." She began to scream hysterically. Linda did not move. The grocer thrust his hands into the till, tossed her a ten-shilling note, and hustled his wife out through the back of the shop. Linda looked the customers over, her eyes sarcastic. The women flinched and looked away. Linda walked out.

Doctor Charles Barton scurried out of court to the shelter of a passing taxi. He fell into the back seat. The driver said: "Where to, mate?" Barton said: "Eh? Oh, I don't know." The driver said, amiably: "If you don't, mate, you can bet your shirt I ain't got no idea." Barton said: "Just drive . . . I'm not sure . . . I'll think of somewhere." The driver shrugged and put in his gears. The cab moved off. When it had travelled about 100 yards Barton said: "Go to the Park. Drive round the Park. Any park." The driver said: "You're paying."

Barton sat back and closed his eyes. His mood was abject misery. Fool, fool, fool! he raved at himself, why couldn't you keep away from the girls? Why couldn't you keep your relationship with prostitutes on a professional footing? Why did you have to use them as well? Why wasn't Dorothy enough? Why did you have to help them when they were in trouble? Why did you have to make that stupid mistake over Watkins? Carelessness, sheer carelessness. Because she had a history of heart weakness you jumped to conclusions. You've ruined yourself by your folly.

A spark of strength struck in his mind. No, he told himself, it wasn't my fault. The Ripper ruined me. I'm no worse than a thousand other men. How many people could stand a searchlight on their private, professional and sex lives? And the Watkins thing was just bad luck. Hundreds of doctors made similar assumptions. You had to make it on the one woman who really mattered.

Barton groaned aloud. The driver glanced at him briefly through his rear-vision mirror. He hoped the bloke wasn't going to be ill. Looked queer. A bit loony, perhaps. Eyes wild, face haggard. Or just in trouble. Money or a woman. They caused most of the trouble in the world.

Barton thought: What does it matter whose fault it is? You're finished. Your practice was going down long before this affair —that's why you had to go in for abortions. Now it will all come out. The Medical Council will investigate. Even if they can prove nothing, you'll lose your remaining patients. Nobody will trust a man who makes such glaring mistakes. Even the girls won't come to you any more. . . . What about Dorothy? What will she think? Why didn't she come to see me in the cells? Why wasn't she in court? He answered himself: You know why. She's done the best she could for you and this is the way you've repaid her. You've destroyed your reputation and your livelihood. Oh God! What hideous luck, falling under suspicion for a crime you'd never even contemplate, let alone commit.

Abruptly, Barton sat upright. He thought suddenly: You can sue them! Sue the police for wrongful arrest! Sue the newspapers for their libellous hints. You'll get damages, big damages.

The spurt of spirit faded. He slumped back. You'll get nothing, he said to himself. Nothing. You'll only spend money you can't afford—money you don't possess—chasing a reputation you can never repair.

Barton leaned forward and gave his address to the driver.

I'll beg Dorothy's forgiveness. I'll promise anything, everything. We'll go away, somewhere where we'll not be known, and try again. I'm not old. Fifty-five isn't old. I feel old but if we get away, Dorothy and I, somewhere clean, and start afresh, everything will be all right. And I *can* claim against the Metropolitan Police. They had no right to arrest me. I'll write to the Commissioner today, making my complaint.

The taxi drew up outside the old Victorian house, consisting of bed-sitters upstairs, and his flat, surgery and waiting-room on the ground floor. He paid the taxi-driver and waved away the change. He let himself in at the front door. Letters and newspapers lay on the mat. He picked them up automatically. He walked on, clutching the bundle. The house was still. He called: "Dorothy! I'm home! I'm free!" Silence replied. Suddenly he glimpsed the significance of the letters and newspapers left unheeded at the front door. He dropped them in panic and ran into the bedroom. He paused in the doorway. He clutched the lintel for support. His eyes filled with tears.

Presently Barton moved back into the lounge, out into the passage and along to the surgery. The lock on the poison cupboard had been forced and the door hung open.

Barton took the stopper off one of the two bottles marked "morphine", shook tablets into the palm of his hand, drew a glass of water from the tap in the surgery, and swallowed his chosen dose. Then he walked back into the bedroom and lay down beside his wife.

CHAPTER ELEVEN

SHORTLY after midday, when Wyndham's report was in sight of completion, his phone range. He swore. He lifted the receiver irritably and heard the irascible voice of Sir Graham Dunstable.

"What's this about the Bartons, Wyndham?"

"The Bartons?" Wyndham wrenched his mind away from the Ripper. "Barton left the court after the formal acquittal. I suppose he went home."

"He's dead. And so's his wife. Suicide. It's in the papers already. What the hell do you think you're doing down there? Brewing tea and playing brag?"

Wyndham said, more tartly than was tactful: "I gave orders not to be disturbed by anything except new Ripper developments. I've been working out emergency measures. My report is almost finished. It'll be ready in about fifteen minutes."

Dunstable said, somewhat mollified: "Get a copy along to me as soon as—no; there's not enough time for that. I'll come down to Albany Street."

He rang off. Wyndham thought: Two more. Two more for the Ripper's score, though they'll never appear on his charge-sheet. Suddenly he felt a spurt of anger against Bennett. Barton and his wife would be alive today if the Super's nerves had held out for a few more hours. Then he felt ashamed. You couldn't blame Bennett. The Ripper frightened people and, scared, they acted too soon or too late. And then he thought: Go further back and blame yourself.

He shook his head. He closed his mind. Such thoughts were crippling. What was done was done. Past errors could not be corrected. The task now was to dam the consequences which flowed from them before they became an untameable flood.

Wyndham warned the duty officer that the A.C.(C.) was on his way, and returned to his report. The interruption had cleared his mind. He wrote rapidly and with a touch of anger.

The conference was held in Superintendent Bennett's room as a matter of form and tact, but Bennett took no part in it. His one contribution was to say to Dunstable: "Wyndham will give you the picture, sir. It's all his. My only intervention was disastrous." Wyndham liked him for that.

Wyndham said: "My report is being typed, but it should be ready in ten minutes." Dunstable said: "Give it to me verbally."

"Very well, sir." Wyndham paused to marshal his thoughts. He said: "The case has now become an emergency, and emergency measures are essential. Therefore I want more men, more cars, more walkie-talkies. I've cancelled all leave in both uniformed and plain-clothes branches and I've asked all men to work at least four hours overtime during the emergency. I've worked out a new beat system designed to cover all the most likely places where he may strike. My existing force is not large enough to do it properly. I'd like men drafted in from other divisions, particularly those who know the division. At least thirty, if possible."

Dunstable made a note.

"This beat system will be reinforced by cars, which will be on patrol constantly, particularly in dimly-lit side streets. They will use their spotlights to illuminate dark places. They will *not*, repeat *not*, patrol regularly. The essence of their work is that they should appear at unexpected times and at irregular intervals. If I could have ten extra cars and crews for this work . . . ?"

"You can have as many men and as much equipment as we can spare." Dunstable made another note.

"All the cars will keep in constant touch with Albany Street by radio. So, too, will uniformed men equipped with walkie-talkies." He turned to the wall-map of the division. "These are the key points," he said, pointing them out.

Dunstable made another note.

"All suspicious characters are to be stopped and interrogated, and if necessary brought in to be searched. The officer who detains a suspect is to go only as far as the nearest walkie-talkie or squad car and report. I will keep two cars in reserve to pick up suspects."

Dunstable said: "A good point."

"I would like additional plain-clothes men—again, those familiar with the district, if possible—who will patrol in the guise of civilians."

The A.C.(C.) nodded.

"Most of my own detectives will be keeping watch on men whom we suspected before the evidence against Barton became overwhelming. They will keep them under surveillance from before dusk until dawn."

"Yes."

"If the Ripper strikes again, the officer who sees the crime, or discovers it, is to report at once to the nearest radio, giving the position where the body was found. If no suspect has been arrested, all cars and men are to move at once to the area, according to instructions issued from here, and to cordon off the area for several streets around. No vehicles or pedestrians will be allowed to enter the area and none will be allowed to leave. Any who attempt to do so will be detained. Finally, if we haven't got the man, a house-to-house search will be instituted."

"You'll need a blank search-warrant," said the A.C.(C.). "I'll make the necessary arrangements. Anything else?"

"These are our own measures. I'd like the public to help, too. The B.B.C. and TV stations should be asked to warn women of all ages not to go out after dark unless it is absolutely necessary, and then only if accompanied. Any woman who cannot find an escort should contact her destination by phone, giving her estimated time of arrival, and route. If she does not turn up prompt to the minute, we must be notified at once."

"*That'll* make a lot of work," said Dunstable. "We'll be inundated with false alarms." He thought for a moment. "I think we'll scrub that one, for two reasons. First, thousands of people haven't got phones. Second, our lines may get jammed with trivial calls at the moment when someone wants to get through with an important message. We must keep in mind the fact that other crooks will be at large in London."

"Very well, sir."

Dunstable said, approvingly: "This is more like it, Wyndham."

Wyndham said, coolly: "Thank you, sir. All the same, I don't think we have a snowball in hell's chance of catching him."

Sir Graham frowned. He said, sharply: "I don't understand you, Wyndham. If there are any flaws in your scheme, plug 'em. You can have the men."

Wyndham said: "If I had ten times as many, sir, they would be too few. You could give me the Guards, the Tank Regiment and the paratroops and, in my considered opinion, if the Ripper wants to go on murdering people he can do so."

Dunstable said, sarcastically: "Just a waste, eh?"

Wyndham said: "Well, not quite, sir. We can hamper him, harass him, perhaps force him to stop his attacks for the time being. And lesser crooks in the division will have one hell of a time. But we won't muzzle him this way."

He hesitated, then went on: "We are up against a clever, cunning and skilful man who works in the dark. Each murder takes him no more than a minute or two to commit. I am convinced that he has no personal contact with his victims except at the moment of murder. He kills in neutral places. He is a faceless man. He walks up a street, or into a cinema, or through a park. We may see him. I've probably seen him. And so what? He is one man, insignificant among millions of men. There is no mark of Cain on his brow. His eyes don't glare crazily and he doesn't foam at the mouth. He is an ordinary little man in everything except his murders. I picture him strolling about London, feeling like God about to launch another thunderbolt. Shall it fall here? Or there? And then, perhaps, he sees a policeman and stops, 'Oh constable, can you tell me the time? My watch has stopped.' 'Certainly, sir. Eleven-fifteen.' 'Thank you, officer. Good night.' And ten minutes later, five streets away, he kills again."

Dunstable said, gruffly: "He'll make a mistake. Murderers

always do. He nearly tripped up with the Childs woman."

"Frankly, sir, that's what we're hoping for, isn't it? All these preventive measures. We've got to take them, if only to reassure the public. But they're not foolproof. We can't watch every rat-hole all the time. Even if these steps are too strong for him, he has only to stop killing until we relax them. Or he could decide to travel farther afield for his victims. I don't suppose a bus-fare to South Kensington or Soho would ruin him. Or he need only wait for a bad fog. November is approaching. What use will our spotlights, headlights, torches and peering eyes be then?"

"I see what you're getting at," said Dunstable, slowly. "You mean we should try to entice him into attempting murder on a victim of our choice?"

"Exactly, sir. It was tried in the Cummins case. It didn't work because he was a much clumsier crook than our man and he was caught another way. But it might work with the Ripper. I'd like to put half a dozen policewomen on the streets, disguised as toms, in the hope that we can draw his fire."

Dunstable nodded. "Yes," he said, "but it's damned risky."

"We all risk our lives," said Wyndham. "Some of us lose them."

"I wasn't thinking of the risk to the girls," snapped Dunstable. "I was thinking of the stink that would blow up if our precautions failed and one of the girls was killed. The Met., offering young women as decoy ducks to lure a raving lunatic—and letting him get away with it."

"It's our only chance, sir."

"Oh, we'll take it. It's a good idea. I'm only warning you that a lot of us will be looking for other jobs if there's any slip up."

He rose.

"Go ahead with your side of the arrangements. I'll have the men, the cars and the radios down here by six o'clock. That suit you?" Wyndham nodded. "The girls, too. Take care of 'em." He put out his hand. "Good luck."

Dunstable paused at the door. "And get some sleep this afternoon, Wyndham. You'll need all your reserves of strength."

CHAPTER TWELVE

WYNDHAM, now in undisputed command, called in his senior officers and issued his orders. It took a fair amount of time. At a quarter to two he decided that he had done everything that could be done, and went out for lunch. Another bunch of sightseers had collected but they offered no demonstration as Wyndham appeared and walked rapidly down the street in quest of food and drink.

He visited the Green Dragon but soon left. Too many people knew him. They wanted to talk. Those who did not know him stared at him, without affection. He tried a licensed restaurant, only to meet the same barrage of half-interested, half-resentful stares, plus infuriating requests from complete strangers for information which he would not have given even if he could. He left without ordering. The brief period of elation he had felt during the interview with the A.C.(C.), and the feeling that he was at last getting to grips with his quarry, had evaporated. He was hungry, thirsty, tired and pessimistic.

Wyndham thought about going home, and discarded the idea. It was too far away. He decided to take a room in a small family hotel. It would be useful during the next days or weeks, when he might have to snatch what sleep he could when he could, as well as being handy in case of an emergency call.

He rang Albany Street with his new address, ate and drank in his room, and read the evening newspapers. He skipped the Ripper case and the Barton suicides and tried to rest his mind with more humdrum news. Newcastle United F.C. (he read without wild enthusiasm) had purchased another defender; the St. Leger winner had been retired to stud; the outlook for the Home Countries in the rugby internationals looked black in the face of the strong French challenge. On the City page he learned that Consols had stiffened (he owned no Consols) and that blue-chip stocks were depressed following adverse news from Wall Street (he had no intention of selling the few blue-chip stocks which he possessed). The general news pages told him that a retired brick manufacturer from Eastbourne had left his entire fortune of £384,721 (net personalty £316,102; tax paid £92,341) to an actors' charity. Wyndham puzzled over likely reasons for such an unlikely source of such a bequest, and gave up, baffled. A titled lady gave her reasons for intending to marry for the fourth time; a visiting Hollywood film star gave her reasons for staying married to one man for thirteen years. The feature pages told him how to keep slim; how to stay happy though married; when to plant seeds he had no intention of planting, since he possessed no garden or even a windowbox, and how to win a fortune on the football pools. The complete irrelevance of all this information amused and relaxed him. He found himself reading, with deeper concentration but without strain, the news items of various crimes: £1,000 stolen from a solicitor's safe; a well-known Communist attacked in daylight in Mile End; a gang-brawl among teddy boys outside a dance-hall in Stratford East; anti-Semitic slogans daubed on two synagogues in Whitechapel and Golders Green; a bank robbery at Perivale, Middlesex; arson suspected after a fire in the City; a company director arrested on fraud charges; three hurt in a daylight brawl between Whites and Coloureds outside a pub in Camden Town. . . .

He allowed the newspaper to slip to the floor. Uneasiness returned. Anti-Semitic activity, racial brawls, a Communist attacked; all in daylight. Did those items add up to anything? He tried to tell himself not to be fanciful. A certain number of these incidents were always being reported. It could be pure coincidence that these had occurred today. It could be, but he felt certain that it was not.

Food, wine, the heat of the room, lack of sleep; all combined to cloud his mind as his brain refused to function. The room blurred. His head nodded. He grunted. He jerked himself awake with an effort, pulled off collar and tie, and flung himself on the bed.

Suddenly his mind was clear. The problem of the Ripper was no problem at all. He could see the murderer distinctly. He was running down Albany Street with a rapier in one hand, waving a Communist Party card in the other. He was a White Irish-Catholic Negro with the nose of a Jew. As he ran he stabbed the men and women he passed with the point of the rapier, not in the abdomen but in the centre of the forehead. He was killing people wholesale and must be stopped. No, when you looked closer you could see that he wasn't killing people at all. The men and women he stabbed had curious bumps on their foreheads, like tiny unicorn horns, and the Ripper was lancing them with his rapier. The lumps, when pierced, oozed streams of foul, multi-coloured material which poured out unceasingly like a strip of ribbon. The colours were congealed-blood red, sulphur yellow, crêpe black and corpse white. The ribbon unwound along Albany Street like a noisome carpet. As it flowed nearer he could see that it smoked and bubbled like the core of a volcano. It smelled, too: a revolting odour compounded of death, corruption and degeneration. It came nearer. Now he could see that it wasn't a ribbon. It was a poisonous mental pus concocted from equal parts of hate, fear, jealousy, envy, greed and lust. The ingredients were bound together with a powder labelled "Ignorance and Stupidity".

Suddenly all the people with the holes in their foreheads ran towards him in a mob, their eyes glaring. They chanted: "We've found the Ripper. We'll kill the Ripper. Get out of the way. You're getting in the way." They surged closer. Soon it was clear that if he did not give ground he would be trampled underfoot. He would suffocate in the stench or strangle in the folds of the ribbon, which had reappeared. There was music, too, now, a hollow drumming like a hideous tom-tom. It grew louder. The people were on him. He was down. He was in the slime and stench. The ribbon was twisting round his throat. The drumming was intolerable. His brain would burst.

Wyndham awoke, his eyes gummy, his mouth fuzzy, his mind reeling. A voice at the door shouted: "Mr. Wyndham! Mr. Wyndham!" A fist banged. Wyndham said: "Hallo! Hallo!" The voice said: "Half-five, Mr. Wyndham. The time you asked to be called."

The voice stopped. Footsteps went away.

Wyndham, still half asleep, rolled off the bed. He almost fell into the remains of his lunch, still littering the table by the bedside. God, he thought, what a hell of a nightmare! Must have been the Stilton. He swayed across the room to the wash-basin and plunged his head under the tap. The icy water ran down his neck and soaked his shirt but it also cleared his mind. Eyes and brain were focusing again as he towelled his hair and wiped his face and neck.

He combed his hair, adjusted his collar and tie, and put on his jacket. As he moved to leave the room his eye fell on the newspaper. He picked it up. The aftermath of the nightmare was still with him. He scanned the suspicious news items and ringed them with a pencil.

He went back to Albany Street, feeling like death.

CHAPTER THIRTEEN

ARTHUR LAIDLAW emerged from the sedatives into a grey and ghastly world. He lay in his bed without speech or movement. The devoted Lise, her plump face lined with shock, tempted him with choice foods and soothing words. He would not eat, he did not listen.

He rose at last, at three o'clock in the afternoon, and shambled about the flat in his pyjamas. The place resembled a shell, a spent cartridge, dead and derelict. The very colours seemed muted as though wall-paint, curtains, cushions and carpets had faded in a night. It was an hour before he could force himself to open the door of Ruth's room. Lise had tidied it with loving, destroying hands. Her clothes had been folded, her books and gramophone records stacked in their places. Ruth's room had never looked like this, so null, so void, as though a stranger had lived there, cool, precise, tidy. Then Laidlaw knew that Ruth was gone, and that he hated Lise and that he was alone with the dreadful loneliness of the creature who has built his life upon a single prop, and lost it.

He left the room, dressed carelessly, and went out, ignoring Lise's protestations. He drove to Albany Street and found out where Ruth had been taken. At five o'clock he looked on her for the last time. Still he could not find her, for her body, too, was null. At six o'clock he began drinking. An hour later he began an aimless peregrination about the streets of London, now walking, now sitting silent in a pub, drinking. There was no clear motive in his movements but deep in the recesses of his stunned brain a thin voice told him that his girl had died by violence, and that the man who had killed her was still at large, and that the killer wandered, as he now wandered, seeking victims.

9 p.m. No mist but heavy cloud scudding before a wind from the north. Presently rain, stinging, chill, penetrating. It blew into faces, dimmed windscreens, slowed traffic. Men turned up coat collars, pulled down hat brims, hunched shoulders. Women— though there were few of these—put up umbrellas and leaned forward blindly against wind and drizzle.

Wyndham swore. Autumn was on the side of murder. He found that he was biting his fingernails, a habit he had never contracted. He pulled in his shoulders. He felt as though walls and ceiling were pressing on him. He wandered into the control-room and read reports of car movements, studied the beats patrolled by his fake toms, listened to radio calls. The station closed on his mind like a clamp. He called for a car and went out. Anything was better than the waiting. . . .

9.15 p.m. The murderer let himself out of his home and strode towards the nearest bus-stop, his hat low on his forehead, his coat collar high, his lapels turned forward, the knife swinging loose in his pocket. He rode, and walked, and changed buses, and all the time his eyes watched, recording thoughts he would later put down in his diary. . . .

A lot more police about. . . . Those black Wolseleys are police cars. . . . The hump under that P.C.'s cloak, I suppose it's what they call a walkie-talkie radio. I've really stirred them up this time! They won't stop me though. How can they? Look at those two P.C.s, supposed to be on watch for me and they're smoking cigarettes surreptitiously in the shelter of a doorway. A filthy habit, smoking. It must be responsible for a lot of inefficiency. . . . The cars are using their spotlights in dark streets. That might be dangerous for me. . . . Why should it be? They can't light all the streets all the time and London was built for concealment. There's always an alley or a deep doorway. . . .

Funny! There seem to be more prostitutes about. That one over there—I've never seen her before. There was another one, way back. They both looked odd, somehow. And there's another. I wonder. . . .

Here I am. I can do with a drink. How much time have I got? About ten minutes. She's usually prompt in her habits. I feel like having a celebratory drink, in anticipation, but I'd better not. might attract attention. I'll take my usual; at least my usual drink in this particular pub. "Pint of mild and bitter, Joe. Thanks." Nod to those men who know you. They're all talking about the Ripper, of course. Listen to that fool in the corner: he belongs to the Nigger school of thought. I wonder what he'd say if I interrupted and told him the truth? I'd like to see his face!

Wyndham noted the signs of care, and of fear. Many fewer people on the streets, and only a handful of unaccompanied women. These he spoke to, and was angry. They were the bold and the foolish. "He can't scare me." "I can take care of myself." "He'd better not try anything with *me*."

Cinemas were almost empty and those courageous spirits who had refused to be daunted sat together in close-knit groups. Café trade was slack, only teds and young Coloureds, each in their preferred places, not mixing, hostile when they passed in the streets. Pub business brisker than usual, though—and almost 100 per cent male. Men, feeling protected by their sex, had left women folk cowering over the telly and gone out in search of comradely conversation. The talk was all about the Ripper. Wyndham didn't like the talk, anywhere he heard it.

"The Ripper's a Jew, mate," said a thin, black-coated, white-collared man at the bar of the King Henry. "Stands to reason, don't it? All the ones he's killed are Gentiles—the paper says so. But why? There's plenty of Jews around—Jewish prostitutes, too. So why's he pick on non-Jews? Because he's a Jew himself and the Jews stick together. . . ."

"He's Coloured!" said a red-faced man in the bar of the Red Lion. "Aren't the Niggers behind all the trouble these days? A Nigger sex-maniac. Everybody knows that the Niggers are hot on sex. It's the sun that does it. Why hasn't he killed a Coloured woman? There's plenty about as deserves it. You see them everywhere, hanging on the arms of White men. Disgusting! If I was in charge of the police I'd pack the lot of them back where they come from, then you'd see. . . ."

"The Ripper's motive is mingled sex and religion," said a pseudo-intellectual in a pub in Swiss Cottage. "He is a strongly religious type—that's a characteristic of all sex-maniacs—who has been jilted. He has sublimated his frustrated ego and sex-urge into a religious mania. He feels called upon to murder, as heretics, all women who are not of his own religion. Now, when we study the list of his victims, what feature stands out most strikingly? *All* are Protestants. Even—and mark this closely—even that Irish girl, Grace Childs. She was that rare bird, a Southern-Irish Protestant. Logically, then, the Ripper *must* be a Catholic. Well, you know how bigoted Catholics are. . . ."

"It's a Communist plot!" shouted an excited little man in a cloth cap, in a pub off the Euston Road. "Don't tell me no different —and don't try to tell me the Ripper's one bloke. He's a Red gang. King Street is fed up. They've tried everything, haven't they? Propaganda, unofficial strikes, rigging Union ballots—and where's it got them? Nowhere. Now they're after direct action. Kill the women. Frighten the public. Start a panic. *That's* when the Reds get into power. If I were Scotland Yard I'd round up the bloody lot. . . ."

Wyndham felt like saying: "My theory is that the Ripper is one-eyed. Have you noticed the striking fact about all the victims? They each had two eyes. Or else he's one-legged. The victims all had two legs. Or—yes, this is more sensible—he had his nose blown off in the last war. All the girls had noses." He also felt like saying: "You bloody fools—there are no facts to argue from. No facts at all. There are two reasonable suppositions, but even *they* are only suppositions, we don't *know*. The first is that the Ripper is a man. The second is that he lives within easy walking distance of Regents Park." He said nothing and presently he went back to Albany Street in time to greet the A.C.(C.).

The Ripper thought: Not long now. Pity the rain's so thick —I can't see out of the window properly. . . . What's that? God, it made me jump! But it's only a police car going down the street with its spotlight flaring. Most obliging! It should have waited a few minutes. I'll bet it won't be back for a long time. . . .

He glanced at the pub clock, deducted the ten minutes which were always added to its time, placed his pint pot on the counter, and went out through the door marked, "There it is, mates." He did not patronize the urinal. He turned left, walked swiftly through the wooden gate which opened on the side street, and slipped into an alley.

Four minutes later he returned to the pub, drank the remainder of his pint without haste, nodded good night to the barman and the few regulars who knew him by sight, and walked out.

The time was ten minutes to ten.

Dunstable looked at Wyndham sharply. He marked the signs of strain around mouth, eyes and cheeks, the lurking weariness behind the gaze, and something else—camouflaged, but not cleverly enough—which might be worry. A bad sign.

He said, genially: " 'Evening, Wyndham. Sit down, man, sit down. You're not on trial for your life!" Wyndham sat. He thought: This sort of forced joviality is not in character. Dunstable's worried. Aren't we all?

Dunstable said: "Just dropped by to see how things are going."

"All quiet, sir. At least . . ." Wyndham hesitated. "Yes," he went on, "all quiet, so far."

Dunstable said, sharply: "You don't sound too sure."

Wyndham said, firmly: "I am—as far as the situation goes up to now."

Dunstable said: "Expecting another attempt tonight?"

"No, sir, not really. He's never yet killed on successive nights." The A.C.(C.) nodded. "Nevertheless, there's something on your mind."

Wyndham accepted the opening. "It's true I'm not so worried about the Ripper, but I'm worried about what he's doing to men's minds." He opened a drawer and dropped the marked newspaper in front of Sir Graham. "These incidents worry me, sir. A Com-

munist attacked, anti-Semitic slogans on synagogues, Whites and
Coloureds brawling."

Dunstable frowned. "We're always getting similar cases."

"In daylight, sir? All on the morning after the Ripper's fifth
and sixth murders? And there's another thing. I've been on patrol
and the talk is nasty. The Ripper is a Jew, a Red, a Nigger, a
Roman Catholic, according to prejudice. It's inflammable stuff,
sir. It reminds me of the tension in Palestine. I have an uneasy
feeling that almost any incident could spark off a lot of trouble."

"A new Ripper crime, you mean?"

"Not necessarily. A Coloured man spilling a White man's beer
in a pub. A Jewish youth in a dance-hall making a pass at a
Gentile's girl-friend. A Communist shouting off his mouth in
the wrong company. An Ulsterman speaking out of turn in an
Irish house. Or some drunken fool somewhere might pull a knife
and spark off a scare."

"Rioting?"

"Yes, sir."

Dunstable shook his head. "You exaggerate the atmosphere,
Wyndham. In any case, this division has no strong centres of
prejudice."

"I wasn't thinking of my division, though the chances of something starting here are highest. But if it starts, it'll spread."

"There may be isolated incidents like those you mention,"
conceded Dunstable, "but we can handle them. London isn't
Palestine, you know, or Little Rock, or Sharpville, or a ghetto.
We don't riot, Wyndham. We're too level-headed."

Wyndham stood his ground. "Nottingham, sir, or Notting
Hill?"

"Isolated incidents," said Dunstable, brushing aside Nottingham and Notting Hill. "A bunch of hot-heads. A few stiff gaol
sentences soon put paid to them."

"They were a shock to public opinion, sir. We didn't think they
would happen here, but they did."

Dunstable rose, abruptly. "Concentrate on catching the Ripper,
Wyndham. That's your immediate task—and so far you haven't
been conspicuously successful."

Wyndham said, formally: "Yes, sir." Dunstable rose and
walked to the door. The telephone rang. Dunstable paused.
Wyndham answered the ring.

"Yes," he said. And again: "Yes . . . yes . . . immediately." He
put down the receiver. His face was grey.

"I was wrong," he said, heavily. "It's number seven, sir. A tom named Florrie Bates. Found in an alley ten yards from her flat. Killed on her way to the local to buy beer, as she did every night at about the same time. Only been dead a few minutes. I'm going down there right away."

The time was 10.17 p.m.

The news swirled through London. TV sets interrupted programmes to flash the information. Radios announced it. Men carried it on foot, by Tube and bus and car. "Another one. Under the eyes of the police. Two minutes after a squad car drove down the street."

Talk intensified. Nerves tightened. Men and women clustered a little closer together in public places. Eyes flickered indecisively over blank faces. Men who ventured from pubs, clubs, cafés and cinemas did so in groups, as though the fear of the Ripper had reached into their own bones.

The client touched Linda's arm. "You can drop me here," he said. Obediently, she pulled the Zephyr into the kerb alongside Camden Town Tube Station. The client said: "Thanks, Linda." She smiled up at him professionally. "Come again," she said. "You have my number." He nodded non-committally and walked away. She watched him disappear into the station.

A man paused, swaying, by the car. She glanced at him casually. He was hatless and without an overcoat. She recognized him. He leaned on the door and pushed his head under the cover. She was shocked by his appearance. He said: "Funny! I knew the car at once. Wasn't thinking about it. Wasn't thinking about anything."

"I'm terribly sorry," she said, and meant it.

He nodded, slowly. "You know my real name now, don't you? From the papers. I wonder if it matters?"

"Not to me," she said. "You'd better come in."

He shook his head. "Not tonight, Linda. Not tonight. I couldn't. Though in a funny sort of way you're the only one I've got left."

"I meant, come in out of the rain."

"Oh!" He looked surprised. "It's raining. I must be wet." He fumbled with the door, opened it, and climbed in. "Yes, that's funny, really funny. How long has it been now, Linda, every week for how long?"

She didn't answer. She said: "A cigarette?"

Laidlaw shook his head. "There's been another murder," he said. "Just heard about it, in a pub. I've been in a lot of pubs. I'm looking for the Ripper."

"I'll take you home," she said. "You're soaking wet. You need dry clothes and a good night's sleep."

"No." He put a hand on her arm as she moved to touch the gear lever. "I'm not drunk. It's not the drink. I could drink London dry tonight and not get drunk. I'm all alone. Come and have a drink with me. That pub over there."

Linda hesitated. He misinterpreted it. He said: "I'll pay for your time, Linda. Time's money."

"I wasn't thinking of that," she said, not offended. "I was thinking that whatever you say I should take you home."

He shrugged. "I shan't stay there," he said. "No one can force me to stay there."

She acquiesced with a nod, wondering why she should play the nursemaid even to an old client. As she drove across the intersection and performed a U-turn to bring them to a stop outside the pub, he said: "Yes, it's funny. The only one I've got left, the only one in the whole wide world."

They walked through the drizzle to the door of the saloon bar. The time was 10.25 p.m.

Ten-thirty. Four men and a woman emerged from the King-fisher. The men surrounded her. They laughed and joked, bawdily, about the Ripper. They told the glistening coldness of the street exactly what they would do to him if they caught him. The girl, whose name was Ellen Foy, added obscene comments of her own.

They reached the door of the Black Boy. One man said: "One for the road, eh?" Ellen Foy said: "Make it two, Ken—but hold on a sec., I must spend a penny. These bloody pubs ought to be rebuilt, specially for dames."

A police constable, standing in a doorway, watched the quintet. He knew the girl as a notorious tom who had been implicated in robbery with violence, and the four men as layabouts and mobsters. Ken, catching the constable's eye, said: "Christ, that flatty gives me the creeps with his fish eyes! I'm going in. See you inside, Ellen."

The girl nodded and ran quickly down the steps of the public convenience. The men jammed themselves into the pub. The constable, recollecting his orders, turned and walked down the street to keep an appointment with his sergeant. Behind him, a man strolled across the road and leaned on the railings at the top of the steps to the toilets.

A flurry of wind and rain, strong and rough, swept down the street. The few passers-by ran for shelter. The man at the railings looked down the steps. His right hand moved. He turned away, fumbling with something under his coat. He dodged across the road, shielding his face from the rain, and leapt on a bus which had been held up at a traffic light.

"Stabbed as she reached the top of the steps," said Follitt, savagely, "and then fell to the bottom. No mutilations, of course." He paused. "He's getting bolder," he said.

The time was 10.50 p.m.

The news of the eighth victim coincided with closing time. It swept into the pub where Linda and Laidlaw sat. Laidlaw stood up, raving obscenely. The barman said: "Naow, naow, I agree with you, but not in front of ladies." Linda pulled his arm. "Sit down and shut up!" she said. The barman said: "Last orders, please, last orders."

By ten minutes past eleven the pubs had emptied. The customers stood on the pavements, their minds flushed with drink, their nerves taut.

And at this moment, in a street off Camden Town, just beyond the confines of D Division, a woman screamed and ran bleeding from the steel blade of her attacker. Ten seconds later she turned into Camden High Road. An enormous Negro pounded behind her, brandishing a razor.

Laidlaw saw them and yelled: "The Ripper! It's the Ripper! The Ripper's a Nigger!" He ran. Hate and the lust for vengeance cleared his mind. He ran fast and steadily, still shouting, towards the fleeing woman and the Negro. Behind him, irresolute men found resolution in his voice and deed and started to follow.

Linda recognized the injured woman and the man who chased her. She shouted: "Stop! Laidlaw, stop! That's not——" Her voice was lost in the growing murmur of angry men. She ran to her car, animated by an impulse to catch Laidlaw. She switched on the engine and looked again. The rain had ceased and the scene was clear under the street-lamps. She sat, a hand to her mouth to stifle a scream, and watched hypnotized.

The Negro saw men running, men who shouted and gesticulated. There was one man ahead of the rest and his face was demented. The Negro tried to halt his headlong gallop and slipped. He fell heavily, the razor still in his hand. He saw the leading pursuer hurl himself forward. He brought up his hands first in defence, then in attack. Bodies fell on him. He squealed, high and scared, like a rabbit. Fists and boots pounded him on head, ribs, belly and groin. Once, he managed to reach his knees. The lamplight shone on his face, greasy with sweat, saliva and blood, as a group of Coloureds swung out of the Tube station. Then he went down again, and this time he did not rise. He did not fall on the pavement. There was a body beneath him, a body that did not move, but whose body it was he did not know. He screamed again. A boot struck his mouth. He was silent.

The Coloureds took in the situation and saw logic. A man of their own colour was being attacked by Whites, and this was something they knew about from way back. They ran, yelling. White men turned to meet them.

The battle raged on pavement and roadway. It spread, it grew, it became more savage. Thugs came with coshes, knives, bicycle chains and knuckledusters. Men ran from side streets, poured out of cars and buses. The air was noisy with screams and shouts. Linda sat in her car, watching in helpless horror. She saw a Coloured woman peer fearfully from a doorway, and a running ted swipe at her with a cosh, and the woman disappear, screaming. She saw a Negro, pursued by half a dozen Whites, climb into his open sports car, and the Whites pull him clear, and trample on him, and turn over the car, and ignite the petrol which flowed from the tank. The petrol burned with a glare which lit the scene with a macabre glow. Its flickering flame lent ghoulish shadows to the frightening faces. She saw shop windows crash under the weight of flailing bodies, and men emerge from the interiors armed with chair-legs and bottles. She saw three Negroes corner a man and his wife, and knock down the man, and kick him, and tear the clothes off the woman until she managed to escape and fled, white-bodied, screaming, down the street. She saw, fitfully through the swirling struggle, the body of the huge Negro spreadeagled on the pavement, his face crushed; and the woman he had attacked, her bare legs grotesque, dead on her face; and Laidlaw, his clothes ripped, his face bloody, sprawled on his side.

And then she saw huge shadows gather round her car, and black faces and white teeth, and voices raging. A hand grabbed at her

shoulder. Her dress tore. Frantic, she slapped the gear lever into
bottom and pressed the accelerator. The faces disappeared. She
felt a bump as the offside wheel ran over something lying in the
road. She saw a turning and swung the wheel. The tyres squealed.
The car lifted ominously on two wheels, then slowly returned to
equilibrium. She did not stop until the drive of Harwell Mansions
came into view, and by that time the inferno was a mile behind.

CHAPTER FOURTEEN

"THREE dead, thirty-five injured, and God knows how many
thousands of pounds worth of damage done," said Follitt, stonily,
wishing Wyndham had not asked for a report, wishing the man
would go home and take some sleep dope instead of sitting there
with his head between his hands. "The dead Coloured boy was
Spade Willy Jameson, a Jamaican pimp. The woman was his tom,
Gladys Poole. Neighbours heard them quarrelling in the street.
Spade wanted money. Gladys refused to give him any and cheeked
him. Spade slashed her—he was probably hopped on reefers.
Gladys ran. Then Laidlaw saw them and jumped to conclusions.
He was stunned by the death of his daughter, he'd been on the
drink, he didn't like Coloureds——"

"He hated them," said Wyndham, unemotionally. "He told me
so. He hated them as I hated toms—probably because he'd never
really known any. So he got himself killed and in doing so egged
a lot of men into committing criminal folly. There's a sort of
insane logic in it, I suppose."

"Blame Spade Willy," said Follitt, quickly. "He was a fool.
All pimps are stupid but Willy was worse than most. He could
have won prizes for it if anyone had thought of putting them up
for competition. Pulling a razor on a girl when the whole town
was blazing with fear! You might say that he got what was coming
to him."

Me, too, thought Wyndham. This is where it ends—if this is
indeed the end. This is where folly and prejudice lead. First it is
people you do not know or care about, and suddenly it is your
friends and their children and all the innocents, who perhaps are
not so guiltless. But there has to be a fountainhead, and that is
the Ripper. I am the faulty jet through which his wickedness has
been allowed to spread.

Follitt leaned across the desk and said, sharply: "Stop it,

David! Stop it, do you hear? If you don't stop blaming yourself you'll go crazy. Take a few days' leave. They'll give it to you."

Wyndham laughed. "They'll give it to me all right. As much as I want. Preferably the rest of my life. Why don't they ask for my resignation or just post me?"

"Don't talk rot!" said Follitt. "The riot didn't occur in our manor. You're doing everything a man can."

"Now," said Wyndham, "too late."

"So we all make mistakes! Forget it. We've got the trap set. He'll fall into it. He'll have to—there are practically no genuine toms on the streets in this area. Believe me, nobody wants you to resign."

"Nobody wants my job!" said Wyndham. "I don't blame them." But he was beginning to feel better under Follitt's firm handling.

"Go home," said Follitt. "Or to your hotel—but take a rest. Sleep today, even if you do feel you must come on duty at night until this period is over. You can't go day and night without sleep."

"No," said Wyndham. "O.K., I'll stick it out. And thanks, Jim."

"Phooey!" said Follitt.

Wyndham tried. He tried to stop blaming himself. He tried to outface the storm which blew about his head. He tried to persuade himself that his trap would close on the murderer, and soon. But the days passed, and though there were no more murders, the rage of Press and public did not abate. The riot had shocked and shamed them and, human-like, they sought a scapegoat for their sins. Wyndham was the man.

On the morning of the fourth day after the riot he was ready to throw in his hand. He reached his office that morning to find a missive waiting for him. It was a plain brown foolscap envelope. His name and address and the word "personal" in the top left-hand corner were printed in block letters. The postmark showed that it had been collected locally at 11.15 on the previous evening.

He slit the envelope without interest, expecting to find that it was another of the many letters he had received from abusive cranks. He extracted a single sheet of thin quarto typing-paper. The letter, which was also printed in block capitals, carried no salutation and no signature. It said:

SEND YOUR FAKE PROSTITUTES BACK TO THEIR

USUAL BEATS. YOU DID NOT REALLY BELIEVE THEY WOULD FOOL ME?

Wyndham stared at it for a long time. At first he thought it must be a hoax. Then he realized that it could only be genuine, and his last defence went down. His trap had been spotted. The Ripper had outwitted him once more.

Automatically, he arranged for the envelope and letter to be tested and gave orders for any similar communications to be handled carefully and brought straight to him; but personally he was without hope. His prejudice had caused him to miss his best chance of muzzling the Ripper; since then he had been led a dance. He would never catch him, never.

It was at this point that he began to write his letter of resignation, and it was an hour later that the diary was brought to him, and he began to read.

Wyndham read the remainder of the diary rapidly skipping large sections since it dealt, in the main, with matters he already knew from the official angle. He picked out the personal items: the arrogant boasting, the sneers at the police in general and himself in particular, the diatribes against prostitutes, the explanations of a few things that were obscure, the statements of movements. The reason for the mutilations became clear in a paragraph which read: "I'm glad I decided to mark my victims for warning, otherwise I'm sure the police would believe that prostitutes were dropping dead in the Park from heart failure or the plague or something!" On September 9th, after killing Jopson and Metcalfe, he had written: "I went to the Park today to see what it looks like in daylight. I took no risk. Hundreds of ghouls have done the same. The two areas where the bodies were found have been roped off, but as far as I could see everything else looked normal. Admittedly, I could not see very well among all the people and with policemen moving us along. . . ." On September 14th he had written: "The Park is now useless to me. All the girls have fled! One of the lungs of London has been cleansed of its impurities. My scheme works, and works well. I will yet make London a city fit for men to walk in. And to do this it is not merely desirable but essential for me to work elsewhere."

More significant still, he had written within hours of killing Ruth Laidlaw: "I have been arrested! I heard the news in a public house at one o'clock when a man rushed in, shouting the news. The name of the suspect was not mentioned but I overheard that detective tell it to the woman, Linda Ward. They have arrested Barton! Barton! They have mistaken that bungling, ineffectual creature for *me*. I suppose I should feel pleased that their suspicions are so wide of the mark, but I cannot. It is an insult to me to imagine that such a weak-kneed creature could possess *my* selfless skill, courage and daring.

"The discovery that Linda Ward is a common prostitute is another shock. When I first saw her with the policeman Wyndham (a real bungler if ever there was one), I thought she must be his fiancée, they were so intimate. Later I heard a man at the bar whispering about her. I am more than shocked. I am dismayed. I had no idea that women of breeding and intelligence take to the streets. I would like to put her on my list of examples but I don't know how. It would be too dangerous for me to approach her. . . ."

The final entries read: "I had a good deal of fun with my two examples tonight, but it was clouded by the dreadful rioting in Camden Town. I was on my way home and my bus was held up in the traffic jam it caused. People were talking and they all blamed me. But it's not my fault. It's all the fault of the newspapers, with their idiotic theories. The lunatic idea I have got used to; I suppose their stupid minds reach no higher. But I cannot tolerate being called Jew, Negro, Catholic or Communist. Can't they understand that *only* a right-thinking Englishman could possess the nerve, brain and selflessness to commit such deeds?

"I must, of course, make allowance for the fact that they are in ignorance of my true reasons. Also, my mistake over the Laidlaw girl has confused the issue. No, not a mistake—that implies that I do not know a prostitute, which is quite absurd. She had not yet gone on the street, that is all. It was obvious that her morals were loose and that the final step was only a matter of time. The newspapers also helped to cloud the issue by refusing to describe the Marshall woman in her true light, with the result that decent people have become afraid. I did not want this. It hurts and worries me. I wish only to cleanse the city of its human filth, not to terrify everyone indiscriminately. Besides, these misconceptions blur my real purpose. Unless prostitutes know that I seek only to destroy *them*, they will not take proper warning.

"Yet what can I do . . . ?"

The following day he had written: "I have had a brilliant idea! I will send this diary to the Chief Inspector! Not quite as it is written, of course. I must remove all names, my place of business, anything which might identify me, etc., etc. And I will slip in a few misleading references here and there, just like a crime writer putting in the red herrings! But I shall leave the bulk of it intact, and particularly those sections which deal with my mission. I will type it. . . .

"Another thing. I've just realized that those odd-looking prostitutes must be policewomen, put out as decoys. Really, Wyndham's intelligence must be zero. Does he really think I don't know a genuine prostitute when I see one . . . ?"

Wyndham reached the end of the final sheet. He felt sick. He wanted a bath. He had looked into the mind of a murderer and he decided that he would never feel clean again. His abhorrence was complete. Here in black and white were the thought processes of a man who was extraordinary in only one thing: his murders. For the rest, it revealed the pattern of the thoughts of a thousand ineffectual men whose egos outweighed their abilities; the minds of cowards who peered out meanly at a world which refused to reward them for services they did not perform; the minds of men without moral courage, whose every action and every fear took them deeper into corroding hatred. Even the Ripper's sublimation of his fear and hate into a mission to cleanse the world was not unique or even unusual. It was the mind of the bigot who commits evil in the name of good and of God. The Ripper should take his place in the long line of the persecutors. His knife should stand in the same gallery as rack and thumb-screw, stake and gas-chamber, Inquisition and Index, Purge and Witch-hunt, the Holy War and "The Native Question", as one of the engines employed by zealots in their ceaseless, bitter, slaughterous and finally futile task of trying to force the minds and deeds of men into an unbreakable mould of prejudiced conformity.

Wyndham knew then that he hated the Ripper with an intensity which went far beyond the call of law and duty, of sympathy for the victims, or even his own sense of guilty complicity. It reached deep into the essential honesty of his being and cried out to him: Destroy this man.

Wyndham reached into his pocket. He took out his letter of resignation. Deliberately, he tore it into little pieces and dropped the wreckage in the wastepaper basket. Then he picked up the diary and commenced to re-read. From time to time he underlined a passage or made a marginal note. By the time he had reached the end, the faceless man behind the knife had begun to take shape.

PART THREE

Ploughing In

CHAPTER ONE

ONE week later, when an augmented force of detectives and desk-
men had completed their inquiries into the hidden clues in the
diary, Detective-Chief-Inspector David Wyndham drove a hired
car south-westwards out of London to keep a secret rendezvous
with Linda Ward. He left the capital by a devious route and
stopped several times to make sure that he was not being followed.
When he reached the appointed place—a remote hotel-pub in
Kent—he looked in all the public rooms and checked the names in
the hotel register before he allowed himself to be satisfied. He was
not afraid that they would be seen by the Ripper, who should be
at his office desk among the giggling typists who did not like him
to touch them, sensible girls; but Wyndham did not want even a
casual acquaintance to see them together, in case a subsequent
word in a pub, or a ribald joke, should get back to the Ripper's
long ears.

He took a high stool at the bar, ordered a whisky and soda,
and resisted an impulse to take it over to a window-seat from
where he could watch Linda approach. You're a bloody fool,
he told himself, gloomily. When will you learn to wipe the woman
off the emotional slate and stick to your job?

Linda arrived, punctual to the second, and Wyndham felt a
pang of mingled affection and irritation. She possessed so much
of what he wanted in a woman; poise, intelligence, independence,
the courage to run counter to public opinion. She lacked the one
quality which would have made her a desirable mate. Oh well,
that's the way it is, he thought, and no use brooding over it.

Wyndham took her coat and escorted her to a corner seat where
they could talk in privacy. She sat down, opened her handbag,
and dropped a bulky brown octavo envelope on the table. It was a
copy of the Ripper's diary. She said: "I love saying, 'I told you
so'."

Wyndham did not hesitate. "I owe you an apology," he said,

sincerely. "You were absolutely right. I shall never challenge your word again—at least, not on these matters." She smiled, for once without mockery. "Handsome," she said. "Very handsome." The smile faded. The hardness under the make-up lifted to the surface. There was cruelty in her face, and bitterness. She said: "All the same, I don't see that the diary gets you any further. There's no name, no address, no face except a blur. It could still be one of a million men. I can't see that it's told you a damn thing except his mental processes."

"It told us a great deal," said Wyndham. She had made him feel small so often that he could not resist the opportunity to parade his knowledge. "It told us that he is between five feet seven inches and five-nine in height; that he lives—probably in a Victorian house converted into flats—within twenty minutes' walk of Regents Park, to the north-west. He is married without children, a non-smoker, and does not own a car. He was almost certainly educated at a State grammar school before the war. He is the head—chief clerk, I'd guess—of a small department in an office, probably somewhere in the City. I think he went to night school or Pitman's College. He is between thirty-five and forty-five years of age, indisputably lower-middle-class, a snob as well as an egotist, and drinks lager."

He stopped. The mockery was back in her eyes. He said, grinning: "Sorry, I'm showing off again." She shook her head. "No, please, I really *am* impressed. Did you get *all* that out of the diary?"

"We got a lot more, actually, and though I've made it sound like a conjuring trick, it wasn't really difficult."

"I can see that you've done some guessing," she said, hesitantly.

"Not entirely," he said, amused to see her groping in an unfamiliar field. "Let's take the indisputable facts. He talks about smoking as a filthy habit and cannot provide Rosie with a light. So he's a non-smoker. He makes two references to Watkins looking up to him. She was five-feet two; yet he is not so tall that he can see over the heads of the crowd at the murder scene. Therefore he is of medium height.

"Yes," she said, nodding.

"He gives us detailed times for his first encounter with Watkins. We know where she usually solicited and where she lived. We timed the walking distance from her home to the Park, deducted the few minutes he spent in her room, worked out an estimate of the time they spent talking together—and forty or so minutes are left. That means he must live within a twenty-minute walk of the Park. Now, he mentions that they came out of the Park together on the east, which he did not know. So he doesn't live there. South and south-west of the Park are too expensive for him. Therefore he lives north-west—the Swiss Cottage area—with a 'saver', as the punters say, on the smaller streets behind Lord's Cricket Ground."

"But why a house and not a flat?"

"He talks of going upstairs. It *could* be a maisonette, but I think that he'd have said so—the word has got the sort of snob appeal which he'd like. So it's a house. But newly-built houses are scarce and expensive in that area and the older houses are too big for him and his wife to keep up alone. Q.E.D., as Euclid used to say, I deduce that he occupies two floors and the rest is converted."

"You're starting my mind working, too," she said. "You deduce the childlessness from the fact that he never mentions a family and no car because he walks or uses public transport."

"Car owners rarely walk, even when they're upset. They go for a drive."

"The lower-middle-class, schooling and snobbish angles—how do you get those?"

"They're inference, but the diary reeks of them. His idea of virtue is essentially lower-middle- or upper-working-class, but we know he isn't an artisan. He reads the *Telegraph* rather than the *Express* or *Mail*, which argues snobbishness—the 'City' type. He can make a fair stab at the *Telegraph* crossword, which argues a bit of education, yet he doesn't know enough to refer to Bordeaux wine as Bordeaux without the wine, which anyone who had been to a decent school would know by reason of his background. State schools don't teach such things—or at least they didn't when he went to school. Besides, nobody with any knowledge would visit a pseudo-French restaurant to learn correct table manners and menu French. '*Bouillon Windsor*!' 'Chicken *rôti*!' For God's sake!"

Linda smiled at his outraged voice.

"Also, he can type. He might have picked it up, four-fingered style, in the office, but I doubt it. It seems too competent. Therefore I infer night school or Pitman's. The lager—frankly, that's a guess. He talks about drinking bottled beer, and lager is the fashionable bottled beer these days. He'll be fashionable if it doesn't cost him too much."

She nodded, thoughtfully. "It fits," she said. "Anything else?"

"Yes. I've left the most important to the last. He tells us that he won a specified sum on a summer pool on a given date. It was his biggest mistake. He forgot—or didn't know—that the pools companies keep records of all winners of substantial amounts. We checked back at the published dividends, contacted the firm which paid that sum, and they supplied a list of the winners.

She leaned forward, suddenly tense. "And only one of the names fits all the other facts, so you know who the Ripper is?"

He shook his head. "Unfortunately, no. There were six hundred and eighty-three winners of that amount that day. Five of them fit all or most of the facts we have deduced."

A sudden thought occurred to her. "But all your deductions may be wrong. He admits that he's altered the diary."

"Not all wrong," he insisted, "but I'll agree to some. That's why the diary as it stands is useless as evidence. The defence would trample on it. Nevertheless, I'll bet my hopes of Heaven that I'm eighty per cent right."

"All the same," she persisted, "he could have won a different sum on the pools and faked the amount by doing what you've done: check back on the sums paid that week and select one that suited him."

"He could," agreed Wyndham. "I don't think he did, but that's only a guess. However, we checked other pools which had paid between one hundred and three hundred pounds that day and got their lists."

"Why those limits? Why not a thousand, say?"

"Because I think that a man of the Ripper's calibre would have acted differently if he'd won a much larger sum. The amount he gives is sufficient for a slap-up holiday, a spree on the town, a deposit on a car, or the price of a TV set. A thousand would be a fortune to a man like the Ripper."

She found his analysis irrefutable. "Yes, I suppose so."

"We checked through the other lists and were able to eliminate all except two."

"So you have seven men, any one of which might be the Ripper. That's not bad."

"It's better, yes; and I've got my own favourite. So have you, I'm sure. He was with us in the Green Dragon that day. But as evidence it's not conclusive." Wyndham hesitated and then made up his mind. She deserved to know everything. "We have searched the homes of all those seven men at a time when they were absent. We used the best men in the Force so that no traces of entry should be left. We found nothing. No original diary. No typing-paper or envelopes of the type he sent. No typewriter. And seven kitchen-knives. Seven damned kitchen-knives, any one of which could be the murder weapon."

"Bloodstains?"

"Clever girl!" he said. "Yes, there were traces of blood on all of them at the place where the blades joined the handles. Specimens were taken and analysed. Beef blood, Linda. The Sunday joint of beef. The bloody British institution."

"The typewriter—couldn't he have used an office machine?"

"I think not—that diary took a long time to type. He'd have had to stay late on several evenings and I doubt if he'd risk it. Nevertheless, we investigated the offices where they work. We sent in a fake typewriter mechanic—he pretended to be offering a free service in order to attract new business. We didn't find the typewriter."

Linda leaned back, her questions exhausted. "I see." She stared at him. Her gaze was hard, cold and calculating. "So where do I come in?" she asked. "Imagine you didn't bring me down here to ruin my health with all this fresh air just to parade your deductions."

"No," he said, his voice and face grave. "The Ripper would like to kill you, Linda. He's too scared to try it. But if you offered him the chance . . . ?"

She said, bitingly: "Another decoy duck, but a real one this time. A genuine, dyed-in-the-wool, cheap lousy tom."

"I'm sorry," he said. "I deserve that."

He returned her stare, searchingly. Suddenly he felt like saying: "Scrub it, Linda. Do yourself a favour and take another holiday in the sun in case he screws up his courage to have a go at you. We'll catch him some other way." The words remained unspoken. Instead he said: "I shan't blame you if you say no. I'm asking you to risk your life. You may well lose it. All seven suspects are under observation twenty-four hours a day but I won't kid you that we can tail him if he wants to throw us off. We can keep you under observation, too, but it will need to be so discreet that it might be useless as protection at the moment of attack. We would muzzle him afterwards, of course, but that wouldn't do you any good. And yet I see no other way of catching him before he commits more crimes. We can't watch every girl in London. We can't stop these men every time they go out at night in the hope of finding the weapon. He carries it only when he needs it and we never know in advance when he is on a murder walk. One abortive search of the real man and he'd go to ground. Sure, we'd stop any further murders but that's not good enough. We don't want another Jack the Ripper in our unsolved files. Yet if we don't lure him into striking at a target of our choice, he might kill anyone. He is mad, Linda. He believes that he can kill and kill and kill again, with impunity, whenever, wherever and however he chooses. And I tell you frankly, Linda, that barring accidents he can. I live in dread of the first foggy night. It could come at any time now. And beyond that is the new-moon period."

He paused. She said nothing. Her gaze did not falter from his face. He gestured helplessly. "If you say yes, and the luck of the weather goes with us, we may have two to two and a half weeks in which you can trail your coat. Madden him, taunt him, flaunt your wickedness, as he calls it, until he is blind with the lust to destroy you." He rubbed his eyes. "What am I saying? I'm inviting you to be murdered. The trick would need to be done so cleverly that he would not suspect—and every precaution would make safety for you less possible. You'd have to be on your guard day and night. There's no knowing what he might try. It's not even certain that he would strike at night." He paused. He added, hopefully: "You could wear a bullet-proof vest, perhaps?"

She laughed, harshly, "With my figure? What do you think my silhouette would look like? He'd smell a rat at once. That swine knows a woman's figure when he sees one. So he should—he's been peeping at them long enough."

Wyndham spread his hands. The gesture revealed despair, hope, supplication. He said: "Let's have lunch and talk about something else. They're offering some splendid winter cruises to the sun this year."

Linda did not move. She said slowly, with venom: "I hate him! I hate him and all men like him. I hate them because they're creeping, slimy, gutless beasts. Why didn't he lay a complaint to the police when that fool Rosie tried to blackmail him? Because he was too damned respectable. Murder was easier. Why didn't he walk out on his wife when she got fed-up with his bed manners? Because of his bloody respectability. They hate each other, but they're an ever-loving couple. Prostitutes are filthy, but go to them just the same. Shop-keepers borrow money from us and short-change us because they know that most of us dare not make a fuss. They're glad of our custom, but they keep us waiting at the back of the shop until all the respectable women have gone. 'Nice' women spit at us in the street, and go home to their furtive affairs with men friends or to keep their husbands out of their beds. Nice, nice people, wonderful people, charming, stinking, rotten people because they're cowards; they're liars and cowards to the bottom of their wretched little souls.'

She paused to draw breath, her face cruel, her fingers flexing. Wyndham felt repelled. His own hatred for the Ripper was rooted in moral purpose. Hers was set in vengeance for wrongs committed against her sisterhood. It was not even directed specifically against the Ripper. He was only the symbol, the prototype projected to its logical conclusion in wholesale murder. Her hate was directed against the society which nourished him, cherished him, took off its hat to him, opened its places to him, while it kept her on the outside, looking in.

Wyndham knew that though he might go on loving her, because love is independent of aversion, he would never like her again. She had exposed a segment of her soul which was as hateful as the soul of the Ripper. And yet he also felt sympathy for her. Her hatefulness had bred within her because society would not permit her the right to enter fully into it: which used her and despised her because it despised itself for using her. In that moment Wyndham understood the wrath of the oppressed and the atrocities they commit against the governors who refuse them the right to live as men.

He also knew that his private problem was solved. She would offer herself in his service even if it led to her death.

CHAPTER TWO

THE clock on the office wall jerked its minute-hand forward to five o'clock. Desk drawers slammed, typewriters stopped clicking, men and girls rose hastily, calling, "Good night. 'Night. See you tomorrow. Goo'night."

Mr. Edgar Horncastle, chief clerk in the Mailing Department of the Baltic-Far East Steam Navigation Company (passengers and freight), of Fenchurch Street, rose from his desk punctually on the hour, extracted towel and soap-holder from a drawer, and proceeded to the gentlemen's washroom. By the time he returned the office was deserted. He put on his nondescript overcoat and hat and walked downstairs. He paused at the entrance to the office block and sniffed the dank November air joyously. Dusk was falling fast and fog was rising from the river. This looked like being his night.

A girl waiting in the doorway said: "Good night, Mr. Horncastle." He said, condescendingly: "Good night, Miss Griggs." A youth emerged from the murk. He said: "Hi-ya honey-chile. Ain't this a stinking night?" Miss Griggs giggled. "Oh, Charlie!" she said. "The things you *say*!" They linked arms happily and moved off. Horncastle frowned. Irene Griggs was definitely *not* the girl she used to be. A shy, young (though well-developed) girl when she had joined his department six months earlier, she was now pert, even insolent. And surely this Charlie was not the boy who had called for her last week? He hadn't looked too closely at the youth but he was almost sure that the other one had been named Ted. He would have to keep an eye on Irene Griggs. If she were playing fast and loose with all the youths in the district it could mean only one thing.

He sighed and, feeling momentarily discouraged, turned into Fenchurch Street and made his way towards the Tube. There was a lot of wickedness in the world. Morality was crumbling fast. England seethed with illicit sex, like an evil cauldron. How many more evil-doers must he remove before the country began to take heed? Then his mood brightened. What did it matter? There was plenty of time before him. Generals did not count the cost in human lives before they joined battle. There was no nobler, cleaner fight than the one he had voluntarily undertaken to wage, and he would fight it to the bitter end. What had Napoleon thought of the millions of men and women who lay dead and dying after his campaigns? Nothing. And Napoleon had conquered most of Europe before making his Russian mistake, an error of over-confidence. Well, that was a mistake *he* would not make. Prudence in day-to-day life; care in planning; speed and skill in execution; these were his watch-words. He would root out evil wherever it could be found, at the times and places of his own choosing. He need not stop at sex, either. There were other evils in the world.

A thought drew sober lines on his forehead. What a nuisance! If he widened his sphere of activities, would he not be going outside his own terms of reference? There could be no gainsaying the change in the public attitude towards him since extracts from his diary had been published. Still, if he *did* decide to widen his scope, he could easily write another note. It would mean acquiring another typewriter and then disposing of it afterwards, and that was extravagant. Perhaps he had been over-cautious in dropping it into the Thames with the remainder of the paper and the envelopes tucked inside its case? But no. He had acted correctly. Typewriters could be traced. Prudence, care, all the time. . . .

Mr. Horncastle emerged from Regents Park Underground and walked slowly towards the Green Dragon. It was a detour which he made fairly regularly these days. He noticed that the fog had thickened. By ten o'clock it should be the worst of the autumn so far; not a pea-souper, but with visibility down to a few yards.

The Green Dragon, as usual, was crowded. Mr. Horncastle passed a remark about the weather to Jimmy Leech, and retired with his lager to a quiet corner. Presently Linda Ward came in, alone, and drank one gin and lime before leaving again. Mr. Horncastle finished his drink leisurely, his thoughts burning. Incredible! Disgusting! Revolting! That woman—a prostitute! How could men guard themselves against vice when it appeared dressed in such fashion? She and her sisters were far, far worse than the drabs at the street corners. Those, men could recognize and be warned. But *her*, with her smart car and her ogling looks and expensive clothes. She would delude most men, as she almost deluded me. . . . Well, not for long now. How very convenient for me that lately she has taken to dropping into the Green Dragon at six-thirty, and again around ten o'clock for a drink between clients. And how much more fortunate that she cannot park her car nearer than sixty yards away. Clearly she is not going to change her routine tonight, despite the fog. How very obliging of her!

Mr. Horncastle went home to high tea.

Linda Ward phoned David Wyndham. Wyndham listened, his face impassive. He said at length, softly: "So he was there. Then there's no longer any doubt about it. Horncastle is the Ripper and tonight's the night. Now listen carefully, Linda. We've gone over this before but I want no slip-ups, for your sake as well as our own. My reasoning is that he will leave the pub a little before you do, as he normally does. He'll go for you somewhere between the pub and your car—almost certainly at the car, when he can hope that you'll be off-guard. Sergeant Green—you know him—will be tailing him as closely as he dare—and that, if this fog continues to thicken, will be about three paces behind. Green's instructions are to muzzle Horncastle the moment he draws the knife, but you mustn't bank on it. If you hear any ominous sound, dodge like a hare. Get your torch on his face if you can. And scream. Scream the bloody street down. When he bolts for it there'll be a dozen men within call to nab him. If he slips *them*, which is unlikely, he'll run into a cordon within two hundred yards." He paused, thinking. Was there any more that he could do or say? He added: "And for God's sake, Linda, take care of yourself." Then he realized that the warning was futile. In his heart Wyndham felt certain that despite all the precautions he could devise, action to aid her would come too late. He was sending her to her death in order to prevent more deaths.

He pulled himself together. "How do you feel?" She said: "Lousy." He said, impulsively: "Christ, you've got guts!" She laughed. He fancied that the note was shaky. She said: "Guts? It feels as though I haven't got any at all. S'long." He was about to say "good-bye" when the finality of the salutation rebuked him. He said: "*Au revoir,* Linda. Be seeing you."

"I hope," she said.

The phone rang again. Wyndham listened. He said: "Thanks. Your relief is on the way." He hung up. He said to Follitt: "Horncastle's just got home, after inspecting the Green Dragon to see if Linda was there. Get Green, Jim, will you?"

Detective-Sergeant (first-class) Harry Green listened attentively to Wyndham's instructions. "We are certain now that Horncastle is the Ripper and equally certain that he will try for the girl tonight. Your task is the most difficult and important of all. First, we want the Ripper. Second, we don't want the girl killed." He noticed the order in which he had placed them and hoped that there would be no need for priorities. "You will go to the Green Dragon at nine-thirty. Horncastle should be there, or will enter soon after. While he's been watching the girl he's adopted the procedure of leaving the pub before she does. We think he'll do the same tonight so that he can lie in ambush for her between the pub and her car. Personally, I think the car is the most likely place for the attack, but it's not certain. So when Horncastle leaves, you leave, without giving him a hint that he's being tailed. When he holes up to wait for her, you wait, too, within three or four yards if you can. The moment you can see him draw his knife, spring him. If he should slip you, blow your whistle and there'll be plenty of reinforcements on hand. Got that? Repeat. . . . Fine." He paused. He said, levelly: "I don't pretend that this job is going to be easy, Green. The fog may help or it may hinder. If he gets the slightest suspicion that he is being watched he'll go to ground. On the other hand, if you act too late the girl will die."

"I understand, sir. I'll do my best."

"I'm sure you will. And remember—when you nab him, make sure you get the knife."

"Yes, sir."

"Good. Go and get an hour's rest. Wear any clothes you think will help you, provided they don't shriek 'copper'. And no drinking until you get to the Green Dragon, and then only one."

Green thought, resentfully: Who does he think I am? He said: "Yes, sir."

"Then off you go. Good luck." Wyndham turned to Follitt as the sergeant went out. "Now, Jim, it's your turn. Give me back all the other dispositions."

"Harris and Barker are watching Horncastle's house. When he leaves, Barker will tail him, Harris will phone us. Green will be on duty in the Green Dragon, with Atkins. When Horncastle enters Atkins will leave the sus to Green and phone us. Then Harris, Barker, Atkins, Borden, French, Curtis, Martin, Vaughan, Gooch and Purdom will take up their positions." Follitt pointed them out on the map. "On receipt of Atkins's message that the sus is in the pub, we shall notify the radio cars, which will move into position ready to cordon off the area. At the first sound of trouble—the woman screaming or police whistles—all roads will be blocked. No traffic, wheeled or on foot, will be allowed to enter. All vehicles and pedestrians attempting to leave will be checked. All our men have seen the sus in person, or the photographs we have had taken of him, and if he is seen he will be detained on suspicion. I think that's all, sir."

"Good man!" said Wyndham. He sat back. The calm recital of the precautions had soothed him. "If Horncastle makes the attempt, we'll get him. Of that I'm certain." His face clouded. "I wish I were as certain as that . . ."

He broke off. Follitt said: "Yes, sir. For a tom, Linda's got a lot of nerve. A lot of nerve."

By 9.30 p.m. the fog had thickened so deeply that in patches it was impossible to see more than two paces. Edgar Horncastle, groping along familiar streets, wondered fretfully whether it might not hinder rather than help. Then he remembered that his home stood on lower ground than the pub. Around the Green Dragon the fog should be thinner; a shield and a cloak but not a fetter. His spirits rose when he discovered that he was right.

The saloon bar was more empty than he had ever seen it. The fog had kept a lot of *habitués* away. A few regulars stood idly around, and two men he had never seen before were chatting desultorily at the bar. One of them left almost at once.

Jimmy Leech said: "Managed to make it, eh, Mr. Horncastle?" Horncastle said: "Nearly didn't, Mr. Leech. Very thick down my way. Better up here, though—higher ground." He took his drink, nodded to a couple of the regulars, and found his corner. He hoped that no one would talk to him. He need not have worried. He had built a reputation for solitariness and the regulars left him alone.

Linda Ward usually came in at about ten o'clock. Tonight she was late. By a quarter-past Edgar Horncastle began to worry. He tried to argue that she had been held up by the fog, but his mind persisted in saying that because of the fog she would not come at all.

She entered at 10.20. She wore a loose coat over a sweater and skirt. She put her handbag on the table and turned to hang the coat on a peg. Horncastle saw her back, smooth under the expensive wool. He saw the spot he must aim at, and then, as she turned, he hid his face in his glass in case his eyes betrayed him.

Horncastle finished his drink leisurely, placed his glass on the bar-counter, and said good night to Leech. As he opened the street door he noticed the second of the two strangers also put down his glass and make a motion to leave. Horncastle allowed the door to close behind him, and suddenly ran. He had no desire to have his direction noticed by even the most harmless customer who might remember it when inquiries were made. So he turned left instead of right, left again at the first turning, left yet again along the street behind the Green Dragon, and then, cautiously, left once more to bring him into the side street in which Linda Ward parked her car.

Horncastle peered at the vehicles and his nerves jumped irritably. Three cars stood by the kerb. He recognized none. They were a black Humber Hawk, a red M.G. with a black hard-top, and a green Consul. Damn the woman! Had she parked her car somewhere else on this night of nights or—a sudden thought—had she changed it? She hired them; that he knew. If she had chosen another make tonight the M.G. was the most likely to be hers, but he dare not take the chance. He must alter his plans slightly and strike nearer to the Green Dragon.

Footsteps sounded in the street. Horncastle shrank down almost to his knees in the road behind the Hawk. A man appeared. He looked worried. He peered about him anxiously, as though he were short-sighted and the fog bothered him. Horncastle recognized the second of the two drinkers and was glad that he had acted quickly. The man continued on down the street.

Horncastle slid from behind the Hawk and walked the other way. He turned into the street which housed the Green Dragon and retreated into a shop doorway. He could just make out the illuminated sign outside the pub, a yellow blur in the murk, and the square lightness which was the saloon-bar window.

The bar door opened. A woman's form appeared, and paused. Linda Ward's voice said: "Good Heavens, it's only fifty yards! Besides, the Ripper isn't after decent women." In the Green Dragon she kept up the pose of respectability. The hypocrite!

The door closed. She moved towards him. She walked on the edge of the pavement, taking the line of the kerbstone as her guide. She came nearer. Her heels tapped faintly on the stone. All sound was muted in the fog.

She came abreast, went past. Silently, Horncastle stepped from his refuge. He moved swiftly, without attempting to deaden his footsteps, but she did not hear him. She continued to walk, head down, absorbed in following the kerbstone.

Horncastle drew his right hand from his pocket, lifted the knife, and struck at her heart.

Shock travelled up the knife blade. It hurt the muscles of his wrist and biceps. He stood, bewildered. The girl staggered, recovered herself, swung round and flashed a torch on his face, the torch she had not used to find her way in the fog. Horncastle turned and ran. Linda Ward began to scream.

CHAPTER THREE

HORNCASTLE ran without thought of direction. He ran in blind fear and panic. He must get away. He had walked into a trap. Get away. Get home. Keep away from people. Run, run, run. Police whistles now. Forms shadowy in the fog. Turn off. Run right. Run left. More figures. Run left. Turn here. Twist there.

Get away. Get home. Turn again. Twist again. Keep going. Keep going.

He tripped and stumbled. He changed direction. His route, drawn as a graph, was a crazy squiggle of lines crossing and re-crossing. The fog both hindered and helped. Once he almost ran into a car and doubled back only just in time. Several times he flitted within yards of the hunters and they neither saw nor heard him.

A wall. A gap in the wall. A final turn. A different paving surface under his feet. A wall beside him. A lighted window in front of him, dim in the haze. Noise in the street, cutting off retreat. He had trapped himself. Horncastle sobbed. He stopped running. There was no longer anywhere to run to. His lungs heaved, leg and calf muscles ached, his chest pained. He stood crouching, his eyes wild, his teeth bared like an animal, the knife still in his hand.

He was in a yard. An open gateway had misled him. Whose yard, and where, he did not know. A door opened and he shrank against a wall as an oblong of light filtered into the yard. A man dumped something by the door, something wooden which also clinked like glass. Before the door closed again Horncastle heard excited voices and the rattle of glasses. He knew then that he was in the yard of a pub. The man had put out a crate of empties. And then he knew the name of the pub. His crazy, zig-zag, doubling flight had brought him to the back door of the Green Dragon.

Horncastle's heart and bowels contracted, then eased. His breath slowed. His mind began to work again, fitfully at first and then with more clarity. He had walked into a trap. The girl had worn some sort of metal protection under her clothes. But what? He had seen her body under the tight-fitting clothes. She must have put it on after his departure. Changed in the Ladies' toilet, of course. He pulled himself together. What the hell did it matter what she had worn? She had protected herself and carried a torch to shine on him. The police had lured him into a trap. All those police whistles. That car drawn up across the street to bar traffic. A net had been drawn around him and he would never escape.

Wait! Couldn't he escape, though? If he were bold, might he not slip the noose? What evidence had they against him? None to arrest him until tonight, otherwise they'd never have used the girl as a decoy. What had they now? He had left the pub. The girl had left later. She had been attacked. They couldn't prove it was him. Except for the knife. He had to get rid of the knife. Get rid of it so that they could never find it and trace it back to him. But the girl had seen his face. Did that matter? It was his word against hers. No one else had seen him. They couldn't hang him on the unsupported word of a prostitute. The diary, though. They'd search the house for the diary. Safe there; they'd never find it, not if they pulled the house down brick by brick. One thing at a time. Get rid of the knife. With the knife he was a dead man dangling on a hempen rope in a wooden shed. Without it, there was a chance.

He was still crouching, unconscious of his stance, peering about him. Inspiration dawned. He laughed silently. He was standing on cobbles, and grass grew between the stones. The perfect hiding place! He bent down, inserted the point of the knife between two cobbles, and pressed. The blade slid into the earth up to its haft. Horncastle stood up. He placed one foot against the haft and stamped hard at an angle. The blade snapped off clean at the point where it joined the handle. Horncastle picked up the piece of wood and crept over to a pile of miscellaneous refuse; crates of empties, piles of bottles, pieces of tin, boxes, broken spirit-measures; all the paraphernalia of a busy public house. He thrust the knife handle among the odds and ends. The police would look for a knife. What would it matter if they found a piece of wood?

Horncastle expelled breath in a great sigh of relief. He straightened his hair and tie, brushed at his coat, stepped out into the street, and a few moments later he pushed open the door of the saloon bar.

Wyndham's phone rang. He grabbed the receiver. Follitt's voice said: "Follitt here, sir. The sus gave our man the slip. He made the attack and disappeared into the fog."

Wyndham felt a wave of nausea sweep over him: a compound of rage, worry and acute distress amounting to despair. He said, in a stifled voice: "So the girl's dead?"

"Dead, sir?" Follitt sounded surprised. "Good lord, no! Right as rain. A bit shaken up, of course, and in a couple of hours or so she'll have a bruise as big as a half-dollar on her back, over her heart. But just now she's lapping up brandy in the Green Dragon. That's where I'm phoning from."

Wyndham, struggling with joy mixed with anxiety and bewilderment, said, faintly: "I don't understand. You mean that the Ripper actually stabbed her?"

"Bang on the target. I thought you knew the gag. When Horncastle left the pub she went to the Ladies and put on a sort of small harness she'd carried in her handbag. Two pieces of thin steel, circular, about eight inches across, worn under her sweater and over her heart, back and front. In the fog, under her coat, it couldn't be seen. You mean to say she thought it all up by herself?" Follitt's voice was admiring. "What a woman! If she wasn't a tom I'd leave my happy home for her."

Wyndham said: "Yes. Give me the dope. How did Green lose him?"

"God alone knows. He swears he was only four paces behind Horncastle when he left the pub but by the time he got to the door the sus had vanished. Then," said Follitt, grimly, "the fool lost his head. Instead of warning the girl to stay put until he'd located Horncastle, he decided to stand guard over the M.G."

"M.G.?" said Wyndham, sharply. "Why not the Zephyr?"

"Side-swiped in the fog on the way to the pub. Not much damage but enough to put it out of action. It was all Linda could do to warn Green in time. Anyway, Green hung round the car. Next thing, he heard the girl screaming only thirty yards from the pub door. By the time he got there the Ripper had gone."

Wyndham glanced at the clock. "How long ago did all this happen?"

"Twenty-five minutes, guv. Couldn't call you earlier."

Wyndham said, slowly: "It's a bad show, Jim."

"Not too good, guv, no, but we'll nab him, don't worry. Even with this fog, I defy anything to get through the cordon." His voice changed. He said, his voice faint as though he had taken his mouth from the transmitter: "Jesus Christ Almighty!" Wyndham felt a thrill of uneasiness: Follitt never blasphemed. Follitt's voice gathered strength. "He's just walked in, guv! The sus has just walked in, as large as life and twice as natural." He sounded dazed.

"Muzzle him, you fool!" shouted Wyndham. "Detain him on suspicion and search him. I'll hang on."

"Right, guv."

The receiver thudded, Wyndham sat, his emotions a swirling tide. Relief at Linda's safety, admiration for her ingenuity, the emotion he now recognized as a love she would never reciprocate, anger at Green's incompetence, a dull fear that the Ripper had out-manoeuvred them again; all these thoughts and feelings thrashed inside him in a frightful storm.

The phone said, subdued: "You there, guv? We've searched him. He's got rid of the knife."

CHAPTER FOUR

MRS. LILLIAN HORNCASTLE, lying sleepless in her bed at midnight, heard the click of the gate, the unfamiliar footsteps, and the ominous ring at the front door which she had dreaded. She did not move. She thought vaguely that if she did not answer the men would decide that they had come to the wrong house and go away. The ring was repeated, more authoritatively. She rose, put on a dressing-gown over her nightdress, and went downstairs.

Wyndham waited without impatience outside the grimy, four-storied terrace house in a street behind Lord's. Three sergeants, including the two men who had searched the house three weeks earlier, waited with him. There was a long delay before they heard shuffling footsteps behind the door. A woman's voice called out: "Is that you, Edgar? Have you lost your key?" Wyndham said: "No, Mrs. Horncastle. We are police officers."

Silence. The door opened. A frightened face under hair in curlers and a net peered at them through a narrow gap. She said: "What do you want?" Wyndham said: "May we come in, please? I have a few questions I would like to ask."

She opened the door wider. She was thin. She wore a long, faded dressing-gown of pale blue quilt over an ankle-length nightdress of pink wool. Her feet were shod in old blue slippers which had once possessed fluffy pompons. Wyndham thought, uncharitably, that the Ripper's comments on his wife had been accurate.

She admitted them to a small, over-furnished lounge with curtains and table runners as faded as herself. Wyndham said, producing a piece of paper: "I have a search-warrant authorizing us to look over this house."

Mrs. Horncastle said nothing. Wyndham thought: She knows, or at least guesses, that her husband is the Ripper. Her silence proves it. I wonder which way she'll jump? She ought to be glad to see the back of him, but wives are curious people.

He nodded to the men who had searched the house before. They went away to look for the knife, which they did not want to find, and the original of the diary, which they hoped that this time they would. One returned almost at once and shook his head negatively from the doorway. The knife had gone. Wyndham had expected nothing else. He nodded. The sergeant went away again. Wyndham looked at the woman, sitting blinking and fearful. He said, pleasantly: "Mrs. Horncastle, do you own a kitchen-knife?"

She looked up, startled, the fear lively in her nervous eyes. She said: "I . . . I . . . why do you ask?"

"Answer my question, please."

She looked away. She said: "No."

"You have never owned one?"

She hesitated. She said: "I . . . I . . . yes, we did have one, I think."

He said: "Most households do, Mrs. Horncastle."

She said: "Yes, yes, they do, don't they?" He waited. She thought. Suddenly she straightened in her seat. She said, firmly: "I gave it away. Or threw it away. I can't remember."

Wyndham thought: So it's defence. He said: "When was it, this throwing or giving?"

"I don't remember. Not long."

"Can you give me the approximate date?"

"I don't think so. I was doing some cleaning out. When was it? It was getting old and blunt. Very worn. I thought it was too old to be worth keeping. I meant to buy another but I forgot. It must have been about two weeks ago. Perhaps a little less, perhaps a little more. It's difficult to remember."

"Why is it difficult to remember, Mrs. Horncastle? Are you always throwing stuff away?"

"No, of course not. I'm not good on dates and things."

Wyndham thought: She's groping, but she's doing well, blast her! He said, patiently: "What else did you throw or give away, Mrs. Horncastle?"

She asked: "Why do you want to know these silly things?"

"I am asking the questions. What else did you throw or give away?"

"Oh, pictures and things. Junk. It's amazing how things accumulate in a house like this. Really, I can't think where some of the things come from."

Wyndham said: "If you threw them away, they would have been collected by the dustman?"

She looked at him, sideways. "I suppose so."

"On the other hand, if you gave them away, you will give them to a specific person."

She said: "I remember now. Some I gave away, some I threw away. I gave stuff to a rag-and-bone man. You don't often see them nowadays, do you?"

"You gave him the knife?"

"Yes, I did. I remember quite clearly now."

Wyndham fought down a feeling that he was trying to burst a balloon with a feather duster and changed his tack. "I understand that you and your husband are not on good terms."

She said, instantly: "It's a lie! I don't know where you heard it but if the neighbours told you, it's a wicked, wicked lie."

"Is your husband often home late?"

"No. Not as late as this."

"He often goes out in the evening?"

"Quite often."

"Where does he go?"

"I don't know. For a drink, I suppose. That's where most men go at night, isn't it?"

"You don't know?"

"No, and I don't ask."

"Yet you are on good terms with him?"

She stared at him straight. "I trust my husband," she said. She stood up. "I have answered a lot of questions. I demand to know your name and why I am being pestered."

"My name is Wyndham," he said, watching her narrowly. "Detective-Chief-Inspector Wyndham." She sat down abruptly but he knew that she was not surprised. The fear, which had ebbed from her eyes during her last few replies, returned more stark than ever. "I have to tell you that your husband has been detained on suspicion of being the murderer nicknamed The Ripper of Regents Park."

She began to laugh. He said, sharply: "Your husband was in the vicinity of an attempt at murder tonight. We know that you possessed a knife of the type used by the Ripper. That knife is no longer in your possession." He leaned forward. "Mrs. Horncastle, I realize the appalling position you are in, as his wife. But this man has killed eight people, including a young and charming girl. I beg you to be truthful with me. When did you last see that kitchen-knife?"

She had stopped laughing. She said, stonily: "I gave it away. I've told you the truth." Wyndham opened his mouth. She said, fiercely: "It's absurd, ridiculous, outrageous! Do you think that I, his wife, wouldn't know if Edgar was that terrible man?"

Wyndham said: "The Ripper has killed eight times. Five other people are dead as a result of the terror he inspired. Tonight he tried again. He failed, but tomorrow he might succeed."

She said, spitefully: "They deserve all they get. Filthy, dirty creatures." Wyndham felt sick.

The sergeants returned, bitter with frustration. Wyndham's low spirits sagged lower. He said, formally: "Thank you, Mrs. Horncastle. That will be all for now. I'm afraid we shall need to detain your husband for a little longer, so don't expect him home tonight." He added to himself: Or ever, I hope. "In the meantime if you should wish to change anything of what you have told me, you can reach me through Albany Street police station at any time. Good night."

The four men went out. The front door closed behind them. Lillian Horncastle began to cry. Her thoughts said: So I was right. I couldn't believe it. I wouldn't believe it. But I knew. The change in him. The dates when he went out. The knife missing from the drawer. Oh God! I'm married to a murderer! What have I done to deserve this? A murderer in the family. What will my parents think? What will the neighbours say? What is going to happen to me? We've always been so respectable.

She cried into her arms for a long time.

Edgar Horncastle blinked at Wyndham nervously. He said: "I don't understand why you are detaining me like this. I have been searched, stripped and searched. Outrageous!" Wyndham thought: How extraordinarily alike they are, man and wife. He said: "Perhaps you will tell us where you went after leaving the Green Dragon."

"I don't know. I got lost in the fog. I took a wrong turning. I was thinking about a problem at the office—important mail has gone astray and I am being blamed. Then I found I didn't know where I was. I wandered about for a little while. Then I heard police whistles. I'd been hearing them for quite a time without taking any notice but suddenly I realized that if they were police whistles there would be policemen who could tell me where I was. So I walked towards them and discovered that I was back at the Green Dragon. It was still open, so I thought I would have another drink. That's all."

Wyndham asked: "What did you do with the knife?"

Horncastle said: "Knife? What knife? I don't carry a knife. I used to have a penknife but I lost it."

Wyndham said: "The kitchen-knife you carried in your right trouser-pocket."

"What?" Horncastle's eyes widened. "You mean like the Ripper? Oh, you can't think I'm the Ripper!" He laughed.

Wyndham said: "There is a hole in your right trouser-pocket."

"Eh?" (God, I'd forgotten that! Think quickly. . . . Easy!) "So I have. I keep forgetting to ask my wife to mend it. I often drop small change through it. Very annoying."

"It wore through?"

"That's right."

"But it has not worn through, Mr. Horncastle. The stitches have been cut. It is just wide enough to permit the entry of a narrow knife-blade. How do you account for this?"

"I can't. I suppose the stitches broke. Would they do that?"

"I'm asking you."

"Well, I'm sure I don't know. I'm not an authority on how holes appear in garments."

"Did anyone see you while you were lost in the fog?"

"I don't think so. I didn't see anyone to begin with. Later, when the commotion occurred, I caught sight of blurred figures but they all seemed to be hurrying. I thought there had been an accident and that they were going to see it."

"Did you call out to these hurrying figures?"

"No."

"Why not? You were lost."

"They came and went too quickly."

"I see." Wyndham smiled. He asked, pleasantly: "Did you carve the joint last Sunday, Mr. Horncastle?"

Horncastle hesitated. His eyes turned wary. He could not see the relevance of the question. Presently he said: "I suppose so."

Wyndham thought: This is the breakthrough! The knife was given away two weeks ago, but he carved the joint with it two days ago! He said: "You suppose? Don't you know?"

Horncastle's face cleared. "No, I didn't," he said. "We didn't have beef. Friends came to lunch and my wife decided to give them a treat so we had roast chicken."

"Well," said Wyndham, trying to keep his patience, "I hope the knife was sharp when you carved the chicken."

"Oh, but I didn't carve it. I'm all right with a joint but I make a terrible mess of chicken. It slides all over the dish and gravy splashes everywhere, so my wife buys it ready cut up."

Wyndham said, politely: "Then the Sunday before?"

"We didn't lunch at home that week. We went out to these friends. This week they came to us."

It sounded like the truth. Wyndham felt like screaming. Of all the lousy luck! The damned Horncastles probably ate beef on fifty Sundays in the year—and had to change their bloody habits on these two. He said: "Thank you. We shall have to detain you until the morning." He nodded to the officer standing by the door, "Take him away."

Horncastle said: "This is an outrage! I demand——"

Wyndham said, wearily: "We are within our rights. You will be granted the opportunity to contact your wife, your solicitor, or anyone else you think fit, but you will be detained until the morning."

"The bloody knife must be *somewhere*," said Wyndham, ferociously, to Follitt at ten o'clock in the morning. "It can't have disappeared into thin air and there are only a limited number of places where he could have got rid of it: a few front gardens, or over someone's wall, or down a drain."

"We've searched the sewers," said Follitt. "We've searched everywhere."

"Well, search some more!" said Wyndham, crossly. He rose as the door opened and Linda Ward was ushered in. He said: "Nice to see you, Linda. How do you feel?" She smiled wryly. "Wrung out," she said, "like an old dish-cloth. And my back is giving me hell."

They sat down. Wyndham said: "Thank God he didn't decide to change his tactics and cut your throat instead." Linda shivered. "Don't remind me! I couldn't think of anything else. When I heard him running behind me I nearly passed out. It took all I'd got to keep on walking. I didn't want to make a sudden move and force him to miss." She shuddered. "Afterwards I needed half a dozen brandies, and I loathe brandy."

Wyndham smiled. "Well, it's all over now, bar the shouting. Your identification, plus the knife when we find it, will be enough to hang him. Did you get a good look at him?"

She said: "You haven't found the knife?"

"Not yet, but we shall. It's missing from the house, of course, which is a point in our favour, but his wife is standing by him and swears she gave it away weeks ago. It all makes life extra difficult, but we're used to that." He said again: "Did you get a good look at him?"

She hesitated. "I got his face in the beam but it was pretty well distorted. It gave him an awful shock, you know. Must have nearly sprained his wrist."

Wyndham said, thoughtfully: "That's a point. I'll have the doctor look for damage." He went on: "Anyway, we've arranged a formal identification parade so that you can pick him out and go on record as saying, 'That's him. It's him what done it'."

She smiled at his humour but her eyes were thoughtful. Wyndham rose. He said: "I'm not allowed to come with you, in case I'm a nasty type and tip you the wink which chap we want you to pick out, but Inspector Grove will look after you." He ushered her to the door. "How I hate identification parades!" he said, with a sigh. "It's a sign of weakness in a case."

He beckoned to a uniformed officer. "Inspector Grove, Miss Linda Ward. Your boys all ready, Jack?" Grove said: "Lined up and waiting, sir." Wyndham said: "Good! Off you go."

They went out. Wyndham moved over to a window from which he could watch the parade. Nine men and Horncastle stood in a row. All bore a superficial likeness to one another. Horncastle was ninth in the row.

Wyndham watched Linda walk slowly down the file, looking intently into each face in turn. Six, seven, eight, nine. . . . Wyndham's face turned white. Ten! Linda turned away, shaking her head. She said something to Grove. Wyndham could not hear the words but her actions betrayed them. She was saying: "The man who attacked me is not here."

Wyndham turned away from the window and sat down, incredulous and dismayed. His case, already too tenuous for comfort, lay in ruins.

CHAPTER FIVE

EDGAR HORNCASTLE'S eyes glazed. His knees trembled. Muscles jerked at the corners of his mouth. His bowels threatened to betray him. He stared in a daze at Linda Ward as she retreated with the Inspector. She hadn't recognized him! She hadn't recognized him! She hadn't recognized him! She had shone her torch-beam full in his face and yet had failed to recognize him!

The parade fell out. Men walked away, talking animatedly, glancing at him curiously. A policeman touched him on the elbow. "Will you come this way, please?" The touch cleared Horncastle's mind. "Keep your hands off me, my man!" he snapped. The policeman looked at him without affection. He said: "This way."

Wyndham looked at Horncastle coldly. He said, formally: "You may go. I regret any inconvenience we have caused you."

Horncastle said: "Outrageous! You have kept me here all night. I have spent a night in the cells. Me, a respectable citizen! I have been stripped and brutally searched. Questioned, too. Monstrous allegations have been made against me. You won't get away with this. I shall consult a solicitor about an action for wrongful arrest."

Wyndham said: "You have not been arrested, Mr. Horn-castle. You have merely been detained on suspicion of being implicated in a crime which took place last night. Neither have you been treated brutally. You have received every consideration."

"I shall write to my M.P. I shall demand an inquiry into police methods. I shall——"

"Writing to his M.P. is the right of every Englishman."

"What about my job? It's nearly eleven o'clock. I am already two hours late. What do you think has happened to my work? I have to trace that important mail."

Wyndham said, before he could stop himself: "I imagine that in your absence the mail reached its correct destination."

Horncastle's face turned evil. His lips disappeared. The skin tightened across cheeks and jawbone. A vein throbbed in his temples. Hatred blazed from his slightly bulging eyes. Wynd-ham thought, with a stab of fear which he could not suppress: The man's a raving lunatic. He'd like to go for me next. I hope to God he does. I'd like to strangle the sod.

He pulled himself together. "I'm a busy man," he said. "The door is behind you. Don't bother to slam it—the patent thing-ummybob will close it." Horncastle rose without a word and went out.

Wyndham thought: There he goes, a multiple murderer, and I can't hold him. A detective makes an error of judgement at a vital moment; a wife lies for a husband she hates; a clever man gets rid of the weapon; and Linda fails to identify him. Four small items in a long catalogue, but they are the vital ones, the irrefutable items which would convince a jury. Oh, Linda, why did you fail to identify him? You must have recognized him, you *must*. You couldn't mistake him, even in your terror and his bewilderment. Of course you recognized him. . . .

The new thought rocketed him. In his immediate despair he had almost concluded that he had made a mistake, that Horncastle was not the Ripper. Afterwards, he had decided that in her fear and shock, plus the distortion on Horncastle's face, she had been genuinely unable to say: "This is the man." But suppose . . .

Follitt came in. "Not a sausage," he said, gloomily. "Do you think he's a confounded sword-swallower?"

"It's too late to find out, even if he is," said Wyndham. "Linda failed to identify him."

"*What?*" Follitt looked incredulous. "But she said last night . . ." He stopped. "No," he said, "she didn't. I didn't ask her positively if her attacker was Horncastle. Did you?"

"No. We both took it for granted." Wyndham grinned ruefully. "So she didn't have to contradict herself today."

Follitt said, puzzled: "But we *know* he's our man. So does she. Why——"

Wyndham said: "We hadn't much of a case without the knife or the diary. She knew that."

Follitt said, slowly: "I suppose she realized that we'd have had a tough job to make it stick, and *she'd* have had a hell of a time under cross-examination. A tom against respectability." His voice trailed away. He said, presently: "She's a clever girl. I wonder . . .?"

Linda Ward slipped into the driving seat of the M.G. She did not immediately drive away. She lit a cigarette with trembling fingers and sat, smoking quietly. She rarely smoked, but this, she felt, was a moment to indulge. Her emotions were not under control. She needed calm before she could trust herself in the rush of morning traffic.

Her decision had been taken on the spur of the moment. She had recognized Horncastle in the beam of her torch; she had recognized him again the moment she stepped on the parade ground. She had lingered over the faces that held no interest for her to give her mind time to work. Her chief emotion had been rage against the police. They had permitted the attack upon her, failed to catch Horncastle with the knife, and couldn't break his wife's lies. What the hell good were they? And what would her identification mean? It would be Horncastle's word against hers. She could imagine defending counsel's scorn and loathing: "Ladies and gentlemen of the jury, this man's life is in your hands. Virtually the whole body of the case against him rests on the testimony of one woman, the witness Ward, a woman who has confessed in open court that she is a common prostitute with fifteen convictions. What sort of confidence can you repose in the word of a woman of her type?" And so on and so on. The prosecution might prove that Horncastle has gone out on the nights of the murders. They might show that he had won money on the pools. They might offer the evidence of the missing knife, of the number of times he had been seen in the Green Dragon when she was there, and they would offer identification. And so what? Thousands of men had gone out on the nights of the murders; his wife swore that she had given the knife away; the author of the diary admitted falsifying certain—unspecified—items. And the identification lay in the words of a prostitute, a harlot, a whore.

At this point in her thoughts Linda Ward came face to face with Horncastle and looked through his eyes into his soul. She had tried to keep emotion out of her face, to impose tranquillity on her leaping muscles, while hatred engulfed her like a tidal wave. She had seen this man many times and disliked him on sight; but now she *knew*. She saw in his eyes the craven fear of the moral coward who has been caught, and mirrored in them she seemed to see the bodies of all his victims, seven of them women who had been as she was, a whore. She had known them all, and one or two she had not liked, but in one sense they had all been part of her: outcasts as she was, inhabitants of the half-world which lay midway between the respectable who hired her and the underworld which provided her only companionship. In that moment her mind said: I do not know this man. I must not know him. I must deal with him myself.

She did not know what she would do, or what she could do. She could only sum up her feelings in the common phrase, used about criminals whose crimes are beyond the comprehension of the compassionate: "Hanging's too good for him."

Linda threw away the cigarette-end, switched on the ignition, and drove back to her working flat. She parked the car in the driveway and took the lift to her apartment. Martha, her maid, clucked compassionately at her pale, haggard face, and insisted that she lay down. Linda obeyed. She needed comfort and only

Martha could give it. Martha, a widow with two sons, had worked for Linda for ten years. She was large, loud of voice, bawdily jolly, and terrified of nothing and nobody. She cooked for Linda, kept watch against violent customers, and gave her the devotion of a good servant and a little of a mother's love.

She massaged Linda's bruised back with rough, gentle fingers. Linda relaxed. Her brain, freed from the paralysis of intense hatred, began to move again. It slid over various ideas, discarding, rejecting, selecting. Presently she began to laugh. Martha thought it was hysteria and tried to calm her. Linda shook her head. She sat up, her hair falling over her bare shoulders, her eye malicious.

"I'm all right now, Martha," she said. She put her arms round the stout figure and pressed her face into the massive bosom. "I'm all right," she repeated. "Send for Harry and Joe."

Martha hesitated. Harry and Joe were the two layabouts whom Linda employed as protectors and touts. Martha said, dubiously: "I don't think you oughta work today, love." Linda said: "I'm not going to work. I just want Harry and Joe."

Harry and Joe came to the flat, listened, and departed. They were not puzzled. They simply obeyed orders. Thinking was a task best left to those more fitted for it. They went into various parts of central London and spoke to a number of women, all toms.

At three o'clock that afternoon Linda's flat was full. Women stood or sat or squatted cross-legged on the floor. They were of all ages, shapes and sizes. Some were young and still fresh-faced, wearing short skirts and tight sweaters; some were middle-aged, heavily made up, trying to beat back the tide of the years; and some were old beyond their years. Their origins lay in the North Country, in Ireland, in South Wales, in London and at least one of them came from the West Indies. They were garrulous or taciturn, prissy or foul-mouthed, hard or generous. Some disliked Linda Ward intensely because she was rich, successful and "a cut above the likes of us." Others liked her because she was all these things. But all respected her and the power of command which she wielded so effortlessly.

They smoked her cigarettes, they drank her liquor, they laughed and chattered and swapped stories of clients, of pimps, of jazz musicians, crooks, gamblers, drug addicts, club proprietors and the flatties who pinched them. Then they listened to Linda, and as she spoke the faces broke into smiles, and the smiles turned into grins, and the grins burst into a storm of laughter. The only discordant note was expressed by those who, for various reasons, could not be in on the scheme right from the start.

CHAPTER SIX

EDGAR HORNCASTLE'S hours, like Linda's, were also full of hate; and this, in view of the peril from which he had so narrowly escaped, was curious. A more humble man would have thanked his lucky stars (or God); a more rational one would have examined the facts and shuddered at the ominous picture they revealed. In either case, he would have walked circumspectly. Horncastle was neither humble nor rational; had he been there would have been no Ripper of Regents Park. His arrogance filled the void when his terror departed, and the arrogance turned to hate. He left Albany Street hating Wyndham; soon it spread to envelop his wife; then he drew his colleagues into its all-embracing net. Finally, since diffused hatred is an impotent, frustrating thing, he concentrated his venom upon one objective: Linda Ward.

Lillian Horncastle heard the garden gate squeak and the scratching of her husband's key in the lock. She rose from her bed, gathered her shaking nerves, unlocked the bedroom door and went to the head of the stairs. Horncastle paused in the hall. He peered up at her—the house was always dim—and said: "Oh, Lillian, there you are! I've had a terrible time, terrible! The police——"

"The police came," she said, icily. "I lied to them. I told them I'd got rid of the knife about two weeks ago. I told them because I won't be ruined. I won't have my parents hurt. I won't have the neighbours pointing fingers at me. I won't, I won't, I won't!" She paused for breath. Horncastle took a step forward. "Don't you dare come near me! That's all I'll do for you. I won't speak to you again. I won't see you if I can help it. I can't go away because people will suspect, but I won't cook or sew or see you or speak to you, you wicked, wicked man! How could you do this to me? How *could* you?"

She turned and went back into the bedroom. The key clicked. Edgar Horncastle stood in the hall, his shoulders slightly bowed, his rage mounting. Then, wordlessly, he turned and walked out of the house.

He ate an early lunch at a nearby tea-shop, made a telephone call to Y (John Harris, office manager) to explain his non-appearance, and promised to turn up after lunch and make good the lost time. He arrived at the office at two o'clock, and for a little time he basked in the awed respect of juniors and the fascinated interest of his seniors. For an hour Edgar Horncastle tasted the intoxicating atmosphere of greatness. He had been on the scene of another Ripper crime—an attempted one, at any rate. More, he had been detained by the police on suspicion of being the Ripper himself. Horncastle dwelt at length on the details, uninterrupted, uncorrected. He expatiated on the brutality of the police, the ugliness of the search, the discomfort of the cell. They asked him questions. He must have seen the Ripper, who must have been in the Green Dragon at the same time, mustn't he? Who did he think it was? Or had the Ripper been lurking outside in the street all the time? Or, or, or? And as Horncastle invented and improvised a curious change came over his listeners. Respect gave way to sidelong stares, attentiveness to a tendency to fidget, close companionship to withdrawal. Finally, a young typist had a fit of hysteria. It gave Harris the chance to break up the party. The typist was sent home. Men and girls went back to their desks. Harris went to see Charles Hardman, the general manager. Horncastle, baffled and annoyed by the reaction, could not make sense of it until a little later when, leaving the men's washroom, he passed the door of the Ladies. Someone inside was holding it slightly open and he heard one of the older women, a secretary, say firmly: "What I say is: there's no smoke without fire. We've still got the best police force in the world and if they——" The door closed. Edgar Horncastle passed on, raving at the injustice. A man was presumed innocent until he was proved guilty, wasn't he? The police had let him go, hadn't they? What right had others to suspect him? They'd better look out, the whole lot of them. They'd better look out.

In the general manager's office, Harris said: "I don't like it, Mr. Hardman. There's something funny about him. He's been acting strangely for weeks. And then, there was that diary which the papers published. I thought some of it sounded a bit familiar at the time, but naturally I didn't pay too much attention. I mean things like that happen in hundreds of offices all the time."

Hardman said, irritably: "What things?"

"Promotions, sir. You remember. When my present post became vacant, I'll swear Horncastle thought *he* was going to get it, like the man in the diary."

Hardman said, uncomfortably: "Nonsense, Harris!"

Harris said: "The dates coincide, sir. I noticed it at the time, without noticing, if you know what I mean."

"It's ridiculous! You're saying we've got the Ripper working in *our* office. Absurd!"

"He's working in somebody's office, sir."

Hardman cleared his throat, abruptly. "The police let him go. Obviously they couldn't prove anything."

"No, sir," said Harris, unhappily.

"I think you're linking up too many vague ideas, Harris," said Hardman, with finality. "But leave it to me. I'll think about it."

"Yes, sir," said Harris, dissatisfied. He went back to his office. On the way he looked in at the Mailing Department. Wasn't there something sinister in the back of Horncastle's head?

Hardman sat for a long time, frowning. Finally he sent for his secretary. "Bring me the phone book, Miss Ellerman," he said. "Letter P." Miss Ellerman was surprised. Mr. Hardman never looked up his own numbers. Hardman opened his morning newspaper and re-read the story of the Ripper's attack until he came to Wyndham's name. When the secretary returned he looked up the number of Albany Street Police Station.

Wyndham said: "It's another link in the chain, Jim, but by itself it's not strong enough to justify an arrest. You can hear the defence, can't you? 'Why did the firm not think of this *before* suspicion fell on the accused? Because they considered—and rightly—that similar events were occurring in thousands of similar offices all over London.' I told the chap to report anything unusual. I didn't tell him that we're keeping Horncastle under observation. Though a fat lot of good *that* will do. He'll go to ground now, with a vengeance." Wyndham sighed. "What the hell *did* he do with that bloody knife?"

CHAPTER SEVEN

EDGAR HORNCASTLE went home without stopping off at the Green Dragon. The house was cold. The fire in the sitting-room had not been lit. The grate in the kitchen was dull with dead ash. The boiler in the basement had been allowed to go out. Furious, he climbed the stairs to the first floor and listened outside his wife's room. He heard the faint, involuntary movements of someone trying to keep absolutely still, and the light hiss of the gasfire. Of course, *she* would look after herself while *he* could freeze.

He straightened up at the sound of footsteps. The tenant of the top-storey flat ran lightly downstairs, called a cheerful, "Good evening, Mr. Horncastle," galloped down to the hall, and went out. Horncastle, following a few moments later, saw a white envelope lying on the hallstand. It was addressed to his wife and was unstamped. He knew that it contained the week's rent. Out of habit he allowed it to lie. The house belonged to his wife. She took the rent, paid all the outgoings, and kept the small balance for herself. The arrangement meant that Horncastle did not have to find rent and rates out of his income. He had never paid rent or rates, for he had married from his parents' home; and, never having paid them, he had no idea of the difference this made to his standard of living. Indeed, he had always resented the arrangement, partly because he thought that his wife made a good thing out of it, but chiefly because he resented the independence it gave her. He held the view that money and business are the man's prerogative.

Horncastle searched the kitchen for food, in vain. Slowly it dawned on him that his wife meant exactly what she said. He would have to do his own shopping, laundry, mending, cooking—or arrange for these things to be done. The deprivation of these comforts, so long taken for granted, incensed him. He slammed the door of the kitchen cupboard so hard that he broke one of the glass panels, stamped back into the hall and picked up the envelope. If he must pay for restaurant meals because his wife had abandoned her marital duties, then his wife could damn well help to pay for them. He ripped the envelope open, tipped out the five guineas and crushed the notes into his pocket. Then, jingling the coins defiantly in his palm, he went out.

He dined, fairly expansively for him, in a modest restaurant off Baker Street. He topped the meal with a last act of defiance: coffee and brandy. By the time he finished, at nine-thirty, he was warm, replete and content. The thought of facing the chill house in St. John's Wood curled his stomach. He decided to have a drink at the Green Dragon instead. This, he felt, would be an act of extreme cunning. After all, he had been a regular for several weeks. It would look odd if, after last night, he ceased to go there.

Horncastle entered the saloon bar and, full of food, wine, brandy and self-assurance, failed to detect the chill pause, mixed with astonishment ("appalling gall," as one of the regulars put it), which greeted his entrance. The reaction was as illogical as the secretary's comment. It is doubtful whether anybody in the pub really believed that he was the Ripper, but there was no doubt that they felt uncomfortable in his presence. Jimmy Leech, in particular, needed several seconds in which to produce his genial smile, and even then it looked slightly strained.

Horncastle said, breezily: "'Evening, Mr. Leech. Bit better night tonight." Leech said: "'Evening, Mr. Horncastle. Lager and lime as usual?" Horncastle shook his head. "Not tonight, Mr. Leech. I think I'll have a brandy. Must celebrate my release from durance vile, eh?" He laughed. "They didn't keep me, you see." Leech said, a shade tartly: "I should hope not. Wouldn't like to think I had the Ripper among my customers." He poured the brandy, pretended that his services were needed elsewhere, and moved away.

Horncastle, feeling a little peevish, found his corner. He wished that he had not been so stand-offish on previous visits. He wanted to relate his experiences to such of the regulars as he knew by sight, but they, as usual, did not approach him. He considered strolling over to a small group and broaching the subject. He had almost decided to do so when Linda Ward came in.

Horncastle had temporarily forgotten her and the sight of her came as a shock. She looked at him levelly, without expression, and sat down. Leech bustled across with her drink, smiling, sympathetic. She was quite all right? No after-effects? Bruise fading? Good! Good! Wonderful! Leech knew Linda's profession and didn't care a tuppenny damn. She was a good and decorative customer, she never abused the hospitality of the house by attempting to ply her trade there, and, in Leech's private thought: I have a sight less trouble with her than some others I could name who'd have me chuck her out if they knew what she was.

Five minutes after the arrival of Linda Ward, Toots McBride walked in. Jimmy Leech stiffened in horror. Linda Ward was one thing, Toots was quite another. The most naïve youth could guess Toots's profession at a glance. She looked terrible. Her eyes were black pools of mascara; her cheeks blushed with rouge; her lipstick, a ghastly mauve, was spread as thick as margarine in a magazine advertisement, and her hair was henna with black roots. Ivory nail-varnish, chipped with wear, decorated her none-too-clean fingernails. Her blouse lacked the two top buttons and fell open in what Toots imagined, erroneously, a suggestive fashion. Her skirt swept tightly under her buttocks and her high-heeled shoes, worn down perilously by her sloppy gait, threw her body forward. She called for a gin in a loud, husky voice, ran her eyes over the male occupants of the bar, winked outrageously at a red-faced man, who spluttered and turned away, and caught sight of Horncastle.

Leech said: "Sorry, madam, no ladies served unless accompanied by a gentleman." Normally Toots would have said: "That's O.K., dearie, I'm no lady." But she was absorbed in a study of Horncastle. Suddenly she pointed a dramatic finger. She took two outraged steps forward. "That's 'im!" she said.

Every eye in the bar followed her accusing gesture. She said: "Give me me money! Four quid was what we agreed. Four quid, and you bleeding well bilked me. Give me me money, you lousy bilker. Doing an honest girl out of her rights." She banged a fist on the counter. Horncastle, horrified, turned a guilty red. Leech came from behind the counter, and took Toots by the arm. "None of that there 'ere," he said, lapsing into the Cockney which afflicted him in times of stress. "Four quid," said Toots, indignantly. "The lousy thief! 'Four quid in me room,' I said to 'im—and it's a nice room, though I says it who shouldn't—'fifty bob under the arches.' 'In your room,' he said, 'it's a bit draughty outside'." A man at the back of the pub guffawed uncontrollably and was suppressed by glares. Leech said: "If you have any argument with this gentleman, finish it outside. Not in *my* pub." He propelled the protesting Toots towards the door. Toots screamed over her shoulder: "I want me dough, you lousy bastard, robbing a poor working girl. Four quid he agreed and put it on the mantelpiece. When he went out he picked it up again when I wasn't looking."

The door closed behind her. Jimmy Leech returned to the bar, perspiring. Horncastle, finding at last that his vocal chords were still in working order, said: "It's a lie! I never saw the woman before in my life. I don't go with women like that. Do I look like a man who goes with women like that?"

Men turned their backs on him. Linda Ward surveyed him coldly. Horncastle started to rage. "It's a lie—a mistake—I never saw her before. You've got to believe me. You've got to."

Leech said, in a hard voice which few in the bar had ever heard him use before: "I'd be obliged if you would drink up, Mr. Horncastle, and take your custom elsewhere."

Horncastle stared. "I'll do nothing of the sort," he shouted. "I'll drink up when and where I please. You're obliged by law to serve me. I know my rights."

Leech took an angry step forward. He said: "Get out! Get out before I throw you out. And don't come back!"

Horncastle put the glass to his lips with a hand that shook, drank the rest of the brandy, and tottered to the door. As he passed Linda Ward she looked straight at him. Her eyes smiled maliciously.

Horncastle walked out. The prostitute had gone. Thankful for this mercy, he started on his way home. Linda Ward's smile remained fixed in his memory and presently a vague terror gripped him, a terror to which he could not put a name.

At a little after nine o'clock the next morning, Miss Griggs, temporarily seconded from Mailing to Inquiries, said to the salesman, desperately: "No, *thank* you! No, I've told you. No typewriter ribbons, no ball-point pens, no carbon or typing-papers, no rubbers. We have our own suppliers." The salesman closed his attaché-case with a sigh. "How about a date, then, honey?" Miss Griggs flushed. "Certainly not!" she said. The man grinned, unabashed. "S'long, dearie," he said. He went out. Miss Griggs tossed her pretty little head. "Really!" she said to the room at large, "the *sauce* of some people."

The man ran lightly downstairs without attempting to sell to any other office in the building and joined two women and a three-months-old baby in a nearby tea-shop. The younger woman said: "Whaddyer get, Harry?" Harry said: "Second floor. Inquiry counter—he works way back at the far end of the room, facing the door." The younger woman said: "O.K. Here goes." She had big black eyes, and the soft face of the Southern Irish. Her hair was drawn back from her forehead and fastened at the back in a pony-tail. She bore a faint resemblance to a back-street Madonna, somewhat shop-soiled. She took the baby awkwardly. Her sister said, threateningly: "You drop him, Maureen, and I'll skin you with a blunt knife." Maureen said: "I won't drop him. I only hope to hell he doesn't scream the place down." She went out.

Miss Griggs looked up in surprise. Working-class women with babies were not common visitors to the office of the Baltic-Far East Steam Navigation Company. She did not look the type who would book a sea passage in a cargo-passenger liner, and still less like a potential consignor of freight to Penang, Kobe or Hong Kong. Beggars, too, were out of date these days.

The woman smiled amiably. "Hello, dearie," she said. "Have

you got a chap working here . . .?" Her eyes were busy round the room. She interrupted herself. She said, triumphantly: "Yes, you have! There he is!" She pointed. She called out: "Hey—you over there! What about my kid?" Heads turned. Miss Griggs resisted an impulse to giggle. The girl said: "What's his name, love?" Miss Griggs said: "Do you mean Mr. Horncastle?" "Ah!" said the girl, *now* I've got him!" She yelled again: "Here, you— Hornchurch or whatever your lying name is—what about your kid? If you won't pay for him you can perishing well have him." Horncastle looked everywhere, but principally at his desk. He did not rise. The girl, her lips tight, said to Miss Griggs confidingly: "A year I've been looking for him. Saw him come in here this morning. A year! Thought I'd never find him. Gave me a false name, he did, when he took me out and did me wrong." Miss Griggs's eyes were wide. The girl went on: "Promises—oh yes!—loads of promises. Marriage, a car, the lot! And I trusted him."

Maureen's large eyes filled with tears. She found her performance most moving. She said, brokenly: "Left me to go through with it all alone." She sobbed loudly. She said, even more loudly, through her tears: "Take care of me and the kid, you. Now I've found you, give us both a proper home." She wailed *fortissimo*.

Harris came out of his office, looking bewildered. He said: "What's going on, Miss Griggs?" The "mother" thrust the baby at him. Harris recoiled. She said: "Go on—take it. Give it to the bloke what's responsible. A year ago last Wednesday, after a few drinks in a pub, and him after me for weeks beforehand." Harris glanced at Horncastle, frowning. He said to the girl: "You'd better come into my office." He lifted the counter flap. The girl walked through and went straight over to Horncastle. She held the baby out. It began to cry. She said: "Don't try and deny it, now. I've got plenty of witnesses. People what saw us together. They'll remember."

Horncastle said: "Take her away! I don't know what she's talking about. I've never seen her before." The girl wailed again. The baby lifted its voice. Harris, distracted, said: "Please Miss . . . er . . . Miss, into my office. You, too, Horncastle." Horncastle shouted: "I don't know her! I've never seen her before!" Harris said: "I gave you an order, Horncastle."

He ushered woman and baby into his office. Horncastle, after a hesitation, followed him, as Mr. Hardman's secretary came in and asked for information on the cause of the disturbance.

The office told her. "Wow!" she said. She scuttled back to tell Mr. Hardman.

The office listened, breathless, to the noises from Harris's office: the girl alternately wailing and declaiming, Horncastle denying, the baby howling, Harris vainly trying to restore order. Presently they heard the girl say: "All right, all right, I know you now. I know where to find you. I'll go to the police, I will. I'll make you pay. Says he doesn't know me! He'll soon see whether he knows me or not."

The outer door of Harris's office opened and closed. Heels tapped down the stairs. The baby's cries receded. Heads went hastily down over desks as Horncastle emerged, his face livid. Presently Harris was heard going down the corridor towards Hardman's room. The breathless silence in Mailing and Inquiries was complete.

A little later, Harris returned to his office. A few minutes afterwards, Hardman's secretary bustled through to the Cashier's Department, throwing an amazed look at Horncastle as she went. She returned within seconds. Presently the intercom buzzed on Horncastle's desk. They heard him say, "Yes, sir." He rose and went through to Hardman's office. The straining ears in Mailing and Inquiries heard nothing for several minutes. Then, suddenly, there was another disturbance, this time the high, shrieking voice of Horncastle, almost unrecognizable and entirely incoherent, until one phrase stood out, a phrase repeated over and over again: "Don't cross me, Hardman. Don't cross me, Hardman." And then: "I'm a dangerous man to cross, Hardman." Hardman's voice answered, a deep bellow. Silence fell.

Horncastle returned. He carried a slip of paper. He went to his desk, not looking at anyone, and opened drawers. He pulled out odds and ends of personal belongings: old letters, photographs, towel, soap-holder, two paperback novels, all the miscellany which a man collects when he works in an office for any length of time. He stuffed them into his briefcase, put on his hat and overcoat, and walked through to Cashier's. Oddly, the sight of a man tidying up in the place he had occupied for fifteen years touched none of them with sympathy. Those who saw his face described it afterwards as indescribable.

A few minutes later they heard his footsteps in the corridor, descending the stairs, fading. Whispering began as news filtered through from Cashier's and General Manager's. "On the spot."

"A week's pay for each year in lieu of notice." "Abused Mr. Hardman dreadfully." "Terrible." "Never liked him." "Creepy, somehow." "Out on his ear and good riddance."

Slowly, very slowly, the office resumed an aspect of normality.

Wyndham said: "Yes, Mr. Hardman, I appreciate your motives, and I may say I don't blame you. Thank you for keeping me informed." He replaced the receiver and went on with his paperwork. Presently the duty officer announced that Mr. Edgar Horncastle wanted to see him. Wyndham lifted his eyebrows but said: "Show him in."

Horncastle burst in. He placed his hands on Wyndham's desk and leaned forward. "I'm being persecuted!" he shouted. "Prostitutes are following me about, telling lies about me. I've lost my job. I've been banned from a pub. I——"

Wyndham said: "How very curious, Mr. Horncastle! I wonder why?"

They looked at each other. Horncastle's face changed. His eyes turned vicious. He went out abruptly, without another word. Wyndham watched him thoughtfully. Presently he took up the phone and dialled a number. He said: "Linda? Wyndham. Go easy on that chap Horncastle. I don't know what you're up to, and I don't want to know, but go easy."

Linda said: "I haven't finished with him yet." She put down the receiver. Wyndham looked worried, but his concern was not for the future of Edgar Horncastle.

At 12.30 p.m. Lillian Horncastle heard her husband's footsteps on the short path to the front door. Startled, she glanced at the clock. This was no time for him to come home. She scuttled upstairs as the key scraped. Horncastle heard her and smiled unpleasantly. He went into the kitchen, saw the meal she had cooked for herself, and ate it. An hour later his wife heard him go out again. When she thought that he was safely away she crept downstairs, saw the soiled dishes, and started to cry. She was beginning to realize that her situation was untenable. She was also beginning to feel afraid. It had not occurred to her that she might be one of her husband's victims, but in the long hours of loneliness the fear had crept into her brain. The theft of the rent, too, caused her concern. She had been relying on it to pay her expenses. She had a small nest egg, and no doubt she could arrange to receive further rents at a time when her husband could not lay his hands on them. But now she looked at her position from a long-term view and wondered.

Her afternoon and evening passed slowly. Her husband did not come home. She went out, bought more food, and was able to eat lunch and dinner without molestation. After dinner, expecting to hear from him at any time, she retreated to her room.

Shortly before ten o'clock she heard the sound of shouting in the distance. She took no notice. Other people's problems were too trivial to engage her attention. The noises grew louder. They sounded like the voices of angry women. . . . Nearer, nearer. The voices were quite close now, almost in the street. She was drawn to the window in spite of herself.

A man ran round the corner. She recognized her husband. Behind him came a pack of women, cheap women, women with raddled, furious faces and indecent clothing. They looked like prostitutes and there were three, four, six—no, eight—of them. They were shouting. She heard the words: "Pay up! We know you! Pay up! Pay up! Dirty bilker! We know you!"

Her husband reached the door. He fitted the key in the lock with trembling fingers and ran inside. The door slammed. The women, baulked of their prey, gathered at the door, hammering and shouting. Heads appeared at neighbouring windows. Voices asked questions and received answers. "Been robbing us for weeks. Lying cheating swine! If he likes us why don't he pay us? Cunning bastard! Taken us weeks to trace him." A constable appeared and tried to pacify them. The shouting continued for some time but at length he managed to calm them. The women shuffled away, calling imprecations, threatening reprisals. The neighbours hung out of their windows for a long time after the women had gone, discussing the reprehensible conduct of Edgar Horncastle.

Lillian Horncastle, listening at her keyhole, heard her husband come upstairs and enter his room. His door closed. She could hear no movement. As quickly as she could in her emotional state, she plucked clothes from drawers and filled a suitcase. She took money from her private cache. Her preparations complete, she put on her coat and stealthily opened the door. There were no sounds from her husband's room. She tiptoed down the stairs. She was almost at the bottom when her husband's door opened. He shouted: "Lillian! Where are you going?" She ran, the heavy suitcase banging against her legs. She slammed the front door and struggled round the corner, expecting to hear his running footsteps behind her. The cruising taxi seemed to her stricken eyes to be a haven from fear. She snatched open the door and fell inside. She said, gasping: "Euston Station." She would be safe only among her own people.

CHAPTER EIGHT

HORNCASTLE stood at the top of the stairs. He did not think about his wife. The whore, he thought, the whore, that whore, that whore has done this to me. She planned it, she organized it, she's paid the women to carry it out. My wife, my job, my respectability —they've all gone. All through her. That whore. I know her. I know where she lives. She's crossed me and I'm a dangerous man to cross. I'll show her. I'll teach her, like I taught the others. She won't escape this time. . . . I have no knife. The knife is buried. Why worry? There are plenty of weapons in the world. I'll find something. I know where to strike. What does it matter what I use? I'll strike differently this time, too. I'll make her suffer as I'm suffering. I know. I know the very thing.

He turned along the landing and entered his wife's room. He went to her sewing-machine and opened the wicker work-basket which stood alongside. He did not immediately see what he was looking for and up-ended the basket with an impatient grunt. Reels of cotton, packets of pins, needles threaded with lengths of cotton, remnants of material, all fell out, and among them the object he was seeking.

He picked up the pair of dressmaking shears and put them into a trouser pocket. He went downstairs, grabbed his coat and hat, and went out. He strode rapidly down the path, still struggling into the sleeves of his coat, the women who had pursued him entirely forgotten. He opened the gate and hurried down the road, half walking, half running.

Behind him, a dark figure detached itself from the shadows and hurried in pursuit.

Wyndham's phone rang. He turned back from the door, his coat half on his back. The voice said: "Baxter here, sir. Our man's on the prowl. He's having a drink in the White Horse, St. John's Wood Village. I don't like the look of him." He caught his breath and spoke again before Wyndham could say anything. "Christ, that was a quick one! He's coming out at a rate of knots, turning north. I'm off."

Wyndham said, sharply: "Lose him and you lose your stripes!" He spoke to a deaf instrument. He slammed down the receiver. The White Horse. Two minutes' brisk walk to Harwell Mansions. First step: warn Linda. He dialled her number. He said to the woman's voice: "Linda?" The voice said, sweetly: "I'm sorry, sir. Miss Linda is out just now. It's her maid speaking. Can I ——?" Wyndham said: "Listen carefully. Martha. This is Chief-Inspector Wyndham speaking—you know me. We have reason to believe that Linda is in danger. Can we get in touch with her?"

"No, sir," said Martha, worried. "She'll be in the car in Soho or Mayfair, but I don't know exactly where. But she'll be back in about half an hour—she has an appointment."

"We'll try to intercept her. Meanwhile, this man may try to get into the flat. You are not to open up for anybody. *Anybody*, understand?"

"That's difficult, sir. There are clients and——"

"For nobody, Martha. *Nobody*. Nobody at all."

Martha said: "Very well, sir, I'll do as you say. Miss Linda's got her own key. I'll wait for her."

"Thanks." Wyndham rang off. He went to the door and called: "Follitt!" Follitt came running. "Horncastle's on the loose, heading towards Linda's place. Get a squad car there right away. Fortunately, Linda's not there, but they're to grab him and hold him on suspicion. If Horncastle gets into the block first, they're to cover all exits and beat the block until they flush him out. I've warned the maid not to open up."

Follitt hurried out. Wyndham sent for Grove.

"Jack, get on to West End Central. Ask them to find Linda Ward—they know her. Probably soliciting from a red M.G. with a black hardtop, registration number HCRZ 2077. She is not to return home without a police escort. If she has left their area, warn all uniformed men and cars on likely routes into our manor to stop her." He turned to the wall-map. "She'll probably come this way, or this. . . ."

Follitt came back as Grove departed at the double. "Jameson's car is on the way. Ought to be there within five minutes."

"Good!" Wyndham paced the room. What else? What else? His phone rang. It was Baxter again. "The sus has entered a block of flats, Harwell Mansions. Walked in the front way."

Wyndham said: "He's after the tenant of number fourteen on the fourth floor, Miss Linda Ward. Sergeant Jameson will join you at any minute now with a squad car. Work with him. Whatever happens Horncastle's not to get away. He's in the open now, with a vengeance, and I'm taking no chances."

Martha put down the telephone, frowning. It was all right for the Inspector to say, "Don't open the door," but there was business to be thought of. Besides, Miss Linda wasn't in, and this man had no quarrel with her. On the other hand, Mr. Wyndham had sounded upset and she'd promised him.

The flat door-bell shrilled.

Martha jumped. She stood for a second, listening. She glanced at the clock on the lounge mantelpiece. It wasn't yet time for the client. He was always a few minutes early, but not as early as this.

The bell rang again. Martha tiptoed across the thick carpet and put her ear to the door. Silence. Then, very quietly, knuckles rapped on the wood, tap, tap, tap, soft and gentle. A voice spoke. She could hear it whispering through the keyhole of the mortice lock which acted as double protection with the Yale. The voice said: "Let me in, Linda. Please let me in. Let me in, Linda. I've a lovely present for you. It's a beautiful present, specially for you. Let me in. Please, Linda, let me in."

The mad tones chilled her. She stood, trembling violently, listening to the whisper and the punctuating tap, tap, tap until they stopped. The hush sounded uncanny.

Movements rustled through the keyhole; sounds diminished outside. Martha uttered an audible sigh of relief. He'd gone! Thank God! What an awful voice!

She returned to the lounge. She poured herself a dose of whisky from the bottle which Linda kept for valued clients, and drank it in a gulp. She sat down. Slowly her nerves recovered.

Presently the bell rang again. She jumped, and then looked at the clock. Time for the client.

Martha padded across the room. She called: "Coming, sir, coming!" She opened the door.

Grove said: "We've found Miss Ward, sir. Stopped her on her way home. One of our men is with her. They'll contact Jameson when they reach the flats."

"Good!" Grove went out. Wyndham looked at Follitt. "We should have him now," he said. Follitt nodded. The phone rang. "Baxter again, sir. Reporting for Jameson. No sign of the sus inside the building. We looked everywhere—not that there are many places where he can hide. Most of the flats are unoccupied tonight. People at home have noticed nothing suspicious."

Wyndham said, slowly: "What about number fourteen?"

"No one in, sir. We knocked and rang but got no answer. I think it's fairly clear, sir, that he went inside, got no answer from number fourteen, and went straight out again in the few minutes before Sergeant Jameson arrived and we could seal off the building."

"Yes," said Wyndham. It sounded plausible, yet doubt contradicted the affirmative. He tried to imagine Martha's reaction to the official knock—any knock—after his warning. Would she call out? Or would she keep silent until she heard Linda's key in the lock? He said, uneasily: "No signs that the door had been tampered with or the windows forced?"

"No, sir," said Baxter, surprised. "Door was O.K., and the window to the fire-escape was closed and latched."

"Yes," said Wyndham, again. His questions were idiotic. Horncastle couldn't have picked the lock or opened the window catch—he wasn't that sort of a crook. He couldn't have broken the door down. Clearly Martha had decided that her best plan was to ignore all callers until Linda returned. It occurred to him that there was a simple way of resolving his doubts. He said: "Hang on, Baxter." He laid the receiver on the desk and went out to another phone. He dialled Linda's number. The burr-burr mocked him for a long time before he abandoned the call.

Wyndham ran back into his own room. He said: "Baxter, get this clear—somehow Horncastle's got inside number fourteen. There's no reply to her number and there should be—her maid's there. I spoke to her myself not fifteen minutes ago and she was waiting for Miss Ward to get home. Tell Jameson he's to go up with as many men as he can spare. And he's to send a man up the fire-escape to make sure Horncastle doesn't bolt out the back way. Now get going!"

He dropped the receiver with a bang. He ran nervous fingers through his hair. The Ripper's score was nine now, for a certainty, and the fact that he would now be caught red-handed did not ease Wyndham's anguish. He said to Follitt in a strained, anxious voice: "Why in hell did she have to open the door?"

CHAPTER NINE

Edgar Horncastle stood at the window of the flat, looking down into the courtyard, waiting for the M.G. He snipped the bloodstained scissors aimlessly in his right hand. It had all been too easy, as it always was. He had not reckoned on the maid, but she had proved no obstacle. No noise; anyway not enough to penetrate the discreet walls of this luxury block, where neighbours did not need to live in their neighbours' pockets. Now he had only to wait for the girl to come home.

Movement in the courtyard attracted his attention. He frowned. He peered more intently through the window. The black car with the ant-like figures clustered around it looked familiar. Where had he seen it before? Then he knew. It was a police car. He had been followed. So that was why the maid had not answered the door the first time. She must have been warned. His face turned petulant. Why didn't they leave him alone? They were always pestering him. Everybody pestered him. It was really too bad. Nobody was free from interference these days. He would really have to write to the papers about it. He looked again. The figures had disappeared beyond his range of vision. He shook his head fretfully, and his brain cleared. He was in danger.

Horncastle moved across the room, stepped over the body, and quietly slipped back the latch on the door. He listened through a crack. He heard the lift whirring. Light gleamed through opaque glass as it stopped on his floor. He closed the door, switched off the light, and went through to the back of the apartment. The door-bell shrilled once, twice, three times. He took no notice.

The man climbing the fire-escape was only one floor below. Horncastle ducked back into the room. He watched from behind a wardrobe. A face appeared. A hand rattled the windows. He heard a muffled grunt. The man's head and shoulders sank out of sight.

The ringing had stopped. Horncastle wandered aimlessly through the flat, trying to think, his nervous fingers still snipping the scissors thoughtlessly. He listened at the door. Silence. He looked out of the front window. The figures were back at the car. He counted them. Five. Was that the lot? Hadn't there been six? He walked some more, back and forth in the dark, picking his way among the furniture. He looked out of the back window, screwing his neck to see as far as possible down the fire-escape. It was empty.

The telephone rang in the darkness. His nerves leaped. He resisted an impulse to take up the receiver and say: "Horncastle here, Mailing." The ringing went on for a long time before it ceased.

He returned to his view of the courtyard. The men were still there. Presently the sixth man joined them. He gesticulated. They all looked upwards. Horncastle shrank back, though they could not possibly see him. When he looked again the men were moving purposefully towards front and rear.

Horncastle acted at last. He opened the front door and listened. The lift was moving upwards, fast. He did not return inside the flat. He closed the door behind him. It locked on its Yale fastener. He ran upstairs to the fifth floor and stood by the lift doors, waiting. The lift stopped at the fourth. Men got out, only fifteen feet below him but concealed by the twist in the stairs. The lift gates closed automatically as knocking began on the door of number fourteen. A voice said: "Open up! Police!"

Horncastle pressed the lift button. He waited, in agony. A sudden anxious voice said: "See who called the lift." Horncastle wrenched the doors open as footsteps started up the stairs. The doors closed. He pressed a button and sank out of sight.

The lift stopped. Horncastle darted out and paused, momentarily at a loss. This was not the ground floor. He had pressed the wrong button. He heard footsteps pounding down the stairs. An open window opposite the lift beckoned him. He climbed through it to the fire-escape. He looked upwards. A man on the fourth floor was fiddling with a window. Horncastle ran to the ground. Vibration travelled up the metal. The man above shouted. Footsteps clanged on the fire-escape. Horncastle hit the ground and ran into shadow.

Horncastle crouched, looking this way and that. He had no chance. They'd get him and hang him. The evidence was all there this time.

He moved forward. He worked his way round towards the courtyard under cover of the shadows and the pillars which supported the overhang of the building. He had no plan, only desperation. He stopped as the driveway came into view. Linda Ward was standing not ten yards from him. A uniformed man stood with her. Their backs were towards him. Linda's left hand rested on the open door of the M.G., and its engine was running.

Horncastle snipped his fingers together, and realized that he no longer held the scissors. He could have cried. Then he saw his way to freedom. He had not driven a car for two years, and then only a hired one during a holiday at Bournemouth, but he did not think of this. He leaped from the shadows. A man's voice shouted. Linda started to turn. He struck at her frenziedly. She reeled against the man. Horncastle leaped into the car and fumbled with gear-lever and brake. Linda came at him, groping into her handbag. She struck at him. Pain coursed down Horncastle's cheek as he accelerated and swung the wheel. Linda disappeared. He hoped he had run her down. The M.G. howled out of the driveway into the streets of London.

The car was found abandoned in a side street in Holborn shortly before midnight, but by that time the call had gone out for Edgar Horncastle, wanted for questioning in connection with the murder of a maid in a block of flats in St. John's Wood. Every policeman in England was on the look-out for him. Hotels and boarding-houses were warned to watch for a man with a fresh wound on his left cheek, perhaps covered with sticking plaster, who might attempt to obtain a night's lodging. Police cars hunted him. Ports and airports were closed to him. In the morning every newspaper would carry his picture, his face would be shown on every television screen, sound radio would broadcast his description. The official net was out for Edgar Horncastle and a price was put upon his head.

Beyond and beneath the official snare, another trap was set. It was set by an army which owed no allegiance to the law; which hated, feared and despised the law; which wanted nothing to do with the law. The word had gone out to prostitutes and pimps, to crooks, gamblers, tearaways and layabouts, to the proprietors of sleazy cafés and shady clubs; out to all the inhabitants of the un-underworld: Find Edgar Horncastle, and find him *first*.

In the centre of this web sat Linda Ward, cold, haggard and merciless.

The underworld found him first, as they were bound to do. The avenues of respectability were barred to Horncastle. His only hope of freedom was to burrow among the people who shunned the police and pray that he could walk unknown among them. Edgar Horncastle considered that his unsatisfactory story could pass unchallenged only among the shady and the shiftless. He believed that there is honour among thieves, and that even if they knew him for what he was their code would protect him. It never occurred to him that there is no honour among thieves or that, even if there had been, he had transgressed it by selecting his victims from among those who walked with thieves.

And so, at ten o'clock on the morning after the ninth Ripper murder, a telephone call went out to Linda Ward. Subsequently she drove to an obscure café in Bethnal Green, taking care that she was not followed. In the café she talked to Edna Lucas, a young tom.

Edna said: "I dunno where he spent the night, but at eight o'clock this morning up he comes, as bold as brass, sticking-plaster and all, and asks my mum if she has a room and can give him all his meals. An inventor, he says he is, just come back from abroad, who needs peace and quiet. Inventor! I'll say he's a bleeding inventor. Inventor of perishing lies." She added, in response to Linda's question: "It's him all right. No doubt about it. Wasn't I one of the girls who chased him home last night? Lucky he didn't see me—and I've kept out of his way since." She looked at the ravaged Linda, curiously: "What're you going to do, love?"

Linda smiled, cruelly. She said, softly: "I think we'll have a party. A party for the whole street." She laughed in Edna's baffled face. "A big, noisy party, with lots of booze and singing. Yes, we must have a lot of noise."

CHAPTER TEN

THE house stood in a cul-de-sac in one of the dingier districts of Bethnal Green. The railway ran behind the closed end of the street and its intermittent rattle matched the turbulence of Horncastle's thoughts. They shook about in his head like pieces of mosaic in a tin. Nothing was clear to him; neither his past, his present, nor his future. His past was behind him, shining with pure endeavour; his present was about him, bleak and broken, owing to that harlot; his future . . . he had no thoughts about his future beyond the hope that he could stay here for days or weeks if necessary until the hue and cry faded and it would be safe for him to emerge and take up some other identity. The fact that he had no clothes beyond those he was wearing, and little money, did not worry him because he was incapable of thought. The shattering experiences of the past few days had unbalanced him in a sense which was quite different from the imbalance behind his insane murder plan. His mind was almost completely in ruins.

The day passed in a mood of torpor. Mrs. Lucas, a large, blowsy woman who had once been a tom and had saved enough at the game to buy this house, brought him his meals and the newspapers. The food was hot, wholesome and satisfying. The newspapers made no impression on him. He read them from front page to back, including the advertisements, with childlike intensity. The only item which aroused even a flicker of emotion was the name of Linda Ward. He felt a touch of anger, combined with a sense of a task unfinished. After much rambling thought he tracked down the source of incompleteness: he had failed to kill her. He looked uncertainly round the small dark room, as though expecting to see his knife or the shears. They were not there. Of course not. He had buried the knife. He could not remember what he had done with the shears. Dropped them somewhere, he supposed. It didn't matter. He could get others later and finish the job. . . . The short burst of lucidity faded and he resumed his perusal of news items which held neither interest nor meaning for him.

After lunch he slept for a couple of hours. Towards late afternoon he became conscious of noise outside. He rose, alarmed, and peered through the small window down into the street, four storeys below. He saw men and women erecting trestle tables in the open. Yards of bunting—incongruous stuff kept in mysterious drawers after previous celebrations—were strung on house fronts and between lamp-posts. Lines of coloured electric bulbs were fixed by expert hands. Cases of beer arrived on a lorry. Bottles of gin, whisky, rum, port and sherry made their appearance. Buns, cakes and sandwiches, with bottles of lemonade and Coca Cola for the young people, were stacked high on the wooden boards. Braziers were lugged out and filled with coke. When Mrs. Lucas brought his dinner at six o'clock—she called it tea and had promised him supper at nine-thirty—he asked the reason for the preparations.

"A party," said Mrs. Lucas, unnecessarily. "Young chap down the street just got home from the navy, *and* he's got engaged, *and* it's the girl's birthday, so we thought it'd be nice to have a treat for them. Haven't had a real good binge since the Coronation." Horncastle knew nothing of working-class habits and did not notice Mrs. Lucas's slightly anxious look, as if to see how he would swallow it. When he made no comment, the anxiety disappeared. She said, expansively: "How about joining us, Mr. Jackson? It's a free-for-all. As you're one of the street now, as you might say, you'd be welcome." He shrank. He said: "No, thank you, Mrs. Lucas. I . . . I don't care much for mixing with people." Mrs. Lucas said: "I'll tell you what: I'll bring you a couple of bottles of beer to drink with your supper." He said: "That would be very kind of you."

It was dark now. The street looked festive under its coloured bulbs. The light fell in pools on pavements and roadway, lending a harlequinesque appearance to the drabness. The braziers glowed red and smoke drifted lazily over the scene. Men, women and children moved in and out of the light, laughing, talking, shouting. Bottles clinked against glasses. Children ran shrieking between the trestles. The laughter grew louder. Horncastle, watching periodically from his eyrie, noticed that there seemed to be a lot of women among the guests and not all of them, he thought, were of good character. Still, he could hardly complain. He had sought refuge in this part of London precisely for that reason. And if the women looked coarse and the men brutal, that was to be expected in the area.

The singing began shortly before eight o'clock. Mrs. Lucas started it. She was in her element: huge, jolly, bawdy, the life and soul of the party. She started them off on the right note with "Knees up, Mother Brown". Soon she had men and women of all ages cavorting, lifting their knees high. When, temporarily exhausted, they abandoned prancing in favour of more drink, she led them in old favourites: "Down at the Old Bull and Bush", "Daisy, Daisy", "It's a Long Way to Tipperary", "Pack up your Troubles". More modern community songs followed: "Run, Rabbit, Run"; "Roll Out the Barrel". Then, in deference to the younger generation, some rock'n'roll and cha-cha mingled with sentimental moon-June pop songs. Musical instruments appeared and multiplied: mouth-organs, guitars, squeeze-boxes, even a tenor saxophone.

Presently a Coloured girl took the centre of the stage. She apparently enjoyed a local reputation, for she was accorded an unusual degree of respect. An enormous West Indian accompanied her on a guitar. She sang calypso songs, some of them well

known like "Jamaica Farewell" and "The Banana Boat Song".
Some she improvised with—to judge from the laughter and
applause—references to people present.

She fell out at last and the entire community took up "John
Brown's Body". The scene was riotous now. Many of the guests
were drunk, or nearly so, and the noise was deafening. When the
trains went by the cacophony, even up in Horncastle's room, was
almost unbearable. He felt disgust. Then, noticing that Mrs.
Lucas had disappeared, he turned from the window. She must
have gone inside to prepare his supper. He hoped she would not
forget the beer. As he turned away a slim, fair-haired girl skirted
swiftly past a pool of light. Horncastle had reached his chair and
was about to sit down when recognition struck him. He ran back
to the window, his heart pounding. The girl had gone. Had he
been mistaken? And was he mistaken in thinking that though the
noise was as loud as ever, the number of people in the street had
diminished?

Horncastle stood by the window, trying to master his emotions,
trying to work out the implications, doubting, fearing, hating,
worrying. He saw the Coloured girl dart into the middle of the
street as "John Brown's Body" faded away. She led them in another song, a dirge he did not know.

He turned from the window. The song rose to his brain,
beat there, throbbed there, strummed there. Presently it made
sense. Fear struck at his bowels. The revellers were singing a
parody of "Tom Dooley". He listened. They sang:

> Hang down your head, old Ripper.
> Hang down your head, and cry.
>
> Hang down your head, old Ripper,
> For now you are bound to die. . . .

Horncastle leapt for the door. He wrenched it open. He stood
shivering on the landing. The words came more faintly:

> Hang down your head, old Ripper,
> For now you are bound to die. . . .

Well, why shouldn't they sing? The Ripper was news. The
Ripper had been the subject of macabre songs and jokes on radio
and television.

Below, the street door opened. The song welled in:

Took her in a park-way.
There I took her life.
Took her in a park-way,
Stuck her with me knife. . . .

Women were moving in the hall. They were climbing the stairs.
As they walked they chanted:

Took her in a park-way,
Stuck her with me knife. . . .

They had reached the first-floor landing. Now the stairs. The
second-floor landing. He could see them now. *She* was the leader.
What was she carrying in her hand?

Horncastle screamed in the back of his throat. He retreated
into his room. He shut the door. He discovered, too late, that the
key was missing. He stood with his back to the door, panting,
until he was visited with a memory of a girl in a cinema, a girl
sitting pressed against the back of her seat, but still vulnerable to
his attack.

He ran beyond the bed to the other side of the room. He
saw the door handle turn. The door swung open. The woman
entered alone. Her face was as still as a loch, empty, expressionless,
blind, without hate or mercy.

She came round the bed. A train rattled beyond the end of the
street. Horncastle screamed to the bottom of his demented soul. . . .

The door of his room closed, gently. The woman went downstairs. The song continued to float into the top-floor room:

Hang down your head, old Ripper.
Hang down your head and cry.
Hang down your head, old Ripper,
For now you are bound to die. . . .

CHAPTER ELEVEN

DAVID WYNDHAM looked with undisguised interest around Linda
Ward's bachelor-girl flat overlooking Hampstead Heath. There
was money in it, and more than money, taste. It fits her, he
thought, his mind temporarily diverted from his errand. Everything was cool, elegant and functional in a style that was modern

without being aggressive. Books lined the walls, gramophone records stood in racks. Her taste in literature was dry, almost ascetic: mostly non-fiction. There were a few novels but none, he noticed without surprise, with a strong romantic theme. If he had known more about music he would have realized that the same attitude was dominant there.

She entered from the bedroom, dressed for the street in a severely cut suit. She dropped her handbag on a coffee table. "Sorry I kept you waiting," she said, politely. "Thank you for allowing me to come," he replied. He felt stiff and formal.

She laughed, abruptly, at their self-consciousness. "This is ridiculous!" she said. "Sit down, man. Will you have a drink? It's almost noon."

Wyndham relaxed. "Whisky and soda, please." He sat down and felt immediately at ease. He stretched his legs. She said as she handed him a glass: "You sounded very mysterious on the phone."

"Did I? You surprise me. I only thought that I would like to bring you the news in person. We have found the Ripper. He's dead."

She said, caustically: "I'm sorry. I shall cry my eyes out. He should have been hanged." She sipped her drink. "How, when and where?"

"A woman telephoned me late last night, a Mrs. Lucas, owns a boarding-house in Bethnal Green. Said a man had killed himself in an upstairs room. She hadn't recognized him when he took the room but now she thought he might be the Ripper."

"You went along?"

"It isn't my manor, of course, but the local chaps were glad to have me. I went there with them. It was Horncastle all right."

"How had he died?"

"A single knife-thrust through the heart."

"Suicide?"

"It seems so. The knife was in his hand, the wound could have been self-inflicted. The knife belonged to Mrs. Lucas. He must have sneaked downstairs sometime during the day and nicked it from the kitchen drawer."

"A fixation about kitchen-knives, isn't that what the psychiatrists would call it?"

"Probably. Funny way to kill himself, though. Samurai stuff. *Hara-kiri* and all that."

"No doubt he'd got so used to killing people that he couldn't stop, and as there was no one else around he had to kill himself."

He smiled at the imagery, without mirth. "Anyway, that's the way it is. His wife's talked, too, now that it no longer matters."

Linda said, nastily: "A pity she didn't talk earlier. Martha would be still alive."

"A lot of others, too," said Wyndham, soberly. "God knows how long she'd known, or guessed, but she must have had her suspicions fairly early on." He shrugged, wearily. "Oh, well, let's not start throwing blame around or few of us will escape, me least of all."

"You?" she said. She glanced at him appraisingly. "You won't get the blame, surely. You'll get the kudos. More promotion?"

"No," he said. "There's nothing in it for me. As a matter of fact, I've put in my resignation."

She was genuinely surprised. "You're quitting? Why?"

"I've decided that I'm not cut out for the game."

"Isn't it a bit late to find that out?"

"Perhaps. I had a phenomenal run of luck. It had to end sometime."

"Have you done so badly on this case?"

"From beginning to end. You don't know how badly."

She shrugged. "It's your conscience," she said. "What will you do now?"

"Try my hand at being a bum."

"Oh, don't be a fool!" she said, snappishly.

"I'm not. I mean it. I leave the Met. at the end of next month. I shall go abroad, travel Europe, North Africa, the Middle East. I may have a shot at driving to Singapore. I'll pick up jobs on the way. There's a lot of work lying about for men like me. But that's in the future. I shall head for the South of Spain and Morocco first. Go down as far as Marrakesh and into the Blue Men's country. That will occupy me for the winter."

He rose. He stood over her, his pose lazy, his eyes veiled. "Maybe we'll meet again in Tangier?" The veil lifted for a second and the man shone through, hungry, yearning, desperate.

She lowered her eyes, shaken. Her lips trembled against her will. She said, coolly: "Tangier is very dull these days, don't you think? I shan't go there again."

"No," he said. "No. Well, it's good-bye then." He put out his hand. "Take care of yourself."

"Good-bye." Her grip was cool and firm. He nodded. He turned away. He paused momentarily, one hand on the top of the sideboard, and she thought he was going to speak again, an appeal, a hope. He did not. The door closed behind him.

Linda Ward lit a cigarette. The grey eyes haunted her. There had never been a man in her life quite like him. If only . . .

Her thoughts paused. She saw a square of white material lying on the sideboard. It had not been there when Wyndham entered. She picked it up. It was a square of cambric, soft and delicate. She recognized it even before she saw her initials in the corner. Where had she dropped it? She had used it to wipe the knife-handle before implanting the Ripper's dead fingers on it. Then she had thrust it into the pocket of her skirt. Only she must have been careless. Wyndham had found it. He knew.

Linda Ward drew a deep breath. For the first and only time in her life she felt a stab of genuine affection for a man. It swept over her and passed on, leaving a lingering after-effect of indescribable longing and a sense of loss. Then these, too, faded.

She put the handkerchief in her bag and went out to her car. She drove south to the new working flat she had rented in another part of St. John's Wood.

Linda Ward was back in business.

THE EDUCATION COMMITTEE OF BANFF COUNTY COUNCIL.

....School.

1. This book is the property of the Banffshire Education Committee.
2. The pupil to whom it is issued or his parents will be held responsible for its safe keeping and good condition.
3. Loss of or damage to the book should be reported immediately to the Headmaster. The parent or guardian of a pupil losing or misusing a book will be required either to replace it or to refund the value of the book to the Education Committee.
4. The fact that the pupil or another member of his/her household is suffering from infectious or contagious disease should be reported immediately to the headmaster.
5. This book must be covered by the pupil to whom it is issued.
6. Any person finding this book is requested to return it to the nearest school.

Date of Issue	Name of Pupil	Class
Feb. 1964.	ALAN GEDDES.	1A

J. M. & S., K.

THE OUIDE NOVELS
Edited by N. L. Clay

GULLIVER'S
TRAVELS

The Guide Novel Series

GULLIVER'S TRAVELS

THE FIRST THREE PARTS

by

JONATHAN SWIFT

Edited by

JAMES REEVES

WILLIAM HEINEMANN LTD
MELBOURNE :: LONDON :: TORONTO

FIRST PUBLISHED IN GUIDE NOVELS

1955

PUBLISHED BY

WILLIAM HEINEMANN LTD.

99 GREAT RUSSELL STREET, LONDON, W.C.I

PRINTED IN GREAT BRITAIN BY MORRISON AND GIBB LTD.

LONDON AND EDINBURGH

CONTENTS

GULLIVER'S TRAVELS

PART I: A VOYAGE TO LILLIPUT

PART II: A VOYAGE TO BROBDINGNAG

Contents

PART III : A VOYAGE TO LAPUTA, BALNIBARBI, LUGGNAGG, GLUBBDUBDRIB, AND JAPAN

Contents

TO GUIDE THE READER

THE PUBLISHER TO THE READER

THE author of these Travels, Mr. Lemuel Gulliver, is my ancient and intimate friend; there is likewise some relation between us by the mother's side. About three years ago, Mr. Gulliver, growing weary of the concourse of curious people coming to him at his house in Redriff, made a small purchase of land, with a convenient house, near Newark, in Nottinghamshire, his native country; where he now lived retired, yet in good esteem among his neighbours.

Although Mr. Gulliver was born in Nottinghamshire, where his father dwelt, yet I have heard him say his family came from Oxfordshire; to confirm which, I have observed in the church-yard at Banbury, in that county, several tombs and monuments of the Gullivers.

Before he quitted Redriff, he left the custody of the following papers in my hands, with the liberty to dispose of them as I should think fit. I have carefully perused them three times: the style is very plain and simple; and the only fault I find is, that the author, after the manner of travellers, is a little too circumstantial. There is an air of truth apparent through the whole; and indeed the author was so distinguished for his veracity, that it became a sort of proverb among his neighbours at Redriff, when any one affirmed a thing, to say it was as true as if Mr. Gulliver had spoke it.

By the advice of several worthy persons, to whom, with the author's permission, I communicated these papers, I now venture to send them into the world, hoping they may be at least, for some time, a better entertainment to our young noblemen, than the common scribbles of politics and party.

This volume would have been at least twice as large, if I had not made bold to strike out innumerable passages relating to the winds and tides, as well as to the variations and bearings in the several voyages; together with the minute descriptions of the management of the ship in storms, in the style of sailors: likewise the account of longitudes and latitudes; wherein I have reason to apprehend that Mr. Gulliver may be a little dissatisfied: but I was resolved to fit the work as much as possible to the general capacity of readers. However, if my own ignorance in sea-affairs shall have led me to commit some mistakes, I alone am answerable for them: and if any traveller hath a curiosity to see the whole work at large, as it came from the hand of the author, I will be ready to gratify him.

As for any further particulars relating to the author, the reader will receive satisfaction from the first pages of the book.

RICHARD SYMPSON

PART I

A VOYAGE TO LILLIPUT

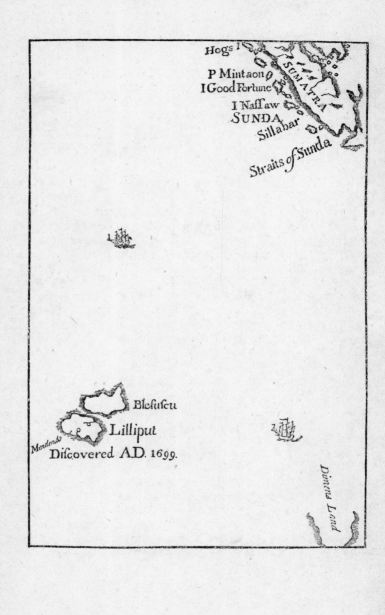

Hogs I

P Mint aon
I Good Fortune

I Nassaw
SUNDA
Sillabar

SUMATRA

Straits of Sunda

Blefuscu

Mendendo Lilliput
Discovered AD. 1699.

Dinena Land

CHAPTER I

The Author gives some account of himself and family, his first induce-
ments to travel. He is shipwrecked, and swims for his life, gets
safe on shore in the country of Lilliput, *is made a prisoner, and*
is carried up country.

MY father had a small estate in Nottinghamshire; I was
the third of five sons. He sent me to Emanuel
College in Cambridge, at fourteen years old, where I resided
three years, and applied myself close to my studies; but the
charge of maintaining me (although I had a very scanty
allowance) being too great for a narrow fortune, I was bound
apprentice to Mr. James Bates, an eminent surgeon in
London, with whom I continued four years; and my father
now and then sending me small sums of money, I laid them
out in learning navigation, and other parts of the mathematics, useful to those who intend to travel, as I always
believed it would be some time or other my fortune to do.
When I left Mr. Bates, I went down to my father; where,
by the assistance of him and my uncle John, and some
other relations, I got forty pounds, and a promise of thirty
pounds a year to maintain me at Leyden: there I studied
physic two years and seven months, knowing it would be
useful in long voyages.

Soon after my return from Leyden, I was recommended
by my good master, Mr. Bates, to be surgeon to the *Swallow*,
Captain Abraham Pannell, commander; with whom I continued three years and a half, making a voyage or two into
the Levant, and some other parts. When I came back I
resolved to settle in London, to which Mr. Bates, my master,
encouraged me, and by him I was recommended to several
patients. I took part of a small house in the Old Jury; and
being advised to alter my condition, I married Mrs. Mary

Burton, second daughter to Mr. Edmund Burton, hosier, in Newgate Street, with whom I received four hundred pounds for a portion.

But, my good master Bates dying in two years after, and I having few friends, my business began to fail; for my conscience would not suffer me to imitate the bad practice of too many among my brethren. Having therefore consulted with my wife, and some of my acquaintances, I determined to go again to sea. I was surgeon successively in two ships, and made several voyages, for six years, to the East and West-Indies, by which I got some addition to my fortune. My hours of leisure I spent in reading the best authors, ancient and modern, being always provided with a good number of books; and when I was ashore, in observing the manners and dispositions of the people, as well as learning their language, wherein I had a great facility by the strength of my memory.

The last of these voyages not proving very fortunate, I grew weary of the sea, and intended to stay at home with my wife and family. I removed from the Old Jury to Fetter Lane, and from thence to Wapping, hoping to get business among the sailors; but it would not turn to account. After three years' expectation that things would mend, I accepted an advantageous offer from Captain William Pritchard, master of the *Antelope*, who was making a voyage to the South-Sea. We set sail from Bristol, May 4, 1699, and our voyage at first was very prosperous.

It would not be proper, for some reasons, to trouble the reader with the particulars of our adventures in those seas; let it suffice to inform him, that in our passage from thence to the East-Indies, we were driven by a violent storm to the north-west of Van Diemen's Land. By an observation, we found ourselves in the latitude of 30 degrees 2 minutes south. Twelve of our crew were dead by immoderate labour, and ill food, the rest were in a very weak condition. On the fifth of November, which was the beginning of summer in those parts, the weather being very hazy, the seamen spied a rock, within half a cable's length of the ship; but the wind was so strong, that we were driven directly upon it, and immediately split. Six of the crew, of whom I was one, having let down the boat into the sea, made a shift to get clear of the ship, and the rock. We rowed, by my computation, about three leagues, till we were able to work no longer, being already spent with labour while we were in the ship. We therefore trusted ourselves to the mercy of the waves, and in about half an hour the boat was overset by a sudden flurry from the north. What became of my companions in the boat, as well as of those who escaped on the rock, or were left in the vessel, I cannot tell; but conclude they were all lost. For my own part, I swam as fortune directed me, and was pushed forward by wind and tide. I often let my legs drop, and could feel no bottom: but when I was almost gone, and able to struggle no longer, I found myself within my depth; and by this time the storm was much abated. The declivity was so small, that I walked near a mile before I got to the shore, which I conjectured was about eight o'clock in the evening. I then advanced forward near half a mile, but could not discover any sign of houses or inhabitants; at least I was in so weak a condition, that I did not observe them. I was extremely tired, and with that, and the heat of the weather, and about half a pint of brandy that I drank as I left the ship, I found myself much inclined to sleep. I lay down on the grass, which was very short and soft, where I slept sounder than ever I remember to have done in my life, and, as I reckoned, about nine hours; for when I awaked, it was just day-light. I attempted to rise, but was not able to stir: for as I happened to lie on my back, I found my arms and legs were strongly fastened on each side to the ground; and my hair, which was long and thick, tied down in the same manner. I likewise felt several slender ligatures across my body, from my arm-pits to my thighs. I could only look upwards, the sun began to grow hot, and the light offended my eyes. I heard a confused noise about me, but in the posture I lay, could see nothing except the sky. In a little time I felt something alive moving on my left leg, which advancing gently forward over my breast, came almost up to my chin; when bending my eyes downwards as much as I could, I perceived it to be a human creature not six inches high, with a bow and arrow in his hands, and a quiver at his back. In the meantime, I felt at least forty more of the same kind (as I conjectured) following the first. I was in the utmost astonishment, and roared so loud, that they all ran back in a fright; and some of them, as I was afterwards told, were hurt with the falls they got by leaping from my sides upon the ground. However, they soon returned, and one of them, who ventured so far as to get a full sight of my face, lifting up his hands and eyes by way of admiration, cried out in a shrill, but distinct voice, *Hekinah degul:* the others repeated the same words several times, but then I knew not what they meant. I lay all this while, as the reader may believe, in great uneasiness: at length, struggling to get loose, I had the fortune to break the strings, and wrench out the pegs that fastened my left arm to the ground; for, by lifting it up to my face, I discovered the methods they had taken to bind me, and at the same time with a violent pull, which gave me excessive pain, I a little loosened the strings that tied down my hair on the left side, so that I was just able to turn my head about two inches. But the creatures ran off a second time, before I could seize them; whereupon there was a great shout in a very shrill accent, and after it ceased, I heard one of them cry aloud *Tolga phonac;* when in an instant I felt above an hundred arrows discharged on my left hand, which pricked me like so many needles; and besides, they shot another flight into the air, as we do bombs in Europe, whereof many, I suppose, fell on my body (though I felt them not), and some on my face, which I immediately covered with my left hand. When this shower of arrows was over, I fell a groaning with grief and pain, and then striving again to get loose, they discharged another volley larger than the first, and some of them attempted with spears to stick me in the sides; but, by good luck, I had on a buff jerkin, which they could not pierce. I thought it the most prudent method to lie still, and my design was to continue so till night, when, my left hand being already loose, I could easily free myself: and as for the inhabitants, I had reason to believe I might be a match for the greatest armies they could bring against me, if they were all of the same size with him that I saw. But fortune disposed otherwise of me. When the people observed I was quiet, they discharged no more arrows; but, by the noise I heard, I knew their numbers increased; and about four yards from me, over-against my right ear, I heard a knocking for above an hour, like that of people at work; when turning my head that way, as well as the pegs and strings would permit me, I saw a stage erected, about a foot and a half from the ground, capable of holding four of the inhabitants, with two or three ladders to mount it: from whence one of them, who seemed to be a person of quality, made me a long speech, whereof I understood not one syllable. But I should have mentioned, that before the principal person began his oration, he cried out three times, *Langro dehul san:* (these words and the former were afterwards repeated and explained to me). Whereupon immediately about fifty of the inhabitants came and cut the strings that fastened the left side of my head, which gave me the liberty of turning it to the right, and of observing the person and gesture of him that was to speak. He appeared to be of a middle age, and taller than any of the other three who attended him, whereof one was a page that held up his train, and seemed to be somewhat longer than my middle finger; the other two stood one on each side to support him. He acted every part of an orator, and I could observe many periods of threatenings, and others of promises, pity and kindness. I answered in a few words, but in the most submissive manner, lifting up my left hand, and both my eyes to the sun, as calling him for a witness; and being almost famished with hunger, having not eaten a morsel for some hours before I left the ship, I found the demands of nature so strong upon me, that I could not forbear showing my impatience (perhaps against the strict rules of decency) by putting my finger frequently on my mouth, to signify that I wanted food. The

2

Hurgo (for so they call a great lord, as I afterwards learnt)
understood me very well. He descended from the stage,
and commanded that several ladders should be applied to
my sides, on which above an hundred of the inhabitants
mounted and walked towards my mouth, laden with baskets
full of meat, which had been provided and sent thither by
the King's orders, upon the first intelligence he received of
me. I observed there was the flesh of several animals, but
could not distinguish them by the taste. There were
shoulders, legs, and loins, shaped like those of mutton, and
very well dressed, but smaller than the wings of a lark. I eat
them by two or three at a mouthful, and took three loaves
at a time, about the bigness of musket bullets. They
supplied me as fast as they could, showing a thousand marks
of wonder and astonishment at my bulk and appetite. I then
made another sign that I wanted drink. They found by my
eating, that a small quantity would not suffice me; and
being a most ingenious people, they slung up with great
dexterity one of their largest hogsheads, then rolled it
towards my hand, and beat out the top; I drank it off at a
draught, which I might well do, for it did not hold half a
pint, and tasted like a small wine of Burgundy, but much
more delicious. They brought me a second hogshead, which
I drank in the same manner, and made signs for more, but
they had none to give me. When I had performed these
wonders, they shouted for joy, and danced upon my breast,
repeating several times as they did at first, *Hekinah degul*.
They made me a sign that I should throw down the two
hogsheads, but first warning the people below to stand out
of the way, crying aloud, *Borach mivola*, and when they saw
the vessels in the air, there was an universal shout of *Hekinah
degul*. I confess I was often tempted, while they were passing
backwards and forwards on my body, to seize forty or
fifty of the first that came in my reach, and dash them
against the ground. But the remembrance of what I had felt,
which probably might not be the worst they could do, and
the promise of honour I made them, for so I interpreted my
submissive behaviour, soon drove out these imaginations.

Besides, I now considered myself as bound by the laws of hospitality to a people who had treated me with so much expense and magnificence. However, in my thoughts, I could not sufficiently wonder at the intrepidity of these diminutive mortals, who durst venture to mount and walk upon my body, while one of my hands was at liberty, without trembling at the very sight of so prodigious a creature as I must appear to them. After some time, when they observed that I made no more demands for meat, there appeared before me a person of high rank from his Imperial Majesty. His Excellency, having mounted on the small of my right leg, advanced forwards up to my face, with about a dozen of his retinue. And producing his credentials under the Signet Royal, which he applied close to my eyes, spoke about ten minutes, without any signs of anger, but with a kind of determinate resolution; often pointing forwards, which, as I afterwards found, was towards the capital city, about half a mile distant, whither it was agreed by his Majesty in council that I must be conveyed. I answered in few words, but to no purpose, and made a sign with my hand that was loose, putting it to the other (but over his Excellency's head for fear of hurting him or his train) and then to my own head and body, to signify that I desired my liberty. It appeared that he understood me well enough, for he shook his head by way of disapprobation, and held his hand in a posture to show that I must be carried as a prisoner. However, he made other signs to let me understand that I should have meat and drink enough, and very good treatment. Whereupon I once more thought of attempting to break my bonds; but again, when I felt the smart of their arrows, upon my face and hands, which were all in blisters, and many of the darts still sticking in them, and observing likewise that the number of my enemies increased, I gave tokens to let them know that they might do with me what they pleased. Upon this, the *Hurgo* and his train withdrew, with much civility and cheerful countenances. Soon after I heard a general shout, with frequent repetitions of the words, *Peplom selan*, and I felt great numbers of people on my left side relaxing the cords to such a degree, that I was able to turn upon my right, and to ease myself with making water; which I very plentifully did, to the great astonishment of the people, who conjecturing by my motions what I was going to do, immediately opened to the right and left on that side, to avoid the torrent which fell with such noise and violence from me. But before this, they had daubed my face and both my hands with a sort of ointment very pleasant to the smell, which in a few minutes removed all the smart of their arrows. These circumstances, added to the refreshment I had received by their victuals and drink, which were very nourishing, disposed me to sleep. I slept about eight hours, as I was afterwards assured; and it was no wonder, for the physicians, by the Emperor's order, had mingled a sleepy potion in the hogshead of wine.

It seems that upon the first moment I was discovered sleeping on the ground after my landing, the Emperor had early notice of it by an express; and determined in council that I should be tied in the manner I have related (which was done in the night while I slept), that plenty of meat and drink should be sent to me, and a machine prepared to carry me to the capital city.

This resolution perhaps may appear very bold and dangerous, and I am confident would not be imitated by any prince in Europe on the like occasion; however, in my opinion, it was extremely prudent, as well as generous: for supposing these people had endeavoured to kill me with their spears and arrows while I was asleep, I should certainly have awakened with the first sense of smart, which might so far have roused my rage and strength, as to have enabled me to break the strings wherewith I was tied; after which, as they were not able to make resistance, so they could expect no mercy.

These people are most excellent mathematicians, and arrived to a great perfection in mechanics, by the countenance and encouragement of the Emperor, who is a renowned patron of learning. This prince hath several machines fixed in wheels, for the carriage of trees and other great weights.

He often builds his largest men of war, whereof some are nine foot long, in the woods where the timber grows, and has them carried on these engines three or four hundred yards to the sea. Five hundred carpenters and engineers were immediately set at work to prepare the greatest engine they had. It was a frame of wood raised three inches from the ground, about seven foot long and four wide, moving upon twenty-two wheels. The shout I heard was upon the arrival of this engine, which it seems set out in four hours after my landing. It was brought parallel to me as I lay. But the principal difficulty was to raise and place me in this vehicle. Eighty poles, each of one foot high, were erected for this purpose, and very strong cords of the bigness of packthread were fastened by hooks to many bandages, which the workmen had girt round my neck, my hands, my body, and my legs. Nine hundred of the strongest men were employed to draw up these cords by many pulleys fastened on the poles, and thus, in less than three hours, I was raised and slung into the engine, and there tied fast. All this I was told, for, while the whole operation was performing, I lay in a profound sleep, by the force of that soporiferous medicine infused into my liquor. Fifteen hundred of the Emperor's largest horses, each about four inches and a half high, were employed to draw me towards the metropolis, which, as I said, was half a mile distant.

About four hours after we began our journey, I awaked by a very ridiculous accident; for the carriage being stopped a while to adjust something that was out of order, two or three of the young natives had the curiosity to see how I looked when I was asleep; they climbed up into the engine, and advancing very softly to my face, one of them, an officer in the guards, put the sharp end of his half-pike a good way up into my left nostril, which tickled my nose like a straw, and made me sneeze violently: whereupon they stole off unperceived, and it was three weeks before I knew the cause of my awaking so suddenly. We made a long march the remaining part of that day, and rested at night with five hundred guards on each side of me, half with

torches, and half with bows and arrows, ready to shoot me
if I should offer to stir. The next morning at sun-rise we
continued our march, and arrived within two hundred yards
of the city gates about noon. The Emperor, and all his
court, came out to meet us; but his great officers would by
no means suffer his Majesty to endanger his person by
mounting on my body.

At the place where the carriage stopped, there stood an
ancient temple, esteemed to be the largest in the whole
kingdom; which having been polluted some years before
by an unnatural murder, was, according to the zeal of those
people, looked upon as profane, and therefore had been
applied to common uses, and all the ornaments and furniture
carried away. In this edifice it was determined I should
lodge. The great gate fronting to the north was about
four foot high, and almost two foot wide, through which
I could easily creep. On each side of the gate was a small
window not above six inches from the ground: into that
on the left side, the King's smiths conveyed fourscore and
eleven chains, like those that hang to a lady's watch in
Europe, and almost as large, which were locked to my left
leg with six and thirty padlocks. Over-against this temple,
on t'other side of the great highway, at twenty foot distance,
there was a turret at least five foot high. Here the Emperor
ascended, with many principal lords of his court, to have
an opportunity of viewing me, as I was told, for I could not
see them. It was reckoned that above an hundred thousand
inhabitants come out of the town upon the same errand;
and, in spite of my guards, I believe there could not be
fewer than ten thousand at several times, who mounted my
body by the help of ladders. But a proclamation was soon
issued to forbid it upon pain of death. When the workmen
found it was impossible for me to break loose, they cut all
the strings that bound me; whereupon I rose up, with as
melancholy a disposition as ever I had in my life. But the
noise and astonishment of the people at seeing me rise and
walk, are not to be expressed. The chains that held my
left leg were about two yards long, and gave me not only

the liberty of walking backwards and forwards in a semi-circle; but, being fixed within four inches of the gate, allowed me to creep in, and lie at my full length in the temple.

CHAPTER II

The Emperor of Lilliput, *attended by several of the nobility, comes to see the Author in his confinement. The Emperor's person and habit described. Learned men appointed to teach the Author their language. He gains favour by his mild disposition. His pockets are searched, and his sword and pistols taken from him.*

WHEN I found myself on my feet, I looked about me, and must confess I never beheld a more entertaining prospect. The country round appeared like a continued garden, and the inclosed fields, which were generally forty foot square, resembled so many beds of flowers. These fields were intermingled with woods of half a stang, and the tallest trees, as I could judge, appeared to be seven foot high. I viewed the town on my left hand, which looked like the painted scene of a city in a theatre.

I had been for some hours extremely pressed by the necessities of nature; which was no wonder, it being almost two days since I had last disburthened myself. I was under great difficulties between urgency and shame. The best expedient I could think on, was to creep into my house, which I accordingly did; and shutting the gate after me, I went as far as the length of my chain would suffer, and discharged my body of that uneasy load. But this was the only time I was ever guilty of so uncleanly an action; for which I cannot but hope the candid reader will give some allowance, after he hath maturely and impartially considered my case, and the distress I was in. From this time my constant practice was, as soon as I rose, to perform that business in open air, at the full extent of my chain, and due care was taken every morning before company came, that the offensive matter should be carried off in wheel-barrows, by two servants appointed for that purpose. I would not have dwelt so long upon a circumstance, that perhaps at first sight may appear not very momentous, if I had not thought it necessary to justify my character in point of cleanliness to the world; which I am told some of my maligners have been pleased, upon this and other occasions, to call in question.

When this adventure was at an end, I came back out of my house, having occasion for fresh air. The Emperor was already descended from the tower, and advancing on horseback towards me, which had like to have cost him dear; for the beast, though very well trained, yet wholly unused to such a sight, which appeared as if a mountain moved before him, reared up on his hinder feet: but that prince, who is an excellent horseman, kept his seat, till his attendants ran in, and held the bridle, while his Majesty had time to dismount. When he alighted, he surveyed me round with great admiration, but kept beyond the length of my chain. He ordered his cooks and butlers, who were already prepared, to give me victuals and drink, which they pushed forward in a sort of vehicles upon wheels, till I could reach them. I took these vehicles, and soon emptied them all; twenty of them were filled with meat, and ten with liquor; each of the former afforded me two or three good mouthfuls, and I emptied the liquor of ten vessels, which was contained in earthen vials, into one vehicle, drinking it off at a draught; and so I did with the rest. The Empress, and young Princes of the blood of both sexes, attended by many ladies, sat at some distance in their chairs; but upon the accident that happened to the Emperor's horse, they alighted, and came near his person, which I am now going to describe. He is taller by almost the breadth of my nail, than any of his court; which alone is enough to strike an awe into the beholders. His features are strong and masculine, with an Austrian lip and arched nose, his complexion olive, his countenance erect, his body and limbs well proportioned, all his motions graceful, and his deportment majestic. He was then past his prime, being twenty-eight years and three quarters old, of which he had reigned about seven, in great felicity, and generally victorious. For the better convenience of beholding him, I lay on my side, so that my face was parallel to his, and he stood but three yards off: however, I have had him since many times in my hand, and therefore cannot be deceived in the description. His dress was very plain and simple, and the fashion of it between the Asiatic and the European: but he had on his head a light helmet of gold, adorned with jewels, and a plume on the crest. He held his sword drawn in his hand, to defend himself, if I should happen to break loose; it was almost three inches long, the hilt and scabbard were gold enriched with diamonds. His voice was shrill, but very clear and articulate, and I could distinctly hear it when I stood up. The ladies and courtiers were all most magnificently clad, so that the spot they stood upon seemed to resemble a petticoat spread on the ground, embroidered with figures of gold and silver. His Imperial Majesty spoke often to me, and I returned answers, but neither of us could understand a syllable. There were several of his priests and lawyers present (as I conjectured by their habits) who were commanded to address themselves to me, and I spoke to them in as many languages as I had the least smattering of, which were High and Low Dutch, Latin, French, Spanish, Italian, and Lingua Franca; but all to no purpose. After about two hours the court retired, and I was left with a strong guard, to prevent the impertinence, and probably the malice of the rabble, who were very impatient to crowd about me as near as they durst and some of them had the impudence to shoot their arrows at me as I sat on the ground by the door of my house, whereof one very narrowly missed my left eye. But the colonel ordered six of the ringleaders to be seized, and thought no punishment so proper as to deliver them bound into my hands, which some of his soldiers accordingly did, pushing them forward with the butt-ends of their pikes into my reach; I took them all in my right hand, put five of them into my coat-pocket, and as to the sixth, I made a countenance as if I would eat him alive. The poor man squalled terribly, and the colonel and his officers were in much pain, especially when they saw me take out my penknife: but I soon put them out of fear: for, looking mildly, and immediately cutting the strings he was bound with, I set him gently on the ground, and away he ran. I treated the rest in the same manner, taking them one by one out of my pocket, and I observed both the soldiers and people were highly obliged at this mark of my clemency, which was represented very much to my advantage at court.

Towards night I got with some difficulty into my house, where I lay on the ground, and continued to do so about a fortnight; during which time the Emperor gave orders to have a bed prepared for me. Six hundred beds of the common measure were brought in carriages, and worked up in my house; an hundred and fifty of their beds sewn together made up the breadth and length, and these were four double, which however kept me but very indifferently from the hardness of the floor, that was of smooth stone. By the same computation they provided me with sheets, blankets, and coverlets, tolerable enough for one who had been so long inured to hardships as I.

As the news of my arrival spread through the kingdom, it brought prodigious numbers of rich, idle, and curious people to see me; so that the villages were almost emptied, and great neglect of tillage and household affairs must have ensued, if his Imperial Majesty had not provided, by several proclamations and orders of state, against this inconveniency. He directed that those who had already beheld me should return home, and not presume to come within fifty yards of my house without licence from court; whereby the secretaries of state got considerable fees.

In the meantime, the Emperor held frequent councils to debate what course should be taken with me; and I was afterwards assured by a particular friend, a person of great quality, who was looked upon to be as much in the secret as any, that the court was under many difficulties concerning me. They apprehended my breaking loose, that my diet would be very expensive, and might cause a famine. Sometimes they determined to starve me, or at least to shoot me in the face and hands with poisoned arrows, which would soon dispatch me; but again they considered, that the stench of so large a carcass might produce a plague in the metropolis, and probably spread through the whole kingdom. In the midst of these consultations, several officers of the army went to the door of the great council-chamber; two of them being admitted, gave an account of my behaviour to the six criminals above-mentioned, which made so favourable an impression in the breast of his Majesty and the whole board, in my behalf, that an Imperial Commission was issued out, obliging all the villages nine hundred yards round the city, to deliver in every morning six beeves, forty sheep, and other victuals for my sustenance; together with a proportionate quantity of bread, and wine, and other liquors; for the due payment of which his Majesty gave assignments upon his treasury. For this prince lives chiefly upon his own demesnes, seldom, except upon great occasions, raising any subsidies upon his subjects, who are bound to attend him in his wars at their own expense. An establishment was also made of six hundred persons to be my domestics, who had board-wages allowed for their maintenance, and tents built for them very conveniently on each side of my door. It was likewise ordered, that three hundred tailors should make me a suit of clothes after the fashion of the country: that six of his Majesty's greatest scholars should be employed to instruct me in their language: and, lastly, that the Emperor's horses, and those of the nobility, and troops of guards, should be frequently exercised in my sight, to accustom themselves to me. All these orders were duly put in execution, and in about three weeks I made a great progress in learning their language; during which time, the Emperor frequently honoured me with his visits, and was pleased to assist my masters in teaching me. We began already to converse together in some sort; and the first words I learnt were to express my desire that he would please give me my liberty, which I every day repeated on my knees. His answer, as I could comprehend it, was, that this must be a work of time, not to be thought on without the advice of his council, and that first I must *Lumos kelmin pesso desmar lon Emposo;* that is, swear a peace with him and his kingdom. However, that I should be used with all kindness; and he advised me to acquire, by my patience and discreet behaviour, the good opinion of himself and his subjects. He desired I would not take it ill, if he gave order to certain proper officers to search me; for probably I might carry about me several weapons, which must needs be dangerous things, if they answered the bulk of so prodigious a person. I said, his Majesty should be satisfied, for I was ready to strip myself, and turn up my pockets before him. This I delivered part in words, and part in signs. He replied, that by the laws of the kingdom I must be searched by two of his officers; that he knew this could not be done without my consent and assistance; that he had so good an opinion of my generosity and justice, as to trust their persons in my hands: that whatever they took from me should be returned when I left the country, or paid for at the rate which I would set upon them. I took up the two officers in my hands, put them first into my coat-pockets, and then into every other pocket about me, except my two fobs, and another secret pocket which I had no mind should be searched, where in I had some little necessaries that were of no consequence to any but myself. In one of my fobs there was a silver watch, and in the other a small quantity of gold in a purse. These gentlemen, having pen, ink, and paper about them, made an exact inventory of everything they saw; and when they had done, desired I would set them down, that they might deliver it to the Emperor. This inventory I afterwards translated into English, and is word for word as follows.

Imprimis, In the right coat-pocket of the Great Man-Mountain (for so I interpret the words *Quinbus Flestrin*) after the strictest search, we found only one great piece of coarse cloth, large enough to be a foot-cloth for your

Majesty's chief room of state. In the left pocket we saw a huge silver chest, with a cover of the same metal, which we, the searchers, were not able to lift. We desired it should be opened, and one of us stepped into it, found himself up to the mid leg in a sort of dust, some part whereof flying up to our faces, set us both a sneezing for several times together. In his right waistcoat-pocket we found a prodigious bundle of white thin substances, folded one over another, about the bigness of three men, tied with a strong cable, and marked with black figures; which we humbly conceive to be writings, every letter almost half as large as the palm of our hands. In the left there was a sort of engine, from the back of which were extended twenty long poles, resembling the pallisados before your Majesty's court; where we conjecture the Man-Mountain combs his head; for we did not always trouble him with questions, because we found it a great difficulty to make him understand us. In the large pocket on the right side of his middle cover (so I translate the word *ranfu-lo*, by which they meant my breeches) we saw a hollow pillar of iron, about the length of a man, fastened to a strong piece of timber, larger than the pillar; and upon one side of the pillar were huge pieces of iron sticking out, cut into strange figures, which we know not what to make of. In the left pocket, another engine of the same kind. In the smaller pocket on the right side, were several round flat pieces of white and red metal, of different bulk; some of the white, which seemed to be silver, were so large and heavy, that my comrade and I could hardly lift them. In the left pocket were two black pillars irregularly shaped: we could not, without difficulty, reach the top of them as we stood at the bottom of his pocket. One of them was covered, and seemed all of a piece: but at the upper end of the other, there appeared a white round substance, about twice the bigness of our heads. Within each of these was enclosed a prodigious plate of steel; which, by our orders, we obliged him to show us, because we apprehended they might be dangerous engines. He took them out of their cases, and told us, that in his own country his practice was to shave his beard with one of these, and cut his meat with the other. There were two pockets which we could not enter: these he called his fobs; they were two large slits cut into the top of his middle cover, but squeezed close by the pressure of his belly. Out of the right fob hung a great silver chain, with a wonderful kind of engine at the bottom. We directed him to draw out whatever was fastened to that chain; which appeared to be a globe, half silver, and half of some transparent metal; for, on the transparent side, we saw certain strange figures circularly drawn, and thought we could touch them, till we found our fingers stopped by that lucid substance. He put his engine to our ears, which made an incessant noise like that of a water-mill. And we conjecture it is either some unknown animal, or the god that he worships; but we are more inclined to the latter opinion, because he assured us (if we understood him right, for he expressed himself very imperfectly), that he seldom did anything without consulting it. He called it his oracle, and said it pointed out the time for every action of his life. From the left fob he took out a net almost large enough for a fisherman, but contrived to open and shut like a purse, and served him for the same use: we found therein several massy pieces of yellow metal, which, if they be real gold, must be of immense value.

Having thus, in obedience to your Majesty's commands, diligently searched all his pockets, we observed a girdle about his waist made of the hide of some prodigious animal; from which, on the left side, hung a sword of the length of five men; and on the right, a bag or pouch divided into two cells, each cell capable of holding three of your Majesty's subjects. In one of these cells were several globes or balls of a most ponderous metal, about the bigness of our heads, and requiring a strong hand to lift them: the other cell contained a heap of certain black grains, but of no great bulk or weight, for we could hold above fifty of them in the palms of our hands.

This is an exact inventory of what we found about the

body of the Man-Mountain, who used us with great civility, and due respect to your Majesty's Commission. Signed and sealed on the fourth day of the eighty-ninth moon of your Majesty's auspicious reign.

CLEFRIN FRELOCK, MARSI FRELOCK.

When this inventory was read over to the Emperor, he directed me, although in very gentle terms, to deliver up the several particulars. He first called for my scimitar, which I took out, scabbard and all. In the meantime he ordered three thousand of his choicest troops (who then attended him) to surround me at a distance, with their bows and arrows just ready to discharge: but I did not observe it, for my eyes were wholly fixed upon his Majesty. He then desired me to draw my scimitar, which, although it had got some rust by the sea-water, was in most parts exceeding bright. I did so, and immediately all the troops give a shout between terror and surprise; for the sun shone clear, and the reflection dazzled their eyes, as I waved the scimitar to and fro in my hand. His Majesty, who is a most magnanimous prince, was less daunted than I could expect; he ordered me to return it into the scabbard, and cast it on the ground as gently as I could, about six foot from the end of my chain. The next thing he demanded, was one of the hollow iron pillars, by which he meant my pocket-pistols. I drew it out, and at his desire, as well as I could, expressed to him the use of it; and charging it only with powder, which, by the closeness of my pouch, happened to escape wetting in the sea (an inconvenience against which all prudent mariners take special care to provide), I first cautioned the Emperor not to be afraid, and then I let it off in the air. The astonishment here was much greater than at the sight of my scimitar. Hundreds fell down as if they had been struck dead; and even the Emperor, although he stood his ground, could not recover himself in some time. I delivered up both my pistols in the same manner as I had done my scimitar, and then my pouch of powder and bullets; begging him that the former might be kept from fire, for it would kindle with the smallest spark, and blow up his imperial palace into the air. I likewise delivered up my watch, which the Emperor was very curious to see, and commanded two of his tallest yeomen of the guards to bear it on a pole upon their shoulders, as draymen in England do a barrel of ale. He was amazed at the continual noise it made, and the motion of the minute-hand, which he could easily discern; for their sight is much more acute than ours: and asked the opinions of his learned men about him, which were various and remote, as the reader may well imagine without my repeating; although indeed I could not very perfectly understand them. I then gave up my silver and copper money, my purse, with nine large pieces of gold, and some smaller ones; my knife and razor, my comb and silver snuff-box, my handkerchief and journal-book. My scimitar, pistols, and pouch, were conveyed in carriages to his Majesty's stores; but the rest of my goods were returned to me.

I had, as I before observed, one private pocket which escaped their search, wherein there was a pair of spectacles, (which I sometimes use for the weakness of my eyes) a pocket perspective, and several other little conveniences; which being of no consequence to the Emperor, I did not think myself bound in honour to discover, and I apprehended they might be lost or spoiled if I ventured them out of my possession.

CHAPTER III

The Author diverts the Emperor, and his nobility of both sexes, in a very uncommon manner. The diversions of the court of Lilliput described. The Author has his liberty granted him upon certain conditions.

MY gentleness and good behaviour had gained so far on the Emperor and his court, and indeed upon the army and people in general, that I began to conceive hopes of getting my liberty in a short time. I took all possible methods to cultivate this favourable disposition. The natives came by degrees to be less apprehensive of any danger from me. I would sometimes lie down, and let five or six of them dance on my hand. And at last the boys and girls would venture to come and play at hide and seek in my hair. I had now made a good progress in understanding and speaking their language. The Emperor had a mind one day to entertain me with several of the country shows, wherein they exceed all nations I have known, both for dexterity and magnificence. I was diverted with none so much as that of the rope-dancers, performed upon a slender white thread, extending about two foot, and twelve inches from the ground. Upon which I shall desire liberty, with the reader's patience, to enlarge a little.

This diversion is only practised by those persons who are candidates for great employments, and high favour, at court. They are trained in this art from their youth, and are not always of noble birth, or liberal education. When a great office is vacant, either by death or disgrace (which often happens), five or six of those candidates petition the Emperor to entertain his Majesty and the court with a dance on the rope, and whoever jumps the highest without falling, succeeds in the office. Very often the chief ministers themselves are commanded to show their skill, and to convince the Emperor that they have not lost their faculty. Flimnap, the Treasurer, is allowed to cut a caper on the straight rope, at least an inch higher than any other lord in the whole empire. I have seen him do the summerset several times together upon a trencher fixed on the rope, which is no thicker than a common pack-thread in England. My friend Reldresal, principal Secretary for Private Affairs, is, in my opinion, if I am not partial, the second after the Treasurer; the rest of the great officers are much upon a par.

These diversions are often attended with fatal accidents, whereof great numbers are on record. I myself have seen two or three candidates break a limb. But the danger is much greater when the ministers themselves are commanded to show their dexterity; for, by contending to excel them-

3

selves and their fellows, they strain so far, that there is hardly one of them who hath not received a fall, and some of them two or three. I was assured that a year or two before my arrival, Flimnap would have infallibly broke his neck, if one of the King's cushions, that accidentally lay on the ground, had not weakened the force of his fall.

There is likewise another diversion, which is only shown before the Emperor and Empress, and first minister, upon particular occasions. The Emperor lays on the table three fine silken threads of six inches long. One is blue, the other red, and the third green. These threads are proposed as prizes for those persons whom the Emperor hath a mind to distinguish by a peculiar mark of his favour. The ceremony is performed in his Majesty's great chamber of state, where the candidates are to undergo a trial of dexterity very different from the former, and such as I have not observed the least resemblance of in any other country of the old or the new world. The Emperor holds a stick in his hands, both ends parallel to the horizon, while the candidates advancing one by one, sometimes leap over the stick, sometimes creep under it backwards and forwards several times, according as the stick is advanced or depressed. Sometimes the Emperor holds one end of the stick, and his first minister the other; sometimes the minister has it entirely to himself. Whoever performs his part with most agility, and holds out the longest in leaping and creeping, is rewarded with the blue-coloured silk; the red is given to the next, and the green to the third, which they all wear girt twice round about the middle; and you see few great persons about this court, who are not adorned with one of these girdles.

The horses of the army, and those of the royal stables, having been daily led before me, were no longer shy, but would come up to my very feet without starting. The riders would leap them over my hand as I held it on the ground, and one of the Emperor's huntsmen, upon a large courser, took my foot, shoe and all; which was indeed a prodigious leap. I had the good fortune to divert the Emperor one day after a very extraordinary manner. I desired he would order several sticks of two foot high, and the thickness of an ordinary cane, to be brought me; whereupon his Majesty commanded the master of his woods to give directions accordingly; and the next morning six woodmen arrived with as many carriages, drawn by eight horses to each. I took nine of these sticks, fixing them firmly in the ground in a quadrangle figure, two foot and a half square. I took four other sticks, and tied them parallel at each corner, about two foot from the ground; then I fastened my hand-kerchief to the nine sticks that stood erect, and extended it on all sides, till it was tight as the top of a drum; and the four parallel sticks rising about five inches higher than the handkerchief, served as ledges on each side. When I had finished my work, I desired the Emperor to let a troop of his best horse, twenty-four in number, come and exercise upon this plain. His Majesty approved of the proposal, and I took them up, one by one, in my hands, ready mounted and armed, with the proper officers to exercise them. As soon as they got into order, they divided into two parties, performed mock skirmishes, discharged blunt arrows, drew their swords, fled and pursued, attacked and retired, and in short discovered the best military discipline I ever beheld. The parallel sticks secured them and their horses from falling over the stage; and the Emperor was so much delighted, that he ordered this entertainment to be repeated several days, and once was pleased to be lifted up and give the word of command; and, with great difficulty, persuaded even the Empress herself to let me hold her in her close chair within two yards of the stage, from whence she was able to take a full view of the whole performance. It was my good fortune that no ill accident happened in these entertainments, only once a fiery horse, that belonged to one of the captains, pawing with his hoof, struck a hole in my handkerchief, and his foot slipping, he overthrew his rider and himself; but I immediately relieved them both, and covering the hole with one hand, I set down the troop with the other, in the same manner as I took them up. The horse that fell was strained in the left shoulder, but the rider got no hurt, and I repaired my handkerchief as well as I could: however, I would not trust to the strength of it any more in such dangerous enterprises.

About two or three days before I was set at liberty, as I was entertaining the court with these kind of feats, there arrived an express to inform his Majesty, that some of his subjects riding near the place where I was first taken up, had seen a great black substance lying on the ground, very oddly shaped, extending its edges round as wide as his Majesty's bedchamber, and rising up in the middle as high as a man; that it was no living creature, as they at first apprehended, for it lay on the grass without motion, and some of them had walked round it several times: that by mounting upon each other's shoulders, they had got to the top, which was flat and even, and stamping upon it they found it was hollow within; that they humbly conceived it might be something belonging to the Man-Mountain; and if his Majesty pleased, they would undertake to bring it with only five horses. I presently knew what they meant, and was glad at heart to receive this intelligence. It seems upon my first reaching the shore after our shipwreck, I was in such confusion, that before I came to the place where I went to sleep, my hat, which I had fastened with a string to my head while I was rowing, and had stuck on all the time I was swimming, fell off after I came to land; the string, as I conjecture, breaking by some accident which I never observed, but thought my hat had been lost at sea. I intreated his Imperial Majesty to give orders it might be brought to me as soon as possible, describing to him the use and the nature of it: and the next day the waggoners arrived with it, but not in a very good condition; they had bored two holes in the brim, within an inch and half of the edge, and fastened two hooks in the holes; these hooks were tied by a long cord to the harness, and thus my hat was dragged along for above half an English mile; but the ground in that country being extremely smooth and level, it received less damage than I expected.

Two days after this adventure, the Emperor having

ordered that part of his army which quarters in and about his metropolis to be in readiness, took a fancy of diverting himself in a very singular manner. He desired I would stand like a Colossus, with my legs as far asunder as I conveniently could. He then commanded his General (who was an old experienced leader, and a great patron of mine) to draw up the troops in close order, and march them under me; the foot by twenty-four in a breast, and the horse by sixteen, with drums beating, colours flying, and pikes advanced. This body consisted of three thousand foot, and a thousand horse. His Majesty gave orders, upon pain of death, that every soldier in his march should observe the strictest decency with regard to my person; which, however, could not prevent some of the younger officers from turning up their eyes as they passed under me. And, to confess the that truth, my breeches were at that time in so ill a condition, they afforded some opportunities for laughter and admiration.

I had sent so many memorials and petitions for my liberty, that his Majesty at length mentioned the matter, first in the cabinet, and then in a full council; where it was opposed by none, except Skyresh Bolgolam, who was pleased, without any provocation, to be my mortal enemy. But it was carried against him by the whole board, and confirmed by the Emperor. That minister was *Galbet*, or Admiral of the Realm, very much in his master's confidence, and a person well versed in affairs, but of a morose and sour complexion. However, he was at length persuaded to comply; but prevailed that the articles and conditions upon which I should be set free, and to which I must swear, should be drawn up by himself. These articles were brought to me by Skyresh Bolgolam in person, attended by two under-secretaries, and several persons of distinction. After they were read, I was demanded to swear to the performance of them; first in the manner of my own country, and afterwards in the method prescribed by their laws; which was to hold my right foot in my left hand, to place the middle finger of my right hand on the crown of my head, and my thumb on the tip of my right ear. But because the reader may be curious to have some idea of the style and manner of expression peculiar to that people, as well as to know the articles upon which I recovered my liberty, I have made a translation of the whole instrument word for word, as near as I was able, which I here offer to the public.

GOLBASTO MOMAREM EVLAME GURDILO SHEFIN MULLY ULLY GUE, most mighty Emperor of Lilliput, delight and terror of the universe, whose dominions extend five thousand *blustrugs* (about twelve miles in circumference) to the extremities of the globe; monarch of all monarchs, taller than the sons of men; whose feet press down to the centre, and whose head strikes against the sun; at whose nod the princes of the earth shake their knees; pleasant as the spring, comfortable as the summer, fruitful as autumn, dreadful as winter. His most sublime Majesty proposeth to the Man-Mountain, lately arrived to our celestial dominions, the following articles, which by a solemn oath he shall be obliged to perform.

1st, The Man-Mountain shall not depart from our dominions, without our licence under our great seal.

2d, He shall not presume to come into our metropolis, without our express order; at which time, the inhabitants shall have two hours warning to keep within their doors.

3d, The said Man-Mountain shall confine his walks to our principal high roads, and not offer to walk or lie down in a meadow or field of corn.

4th, As he walks the said roads, he shall take the utmost care not to trample upon the bodies of any of our loving subjects, their horses, or carriages, nor take any of our subjects into his hands, without their own consent.

5th, If an express requires extraordinary dispatch, the Man-Mountain shall be obliged to carry in his pocket the messenger and horse a six days journey once in every moon, and return the said messenger back (if so required) safe to our Imperial Presence.

6th, He shall be our ally against our enemies in the Island of Blefuscu, and do his utmost to destroy their fleet, which is now preparing to invade us.

7th, That the said Man-Mountain shall, at his times of leisure, be aiding and assisting to our workmen, in helping to raise certain great stones, towards covering the wall of the principal park, and other our royal buildings.

8th, That the said Man-Mountain shall, in two moons' time, deliver in an exact survey of the circumference of our dominions by a computation of his own paces round the coast.

Lastly, That upon his solemn oath to observe all the above articles, the said Man-Mountain shall have a daily allowance of meat and drink sufficient for the support of 1728 of our subjects, with free access to our Royal Person, and other marks of our favour. Given at our Palace at Belfaborac the twelfth day of the ninety-first moon of our reign.

I swore and subscribed to these articles with great cheerfulness and content, although some of them were not so honourable as I could have wished; which proceeded wholly from the malice of Skyresh Bolgolam, the High-Admiral: whereupon my chains were immediately unlocked, and I was at full liberty; the Emperor himself in person did me the honour to be by at the whole ceremony. I make my acknowledgements by prostrating myself at his Majesty's feet: but he commanded me to rise; and after many gracious expressions, which, to avoid the censure of vanity, I shall not repeat, he added, that he hoped I should prove a useful servant, and well deserve all the favours he had already conferred upon me, or might do for the future.

The reader may please to observe, that in the last article for the recovery of my liberty, the Emperor stipulates to allow me a quantity of meat and drink sufficient for the support of 1728 Lilliputians. Some time after, asking a friend at court how they came to fix on that determinate number; he told me that his Majesty's mathematicians, having taken the height of my body by the help of a quadrant, and finding it to exceed theirs in the proportion of twelve to one, they concluded from the similarity of their bodies, that mine must contain at least 1728 of theirs, and consequently would require as much food as was necessary to support that number of Lilliputians. By which, the reader may conceive an idea of the ingenuity of that people, as well as the prudent and exact economy of so great a prince.

CHAPTER IV

Mildendo, *the metropolis of* Lilliput, *described, together with the Emperor's palace. A conversation between the Author and a principal Secretary, concerning the affairs of that empire. The Author's offers to serve the Emperor in his wars.*

THE first request I made after I had obtained my liberty, was, that I might have licence to see Mildendo, the metropolis; which the Emperor easily granted me, but with a special charge to do no hurt either to the inhabitants or their houses. The people had notice by proclamation of my design to visit the town. The wall which encompassed it, is two foot and a half high, and at least eleven inches broad, so that a coach and horses may be driven very safely round it; and it is flanked with strong towers at ten foot distance. I stepped over the great Western Gate, and passed very gently, and sideling through the two principal streets, only in my short waistcoat, for fear of damaging the roofs and eaves of the houses with the skirts of my coat. I walked with the utmost circumspection, to avoid treading on any stragglers, that might remain in the streets, although the orders were very strict, that all people should keep in their houses, at their own peril. The garret windows and tops of houses were so crowded with spectators, that I thought in all my travels I had not seen a more populous place. The city is an exact square, each side of the wall being five hundred foot long. The two great streets, which run cross and divide it into four quarters, are five foot wide.

The lanes and alleys, which I could not enter, but only viewed them as I passed, are from twelve to eighteen inches. The town is capable of holding five hundred thousand souls. The houses are from three to five stories The shops and markets well provided.

The Emperor's palace is in the centre of the city, where the two great streets meet. It is inclosed by a wall of two foot high, and twenty foot distant from the buildings. I had his Majesty's permission to step over this wall; and the space being so wide between that and the palace, I could easily view it on every side. The outward court is a square of forty foot, and includes two other courts: in the inmost are the royal apartments, which I was very desirous to see, but found it extremely difficult; for the great gates, from one square into another, were but eighteen inches high, and seven inches wide. Now the buildings of the outer court were at least five foot high, and it was impossible for me to stride over them without infinite damage to the pile, though the walls were strongly built of hewn stone, and four inches thick. At the same time the Emperor had a great desire that I should see the magnificence of his palace; but this I was not able to do till three days after, which I spent in cutting down with my knife some of the largest trees in the royal park, about an hundred yards distant from the city. Of these trees I made two stools, each about three foot high, and strong enough to bear my weight. The people having received notice a second time, I went again through the city to the palace, with my two stools in my hands. When I came to the side of the outer court, I stood upon one stool, and took the other in my hand: this I lifted over the roof, and gently set it down on the space between the first and second court, which was eight foot wide. I then stept over the buildings very conveniently from one stool to the other, and drew up the first after me with a hooked stick. By this contrivance I got into the inmost court; and lying down upon my side, I applied my face to the windows of the middle stories, which were left open on purpose, and discovered the most splendid apartments that can be imagined. There I saw the Empress and the young Princes, in their several lodgings, with their chief attendants about them. Her Imperial Majesty was pleased to smile very graciously upon me, and gave me out of the window her hand to kiss.

But I shall not anticipate the reader with farther descriptions of this kind, because I reserve them for a greater work, which is now almost ready for the press, containing a general description of this empire, from its first erection, through a long series of princes, with a particular account of their wars and politics, law, learning, and religion: their plants and animals, their peculiar manners and customs, with other matters very curious and useful; my chief design at present being only to relate such events and transactions as happened to the public, or to myself, during a residence of about nine months in that empire.

One morning, about a fortnight after I had obtained my liberty, Reldresal, principal Secretary (as they style him) of private Affairs, came to my house attended only by one servant. He ordered his coach to wait at a distance, and desired I would give him an hour's audience; which I readily consented to, on account of his quality and personal merits, as well as the many good offices he had done me during my solicitations at court. I offered to lie down, that he might the more conveniently reach my ear; but he chose rather to let me hold him in my hand during our conversation. He began with compliments on my liberty; said he might pretent to some merit in it: but, however, added, that if it had not been for the present situation of things at court, perhaps I might not have obtained it so soon. For, said he, as flourishing a condition as we may appear to be in to foreigners, we labour under two mighty evils; a violent faction at home, and the danger of an invasion by a most potent enemy from abroad. As to the first, you are to understand, that for about seventy moons past there have been two struggling parties in this empire, under the names of *Tramecksan* and *Slamecksan*, from the high and low heels on their shoes, by which they distinguish themselves. It is alleged indeed, that the high heels are most agreeable to our ancient constitution: but however this be, his Majesty hath determined to make use of only low heels in the administration of the government, and all offices in the gift of the Crown, as you cannot but observe; and particularly, that his Majesty's Imperial heels are lower at least by a *drurr* than any of his court; (*drurr* is a measure about the fourteenth part of an inch). The animosities between these two parties run so high, that they will neither eat nor drink, nor talk with each other. We compute the *Tramecksan*, or High-Heels, to exceed us in number; but the power is wholly on our side. We apprehend his Imperial Highness, the Heir to the Crown, to have some tendency towards the High-Heels; at least we can plainly discover one of his heels higher than the other, which gives him a hobble in his gait. Now, in the midst of these intestine disquiets, we are threatened with an invasion from the Island of Blefuscu, which is the other great empire of the universe, almost as large and powerful as this of his Majesty. For as to what we have heard you affirm, that there are other kingdoms and states in the world inhabited by human creatures as large as yourself, our philosophers are in much doubt, and would rather conjecture that you dropped from the moon, or one of the stars; because it is certain, that an hundred mortals of your bulk would, in a short time, destroy all the fruits and cattle of his Majesty's dominions. Besides, our histories of six thousand moons make no mention of any other regions, than the two great empires of Lilliput and Blefuscu. Which two mighty powers have, as I was going to tell you, been engaged in a most obstinate war for six and thirty moons past. It began upon the following occasion. It is allowed on all hands, that the primitive way of breaking eggs before we eat them, was upon the larger end: but his present Majesty's grandfather, while he was a boy, going to eat an egg, and breaking it according to the ancient practice, happened to cut one of his fingers. Whereupon the Emperor his father published an edict, commanding all his subjects, upon great penalties, to break the smaller end of their eggs. The people so highly resented this law, that our histories tell us there have been six rebellions raised on that account; wherein one Emperor lost his life, and another his crown. These civil commotions were constantly fomented by the monarchs of Blefuscu; and when they were quelled, the exiles always fled for refuge to that empire. It is computed, that eleven thousand persons have, at several times, suffered death, rather than submit to break their eggs at the smaller end. Many hundred large volumes have been published upon this controversy: but the books of the Big-Endians have been long forbidden, and the whole party rendered incapable by law of holding employments. During the course of these troubles, the Emperors of Blefuscu did frequently expostulate by the ambassadors, accusing us of making a schism in religion, by offending against a funda-mental doctrine of our great prophet Lustrog, in the fifty-fourth chapter of the Blundecral (which is their Alcoran). This, however, is thought to be a mere strain upon the text: for the words are these; *That all true believers break their eggs at the convenient end:* and which is the convenient end, seems, in my humble opinion, to be left to every man's conscience, or at least in the power of the chief magistrate to determine. Now the Big-Endian exiles have found so much credit in the Emperor of Blefuscu's court, and so much private assistance and encouragement from their party here at home, that a bloody war has been carried on between the two empires for six and thirty moons with various success; during which time we have lost forty capital ships, and a much greater number of smaller vessels, together with thirty thousand of our best seamen and soldiers; and the damage received by the enemy is reckoned to be somewhat greater than ours. However, they have now equipped a numerous fleet, and are just preparing to make a descent upon us; and his Imperial Majesty, placing great confidence in your valour and strength, has commanded me to lay this account of his affairs before you.

I desired the Secretary to present my humble duty to the Emperor, and to let him know, that I thought it would not become me, who was a foreigner, to interfere with parties; but I was ready, with the hazard of my life, to defend his person and state against all invaders.

CHAPTER V

The Author, by an extraordinary stratagem, prevents an invasion. A high title of honour is conferred upon him. Ambassadors arrive from the Emperor of Blefuscu, and sue for peace. The Empress's apartment on fire by an accident, the Author instrumental in saving the rest of the palace.

THE Empire of Blefuscu is an island situated to the north north-east side of Lilliput, from whence it is parted only by a channel of eight hundred yards wide. I had not yet seen it, and upon this notice of an intended invasion, I avoided appearing on that side of the coast, for fear of being discovered by some of the enemy's ships, who had received no intelligence of me, all intercourse between the two empires having been strictly forbidden during the war, upon pain of death, and an embargo laid by our Emperor upon all vessels whatsoever. I communicated to his Majesty a project I had formed of seizing the enemy's whole fleet: which, as our scouts assured us, lay at anchor in the harbour ready to sail with the first fair wind. I consulted the most experienced seamen, upon the depth of the channel, which they had often plumbed, who told me, that in the middle at high-water it was seventy *glumgluffs* deep, which is about six foot of European measure; and the rest of it fifty *glumgluffs* at most. I walked towards the north-east coast over against Blefuscu; and lying down behind a hillock, took out my small pocket perspective-glass, and viewed the enemy's fleet at anchor, consisting of about fifty men of war, and a great number of transports: I then came back to my house, and gave order (for which I had a warrant) for a great quantity of the strongest cable and bars of iron. The cable was about as thick as packthread, and the bars of the length and size of a knitting-needle. I trebled the cable to make it stronger, and for the same reason I twisted three of the iron bars together, binding the extremities into a hook. Having thus fixed fifty hooks to as many cables, I went back to the north-east coast, and putting off my coat, shoes, and stockings, walked into the sea in my leathern jerkin, about half an hour before high water. I waded with what haste I could, and swam in the middle about thirty yards till I felt ground; I arrived at the fleet in less than half an hour. The enemy was so frightened when they saw me, that they leaped out of their ships, and swam to shore, where there could not be fewer than thirty thousand souls. I then took my tackling, and fastening a hook to the hole at the prow of each, I tied all the cords together at the end. While I was thus employed, the enemy discharged several thousand arrows, many of which stuck in my hands and face; and besides the excessive smart, gave me much disturbance in my work. My greatest apprehension was for my eyes, which I should have infallibly lost, if I had not suddenly thought of an expedient. I kept among other little necessaries a pair of spectacles in a private pocket, which, as I observed before, had scaped the Emperor's searchers. These I took out and fastened as strongly as I could upon my nose, and thus armed went on boldly with my work in spite of the enemy's arrows, many of which struck against the glasses of my spectacles, but without any other effect, further than a little to discompose them. I had now fastened all the hooks, and taking the knot in my hand, began to pull; but not a ship would stir, for they were all too fast held by their anchors, so that the boldest part of my enterprise remained. I therefore let go the cord, and leaving the hooks fixed to the ships, I resolutely cut with my knife the cables that fastened the anchors, receiving about two hundred shots in my face and hands; then I took up the knotted end of the cables, to which my hooks were tied, and with great ease drew fifty of the enemy's largest men of war after me.

The Blefuscudians, who had not the least imagination of what I intended, were at first confounded with astonishment.

They had seen me cut the cables, and thought my design was only to let the ships run a-drift, or fall foul on each other: but when they perceived the whole fleet moving in order, and saw me pulling at the end, they set up such a scream of grief and despair, that it is almost impossible to describe or conceive. When I had got out of danger, I stopped awhile to pick out the arrows that stuck in my hands and face; and rubbed on some of the same ointment that was given me at my first arrival, as I have formerly mentioned. I then took off my spectacles, and waiting about an hour, till the tide was a little fallen, I waded through the middle with my cargo, and arrived safe at the royal port of Lilliput.

The Emperor and his whole court stood on the shore, expecting the issue of this great adventure. They saw the ships move forward in a large half-moon, but could not discern me, who was up to my breast in water. When I advanced to the middle of the channel, they were yet in more pain, because I was under water to my neck. The Emperor concluded me to be drowned, and that the enemy's fleet was approaching in a hostile manner: but he was soon eased of his fears, for the channel growing shallower every step I made, I came in a short time within hearing, and holding up the end of the cable by which the fleet was fastened, I cried in a loud voice, *Long live the most puissant Emperor of Lilliput!* This great prince received me at my landing with all possible encomiums, and created me a *Nardac* upon the spot, which is the highest title of honour among them.

His Majesty desired I would take some other opportunity of bringing all the rest of his enemy's ships into his ports. And so unmeasurable is the ambition of princes, that he seemed to think of nothing less than reducing the whole empire of Blefuscu into a province, and governing it by a viceroy; of destroying the Big-Endian exiles, and compelling that people to break the smaller end of their eggs, by which he would remain the sole monarch of the whole world. But I endeavoured to divert him from this design, by many arguments drawn from the topics of policy as well as justice; and I plainly protested, that I would never be an instrument of bringing a free and brave people into slavery. And when the matter was debated in council, the wisest part of the ministry were of my opinion.

This open bold declaration of mine was so opposite to the schemes and politics of his Imperial Majesty, that he could never forgive it; he mentioned it in a very artful manner at council, where I was told that some of the wisest appeared, at least by their silence, to be of my opinion; but others, who were my secret enemies, could not forbear some expressions, which by a side-wind reflected on me. And from this time began an intrigue between his Majesty and a junto of ministers maliciously bent against me, which broke out in less than two months, and had like to have ended in my utter destruction. Of so little weight are the greatest services to princes, when put into the balance with a refusal to gratify their passions.

About three weeks after this exploit, there arrived a solemn embassy from Blefuscu, with humble offers of a peace; which was soon concluded upon conditions very advantageous to our Emperor, wherewith I shall not trouble the reader. There were six ambassadors, with a train of about five hundred persons, and their entry was very magnificent, suitable to the grandeur of their master, and the importance of their business. When their treaty was finished, wherein I did them several good offices by the credit I now had, or at least appeared to have at court, their Excellencies, who were privately told how much I had been their friend, made me a visit in form. They began with many compliments upon my valour and generosity, invited me to that kingdom in the Emperor their master's name, and desired me to show them some proofs of my prodigious strength, of which they had heard so many wonders; wherein I readily obliged them, but shall not trouble the reader with the particulars.

When I had for some time entertained their Excellencies, to their infinite satisfaction and surprise, I desired they would do me the honour to present my most humble respect to the Emperor their master, the renown of whose virtues had so justly filled the whole world with admiration, and whose royal person I resolved to attend before I returned to my own country: accordingly, the next time I had the honour to see our Emperor, I desired his general licence to wait on the Blefuscudian monarch, which he was pleased to grant me, as I could perceive, in a very cold manner; but could not guess the reason, till I had a whisper from a certain person, that Flimnap and Bolgolam had represented my intercourse with those ambassadors as a mark of disaffection, from which I am sure my heart was wholly free. And this was the first time I began to conceive some imperfect idea of courts and ministers.

It is to be observed, that these ambassadors spoke to me by an interpreter, the languages of both empires differing as much from each other as any two in Europe, and each nation priding itself upon the antiquity, beauty, and energy of their own tongues, with an avowed contempt for that of their neighbour; yet our Emperor, standing upon the advantage he had got by the seizure of their fleet, obliged them to deliver their credentials, and make their speech in the Lilliputian tongue. And it must be confessed, that from the great intercourse of trade and commence between both realms, from the continual reception of exiles, which is mutual among them, and from the custom in each empire to send their young nobility and richer gentry to the others, in order to polish themselves by seeing the world, and understanding men and manners; there are few persons of distinction, or merchants, or seamen, who dwell in the maritime parts, but what can hold conversation in both tongues; as I found some weeks after, when I went to pay my respects to the Emperor of Blefuscu, which in the midst of great misfortune, through the malice of my enemies, proved a very happy adventure to me, as I shall relate in its proper place.

The reader may remember, that when I signed those articles upon which I recovered my liberty, there were some which I disliked upon account of their being too servile, neither could anything but an extreme necessity have forced me to submit. But being now a *Nardac* of the highest rank

4

in that empire, such offices were looked upon as below my dignity, and the Emperor (to do him justice) never once mentioned them to me. However, it was not long before I had an opportunity of doing his Majesty, at least, as I then thought, a most signal service. I was alarmed at midnight with the cries of many hundred people at my door; by which being suddenly awaked, I was in some kind of terror. I heard the word *burglum* repeated incessantly: several of the Emperor's court, making their way through the crowd, entreated me to come immediately to the palace, where her Imperial Majesty's apartment was on fire, by the carelessness of a maid of honour, who fell asleep while she was reading a romance. I got up in an instant; and orders being given to clear the way before me, and it being likewise a moonshine night, I made a shift to get to the Palace without trampling on any of the people. I found they had already applied ladders to the walls of the apartment, and were well provided with buckets, but the water was at some distance. These buckets were about the size of a large thimble, and the poor people supplied me with them as fast as they could; but the flame was so violent that they did little good. I might easily have stifled it with my coat, which I unfortunately left behind me for haste, and came away only in my leathern jerkin. The case seemed wholly desperate and deplorable; and this magnificent palace would have infallibly been burnt down to the ground, if, by a presence of mind, unusual to me, I had not suddenly thought of an expedient. I had the evening before drunk plentifully of a most delicious wine, called *glimigrim*, (the Blefuscudians call it *flunec*, but ours is esteemed the better sort) which is very diuretic. By the luckiest chance in the world, I had not discharged myself of any part of it. The heat I had contracted by coming very near the flames, and by labouring to quench them, made the wine begin to operate by urine; which I voided in such a quantity, and applied so well to the proper places, that in three minutes the fire was wholly extinguished, and the rest of that noble pile, which had cost so many ages in erecting, preserved from destruction.

It was now day-light, and I returned to my house without waiting to congratulate with the Emperor: because, although I had done a very eminent piece of service, yet I could not tell how his Majesty might resent the manner by which I had performed it: for, by the fundamental laws of the realm, it is capital in any person, of what quality soever, to make water within the precincts of the palace. But I was a little comforted by a message from his Majesty, that he would give orders to the Grand Justiciary for passing my pardon in form; which, however, I could not obtain. And I was privately assured, that the Empress, conceiving the greatest abhorrence of what I had done, removed to the most distant side of the court, firmly resolved that those buildings should never be repaired for her use: and, in the presence of her chief confidents could not forbear vowing revenge.

CHAPTER VI

Of the inhabitants of Lilliput; *their learning, laws, and customs, the manner of educating their children. The Author's way of living in that country. His vindication of a great lady.*

ALTHOUGH I intend to leave the description of this empire to a particular treatise, yet in the mean time I am content to gratify the curious reader with some general ideas. As the common size of the natives is somewhat under six inches high, so there is an exact proportion in all other animals, as well as plants and trees: for instance, the tallest horses and oxen are between four and five inches in height, the sheep an inch and a half, more or less: their geese about the bigness of a sparrow, and so the several gradations downwards till you come to the smallest, which, to my sight, were almost invisible; but nature hath adapted the eyes of the Lilliputians to all objects proper for their view: they see with great exactness, but at no great distance. And to show the sharpness of their sight towards objects that are near, I have been much pleased with observing a

cook pulling a lark, which was not so large as a common
fly; and a young girl threading an invisible needle with
invisible silk. Their tallest trees are about seven foot high:
I mean some of those in the great royal park, the tops
whereof I could but just reach with my fist clinched. The
other vegetables are in the same proportion; but this I
leave to the reader's imagination.

I shall say but little at present of their learning, which
for many ages hath flourished in all its branches among
them: but their manner of writing is very peculiar, being
neither from the left to the right, like the Europeans; nor
from the right to the left, like the Arabians; nor from up
to down, like the Chinese; nor from down to up, like the
Cascagians; but aslant from one corner of the paper to the
other, like ladies in England.

They bury their dead with their heads directly downwards,
because they hold an opinion, that in eleven thousand
moons they are all to rise again, in which period the earth
(which they conceive to be flat) will turn upside down, and
by this means they shall, at their resurrection, be found
ready standing on their feet. The learned among them
confess the absurdity of this doctrine, but the practice still
continues, in compliance to the vulgar.

There are some laws and customs in this empire very
peculiar; and if they were not so directly contrary to those
of my own dear country, I should be tempted to say a
little in their justification. It is only to be wished, that
they were as well executed. The first I shall mention,
related to informers. All crimes against the state are
punished here with the utmost severity; but if the person
accused maketh his innocence plainly to appear upon his
trial, the accuser is immediately put to an ignominious
death; and out of his goods or lands, the innocent person
is quadruply recompensed for the loss of his time, for the
danger he underwent, for the hardship of his imprisonment,
and for all the charges he hath been at in making his defence.
Or, if that fund be deficient, it is largely supplied by the
Crown. The Emperor does also confer on him some

public mark of his favour, and proclamation is made of his innocence through the whole city.

They look upon fraud as a greater crime than theft, and therefore seldom fail to punish it with death; for they allege, that care and vigilance, with a very common under-standing, may preserve a man's goods from thieves, but honesty has no fence against superior cunning; and since it is necessary that there should be a perpetual intercourse of buying and selling, and dealing upon credit, where fraud is permitted and connived at, or hath no law to punish it, the honest dealer is always undone, and the knave gets the advantage. I remember when I was once interceding with the Emperor for a criminal who had wronged his master of a great sum of money, which he had received by order, and ran away with; and happening to tell his Majesty, by way of extenuation, that it was only a breach of trust; the Emperor thought it monstrous in me to offer, as a defence, the greatest aggravation of the crime: and truly I had little to say in return, farther than the common answer, that different nations had different customs; for, I confess, I was heartily ashamed.

Although we usually call reward and punishment the two hinges upon which all government turns, yet I could never observe this maxim to be put in practice by any nation except that of Lilliput. Whoever can there bring sufficient proof that he had strictly observed the laws of his country for seventy three moons, hath a claim to certain privileges, according to his quality and condition of life, with a proportionate sum of money out of a fund appro-priated for that use; he likewise acquires the title of *Snilpall*, or Legal, which is added to his name, but does not descend to his posterity. And these people thought it a prodigious defect of policy among us, when I told them that our laws were enforced only by penalties, without any mention of reward. It is upon this account that the image of Justice, in their courts of judicature, is formed with six eyes, two before, as many behind, and on each side one, to signify circumspection; with a bag of gold open in her right hand,

and a sword sheathed in her left, to show she is more disposed to reward than to punish.

In choosing persons for all employments, they have more regard to good morals than to great abilities; for, since government is necessary to mankind, they believe that the common size of human understandings is fitted to some station or other, and that Providence never intended to make the management of public affairs a mystery, to be comprehended only by a few persons of sublime genius, of which there seldom are three born in an age: but they suppose truth, justice, temperance, and the like, to be in every man's power; the practice of which virtues, assisted by experience and a good intention, would qualify any man for the service of his country, except where a course of study is required. But they thought the want of moral virtues was so far from being supplied by superior endowments of the mind, that employments could never be put into such dangerous hands as those of persons so qualified and at least, that the mistakes committed by ignorance in a virtuous disposition, would never be of such fatal consequence to the public weal, as the practices of a man whose inclinations led him to be corrupt, and had great abilities to manage, and multiply, and defend his corruptions.

In like manner the disbelief of a Divine Providence renders a man uncapable of holding any public station; for, since kings avow themselves to be the deputies of Providence the Lilliputians think nothing can be more absurd than for a prince to employ such men as disown the authority under which he acts.

In relating these and the following laws, I would only be understood to mean the original institutions, and not the most scandalous corruptions into which these people are fallen by the degenerate nature of man. For as to that infamous practice of acquiring great employments by dancing on the ropes, or badges of favour and distinction by leaping over sticks and creeping under them, the reader is to observe, that they were first introduced by the grandfather of the Emperor now reigning, and grew to the present height, by the gradual increase of party and faction.

Ingratitude is among them a capital crime, as we read it to have been in some other countries: for they reason thus, that whoever makes ill returns to his benefactor, must needs be a common enemy to the rest of mankind, from whom he hath received no obligation, and therefore such a man is not fit to live.

Their notions relating to the duties of parents and children differ extremely from ours. For, since the conjunction of male and female is founded upon the great law of nature, in order to propagate and continue the species, the Lilliputians will needs have it, that men and women are joined together like other animals, by the motives of concupiscence; and that their tenderness towards their young proceeds from the like natural principle: for which reason they will never allow, that a child is under any obligation to his father for begetting him, or to his mother for bringing him into the world, which, considering the miseries of human life, was neither a benefit in itself, nor intended so by his parents, whose thoughts in their love-encounters were otherwise employed. Upon these, and the like reasonings, their opinion is, that parents are the last of all others to be trusted with the education of their own children; and therefore they have in every town public nurseries, where all parents, except cottagers and labourers, are obliged to send their infants of both sexes to be reared and educated when they come to the age of twenty moons, at which time they are supposed to have some rudiments of docility. These schools are of several kinds, suited to different qualities, and to both sexes. They have certain professors well skilled in preparing children for such a condition of life as befits the rank of their parents, and their own capacities as well as inclinations. I shall first say something of the male nurseries, and then of the female.

The nurseries for males of noble or eminent birth, are provided with grave and learned professors, and their several deputies. The clothes and food of the children are plain and simple. They are bred up in the principles of honour, justice, courage, modesty, clemency, religion, and love of their country; they are always employed in some business, except in the times of eating and sleeping, which are very short, and two hours for diversions, consisting of bodily exercises. They are dressed by men till four years of age, and then are obliged to dress themselves, although their quality be ever so great; and the women attendants, who are aged proportionably to ours at fifty, perform only the most menial offices. They are never suffered to converse with servants, but go together in small or greater numbers to take their diversions, and always in the presence of a professor, or one of his deputies; whereby they avoid those early bad impressions of folly and vice to which our children are subject. Their parents are suffered to see them only twice a year; the visit is to last but an hour. They are allowed to kiss the child at meeting and parting; but a professor, who always stands by on those occasions, will not suffer them to whisper, or use any fondling expressions, or bring any presents of toys, sweetmeats, and the like.

The pension from each family for the education and entertainment of a child, upon failure of due payment, is levied by the Emperor's officers.

The nurseries for children of ordinary gentlemen, merchants, traders, and handicrafts, are managed proportionably after the same manner; only those designed for trades, are put out apprentices at eleven years old, whereas those of persons of quality continue in their exercises till fifteen, which answers to one and twenty with us: but the confinement is gradually lessened for the last three years.

In the female nurseries, the young girls of quality are educated much like the males, only they are dressed by orderly servants of their own sex; but always in the presence of a professor or deputy, till they come to dress themselves, which is at five years old. And if it be found that these nurses ever presume to entertain the girls with frightful or foolish stories, or the common follies practised by chambermaids among us, they are publicly whipped thrice about the city, imprisoned for a year, and banished for life to the most desolate part of the country. Thus the young ladies there are as much ashamed of being cowards and fools, as the men, and despite all personal ornaments beyond decency and cleanliness: neither did I perceive any difference in their education, made by the difference of sex, only that the exercises of the females were not altogether so robust; and that some rules were given them relating to domestic life, and a smaller compass of learning was enjoined them: for their maxim is, that among people of quality, a wife should be always a reasonable and agreeable companion, because she cannot always be young. When the girls are twelve years old, which among them is the marriageable age, their parents or guardians take them home, with great expressions of gratitude to the professors, and seldom without tears of the young lady and her companions.

In the nurseries of females of the meaner sort, the children are instructed in all kinds of works proper for their sex, and their several degrees: those intended for apprentices, are dismissed at seven years old, the rest are kept to eleven.

The meaner families who have children at these nurseries, are obliged, besides their annual pension, which is as low as possible, to return to the steward of the nursery a small monthly share of their gettings, to be a portion for the child; and therefore all parents are limited in their expenses by the law. For the Lilliputians think nothing can be more unjust, than for people, in subservience to their own appetites, to bring children into the world, and leave the burthen of supporting them on the public. As to persons of quality, they give security to appropriate a certain sum for each child, suitable to their condition; and these funds are always managed with good husbandry, and the most exact justice.

The cottagers and labourers keep their children at home, their business being only to till and cultivate the earth, and therefore their education is of little consequence to the public; but the old and diseased among them are supported by hospitals: for begging is a trade unknown in this empire.

And here it may perhaps divert the curious reader, to give some account of my domestic, and my manner of living in this country, during a residence of nine months and thirteen days. Having a head mechanically turned, and being likewise forced by necessity, I had made for myself a table and chair convenient enough, out of the largest trees in the royal park. Two hundred sempstresses were employed to make me shirts, and linen for my bed and table, all of the strongest and coarsest kind they could get; which, however, they were forced to quilt together in several folds, for the thickest was some degrees finer than lawn. Their linen is usually three inches wide, and three foot make a piece. The sempstresses took my measure as I lay on the ground, one standing at my neck, and another at my mid-leg, with a strong cord extended, that each held by the end, while the third measured the length of the cord with a rule of an inch long. Then they measured my right thumb, and desired no more; for by a mathematical computation, that twice round the thumb is once round the wrist, and so on to the neck and the waist, and by the help of my old shirt, which I displayed on the ground before them for a pattern, they fitted me exactly. Three hundred tailors were employed in the same manner to make me clothes; but they had another contrivance for taking my measure. I kneeled down, and they raised a ladder from the ground to my neck; upon this ladder one of them mounted, and let fall a plumb-line from my collar to the floor, which just answered the length of my coat: but my waist and arms I measured myself. When my clothes were finished, which was done in my house (for the largest of theirs would not have been able to hold them), they looked like the patch-work made by the ladies in England, only that mine were all of a colour.

I had three hundred cooks to dress my victuals, in little convenient huts built about my house, where they and their families lived, and prepared me two dishes a-piece. I took up twenty waiters in my hand, and placed them on the table: an hundred more attended below on the ground, some with dishes of meat, and some with barrels of wine, and other liquors, slung on their shoulders; all which the waiters above drew up as I wanted, in a very ingenious manner, by certain cords, as we draw the bucket up a well in Europe. A dish of their meat was a good mouthful, and a barrel of the liquor a reasonable draught. Their mutton yields to ours, but their beef is excellent. I have had a sirloin so large, that I have been forced to make three bits of it; but this is rare. My servants were astonished to see me eat it bones and all, as in our country we do the leg of a lark. Their geese and turkeys I usually eat at a mouthful, and I must confess they far exceed ours. Of their smaller fowl I could take up twenty or thirty at the end of my knife.

One day his Imperial Majesty, being informed of my way of living, desired that himself and his Royal Consort, with the young Princes of the blood of both sexes, might have the happiness (as he was pleased to call it) of dining with me. They came accordingly, and I placed them in chairs of state on my table, just over against me, with their guards about them. Flimnap, the Lord High Treasurer, attended there likewise with his white staff; and I observed he often looked on me with a sour countenance, which I would not seem to regard, but eat more than usual, in honour to my dear country, as well as to fill the court with admiration. I have some private reasons to believe, that this visit from his Majesty gave Flimnap an opportunity of doing me ill offices to his master. That minister had always been my secret enemy, though he outwardly caressed me more than was usual to the moroseness of his nature. He represented to the Emperor the low condition of his treasury; that he was forced to take up money at great discount; that exchequer bills would not circulate under nine per cent. below par; that in sport I had cost his Majesty above a million and a half of *sprugs* (their greatest gold coin, about the bigness of a spangle); and upon the whole, that it would be advisable in the Emperor to take the first fair occasion of dismissing me.

I am here obliged to vindicate the reputation of an excellent lady, who was an innocent sufferer upon my account. The Treasurer took a fancy to be jealous of his wife, from the malice of some evil tongues, who informed him that her Grace had taken a violent affection for my person; and the court-scandal ran for some time, that she once came privately to my lodging. This I solemnly declare to be a most infamous falsehood, without any grounds, farther than that her Grace was pleased to treat me with all innocent marks of freedom and friendship. I owe she came often to my house, but always publicly, nor ever without three more in the coach, who were usually her sister and young daughter, and some particular acquaintance; but this was common to many other ladies of the court. And I still appeal to my servants round, whether they at any time saw a coach at my door without knowing what persons were in it. On those occasions, when a servant had given me notice, my custom was to go immediately to the door; and, after paying my respects, to take up the coach and two horses very carefully in my hands (for, if there were six horses, the postillion always unharnessed four), and place them on a table, where I had fixed a moveable rim quite round, of five inches high, to prevent accidents. And I have often had four coaches and horses at once on my table full of company, while I sat in my chair leaning my face towards them; and when I was engaged with one set, the coachmen would gently drive the others round my table. I have passed many an afternoon very agreeably in these conversations. But I defy the Treasurer, or his two informers (I will name them, and let them make their best of it) Clustril and Drunlo, to prove that any person ever came to me *incognito*, except the secretary Reldresal, who was sent by express command of his Imperial Majesty, as I have before related. I should not have dwelt so long upon this particular, if it had not been a point wherein the reputation of a great lady is so nearly concerned, to say nothing of my own; though I then had the honour to be a *Nardac*, which the Treasurer himself is not; for all the world knows he is only a *Glumglum*, a title inferior by one degree, as that of a Marquis is to a Duke in England, although I allow he preceded me in right of his post. These false informations,

which I afterwards came to the knowledge of, by an accident
not proper to mention, made Flimnap, the Treasurer, show
his lady for some time an ill countenance, and me a worse;
and although he were at last undeceived and reconciled
to her, yet I lost all credit with him, and found my interest
decline very fast with the Emperor himself, who was indeed
too much governed by that favourite.

CHAPTER VII

*The Author, being informed of a design to accuse him of high-treason,
makes his escape to Blefuscu. His reception there.*

BEFORE I proceed to give an account of my leaving
this kingdom, it may be proper to inform the reader
of a private intrigue which had been for two months forming
against me.

I had been hitherto all my life a stranger to courts, for
which I was unqualified by the meanness of my condition.
I had indeed heard and read enough of the dispositions of
great princes and ministers; but never expected to have
found such terrible effects of them in so remote a country,
governed, as I thought, by very different maxims from those
in Europe.

When I was just preparing to pay my attendance on the
Emperor of Blefuscu, a considerable person at court (to
whom I had been very serviceable at a time when he lay
under the highest displeasure of his Imperial Majesty) came
to my house very privately at night in a close chair, and
without sending his name, desired admittance. The chairmen
were dismissed; I put the chair, with his Lordship in it,
into my coat-pocket: and giving orders to a trusty servant
to say I was indisposed and gone to sleep, I fastened the
door of my house, placed the chair on the table, according
to my usual custom, and sat down by it. After the common
salutations were over, observing his Lordship's countenance

full of concern, and enquiring into the reason, he desired I would hear him with patience in a matter that highly concerned my honour and my life. His speech was to the following effect, for I took notes of it as soon as he left me.

You are to know, said he, that several Committees of Council have been lately called in the most private manner on your account; but it is but two days since his Majesty came to a full resolution.

You are very sensible that Skyresh Bolgolam (*Galbet*, or High-Admiral) hath been your mortal enemy almost ever since your arrival. His original reasons I know not; but his hatred is much increased since your great success against Blefuscu, by which his glory, as Admiral, is obscured. This Lord, in conjunction with Flimnap the High-Treasurer, whose enmity against you is notorious on account of his lady, Limtoc the General, Lalcon the Chamberlain, and Balmuff the Grand Justiciary, have prepared articles of impeachment against you, for treason, and other capital crimes.

This preface made me so impatient, being conscious of my own merits and innocence, that I was going to interrupt; when he entreated me to be silent, and thus proceeded.

Out of gratitude for the favours you have done me, I procured information of the whole proceedings, and a copy of the articles, wherein I venture my head for your service.

Articles of Impeachment against Quinbus Flestrin
(*the* Man-Mountain.)

ARTICLE I

Whereas, by a statute made in the reign of his Imperial Majesty Calin Deffar Plune, it is enacted, that whoever shall make water within the precincts of the royal palace, shall be liable to the pains and penalties of high treason; notwithstanding, the said Quinbus Flestrin, in open breach of the said law, under colour of extinguishing the fire kindled in the apartment of his Majesty's most dear Imperial Consort, did maliciously, traitorously, and devilishly, by discharge of his urine, put out the said fire kindled in the said apartment, lying and being within the precincts of the said royal palace, against the statute in that case provided, *etc.* against the duty, *etc.*

ARTICLE II

That the said Quinbus Flestrin having brought the imperial fleet of Blefuscu into the royal port, and being afterwards commanded by his Imperial Majesty to seize all the other ships of the said empire of Blefuscu, and reduce that empire to a province, to be governed by a viceroy from hence, and to destroy and put to death not only all the Big-Endian exiles, but likewise all the people of that empire, who would not immediately forsake the Big-Endian heresy: He, the said Flestrin, like a false traitor against his most Auspicious, Serene, Imperial Majesty, did petition to be excused from the said service, upon pretence of unwillingness to force the consciences, or destroy the liberties and lives of an innocent people.

ARTICLE III

That, whereas certain ambassadors arrived from the court of Blefuscu, to sue for peace in his Majesty's court: He, the said Flestrin, did, like a false traitor, aid, abet, comfort, and divert the said ambassadors, although he knew them to be servants to a Prince who was lately an open enemy to his Imperial Majesty, and in open war against his said Majesty.

ARTICLE IV

That the said Quinbus Flestrin, contrary to the duty of a faithful subject, is now preparing to make a voyage to the court and empire of Blefuscu, for which he hath received only verbal licence from his Imperial Majesty; and under colour of the said licence, doth falsely and traitorously intend to take the said voyage, and thereby to aid, comfort, and abet the Emperor of Blefuscu, so late an enemy, and in open war with his Imperial Majesty aforesaid.

There are some other articles, but these are the most important, of which I have read you an abstract.

In the several debates upon this impeachment, it must be confessed that his Majesty gave many marks of his great lenity, often urging the services you had done him, and endeavouring to extenuate your crimes. The Treasurer and Admiral insisted that you should be put to the most painful and ignominious death, by setting fire on your house at night, and the General was to attend with twenty thousand men armed with poisoned arrows to shoot you on the face and hands. Some of your servants were to have private orders to strew a poisonous juice on your shirts, which would soon make you tear your own flesh, and die in the utmost torture. The General came into the same opinion; so that for a long time there was a majority against you. But his Majesty resolving, if possible, to spare your life, at last brought off the Chamberlain.

Upon this incident, Reldresel, principal Secretary for private Affairs, who always approved himself your true friend, was commanded by the Emperor to deliver his opinion, which he accordingly did; and therein justified the good thoughts you have of him. He allowed your crimes to be great, but that still there was room for mercy, the most commendable virtue in a prince, and for which his Majesty was so justly celebrated. He said, the friendship between you and him was so well known to the world, that perhaps the most honourable board might think him partial: however, in obedience to the command he had received, he would freely offer his sentiments. That if his Majesty, in consideration of your services, and pursuant to his own merciful disposition, would please to spare your life, and only give orders to put out both your eyes, he humbly conceived, that by this expedient, justice might in some measure be satisfied, and all the world would applaud the lenity of the Emperor, as well as the fair and generous proceedings of those who have the honour to be his counsellors. That the loss of your eyes would be no impediment to your bodily strength, by which you might still be useful to his Majesty. That blindness is an addition to courage, by concealing dangers from us; that the fear you had for your eyes, was the greatest difficulty in bringing over the enemy's fleet, and it would be sufficient for you to see by the eyes of the ministers, since the greatest princes do no more.

This proposal was received with the utmost disapprobation by the whole board. Bolgolam, the Admiral, could not preserve his temper; but rising up in fury, said, he wondered how the Secretary durst presume to give his opinion for preserving the life of a traitor: that the services you had performed, were, by all true reasons of state, the great aggravation of your crimes; that you, who were able to extinguish the fire, by discharge of urine in her Majesty's apartment (which he mentioned with horror), might, at another time, raise an inundation by the same means, to drown the whole palace; and the same strength which enabled you to bring over the enemy's fleet, might serve, upon the first discontent, to carry it back: that he had good reasons to think you were a Big-Endian in your heart; and as treason begins in the heart, before it appears in overt-acts, so he accused you as a traitor on that account, and therefore insisted you should be put to death.

The Treasurer was of the same opinion; he showed to what straits his Majesty's revenue was reduced by the charge of maintaining you, which would soon grow insupportable: that the Secretary's expedient of putting out your eyes was so far from being a remedy against this evil, that it would probably increase it, as it is manifest from the common practice of blinding some kind of fowl, after which they fed the faster, and grew sooner fat: that his sacred Majesty and the Council, who are your judges, were in their own consciences fully convinced of your guilt, which

5

was a sufficient argument to condemn you to death, without the formal proofs required by the strict letter of the law.

But his Imperial Majesty, fully determined against capital punishment, was graciously pleased to say, that since the Council thought the loss of your eyes too easy a censure, some other may be inflicted hereafter. And your friend the Secretary humbly desiring to be heard again, in answer to what the Treasurer had objected concerning the great charge his Majesty was at in maintaining you, said, that his Excellency, who had the sole disposal of the Emperor's revenue might easily provide against that evil, by gradually lessening your establishment; by which, for want of sufficient food, you would grow weak and faint, and lose your appetite, and consequently decay and consume in a few months; neither would the stench of your carcass be then so dangerous, when it should become more than half diminished; and immediately upon your death, five or six thousand of his Majesty's subjects might, in two or three days, cut your flesh from your bones, take it away by cart-loads, and bury it in distant parts to prevent infection, leaving the skeleton as a monument of admiration to posterity.

Thus by the great friendship of the Secretary, the whole affair was compromised. It was strictly enjoined, that the project of starving you by degrees should be kept a secret, but the sentence of putting out your eyes was entered on the books; none dissenting except Bolgolam the Admiral, who, being a creature of the Empress, was perpetually instigated by her Majesty to insist upon your death, she having borne perpetual malice against you, on account of that infamous and illegal method you took to extinguish the fire in her apartment.

In three days your friend the Secretary will be directed to come to your house, and read before you the articles of impeachment; and then to signify the great lenity and favour of his Majesty and Council, whereby you are only condemned to the loss of your eyes, which his Majesty doth not question you will gratefully and humbly submit to; and twenty of his Majesty's surgeons will attend, in order to see the operation well performed, by discharging very sharp-pointed arrows into the balls of your eyes, as you lie on the ground.

I leave to your prudence what measures you will take; and to avoid suspicion, I must immediately return in as private a manner as I came.

His Lordship did so, and I remained alone, under many doubts and perplexities of mind.

It was a custom introduced by this prince that his ministry (very different, as I have been assured, from the practices of former times,) that after the court had decreed any cruel execution, either to gratify the monarch's resentment, or the malice of a favourite, the Emperor always made a speech to his whole Council, expressing his great lenity and tenderness, as qualities known and confessed by all the world. This speech was immediately published through the kingdom; nor did any thing terrify the people so much as those encomiums on his Majesty's mercy; because it was observed, that the more these praises were enlarged and insisted on, the more inhuman was the punishment, and the sufferer more innocent. And as to myself, I must confess, having never been designed for a courtier either by my birth or education, I was so ill a judge of things, that I could not discover the lenity and favour of this sentence, but conceived it (perhaps erroneously) rather to be rigorous than gentle. I sometimes thought of standing my trial, for although I could not deny the facts alleged in the several articles, yet I hoped they would admit of some extenuations. But having in my life perused many state-trials, which I ever observed to terminate as the judges thought fit to direct, I durst not rely on so dangerous a decision, in so critical a juncture, and against such powerful enemies. Once I was strongly bent upon resistance, for while I had liberty, the whole strength of that empire could hardly subdue me, and I might easily with stones pelt the metropolis to pieces; but I soon rejected that project with horror, by remembering the oath I had made to the Emperor, the favours I received from him, and the high title of *Nardac* he conferred upon me.

Neither had I so soon learned the gratitude of courtiers, to persuade myself that his Majesty's present severities acquitted me of all past obligations.

At last I fixed upon a resolution, for which it is probable I may incur some censure, and not unjustly; for I confess I owe the preserving my eyes, and consequently my liberty, to my own great rashness and want of experience: because if I had then known the nature of princes and ministers, which I have since observed in many other courts, and their methods of treating criminals less obnoxious than myself, I should with great alacrity and readiness have submitted to so easy a punishment. But hurried on by the precipitancy of youth, and having his Imperial Majesty's licence to pay my attendance upon the Emperor of Blefuscu, I took this opportunity, before the three days were elapsed, to send a letter to my friend the Secretary, signifying my resolution of setting out that morning for Blefuscu pursuant to the leave I had got; and without waiting for an answer, I went to that side of the island where our fleet lay. I seized a large man of war, tied a cable to the prow, and, lifting up the anchors, I stripped myself, put my clothes (together with my coverlet, which I brought under my arm) into the vessel, and drawing it after me between wading and swimming, arrived at the royal port of Blefuscu, where the people had long expected me: they lent me two guides to direct me to the capital city, which is of the same name. I held them in my hands till I came within two hundred yards of the gate, and desired them to signify my arrival to one of the secretaries, and let him know, I there waited his Majesty's command. I had an answer in about an hour, that his Majesty, attended by the Royal Family, and great officers of the court, was coming out to receive me. I advanced a hundred yards. The Emperor and his train alighted from their horses, the Empress and ladies from their coaches, and I did not perceive they were in any fright or concern. I lay on the ground to kiss his Majesty's and the Empress's hands. I told his Majesty, that I was come according to my promise, and with the licence of the Emperor my master, to have the honour of seeing so mighty a monarch, and to offer him any service in my power, consistent with my duty to my own prince; not mentioning a word of my disgrace, because I had hitherto no regular information of it, and might suppose myself wholly ignorant of any such design; neither could I reasonably conceive that the Emperor would discover the secret while I was out of his power: wherein, however, it soon appeared I was deceived.

I shall not trouble the reader with the particular account of my reception at this court, which was suitable to the generosity of so great a prince; nor of the difficulties I was in for want of a house and bed, being forced to lie on the ground, wrapped up in my coverlet.

CHAPTER VIII

The Author, by a lucky accident, finds means to leave Blefuscu; and after some difficulties, returns safe to his native country.

THREE days after my arrival, walking out of curiosity to the north-east coast of the island, I observed, about half a league off, in the sea, somewhat that looked like a boat overturned. I pulled off my shoes and stockings, and wading two or three hundred yards, I found the object to approach nearer by force of the tide; and then plainly saw it to be a real boat, which I supposed might, by some tempest, have been driven from a ship; whereupon I returned immediately towards the city, and desired his Imperial Majesty to lend me twenty of the tallest vessels he had left after the loss of his fleet, and three thousand seamen under the command of his Vice-Admiral. This fleet sailed round, while I went back the shortest way to the coast where I first discovered the boat; I found the tide had driven it still nearer. The seamen were all provided with cordage, which I had beforehand twisted to a sufficient strength. When the ships came up, I stripped myself, and waded till I came within an hundred yards of the boat, after which I was forced to swim till I got up to it. The seamen threw me the end of the cord, which I fastened to a hole in the fore-part of the boat, and the other end to a man of war; but I found all my labour to little purpose; for being out of my depth, I was not able to work. In this necessity, I was forced to swim behind, and push the boat forwards as often as I could, with one of my hands; and the tide favouring me, I advanced so far, that I could just hold up my chin and feel the ground. I rested two or three minutes, and then gave the boat another shove, and so on till the sea was no higher than my arm-pits; and now the most laborious part being over, I took out my other cables, which were stowed in one of the ships, and fastening them first to the boat, and then to nine of the vessels which attended me; the wind being favourable, the seamen towed, and I shoved till we arrived within forty yards of the shore; and waiting till the tide was out, I got dry to the boat, and by the assistance of two thousand men, with ropes and engines, I made a shift to turn it on its bottom, and found it was but little damaged.

I shall not trouble the reader with the difficulties I was under by the help of certain paddles, which cost me ten days making, to get my boat to the royal port of Blefuscu, where a mighty concourse of people appeared upon my arrival, full of wonder at the sight of so prodigious a vessel. I told the Emperor that my good fortune had thrown this boat in my way, to carry me to some place from whence I might return into my native country, and begged his Majesty's orders for getting materials to fit it up, together with his licence to depart; which, after some kind expostulations, he was pleased to grant.

I did very much wonder, in all this time, not to have heard of any express relating to me from our Emperor to the court of Blefuscu. But I was afterwards given privately to understand, that his Imperial Majesty, never imagining I had the least notice of his designs, believed I was only gone to Blefuscu in performance of my promise, according to the licence he had given me, which was well known at our court, and would return in a few days when that ceremony was ended. But he was at last in pain at my long absence; and after consulting with the Treasurer, and the rest of that cabal, a person of quality was dispatched with the copy of the articles against me. This envoy had instructions to represent to the monarch of Blefuscu, the great lenity of his master, who was content to punish me no farther than with the loss of my eyes; that I had fled from justice, and if I did not return in two hours, I should be deprived of my title of *Nardac*, and declared a traitor. The envoy further added, that in order to maintain the peace and amity between both empires, his master expected, that his brother of Blefuscu would give orders to have me sent back to Lilliput, bound hand and foot, to be punished as a traitor.

The Emperor of Blefuscu having taken three days to consult, returned an answer consisting of many civilities and excuses. He said, that as for sending me bound, his brother knew it was impossible; that although I had deprived him of his fleet, yet he owed great obligations to me for many good offices I had done him in making the peace. That however both their Majesties would soon be made easy; for I had found a prodigious vessel on the shore, able to carry me on the sea, which he had given order to fit up with my own assistance and direction; and he hoped in a few weeks both empires would be freed from so insupportable an incumbrance.

With this answer the envoy returned to Lilliput, and the monarch of Blefuscu related to me all that had passed; offering me at the same time (but under the strictest confidence) his gracious protection, if I would continue in his service; wherein although I believed him sincere, yet I resolved never more to put my confidence in princes or ministers, where I could possibly avoid it; and therefore, with all due acknowledgments for his favourable intentions, I humbly begged to be excused. I told him, that since fortune, whether good or evil, had thrown a vessel in my way, I was resolved to venture myself in the ocean, rather than be an occasion of difference between two such mighty monarchs. Neither did I find the Emperor at all displeased; and I discovered by a certain accident, that he was very glad of my resolution, and so were most of his ministers.

These considerations moved me to hasten my departure somewhat sooner than I intended; to which the court, impatient to have me gone, very readily contributed. Five hundred workmen were employed to make two sails to my boat, according to my directions, by quilting thirteen fold of their strongest linen together. I was at the pains of making ropes and cables, by twisting ten, twenty or thirty of the thickest and strongest of theirs. A great stone that I happened to find, after a long search, by the sea-shore, served me for an anchor. I had the tallow of three hundred cows for greasing my boat, and other uses. I was at incredible pains in cutting down some of the largest timber-trees for oars and masts, wherein I was, however, much assisted by his Majesty's ship-carpenters, who helped me in smoothing them, after I had done the rough work.

In about a month, when all was prepared, I sent to receive his Majesty's commands, and to take my leave. The Emperor and Royal Family came out of the palace; I lay down on my face to kiss his hand, which he very graciously gave me: so did the Empress and young Princes of the blood. His majesty presented me with fifty purses of two hundred *sprugs* a-piece, together with his picture at full length, which I put immediately into one of my gloves, to keep it from being hurt. The ceremonies at my departure were too many to trouble the reader with at this time.

I stored the boat with the carcases of an hundred oxen, and three hundred sheep, with bread and drink proportionable, and as much meat ready dressed as four hundred cooks could provide. I took with me six cows and two bulls alive, with as many ewes and rams, intending to carry them into my own country, and propagate the breed. And to feed them on board, I had a good bundle of hay, and a bag of corn. I would gladly have taken a dozen of the natives, but this was a thing the Emperor would by no means permit; and besides a diligent search into my pockets, his

Majesty engaged my honour not to carry away any of his subjects, although with their own consent and desire.

Having thus prepared all things as well as I was able, I set sail on the twenty-fourth day of September, 1701, at six in the morning; and when I had gone about four leagues to the northward, the wind being at south-east, at six in the evening I descried a small island about half a league to the north-west. I advanced forward, and cast anchor on the lee-side of the island, which seemed to be uninhabited. I then took some refreshment, and went to my rest. I slept well, and as I conjectured at least six hours, for I found the day broke in two hours after I awaked. It was a clear night. I eat my breakfast, before the sun was up; and heaving anchor, the wind being favourable, I steered the same course that I had done the day before, wherein I was directed by my pocket-compass. My intention was to reach, if possible, one of those islands, which I had reason to believe lay to the north-east of Van Diemen's Land. I discovered nothing all that day; but upon the next, about three in the afternoon, when I had by my computation made twenty-four leagues from Blefuscu, I descried a sail steering to the south-east; my course was due east. I hailed her, but could get no answer; yet I found I gained upon her, for the wind slackened. I made all the sail I could, and in half an hour she spied me, then hung out her ancient, and discharged a gun. It is not easy to express the joy I was in upon the unexpected hope of once more seeing my beloved country, and the dear pledges I had left in it. The ship slackened her sails, and I came up with her between five and six in the evening, September 26; but my heart leaped within me to see her English colours. I put my cows and sheep into my coat-pocket, and got on board with all my little cargo of provisions. The vessel was an English merchant-man, returning from Japan by the North and South Seas; the Captain, Mr. John Biddel of Deptford, a very civil man, and an excellent sailor. We were now in the latitude of 30 degrees south; there were about fifty men in the ship; and here I met an old comrade of mine, one Peter Williams,

who gave me a good character to the Captain. This gentleman treated me with kindness, and desired I would let him
know what place I came from last, and whither I was bound;
which I did in a few words, but he thought I was raving,
and that the dangers I underwent had disturbed my head;
whereupon I took my black cattle and sheep out of my
pocket, which, after great astonishment, clearly convinced
him of my veracity. I then showed him the gold given me
by the Emperor of Blefuscu, together with his Majesty's
picture at full length, and some other rarities of that country.
I gave him two purses of two hundred *sprugs* each, and
promised, when we arrived in England, to make him a
present of a cow and sheep big with young.

I shall not trouble the reader with a particular account
of this voyage, which was very prosperous for the most part.
We arrived in the Downs on the 13th of April, 1702. I
had only one misfortune, that the rats on board carried
away one of my sheep; I found her bones in a hole, picked
clean from the flesh. The rest of my cattle I got safe on
shore, and set them a grazing in a bowling-green at Green-
wich, where the fineness of the grass made them feed very
heartily, though I had always feared the contrary: neither
could I possibly have preserved them in so long a voyage,
if the Captain had not allowed me some of his best biscuit,
which, rubbed to powder, and mingled with water, was their
constant food. The short time I continued in England, I
made a considerable profit by showing my cattle to many
persons of quality, and others: and before I began my
second voyage, I sold them for six hundred pounds. Since
my last return, I find the breed is considerably increased,
especially the sheep; which I hope will prove much to the
advantage of the woollen manufacture, by the fineness of
the fleeces.

I stayed but two months with my wife and family; for
my insatiable desire of seeing foreign countries would suffer
me to continue no longer. I left fifteen hundred pounds
with my wife, and fixed her in a good house at Redriff. My
remaining stock I carried with me, part in money, and part

in goods, in hopes to improve my fortunes. My eldest uncle John had left me an estate in land, near Epping, of about thirty pounds a year; and I had a long lease of the Black Bull in Fetter-Lane, which yielded me as much more; so that I was not in any danger of leaving my family upon the parish. My son Johnny, named so after his uncle, was at the Grammar School, and a towardly child. My daughter Betty (who is now well married, and has children) was then at her needle-work. I took leave of my wife, and boy and girl, with tears on both sides, and went on board the *Adventure*, a merchant-ship of three hundred tons, bound for Surat, Captain John Nicholas, of Liverpool, Commander. But my account of this voyage must be referred to the second part of my Travels.

The End of the First Part.

PART II

A VOYAGE TO BROBDINGNAG

BROBDINGNAG

Flanſtaſnic

Lorbrulgrud

Diſcovered A.D. 1703

NORTH AMERICA

Streights of Annian

C. Blanco

St Sebaſtian

C. Mendocino

Pt.o St. Francis Drake

NEW ALBION

Mount St Martin

P Monterey

CHAPTER I

A great storm described, the long-boat sent to fetch water, the Author goes with it to discover the country. He is left on shore, is seized by one of the natives, and carried to a farmer's house. His reception there, with several accidents that happened there. A description of the inhabitants.

HAVING been condemned by nature and fortune to an active and restless life, in two months after my return, I again left my native country, and took shipping in the Downs on the 20th day of June, 1702, in the *Adventure*, Captain John Nicholas, a Cornish man, Commander, bound for Surat. We had a very prosperous gale till we arrived at the Cape of Good Hope, where we landed for fresh water, but discovering a leak we unshipped our goods and wintered there; for the Captain falling sick of an ague, we could not leave the Cape till the end of March. We then set sail, and had a good voyage till we passed the Straits of Madagascar; but having got northward of that island, and to about five degrees south latitude, the winds, which in those seas are observed to blow a constant equal gale between the north and west from the beginning of December to the beginning of May, on the 19th of April began to blow with much greater violence, and more westerly than usual, continuing so for twenty days together, during which time we were driven a little to the east of the Molucca Islands, and about three degrees northward of the Line, as our Captain found by an observation he took the 2nd of May, at which time the wind ceased, and it was a perfect calm, whereas I was not a little rejoiced. But he, being a man well experienced in the navigation of those seas, bid us all prepare against a storm, which accordingly happened the day following: for a southern wind, called the southern monsoon, began to set in.

Finding it was likely to overblow, we took in our spritsail, and stood by to hand the fore-sail; but making foul weather, we looked the guns were all fast, and handed the mizen. The ship lay very broad off, so we thought it better spooning before the sea, than trying or hulling. We reefed the fore-sail and set him, we hawled aft the fore-sheet; the helm was hard a weather. The ship wore bravely. We belayed the fore-down-hall; but the sail was split, and we hawled down the yard, and got the sail into the ship, and unbound all the things clear of it. It was a very fierce storm; the sea broke strange and dangerous. We hawled off upon the laniard of the whipstaff, and helped the man at helm. We would not get down our top-mast, but let all stand, because she scudded before the sea very well, and we knew that the top-mast being aloft, the ship was the wholesomer, and made better way through the sea, seeing we had sea-room. When the storm was over, we set fore-sail and main-sail, and brought the ship to. Then we set the mizen, main-top-sail, and fore-top-sail. Our course was east north-east, the wind was at south-west. We got the starboard tacks aboard, we cast off our weather-braces and lifts; we set in the lee-braces, and hawled forward by the weather-bowlings, and hawled them tight, and belayed them, and hawled over the mizen tack to windward, and kept her full and by as near as she would lie.

During this storm, which was followed by a strong wind west south-west, we were carried by my computation about five hundred leagues to the east, so that the oldest sailor on board could not tell in what part of the world we were. Our provisions held out well, our ship was staunch, and our crew all in good health; but we lay in the utmost distress for water. We thought it best to hold on the same course, rather than turn more northerly, which might have brought us to the north-west parts of Great Tartary, and into the frozen sea.

On the 16th day of June, 1703, a boy on the top-mast discovered land. On the 17th we came in full view of a great island or continent (for we knew not whether) on the south side whereof was a small neck of land jutting out into the sea, and a creek too shallow to hold a ship of above one hundred tons. We cast anchor within a league of this creek, and our Captain sent a dozen of his men well armed in the long-boat, with vessels for water if any could be found. I desired his leave to go with them, that I might see the country, and make what discoveries I could. When we came to land we saw no river or spring, nor any sign of inhabitants. Our men therefore wandered on the shore to find out some fresh water near the sea, and I walked alone about a mile on the other side, where I observed the country all barren and rocky. I now began to be weary, and seeing nothing to entertain my curiosity, I returned gently down towards the creek; and the sea being full in my view, I saw our men already got into the boat, and rowing for life to the ship. I was going to hollow after them, although it had been to little purpose, when I observed a huge creature walking after them in the sea, as fast as he could: he waded not much deeper than his knees, and took prodigious strides: but our men had the start of him half a league, and the sea thereabouts being full of sharp-pointed rocks, the monster was not able to overtake the boat. This I was afterwards told, for I durst not stay to see the issue of that adventure; but ran as fast as I could the way I first went, and then climbed up a steep hill, which gave me some prospect of the country. I found it fully cultivated; but that which first surprised me was the length of the grass, which in those grounds that seemed to be kept for hay, was about twenty foot high.

I fell into a high road, for so I took it to be, though it served to the inhabitants only as a foot-path through a field of barley. Here I walked on for some time, but could see little on either side, it being now near harvest, and the corn rising at least forty foot. I was an hour walking to the end of this field, which was fenced in with a hedge of at least one hundred and twenty foot high, and the trees so lofty that I could make no computation of their altitude. There was a stile to pass from this field into the next. It had four steps, and a stone to cross over when you came to the

6

uppermost. It was impossible for me to climb this stile, because every step was six foot high, and the upper stone about twenty. I was endeavouring to find some gaps in the hedge, when I discovered one of the inhabitants in the next field, advancing towards the stile, of the same size with him whom I saw in the sea pursuing our boat. He appeared as tall as an ordinary spire-steeple, and took about ten yards at every stride, as near as I could guess. I was struck with the utmost fear and astonishment, and ran to hide myself in the corn, from whence I saw him at the top of the stile, looking back into the next field on the right hand, and heard him call in a voice many degrees louder than a speaking-trumpet: but the noise was so high in the air, that at first I certainly thought it was thunder. Whereupon seven monsters like himself came towards him with reaping-hooks in their hands, each hook about the largeness of six scythes. These people were not so well clad as the first, whose servants or labourers they seemed to be: for, upon some words he spoke, they went to reap the corn in the field where I lay. I kept from them at as great a distance as I could, but was forced to move with extreme difficulty, for the stalks of the corn were sometimes not above a foot distant, so that I could hardly squeeze my body betwixt them. However, I made a shift to go forward till I came to a part of the field where the corn had been laid by the rain and wind. Here it was impossible for me to advance a step; for the stalks were so interwoven that I could not creep through, and the beards of the fallen ears so strong and pointed that they pierced through my clothes into my flesh. At the same time I heard the reapers not above an hundred yards behind me. Being quite dispirited with toil, and wholly overcome by grief and despair, I lay down between two ridges, and heartily wished I might there end my days. I bemoaned my desolate widow, and fatherless children. I lamented my own folly and wilfulness in attempting a second voyage against the advice of all my friends and relations. In this terrible agitation of mind I could not forbear thinking of Lilliput, whose inhabitants looked upon me at the greatest prodigy that ever appeared in the world; where I was able to draw an Imperial Fleet in my hand, and perform those other actions which will be recorded for ever in the chronicles of that empire, while posterity shall hardly believe them, although attested by millions. I reflected what a mortification it must prove to me to appear as inconsiderable in this nation as one single Lilliputian would be among us. But this I conceived was to be the least of my misfortunes: for, as human creatures are observed to be more savage and cruel in proportion to their bulk, what could I expect but to be a morsel in the mouth of the first among these enormous barbarians that should happen to seize me? Undoubtedly philosophers are in the right when they tell us, that nothing is great or little otherwise than by comparison. It might have pleased fortune to have let the Lilliputian find some nation, where the people were as diminutive with respect to them, as they were to me. And who knows but that even this prodigious race of mortals might be equally overmatched in some distant part of the world, whereof we have yet no discovery?

Scared and confounded as I was, I could not forbear going on with these reflections, when one of the reapers approaching within ten yards of the ridge where I lay, made me apprehend that with the next step I should be squashed to death under his foot, or cut in two with his reaping-hook. And therefore when he was again about to move, I screamed as loud as fear could make me. Whereupon the huge creature trod short, and looking round about under him for some time, at last espied me as I lay on the ground. He considered a while with the caution of one who endeavours to lay hold on a small dangerous animal in such a manner that it shall not be able either to scratch or bite him, as I myself have sometimes done with a weasel in England. At length he ventured to take me up behind by the middle between his forefinger and thumb, and brought me within three yards of his eyes, that he might behold my shape more perfectly. I guessed his meaning, and my good fortune gave me so much presence of mind, that I resolved not to struggle in the least as he held me in the air about sixty foot from the ground, although he grievously pinched my sides, for fear I should slip through his fingers. All I ventured was to raise my eyes towards the sun, and place my hands together in a supplicating posture, and to speak some words in an humble melancholy tone, suitable to the condition I then was in. For I apprehended every moment that he would dash me against the ground, as we usually do any little hateful animal which we have a mind to destroy. But my good star would have it, that he appeared pleased with my voice and gestures, and began to look upon me as a curiosity, much wondering to hear me pronounce articulate words, although he could not understand them. In the mean time I was not able to forbear groaning and shedding tears, and turning my head towards my sides; letting him know, as well as I could, how cruelly I was hurt by the pressure of his thumb and finger. He seemed to apprehend my meaning; for, lifting up the lappet of his coat, he put me gently into it, and immediately ran along with me to his master, who was a substantial farmer, and the same person I had first seen in the field.

The farmer having (as I supposed by their talk) received such an account of me as his servant could give him, took a piece of a small straw, about the size of a walking staff, and therewith lifted up the lappets of my coat; which it seems he thought to be some kind of covering that nature had given me. He blew my hairs aside to take a better view of my face. He called his hinds about him, and asked them (as I afterwards learned) whether they had ever seen in the fields any little creature that resembled me. He then placed me softly on the ground upon all four, but I got immediately up, and walked slowly backwards and forwards, to let those people see I had no intent to run away. They all sat down in a circle about me, the better to observe my motions. I pulled off my hat, and made a low bow towards the farmer. I fell on my knees, and lifted up my hands and eyes, and spoke several words as loud as I could: I took a purse of gold out of my pocket, and humbly presented it to him. He received it on the palm of his hand, then applied it close to his eye, to see what it was, and afterwards turned it several times with the point of a pin (which he took out of his sleeve), but could make nothing of it. Whereupon I made a sign that he should place his hand on the ground. I then took the purse, and opening it, poured all the gold into his palm. There were six Spanish pieces of four pistoles each, beside twenty or thirty smaller coins. I saw him wet the tip of his little finger upon his tongue, and take up one of my largest pieces, and then another, but he seemed to be wholly ignorant what they were. He made me a sign to put them again into my purse, and the purse again into my pocket, which after offering to him several times, I thought it best to do.

The farmer by this time was convinced I must be a rational creature. He spoke often to me, but the sound of his voice pierced my ears like that of a water-mill, yet his words were articulate enough. I answered as loud as I could, in several languages, and he often laid his ear within two yards of me, but all in vain, for we were wholly unintelligible to each other. He then sent his servants to their work, and taking his handkerchief out of his pocket, he doubled and spread it on his left hand, which he placed flat on the ground, with the palm upwards, making me a sign to step into it, as I could easily do, for it was not above a foot in thickness. I thought it my part to obey, and for fear of falling, laid myself at length upon the handkerchief, with the remainder of which he lapped me up to the head for further security, and in this manner carried me home to his house. There he called his wife, and showed me to her; but she screamed and ran back, as women in England do at the sight of a toad or a spider. However, when she had a while seen my behaviour, and how well I observed the signs her husband made, she was soon reconciled, and by degrees grew extremely tender of me.

It was about twelve at noon, and a servant brought in dinner. It was only one substantial dish of meat (fit for the plain condition of an husbandman) in a dish of abou four-and-twenty foot diameter. The company were the farmer and his wife, three children, and an old grandmother. When they were sat down, the farmer placed me at some distance from him on the table, which was thirty foot high from the floor. I was in a terrible fright, and kept as far as I could from the edge for fear of falling. The wife minced a bit of meat, then crumbled some bread on a trencher, and placed it before me. I made her a low bow, took out my knife and fork, and fell to eat, which gave them exceeding delight. The mistress sent her maid for a small dram cup, which held about two gallons, and filled it with drink; I took up the vessel with much difficulty in both hands, and in a most respectful manner drank to her ladyship's health, expressing the words as loud as I could in English, which made the company laugh so heartily, that I was almost deafened with the noise. This liquor tasted like a small cyder, and was not unpleasant. Then the master made me a sign to come to his trencher side; but as I walked on the table, being in great surprise all the time, as the indulgent reader will easily conceive and excuse, I happened to stumble against a crust, and fell flat on my face, but received no hurt. I got up immediately, and observing the good people to be in much concern, I took my hat (which I held under my arm out of good manners) and waving it over my head, made three huzzas, to show I had got no mischief by my fall. But advancing forwards toward my master (as I shall henceforth call him) his youngest son who sat next him, an arch boy of about ten years old, took me up by the legs, and held me so high in the air, that I trembled every limb; but his father snatched me from him, and at the same time gave him such a box on the left ear, as would have felled an European troop of horse to the earth, ordering him to be taken from the table. But being afraid the boy might owe me a spite, and well remembering how mischievous all children among us naturally are to sparrows, rabbits, young kittens, and puppy dogs, I fell on my knees, and pointing to the boy, made my master to understand, as well as I could, that I desired his son might be pardoned. The father complied, and the lad took his seat again; whereupon I went to him and kissed his hand, which my master took, and made him stroke me gently with it.

In the midst of dinner, my mistress's favourite cat leapt into her lap. I heard a noise behind me like that of a dozen stocking weavers at work; and turning my head, I found it proceeded from the purring of this animal, who seemed to be three times larger than an ox, as I computed by the view of her head, and one of her paws, while her mistress was feeding and stroking her. The fierceness of this creature's countenance altogether discomposed me; though I stood at the farther end of the table, above fifty foot off; and although my mistress held her fast for fear she might give a spring, and seize me in her talons. But it happened there was no danger; for the cat took not the least notice of me when my master placed me within three yards of her. And as I have been always told and found true by experience in my travels, that flying, or discovering fear before a fierce animal, is a certain way to make it pursue or attack you, so I resolved in this dangerous juncture to show no manner of concern. I walked with intrepidity five or six times before the very head of the cat, and came within half a yard of her; whereupon she drew herself back, as if she were more afraid of me: I had less apprehension concerning the dogs, whereof three or four came into the room, as it is usual in farmers' houses; one of which was a mastiff, equal in bulk to four elephants, and a greyhound, somewhat taller than the mastiff, but not so large.

When dinner was almost done, the nurse came in with a child of a year old in her arms, who immediately spied me, and began a squall that you might have heard from London-Bridge to Chelsea, after the usual oratory of infants, to get me for a plaything. The mother out of pure indulgence took me up, and put me towards the child, who presently seized me by the middle, and got my head in his mouth, where I roared so loud that the urchin was frighted, and let me drop; and I should infallibly have broke my neck if the mother had not held her apron under me. The nurse to quiet her babe made use of a rattle, which was a kind of hollow vessel filled with great stones, and fastened by a cable to the child's waist: but all in vain, so that she was forced to apply the last remedy by giving it suck. I must confess no object ever disgusted me so much as the sight of her monstrous breast, which I cannot tell what to compare with, so as to give the curious reader an idea of its bulk, shape and colour. It stood prominent six foot, and could not be less than sixteen in circumference. The nipple was about half the bigness of my head, and the hue both of that and the dug so varified with spots, pimples and freckles, that nothing could appear more nauseous: for I had a near sight of her, she sitting down the more conveniently to give suck, and I standing on the table. This made me reflect upon the fair skins of our English ladies, who appear so beautiful to us, only because they are of our own size, and their defects not to be seen but through a magnifying glass, where we find by experiment that the smoothness and whitest skins look rough and coarse, and ill coloured.

I remember when I was at Lilliput, the complexion of those diminutive people appeared to me the fairest in the world; and talking upon this subject with a person of learning there, who was an intimate friend of mine, he said that my face appeared much fairer and smoother when he looked on me from the ground, than it did upon a nearer view when I took him up in my hand and brought him close, which he confessed was at first a very shocking sight. He said he could discover great holes in my skin; that the stumps of my beard were ten times stronger than the bristles of a boar, and my complexion made up of several colours altogether disagreeable: although I must beg leave to say for myself, that I am as fair as most of my sex and country, and very little sunburnt by all my travels. On the other side, discoursing of the ladies in that Emperor's court, he used to tell me, one had freckles, another too wide a mouth, a third too large a nose, nothing of which I was able to distinguish. I confess this reflection was obvious enough; which however I could not forbear, lest the reader might think those vast creatures were actually deformed for I must do them justice to say they are a comely race of people; and particularly the features of my master's countenance, although he were but a farmer, when I beheld him from the height of sixty foot, appeared very well proportioned.

When dinner was done, my master went out to his labourers, and as I could discover by his voice and gesture, gave his wife a strict charge to take care of me. I was very much tired, and disposed to sleep, which my mistress perceiving, she put me on her own bed, and covered me with a clean white handkerchief, but larger and coarser than the mainsail of a man of war.

I slept about two hours, and dreamed I was at home with my wife and children, which aggravated my sorrows when I awaked and found myself alone in a vast room, between two and three hundred foot wide, and above two hundred high, lying in a bed twenty yards wide. My mistress was gone about her household affairs, and had locked me in. The bed was eight yards from the floor. Some natural necessities required me to get down; I durst not presume to call, and if I had, it would have been in vain, with such a voice as mine, at so great a distance as from the room where I lay to the kitchen where the family kept. While I was under these circumstances, two rats crept up the curtains, and ran smelling backwards and forwards on the bed. One of them came up almost to my face, whereupon I rose in a fright, and drew out my hanger to defend myself. These horrible animals had the boldness to attack me on both sides, and one of them held his fore-feet at my collar; but I had the good fortune to rip up his belly before he could do me any mischief. He fell down at my feet, and the other seeing the fate of his comrade, made his escape, but not without one good wound on the back, which I gave him as he fled, and made the blood run trickling from him. After this exploit, I walked gently to and fro on the bed, to recover my breath and loss of spirits. These creatures were of the size of a large mastiff, but infinitely more nimble and fierce, so that if I had taken off my belt before I went to sleep, I must have infallibly been torn to pieces and devoured. I measured the tail of the dead rat, and found it to be two yards long, wanting an inch; but it went against my stomach to drag the carcass off the bed, where it lay still bleeding; I observed it had yet some life, but with a strong slash across the neck, I thoroughly dispatched it.

Soon after my mistress came into the room, who seeing me all bloody, ran and took me up in her hand. I pointed to the dead rat, smiling and making other signs to show I was not hurt, whereat she was extremely rejoiced, calling the maid to take up the dead rat with a pair of tongs, and throw it out of the window. Then she set me on a table, where I showed her my hanger all bloody, and wiping it on the lappet of my coat, returned it to the scabbard. I was pressed to do more than one thing, which another could not do for me, and therefore endeavoured to make my mistress understand that I desired to be set down on the floor; which after she had done, my bashfulness would not suffer me to express myself further than by pointing to the door, and bowing several times. The good woman with much difficulty at last perceived what I would be at, and taking me up again in her hand, walked into the garden, where she set me down. I went on one side about two hundred yards, and beckoning to her not to look or to follow me, I hid myself between two leaves of sorrel, and there discharged the necessities of nature.

I hope the gentle reader will excuse me for dwelling on these and the like particulars, which however insignificant they may appear to grovelling vulgar minds, yet will certainly help a philosopher to enlarge his thoughts and imagination, and apply them to the benefit of public as well as private life, which was my sole design in presenting this and other accounts of my travels to the world; wherein I have been chiefly studious of truth, without affecting any ornaments of learning or of style. But the whole scene of this voyage made so strong an impression on my mind, and is so deeply fixed in my memory, that in committing it to paper I did not omit one material circumstance: however, upon a strict review, I blotted out several passages of less moment which were in my first copy, for fear of being censured as tedious and trifling, whereof travellers are often, perhaps not without justice, accused.

CHAPTER II

A description of the farmer's daughter. The Author carried to a market-town, and then to the metropolis. The particulars of his journey.

MY mistress had a daughter of nine years old, a child of forward parts for her age, very dexterous at her needle, and skilful in dressing her baby. Her mother and she contrived to fit up the baby's cradle for me against night: the cradle was put into a small drawer of a cabinet, and the drawer placed upon a hanging shelf for fear of the rats. This was my bed all the time I stayed with those people, though made more convenient by degrees, as I began to learn their language, and make my wants known. This young girl was so handy, that after I had once or twice pulled off my clothes before her, she was able to dress and undress me, though I never gave her that trouble when she would let me do either myself. She made me seven shirts, and some other linen, of as fine cloth as could be got, which indeed was coarser than sackcloth; and these she constantly washed for me with her own hands. She was likewise my school-mistress to teach me the language: when I pointed to any thing, she told me the name of it in her own tongue, so that in a few days I was able to call for whatever I had a mind to. She was very good-natured, and not above forty foot high, being little for her age. She gave me the name of *Grildrig*, which the family took up, and afterwards the whole kingdom. The word imports what the Latins call *nanunculus*, the Italians *homunceletino*, and the English *mannikin*. To her I chiefly owe my preservation in that country: we never parted while I was there; I called her my *Glumdalclitch*, or little nurse: and I should be guilty of great ingratitude, if I omitted this honourable mention of her care and affection towards me, which I heartily wish it lay in my power to requite as she deserves, instead of being the innocent but unhappy instrument of her disgrace, as I have too much reason to fear.

It now began to be known and talked of in the neighbourhood, that my master had found a strange animal in the field, about the bigness of a *splacknuck*, but exactly shaped in every part like a human creature; which it likewise imitated in all its actions; seemed to speak in a little language of its own, had already learned several words of theirs, went erect upon two legs, was tame and gentle, would come when it was called, do whatever it was bid, had the finest limbs in the world, and a complexion fairer than a nobleman's daughter of three years old. Another farmer who lived hard by, and was a particular friend of my master, came on a visit on purpose to enquire into the truth of this story. I was immediately produced, and placed upon a table, where I walked as I was commanded, drew my hanger, put it up again, made my reverence to my master's guest, asked him in his own language how he did, and told him he was welcome, just as my little nurse had instructed me. This man, who was old and dim-sighted, put on his spectacles to behold me better, at which I could not forbear laughing very heartily, for his eyes appeared like the full moon shining into a chamber at two windows. Our people, who discovered the cause of my mirth, bore me company in laughing, at which the old fellow was fool enough to be angry and out of countenance. He had the character of a great miser, and to my misfortune he well deserved it, by the cursed advice he gave my master to show me as a sight upon a market-day in the next town, which was half an hour's riding, about two and twenty miles from our house. I guessed there was some mischief contriving, when I observed my master and his friend whispering long together, sometimes pointing at me; and my fears made me fancy that I overheard and understood some of their words. But the next morning Glumdalclitch, my little nurse, told me the whole matter, which she had cunningly picked out from her mother. The poor girl laid me on her bosom, and fell a weeping with shame and grief. She apprehended some mischief would happen to me from rude vulgar folks, who might squeeze me to death, or break one of my limbs by taking me in their hands. She had also observed how modest I was in my nature, how nicely I regarded my honour, and what an indignity I should conceive it to be exposed for money as a public spectacle to the meanest of the people. She said, her papa and mamma had promised that Grildrig should be hers, but now she found they meant to serve her as they did last year, when they pretended to give her a lamb, and yet, as soon as it was fat, sold it to a butcher. For my own part, I may truly affirm that I was less concerned than my nurse. I had a strong hope which never left me, that I should one day recover my liberty; and as to the ignominy of being carried about for a monster, I considered myself to be a perfect stranger in the country, and that such a misfortune could never be charged upon me as a reproach, if ever I should return to England; since the King of Great Britain himself, in my condition, must have undergone the same distress.

My master, pursuant to the advice of his friend, carried me in a box the next market-day to the neighbouring town, and took along with him his little daughter, my nurse, upon a pillion behind him. The box was close on every side, with a little door for me to go in and out, and a few gimlet-holes to let in air. The girl had been so careful to put the quilt of her baby's bed into it, for me to lie down on. However, I was terribly shaken and discomposed in this journey, though it were but of half an hour. For the horse went about forty foot at every step, and trotted so high, that the agitation was equal to the rising and falling of a ship in a great storm, but much more frequent. Our journey was somewhat farther than from London to St. Albans. My master alighted at an inn which he used to frequent; and after consulting a while with the inn-keeper, and making some necessary preparations, he hired the *Grultrud*, or crier, to give notice through the town of a strange creature to be seen at the Sign of the Green Eagle, not so big as a *splacknuck* (an animal in that country very finely shaped, about six foot long), and in every part of the body resembling an human creature, could speak several words, and perform an hundred diverting tricks.

I was placed upon a table in the largest room of the inn, which might be near three hundred foot square. My little nurse stood on a low stool close to the table, to take care of me, and direct what I should do. My master, to avoid a crowd, would suffer only thirty people at a time to see me. I walked about on the table as the girl commanded: she asked me questions as far as she knew my understanding of the language reached, and I answered them as loud as I could. I turned about several times to the company, paid my humble respects, said they were welcome, and used some other speeches I had been taught. I took up a thimble filled with liquor, which Glumdalclitch had given me for a cup, and drank their health. I drew out my hanger, and flourished with it after the manner of fencers in England. My nurse gave me part of a straw, which I exercised as a pike, having learned the art in my youth. I was that day shown to twelve sets of company, and as often forced to go over again with the same fopperies, till I was half dead with weariness and vexation. For those who had seen me made such wonderful reports, that the people were ready to break down the doors to come in. My master for his own interest would not suffer any one to touch me except my nurse; and, to prevent danger, benches were set round the table at such a distance as put me out of every body's reach. However, an unlucky school-boy aimed a hazel nut directly at my head, which very narrowly missed me; otherwise, it came with so much violence, that it would have infallibly knocked out my brains, for it was almost as large as a small pumpion: but I had the satisfaction to see the young rogue well beaten, and turned out of the room.

My master gave public notice, that he would show me again the next market-day, and in the meantime he prepared a more convenient vehicle for me, which he had reason enough to do; for I was so tired with my first journey, and with entertaining company for eight hours together, that I could hardly stand upon my legs, or speak a word. It was at least three days before I recovered my strength; and that I might have no rest at home, all the neighbouring gentlemen from an hundred miles round, hearing of my fame, came to see me at my master's own house. There could not be fewer than thirty persons with their wives and children (for the country is very populous); and my master demanded the rate of a full room whenever he showed me at home, although it were only to a single family; so that for some time I had but little ease every day of the week (except Wednesday, which is their Sabbath) although I were not carried to the town.

My master finding how profitable I was likely to be, resolved to carry me to the most considerable cities of the kingdom. Having therefore provided himself with all things necessary for a long journey, and settled his affairs at home, he took leave of his wife, and upon the 17th of August, 1703, about two months after my arrival, we set out for the metropolis, situated near the middle of that empire, and about three thousand miles distance from our house. My master made his daughter Glumdalclitch ride behind him. She carried me on her lap in a box tied about her waist. The girl had lined it on all sides with the softest cloth she could get, well quilted underneath, furnished it with her baby's bed, provided me with linen and other necessaries, and made everything as convenient as she could. We had no other company but a boy of the house, who rode after us with the luggage.

My master's design was to show me in all the towns by the way, and to step out of the road for fifty or an hundred miles, to any village or person of quality's house where he might expect custom. We made easy journeys of not above seven or eight score miles a day: for Glumdalclitch, on purpose to spare me, complained she was tired with the trotting of the horse. She often took me out of my box, at my own desire, to give me air, and show me the country, but always held me fast by a leading-string. We passed over five or six rivers many degrees broader and deeper than the Nile or the Ganges; and there was hardly a rivulet so small as the Thames at London-Bridge. We were ten weeks in our journey, and I was shown in eighteen large towns besides many villages and private families.

On the 26th day of October, we arrived at the metropolis, called in their language *Lorbrulgrud*, or Pride of the Universe. My master took a lodging in the principal street of the city, not far from the royal palace, and put out bills in the usual form, containing an exact description of my person and parts. He hired a large room between three and four hundred foot wide. He provided a table sixty foot in diameter, upon which I was to act my part, and pallisadoed it round three foot from the edge, and as many high, to prevent my falling over. I was shown ten times a day to the wonder and satisfaction of all people. I could now speak the language tolerably well, and perfectly understood every word that was spoken to me. Besides, I had learnt their alphabet, and could make a shift to explain a sentence here and there; for Glumdalclitch had been my instructor while we were at home, and at leisure hours during our journey. She carried a little book in her pocket, not much larger than a Sanson's Atlas; it was a common treatise for the use of young girls, giving a short account of their religion: out of this she taught me my letters, and interpreted the words.

CHAPTER III

The Author sent for to Court. The Queen buys him of his master the farmer, and presents him to the King. He disputes with his Majesty's great scholars. An apartment at Court provided for the Author. He is in high favour with the Queen. He stands up for the honour of his own country. His quarrels with the Queen's dwarf.

THE frequent labours I underwent every day made in a few weeks a very considerable change in my health: the more my master got by me, the more insatiable he grew. I had quite lost my stomach, and was almost reduced to a skeleton. The farmer observed it, and concluding I soon must die, resolved to make as good a hand of me as he could. While he was thus reasoning and resolving with himself, a *Slardral*, or Gentleman Usher, came from court, commanding my master to carry me immediately thither for the diversion of the Queen and her ladies. Some of the latter had already been to see me, and reported strange things of my beauty, behaviour, and good sense. Her Majesty and those who attended her were beyond measure delighted with my demeanour. I fell on my knees, and begged the honour of kissing her Imperial foot; but this gracious princess held out her little finger towards me (after I was set on a table) which I embraced in both my arms, and put the tip of it, with the utmost respect, to my lip. She made me some general questions about my country and my travels, which I answered as distinctly and in as few words as I could. She asked whether I would be content to live at court. I bowed down to the board of the table, and humbly answered, that I was my master's slave, but if I were at my own disposal, I should be proud to devote my life to her Majesty's service. She then asked my master whether he were willing to sell me at a good price. He, who apprehended I could not live a month, was ready enough to part with me, and demanded a thousand pieces of gold, which were ordered him on the spot, each piece being about the bigness of eight hundred moidores; but, allowing for the proportion of all things between that country and Europe, and the high price of gold among them, was hardly so great a sum as a thousand guineas would be in England. I then said to the Queen, since I was now her Majesty's most humble creature and vassal, I must beg the favour, that Glumdalclitch, who had always tended me with so much care and kindness, and understood to do it so well, might be admitted into her service, and continue to be my nurse and instructor. Her Majesty agreed to my petition, and easily got the farmer's consent, who was glad enough to have his daughter preferred at court: and the poor girl herself was not able to hide her joy. My late master withdrew, bidding me farewell, and saying he had left me in a good service; to which I replied not a word, only making him a slight bow.

The Queen observed my coldness, and when the farmer was gone out of the apartment, asked me the reason. I made bold to tell her Majesty that I owed no other obligation to my late master, than his not dashing out the brains of a poor harmless creature found by chance in his field; which obligation was amply recompensed by the gain he had made in showing me through half the kingdom, and the price he had now sold me for. That the life I had since led, was laborious enough to kill an animal of ten times my strength. That my health was much impaired by the continual drudgery of entertaining the rabble every hour of the day, and that if my master had not thought my life in danger, her Majesty perhaps would not have got so cheap a bargain. But as I was out of all fear of being ill treated under the protection of so great and good an Empress, the Ornament of Nature, the Darling of the World, the Delight of her Subjects, the Phoenix of the Creation; so I hoped my late master's apprehensions would appear to be groundless, for I already found my spirits to revive by the influence of her most august presence.

This was the sum of my speech, delivered with great improprieties and hesitation; the latter part was altogether framed in the style peculiar to that people, whereof I learned some phrases from Glumdalclitch, while she was carrying me to court.

The Queen giving great allowance for my defectiveness in speaking, was however surprised at so much wit and good sense in so diminutive an animal. She took me in her own hand, and carried me to the King, who was then retired to his cabinet. His Majesty, a prince of much gravity, and austere countenance, not well observing my shape at first view, asked the Queen after a cold manner, how long it was since she grew fond of a *splacknuck*; for such it seems he took me to be, as I lay upon my breast in her Majesty's right hand. But this princess, who hath an infinite deal of wit and humour, set me gently on my feet upon the scrutore, and commanded me to give his Majesty an account of myself, which I did in a very few words; and Glumdalclitch, who attended at the cabinet door, and could not endure I should be out of her sight, being admitted, confirmed all that had passed from my arrival at her father's house.

The King, although he be as learned a person as any in his dominions, and had been educated in the study of philosophy, and particularly mathematics; yet when he observed my shape exactly, and saw me walk erect, before I began to speak, conceived I might be a piece of clock-work (which is in that country arrived to a very great perfection), contrived by some ingenious artist. But when he heard my voice, and found what I delivered to be regular and rational, he could not conceal his astonishment. He was by no means satisfied with the relation I gave him of the manner I came into his kingdom, but thought it a story concerted between Glumdalclitch and her father, who had taught me a set of words to make me sell at a higher price. Upon this imagination he put several other questions to me, and still received rational answers, no otherwise defective than by a foreign accent, and an imperfect knowledge in the language, with some rustic phrases which I had learned at the farmer's house, and did not suit the polite style of a court.

His Majesty sent for three great scholars who were then in their weekly waiting, according to the custom in that country. These gentlemen, after they had a while examined my shape with much nicety, were of different opinions concerning me. They all agreed that I could not be produced according to the regular laws of nature, because I was not framed with a capacity of preserving my life, either by swiftness, or climbing of trees, or digging holes in the earth. They observed by my teeth, which they viewed with great exactness, that I was a carnivorous animal; yet most quadrupeds being an overmatch for me, and field mice, with some others, too nimble, they could not imagine how I should be able to support myself, unless I fed upon snails and other insects, which they offered, by many learned arguments, to evince that I could not possibly do. One of these virtuosi seemed to think that I might be an embryo, or abortive birth. But this opinion was rejected by the other two, who observed my limbs to be perfect and finished, and that I had lived several years, as it was manifest from my beard, the stumps thereof they plainly discovered through a magnifying-glass. They would not allow me to be a dwarf, because my littleness was beyond all degrees of comparison; for the Queen's favourite dwarf, the smallest ever known in that kingdom, was near thirty foot high. After much debate, they concluded unanimously that I was only *relplum scalcath*, which is interpreted literally, *lusus naturae*; a determination exactly agreeable to the modern philosophy of Europe, whose professors, disdaining the old evasion of *occult causes*, whereby the followers of Aristotle endeavour in vain to disguise their ignorance, have invented this wonderful solution of all difficulties, to the unspeakable advancement of human knowledge.

After this decisive conclusion, I entreated to be heard a word or two. I applied myself to the King, and assured his Majesty, that I came from a country which abounded with several millions of both sexes, and of my own stature; where the animals, trees, and houses were all in proportion, and where by consequence I might be as able to defend myself, and to find sustenance, as any of his Majesty's subjects could do here; which I took for a full answer to those gentleman's arguments. To this they only replied with a smile of contempt, saying, that the farmer had instructed me very well in my lesson. The King, who had a much better understanding, dismissed his learned men, sent for the farmer, who by good fortune was not yet gone out of town. Having therefore first examined him privately, and then confronted him with me and the young girl, his Majesty began to think that what we told him might possibly be true. He desired the Queen to order that a particular care should be taken of me, and was of opinion that Glumdalclitch should still continue in her office of tending me, because he observed we had a great affection for each other. A convenient apartment was provided for her at court: she had a sort of governess appointed to take care of her education, a maid to dress her, and two other servants for menial offices; but the care of me was wholly appropriated to herself. The Queen commanded her own cabinet-maker to contrive a box that might serve me for a bed-chamber, after the model that Glumdalclitch and I should agree upon. This man was a most ingenious artist, and according to my directions, in three weeks finished for me a wooden chamber of sixteen foot square, and twelve high, with sash-windows, a door, and two closets, like a London bed-chamber. The board that made the ceiling was to be lifted up and down by two hinges, to put in a bed ready furnished by her Majesty's upholsterer, which Glumdalclitch took out every day to air, made it with her own hands, and letting it down at night, locked up the roof over me. A nice workman, who was famous for little curiosities, undertook to make me two chairs, with backs and frames, of a substance not unlike ivory, and two tables, with a cabinet to put my things in. The room was quilted on all sides, as well as the floor and the ceiling, to prevent any accident from the carelessness of those who carried me, and to break the force of a jolt when I went in a coach. I desired a lock for my door, to prevent rats and mice from coming in: the smith, after several attempts, made the smallest that ever was seen among them, for I have known a larger at the gate of a gentleman's house in England. I made a shift to keep the key in a pocket of my own, fearing Glumdalclitch might lose it. The Queen likewise ordered the thinnest silks that could be gotten, to make me clothes, not much thicker than an English blanket, very cumbersome till I was accustomed to them. They were after the fashion of the kingdom, partly resembling the Persian, and partly the Chinese, and are a very grave and decent habit.

The Queen became so fond of my company, that she could not dine without me. I had a table placed upon the same at which her Majesty eat, just at her left elbow, and a chair to sit on. Glumdalclitch stool upon a stool on the floor, near my table, to assist and take care of me. I had an entire set of silver dishes and plates, and other necessaries, which, in proportion to those of the Queen, were not much bigger than what I have seen of the same kind in a London toy-shop, for the furniture of a baby-house: these my little nurse kept in her pocket, in a silver box, and gave me at meals as I wanted them, always cleaning them herself. No person dined with the Queen but the two Princesses Royal, the elder sixteen years old, and the younger at that time thirteen and a month. Her Majesty used to put a bit of meat upon one of my dishes, out of which I carved for myself, and her diversion was to see me eat in miniature. For the Queen (who had indeed but a weak stomach) took up at one mouthful, as much as a dozen English farmers could eat at a meal, which to me was for some time a very nauseous sight. She would craunch the wing of a lark, bones and all, between her teeth, although it were nine times as large as that of a full-grown turkey; and put a bit of bread into her mouth, as big as two twelve-penny loaves. She drank out of a golden cup, above a hogshead at a draught. Her knives were twice as long as a scythe set straight upon the handle. The spoons, forks, and other instruments were all in the same proportion. I remember when Glumdalclitch carried me out of curiosity to see some of the tables at court, where ten or a dozen of these enormous knives and forks were lifted up together, I thought I had never till then beheld so terrible a sight.

It is the custom that every Wednesday (which, as I have before observed, was their Sabbath) the King and Queen, with the royal issue of both sexes, dine together in the apartment of his Majesty, to whom I was now become a great favourite and at these times my little chair and table were placed at his left hand, before one of the salt-cellars. This prince took a pleasure in conversing with me, enquiring into the manners, religion, laws, government, and learning of Europe; wherein I gave him the best account I was able. His apprehension was so clear, and his judgment so exact, that he made very wise reflections and observations upon all I said. But, I confess, that after I had been a little too copious in talking of my own beloved country, of our trade, and wars by sea and land, of our schisms in religion, and parties in the state; the prejudices of his education prevailed so far, that he could not forbear taking me up in his right hand, and stroking me gently with the other, after an hearty fit of laughing, asked me, whether I were a Whig or a Tory. Then turning to his first minister, who waited behind him with a white staff, near as tall as the mainmast of the *Royal Sovereign*, he observed how contemptible a thing was human grandeur, which could be mimicked by such diminutive insects as I: and yet, said he, I dare engage, these creatures have their titles and distinctions of honour, they contrive little nests and burrows, that they call houses and cities; they make a figure in dress and equipage; they love, they fight, they dispute, they cheat, they betray. And thus he continued on, while my colour came and went several times, with indignation to hear our noble country, the mistress of arts and arms, the scourge of France, the arbitress of Europe, the seat of virtue, piety, honour and truth, the pride and envy of the world, so contemptuously treated.

But as I was not in a condition to resent injuries, so, upon mature thoughts, I began to doubt whether I were injured or no. For, after having been accustomed several months to the sight and converse of this people, and observed every object upon whicn I cast my eyes, to be of proportionable magnitude, the horror I had first conceived from their bulk and aspect was so far worn off, that if I had then beheld a company of English lords and ladies in their finery and birth-day clothes, acting their several parts in the most courtly manner, of strutting, and bowing, and prating; to say the truth, I should have been strongly tempted to laugh as much at them as the King and his grandees did at me. Neither indeed could I forbear smiling at myself, when the Queen used to place me upon her hand towards a looking-glass, by which both our persons appeared before me in full view together; and there could be nothing more ridiculous than the comparison; so that I really began to imagine myself dwindled many degrees below my usual size.

Nothing angered and mortified me so much as the Queen's dwarf, who being of the lowest stature that was ever in that country (for I verily think he was not full thirty foot high) became insolent at seeing a creature so much beneath him, that he would always affect to swagger and look big as he passed by me in the Queen's antechamber, while I was standing on some table talking with the lords or ladies of the court, and he seldom failed of a smart word or two upon my littleness; against which I could only revenge myself by calling him brother, challenging him to wrestle, and such repartees as are usual in the mouths of court pages. One day at dinner this malicious little cub was so nettled with something I had said to him, that raising himself upon the frame of her Majesty's chair, he took me up by the middle, as I was sitting down, not thinking any harm, and let me drop into a large silver bowl of cream, and then ran away as fast as he could. I fell over head and ears, and if I had not been a good swimmer, it might have gone very hard with me; for Glumdalclitch in that instant happened to be at the other end of the room, and the Queen was in such a fright that she wanted presence of mind to assist me. But my little nurse ran to my relief, and took me out, after

I had swallowed above a quart of cream. I was put to bed; however I received no other damage than the loss of a suit of clothes, which was utterly spoiled. The dwarf was soundly whipped, and as a farther punishment, forced to drink up the bowl of cream, into which he had thrown me: neither was he ever restored to favour: for, soon after the Queen bestowed him on a lady of high quality, so that I saw him no more, to my very great satisfaction; for I could not tell to what extremity such a malicious urchin might have carried his resentment.

He had before served me a scurvy trick, which set the Queen a laughing, although at the same time she was heartily vexed, and would have immediately cashiered him, if I had not been so generous as to intercede. Her Majesty had taken a marrow-bone upon her plate, and after knocking out the marrow, placed the bone again in the dish erect as it stood before; the dwarf watching his opportunity, while Glumdalclitch was gone to the sideboard, mounted the stool she stood on to take care of me at meals, took me up in both hands, and squeezing my legs together, wedged them into the marrow bone above my waist, where I stuck for some time, and made a very ridiculous figure. I believe it was near a minute before any one knew what was become of me, for I thought it below me to cry out. But, as princes seldom get their meat hot, my legs were not scalded, only my stocking and breeches in a sad condition. The dwarf, at my entreaty, had no other punishment than a sound whipping.

I was frequently rallied by the Queen upon account of my fearfulness, and she used to ask me whether the people of my country were as great cowards as myself. The occasion was this: the kingdom is much pestered with flies in summer; and these odious insects, each of them as big as a Dunstable lark, hardly gave me any rest while I sat at dinner, with their continuous humming and buzzing about my ears. They would sometimes alight upon my victuals, and leave their loathsome excrement or spawn behind, which to me was very visible, though not to the natives of that country, whose large optics were not so acute as mine in viewing smaller objects. Sometimes they would fix upon my nose or forehead, where they stung me to the quick, smelling very offensively, and I could easily trace that viscous matter, which our naturalists tell us enables those creatures to walk with their feet upwards upon a ceiling. I had much ado to defend myself against these detestable animals, and could not forbear starting when they came on my face. It was the common practice of the dwarf to catch a number of these insects in his hand, as schoolboys do among us, and let them out suddenly under my nose, on purpose to frighten me, and divert the Queen. My remedy was to cut them in pieces with my knife as they flew in the air, wherein my dexterity was much admired.

I remember one morning when Glumdalclitch had set me in my box upon a window, as she usually did in fair days to give me air (for I durst not venture to let the box be hung on a nail out of the window, as we do with cages in England) after I had lifted up one of my sashes, and sat down at my table to eat a piece of sweet cake for my breakfast, above twenty wasps, allured by the smell, came flying into the room, humming louder than the drones of as many bagpipes. Some of them seized my cake, and carried it piecemeal away, others flew about my head and face, confounding me with the noise, and putting me in the utmost terror of their stings. However I had the courage to rise and draw my hanger, and attack them in the air. I dispatched four of them, but the rest got away, and I presently shut my windows. These insects were as large as partridges: I took out their stings, found them an inch and a half long, and as sharp as needles. I carefully preserved them all, and having since shown them with some other curiosities in several parts of Europe; upon my return to England I gave three of them to Gresham College, and kept the fourth for myself.

CHAPTER IV

The country described. A proposal for correcting modern maps. The King's palace, and some account of the metropolis. The Author's way of travelling. The chief temple described.

I NOW intend to give the reader a short description of this country, as far as I travelled in it, which was not above two thousand miles round Lorbrulgrud the metropolis. For the Queen, whom I always attended, never went further when she accompanied the King in his progresses, and there stayed till his Majesty returned from viewing his frontiers. The whole extent of this prince's dominions reacheth about six thousand miles in length, and from three to five in breadth. From whence I cannot but conclude that our geographers of Europe are in a great error, by supposing nothing but sea between Japan and California; for it was ever my opinion that there must be a balance of earth to counterpoise the great continent of Tartary; and therefore they ought to correct their maps and charts, by joining this vast tract of land to the north-west parts of America, wherein I shall be ready to lend them my assistance.

The kingdom is a peninsula, terminated to the north-east by a ridge of mountains thirty miles high, which are altogether impassable by reason of the volcanoes upon the tops. Neither do the most learned know what sort of mortals inhabit beyond those mountains, or whether they be inhabited at all. On the three other sides it is bounded by the ocean. There is not one sea-port in the whole kingdom, and those parts of the coasts into which the rivers issue are so full of pointed rocks, and the sea generally so rough, that there is no venturing with the smallest of their boats, so that these people are wholly excluded from any commerce with the rest of the world. But the large rivers are full of vessels, and abound with excellent fish, for they seldom get any from the sea, because the sea-fish are of the

same size with those in Europe, and consequently not worth
catching; whereby it is manifest, that nature, in the pro-
duction of plants and animals of so extraordinary a bulk,
is wholly confined to this continent, of which I leave the
reasons to be determined by philosophers. However, now
and then they take a whale that happens to be dashed
against the rocks, which the common people feed on heartily.
These whales I have known so large that a man could hardly
carry one upon his shoulders; and sometimes for curiosity
they are brought in hampers to Lorbrulgrud: I saw one of
them in a dish at the King's table, which passed for a rarity,
but I did not observe he was fond of it; for I think indeed
the bigness disgusted him, although I have seen one some
what larger in Greenland.

The country is well inhabited, for it contains fifty-one
cities, near an hundred walled towns, and a great number
of villages. To satisfy my curious reader, it may be
sufficient to describe Lorbrulgrud. This city stands upon
almost two equal parts on each side the river that passes
through. It contains above eighty thousand houses, and
about six hundred thousand inhabitants. It is in length
three *glonglungs* (which make about fifty-four English miles)
and two and a half in breadth, as I measured it myself in
the royal map made by the King's order, which was laid on
the ground on purpose for me, and extended an hundred
feet: I paced the diameter and circumference several times
bare-foot, and computing by the scale, measured it pretty
exactly.

The King's palace is no regular edifice, but an heap of
buildings about seven miles round: the chief rooms are
generally two hundred and forty foot high, and broad and
long in proportion. A coach was allowed to Glumdalclitch
and me, wherein her governess frequently took her out to
see the town, or go among the shops; and I was always of
the party, carried in my box; although the girl at my own
desire would often take me out, and hold me in her hand,
that I might more conveniently view the houses and the
people, as we passed along the streets. I reckoned our

coach to be about a square of Westminster-Hall, but not altogether so high; however, I cannot be very exact. One day the governess ordered our coachman to stop at several shops, where the beggars, watching their opportunity, crowded to the sides of the coach, and gave me the most horrible spectacle that ever an European eye beheld.

Besides the large box in which I was usually carried, the Queen ordered a smaller one to be made for me, of about twelve foot square, and ten high, for the convenience of travelling, because the other was somewhat too large for Glumdalclitch's lap, and cumbersome in the coach; it was made by the same artist, whom I directed in the whole contrivance. This travelling closet was an exact square with a window in the middle of three of the squares, and each window was latticed with iron wire on the outside, to prevent accidents in long journeys. On the fourth side, which had no window, two strong staples were fixed, through which the person that carried me, when I had a mind to be on horseback, put in a leathern belt, and buckled it about his waist. This was always the office of some grave trusty servant in whom I could confide, whether I attended the King and Queen in their progresses, or were disposed to see the gardens, or pay a visit to some great lady or minister of state in the court, when Glumdalclitch happened to be out of order: for I soon began to be known and esteemed among the greatest officers, I suppose more upon account of their Majesties' favour, than any merit of my own. In journeys, when I was weary of the coach, a servant on horseback would buckle on my box, and place it on a cushion before him; and there I had a full prospect of the country on three sides from my three windows. I had in this closet a field-bed and a hammock hung from the ceiling, two chairs and a table, neatly screwed to the floor, to prevent being tossed about by the agitation of the horse or the coach. And having been long used to sea-voyages, those motions, although sometimes very violent, did not much discompose me.

Whenever I had a mind to see the town, it was always in

my travelling-closet, which Glumdalclitch held in her lap in a kind of open sedan, after the fashion of the country, borne by four men, and attended by two others in the Queen's livery. The people who had often heard of me, were very curious to crowd about the sedan, and the girl was complaisant enough to make the bearers stop, and to take me in her hand that I might be more conveniently seen.

I was very desirous to see the chief temple, and particularly the tower belonging to it, which is reckoned the highest in the kingdom. Accordingly one day my nurse carried me thither, but I may truly say I came back disappointed; for the height is not above three thousand foot, reckoning from the ground to the highest pinnacle top; which allowing for the difference between the size of those people, and us in Europe, is no great matter for admiration, nor at all equal in proportion (if I rightly remember) to Salisbury steeple. But, not to detract from a nation to which during my life I shall acknowledge myself extremely obliged, it must be allowed, that whatever this famous tower wants in height is amply made up in beauty and strength. For the walls are near an hundred foot thick, built of hewn stone, whereof each is about forty foot square, and adorned on all sides with statues of Gods and Emperors cut in marble larger than the life, placed in their several niches. I measured a little finger which had fallen down from one of these statues, and lay unperceived among some rubbish, and found it exactly four foot and an inch in length. Glumdalclitch wrapped it up in a handkerchief, and carried it home in her pocket to keep among other trinkets, of which the girl was very fond, as children at her age usually are.

The King's kitchen is indeed a noble building, vaulted at top, and about six hundred foot high. The great oven is not so wide by ten paces as the cupola at St. Paul's: for I measured the latter on purpose after my return. But if I should describe the kitchen-grate, the prodigious pots and kettles, the joints of meat turning on the spits, with many other particulars, perhaps I should be hardly believed;

at least a severe critic would be apt to think I enlarged a little, as travellers are often suspected to do. To avoid which censure, I fear I have run too much into the other extreme; and that if this treatise should happen to be translated into the language of Brobdingnag (which is the general name of that kingdom) and transmitted thither, the King and his people would have reason to complain that I had done them an injury by a false and diminutive representation.

His Majesty seldom keeps above six hundred horses in his stables: they are generally from fifty-four to sixty foot high. But when he goes abroad on solemn days, he is attended for state by a militia guard of five hundred horse, which indeed I thought was the most splendid sight that could be ever beheld, till I saw part of his army in battalia, whereof I shall find another occasion to speak.

CHAPTER V

Several adventures that happened to the Author. The execution of a criminal. The Author shows his skill in navigation.

I SHOULD have lived happy enough in that country, if my littleness had not exposed me to several ridiculous and troublesome accidents: some of which I shall venture to relate. Glumdalclitch often carried me into the gardens of the court in my smaller box, and would sometimes take me out of it and hold me in her hand, or set me down to walk. I remember, before the dwarf left the Queen, he followed us one day into those gardens, and my nurse having set me down, he and I being close together, near some dwarf apple-trees, I must need show my wit by a silly allusion between him and the trees, which happens to hold in their language as it doth in ours. Whereupon, the malicious rogue watching his opportunity, when I was walking under one of them, shook it directly over my head, by which a dozen apples, each of them near as large as a Bristol barrel, came tumbling about my ears; one of them hit me on the back as I chanced to stoop, and knocked me down flat on my face, but I received no other hurt, and the dwarf was pardoned at my desire, because I had given the provocation.

Another day Glumdalclitch left me on a smooth grass-plot to divert myself while she walked at some distance with her governess. In the meantime there suddenly fell such a violent shower of hail, that I was immediately by the force of it struck to the ground: and when I was down, the hail-stones gave me such cruel bangs all over the body, as if I had been pelted with tennis-balls; however I made a shift to creep on all four, and shelter myself by lying flat on my face on the lee-side of a border of lemon thyme, but so bruised from head to foot that I could not go abroad in ten days. Neither is this at all to be wondered at, because nature in that country observing the same proportion through all her operations, a hailstone is near eighteen hundred times as large as one in Europe, which I can assert upon experience, having been so curious to weigh and measure them.

But a more dangerous accident happened to me in the same garden, when my little nurse believing she had put me in a secure place, which I often entreated her to do, that I might enjoy my own thoughts, and having left my box at home to avoid the trouble of carrying it, went to another part of the garden with her governess and some ladies of her acquaintance. While she was absent, and out of hearing, a small white spaniel belonging to one of the chief gardeners, having got by accident into the garden, happened to range near the place where I lay. The dog followed the scent, came directly up, and taking me in his mouth, ran straight to his master, wagging his tail, and set me gently on the ground. By good fortune he had been so well taught, that I was carried between his teeth without the least hurt, or even tearing my clothes. But the poor gardener, who knew me well, and had a great kindness for me, was in a terrible fright. He gently took me up in both his hands, and asked me how I did; but I was so amazed and out of breath, that I could not speak a word. In a few minutes I came to myself, and he carried me safe to my little nurse, who by this time had returned to the place where she left me, and was in cruel agonies when I did not appear, nor answer when she called: she severely reprimanded the gardener on account of his dog. But the thing was hushed up, and never known at court; for the girl was afraid of the Queen's anger, and truly as to myself, I thought it would not be for my reputation that such a story should go about.

This accident absolutely determined Glumdalclitch never to trust me abroad for the future out of her sight. I had been long afraid of this resolution, and therefore concealed from her some little unlucky adventures that happened in those times when I was left by myself. Once a kite hovering

8

over the garden made a stoop at me, and if I had not resolutely drawn my hanger, and run under a thick espalier, he would have certainly carried me away in his talons. Another time walking to the top of a fresh mole-hill, I fell to my neck in the hole through which that animal had cast up the earth, and coined some lie, not worth remembering, to excuse myself for spoiling my clothes. I likewise broke my right shin against the shell of a snail, which I happened to stumble over, as I was walking alone, and thinking on poor England.

I cannot tell whether I were more pleased or mortified, to observe in those solitary walks, that the smaller birds did not appear to be at all afraid of me, but would hop about within a yard distance, looking for worms, and other food, with as much indifference and security, as if no creature at all were near them. I remember, a thrush had the confidence to snatch out of my hand, with his bill, a piece of cake that Glumdalclitch had just given me for my breakfast. When I attempted to catch any of these birds, they would boldly turn against me, endeavouring to pick my fingers, which I durst not venture within their reach; and then they would hop back unconcerned, to hunt for worms or snails, as they did before. But one day I took a thick cudgel, and threw it with all my strength so luckily at a linnet, that I knocked him down, and seizing him by the neck with both my hands, ran with him in triumph to my nurse. However, the bird, who had only been stunned, recovering himself, gave me so many boxes with his wings on both sides of my head and body, though I held him at arm's length, and was out of the reach of his claws, that I was twenty times thinking to let him go. But I was soon relieved by one of our servants, who wrung off the bird's neck, and I had him next day for dinner, by the Queen's command. This linnet, as near as I can remember, seemed to be somewhat larger than an English swan.

One day a young gentleman, who was nephew to my nurse's governess, came and pressed them both to see an execution. It was of a man who had murdered one of that gentleman's intimate acquaintance. Glumdalclitch was prevailed on to be of the company, very much against her inclination, for she was naturally tender-hearted: and as for myself, although I abhorred such kind of spectacles, yet my curiosity tempted me to see something that I thought must be extraordinary. The malefactor was fixed in a chair upon a scaffold erected for the purpose, and his head cut off at a blow with a sword of about forty foot long. The veins and arteries spouted up such a prodigious quantity of blood, and so high in the air, that the great *jet d'eau* at Versailles was not equal for the time it lasted; and the head, when it fell on the scaffold floor, gave such a bounce, as made me start, although I were at least half an English mile distant.

The Queen, who often used to hear me talk of my sea-voyages, and took all occasions to divert me when I was melancholy, asked me whether I understood how to handle a sail, or an oar, and whether a little exercise of rowing might not be convenient for my health. I answered, that I understood both very well: for although my proper employment had been to be surgeon or doctor to the ship, yet often, upon a pinch, I was forced to work like a common mariner. But I could not see how this could be done in their country, where the smallest wherry was equal to a first-rate man of war among us, and such a boat as I could manage would never live in any of their rivers. Her Majesty said, if I would contrive a boat, her own joiner should make it, and she would provide a place for me to sail in. The fellow was an ingenious workman, and, by my instructions, in ten days finished a pleasure-boat, with all its tackling, able conveniently to hold eight Europeans. When it was finished, the Queen was so delighted, that she run with it in her lap to the King, who ordered it to be put in a cistern full of water, with me in it, by way of trial; where I could not manage my two sculls, or little oars, for want of room. But the Queen had before contrived another project. She ordered the joiner to make a wooden trough of three hundred foot long, fifty broad, and eight deep; which being well pitched to prevent leaking, was placed on the floor along the wall, in an outer room of the palace. It had a cock near the bottom to let out the water when it began to grow stale, and two servants could easily fill it in half an hour. Here I often used to row for my own diversion, as well as that of the Queen and her ladies, who thought themselves well entertained with my skill and agility. Sometimes I would put up my sail, and then my business was only to steer, while the ladies gave me a gale with their fans; and when they were weary, some of the pages would blow my sail forward with their breath, while I showed my art by steering starboard or larboard as I pleased. When I had done, Glumdalclitch always carried my boat into her closet, and hung it on a nail to dry.

In this exercise I once met an accident which had like to have cost me my life: for, one of the pages having put my boat into the trough, the governess, who attended Glumdalclitch, very officiously lifted me up to place me in the boat, but I happened to slip through her fingers, and should have infallibly fallen down forty feet upon the floor, if by the luckiest chance in the world, I had not been stopped by a corking-pin that stuck in the good gentlewoman's stomacher; the head of the pin passed between my shirt and the waistband of my breeches, and thus I was held by the middle in the air till Glumdalclitch ran to my relief.

Another time, one of the servants, whose office it was to fill my trough every third day with fresh water, was so careless to let a huge frog (not perceiving it) slip out of his pail. The frog lay concealed till I was put into my boat, but then seeing a resting-place, climbed up, and made it lean so much on one side, that I was forced to balance it with all my weight on the other, to prevent overturning. When the frog was got in, it hopped at once half the length of the boat, and then over my head, backwards and forwards, daubing my face and clothes with its odious slime. The largeness of its features made it appear the most deformed animal that can be conceived. However, I desired Glumdalclitch to let me deal with it alone. I banged it a good while with one of my sculls, and at last forced it to leap out of the boat.

But the greatest danger I ever underwent in that kingdom, was from a monkey, who belonged to one of the clerks of the kitchen. Glumdalclitch had locked me up in her closet, while she went somewhere upon business, or a visit. The weather being very warm, the closet-window was left open, as well as the windows and the door of my bigger box, in which I usually lived, because of its largeness and conveniency. As I sat quietly meditating at my table, I heard something bounce in at the closet-window, and skip about from one side to the other; whereat, although I were much alarmed, yet I ventured to look out, but not stirring from my seat; and then I saw this frolicsome animal, frisking and leaping up and down, till at last he came to my box which he seemed to view with great pleasure and curiosity, peeping in at the door and every window. I retreated to the farther corner of my room, or box, but the monkey looking in at every side, put me into such a fright, that I wanted presence of mind to conceal myself under the bed, as I might easily have done. After some time spent in peeping, grinning, and chattering, he at last espied me and reaching one of his paws in at the door, as a cat does when she plays with a mouse, although I often shifted place to avoid him, he at length seized the lappet of my coat (which being made of that country silk, was very thick and strong) and dragged me out. He took me up in his right fore-foot, and held me as a nurse does a child she is going to suckle, just as I have seen the same sort of creature do with a kitten in Europe and when I offered to struggle, he squeezed me so hard, that I thought it more prudent to submit. I have good reason to believe that he took me for a young one of his own species, by his often stroking my face very gently with his other paw. In these diversions he was interrupted by a noise at the closet door, as if somebody was opening it; whereupon he suddenly leaped up to the window, at which he had come in, and thence upon the leads and gutters, walking upon three legs, and holding me in the fourth, till he clambered up to a roof that was next to ours. I heard Glumdalclitch give a shriek at the moment he was carrying me out. The poor girl was almost distracted: that quarter of the palace was all in an uproar; the servants ran for ladders; the monkey was seen by hundreds in the court, sitting upon the ridge of a building, holding me like a baby in one of his fore-paws, and feeding me with the other, by cramming into my mouth some victuals he had squeezed out of the bag on one side of his chaps, and patting me when I would not eat; wherat many of the rabble below could not forbear laughing; neither do I think they justly ought to be blamed, for without question the sight was ridiculous enough to every body but myself. Some of the people threw up stones, hoping to drive the monkey down but this was strictly forbidden, or else very probably my brains had been dashed out.

The ladders were now applied, and mounted by several men, which the monkey observing, and finding himself almost encompassed; not being able to make speed enough with his three legs, let me drop on a ridge tile, and made his escape. Here I sat for some time three hundred yards from the ground, expecting every moment to be blown down by the wind, or to fall by my own giddiness, and come tumbling over and over from the ridge to the eaves; but an honest lad, one of my nurse's footmen, climbed up, and putting me into his breeches pocket, brought me down safe.

I was almost choked with the filthy stuff the monkey had crammed down my throat: but my dear little nurse picked it out of my mouth with a small needle, and then I fell a vomiting, which gave me great relief. Yet I was so weak and bruised in the sides with the squeezes given me by this odious animal, that I was forced to keep my bed a fortnight. The King, Queen, and all the court, sent every day to enquire after my health, and her Majesty made me several visits during my sickness. The monkey was killed and an order made that no such animal should be kept about the palace.

When I attended the King after my recovery, to return him thanks for his favours, he was pleased to rally me a good deal upon this adventure. He asked me what my thoughts and speculations were while I lay in the monkey's paw; how I liked the victuals he gave me; his manner of feeding; and whether the fresh air on the roof had sharpened my stomach. He desired to know what I would have done upon such an occasion in my own country. I told his Majesty, that in Europe we had no monkeys, except such as were brought for curiosities from other places, and so small, that I could deal with a dozen of them together, if they presumed to attack me. And as for that monstrous animal with whom I was so lately engaged, (it was indeed as large as an elephant) if my fears had suffered me to think so far as to make use of my hanger, (looking fiercely and clapping my hand upon the hilt as I spoke) when he poked his paw into my chamber, perhaps I should have given him such a wound, as would have made him glad to withdraw it with more haste than he put it in. This I delivered in a firm tone, like a person who was jealous lest his courage should be called in question. However, my speech produced nothing else besides a loud laughter, which all the respect due to his Majesty from those about him could not make then contain. This made me reflect how vain an attempt it is for a man to endeavour doing himself honour among those who are out of all degree of equality or comparison with him. And yet I have seen the moral of my own behaviour very frequent in England since my return, where a little contemptible varlet, without the least title to birth, person, wit, or common sense, shall presume to look with importance, and put himself upon a foot with the greatest persons of the kingdom.

I was every day furnishing the court with some ridiculous story: and Glumdalclitch, although she loved me to excess, yet was arch enough to inform the Queen, whenever I committed any folly that she thought would be diverting to her Majesty. The girl, who had been out of order, was carried by her governess to take the air about an hour's distance, or thirty miles from town. They alighted out of the coach near a small foot-path in a field, and Glumdalclitch setting down my travelling box, I went out of it to walk. There was a cow-dung in the path, and I must needs try my activity by attempting to leap over it. I took a run, but unfortunately jumped short, and found myself just in the middle up to my knees. I waded through with some difficulty, and one of the footmen wiped me as clean as he could with his handkerchief; for I was filthily bemired, and my nurse confined me to my box till we returned home; where the Queen was soon informed of what had passed, and the footmen spread it about the court: so that all the mirth, for some days, was at my expense.

CHAPTER VI

Several contrivances of the Author to please the King and Queen. He shows his skill in music. The King enquires into the state of Europe, which the Author relates to him. The King's observations thereon.

I USED to attend the King's levee once or twice a week, and had often seen him under the barber's hand, which indeed was at first very terrible to behold: for the razor was almost twice as long as an ordinary scythe. His Majesty, according to the custom of the country, was only shaved twice a week. I once prevailed on the barber to give me some of the suds or lather, out of which I picked forty or fifty of the strongest stumps of hair. I then took a piece of fine wood, and cut it like the back of a comb, making several holes in it at equal distance with as small a needle as I could get from Glumdalclitch. I fixed in the stumps so artificially, scraping and sloping them with my knife toward the points, that I made a very tolerable comb; which was a seasonable supply, my own being so much broken in the teeth, that it was almost useless: neither did I know any artist in that country so nice and exact, as would undertake to make me another.

And this puts me in mind of an amusement wherein I spend many of my leisure hours. I desired the Queen's woman to save for me the combings of her Majesty's hair, whereof in time I got a good quantity, and consulting with my friend the cabinet-maker, who had received general orders to do little jobs for me, I directed him to make two chair-frames, no larger than those I had in my box, and then to bore little holes with a fine awl round those parts where I designed the backs and seats; through these holes I wove the strongest hairs I could pick out, just after the manner of cane-chairs in England. When they were finished, I made a present of them to her Majesty, who kept them in her cabinet, and used to show them for curiosities, as indeed they were the wonder of every one that beheld them. The Queen would have had me sit upon one of these chairs, but I absolutely refused to obey her, protesting I would rather die a thousand deaths than place a dishonourable part of my body on those precious hairs that once adorned her Majesty's head. Of these hairs (as I had always a mechanical genius) I likewise made a neat little purse about five foot long, with her Majesty's name deciphered in gold letters, which I gave to Glumdalclitch, by the Queen's consent. To say the truth, it was more for show than use, being not of strength to bear the weight of the larger coins, and therefore she kept nothing in it but some little toys that girls are fond of.

The King, who delighted in music, had frequent concerts at court, to which I was sometimes carried, and set in my box on a table to hear them: but the noise was so great, that I could hardly distinguish the tunes. I am confident that all the drums and trumpets of a royal army, beating and sounding together just at your ears, could not equal it. My practice was to have my box removed from the places where the performers sat, as far as I could, then to shut the doors and windows of it, and draw the window curtains; after which I found their music not disagreeable.

I had learned in my youth to play a little upon the spinet. Glumdalclitch kept one in her chamber, and a master attended twice a week to teach her: I call it a spinet, because it somewhat resembled that instrument, and was played upon in the same manner. A fancy came into my head that I would entertain the King and Queen with an English tune upon this instrument. But this appeared extremely difficult: for the spinet was near sixty foot long, each key being almost a foot wide, so that, with my arms extended, I could not reach to above five keys, and to press them down required a good smart stroke with my fist, which would be too great a labour, and to no purpose. The method I contrived was this. I prepared two round sticks about the bigness of common cudgels; they were thicker at one end than the other, and I covered the thicker ends with a piece of a mouse's skin, that by rapping on them I might neither damage the top of the keys, nor interrupt the sound. Before the spinet a bench was placed, about four foot below the keys, and I was put upon the bench. I ran sideling upon it that way and this, as fast as I could, banging the proper keys with my two sticks, and made a shift to play a jig, to the great satisfaction of both their Majesties: but it was the most violent exercise I ever underwent, and yet I could not strike above sixteen keys, nor, consequently, play the bass and treble together, as other artists do; which was a great disadvantage to my performance.

The King, who, as I before observed, was a prince of excellent understanding, would frequently order that I should be brought in my box, and set upon the table in his closet. He would then command me to bring one of my chairs out of the box, and sit down within three yards distance upon the top of the cabinet, which brought me almost to a level with his face. In this manner I had several conversations with him. I one day took the freedom to tell his Majesty, that the contempt he discovered towards Europe, and the rest of the world, did not seem answerable to these excellent qualities of the mind he was master of. That reason did not extend itself with the bulk of the body: on the contrary, we observed in our country, that the tallest persons were usually least provided with it. That among other animals, bees and ants had the reputation of more industry, art and sagacity, than many of the larger kinds. And that, as inconsiderable as he took me to be, I hoped I might live to do his Majesty some signal service. The King heard me with attention, and began to conceive a much better opinion of me than he had ever before. He desired I would give him as exact an account of the government of England as I possibly could; because, as fond as princes commonly are of their own customs (for so he conjectured of other monarchs, by my former discourses), he should be glad to hear of any thing that might deserve imitation.

Imagine with thyself, courteous reader, how often I then wished for the tongue of Demosthenes or Cicero, that might have enabled me to celebrate the praise of my own dear native country in a style equal to its merits and felicity.

I began my discourse by informing his Majesty, that our dominions consisted of two islands, which composed three mighty kingdoms under one sovereign, beside our plantations in America. I dwelt long upon the fertility of our soil, and the temperature of our climate. I then spoke at large upon the constitution of an English Parliament, partly made up of an illustrious body called the House of Peers, persons of the noblest blood, and of the most ancient and ample patrimonies. I described that extraordinary care always taken of their education in arts and arms, to qualify them for being counsellers born to the king and kingdom; to have a share in the legislature; to be members of the highest Court of Judicature, from whence there could be no appeal; and to be champions always ready for the defence of their prince and country, by their valour, conduct, and fidelity. That these were the ornament and bulwark of the kingdom, worthy followers of their most renowned ancestors whose honour had been the reward of their virtue, from which their posterity were never once known to degenerate. To these were joined several holy persons, as part of that assembly, under the title of Bishops, whose peculiar business it is to take care of religion, and of those who instruct the people therein. These were searched and sought out through the whole nation, by the prince and his wisest counsellors, among such of the priesthood as were most deservedly distinguished by the sanctity of their lives, and the depth of their erudition; who were indeed the spiritual father of the clergy and the people.

That the other part of the Parliament consisted of an assembly called the House of Commons, who were all principal gentlemen, freely picked and culled out by the people themselves, for their great abilities and love of their country, to represent the wisdom of the whole nation. And these two bodies make up the most august assembly in Europe, to whom, in conjunction with the prince, the whole legislature is committed.

I then descended to the Courts of Justice, over which the Judges, those venerable sages and interpreters of the law presided, for determining the disputed rights and properties of men, as well as for the punishment of vice, and protection of innocence. I mentioned the prudent management of our treasury; the valour and achievements of our forces by sea and land. I computed the number of our people, by reckoning how many millions there might be of each religious sect, or political party among us. I did not omit even our sports and pastimes, or any other particular which I thought might redound to the honour of my country. And I finished all with a brief historical account of affairs and events in England for about an hundred years past.

This conversation was not ended under five audiences, each of several hours, and the King heard the whole with great attention, frequently taking notes of what I spoke, as well as memorandums of what questions he intended to ask me.

When I had put an end to these long discourses, his Majesty in a sixth audience consulting his notes, proposed many doubts, queries, and objections, upon every article. He asked what methods were used to cultivate the minds and bodies of our young nobility, and in what kind of business they commonly spent the first and teachable part of their lives. What course was taken to supply that assembly when any noble family became extinct. What qualifications were necessary in those who are to be created new lords: whether the humour of the prince, a sum of money to a court lady, or a prime minister, or a design of strengthening a party opposite to the public interest, ever happened to be motives in those advancements. What share of knowledge these lords had in the laws of their country, and how they came by it, so as to enable them to decide the properties of their fellow-subjects in the last resort. Whether they were always so free from avarice, partialities, or want, that a bribe, or some other sinister view, could have no place among them. Whether those holy lords I spoke of were always promoted to that rank upon account of their knowledge in religious matters, and the sanctity of their lives, had never been compliers with the times, while they were common priests, or slavish prostitute chaplains to some nobleman, whose opinions they continued servilely to follow after they were admitted into that assembly.

He then desired to know what arts were practised in electing those whom I called commoners: whether a stranger with a strong purse might not influence the vulgar voters to choose him before their own landlord, or the most considerable gentleman in the neighbourhood. How it came to pass, that people were so violently bent upon getting into this assembly, which I allowed to be a great trouble and expense, often to the ruin of their families, without any salary or pension: because this appeared such an exalted strain of virtue and public spirit, that his Majesty seemed to doubt it might possibly not be always sincere: and he desired to know whether such zealous gentlemen could have any views of refunding themselves for the charges and trouble they were at, by sacrificing the public good to the designs of a weak and vicious prince in conjunction with a corrupted ministry. He multiplied his questions, and sifted me thoroughly upon every part of his head, proposing numberless enquiries and objections, which I think it not prudent or convenient to repeat.

Upon what I said in relation to our Courts of Justice, his Majesty desired to be satisfied in several points: and this I was the better able to do, having been formerly almost ruined by a long suit in chancery, which was decreed for me with costs. He asked, what time was usually spent in determining between right and wrong, and what degree of expense. Whether advocates and orators had liberty to plead in causes manifestly known to be unjust, vexatious, or oppressive. Whether party in religion or politics were observed to be of any weight in the scale of justice. Whether those pleading orators were persons educated in the general knowledge of equity, or only in provincial, national, and other local customs. Whether they or their judges had any part in penning those laws which they assumed the liberty of interpreting and glossing upon at their pleasure. Whether they had ever at different times pleaded for and against the same cause, and cited precedents to prove contrary opinions. Whether they were a rich or a poor corporation. Whether they received any pecuniary reward for pleading or delivering their opinions. And particularly, whether they were ever admitted as members in the lower senate.

He fell next upon the management of our treasury; and said, he thought my memory had failed me, because I computed our taxes at about five or six million a year, and when I came to mention the issues, he found they sometimes amounted to more than double; for the notes he had taken were very particular in this point, because he hoped, as he told me, that the knowledge of our conduct might be useful to him, and he could not be deceived in his calculations. But, if what I told him were true, he was still at a loss how a kingdom could run out of its estate like a private person. He asked me, who were our creditors; and where we should find money to pay them. He wondered to hear me talk of such chargeable and expensive wars; that certainly we must be a quarrelsome people, or live among very bad neighbours, and that our generals must needs be richer than our kings. He asked what business we had out of our own islands, unless upon the score of trade or treaty, or to defend the coasts with our fleet. Above all, he was amazed to hear me talk of a mercenary standing army in the midst of peace, and among a free people. He said, if we were governed by our own consent in the persons of our representatives, he could not imagine of whom we were afraid, or against whom we were to fight; and would hear my opinion, whether a private man's house might not better be defended by himself, his children, and family, than by half a dozen rascals picked up at a venture in the streets, for small wages, who might get an hundred times more by cutting their throats.

He laughed at my odd kind of arithmetic (as he was pleased to call it) in reckoning the number of our people by a computation drawn from the several sects among us in religion and politics. He said, he knew no reason, why those who entertain opinions prejudicial to the public, should be obliged to change, or should not be obliged to conceal them. And as it was tyranny in any government to require the first, so it was weakness not to enforce the second: for a man may be allowed to keep poisons in his closet, but not to vend them about for cordials.

He observed, that among the diversions of our nobility and gentry, I had mentioned gaming. He desired to know at what age this entertainment was usually taken up, and when it was laid down; how much of their time it employed; whether it ever went so high as to affect their fortunes; whether mean vicious people, by their dexterity in that art, might not arrive at great riches, and sometimes keep our very nobles in dependence, as well as habituate them to vile companions, wholly take them from the improvement of their minds, and force them, by the losses they have received, to learn and practise that infamous dexterity upon others.

He was perfectly astonished with the historical account I gave him of our affairs during the last century, protesting it was only an heap of conspiracies, rebellions, murders, massacres, revolutions, banishments, the very worst effects that avarice, faction, hypocrisy, perfidiousness, cruelty, rage, madness, hatred, envy, lust, malice, or ambition, could produce.

His Majesty, in another audience, was at the pains to recapitulate the sum of all I had spoken; compared the question he made with the answers I had given; then taking me into his hands, and stroking me gently, delivered himself in these words, which I shall never forget, nor the manner he spoke them in: My little friend Grildrig, you have made a most admirable panegyric upon your country; you have clearly proved that ignorance, idleness, and vice, are the proper ingredients for qualifying a legislator: that laws are best explained, interpreted and applied by those whose interest and abilities lie in perverting, confounding, and eluding them. I observe among you some lines of an institution, which in its original might have been tolerable, but these half erased, and the rest wholly blurred and blotted by corruptions. It doth not appear from all you have said, how any one virtue is required towards the procurement of any one station among you; much less that men are ennobled on account of their virtue, that priests are advanced for their piety or learning, soldiers for their conduct or valour, judges for their integrity, senators for the love of their country, or counsellors for their wisdom. As for yourself (continued the King), who have spent the greatest part of your life travelling, I am well disposed to hope you may hitherto have escaped many vices of your country. But by what I have gathered from your own relation, and the answers I have with much pains wringed and extorted from you, I cannot but conclude the bulk of your natives to be the most pernicious race of little odious vermin that nature ever suffered to crawl upon the surface of the earth.

CHAPTER VII

The Author's love of his country. He makes a proposal of much advantage to the King, which is rejected. The King's great ignorance in politics. The learning of that country very imperfect and confined. Their laws, and military affairs, and parties in the State.

NOTHING but an extreme love of truth could have hindered me from concealing this part of my story. It was in vain to discover my resentments, which were always turned into ridicule; and I was forced to rest with patience while my noble and most beloved country was so injuriously treated. I am heartily sorry as any of my readers can possibly be, that such an occasion was given: but this prince happened to be so curious and inquisitive upon every particular, that it could not consist either with gratitude or good manners to refuse giving him what satisfaction I was able. Yet thus much I may be allowed to say in my own vindication, that I artfully eluded many of his questions, and gave to every point a more favourable turn by many degrees than the strictness of truth would allow. For I have always borne that laudable partiality to my own country, which Dionysius Halicarnassensis with so much justice recommends to an historian: I would hide the frailties and deformities of my political mother, and place her virtues and beauties in the most advantageous light. This was my sincere endeavour in those many discourses I had with that mighty monarch, although it unfortunately failed of success.

But great allowances should be given to a King who lives wholly secluded from the rest of the world, and must therefore be altogether unacquainted with the manners and customs that most prevail in other nations: the want of which knowledge will ever produce many prejudices, and a certain narrowness of thinking, from which we and the politer countries of Europe are wholly exempted. And it would be hard indeed, if so remote a prince's notions of virtue and vice were to be offered as a standard for all mankind.

To confirm what I have now said, and further, to show the miserable effects of a confined education, I shall here insert a passage which will hardly obtain belief. In hopes to ingratiate myself farther into his Majesty's favour, I told him of an invention discovered between three and four hundred years ago, to make a certain powder, into an heap of which the smallest spark of fire falling, would kindle the whole in a moment, although it were as big as a mountain, and make it all fly up in the air together, with a noise and agitation greater than thunder. That a proper quantity of this powder rammed into an hollow tube of brass or iron, according to its bigness, would drive a ball of iron or lead with such violence and speed, as nothing was able to sustain its force. That the largest balls thus discharged, would not only destroy whole ranks of an army at once, but batter the strongest walls to the ground, sink down ships, with a thousand men in each, to the bottom of the sea; and, when linked together by a chain, would cut through masts and rigging, divide hundreds of bodies in the middle, and lay all waste before them. That we often put this powder into large hollow balls of iron, and discharged them by an engine into some city we were besieging, which would rip up the pavements, tear the houses to pieces, burst and throw splinters on every side, dashing out the brains of all who came near. That I knew the ingredients very well, which were cheap, and common; I understood the manner of compounding them, and could direct his workmen how to make those tubes, of a size proportionable to all other things in his Majesty's kingdom, and the largest need not be above an hundred foot long; twenty or thirty of which tubes, charged with the proper quantity of powder and balls, would batter down the walls of the strongest town in his dominions in a few hours, or destroy the whole metropolis, if ever it should pretend to dispute his absolute commands. This I humbly offered to his Majesty, as a small tribute of acknowledgment in return of so many marks that I had received of his royal favour and protection.

The King was struck with horror at the description I had

given of these terrible engines, and the proposal I had made. He was amazed how so impotent and grovelling an insect as I (these were his expressions) could entertain such inhuman ideas, and in so familiar a manner as to appear wholly unmoved at all the scenes of blood and desolation, which I had painted as the common effects of those destructive machines, whereof he said, some evil genius, enemy to mankind, must have been the first contriver. As for himself, he protested, that although few things delighted him so much as new discoveries in art or in nature, yet he would rather lose half his kingdom than be privy to such a secret, which he commanded me, as I valued my life, never to mention any more.

A strange effect of narrow principles and short views! that a prince possessed of every quality which procures veneration, love, and esteem; of strong parts, great wisdom, and profound learning, endued with admirable talents for government, and almost adored by his subjects, should from a nice unnecessary scruple, whereof in Europe we can have no conception, let slip an opportunity put into his hands, that would have made him absolute master of the lives, the liberties, and the fortunes of his people. Neither do I say this with the least intention to detract from the many virtues of that excellent King, whose character I am sensible will on this account be very much lessened in the opinion of an English reader: but I take this defect among them to have risen from their ignorance, they not having hitherto reduced politics into a science, as the more acute wits of Europe have done. For, I remember very well, in a discourse one day with the King, when I happened to say there were several thousand books among us written upon the art of government, it gave him (directly contrary to my intention) a very mean opinion of our understandings. He professed both to abominate and despise all mystery, refinement, and intrigue, either in a prince or a minister. He could not tell what I meant by secrets of state, where an enemy or some rival nation were not in the case. He confined the knowledge of governing within very narrow bounds; to common sense and reason, to justice and lenity, to the speedy determination of civil and criminal causes; with some other obvious topics, which are not worth considering. And he gave it for his opinion, that whoever could make two ears of corn, or two blades of grass to grow upon a spot of ground where only one grew before, would deserve better of mankind, and do more essential service to his country than the whole race of politicians put together.

The learning of this people is very defective, consisting only in morality, history, poetry, and mathematics, wherein they must be allowed to excel. But the last of these is wholly applied to what may be useful in life, to the improvement of agriculture, and all mechanical arts; so that among us it would be little esteemed. And as to ideas, entities, abstractions, and transcendentals, I could never drive the least conception into their heads.

No law of that country must exceed in words the number of letters in their alphabet, which consists only in two and twenty. But, indeed, few of them extend even to that length. They are expressed in the most plain and simple terms, wherein those people are not mercurial enough to discover above one interpretation: and to write a comment upon any law is a capital crime. As to the decision of civil causes, or proceedings against criminals, their precedents are so few, that they have little reason to boast of any extraordinary skill in either.

They have had the art of printing, as well as the Chinese, time out of mind: but their libraries are not very large; for that of the King's, which is reckoned the biggest, doth not amount to above a thousand volumes, placed in a gallery of twelve hundred foot long, from whence I had liberty to borrow what books I pleased. The Queen's joiner had contrived in one of Glumdalclitch's rooms a kind of wooden machine five and twenty foot high, formed like a standing ladder; the steps were each fifty foot long. It was indeed a moveable pair of stairs, the lowest end placed at ten foot distance from the wall of the chamber. The book I had a mind to read was put up leaning against the wall. I first mounted to the upper step of the ladder, and turning my face towards the book, began at the top of the page, and so walking to the right and left about eight or ten paces, according to the length of the lines, till I had gotten a little below the level of my eyes, and then descending gradually till I came to the bottom: after which I mounted again, and began the other page in the same manner, and so turned over the leaf, which I could easily do with both my hands, for it was as thick and stiff as a pasteboard, and in the largest folios not above eighteen or twenty foot long.

Their style is clear, masculine, and smooth, but not florid, for they avoid nothing more than multiplying unnecessary words, or using various expressions. I have perused many of their books, especially those in history and morality. Among the rest, I was much diverted with a little old treatise, which always lay in Glumdalclitch's bed-chamber, and belonged to her governess, a grave elderly gentlewoman, who dealt in writings of morality and devotion. The book treats of the weakness of human kind, and is in little esteem, except among the women and the vulgar. However, I was curious to see what an author of that country could say upon such a subject. This writer went through all the usual topics of European moralists, showing how diminutive, contemptible, and helpless an animal was man in his own nature; how unable to defend himself from the inclemencies of the air, or the fury of wild beasts: how much he was excelled by one creature in strength, by another in speed, by a third in foresight, by a fourth in industry. He added, that nature was degenerated in these latter declining ages of the world, and could now produce only small abortive births in comparison of those in ancient times. He said, it was very reasonable to think, not only that the species of men were originally much larger, but also, that there must have been giants in former ages, which, as it is asserted by histories and traditions, so it hath been confirmed by huge bones and skulls casually dug up in several parts of the kingdom, far exceeding the common dwindled race of man in our days. He argued, that the very laws of nature absolutely required we should have been made in the beginning, of a size more large and robust, not so liable to destruction from every little accident of a tile falling from a house, or a stone cast from the hand of a boy, or of being drowned in a little brook. From this way of reasoning the author drew several moral applications useful in the conduct of life, but needless here to repeat. For my own part, I could not avoid reflecting how universally this talent was spread, of drawing lectures in morality or indeed rather matter of discontent and repining, from the quarrels we raise with nature. And I believe, upon a strict enquiry, those quarrels might be shown as ill grounded among us, as they are among that people.

As to their military affairs, they boast that the King's army consists of an hundred and seventy-six thousand foot, and thirty-two thousand horse: if that may be called an army which is made up of tradesmen in the several cities, and farmers in the country, whose commanders are only the nobility and gentry, without pay or reward. They are indeed perfect enough in their exercises, and under very good discipline, wherein I saw no great merit; for how should it be otherwise, where every farmer is under the command of his own landlord, and every citizen under that of the principal men in his own city, chosen after the manner of Venice by ballot.

I have often seen the militia of Lorbrulgrud drawn out to exercise in a great field near the city of twenty miles square. They were in all not above twenty-five thousand foot, and six thousand horse; but it was impossible for me to compute their number, considering the space of ground they took up. A cavalier mounted on a large steed, might be about an hundred foot high. I have seen this whole body of horse, upon a word of command, draw their swords at once, and brandish them in the air. Imagination can figure nothing so grand, so surprising, and so astonishing! It looked as if ten thousand flashes of lightning were darting at the same time from every quarter of the sky.

I was curious to know how this prince, to whose

dominions there is no access from any other country, came to think of armies, or to teach his people the practice of military discipline. But I was soon informed, both by conversation, and reading their histories. For, in the course of many ages they have been troubled with the same disease to which the whole race of mankind is subject; the nobility often contending for power, the people for liberty, and the King for absolute dominion. All which however happily tempered by the laws of that kingdom, have been sometimes violated by each of the three parties, and have once or more occasioned civil wars, the last whereof was happily put an end to by this prince's grandfather by a general composition; and the militia, then settled with common consent, hath been ever since kept in the strictest duty.

CHAPTER VIII

The King and Queen make a progress to the frontiers. The Author attends them. The manner in which he leaves the country very particularly related. He returns to England.

I HAD always a strong impulse that I should some time recover my liberty, though it was impossible to conjecture by what means, or to form any project with the least hope of succeeding. The ship in which I sailed was the first ever known to be driven within sight of that coast, and the King had given strict orders, that if at any time another appeared, it should be taken ashore, and with all its crew and passengers brought in a tumbril to Lorbrulgrud. He was strongly bent to get me a woman of my own size, by whom I might propagate the breed: but I think I should rather have died than undergone the disgrace of leaving a posterity to be kept in cages like tame canary birds, and perhaps, in time, sold about the kingdom to persons of quality for curiosities. I was, indeed, treated with much kindness: I was the favourite of a great King and Queen, and the delight of the whole court, but it was upon such a foot as ill became the dignity of human kind. I could never forget those domestic pledges I had left behind me. I wanted to be among people with whom I could converse upon even terms, and walk about the streets and fields without fear of being trod to death like a frog or a young puppy. But my deliverance came sooner than I expected, and in a manner not very common: the whole story and circumstances of which I shall faithfully relate.

I had now been two years in this country; and about the beginning of the third, Glumdalclitch and I attended the King and Queen in a progress to the south coast of the kingdom. I was carried, as usual, in my travelling-box, which, as I have already described, was a very convenient closet of twelve foot wide. And I had ordered a hammock to be fixed by silken ropes from the four corners at the top, to break the jolts when a servant carried me before him on horseback, as I sometimes desired, and would often sleep in my hammock while we were upon the road. On the roof of my closet, just over the middle of the hammock, I ordered the joiner to cut out a hole of a foot square, to give me air in hot weather, as I slept; which hole I shut at pleasure with a board that drew backwards and forwards through a groove.

When we came to our journey's end, the King thought proper to pass a few days at a palace he hath near Flanflasnic, a city within eighteen English miles of the sea-side. Glumdalclitch and I were much fatigued; I had gotten a small cold, but the poor girl was so ill as to be confined to her chamber. I longed to see the ocean, which must be the only scene of my escape, if ever it should happen. I pretended to be worse than I really was, and desired leave to take the fresh air of the sea, with a page whom I was very fond of, and who had sometimes been trusted with me. I shall never forget with what unwillingness Glumdalclitch consented, nor the strict charge she gave the page to be careful of me, bursting at the same time into a flood of tears, as if she had some foreboding of what was to happen.

The boy took me out of my box about half an hour's walk from the palace, towards the rocks on the sea-shore. I ordered him to set me down, and lifting up one of my sashes, cast many a wistful melancholy look towards the sea. I found myself not very well, and told the page that I had a mind to take a nap in my hammock, which I hoped would do me good. I got in, and the boy shut the window close down to keep out the cold. I soon fell asleep, and all I can conjecture is, that while I slept, the page, thinking no danger could happen, went among the rocks to look for birds' eggs, having before observed him from my window searching about, and picking up one or two in the clefts. Be that as it will, I found myself suddenly awaked with a violent pull upon the ring which was fastened at the top of my box for the conveniency of carriage. I felt my box raised very high in the air, and then borne forward with pro-digious speed. The first jolt had like to have shaken me out of my hammock, but afterwards the motion was easy enough. I called out several times, as loud as I could raise my voice, but all to no purpose. I looked towards my windows, and could see nothing but the clouds and sky. I heard a noise just over my head like the clapping of wings, and then began to perceive the woeful condition I was in; that some eagle had got the ring of my box in his beak, with an intent to let it fall on a rock like a tortoise in a shell, and then pick out my body, and devour it. For the sagacity and smell of this bird enabled him to discover his quarry at a great distance, though better concealed than I could be within a two-inch board.

In a little time I observed the noise and flutter of wings to increase very fast, and my box was tossed up and down, like a sign-post in a windy day. I heard several bangs or buffets, as I thought, given to the eagle (for such I am certain it must have been that held the ring of my box in his beak), and then all on a sudden felt myself falling perpendicularly down for above a minute, but with such incredible swiftness that I almost lost my breath. My fall was stopped by a terrible squash, that sounded louder to my ears than the cataract of Niagara; after which I was quite in the dark for another minute, and then my box began to rise so high that I could see light from the tops of my windows. I now perceived that I was fallen into the sea. My box, by the weight of my body, the goods that were in, and the broad plates of iron fixed for strength at the four corners of the top and bottom, floated about five foot deep in water. I did then, and do now suppose that the eagle which flew away with my box was pursued by two or three others, and forced to let me drop while he was defending himself against the rest, who hoped to share in the prey. The plates of iron fastened at the bottom of the box (for those were the strongest) preserved the balance while it fell, and hindered it from being broken on the surface of the water. Every joint of it was well grooved, and the door did not move on hinges, but up and down like a sash, which kept my closet so tight that very little water came in. I got with much difficulty out of my hammock, having first ventured to draw back the slip-board on the roof already mentioned, contrived on purpose to let in air, for want of which I found myself almost stifled.

How often did I then wish myself with my dear Glumdalclitch, from whom one single hour had so far divided me. And I may say with truth, that in the midst of my own misfortunes I could not forbear lamenting my poor nurse, the grief she would suffer for my loss, the displeasure of the Queen, and the ruin of her fortune. Perhaps many travellers have not been under greater difficulties and distress than I was at this juncture, expecting every moment to see my box dashed in pieces, or at least overset by the first violent blast, or a rising wave. A breach in one single pane of glass would have been immediate death: nor could any thing have preserved the windows, but the strong lattice wires placed on the outside against accidents in travelling. I saw the water ooze in at several crannies, although the leaks were not considerable, and I endeavoured to stop them as well as I could. I was not able to lift up the roof of my closet, which otherwise I certainly should have done, and sat on the top of it, where I might at least preserve myself some hours longer than by being shut up, as I may call it, in the hold. Or, if I escaped these dangers for a day or two, what could I expect but a miserable death of cold and hunger. I was four hours under these circumstances, expecting and indeed wishing every moment to be my last.

I have already told the reader, that there were two strong staples fixed upon that side of my box which had no window, and into which the servant who used to carry me on horseback would put a leathern belt, and buckle it about his waist. Being in this disconsolate state, I heard or at least thought I heard some kind of grating noise on that side of my box where the staples were fixed, and soon after I began to fancy that the box was pulled or towed along in the sea; for I now and then felt a sort of tugging, which made the waves rise near the tops of my windows, leaving me almost in the dark. This gave me some faint hopes of relief, although I was not able to imagine how it could be brought about. I ventured to unscrew one of my chairs, which were always fastened to the floor; and having made a hard shift to screw it down again directly under the slipping-board that I had lately opened, I mounted on the chair, and putting my mouth as near as I could to the hole, I called for help in a loud voice, and in all the languages I understood. I then fastened my handkerchief to a stick I usually carried, and thrusting it up the hole, waved it several times in the air, that if any boat or ship were near, the seamen might conjecture some unhappy mortal to be shut up in the box.

I found no effect from all I could do, but plainly perceived my closet to be moved along; and in the space of an hour, or better, that side of the box where the staples were, and had no window, struck against something that was hard. I apprehended it to be a rock, and found myself tossed more than ever. I plainly heard a noise upon the cover of my closet, like that of a cable, and the grating of it as it passed through the ring. I then found myself hoisted up by degrees at least three foot higher than I was before. Whereupon I again thrust up my stick and handkerchief, calling for help till I was almost hoarse. In return to which, I heard a great shout repeated three times, giving me such transports of joy, as are not to be conceived bu by those who feel them. I now heard a trampling over my head, and somebody calling through the hole with a loud voice in the English tongue; If there be any body below, let them speak. I answered, I was an Englishman, drawn by ill fortune into the greatest calamity that ever any creature underwent, and begged, by all that was moving, to be delivered out of the dungeon I was in. The voice replied, I was safe, for my box was fastened to their ship; and the carpenter should immediately come and saw an hole in the cover, large enough to pull me out. I answered, that was needless, and would take up too much time, for there was no more to be done, but let one of the crew put his finger into the ring, and take the box out of the sea into the ship, and so into the captain's cabin. Some of them upon hearing me talk so wildly thought I was mad; others laughed; for indeed it never came into my head that I was now got among people of my own stature and strength. The carpenter came, and in a few minutes sawed a passage about four foot square, then let down a small ladder, upon which I mounted, and from thence was taken into the ship in a very weak condition.

The sailors were all in amazement, and asked me a thousand questions, which I had no inclination to answer. I was equally confounded at the sight of so many pigmies, for such I took them to be, after having so long accustomed my eyes to the monstrous objects I had left. But the Captain, Mr. Thomas Wilcocks, an honest worthy Shropshire man, observing I was ready to faint, took me into his cabin, gave me a cordial to comfort me, and made me turn in upon his own bed, advising me to take a little rest, of which I had great need. Before I went to sleep I gave him to understand that I had some valuable furniture in my box, too good to be lost; a fine hammock, an handsome field-bed, two chairs, a table, and a cabinet: that my closet was hung on all sides, or rather quilted, with silk and cotton: that if he would let one of the crew bring my closet into his cabin, I would open it there before him, and show him my goods. The Captain hearing me utter these absurdities, concluded I was raving: however, (I suppose to pacify me) he promised to give order as I desired, and going upon deck sent some of his men down into my closet, from whence (as I afterwards found) they drew up all my goods, and stripped off the quilting: but the chairs, cabinet, and bedstead, being screwed to the floor, were much damaged by the ignorance of the seamen, who tore them up by force. Then they knocked off some of the boards for the use of the ship, and when they had got all they had a mind for, let the hull drop into the sea, which by reason of many breaches made in the bottom and sides, sunk to rights. And indeed I was glad not to have been a spectator of the havoc they made; because I am confident it would have sensibly touched me, by bringing former passages into my mind, which I had rather forget.

I slept some hours, but perpetually disturbed with dreams of the place I had left, and the dangers I had escaped. However, upon waking I found myself much recovered. It was now about eight o'clock at night, and the Captain ordered supper immediately, thinking I had already fasted too long. He entertained me with great kindness, observing me not to look wildly, or talk inconsistently: and when we were left alone, desired I would give him a relation of my travels, and by what accident I came to be set adrift in that monstrous wooden chest. He said, that about twelve o'clock at noon, as he was looking through his glass, he spied it at a distance, and thought it was a sail, which he had a mind to make, being not much out of his course, in hopes of buying some biscuits, his own beginning to fall short. That upon coming nearer, and finding his error, he sent out his long-boat to discover what I was; that his men came back in a fright, swearing they had seen a swimming house. That he laughed at their folly, and went himself in the boat, ordering his men to take a strong cable along with them. That the weather being calm, he rowed round me several times, observed my windows, and the wire lattices that defended them. That he discovered two staples upon one side, which was all of boards, without any passage for light. He then commanded his men to row up to that side, and fastening a cable to one of the staples, ordered them to tow my chest (as he called it), towards the ship. When it was there, he gave directions to fasten another cable to the ring fixed in the cover, and to raise up my chest with pulleys, which all the sailors were not able to do above two or three foot. He said, they saw my stick and hand-kerchief thrust out of the hole, and concluded that some unhappy man must be shut up in the cavity. I asked whether he or the crew had seen any prodigious birds in the air about the time he first discovered me. To which he answered, that discoursing this matter with the sailors while I was asleep, one of them said he had observed three eagles flying towards the north, but remarked nothing of their being larger than the usual size, which I suppose must be imputed to the great height they were at; and he could not guess the reason of my question. I then asked the Captain how far he reckoned we might be from land; he said, by the best computation he could make, we were at least an hundred leagues. I assured him, that he must be mistaken by almost half, for I had not left the country from whence I came above two hours before I dropt into the sea. Whereupon he began again to think that my brain was disturbed, of which he gave me a hint, and advised me to go to bed in a cabin he had provided. I assured him I was well refreshed with his good entertainment and company, and as much in my senses as ever I was in my life. He then grew serious, and desired to ask me freely whether I were not troubled in mind by the consciousness of some enormous crime, for which I was punished at the command of some prince, by exposing me in that chest, as great criminals in other countries have been forced to sea in a leaky vessel without provisions: for, although he should be sorry to have taken so ill a man into his ship, yet he would engage his word to set me safe on shore in the first port where we arrived. He added, that his suspicions were much increased by some very absurd speeches I had delivered at first to the sailors, and afterwards to himself, in relation to my closet or chest, as well as by my odd looks and behaviour while I was at supper.

I begged his patience to hear me tell my story, which I faithfully did from the last time I left England to the moment he first discovered me. And, as truth always forceth its way into rational minds, so this honest worthy gentleman, who had some tincture of learning, and very good sense, was immediately convinced of my candour and veracity. But further to confirm all I had said, I entreated him to give order that my cabinet should be brought, of which I had the key in my pocket, (for he had already informed me how the seamen disposed of my closet). I opened it in his presence, and showed him the small collection of rarities I made in the country from whence I had been so strangely delivered. There was the comb I had contrived out of the stumps of the King's beard, and another of the same materials, but fixed into a paring of her Majesty's thumb-nail, which served for the back. There was a collection of needles and pins from a foot to half a yard long; four wasp-stings, like joiners' tacks; some combings of the Queen's hair; a gold ring which one day she made me a present of in a most obliging manner, taking it from her little finger, and throwing it over my head like a collar. I desired the Captain would please to accept this ring in return of his civilities; which he absolutely refused. I showed him a corn that I had cut off with my own hand, from a maid of honour's toe; it was about the bigness of a Kentish pippin, and grown so hard that when I returned to England, I got it hollowed into a cup, and set in silver. Lastly, I desired him to see the breeches I had then on, which were made of a mouse's skin.

I could force nothing on him but a footman's tooth, which I observed him to examine with great curiosity, and found he had a fancy for it. He received it with abundance of thanks, more than such a trifle could deserve. It was drawn by an unskilled surgeon, in a mistake, from one of Glumdalclitch's men, who was afflicted with the tooth-ache, but it was as sound as any in his head. I got it cleaned, and put it into my cabinet. It was about a foot long, and four inches in diameter.

The Captain was very well satified with this plain relation I had given him, and said, he hoped when we returned to England, I would oblige the world by putting it in paper, and making it public. My answer was, that I thought we were already overstocked with books of travel: that nothing could now pass which was not extraordinary; wherein I doubted some authors less consulted truth than their own vanity, or interest, or the diversion of ignorant readers. That my story could contain little besides common events, without those ornamental descriptions of strange plants, trees, birds, and other animals, or of the barbarous customs and idolatry of savage people, with which most writers abound. However, I thanked him for his good opinion, and promised to take the matter into my thoughts.

He said he wondered at one thing very much, which was, to hear me speak so loud, asking me whether the King or Queen of that country were thick of hearing. I told him, it was what I had been used to for above two years past; and that I admired as much at the voices of him and his men, who seemed to me only to whisper, and yet I could hear them well enough. But when I spoke in that country, it was like a man talking in the street to another looking out from the top of a steeple, unless when I was placed on a table, or held in any person's hand. I told him, I had likewise observed another thing, that when I first got into the ship, and the sailors stood all about me, I thought they were the most little contemptible creatures I had ever beheld. For, indeed, while I was in that prince's country, I could never endure to look in a glass after my eyes had been accustomed to such prodigious objects, because the comparison gave me so despicable a conceit of myself. The Captain said, that while we were at supper, be observed me to look at every thing with a sort of wonder, and

10

that I often seemed hardly able to contain my laughter, which he knew not well how to take, but imputed it to some disorder in my brain. I answered, it was very true; and I wondered how I could forbear, when I saw his dishes of the size of a silver three-pence, a leg of pork hardly a mouthful, a cup not so big as a nut-shell; and so I went on, describing the rest of his household-stuff and provisions after the same manner. For, although the Queen had ordered a little equipage of all things necessary for me while I was in her service, yet my ideas were wholly taken up with what I saw on every side of me, and I winked at my own littleness as people do at their own faults. The Captain understood my raillery very well, and merrily replied with the old English proverb, that he doubted my eyes were bigger than my belly, for he did not observe my stomach so good, although I had fasted all day; and continuing in his mirth, protested he would have gladly given an hundred pounds to have seen my closet in the eagle's bill, and afterwards in its fall from so great an height into the sea; which would certainly have been a most astonishing object, worthy to have the description of it transmitted to future ages: and the comparison of Phaeton was so obvious, that he could not forbear applying it, although I did not much admire the conceit.

The Captain having been at Tonquin, was in his return to England driven north-eastward to the latitude of 44 degrees, and of longitude 143. But meeting a trade-wind two days after I came on board him, we sailed southward a long time, and coasting New Holland kept our course west-south-west, and then south-south-west till we doubled the Cape of Good Hope. Our voyage was very prosperous, but I shall not trouble the reader with a journal of it. The Captain called in at one or two ports, and sent in his long-boat for provisions and fresh water, but I never went out of the ship till we came into the Downs, which was on the third day of June, 1706, about nine months after my escape. I offered to leave my goods in security for payment of my freight: but the Captain protested he would not receive one farthing. We took kind leave of each other, and I made him promise he would come to see me at my house in Redriff. I hired a horse and guide for five shillings, which I borrowed of the Captain.

As I was on the road, observing the littleness of the houses, the trees, the cattle, and the people, I began to think myself in Lilliput. I was afraid of trampling on every traveller I met, and often called aloud to have them stand out of the way, so that I had like to have gotten one or two broken heads for my impertinence.

When I came to my own house, for which I was forced to enquire, one of the servants opening the door, I bent down to go in (like a goose under a gate) for fear of striking my head. My wife ran out to embrace me, but I stooped lower than her knees, thinking she could otherwise never be able to reach my mouth. My daughter kneeled to ask my blessing, but I could not see her till she arose, having been so long used to stand with my head and eyes erect to above sixty foot; and then I went to take her up with one hand, by the waist. I looked down upon the servants and one or two friends who were in the house, as if they had been pigmies, and I a giant. I told my wife, she had been too thrifty, for I found she had starved herself and her daughter to nothing. In short, I behaved myself so unaccountably, that they were all of the Captain's opinion when he first saw me, and concluded I had lost my wits. This I mention as an instance of the great power of habit and prejudice.

In a little time I and my family and friends came to a right understanding: but my wife protested I should never go to sea any more; although my evil destiny so ordered that she had not power to hinder me, as the reader may know hereafter. In the mean time I here conclude the second part of my unfortunate voyages.

The End of the Second Part.

PART III

A VOYAGE TO LAPUTA, BALNIBARBI, LUGGNAGG, GLUBBDUBDRIB, AND JAPAN

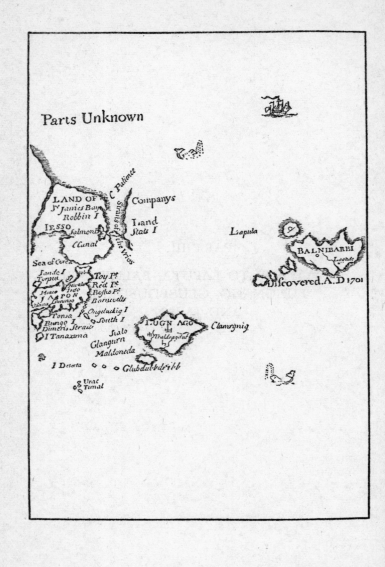

Parts Unknown

LAND OF
Sᵗ James Bay
Robbin I
IESSO
Salmond
Clanal

C Patience

Companys
Land
Stats I

Strait of the Vries

Laputa

BALNIBARBI
Lagado

Discovered. A.D 1701

Sea of Corea
Sande I
Torpta
Nivale
Trido
Meaco
Damasco
PON
Ongeluckig I
South I
Tonsa
Bungo I
Dimeris Strait
I Tanaxima
Scalo
Glangun
Maldoneda
Toy Pt
Red Pt
Bosho Pt
Barnevelt

LUGN AGG
Waldegdub
Clamegnig

I Desata
Glubdubdrib

Urac
Tunal

CHAPTER I

The Author sets out on his third voyage, is taken by pirates. The malice of a Dutchman. *His arrival at an island. He is received into* Laputa.

I HAD not been at home above ten days, when Captain William Robinson, a Cornish man, Commander of the *Hopewell*, a stout ship of three hundred tons, came to my house. I had formerly been surgeon of another ship where he was master, and fourth part owner, in a voyage to the Levant; he had always treated me more like a brother than an inferior officer, and hearing of my arrival made me a visit, as I apprehended only out of friendship, for nothing passed more than what is usual after long absences. But repeating his visits often, expressing his joy to find me in good health, asking whether I were now settled for life, adding that he intended a voyage to the East Indies in two months; at last he plainly invited me, though with some apologies, to be surgeon of the ship; that I should have another surgeon under me besides our two mates; that my salary should be double to the usual pay; and that having experienced my knowledge in sea-affairs to be at least equal to his, he would enter into any engagement to follow my advice, as much as if I had share in the command.

He said so many other obliging things, and I knew him to be so honest a man, that I could not reject his proposal; the thirst I had of seeing the world, not withstanding my past misfortunes, continuing as violent as ever. The only difficulty that remained, was to persuade my wife, whose consent however I at last obtained by the prospect of advantage she proposed to her children.

We set out the 5th day of August, 1706, and arrived at Fort St. George the 11th of April, 1707. We stayed there three weeks to refresh our crew, many of whom were sick. From thence we went to Tonquin, where the Captain resolved to continue some time, because many of the goods

he intended to buy were not ready, nor could he expect to
be dispatched in several months. Therefore, in hopes to
defray some of the charges he must be at, he bought a sloop,
loaded it with several sorts of goods, wherewith the Ton-
quinese usually trade to the neighbouring islands, and
putting fourteen men on board, whereof three were of the
country, he appointed me master of the sloop, and gave me
power to traffic for two months, while he transacted his
affairs at Tonquin.

We had not sailed above three days, when a great storm
arising, we were driven five days to the north-north-east, and
then to the east: after which we had fair weather, but still
with a pretty strong gale from the west. Upon the tenth
day we were chased by two pirates, who soon overtook us;
for my sloop was so deep loaden, that she sailed very slow,
neither were we in a condition to defend ourselves.

We were boarded about the same time by both the
pirates, who entered furiously at the head of their men, but
finding us all prostrate upon our faces (for so I gave order),
they pinioned us with strong ropes, and setting a guard upon
us, went to search the sloop.

I observed among them a Dutchman, who seemed to be
of some authority, though he was not Commander of either
ship. He knew us by our countenances to be Englishmen,
and jabbering to us in his own language, swore we should
be tied back to back, and thrown into the sea. I spoke
Dutch tolerably well; I told him who we were, and begged
him in consideration of our being Christians and Protestants,
of neighbouring countries, in strict alliance, that he would
move the Captains to take some pity on us. This inflamed
his rage; he repeated his threatenings, and turning to his
companions, spoke with great vehemence, in the Japanese
language, as I suppose, often using the word *Christianos*.

The largest of the two pirate ships was commanded by a
Japanese Captain, who spoke a little Dutch, but very
imperfectly. He came up to me, and after several questions,
which I answered in great humility, he said we should not
die. I made the Captain a very low bow, and then turning

to the Dutchman, said, I was sorry to find more mercy in a heathen, than in a brother Christian. But I had soon reason to repent those foolish words: for that malicious reprobate, having often endeavoured in vain to persuade both the Captains that I might be thrown into the sea (which they would not yield to after the promise made me, that I should not die), however prevailed so far as to have a punishment inflicted on me, worse in all human appearance than death itself. My men were sent by an equal division into both the pirate ships, and my sloop new manned. As to myself, it was determined that I should be set a-drift in a small canoe, with paddles and a sail, and four days' provisions, which last the Japanese Captain was so kind to double out of his own stores, and would permit no man to search me. I got down into the canoe, while the Dutchman standing upon the deck, loaded me with all the curses and injurious terms his language could afford.

About an hour before we saw the pirates, I had taken an observation, and found we were in the latitude of 46 N. and of longitute 183. When I was at some distance from the pirates, I discovered by my pocket-glass several islands to the south-east. I set up my sail, the wind being fair, with a design to reach the nearest of those islands, which I made a shift to do in about three hours. It was all rocky; however I got many birds' eggs, and striking fire, I kindled some heath and dry sea-weed, by which I roasted my eggs. I ate no other supper, being resolved to spare my provisions as much as I could. I passed the night under the shelter of a rock, strowing some heath under me, and slept pretty well.

The next day I sailed to another island, and thence to a third and fourth, sometimes using my sail, and sometimes my paddles. But not to trouble the reader with a particular account of my distresses, let it suffice, that on the fifth day I arrived at the last island in my sight, which lay south-south-east to the former.

This island was at a greater distance than I expected, and I did not reach it in less than five hours. I encompassed it almost round, before I could find a convenient place to land in, which was a small creek, about three times the wideness of my canoe. I found the island to be all rocky, only a little intermingled with tufts of grass, and sweet smelling herbs. I took out my small provisions, and after having refreshed myself, I secured the remainder in a cave, whereof there were great numbers. I gathered plenty of eggs upon the rocks, and got a quantity of dry sea-weed, and parched grass, which I designed to kindle the next day, and roast my eggs as well as I could, (for I had about me my flint, steel, match, and burning-glass.) I lay all night in the cave where I had lodged my provisions. My bed was the same dry grass and sea-weed which I intended for fuel. I slept very little, for the disquiets of my mind prevailed over my weariness, and kept me awake. I considered how impossible it was to preserve my life in so desolate a place, and how miserable my end must be. Yet I found myself so listless and desponding, that I had not the heart to rise; and before I could get spirits enough to creep out of my cave, the day was far advanced. I walked a while among the rocks; the sky was perfectly clear, and the sun so hot, that I was forced to turn my face from it: when all on a sudden it became obscured, as I thought, in a manner very different from what happens by the interposition of a cloud. I turned back, and perceived a vast opaque body between me and the sun, moving forwards towards the island: it seemed to be about two miles high, and hid the sun six or seven minutes, but I did not observe the air to be much colder, or the sky more darkened, than if I had stood under the shade of a mountain. As it approached nearer over the place where I was, it appeared to be a firm substance, the bottom flat, smooth, and shining very bright from the reflection of the sea below. I stood upon a height about two hundred yards from the shore, and saw this vast body descending almost to a parallel with me, at less than an English mile distance. I took out my pocket-perspective, and could plainly discover numbers of people moving up and down the sides of it, which appeared to be sloping, but what those people were doing, I was not able to distinguish.

The natural love of life gave me some inward motions of

joy, and I was ready to entertain a hope that this adventure might some way or other help to deliver me from the desolate place and condition I was in. But at the same time the reader can hardly conceive my astonishment, to behold an island in the air, inhabited by men, who were able (as it should seem) to raise or sink, or put it into a progressive motion, as they pleased. But not being at that time in a disposition to philosophise upon this phenomenon, I rather chose to observe what course the island would take, because it seemed for a while to stand still. Yet soon after, it advanced nearer, and I could see the sides of it encompassed with several gradations of galleries and stairs, at certain intervals, to descend from one to the other. In the lowest gallery, I beheld some people fishing with long angling rods, and others looking on. I waved my cap (for my hat was long since worn out) and my handkerchief towards the island; and upon its nearer approach, I called and shouted with the utmost strength of my voice; and then looking circumspectly, I beheld a crowd gather to that side which was most in my view. I found by their pointing towards me and to each other, that they plainly discovered me, although they made no return to my shouting. But I could see four or five men running in great haste up the stairs to the top of the island, who then disappeared. I happened rightly to conjecture, that these were sent for orders to some person in authority upon this occasion.

The number of people increased, and in less than half an hour, the island was moved and raised in such a manner, that the lowest gallery appeared in a parallel of less than an hundred yards distance from the height where I stood. I then put myself into the most supplicating postures, and spoke in the humblest accent, but received no answer. Those who stood nearest over against me, seemed to be persons of distinction, as I supposed by their habit. They conferred earnestly with each other, looking often upon me. At length one of them called out in a clear, polite, smooth dialect, not unlike in sound to the Italian; and therefore I returned an answer in that language, hoping at least that the cadence might be more agreeable to his ears. Although neither of us understood the other, yet my meaning was easily known, for the people saw the distress I was in.

They made signs for me to come down from the rock, and go towards the shore, which I accordingly did; and the flying island being raised to a convenient height, the verge directly over me, a chain was let down from the lowest gallery, with a seat fastened to the bottom, to which I fixed myself, and was drawn up by pulleys.

CHAPTER II

The humours and dispositions of the Laputians *described. An account of their learning. Of the King and his Court. The Author's reception there. The inhabitants subject to fear and disquietudes. An account of the women.*

AT my alighting I was surrounded by a crowd of people, but those who stood nearest seemed to be of better quality. They beheld me with all the marks and circumstances of wonder; neither indeed was I much in their debt, having never till then seen a race of mortals so singular in their shapes, habits, and countenances. Their heads were all reclined either to the right or the left; one of their eyes turned inward, and the other directly up to the zenith. Their outward garments were adorned with the figures of suns, moons, and stars, interwoven with those of fiddles, flutes, harps, trumpets, guitars, harpsichords, and many other instruments of music, unknown to us in Europe. I observed here and there many in the habit of servants, with a blown bladder fastened like a flail to the end of a short stick, which they carried in their hands. In each bladder was a small quantity of dried pease, or little pebbles (as I was afterwards informed). With these bladders they now and then flapped the mouths and ears of those who stood near them, of which practice I could not then conceive the meaning; it seems, the minds of these people are so taken up with intense speculations, that they neither can speak, nor attend to the discourses of others, without being roused by some external taction upon the organs of speech and hearing; for which reason, those persons who are able to afford it always keep a flapper (the original is *climenole*) in their family, as one of their domestics, nor ever walk abroad or make visits without him. And the business of this officer is, when two or more persons are in company, gently to strike with his bladder the mouth of him who is to speak, and the right ear of him or them to whom the speaker addresseth himself. This flapper is likewise employed diligently to attend his master in his walks, and upon occasion to give him a soft flap on his eyes, because he is always so wrapped up in cogitation, that he is in manifest danger of falling down every precipice, and bouncing his head against every post, and in the streets, of justling others, or being justled himself into the kennel.

It was necessary to give the reader this information, without which he would be at the same loss with me, to understand the proceedings of these people, as they conducted me up the stairs, to the top of the island, and from thence to the royal palace. While we were ascending, they forgot several times what they were about, and left me to myself, till their memories were again roused by their flappers; for they appeared altogether unmoved by the sight of my foreign habit and countenance, and by the shouts of the vulgar, whose thoughts and minds were more disengaged.

At last we entered the palace, and proceeded into the chamber of presence, where I saw the King seated on his throne, attended on each side by persons of prime quality. Before the throne, was a large table filled with globes and spheres, and mathematical instruments of all kinds. His Majesty took not the least notice of us, although our entrance was not without sufficient noise, by the concourse of all persons belonging to the court. But he was then deep in a problem, and we attended at least an hour, before he could solve it. There stood by him on each side, a young page, with flaps in their hands, and when they saw he was at leisure, one of them gently struck his mouth, and the other his right ear; at which he started like one awaked on the sudden, and looking towards me, and the company I was in, recollected the occasion of our coming, whereof he had been informed before. He spoke some words, whereupon immediately a young man with a flap came up to my side, and flapped me gently on the right ear; but I made signs, as well as I could, that I had no occasion for such an instrument; which, as I afterwards found, gave his Majesty and the whole court a very mean opinion of my understanding. The King, as far as I could conjecture, asked me several questions, and I addressed myself to him in all the languages I had. When it was found, that I could neither understand nor be understood, I was conducted by his order to an apartment in his palace (this prince being distinguished above all his predecessors for his hospitality to strangers), where two servants were appointed to attend me. My dinner was brought, and four persons of quality, whom I remembered to have seen very near the King's person, did me the honour to dine with me. We had two courses, of three dishes each. In the first course, there was a shoulder of mutton, cut into an equilateral triangle, a piece of beef into a rhomboides, and a pudding into a cycloid. The second course was two ducks, trussed up into the form of fiddles; sausages and puddings resembling flutes and hautboys, and a breast of veal in the shape of a harp. The servants cut our bread into cones, cylinders, parallelograms, and several other mathematical figures.

While we were at dinner, I made bold to ask the names of several things in their language; and those noble persons, by the assistance of their flappers, delighted to give me answers, hoping to raise my admiration of their great abilities, if I could be brought to converse with them. I was soon able to call for bread and drink, or whatever else I wanted.

After dinner my company withdrew, and a person was sent to me by the King's order, attended by a flapper. He brought with him pen, ink, and paper, and three or four books, giving me to understand by signs, that he was sent to teach me the language. We sat together four hours, in which time I wrote down a great number of words in columns, with the translations over against them. I likewise made a shift to learn several short sentences. For my tutor would order one of my servants to fetch something, to turn about, to make a bow, to sit, or stand, or walk, and the like. Then I took down the sentence in writing. He showed me also in one of his books, the figures of the sun, moon, and stars, the zodiac, the tropics, and polar circles, together with the denominations of many planes and solids. He gave me the names and descriptions of all the musical instruments, and the general terms of art in playing on each of them. After he had left me, I placed all my words with their interpretations in alphabetical order. And thus in a few days, by the help of a very faithful memory, I got some insight into their language.

The word, which I interpret the *Flying* or *Floating Island*, is in the original *Laputa*, whereof I could never learn the true etymology. *Lap* in the old obsolete language signifieth *high*, and *untuh*, a *governor*, from which they say, by corruption, was derived *Laputa*, from *Lapuntuh*. But I do not approve of this derivation, which seems to be a little strained. I ventured to offer to the learned among them a conjecture of my own, that *Laputa* was *quasi la pouted*; *lap* signifying properly the dancing of the sunbeams in the sea, and *outed*, a wing, which however I shall not obtrude, but submit to the judicious reader.

Those to whom the King had entrusted me, observing how ill I was clad, ordered a tailor to come next morning, and take my measure for a suit of clothes. This operator did his office after a different manner from those of his trade in Europe. He first took my altitude by a quadrant, and then with a rule and compasses, described the dimensions and outlines of my whole body, all which he entered upon paper, and in six days brought my clothes very ill made, and quite out of shape, by happening to mistake a figure in the calculation. But my comfort was, that I observed such accidents very frequent, and little regarded.

During my confinement for want of clothes, and by an indisposition that held me some days longer, I much enlarged my dictionary; and when I went next to court, was able to understand many things the King spoke, and to return him some kind of answers. His Majesty had given orders that the island should move north-east and by east, to the vertical point over Lagado, the metropolis of the whole kingdom below upon the firm earth. It was about ninety leagues distant, and our voyage lasted four days and an half. I was not in the least sensible of the progressive motion made in the air by the island. On the second morning about eleven o'clock, the King himself in person, attended by his nobility, courtiers, and officers, having prepared all their musical instruments, played on them for three hours without intermission, so that I was quite stunned with the noise; neither could I possibly guess the meaning till my tutor informed me. He said that the people of their island had their ears adapted to hear the music of the spheres, which always played at certain periods, and the court was now prepared to bear their part in whatever instrument they most excelled.

In our journey towards Lagado, the capital city, his Majesty ordered that the island should stop over certain towns and villages, from whence he might receive the petitions of his subjects. And to this purpose several pack-threads were let down with small weights at the bottom. On these packthreads the people strung their petitions, which mounted up directly like the scraps of paper fastened by school-boys at the end of the string that holds their kite. Sometimes we received wine and victuals from below, which were drawn up by pulleys.

The knowledge I had in mathematics gave me great assistance in acquiring their phraseology, which depended much upon that science and music; and in the latter I was not unskilled. Their ideas are perpetually conversant in lines and figures. If they would, for example, praise the beauty of a woman, or any other animal, they describe it by rhombs, circles, parallelograms, ellipses, and other geometrical terms, or by words of art drawn from music, needless here to repeat. I observed in the King's kitchen all sorts of mathematical and musical instruments, after the figures of which they cut up the joints that were served to His Majesty's table.

Their houses are very ill built, the walls bevil, without one right angle in any apartment, and this defect ariseth from the contempt they bear to practical geometry, which they despise as vulgar and mechanic, those instructions they give being too refined for the intellectuals of their workmen, which occasions perpetual mistakes. And although they are dexterous enough upon a piece of paper in the management of the rule, the pencil, and the divider, yet in the common actions and behaviour of life, I have not seen a more clumsy, awkward, and unhandy people, nor so slow and perplexed in their conceptions upon all other subjects, except those of mathematics and music. They are very bad reasoners, and vehemently given to opposition, unless when they happen to be of the right opinion, which is seldom their case. Imagination, fancy, and invention, they are wholly strangers to, nor have any words in their language by which those ideas can be expressed; the whole compass of their thoughts and mind being shut up within the two forementioned sciences.

Most of them, and especially those who deal in the astronomical part, have great faith in judicial astrology, although they are ashamed to own it publicly. But what I chiefly admired, and thought altogether unaccountable, was the strong disposition I observed in them towards news and politics, perpetually enquiring into public affairs, giving their judgments in matters of state, and passionately disputing every inch of a party opinion. I have indeed observed the same disposition among most of the mathematicians I have known in Europe, although I could never discover the least analogy between the two sciences; unless those people suppose, that because the smallest circle hath as many degrees as the largest, therefore the regulation and management of the world require no more abilities than the handling and turning of a globe. But I rather take this quality to spring from a very common infirmity of human nature, inclining us to be more curious and conceited in matters where we have least concern, and for which we are least adapted either by study or nature.

These people are under continual disquietudes, never enjoying a minute's peace of mind; and their disturbances proceed from causes which very little affect the rest of mortals. Their apprehensions arise from several changes they dread in the celestial bodies. For instance; that the earth, by the continual approaches of the sun towards it, must in course of time be absorbed, or swallowed up. That the face of the sun will by degrees be encrusted with its own effluvia, and give no more light to the world. That the earth very narrowly escaped a brush from the tail of the last comet, which would have infallibly reduced it to ashes; and that the next, which they have calculated for one and thirty years hence, will probably destroy us. For, if in its perihelion it should approach within a certain degree of the sun (as by their calculations they have reason to dread) it will receive a degree of heat ten thousand times more intense than that of red-hot glowing iron; and in its absence from the sun, carry a blazing tail ten hundred thousand and fourteen miles long; through which if the earth should pass at the distance of one hundred thousand miles from the nucleus or main body of the comet, it must in its passage be set on fire, and reduced to ashes. That the sun daily spending its rays without any nutriment to supply them, will at last be wholly consumed and annihilated; which must be attended with the destruction of this earth, and of all the planets that receive their light from it.

They are so perpetually alarmed with the apprehensions of these and the like impending dangers, that they can neither sleep quietly in their beds, nor have any relish for the common pleasures or amusements of life. When they meet an acquaintance in the morning, the first question is about the sun's health, how he looked at his setting and rising, and what hopes they have to avoid the stroke of the approaching comet. This conversation they are apt to run into with the same temper that boys discover, in delighting to hear terrible stories of sprites and hobgoblins, which they greedily listen to, and dare not go to bed for fear.

The women of the island have abundance of vivacity: they contemn their husbands, and are exceedingly fond of strangers, whereof there is always a considerable number from the continent below, attending at court, either upon affairs of the several towns and corporations, or their own particular occasions, but are much despised, because they want the same endowments. Among these the ladies choose their gallants: but the vexation is, that they act with too much ease and security, for the husband is always so rapt in speculation, that the mistress and lover may proceed to the greatest familiarities before his face, if he be but provided with paper and implements, and without his flapper at his side.

The wives and daughters lament their confinement to the island, although I think it the most delicious spot of ground in the world; and although they live here in the greatest plenty and magnificence, and are allowed to do whatever they please, they long to see the world, and take the diversions of the metropolis, which they are not allowed to do without a particular licence from the King; and this is not easy to be obtained, because the people of quality have found, by frequent experience, how hard it is to persuade their women to return from below. I was told that a great court lady, who had several children, is married to the prime minister, the richest subject in the kingdom, a very graceful person, extremely fond of her, and lives in the finest palace of the island, went down to Lagado, on the pretence of health, there hid herself for several months, till the King sent a warrant to search for her, and she was found in an obscure eating-house all in rags, having pawned her clothes to maintain an old deformed footman, who beat her every day, and in whose company she was taken much against her will. And although her husband received her with all possible kindness, and without the least reproach, she soon after contrived to steal down again with all her jewels, to the same gallant, and hath not been heard of since.

This may perhaps pass with the reader rather for an European or English story, than for one of a country so remote. But he may please to consider, that the caprices of womankind are not limited by any climate or nation, and that they are much more uniform than can be easily imagined.

In about a month's time I had made a tolerable proficiency in their language, and was able to answer most of the King's questions, when I had the honour to attend him. His Majesty discovered not the least curiosity to enquire into the laws, government, history, religion, or manners of the countries where I had been, but confined his questions to the state of mathematics, and received the account I gave him with great contempt and indifference, though often roused by his flapper on each side.

CHAPTER III

A phenomenon solved by modern philosophy and astronomy. The Laputians' *great improvements in the latter. The King's method of suppressing insurrections.*

I DESIRED leave of this prince to see the curiosities of the island, which he was graciously pleased to grant, and ordered my tutor to attend me. I chiefly wanted to know to what cause in art, or in nature, it owed its several motions, whereof I will now give a philosophical account to the reader.

The Flying or Floating Island is exactly circular, its diameter 7837 yards, or about four miles and a half, and consequently contains ten thousand acres. It is three hundred yards thick. The bottom or under surface, which appears to those who view it below, is one even regular plate of adamant, shooting up to the height of about two hundred yards. Above it lie the several minerals in their usual order, and over all is a coat of rich mould, ten or twelve foot deep. The declivity of the upper surface, from the circumference to the centre, is the natural cause why all the dews and rains which fall upon the island, are conveyed in small rivulets toward the middle, where they are emptied into four large basins, each of about half a mile in circuit, and two hundred yards distant from the centre. From these basins the water is continually exhaled by the sun in the day-time, which effectually prevents their overflowing. Besides, as it is in the power of the monarch to raise the island above the region of clouds and vapours, he can prevent the falling of dews and rains whenever he pleases. For the highest clouds cannot rise above two miles, as naturalists agree, at least they were never known to do so in that country.

At the centre of the island there is a chasm about fifty yards in diameter, from whence the astronomers descend into a large dome, which is therefore called *Flandona Gagnole*, or the Astronomer's Cave, situated at the depth of an hundred yards beneath the upper surface of the adamant. In this cave are twenty lamps continually burning, which from the reflection of the adamant cast a strong light into every part. The place is stored with great variety of sextants, quadrants, telescopes, astrolabes, and other astronomical instruments. But the greatest curiosity, upon which the fate of the island depends, is a loadstone of a prodigious size, in shape resembling a weaver's shuttle. It is in length six yards, and in the thickest part at least three yards over. This magnet is sustained by a very strong axle of adamant passing through its middle, upon which it plays, and is poised so exactly that the weakest hand can turn it. It is hooped round with an hollow cylinder of adamant, four foot deep, as many thick, and twelve yards in diameter, placed horizontally, and supported by eight adamantine feet, each six yards high. In the middle of the concave side there is a groove twelve inches deep, in which the extremities of the axle are lodged, and turned round as there is occasion.

The stone cannot be moved from its place by any force,

because the hoop and its feet are one continued piece with that body of adamant which constitutes the bottom of the island.

By means of this loadstone, the island is made to rise and fall, and move from one place to another. For, with respect to that part of the earth over which the monarch presides, the stone is endued at one of its sides with an attractive power, and at the other with a repulsive. Upon placing the magnet erect with its attracting end towards the earth, the island descends; but when the repelling extremity points downwards, the island mounts directly upwards. When the position of the stone is oblique, the motion of the island is so too. For in this magnet the forces always act in lines parallel to its direction.

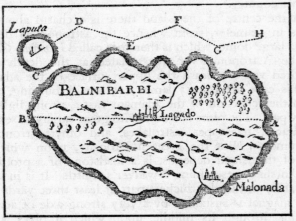

By this oblique motion, the island is conveyed to different parts of the monarch's dominions. To explain the manner of its progress, let *A B* represent a line drawn across the dominions of Balnibarbi, let the line *c d* represent the loadstone, of which let *d* be the repelling end, and *c* the attracting end, the island being over *C;* let the stone be placed in the position *c d*, with its repelling end downwards; then the island will be driven upwards obliquely towards *D*. When it is arrived at *D*, let the stone be turned upon its axle, till its attracting end points towards E, and then the island will be carried obliquely towards $E;$ where if the stone be again turned upon its axle till it stands in the position $E F$, with its repelling point downwards, the island will rise obliquely towards F, where by directing the attracting end towards G, the island may be carried to G, and from G to H, by turning the stone, so as to make its repelling extremity to point directly downwards. And thus by changing the situation of the stone as often as there is occasion, the island is made to rise and fall by turns in an oblique direction, and by those alternate risings and fallings (the obliquity being not considerable) is conveyed from one part of the dominions to the other.

But it must be observed, that this island cannot move beyond the extent of the dominions below, nor can it rise above the height of four miles. For which the astronomers (who have written large systems concerning the stone) assign the following reason: that the magnetic virtue does not extend beyond the distance of four miles, and that the mineral which acts upon the stone in the bowels of the earth, and in the sea about six leagues distant from the shore, is not diffused through the whole globe, but terminated with the limits of the King's dominions; and it was easy from the great advantage of such a superior situation, for a prince to bring under his obedience whatever country lay within the attraction of that magnet.

When the stone is put parallel to the plane of the horizon, the island standeth still; for in that case the extremities of it being at equal distance from the earth, act with equal force, the one in drawing downwards, the other in pushing upwards, and consequently no motion can ensue.

This loadstone is under the care of certain astronomers, who from time to time give it such positions as the monarch directs. They spend the greatest part of their lives in observing the celestial bodies, which they do by the assistance of glasses far exceeding ours in goodness. For although their largest telescopes do not exceed three feet, they magnify much more than those of an hundred among us, and show the stars with greater clearness. This advantage hath enabled them to extend their discoveries much further than our astronomers in Europe; for they have made a catalogue of ten thousand fixed stars, whereas the largest of ours do not contain above one third part of that number. They have likewise discovered two lesser stars, or satellites, which revolve about Mars, whereof the innermost is distant from the centre of the primary planet exactly three of his diameters, and the outermost five; the former revolves in the space of ten hours, and the latter in twenty one and an half; so that the squares of their periodical times are very near in the same proportion with the cubes of their distance from the centre of Mars, which evidently shows them to be governed by the same law of gravitation, that influences the other heavenly bodies.

They have observed ninety-three different comets, and settled their periods with great exactness. If this be true, (and they affirm it with great confidence) it is much to be wished that their observations were made public, whereby the theory of comets, which at present is very lame and defective, might be brought to the same perfection with other parts of astronomy.

The King would be the most absolute prince in the universe, if he could but prevail on a ministry to join with him; but these having their estates below on the continent, and considering that the office of a favourite hath a very uncertain tenure, would never consent to the enslaving their country.

If any town should engage in rebellion or mutiny, fall into violent factions, or refuse to pay the usual tribute, the King hath two methods of reducing them to obedience. The first and the mildest course is by keeping the island hovering over such a town, and the lands about it, whereby he can deprive them of the benefits of the sun and the rain, and consequently afflict the inhabitants with dearth and diseases. And if the crime deserve it, they are at the same time pelted from above with great stones, against which they have no defence but by creeping into cellars or caves, while the roofs of their houses are beaten to pieces. But if they still continue obstinate, or offer to raise insurrections, he proceeds to the last remedy, by letting the island drop directly upon their heads, which makes a universal destruction both of houses and men. However, this is an extremity to which the prince is seldom driven, neither indeed is he willing to put it in execution, nor dare his ministers advise him to an action, which as it would render them odious to the people, so it would be a great damage to their own estates, which lie all below, for the island is the King's demesne.

But there is still indeed a more weighty reason, why the kings of this country have been always averse from executing so terrible an action, unless upon the utmost necessity. For if the town intended to be destroyed should have in it any tall rocks, as it generally falls out in the larger cities, a situation probably chosen at first with a view to prevent such a catastrophe; or if it abound in high spires, or pillars of stone, a sudden fall might endanger the bottom or under surface of the island, which, although it consists, as I have said, of one entire adamant two hundred yards thick, might happen to crack by too great a choque, or burst by approaching too near the fires from the houses below, as the backs both of iron and stone will often do in our chimneys. Of all this the people are well apprised, and understand how far to carry their obstinacy, where their liberty or property is concerned. And the King, when he is highest provoked, and most determined to press a city to rubbish, orders the island to descend with great gentleness, out of a pretence of tenderness to his people, but indeed for fear of breaking the adamantine bottom; in which case, it is the opinion of all their philosophers, that the loadstone could no longer hold it up, and the whole mass would fall to the ground.

About three years before my arrival among them, while the King was in his progress over his dominions, there happened an extraordinary accident which had like to have put a period to the fate of that monarchy, at least as it is now instituted. Lindalino, the second city in the kingdom, was the first his Majesty visited in his progress. Three days after his departure the inhabitants, who had often complained of great oppressions, shut the town gates, seized on the governor, and with incredible speed and labour erected four large towers, one at every corner of the city (which is an exact square), equal in height to the strong pointed rock that stands directly in the centre of the city. Upon the top of each tower, as well as upon the rock, they fixed a great loadstone, and in case their design should fail, they had provided a vast quantity of the most combustible fuel, hoping to burst therewith the adamantine bottom of the island, if the loadstone project should miscarry.

It was eight months before the King had perfect notice that the Lindalinians were in rebellion. He then commanded that the island should be wafted over the city. The people were unanimous, and had laid in store of provisions, and a great river runs through the middle of the town. The King hovered over them several days to deprive them of the sun and the rain. He ordered many pack-threads to be let down, yet not a person offered to send up a petition, but instead thereof, very bold demands, the redress of all their grievances, great immunities, the choice of their own governor, and other the like exorbitances. Upon which his Majesty commanded all the inhabitants of the island to cast great stones from the lower gallery into the town; but the citizens had provided against this mischief by conveying their persons and effects into the four towers, and other strong buildings, and vaults underground.

The King being now determined to reduce this proud people, ordered that the island should descend gently within forty yards of the top of the towers and rock. This was accordingly done; but the officers employed in that work found the descent much speedier than usual, and by turning the loadstone could not without great difficulty keep it in a firm position, but found the island inclining to fall. They sent the King immediate intelligence of this astonishing event, and begged his Majesty's permission to raise the island higher; the King consented, a general council was called, and the officers of the loadstone ordered to attend. One of the oldest and expertest among them obtained leave to try an experiment. He took a strong line of an hundred yards, and the island being raised over the town above the attracting power they had felt, he fastened a piece of adamant to the end of his line, which had in it a mixture of iron mineral, of the same nature with that whereof the bottom or lower surface of the island is composed, and from the lower gallery let it down slowly towards the top of the towers. The adamant was not descended four yards, before the officer felt it drawn so strongly downwards, that he could hardly pull it back. He then threw down several small pieces of adamant, and observed that they were all violently attracted by the top of the tower. The same experiment was made on the other three towers, and on the rock with the same effect.

This incident broke entirely the King's measures, and (to dwell no longer on other circumstances) he was forced to give the town their own conditions.

I was assured by a great minister, that if the island had descended so near the town as not to be able to raise itself, the citizens were determined to fix it for ever, to kill the King and all his servants, and entirely change the government.

By a fundamental law of this realm, neither the king, nor either of his two eldest sons, are permitted to leave the island; nor the queen, till she is past child-bearing.

CHAPTER IV

The Author leaves Laputa; *is conveyed to* Balnibarbi, *arrives at the metropolis. A description of the metropolis, and the country adjoining. The Author hospitably received by a great Lord. His conversation with that Lord.*

ALTHOUGH I cannot say that I was ill treated in this island, yet I must confess I thought myself too much neglected, not without some degree of contempt. For neither prince nor people appeared to be curious in any part of knowledge, except mathematics and music, wherein I was far their inferior, and upon that account very little regarded.

On the other side, after having seen all the curiosities of the island, I was very desirous to leave it, being heartily weary of those people. They were indeed excellent in two sciences for which I have great esteem, and wherein I am not unversed; but at the same time so abstracted and involved in speculation, that I never met with such disagreeable companions. I conversed only with women, tradesmen, flappers, and court-pages, during two months of my abode there, by which, at last, I rendered myself extremely contemptible; yet these were the only people from whom I could ever receive a reasonable answer.

I had obtained, by hard study, a good degree of knowledge in their language; I was weary of being confined to an island where I received so little countenance, and resolved to leave it with the first opportunity.

There was a great lord at court, nearly related to the King, and for that reason alone used with respect. He was universally reckoned the most ignorant and stupid person among them. He had performed many eminent services for the crown, had great natural and acquired parts, adorned with integrity and honour, but so ill an ear for music, that his detractors reported he had been often known to beat time in the wrong place; neither could his tutors, without extreme difficulty, teach him to demonstrate the most easy proposition in the mathematics. He was pleased to show me many marks of favour, often did me the honour of a visit, desired to be informed in the affairs of Europe, the laws and customs, the manners and learning of the several countries where I had travelled. He listened to me with great attention, and made very wise observations on all I spoke. He had two flappers attending him for state, but never made use of them except at court, and in visits of ceremony, and would always command them to withdraw when we were alone together.

I entreated this illustrious person to intercede in my behalf with his Majesty for leave to depart, which he accordingly did, as he was pleased to tell me, with regret: for indeed he had made me several offers very advantageous, which however I refused with expressions of the highest acknowledgment.

On the 16th day of February I took leave of his Majesty and the court. The King made me a present to the value of about two hundred pounds English, and my protector his kinsman as much more, together with a letter of recommendation to a friend of his in Lagado, the metropolis. The island being then hovering over a mountain about two miles from it, I was let down from the lowest gallery, in the same manner as I had been taken up.

The continent, as far as it is subject to the monarch of the Flying Island, passes under the general name of *Balnibarbi*, and the metropolis, as I said before, is called *Lagado*. I felt some little satisfaction in finding myself on firm ground. I walked to the city without any concern, being clad like one of the natives, and sufficiently instructed to converse with them. I soon found out the person's house to whom I was recommended, presented my letter from his friend the grandee in the island, and was received with much kindness. This great lord, whose name was Munodi, ordered me an apartment in his own house, where I continued during my stay, and was entertained in a most hospitable manner.

The next morning after my arrival, he took me in his chariot to see the town, which is about half the bigness of London, but the houses very strangely built, and most of them out of repair. The people in the streets walked fast, looked wild, their eyes fixed, and were generally in rags. We passed through one of the town gates, and went about three miles into the country, where I saw many labourers working with several sorts of tools in the ground, but was not able to conjecture what they were about; neither did I observe any expectations either of corn or grass, although the soil appeared to be excellent. I could not forbear admiring at these odd appearances both in town and country, and I made bold to desire my conductor, that he would be pleased to explain to me what could be meant by so many busy heads, hands, and faces, both in the streets and the fields, because I did not discover any good effects they produced; but on the contrary, I never knew a soil so unhappily cultivated, houses so ill contrived and so ruinous, or a people whose countenances and habit expressed so much misery and want.

This Lord Munodi was a person of the first rank, and had been some years Governor of Lagado; but by a cabal of ministers was discharged for insufficiency. However, the King treated him with tenderness, as a well-meaning man, but of a low contemptible understanding.

When I gave that free censure of the country and its inhabitants, he made no further answer than by telling me, that I had not been long enough among them to form a judgment; and that the different nations of the world had different customs, with other common topics to the same purpose. But when we returned to his palace, he asked me how I liked the building, what absurdities I observed, and what quarrel I had with the dress or looks of his domestics. This he might safely do, because every thing about him was magnificent, regular, and polite. I answered that his Excellency's prudence, quality, and fortune, had exempted him from those defects, which folly and beggary had produced in others. He said if I would go with him to his country-house, about twenty miles distant, where his estate lay, there would be more leisure for this kind of conversation. I told his Excellency that I was entirely at his disposal; and accordingly we set out next morning.

During our journey, he made me observe the several methods used by farmers in managing their lands, which to me were wholly unaccountable; for, except in some very few places, I could not discover one ear of corn or blade of grass. But, in three hours travelling, the scene was wholly altered; we came into a most beautiful country; farmers' houses at small distances, neatly built; the fields enclosed, containing vineyards, corn-grounds, and meadows. Neither do I remember to have seen a more delightful prospect. His Excellency observed my countenance to clear up; he told me, with a sigh, that there his estate began, and would continue the same, till we should come to his house. That his countrymen ridiculed and despised him for managing his affairs no better, and for setting so ill an example to the kingdom, which however was followed by very few, such as were old, and wilful, and weak like himself.

We came at length to the house, which was indeed a noble structure, built according to the best rules of ancient architecture. The fountains, gardens, walks, avenues, and groves, were all disposed with exact judgment and taste. I gave due praises to every thing I saw, whereof his Excellency took not the least notice till after supper, when, there being no third companion, he told me with a very melancholy air, that he doubted he must throw down his houses in town and country, to rebuild them after the present mode, destroy all his plantations, and cast others into such a form as modern usage required, and give the same directions to all his tenants, unless he would submit to incur the censure, of pride, singularity, affectation, ignorance, caprice, and perhaps increase his Majesty's displeasure.

That the admiration I appeared to be under, would cease or diminish when he had informed me of some particulars, which probably I never heard of at court, the people there being too much taken up in their own speculations, to have regard to what passed here below.

The sum of his discourse was to this effect. That about forty years ago, certain persons went up to Laputa, either upon business or diversion, and, after five months continuance, came back with a very little smattering in mathematics, but full of volatile spirits acquired in that airy region. That these persons upon their return began to dislike the management of every thing below, and fell into schemes of putting all arts, sciences, languages, and mechanics upon a new foot. To this end they procured a royal patent for erecting an Academy of Projectors in

Lagado; and the humour prevailed so strongly among the people, that there is not a town of any consequence in the kingdom without such an academy. In these colleges, the professors contrive new rules and methods of agriculture and building, and new instruments and tools for all trades and manufactures, whereby, as they undertake, one man shall do the work of ten; a palace may be built in a week, of materials so durable as to last for ever without repairing. All the fruits of the earth shall come to maturity at whatever season we think fit to choose, and increase an hundred fold more than they do at present, with innumerable other happy proposals. The only inconvenience is, that none of these projects are yet brought to perfection, and in the mean time, the whole country lies miserably waste, the houses in ruins, and the people without food or clothes. By all which, instead of being discouraged, they are fifty times more violently bent upon prosecuting their schemes, driven equally on by hope and despair: that as for himself, being not of an enterprising spirit, he was content to go on in the old forms, to live in the houses his ancestors had built, and act as they did in every part of life without innovation. That some few other persons of quality and gentry had done the same, but were looked on with an eye of contempt and ill-will, as enemies to art, ignorant, and ill commonwealth's-men, preferring their own ease and sloth before the general improvement of their country.

His Lordship added, that he would not by any further particulars prevent the pleasure I should certainly take in viewing the grand Academy, whither he was resolved I should go. He only desired me to observe a ruined building upon the side of a mountain about three miles distant, of which he gave me this account. That he had a very convenient mill within half a mile of his house, turned by a current from a large river, and sufficient for his own family, as well as a great number of his tenants. That about seven years ago, a club of those projectors came to him with proposals to destroy this mill, and build another on the side of that mountain, on the long ridge whereof a long canal must be cut for a repository of water, to be conveyed up by pipes and engines to supply the mill: because the wind and air upon a height agitated the water, and thereby made it fitter for motion: and because the water descending down a declivity would turn the mill with half the current of a river whose course is more upon a level. He said, that being then not very well with the court, and pressed by many of his friends, he complied with the proposal; and after employing an hundred men for two years, the work miscarried, the projectors went off, laying the blame entirely upon him, railing at him ever since, and putting others upon the same experiment, with equal assurance of success, as well as equal disappointment.

In a few days we came back to town, and his Excellency, considering the bad character he had in the Academy, would not go with me himself, but recommended me to a friend of his to bear me company thither. My lord was pleased to represent me as a great admirer of projects, and a person of much curiosity and easy belief; which, indeed, was not without truth; for I had myself been a sort of projector in my younger days.

CHAPTER V

*The Author permitted to see the Grand Academy of Lagado. The
Academy largely described. The Arts wherein the professors
employ themselves.*

THIS Academy is not an entire single building, but a
continuation of several houses on both sides of a
street, which growing waste was purchased and applied to
that use.

I was received very kindly by the Warden, and went for
many days to the Academy. Every room hath in it one or
more projectors, and I believe I could not be in fewer than
five hundred rooms.

The first man I saw was of a meagre aspect, with sooty
hands and face, his hair and beard long, ragged and singed
in several places. His clothes, shirt, and skin, were all of
the same colour. He had been eight years upon a project
for extracting sun-beams out of cucumbers, which were to
be put into vials hermetically sealed, and let out to warm
the air in raw inclement summers. He told me, he did not
doubt, in eight years more, he should be able to supply the
Governor's gardens with sunshine at a reasonable rate; but
he complained that his stock was low, and entreated me to
give him something as an encouragement to ingenuity,
especially since this had been a very dear season for
cucumbers. I made him a small present, for my lord had
furnished me with money on purpose, because he knew
their practice of begging from all who go to see them.

I saw another at work to calcine ice into gunpowder, who
likewise showed me a treatise he had written concerning the
malleability of fire, which he intended to publish.

There was a most ingenious architect who had contrived
a new method for building houses, by beginning at the roof,
and working downwards to the foundation, which he

justified to me by the like practice of those two prudent insects, the bee and the spider.

There was a man born blind, who had several apprentices in his own condition: their employment was to mix colours for painters, which their master taught them to distinguish by feeling and smelling. It was indeed my misfortune to find them at that time not very perfect in their lessons, and the professor himself happened to be generally mistaken: this artist is much encouraged and esteemed by the whole fraternity.

In another apartment I was highly pleased with a projector, who had found a device of ploughing the ground with hogs, to save the charges of ploughs, cattle, and labour. The method is this: in an acre of ground you bury, at six inches distance and eight deep, a quantity of acorns, dates, chestnuts, and other mast or vegetables whereof these animals are fondest; then you drive six hundred or more of them into the field, where in a few days they will root up the whole ground in search of their food, and make it fit for sowing, at the same time manuring it with their dung. It is true, upon experiment they found the charge and trouble very great, and they had little or no crop. However, it is not doubted that this invention may be capable of great improvement.

I went into another room, where the walls and ceiling were all hung round with cobwebs, except a narrow passage for the artist to go in and out. At my entrance he called aloud to me not to disturb his webs. He lamented the fatal mistake the world had been so long in of using silk-worms, while we had such plenty of domestic insects, who infinitely excelled the former, because they understood how to weave as well as spin. And he proposed farther, that by employing spiders, the charge of dyeing silks should be wholly saved, whereof I was fully convinced when he showed me a vast number of flies most beautifully coloured, wherewith he fed his spiders, assuring us, that the webs would take a tincture from them; and as he had them of all hues, he hoped to fit everybody's fancy, as soon as he could find proper food for the flies, of certain gums, oils, and other glutinous matter to give a strength and consistence to the threads.

There was an astronomer who had undertaken to place a sundial upon the great weathercock on the town-house, by adjusting the annual and diurnal motions of the earth and sun, so as to answer and coincide with all accidental turnings by the wind.

I visited many other apartments, but shall not trouble my reader with all the curiosities I observed, being studious of brevity.

I had hitherto seen only one side of the Academy, the other being appropriated to the advancers of speculative learning, of whom I shall say something when I have mentioned one illustrious person more, who is called among them *the universal artist.* He told us he had been thirty years employing his thoughts for the improvement of human life. He had two large rooms full of wonderful curiosities, and fifty men at work. Some were condensing air into a dry tangible substance, by extracting the nitre, and letting the aqueous or fluid particles percolate; others softening marble for pillows and pin-cushions; others petrifying the hoofs of a living horse to preserve them from foundering. The artist himself was at that time busy upon two great designs; the first, to sow land with chaff, wherein he affirmed the true seminal virtue to be contained, as he demonstrated by several experiments which I was not skilful enough to comprehend. The other was, by a certain composition of gums, minerals, and vegetables outwardly applied, to prevent the growth of wool upon two young lambs; and he hoped in a reasonable time to propagate the breed of naked sheep all over the kingdom.

We crossed a walk to the other part of the Academy, where, as I have already said, the projectors in speculative learning resided.

The first professor I saw was in a very large room, with forty pupils about him. After salutation, observing me to look earnestly upon a frame, which took up the greatest part of both the length and breadth of the room, he said perhaps I might wonder to see him employed in a project for improving speculative knowledge by practical and mechanical operations. But the world would soon be sensible of its usefulness, and he flattered himself that a more noble exalted thought never sprang in any other man's head. Every one knew how laborious the usual method is of attaining to arts and sciences; whereas, by his contrivance, the most ignorant person at a reasonable charge, and with a little bodily labour, may write books in philosophy, poetry, politics, law, mathematics, and theology, without the least assistance from genius or study. He then led me to the frame, about the sides whereof all his pupils stood in ranks. It was twenty foot square, placed in the middle of the room. The superficies was composed of several bits of wood, about the bigness of a die, but some larger than others. They were all linked together by slender wires. These bits of wood were covered on every square with paper pasted on them, and on these papers were written all the words of their language, in their several moods, tenses, and declensions, but without any order. The professor then desired me to observe, for he was going to set his engine at work. The pupils at his command took each of them hold of an iron handle, whereof there were forty fixed round the edges of the frame and giving them a sudden turn, the whole disposition of the words was entirely changed. He then commanded six and thirty of the lads to read the several lines softly as they appeared upon the frame; and where they found three or four words together that might make part of a sentence, they dictated to the four remaining boys who were scribes. This work was repeated three or four times, and at every turn the engine was so contrived, that the words shifted into new places, as the square bits of wood moved upside down.

Six hours a day the young students were employed in this labour, and the professor showed me several volumes in large folio already collected, of broken sentences, which he intended to piece together, and out of those rich materials to give the world a complete body of all arts and sciences; which however might be still improved, and much expedited if the public would raise a fund for making and employing five hundred such frames in Lagado, and oblige the managers to contribute in common their several collections.

He assured me, that this invention had employed all his thoughts from his youth, that he had emptied the whole vocabulary into his frame, and made the strictest computation of the general proportion there is in books between the numbers of particles, nouns, and verbs, and other parts of speech.

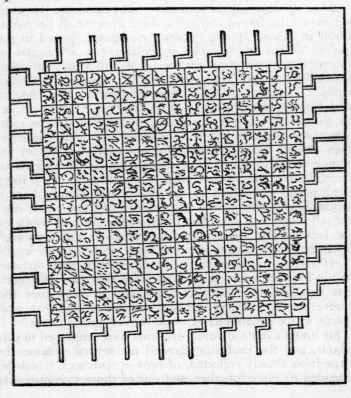

I made my humblest acknowledgment to this illustrious person for his great communicativeness, and promised if ever I had the good fortune to return to my native country, that I would do him justice, as the sole inventor of this wonderful machine; the form and contrivance of which I desired leave to delineate upon paper, as in the figure here annexed. I told him, although it were the custom of our learned in Europe to steal inventions from each other, who had thereby at least this advantage, that it became a controversy which was the right owner, yet I would take such caution, that he should have the honour entire without a rival.

We next went to the school of languages, where three professors sat in consultation upon improving that of their own country.

The first project was to shorten discourse by cutting polysyllables into one, and leaving out verbs and participles, because in reality all things imaginable are but nouns.

The other project was a scheme for entirely abolishing all words whatsoever; and this was urged as a great advantage in point of health as well as brevity. For it is plain, that every word we speak is in some degree a diminution of our lungs by corrosion, and consequently contributes to the shortening of our lives. An expedient was therefore offered, that since words are only names for *things*, it would be more convenient for all men to carry about them such things as were necessary to express the particular business they are to discourse on. And this invention would certainly have taken place, to the great ease as well as health of the subject, if the women, in conjunction with the vulgar and illiterate, had not threatened to raise a rebellion, unless they might be allowed the liberty to speak with their tongues, after the manner of their ancestors; such constant irreconcilable enemies to science are the common people. However, many of the most learned and wise adhere to the new scheme of expressing themselves by things, which hath only this inconvenience attending it, that if a man's business be very great, and of various kinds, he must be obliged in proportion to carry a greater bundle of things upon his back, unless he can afford one or two strong servants to attend him. I have often beheld two of those sages almost sinking under the weight of their packs, like pedlars among us; who, when they met in the streets, would lay down their loads, open their sacks, and hold conversation for an hour together; then put up their implements, help each other to resume their burthens, and take their leave.

But for short conversations a man may carry implements in his pockets and under his arms, enough to supply him, and in his house he cannot be at a loss. Therefore the room where company meet who practise this art, is full of all things ready at hand, requisite to furnish matter for this kind of artificial converse.

Another great advantage proposed by this invention, was that it would serve as an universal language to be understood in all civilised nations, whose goods and utensils are generally of the same kind, or nearly resembling, so that their uses might easily be comprehended. And thus ambassadors would be qualified to treat with foreign princes or ministers of state, to whose tongues they were utter strangers.

I was at the mathematical school, where the master taught his pupils after a method scarce imaginable to us in Europe. The proposition and demonstration were fairly written on a thin wafer, with ink composed of a cephalic tincture. This the student was to swallow upon a fasting stomach, and for three days following eat nothing but bread and water. As the wafer digested, the tincture mounted to his brain, bearing the proposition along with it. But the success hath not hitherto been answerable, partly by some error in the *quantum* or composition, and partly by the perverseness of lads, to whom this bolus is so nauseous, that they generally steal aside, and discharge it upwards before it can operate; neither have they been yet persuaded to use so long an abstinence as the prescription requires.

CHAPTER VI

A further account of the Academy. The Author proposes some improvements, which are honourably received.

IN the school of political projectors I was but ill entertained, the professors appearing in my judgment wholly out of their senses, which is a scene that never fails to make me melancholy. These unhappy people were proposing schemes for persuading monarchs to choose favourites upon the score of their wisdom, capacity, and virtue; of teaching ministers to consult the public good; of rewarding merit, great abilities, eminent services; of instructing princes to know their true interest by placing it on the same foundation with that of their people; of choosing for employments persons qualified to exercise them; with many other wild impossible chimæras, that never entered before into the heart of man to conceive, and confirmed in me the old observation, that there is nothing so extravagant and irrational which some philosophers have not maintained for truth.

But, however, I shall so far do justice to this part of the Academy, as to acknowledge that all of them were not so visionary. There was a most ingenious doctor who seemed to be perfectly versed in the whole nature and system of government. This illustrious person had very usefully employed his studies in finding out effectual remedies for all diseases and corruptions, to which the several kinds of public administration are subject by the vices or infirmities of those who govern, as well as by the licentiousness of those who are to obey. For instance; whereas all writers and reasoners have agreed, that there is a strict universal resemblance between the natural and the political body; can there be any thing more evident, than that the health of both must be preserved, and the diseases cured by the same prescriptions? It is allowed, that senates and great councils are often troubled with redundant, ebullient, and other peccant humours, with many diseases of the head, and more of the heart; with strong convulsions, with grievous contractions of the nerves and sinews in both hands, but especially the right; with spleen, flatus, vertigos, and deliriums; with scrofulous tumours full of fœtid purulent matter; with sour frothy ructations, with canine appetites and crudeness of digestion, besides many other needless to mention. This doctor therefore proposed, that upon the meeting of a senate, certain physicians should attend at the three first days of their sitting, and at the close of each day's debate, feel the pulses of every senator; after which, having maturely considered, and consulted upon the nature of the several maladies, and the methods of cure, they should on the fourth day return to the senate house, attended by their apothecaries stored with proper medicines; and before the members sat, administer to each of them lenitives, aperitives, abstersives, corrosives, restringents, palliatives, laxatives, cephalalgics, icterics, apophlegmatics, acoustics, as their several cases required; and according as these medicines should operate, repeat, alter, or omit them at the next meeting.

This project could not be of any great expense to the public, and would, in my poor opinion, be of much use for the dispatch of business in those countries where senates have any share in the legislative power; beget unanimity, shorten debates, open a few mouths which are now closed, and close many more which are now open; curb the petulancy of the young, and correct the positiveness of the old; rouse the stupid, and damp the pert.

Again; because it is a general complaint, that the favourites of princes are troubled with short and weak memories; the same doctor proposed, that whoever attended a first minister, after having told his business with the utmost brevity and in the plainest words, should at his departure give the said minister a tweak by the nose, or a kick in the belly, or tread on his corns, or lug him thrice by both ears, or run a pin into his breech, or pinch his arm black and blue, to prevent forgetfulness; and at every levee day repeat the same operation, till the business were done or absolutely refused.

He likewise directed, that every senator in the great council of a nation, after he had delivered his opinion, and argued in the defence of it, should be obliged to give his vote directly contrary; because if that were done, the result would infallibly terminate in the good of the public.

When parties in a state are violent, he offered a wonderful contrivance to reconcile them. The method is this. You take a hundred leaders of each party, you dispose them into couples of such whose heads are nearest of a size; then let two nice operators saw off the occiput of each couple at the same time, in such a manner that the brain may be equally divided. Let the occiputs thus cut off be interchanged, applying each to the head of his opposite party-man. It seems indeed to be a work that requireth some exactness, but the professor assured us, that if it were dexterously performed, the cure would be infallible. For he argued thus; that the two half brains being left to debate the matter between themselves within the space of one skull, would soon come to a good understanding, and produce that moderation, as well as regularity of thinking, so much to be wished for in the heads of those, who imagine they come into the world only to watch and govern its motion: and as to the difference of brains in quantity or quality, among those who are directors in faction; the doctor assured us from his own knowledge, that it was a perfect trifle.

I heard a very warm debate between two professors, about the most commodious and effectual ways and means of raising money without grieving the subject. The first affirmed the justest method would be to lay a certain tax upon vices and folly, and the sum fixed upon every man, to be rated after the fairest manner by a jury of his neighbours. The second was of an opinion directly contrary, to tax those qualities of body and mind for which men chiefly value themselves, the rate to be more or less according to the degrees of excelling, the decision whereof should be left entirely to their own breast. The highest tax was upon men who are the greatest favourites of the other sex, and the assessments according to the number and natures of the favours they have received; for which they are allowed to be their own vouchers. Wit, valour, and politeness were likewise proposed to be largely taxed, and collected in the same manner, by every person's giving his own word for the quantum of what he possessed. But as to honour, justice, wisdom, and learning, they should not be taxed at all, because they are qualifications of so singular a kind, that no man will either allow them in his neighbour, or value them in himself.

The women were proposed to be taxed according to their beauty and skill in dressing, wherein they had the same privilege with the men, to be determined by thier own judgment. But constancy, chastity, good sense, and good nature were not rated, because they would not bear the charge of collecting.

To keep senators in the interest of the crown, it was proposed that the members should raffle for employments, every man first taking an oath, and giving security that he would vote for the court, whether he won or no; after which the losers had in their turn the liberty of raffling upon the next vacancy. Thus hope and expectation would be kept alive, none would complain of broken promises, but impute their disappointments wholly to fortune, whose shoulders are broader and stronger than those of a ministry.

Another professor showed me a large paper of instructions for discovering plots and conspiracies against the government. He advised great statesmen to examine into the diet of all suspected persons; their times of eating; upon which side they lay in bed; with which hand they wiped their posteriors; to take a strict view of their excrements, and, from the colour, the odour, the taste, the consistence, the crudeness or maturity of digestion, form a judgment of their thoughts and designs. Because men are never so serious, thoughtful, and intent, as when they are at stool, which he found by frequent experiment; for in such conjunctures, when he used merely as a trial to consider which was the best way of murdering the king, his ordure would have a tincture of green, but quite different when he thought only of raising an insurrection or burning the metropolis.

The whole discourse was written with great acuteness, containing many observations both curious and useful for politicians, but as I conceived not altogether complete. This I ventured to tell the author, and offered if he pleased to supply him with some additions. He received my proposition with more compliance than is usual among writers, especially those of the projecting species, professing he would be glad to receive farther information.

I told him, that in the kingdom of Tribnia, by the natives called Langden, where I had sojourned some time in my travels, the bulk of the people consist in a manner wholly of discoverers, witnesses, informers, accusers, prosecutors, evidences, swearers, together with their several subservient and subaltern instruments, all under the colours and conduct of ministers of state and their deputies. The plots in that kingdom are usually the workmanship of those persons who desire to raise their own characters of profound politicians, to restore new vigour to a crazy administration, to stifle or divert general discontents, to fill their pockets with forfeitures, and raise or sink the opinion of public credit, as either shall best answer their private advantage. It is first agreed and settled among them, what suspected persons shall be accused of a plot; then, effectual care is taken to secure all their letters and papers, and put the criminals in chains. These papers are delivered to a set of artists, very dexterous in finding out the mysterious meanings of words, syllables, and letters. For instance, they can discover a close-stool to signify a privy council; a flock of geese, a senate; a lame god, an invader; a codshead, a ——; the plague, a standing army; a buzzard, a prime minister; the gout, a high priest; a gibbet, a secretary of state; a chamber pot, a committee of grandees; a sieve, a court lady; a broom, a revolution; a mouse-trap, an employment; a bottomless pit, the treasury; a sink, the court; a cap and bells, a favourite; a broken reed, a court of justice; an empty tun, a general; a running sore, the administration.

When this method fails, they have two others more effectual, which the learned among them call acrostics and anagrams. First they can decipher all initial letters into political meanings. Thus, *N.* shall signify a plot; *B.* a regiment of horse; *L.* a fleet at sea; or secondly by transposing the letters of the alphabet in any suspected paper, they can discover the deepest designes of a discontented party. So, for example, if I should say in a letter to a friend, *Our brother* Tom *has just got the piles*, a skilful decipherer would discover, that the same letters which compose that sentence, may be analysed into the following words; *Resist, a plot is brought home; The tour.* And this is the anagrammatic method.

The professor made me great acknowledgments for communicating these observations, and promised to make honourable mention of me in his treatise.

I saw nothing in this country that could invite me to a longer continuance, and began to think of returning home to England.

CHAPTER VII

The Author leaves Lagado, *arrives at* Maldonada. *No ship ready.
He takes a short voyage to* Glubbdubdrib. *His reception by the
Governor.*

THE continent of which this kingdom is a part, extends
itself, as I have reason to believe, eastward to that
unknown tract of America, westward of California, and north
to the Pacific Ocean, which is not above a hundred and fifty
miles from Lagado; where there is a good port and much
commerce with the great island of Luggnagg, situated to the
north-west about 29 degrees north latitude, and 140 longitude, This island of Luggnagg stands south-eastwards of
Japan, about an hundred leagues distant. There is a strict
alliance between the Japanese Emperor and the King of
Luggnagg, which affords frequent opportunities of sailing
from one island to the other. I determined therefore to
direct my course this way, in order to my return to Europe.
I hired two mules with a guide to show me the way, and
carry my small baggage. I took leave of my noble protector,
who had shown me so much favour, and made me a generous
present at my departure.

My journey was without any accident or adventure worth
relating. When I arrived at the port of Maldonada (for
so it is called) there was no ship in the harbour bound for
Luggnagg, nor likely to be in some time. The town is about
as large as Portsmouth. I soon fell into some acquaintance,
and was very hospitably received. A gentleman of distinction said to me, that since the ships bound for Luggnagg
could not be ready in less than a month, it might be no
disagreeable amusement for me to take a trip to the little
island of Glubbdubdrib, about five leagues off to the south-
west. He offered himself and a friend to accompany me,

and that I should be provided with a small convenient barque for the voyage.

Glubbdubdrib, as nearly as I can interpret the word, signifies the Island of *Sorcerers* or *Magicians*. It is about one third as large as the Isle of Wight, and extremely fruitful: it is governed by the head of a certain tribe, who are all magicians. This tribe marries only among each other, and the eldest in succession is Prince or Governor. He hath a noble palace, and a park of about three thousand acres, surrounded by a wall of hewn stone twenty foot high. In this park are several small enclosures for cattle, corn, and gardening.

The Governor and his family are served and attended by domestics of a kind somewhat unusual. By his skill in necromancy, he hath a power of calling whom he pleaseth from the dead, and commanding their service for twenty-four hours, but no longer; nor can he call the same persons up again in less than three months, except upon very extraordinary occasions.

When we arrived at the island, which was about eleven in the morning, one of the gentlemen who accompanied me, went to the Governor, and desired admittance for a stranger, who came on purpose to have the honour of attending on his Highness. This was immediately granted, and we all three entered the gate of the palace between two rows of guards, armed and dressed after a very antic manner, and something in their countenances that made my flesh creep with a horror I cannot express. We passed through several apartments, between servants of the same sort, ranked on each side as before, till we came to the chamber of presence, where after three profound obeisances, and a few general questions, we were permitted to sit on three stools near the lowest step of his Highness's throne. He understood the language of Balnibarbi, although it were different from that of his island. He desired me to give him some account of my travels; and, to let me see that I should be treated without ceremony, he dismissed all his attendants with a turn of his finger, at which to my great astonishment they vanished in an instant, like visions in a dream, when we awake on a sudden. I could not recover myself in some time, till the Governor assured me that I should receive no hurt; and observing my two companions to be under no concern, who had been often entertained in the same manner, I began to take courage, and related to his Highness a short history of my several adventures, yet not without some hesitation, and frequently looking behind me to the place where I had seen those domestic spectres. I had the honour to dine with the Governor, where a new set of ghosts served up the meat, and waited at table. I now observed myself to be less terrified than I had been in the morning. I stayed till sunset, but humbly desired his Highness to excuse me for not accepting his invitation of lodging in the palace. My two friends and I lay at a private house in the town adjoining, which is the capital of this little island; and the next morning we returned to pay our duty to the Governor, as he was pleased to command us.

After this manner we continued in the island for ten days, most part of every day with the Governor, and at night in our lodging. I soon grew so familiarized to the sight of spirits, that after the third or fourth time they gave me no emotion at all; or, if I had any apprehensions left, my curiosity prevailed over them. For his Highness the Governor ordered me to call up whatever persons I would choose to name, and in whatever numbers among all the dead from the beginning of the world to the present time, and command them to answer any questions I should think fit to ask; with this condition, that my questions must be confined within the compass of the times they lived in. And one thing I might depend upon, that they would certainly tell me the truth, for lying was a talent of no use in the lower world.

I made my humble acknowledgment to his Highness for so great a favour. We were in a chamber, from whence there was a fair prospect into the park. And because my first inclination was to be entertained with scenes of pomp and magnificence, I desired to see Alexander the Great, at

13

the head of his army just after the battle of Arbela; which upon a motion of the Governor's finger immediately appeared in a large field under the window, where we stood. Alexander was called up into the room: it was with great difficulty that I understood his Greek, and had but little of my own. He assured me upon his honour that he was not poisoned, but died of a fever by excessive drinking.

Next I saw Hannibal passing the Alps, who told me he had not a drop of vinegar in his camp.

I saw Cæsar and Pompey at the head of their troops, just ready to engage. I saw the former in his last great triumph. I desired that the senate of Rome might appear before me in one large chamber, and a modern representative, in counterview in another. The first seemed to be an assembly of heroes and demi-gods; the other a knot of pedlars, pick-pockets, highway-men, and bullies.

The Governor at my request gave the sign for Cæsar and Brutus to advance towards us. I was struck with a profound veneration at the sight of Brutus, and could easily discover the most consummate virtue, the greatest intrepidity and firmness of mind, the truest love of his country, and general benevolence for mankind in every lineament of his countenance. I observed with much pleasure, that these two persons were in good intelligence with each other, and Cæsar freely confessed to me, that the greatest actions of his own life were not equal by many degrees to the glory of taking it away. I had the honour to have much conversation with Brutus; and was told, that his ancestors Junius, Socrates, Epaminondas, Cato the younger, Sir Thomas More, and himself were perpetually together: a sextumvirate to which all the ages of the world cannot add a seventh.

It would be tedious to trouble the reader with relating what vast numbers of illustrious persons were called up, to gratify that insatiable desire I had to see the world in every period of antiquity placed before me. I chiefly fed my eyes with beholding the destroyers of tyrants and usurpers, and the restorers of liberty to oppressed and injured nations.

But it is impossible to express the satisfaction I received in my own mind, after such a manner as to make it a suitable entertainment to the reader.

CHAPTER VIII

A further account of Glubbdubdrib. *Ancient and modern history corrected.*

HAVING a desire to see those ancients, who were most renowned for wit and learning, I set apart one day on purpose. I proposed that Homer and Aristotle might appear at the head of all their commentators; but these were so numerous that some hundreds were forced to attend in the court, and outward rooms of the palace. I knew and could distinguish those two heroes at first sight, not only from the crowd, but from each other. Homer was the taller and comelier person of the two, walked very erect for one of his age, and his eyes were the most quick and piercing I ever beheld. Aristotle stooped much, and made use of a staff. His visage was meagre, his hair lank and thin, and his voice hollow. I soon discovered that both of them were perfect strangers to the rest of the company, and had never seen or heard of them before. And I had a whisper from a ghost, who shall be nameless, that these commentators always kept in the most distant quarters from their principals in the lower world, through a consciousness of shame and guilt, because they had so horribly misrepresented the meaning of those authors to posterity. I introduced Didymus and Eustathius to Homer, and prevailed on him to treat them better than perhaps they deserved; for he soon found they wanted a genius to enter into the spirit of a poet. But Aristotle was out of all patience with the account I gave him of Scotus and Ramus, as I presented them to him; and he asked them whether the rest of the tribe were as great dunces as themselves.

I then desired the Governor to call up Descartes and Gassendi, with whom I prevailed to explain their systems to Aristotle. This great philosopher freely acknowledged his own mistakes in natural philosophy, because he proceeded in many things upon conjecture, as all men must do; and he found, that Gassendi, who had made the doctrine of Epicurus as palatable as he could, and the *vortices* of Descartes, were equally exploded. He predicted the same fate to *attraction*, whereof the present learned are such zealous asserters. He said, that new systems of nature were but new fashions, which would vary in every age; and even those who pretend to demonstrate them from mathematical principles, would flourish but a short period of time, and be out of vogue when that was determined.

I spent five days in conversing with many others of the ancient learned. I saw most of the first Roman emperors. I prevailed on the Governor to call up Eliogabalus's cooks to dress us a dinner, but they could not show us much of their skill for want of materials. A helot of Agesilaus made us a dish of Spartan broth, but I was not able to get down a second spoonful.

The two gentlemen who conducted me to the island, were pressed by their private affairs to return in three days, which I employed in seeing some of the modern dead, who had made the greatest figure for two or three hundred years past in our own and other countries of Europe; and having been always a great admirer of old illustrious families, I desired the Governor would call up a dozen or two of kings with their ancestors in order for eight or nine generations. But my disappointment was grievous and unexpected. For, instead of a long train with royal diadems, I saw in one family two fiddlers, three spruce courtiers, and an Italian prelate. In another, a barber, an abbot, and two cardinals. I have too great a veneration for crowned heads to dwell any longer on so nice a subject. But as to counts, marquesses, dukes, earls, and the like, I was not so scrupulous. And I confess it was not without some pleasure that I found myself able to trace the particular features, by which certain families are distinguished, up to their originals. I could plainly discover from whence one family derives a long chin, why a second hath abounded with knaves for two generations, and fools for two more; why a third happened to be crack brained, and a fourth to be sharpers. Whence it came what Polydore Virgil says of a certain great house, *Nec vir fortis, nec femina casta.* How cruelty, falsehood, and cowardice grew to be characteristics by which certain families are distinguished as much as by their coat of arms. Who first brought the pox into a noble house, which hath lineally descended in scrofulous tumours to their posterity. Neither could I wonder at all this, when I saw such an interruption of lineages by pages, lackeys, valets, coachmen, gamesters, fiddlers, players, captains and pickpockets.

I was chiefly disgusted with modern history. For having strictly examined all the persons of greatest name in the courts of princes, for an hundred years past, I found how the world had been misled by prostitute writers, to ascribe the greatest exploits in war to cowards, the wisest counsel to fools, sincerity to flatterers, Roman virtue to betrayers of their country, piety to atheists, chastity to sodomites, truth to informers. How many innocent and excellent persons had been condemned to death or banishment, by the practising of great ministers upon the corruption of judges, and the malice of factions. How many villains had been exalted to the highest places of trust, power, dignity, and profit: how great a share in the motions and events of courts, councils, and senates might be challenged by bawds, whores, pimps, parasites, and buffoons. How low an opinion I had of human wisdom and integrity, when I was truly informed of the springs and motives of great enterprizes and revolutions in the world, and of the contemptible accidents to which they owed their success.

Here I discovered the roguery and ignorance of those who pretend to write *anecdotes*, or secret history, who send so many kings to their graves with a cup of poison; will repeat the discourse between a prince and chief minister, where no witness was by; unlock the thoughts and cabinets of

Ambassadors and secretaries of state, and have the perpetual misfortune to be mistaken. Here I discovered the true causes of many great events that have surprised the world, how a whore can govern the back-stairs, the back-stairs a council, and the council a senate. A general confessed in my presence, that he got a victory purely by the force of cowardice and ill conduct; and an admiral, that for want of proper intelligence, he beat the enemy to whom he intended to betray the fleet. Three kings protested to me, that in their whole reigns they never did once prefer any person of merit, unless by mistake or treachery of some minister in whom they confided: neither would they do it if they were to live again: and they showed with great strength of reason, that the royal throne could not be supported without corruption, because that positive, confident, restive temper, which virtue infused into man, was a perpetual clog to public business.

I had the curiosity to enquire in a particular manner, by what method great numbers had procured to themselves high titles of honour, and prodigious estates; and I confined my enquiry to a very modern period: however, without grating upon present times, because I would be sure to give no offence even to foreigners (for I hope the reader need not be told that I do not in the least intend my own country in what I say upon this occasion,) a great number of persons concerned were called up, and upon a very slight examination, discovered such a scene of infamy, that I cannot reflect upon it without some seriousness. Perjury, oppression, subornation, fraud, pandarism, and the like infirmities, were amongst the most excusable arts they had to mention, and for these I gave, as it was reasonable, great allowance. But when some confessed they owed their greatness and wealth to sodomy or incest, others to the prostituting of their own wives and daughters; others to the betraying their country or their prince; some to poisoning, more to the perverting of justice in order to destroy the innocent: I hope I may be pardoned if these discoveries inclined me a little to abate of that profound veneration which I am naturally apt to pay to persons of high rank, who ought to be treated with the utmost respect due to their sublime dignity, by us their inferiors.

I had often read of some great services done to princes and states, and desired to see the persons by whom those services were performed. Upon enquiry I was told that their names were to be found on no record, except a few of them whom history hath represented as the vilest rogues and traitors. As to the rest, I had never once heard of them. They all appeared with dejected looks, and in the meanest habit, most of them telling me they died in poverty and disgrace, and the rest on a scaffold or a gibbet.

Among others there was one person whose case appeared a little singular. He had a youth about eighteen years old standing by his side. He told me he had for many years been commander of a ship, and in the sea fight at Actium, had the good fortune to break through the enemy's great line of battle, sink three of their capital ships, and take a fourth, which was the sole cause of Antony's flight, and of the victory that ensued; that the youth standing by him, his only son, was killed in the action. He added, that upon the confidence of some merit, the war being at an end, he went to Rome, and solicited at the court of Augustus to be preferred to a greater ship, whose commander had been killed; but without any regard to his pretensions, it was given to a youth who had never seen the sea, the son of Libertina, who waited on one of the emperor's mistresses. Returning back to his own vessel, he was charged with neglect of duty, and the ship given to a favourite page of Publicola, the vice-admiral; whereupon he retired to a poor farm at a great distance from Rome, and there ended his life. I was so curious to know the truth of this story, that I desired Agrippa might be called, who was admiral in that fight. He appeared, and confirmed the whole account, but with much more advantage to the captain, whose modesty had extenuated or concealed a great part of his merit.

I was surprised to find corruption grown to high and so quick in that empire, by the force of luxury so lately introduced, which made me less wonder at many parallel cases in other countries, where vices of all kinds have reigned so much longer, and where the whole praise as well as pillage hath been engrossed by the chief commander, who perhaps had the least title to either.

As every person called up made exactly the same appearance he had done in the world, it gave me melancholy reflections to observe how much the race of human kind was degenerated among us, within these hundred years past. How the pox under all its consequences and denominations had altered every lineament of an English countenance, shortened the size of bodies, unbraced the nerves, relaxed the sinews and muscles, introduced a sallow complexion, and rendered the flesh loose and rancid.

I descended so low as to desire some English yeomen of the old stamp might be summoned to appear, once so famous for the simplicity of their manners, diet and dress, for justice in their dealings, for the true spirit of liberty, for their valour and love of their country. Neither could I be wholly unmoved after comparing the living with the dead, when I considered how all these pure native virtues were prostituted for a piece of money by their grand-children, who in selling their votes, and managing at elections, have acquired every vice and corruption that can possibly be learned in a court.

CHAPTER IX

The Author returns to Maldonada. *Sails to the Kingdom of* Luggnagg. *The Author confined. He is sent for to Court. The manner of his admittance. The King's great lenity to his subjects.*

THE day of our departure being come, I took leave of his Highness the Governor of Glubbdubdrib, and returned with my two companions to Maldonada, where after a fortnight's waiting, a ship was ready to sail for Luggnagg. The two gentlemen, and some others, were so generous and kind as to furnish me with provisions, and see me on board. I was a month in this voyage. We had one violent storm, and were under a necessity of steering west-ward to get into the trade wind, which holds for above sixty leagues. On the 21st of April, 1708, we sailed into the river of Clumegnig, which is a seaport town, at the south-east point of Luggnagg. We cast anchor within a league of the town, and made a signal for a pilot. Two of them came on board in less than half an hour, by whom we were guided between certain shoals and rocks, which are very dangerous in the passage to a large basin, where a fleet may ride in safety within a cable's length of the town wall.

Some of our sailors, whether out of treachery or in-advertence, had informed the pilots that I was a stranger and a great traveller, whereof these gave notice to a custom-house officer, by whom I was examined very strictly upon my landing. This officer spoke to me in the language of Balnibarbi, which by the force of much commerce is generally understood in that town, especially by seamen, and those employed in the customs. I gave him a short account of some particulars, and made my story as plausible and consistent as I could; but I thought it necessary to disguise my country, and call myself an Hollander, because my intentions were for Japan, and I knew the Dutch were the only Europeans permitted to enter into that kingdom. I therefore told the officer, that having been shipwrecked on the coast of Balnibarbi, and cast on a rock, I was re-ceived up into Laputa, or the Flying Island (of which he had often heard), and was now endeavouring to get to Japan, from whence I might find a convenience of returning to my own country. The officer said, I must be confined till he could receive orders from court, for which he would write immediately, and hoped to receive an answer in a fortnight. I was carried to a convenient lodging, with a sentry placed at the door; however I had the liberty of a large garden, and was treated with humanity enough, being maintained all the time at the King's charge. I was invited by several persons, chiefly out of curiosity, because it was reported that I came from countries very remote of which they had never heard.

I hired a young man who came in the same ship to be an interpreter; he was a native of Luggnagg, but had lived some years at Maldonada, and was a perfect master of both languages. By his assistance I was able to hold a conversation with those who came to visit me; but this consisted only of their questions, and my answers.

The dispatch came from court about the time we expected. It contained a warrant for conducting me and my retinue to Traldragdubh or Trildrogdrib, for it is pronounced both ways as near as I can remember, by a party of ten horse. All my retinue was that poor lad for an interpreter, whom I persuaded into my service, and at my humble request, we had each of us a mule to ride on. A messenger was dispatched half a day's journey before us, to give the King notice of my approach, and to desire that his Majesty would please to appoint a day and hour, when it would be his gracious pleasure that I might have the honour to *lick the dust before his footstool*. This is the court style, and I found it to be more than matter of form. For upon my admittance two days after my arrival, I was commanded to crawl on my belly, and lick the floor as I advanced; but on account of my being a stranger, care was taken to have it made so clean that the dust was not offensive. However, this was a peculiar grace, not allowed to any but persons of the highest rank, when they desire an admittance. Nay, sometimes the floor is strewed with dust on purpose, when the person to be admitted happens to have powerful enemies at court. And I have seen a great lord with his mouth so crammed, that when he had crept to the proper distance from the throne, he was not able to speak a word. Neither is there any remedy, because it is capital for those who receive an audience to spit or wipe their mouths in his Majesty's presence. There is indeed another custom, which I cannot altogether approve of. When the King hath a mind to put any of his nobles to death in a gentle indulgent manner, he commands to have the floor strowed with a certain brown powder, of a deadly composition, which being licked up infallibly kills him in twenty-four hours. But in justice to this prince's great clemency, and the care he hath of his subjects' lives (wherein it were much to be wished that the monarchs of Europe would imitate him), it must be mentioned for his honour, that strict orders are given to have the infected parts of the floor well washed after every such execution; which if his domestics neglect, they are in danger of incurring his royal displeasure. I myself heard him give directions, that one of his pages should be whipped, whose turn it was to give notice about washing the floor after an execution, but maliciously had omitted it; by which neglect a young lord of great hopes coming to an audience, was unfortunately poisoned, although the King at that time had no design against his life. But this good prince was so gracious, as to forgive the poor page his whipping, upon promise that he would do so no more, without special orders.

To return from this digression; when I had crept within four yards of the throne, I raised myself gently upon my knees, and then striking my forehead seven times on the ground, I pronounced the following words, as they had been taught me the night before, *Ickpling gloffthrobb squutserumm blhiop mlashnalt zwin tnodbalkuffh slhiophad gurdlubh asht.* This is the compliment established by the laws of the land for all persons admitted to the King's presence. It may be rendered into English thus: *May your Celestial Majesty outlive the sun, eleven moons and a half.* To this the King returned some answer, which although I could not understand, yet I replied as I had been directed: *Fluft drin yalerick dwuldom prastrad mirpush,* which properly signifies, *My tongue is in the mouth of my friend,* and by this expression was meant that I desired leave to bring my interpreter; whereupon the young man already mentioned was accordingly introduced, by whose intervention I answered as many questions as his Majesty could put in above an hour. I spoke in the Balnibarbian tongue, and my interpreter delivered my meaning in that of Luggnagg.

The King was much delighted with my company, and ordered his *Bliffmarklub*, or High Chamberlain, to appoint a lodging in the court for me and my interpreter, with a daily allowance for my table, and a large purse of gold for my common expenses.

I stayed three months in this country out of perfect obedience to his Majesty, who was pleased highly to favour me, and made me very honourable offers. But I thought it more consistent with prudence and justice to pass the remainder of my days with my wife and family.

CHAPTER X

The Luggnaggians *commended. A particular description of the* Struldbrugs, *with many conversations between the Author and some eminent persons upon that subject.*

THE Luggnaggians are a polite and generous people, and although they are not without some share of that pride which is peculiar to all Eastern countries, yet they show themselves courteous to strangers, especially such who are countenanced by the court. I had many acquaintances among persons of the best fashion, and being always attended by my interpreter, the conversation we had was not disagreeable.

One day in much good company I was asked by a person of quality, whether I had seen any of their *Struldbrugs*, or *Immortals*. I said I had not, and desired he would explain to me what he meant by such an appellation applied to a mortal creature. He told me, that sometimes, though very rarely, a child happened to be born in a family with a red circular spot in the forehead, directly over the left eyebrow, which was an infallible mark that it should never die. The spot, as he described it, was about the compass of a silver threepence, but in the course of time grew larger, and changed its colour; for at twelve years old it became green, so continued till five and twenty, then turned to a deep blue: at five and forty it grew coal black, and as large as an English shilling, but never admitted any further alteration. He said these births were so rare, that he did not believe there could be above eleven hundred *struldbrugs* of both sexes in the whole kingdom, of which he computed about fifty in the metropolis, and among the rest a young girl born about three years ago. That these productions were not peculiar to any family, but a mere effect of chance; and the children of the *struldbrugs* themselves, were equally mortal with the rest of the people.

I freely own myself to have been struck with inexpressible delight upon hearing this account: and the person who gave it me happening to understand the Balnibarbian language, which I spoke very well, I could not forbear breaking out into expressions perhaps a little too extravagant. I cried out as in a rapture; Happy nation where every child hath at least a chance for being immortal ! Happy people who enjoy so many living examples of ancient virtue, and have masters ready to instruct them in the wisdom of all former ages ! but, happiest beyond all comparison are those excellent *struldbrugs*, who being born exempt from that universal calamity of human nature, have their minds free and disengaged, without the weight and depression of spirits caused by the continual apprehensions of death. I discovered my admiration that I had not observed any of these illustrious persons at court; the black spot on the forehead being so remarkable a distinction, that I could not have easily over-looked it: and it was impossible that his Majesty, a most judicious prince, should not provide himself with a good number of such wise and able counsellors. Yet perhaps the virtue of those reverend sages was too strict for the corrupt and libertine manners of a court. And we often find by experience that young men are too opinionative and volatile to be guided by the sober dictates of their seniors. How-ever, since the King was pleased to allow me access to his royal person, I was resolved upon the very first occasion to deliver my opinion to him on this matter freely, and at large by the help of my interpreter; and whether he would please to take my advice or no, yet in one thing I was determined, that his Majesty having frequently offered me an establishment in this country, I would with great thankfulness accept the favour, and pass my life here in the conversation of those superior beings the *struldbrugs*, if they would please to admit me.

The gentleman to whom I addressed my discourse, because (as I have already observed) he spoke the language of Balnibarbi, said to me with a sort of a smile, which usually ariseth from pity to the ignorant, that he was glad of any occasion to keep me among them, and desired my permission to explain to the company what I had spoke. He did so, and they talked together for some time in their own language, whereof I understood not a syllable, neither could I observe by their countenances what impression my discourse had made on them. After a short silence, the same person told me, that his friends and mine (so he thought fit to express himself) were very much pleased with the judicious remarks I had made on the great happiness and advantages of immortal life; and they were desirous to know in a particular manner, what scheme of living I should have formed to myself, if it had fallen to my lot to have been born a *struldbrug*.

I answered, it was easy to be eloquent on so copious and delightful a subject, especially to me who have been often apt to amuse myself with visions of what I should do if I were a king, a general, or a great lord: and upon this very case I had frequently run over the whole system how I should employ myself, and pass the time if I were sure to live for ever.

That, if it had been my good fortune to come into the world a *struldbrug*, as soon as I could discover my own happiness by understanding the difference between life and death, I would first resolve by all arts and methods whatsoever to procure myself riches. In the pursuit of which by thrift and management, I might reasonably expect in about two hundred years, to be the wealthiest man in the kingdom. In the second place, I would from my earliest youth apply myself to the study of arts and sciences, by which I should arrive in time to excel all others in learning. Lastly, I would carefully record every action and event of consequence that happened in the public, impartially draw the characters of the several successions of princes and great ministers of state, with my own observations on every point. I would exactly set down the several changes in customs, language, fashions of dress, diet and diversions. By all which acquirements, I should be a living treasury of knowledge and wisdom, and certainly become the oracle of the nation.

I would never marry after threescore, but live in an hospitable manner, yet still on the saving side. I would entertain myself in forming and directing the minds of hopeful young men, by convincing them from my own remembrance, experience and observation, fortified by numerous examples, of the usefulness of virtue in public and private life. But my choice and constant companions should be a set of my own immortal brotherhood, among whom I would elect a dozen from the most ancient down to my own contemporaries. Where any of these wanted fortunes, I would provide them with convenient lodges round my own estate, and have some of them always at my table, only mingling a few of the most valuable among you mortals, whom length of time would harden me to lose with little or no reluctance, and treat your posterity after the same manner; just as a man diverts himself with the annual succession of pinks and tulips in his garden, without regretting the loss of those which withered the preceding year.

These *struldbrugs* and I would mutually communicate our observations and memorials through the course of time, remark the several gradations by which corruption steals into the world, and oppose it in every step, by giving perpetual warning and instruction to mankind; which, added to the strong influence of our own example, would probably prevent that continual degeneracy of human nature so justly complained of in all ages.

Add to all this, the pleasure of seeing the various revolutions of states and empires, the changes in the lower and upper world, ancient cities in ruins, and obscure villages become the seats of kings. Famous rivers lessening into shallow brooks, the ocean leaving one coast dry, and overwhelming another: the discovery of many countries yet unknown. Barbarity over-running the politest nations, and the most barbarous become civilized. I should then see the discovery of the longitude, the perpetual motion, the universal medicine, and many other great inventions brought to the utmost perfection.

What wonderful discoveries should we make in astronomy, by outliving and confirming our own predictions, by observing the progress and returns of comets, with the changes of motion in the sun, moon, and stars.

I enlarged upon many other topics, which the natural desire of endless life and sublunary happiness could easily furnish me with. When I had ended, and the sum of my discourse had been interpreted as before, to the rest of the company, there was a good deal of talk among them in the language of the country, not without some laughter at my expense. At last the same gentleman who had been my interpreter said, he was desired by the rest to set me right in a few mistakes, which I had fallen into through the common imbecility of human nature, and upon that allowance was less answerable for them. That this breed of *struldbrugs* was peculiar to their country, for there were no such people either in Balnibarbi or Japan, where he had the honour to be ambassador from his Majesty, and found the natives in both those kingdoms very hard to believe that the fact was possible; and it appeared from my astonishment when he first mentioned the matter to me, that I received it as a thing wholly new, and scarcely to be credited. That in the two kingdoms above mentioned, where during his residence he had conversed very much, he observed long life to be the universal desire and wish of mankind. That whoever had one foot in the grave, was sure to hold back the other as strongly as he could. That the oldest had still hopes of living one day longer, and looked on death as the greatest evil, from which nature always prompted him to retreat; only in this island of Luggnagg the appetite for living was not so eager, from the continual example of the *struldbrugs* before their eyes.

That the system of living contrived by me was unreasonable and unjust, because it supposed a perpetuity of youth, health, and vigour, which no man could be so foolish to hope, however extravagant he may be in his wishes. That the question therefore was not whether a man would choose to be always in the prime of youth, attended with prosperity and health, but how he would pass a perpetual life under all the usual disadvantages which old age brings along with it. For although few men will avow their desires of being immortal upon such hard conditions, yet in the two kingdoms before mentioned of Balnibarbi and Japan, he observed that every man desired to put off death for some time longer, let it approach ever so late; and he rarely heard of any man who died willingly, except he were incited by the extremity of grief or torture. And he appealed to me whether in those countries I had travelled as well as my own, I had not observed the same general disposition.

After this preface, he gave me a particular account of the *struldbrugs* among them. He said they commonly acted like mortals, till about thirty years old, after which by degrees they grew melancholy and dejected, increasing in both till they came to fourscore. This he learned from their own confession: for otherwise there not being above two or three of that species born in an age, they were too few to form a general observation by. When they came to fourscore years, which is reckoned the extremity of living in this country, they had not only all the follies and infirmities of other old men, but many more which arose from the dreadful prospect of never dying. They were not only opinionative, peevish, covetous, morose, vain, talkative, but uncapable of friendship, and dead to all natural affection, which never descended below their grandchildren. Envy and impotent desires are their prevailing passions. But those

14

objects against which their envy seems principally directed, are the vices of the younger sort, and the deaths of the old. By reflecting on the former, they find themselves cut off from all possiblity of pleasure; and whenever they see a funeral, they lament and repine that others have gone to a harbour of rest, to which they themselves never can hope to arrive. They have no remembrance of anything but what they learned and observed in their youth and middle age, and even that is very imperfect. And for the truth or particulars of any fact, it is safer to depend on common traditions than upon their best recollections. The least miserable among them appear to be those who turn to dotage, and entirely lose their memories; these meet with more pity and assistance, because they want many bad qualities which abound in others.

If a *struldbrug* happen to marry one of his own kind, the marriage is dissolved of course by the courtesy of the kingdom, as soon as the younger of the two comes to be fourscore. For the law thinks it a reasonable indulgence, that those who are condemned without any fault of their own to a perpetual continuance in the world, should not have their misery doubled by the load of a wife.

As soon as they have completed the term of eighty years, they are looked on as dead in law; their heirs immediately succeed to their estates, only a small pittance is reserved for their support, and the poor ones are maintained at the public charge. After that period they are held incapable of any employment of trust or profit, they cannot purchase lands or take leases, neither are they allowed to be witnesses in any cause, either civil or criminal, not even for the decision of meers and bounds.

At ninety they lose their teeth and hair, they have at that age no distinction of taste, but eat and drink whatever they can get, without relish or appetite. The diseases they were subject to still continue without increasing or diminishing. In talking they forget the common appellation of things, and the names of persons, even of those who are their nearest friends and relations. For the same reason, they never can amuse themselves with reading, because their memory will not serve to carry them from the beginning of a sentence to the end; and by this defect they are deprived of the only entertainment whereof they might otherwise be capable.

The language of this country being always upon the flux, the *struldbrugs* of one age do not understand those of another, neither are they able after two hundred years to hold any conversation (farther than by a few general words) with their neighbours the mortals; and thus they lie under the disadvantage of living like foreigners in their own country.

This was the account given me of the *struldbrugs*, as near as I can remember. I afterwards saw five or six of different ages, the youngest not above two hundred years old, who were brought to me at several times by some of my friends; but although they were told that I was a great traveller, and had seen all the world, they had not the least curiosity to ask me a question; only desired I would give them *slumskudask*, or a token of remembrance, which is a modest way of begging, to avoid the law that strictly forbids it, because they are provided for by the public, although indeed with a very scanty allowance.

They are despised and hated by all sorts of people; when one of them is born, it is reckoned ominous, and their birth is recorded very particularly: so that you may know their age by consulting the registry, which however hath not been kept above a thousand years past, or at least hath been destroyed by time or public disturbances. But the usual way of computing how old they are, is by asking them what kings or great persons they can remember, and then consulting history, for infallibly the last prince in their mind did not begin his reign after they were fourscore years old.

They were the most mortifying sight I ever beheld, and the women more horrible than the men. Besides the usual deformities in extreme old age, they acquired an additional ghastliness in proportion to their number of years, which is not to be described; and among half a dozen, I soon distinguished which was the eldest, although there was not above a century or two between them.

The reader will easily believe, that from what I had heard and seen, my keen appetite for perpetuity of life was much abated. I grew heartily ashamed of the pleasing visions I had formed, and thought no tyrant could invent a death into which I would not run with pleasure from such a life. The King heard of all that had passed between me and my friends upon this occasion, and rallied me very pleasantly, wishing I would send a couple of *struldbrugs* to my own country to arm our people against the fear of death; but this it seems is forbidden by the fundamental laws of the kingdom, or else I should have been well content with the trouble and expense of transporting them.

I could not but agree that the laws of this kingdom, relating to the *struldbrugs*, were founded upon the strongest reasons, and such as any other country would be under the necessity of enacting in the like circumstances. Otherwise, as avarice is the necessary consequent of old age, those immortals would in time become proprietors of the whole nation, and engross the civil power, which, for want of abilities to manage, must end in the ruin of the public.

CHAPTER XI

The Author leaves Luggnagg, *and sails to* Japan. *From thence he returns in a* Dutch *ship to* Amsterdam, *and from* Amsterdam *to* England.

I THOUGHT this account of the *struldbrugs* might be some entertainment to the reader, because it seems to be a little out of the common way; at least, I do not remember to have met the like in any book of travels that hath come to my hands: and if I am deceived, my excuse must be, that it is necessary for travellers, who describe the same country, very often to agree in dwelling on the same particulars, without deserving the censure of having borrowed or transcribed from those who wrote before them.

There is indeed a perpetual commerce between this kingdom and the great empire of Japan, and it is very probable that the Japanese authors may have given some account of the *struldbrugs*; but my stay in Japan was so short, and I was so entirely a stranger to that language, that I was not qualified to make any enquiries. But I hope the Dutch, upon this notice, will be curious and able enough to supply my defects.

His Majesty having often pressed me to accept some employment in his court, and finding me absolutely determined to return to my native country, was pleased to give me his licence to depart, and honoured me with a letter of recommendation under his own hand to the Emperor of Japan. He likewise presented me with four hundred forty-four large pieces of gold (this nation delighting in even numbers), and a red diamond which I sold in England for eleven hundred pounds.

On the 6th day of May, 1709, I took a solemn leave of his Majesty, and all my friends. This prince was so gracious as to order a guard to conduct me to Glanguenstald, which is a royal port to the south-west part of the island. In six days I found a vessel ready to carry me to Japan, and spent fifteen days in the voyage. We landed at a small port-town called Xamoschi, situated on the southeast part of Japan; the town lies on the western point, where there is a narrow strait, leading northward into a long arm of the sea, upon the north-west part of which, Yedo the metropolis stands. At landing I showed the customhouse officers my letter from the King of Luggnagg to his Imperial Majesty. They knew the seal perfectly well; it was as broad as the palm of my hand. The impression was, *a King lifting up a lame beggar from the earth.* The magistrates of the town hearing of my letter, received me as a public minister. They provided me with carriages and servants, and bore my charges to Yedo, where I was admitted to an audience, and delivered my letter, which was opened with great ceremony, and explained to the Emperor by an interpreter, who then gave me notice by his Majesty's order, that

I should signify my request, and, whatever it were, it should be granted for the sake of his royal brother of Luggnagg. This interpreter was a person employed to transact affairs with the Hollanders; he soon conjectured by my countenance that I was an European, and therefore repeated his Majesty's commands in Low Dutch, which he spoke perfectly well. I answered (as I had before determined), that I was a Dutch merchant, shipwrecked in a very remote country, from whence I had travelled by sea and land to Luggnagg, and then took shipping for Japan, where I knew my countrymen often traded, and with some of these I hoped to get an opportunity of returning into Europe: I therefore most humbly entreated his royal favour, to give order, that I should be conducted in safety to Nangasac. To this I added another petition, that for the sake of my patron the King of Luggnagg, his Majesty would condescend to excuse my performing the ceremony imposed on my countrymen, of trampling upon the crucifix, because I had been thrown into his kingdom by my misfortunes, without any intention of trading. When this latter petition was interpreted to the Emperor, he seemed a little surprised, and said, he believed I was the first of my countrymen who ever made any scruple in this point, and that he began to doubt whether I was a real Hollander, or no, but rather suspected I must be a Christian. However, for the reasons I had offered, but chiefly to gratify the King of Luggnagg by an uncommon mark of his favour, he would comply with the singularity of my humour; but the affair must be managed with dexterity, and his officers should be commanded to let me pass as it were by forgetfulness. For he assured me, that if the secret should be discovered by my countrymen, the Dutch, they would cut my throat in the voyage. I returned my thanks by the interpreter for so unusual a favour, and some troops at that time on their march to Nangasac, the commanding officer had orders to convey me safe thither, with particular instructions about the business of the crucifix.

On the 9th day of June, 1709, I arrived at Nangasac, after a very long and troublesome journey. I soon fell into the company of some Dutch sailors belonging to the *Amboyna*, of Amsterdam, a stout ship of 450 tons. I had lived long in Holland, pursuing my studies at Leyden, and I spoke Dutch well. The seamen soon knew from whence I came last: they were curious to enquire into my voyages and course of life. I made up a story as short and probable as I could, but concealed the greatest part. I knew many persons in Holland; I was able to invent names for my parents, whom I pretended to be obscure people in the province of Guelderland. I would have given the captain (one Theodorus Vangrult) what he pleased to ask for my voyage to Holland; but understanding I was a surgeon, he was contented to take half the usual rate, on condition that I would serve him in the way of my calling. Before we took shipping, I was often asked by some of the crew, whether I had performed the ceremony above-mentioned; I evaded the question by general answers, that I had satisfied the Emperor and court in all particulars. However, a malicious rogue of a skipper went to an officer, and pointing to me, told him I had not yet trampled on the crucifix: but the other, who had received instructions to let me pass, gave the rascal twenty strokes on the shoulders with a bamboo, after which I was no more troubled with such questions.

Nothing happened worth mentioning in this voyage. We sailed with a fair wind to the Cape of Good Hope, where we stayed only to take in fresh water. On the 10th of April, 1710, we arrived safe in Amsterdam, having lost only three men by sickness in the voyage, and a fourth who fell from the foremast into the sea, not far from the coast of Guinea. From Amsterdam I soon after set sail for England in a small vessel belonging to that city.

On the 16th of April we put in at the Downs. I landed the next morning, and saw once more my native country after an absence of five years and six months complete. I went straight to Redriff, where I arrived the same day at two in the afternoon, and found my wife and family in good health.

TO GUIDE THE READER

SWIFT AND HIS AGE

Jonathan Swift was born in Dublin on November 30, 1667. He was descended from an old Yorkshire family of royalist sympathies, and was related by marriage to Dryden, the foremost man of letters of the older generation. His grandfather, the Rev. Thomas Swift, had been ruined during the Civil War owing to his loyalty to the King. His father, in government employment in Dublin, had married a Leicestershire woman, Abigail Erick. Some months before Jonathan's birth his father died; as a baby his nurse kidnapped him and took him to England, and he was not returned to his mother until three years later. To relieve her of domestic and financial care, Jonathan's uncle Godwin charitably maintained him, and at six years old sent him to school at Kilkenny. To this school he was followed, after some years, by Congreve, who became one of the leading wits and dramatists of the day. His mother returned to Leicestershire with the rest of her children.

Brought up virtually as an orphan, Swift long resented the poverty, the lack of a real home, and the air of charity associated with his childhood. It made him bitter and introspective. As a refuge from unhappiness, he read much. His favourite book was the Bible, which he studied without guidance; it may have been this which later made him one of the most original and unorthodox of great churchmen.

His early reading did not, however, make him a successful scholar. In 1682 he began his undistinguished academic career at Trinity College, Dublin, where he found the traditional curriculum irksome. He was granted a degree only through the indulgence of his superiors.

By the Revolution of 1688, James II, becoming increasingly tyrannical and reactionary, was deposed in favour of William of Orange. Swift, now a young man of 21, without means and without prospects, left Ireland to seek employment nearer the centre of government. His mother secured him the post of secretary to Sir William Temple, with whom he had family connections. Sir William, a retired diplomat, lived at Moor

Park in Surrey, and it was here that Swift passed most of the next ten years of his life. He wrote, studied, and performed the duties of something between valet and clerk to his employer; he met the leading political figures of the day, sometimes walking and talking with the King himself. Among the members of the household were Rebecca Dingley, a poor relation, and Esther Johnson, a young girl adopted by Sir William. Fourteen or fifteen years Swift's junior, Esther—or Stella, as he came to call her—became first his pupil and then his companion and chief confidante in Temple's household. Their attachment, which was deep and intimate, lasted until her death. We know nothing of her except what Swift himself tells us, and he never revealed the truth about their supposed marriage. It seems probable that he married her secretly, but the two never lived together openly as man and wife. It was to her that he addressed the famous *Journal* which he began in 1710, relating his part in the affairs of England, and when she died in 1728, Swift was inconsolable and never again mentioned her name.

At Moor Park, Swift fretted for independence and distinction. His subordinate position irked him, although he respected and admired his master.

In 1694 he took holy orders in the hope of making a living for himself in the Church and gaining preferment equal to his talent and ambition. For a short time he became a country clergyman at Kilroot in Ireland, but he was soon back at Moor Park, helping Sir William with his work and himself engaging in the first of the writings for which he was to become famous. He had already written poems which were to earn for him Dryden's remark: "Cousin Swift, you will never be a poet." *A Tale of a Tub* and *The Battle of the Books* were, however, brilliant prose essays in controversy. The former, which was theological in character, was important because it gained Swift a reputation for unorthodox religious views; and he always considered that it was one of the causes of his failure to gain a high place in the Church.

In 1699 occurred the death of Sir William Temple, his master, patron and friend. The various hopes which their association had led Swift to form were destroyed. At thirty-two he was a man with no settled direction in life, no definite prospect of promotion—or indeed of employment, yet a man filled with restless and insatiable ambition, and endowed with great intellectual gifts. He must have appeared to his contemporaries as one not easy to get on with, for his pride and personal integrity made him touchy, even irascible. Yet to those friendships he formed—and they were with some of the greatest intellects and the finest spirits of his day—he was passionately loyal. The age of William and Mary, of Queen Anne, and of George I was one of fierce political warfare, both Whigs and Tories struggling ruthlessly and often unscrupulously for power. Position and influence went to those who could best serve a party or a states-man. A man who might set his own principles above party, justice above expediency, and the interests of his Church above those of individual politicians, might come to be regarded as dangerous.

For the present, however, Swift was almost unknown. Shortly after Temple's death, disappointed in the promise of a position of some influence, he was obliged to accept the obscure living of Laracor, a village twenty miles from Dublin. His congregation was tiny and his duties of the humblest. It is recorded that on one occasion his congregation consisted of his clerk alone, whereupon he began the service with these words: "Dearly beloved Roger, the scripture moveth you and me . . ." The story may not be true, but it is highly characteristic. In Ireland he was forced to see the misery and poverty of the peasants at close quarters. Their condition aroused his fiercest indignation and kept burning in his heart the passion for justice and freedom which never cooled. He loved intelligence and liberty, and loathed stupidity and oppression. All his life he fought against them. His exile in Ireland, relieved as it was by the presence of Stella and Mrs. Dingley, whom he had persuaded to move from England, fretted his restless mind and did nothing to satisfy his ambition. Ambition, we are told, is the sin by which the angels fell; certainly it is a profoundly destructive passion. There is no doubt that Swift longed for power; he was not only a clear and able thinker, a forceful writer, a man of strong conscience and principles, he was also exceedingly practical and methodical. All his writings testify to this. His love of individual men and women—whatever he may have come to feel about mankind in general—made him one of the most consistently charitable and generous of Christians, so far as his poverty and his natural carefulness would allow. Obliged by circumstances to live a sedentary and inactive life, he had the temperament of a man of action. His biographers tell us that he was fond of violent exercise, and this must have been only partly due to the demands

of health. He had mixed with men of power at Moor Park;
power in the life of the nation was something which could come
with promotion in the Church. He schemed, he flattered, he
angled for promotion, as every man at that time was bound to
do who wanted to get on. Of the ten years following 1700 Swift
spent at least four in London. He frequented coffee-house
society and became the friend of wits and writers. He got to
know Addison and Steele, and himself earned a reputation as a
witty pamphleteer and controversialist.

He was taken up by the Whigs, who needed the help of as
many able pens as they could command. When they came into
power in 1708, he had a right to hope that they would relieve
him of his Irish living and give him some position worthy of
his talents and his services to the party. But he found that
the price of preferment was betrayal of his Church. He was
unswervingly loyal to the Church of England and strongly
disapproved of Dissenters. The Whigs needed the support of
the growing body of Dissenters and were prepared to make
concessions to them. Swift could not find it in his conscience
to endorse their religious policy. Accordingly, disappointed and
still unpromoted, he drifted away from the Whigs, and began
to associate with the Tories. In particular, he formed close and
intimate relations with the leaders, Harley (later Lord Oxford)
and St. John (later Lord Bolingbroke).

In 1710 the fall of the Whig ministry and the triumph of the
Tories brought Swift to the zenith of his power and influence.
He was put in charge of the Tory paper, *The Examiner*, and his
advice was sought continually by the most important men in
the government. Oxford and Bolingbroke called him by his
Christian name; he was the prey of suitors for every kind of
favour. He used his influence unsparingly to help those whom he
considered deserving. He betrayed no friend; and he employed
his pen with skill and energy in the service of those principles
in which he believed, and which he believed to be served by the
Tories. He received no money for his writings, and no public
recognition. Men who did far less than he for the party and
the nation were rewarded with high honours; but still promotion
failed to fall upon Swift. Bishoprics were in the gift of the
crown, and Queen Anne and her advisers did not trust this
brilliant but dangerous man.

In 1712 Swift suffered from a temporary breakdown in health.
He was attacked by the fits of giddiness which later became

more frequent and more painful, producing deafness, sickness and the most terrible fits of morbid depression. From now on his health was never good for long. He lived continuously under the fear of insanity, a fear which in the end proved to have been prophetic. At the age of fifty, seeing an ancient elm with its topmost branches withered and leafless, he said to a friend: "I shall be like that tree; I shall die at the top."

An account of Swift's life in outline must to some extent represent him as a gloomy, morbid and dissatisfied man. But if he seems to have failed in all he consciously desired, he fulfilled himself in other ways. He enjoyed the friendship and esteem of the best minds of his time, including Pope, Gay, and Arbuthnot; his intimacy with Addison, broken though it was by his defection from the Whigs, was a real delight to him while it lasted. He knew Congreve and many lesser wits. His writings were highly esteemed by connoisseurs. The years in London must have given him many hours of real happiness and pleasure. One of the less happy incidents which began during his years there was his friendship with Hester Vanhomrigh, whom he christened Vanessa. No doubt he was rash to encourage this passionate young woman in hopes which he could never satisfy. She desired ardently to become his wife, but he would not desert Stella. Yet he loved Vanessa, and her adoration meant much to him.

In 1713 Swift was rewarded with the Deanery of St. Patrick's, the Protestant Cathedral of Dublin. This preferment he regarded as banishment. After a short stay in Ireland, he returned to London; but serious differences between Oxford and Bolingbroke made the fall of the Tories inevitable. In 1714 Queen Anne died, and was succeeded by George I. The Whig ministry was recalled. The Tories were out of office, and Swift's period of public influence came to an end. The remainder of his life is virtually the history of a disappointed man's exile in Ireland, relieved by occasional visits to London and solaced by the friendship of great writers and, for a time, the devotion of admiring women.

In 1723 the death of Vanessa after his final violent rejection of her caused him deep anguish and remorse. The following year he achieved considerable popularity among the Irish for his championship of their rights against the encroachments of English exploiters. The famous anonymous *The Drapier's Letters*, purporting to be the work of a Dublin linen-draper, were directed against the impoverishment of Irish economy by the importation of English coinage known as Wood's halfpence. At all times the condition of the Irish caused him savage indignation, yet he did not love Ireland. He saw too much misery, too much prejudice, and too much stupidity; and so far away from the centre of government he felt powerless to do anything to remedy matters. It was during these years as Dean of St. Patrick's that he wrote the greatest of all his works, *Gulliver's Travels*, which was published in 1726 and earned him the immediate applause of literary and fashionable circles.

Yet it was never literary fame which Swift longed for, it was appointment to a position of power and influence from which he could do direct, practical and lasting good. On the accession of George II in 1727, he went to London in a final attempt to get English preferment. When this failed, he left England, never again to return. The following year, to his lasting sorrow, Stella died. He felt altogether alone in the world. His melancholy, his ill-health, his fear of madness increased. In 1729, in a letter to Bolingbroke, he wrote the terrible words:

> "You think, as I ought to think, that it is time for me to have done with the world; and so I would, if I could get into a better before I was called into the best, and not die here in a rage, like a poisoned rat in a hole."

In 1731 he wrote one of the best known of his poems, the humorous yet bitter *Verses on the Death of Dr. Swift*. Thoughts of his own death increased with age and failing health. For the next ten years he carried on his work as Dean with due regard to the interests of his office and the Church, and with unsurpassed charity towards those in need. His mind gradually gave way, his deafness and giddiness increased, he became more and more isolated from the world, sometimes hardly aware of what he was saying. In 1741 he was put under restraint, and guardians were appointed. Still he lingered on, and it was not till 1745, on October 19th, at the age of 78, that he died at the Deanery in Dublin.

He left about £12,000, with which was endowed a charitable institution in Dublin, St. Patrick's Hospital for Imbeciles. He was buried in St. Patrick's Church, in the grave "where"—to quote his own epitaph, carved on his monument—"where savage indignation could no more tear his heart"—UBI SAEVA INDIGNATIO ULTERIUS COR LACERARE NEQUIT.

GULLIVER'S TRAVELS

Gulliver's Travels is one of the most remarkable, the most popular, and the most original books in English. Like *Robinson Crusoe*, it was not intended for children, but it has been adopted as a universal favourite by young readers; they are fascinated by the bold and simple idea of the Lilliputians, and have of course no notion of the more serious purpose of the book. When it first appeared, Swift's friend Dr. Arbuthnot prophesied that it would have as long a run as *The Pilgrim's Progress*, and so far neither story shows signs of losing favour. The basic idea is so delightful that we are justified in enjoying the story for its own sake; yet something must be said of its deeper import and of Swift's own attitude to his masterpiece.

The germ of *Gulliver* seems to have started in the meetings of an unofficial body known as the Scriblerus Club, which took place in London about 1714. Swift and his friends Arbuthnot, Pope, Gay and Parnell discussed the design of a general satire against dull and pedantic scholarship in the form of an account of an imaginary character, Martinus Scriblerus. The design never materialised, but part of it appeared in Pope's *Dunciad*, while Swift's share took shape in later years as *Gulliver's Travels*. He wrote the first part about 1721, Part II in 1722 and Part IV (not included in the present edition) in 1724. He then returned to the composition of Part III, which he had begun some years earlier. The whole book was published in London in October, 1726, in conditions of the utmost secrecy. Swift was afraid that the satirical allusions to important people would get the printer into serious trouble. In those days the publication of seditious and libellous writings could land a printer in the pillory, where he might lose one or both of his ears. Through Pope's good management, *Gulliver's Travels* was the only one of Swift's books out of which he ever made a penny. In every other case he was content to let the printer keep the profits as a reward for daring to publish dangerous matter.

The success of *Gulliver* was instantaneous. The first impression sold out rapidly, and further impressions followed in quick succession. Arbuthnot wrote to Swift in Dublin describing the delight with which his book had been greeted. Everyone who could read was reading it. Gentlemen in coffee-houses and ladies in drawing-rooms discussed it eagerly with their friends. In France an inferior translation won immediate popularity, and *Gulliver* became all the rage. While everyone enjoyed its novelty, what the people of Swift's time read it for was principally the satire. This was as Swift intended. Neither he nor they could have known then that two hundred years afterwards *Gulliver* would still be read by people who had little knowledge of the political and social conditions which gave rise to the satire.

Swift borrowed material and ideas freely from the Roman writer Lucian, from the Frenchmen Rabelais and Cyrano de Bergerac, and from such English writers as Dampier and Defoe. But what he made out of his various borrowings was entirely his own. It was quite as much his own as *Hamlet* and *Antony and Cleopatra* are Shakespeare's, and Shakespeare certainly borrowed as much as Swift from other sources. *Gulliver* bears the distinctive marks of Swift's own temper and genius: no one else could have written the book. The quality that mainly distinguishes it from other accounts of imaginary voyages is its credibility. As has often been said, once you accept the basic notion of two races of beings, the one twelve times as small and the other twelve times as big as men, everything is possible, nothing fantastic. If in his account of Lilliput and Brobdingnag Swift had allowed himself to stray from his plain, matter-of-fact, circumstantial style of narrative, the plausibility of the simple, basic idea would have broken down, and we would regard the stories as merely ingenious, instead of delightful. Without this quality of delight—which after all constitutes the originality of *Gulliver*—the book could never have been such an inexhaustible favourite for so many generations.

It is difficult to read the beginning of it and realise that it was the work of a bitterly disappointed man who believed himself to be an exile from an ungrateful world. He wished, indeed, as he says, to vex the world; but the poet, the artist in him was too strong. He could not fail to delight it. But let us glance first at the latter part of it. The fourth part is one of the most savage and terrible indictments of mankind ever written. It even shocked Swift's contemporaries, though they were in many ways a tolerant, good-humoured generation, accustomed to savage satire. The third part, dealing with Laputa and other fabulous regions, has always been regarded as the weakest in the whole design. Arbuthnot told Swift so as soon as he read it; and Swift's latest critic, Mr. J. Middleton Murry, echoes him in calling it "Artistically . . . a serious blemish on one of the world's greatest books." It has no central connecting thread, it is not convincing, and, apart from the wonderful passage about the Struldbrugs, or Immortals, it is on a lower imaginative and literary level than the other three parts. Swift hated abstract philosophy and what we should now class under the general heading of Science. He hated scientists, reserving particular venom for Sir Isaac Newton, and he filled his third part with all his unreasoning spite and hatred. Unfortunately he did not not know much about science, and succeeded only too well in exposing his own ignorance rather than theirs. Nevertheless there are some amusing gibes against the more fantastic schemes which led to the South Sea Bubble of 1720, when so many innocent investors were ruined; and we can still smile at the inventor engaged on a project for extracting sunshine from cucumbers.

Turning to Parts I and II, we find Swift taking first, as it were, a bird's eye view of mankind, and then a worm's eye view. Lilliput was England in the reign of Queen Anne. Its enemy, Blefuscu, was France. At first, to gain our interest and sympathy, he represents the Lilliputians rather favourably; only gradually do we realise that he means to belittle their pretensions, to condemn the Lilliputian court as a centre of intrigue, jealousy and corruption. In this book Gulliver is partly Swift himself, and partly his friend, the Tory leader Bolingbroke, whom he considered as one of the noblest and most wronged men of the age. The account of Lilliput is his revenge against the Whigs who exiled Bolingbroke and tried to keep themselves in office by perpetuating the war against France. As for himself, if he had been disappointed in the hopes he had had of the Whigs, he could at least, in his writings, represent himself moving god-like among these diminutive and insignificant little intriguers and war-mongers.

In Part II the satire deepens. In a sense, it is Lilliput over again, but with the hero no bigger than a Lilliputian. The account of Brobdingnag is full of incident depicting the hero in a humiliating situation. It is as if Swift were saying, "You may have thought what a fine and dignified figure a man might cut amidst a race of pygmies; but you were wrong: see what that same man is like amidst a race of giants—how self-important, how defenceless, how ridiculous!"

Swift does not idealise the Brobdingnagians: the farmer who

nearly kills Gulliver by exhibiting him for gain is as mean and grasping as anyone in Europe. But, on the whole, Brobdingnag represents England as it might have been: feudal in social organisation, agricultural in economic character, with the King representing Swift's ideal of political wisdom. Such a king, Swift concludes, could only regard Europeans—to quote the famous peroration to his address to Gulliver in Part III, Chapter VI—as "the most pernicious race of little odious vermin that nature ever suffered to crawl upon the surface of the earth."

The clarity and force of Swift's style are everywhere apparent. They need no illustration. When he wrote *Gulliver*, he was at the height of his creative powers. The style is a reflection of the man. Perhaps the thing which impresses us most about the book, after full consideration, is the way in which the writer's personality is stamped upon it, even though he is disguised as a ship's surgeon. Swift's character was full of violent contradictions; a man of intense feeling, he experienced everything by extremes. In *Gulliver* he expresses intense hatred of mankind: such hatred can only be what one must call the reverse side of love. It arises from a passionate concern for humanity, which is the very opposite of indifference; such concern we can only regard as love, even if it is love transmuted by circumstances into its opposite. The degradation, the vileness, which Swift ascribes to man could not have been conceived but as the corruption of noble qualities. Swift himself left no doubt of his meaning in *Gulliver*; writing to Pope, he said:

"The chief end I propose to myself in all my labours, is to vex the world rather than divert it, and if I could compass that design without hurting my own person or fortune, I would be the most indefatigable writer you have ever seen. . . . I have ever hated all nations, professions and communities, and all my love is towards individuals; for instance, I hate the tribe of lawyers, but I love Counsellor Such-a-one and Judge Such-a-one; so with physicians—I will not speak of my own trade—soldiers, English, Scotch, French, and the rest. But principally I hate and detest that animal called man, although I heartily love John, Peter Thomas, and so forth. This is the system upon which I have governed myself many years, but do not tell, and so I shall go on till I have done with them. . . . Upon this great foundation of misanthropy, though not in Timon's manner, the whole building of my 'Travels' is erected; and

I never will have peace of mind, till all honest men are of my opinion."

To love individuals and hate mankind—that was the curious fate to which Swift's circumstances had driven him. Yet there is something slightly illogical about his protestations of misanthropy. If he had hated mankind so vehemently, could he have worked so vehemently for its good? At all events, there is something strange about the fact that a book which was written out of hatred for mankind should have been accepted by so many of the race as a masterpiece, whether as an adventure story for children or a satire to make adults think about themselves and their institutions.

NOTES

THE PUBLISHER TO THE READER

Great pains were taken to conceal the identity of the author of *Gulliver's Travels*, since at that time the writer and the printer of political satires were liable to severe penalties. Swift's fears, in fact, proved groundless, but he evidently took pleasure in concealing his identity, even when the whole fashionable world knew of the pretence. The manuscript was delivered secretly to the printer, Mott, and was supposed to come from an imaginary cousin of Captain Gulliver, Richard Sympson. Notice how in this prefatory letter he conveniently explains why the book contains so little of the technical information and nautical jargon which the public would expect from a ship's captain, but which was beyond Swift's scope.

PART I

CHAPTER I

3. *Leyden:* a university in Holland, noted throughout Europe for its Medical School.
the Levant: the eastern Mediterranean.

4. *Van Diemen's Land:* Swift means Tasmania but his engraver means the mainland of Australia.   In either case the geography is inaccurate, and the position of Lilliput obscure.

5. *ligatures:* cords or strands used for binding.

6. *not six inches high:* i.e. just short of six inches.   The scale of Lilliput is one inch to a foot as compared with the world of ordinary people.   In Brobdingnag the scale is reversed.

bombs: hand grenades.

buff jerkin: leather waistcoat.

10. *express:* special messenger.

CHAPTER II

14. The Emperor of Lilliput bears some resemblance to George I.

an Austrian lip: the royal house of Hapsburg was noted for a thick, hanging under-lip.

The best essay on political allusions in *Gulliver's Travels* is Sir Charles Firth's *The Political Significance of "Gulliver's Travels"* in his *Essays, Historical and Literary* (1938).

15. *lingua franca:* free language; a mixed tongue of medieval origin, based on English and French, with scraps of other tongues, and spoken by traders and sailors on the shore of the Mediterranean.

19. *a hollow pillar of iron . . . fastened to a strong piece of timber:* i.e. Gulliver's pistol.

21. *I did not observe it:* this refers to the excessive precautions taken by the Whigs against those who were suspected of Jacobite leanings.

22. *perspective:* telescope.

CHAPTER III

23. *the rope-dancers:* this passage is a satire on the difficulties of public men in obtaining and keeping high offices in Swift's time.

Flimnap, the Treasurer, is allowed to cut a caper: i.e. admitted, granted.   Flimnap represents Sir Robert Walpole.

24. *one of the King's cushions:* this refers to the resignation of Walpole in 1717, and his subsequent restoration to favour by the influence of the Duchess of Kendal.

24. *three fine silken threads:* these represent the Orders of the Garter (blue), the Bath (red), and the Thistle (green).

25. *discovered:* revealed, exhibited.

close chair: Sedan chair.

27. *Skyresh Bolgolam:* thought by some editors to be the Duke of Argyle, one of Swift's bitterest opponents.

Chapter IV

32. *he might pretend to some merit in it:* he might claim a share in my gratitude (for having been instrumental in getting me released).

two struggling parties: Tramecksan represents the High Church or Tory party, Slamecksan the Low Church or Whig party.

33. *His Imperial Highness, the Heir to the Crown:* the Prince of Wales, afterwards George II, gave cause for doubt as to which party he supported.

the primitive way of breaking eggs: the Big-Endians represent the Roman Catholics, the Little-Endians the Protestants.

the Emperor his father: Henry VIII, whose "edict" establishing Protestantism in England was the Act of Supremacy of 1534.

His present Majesty's grandfather: no exact historical parallel. Here, as elsewhere in the satire, exact parallels are not to be looked for. The point is that the triviality of the traditional enmity of Lilliput and Blefuscu, and its cause, is compared by Swift to the triviality of the age-long enmity between England and France.

34. *one Emperor lost his life, and another his crown:* Charles I and James II.

Alcoran: the Koran is the bible of the Mohammedans.

Chapter V

36. *with great ease drew fifty of the enemy's largest men of war:* here Gulliver undoubtedly overestimated his strength. The whole incident of the capture of the Blefuscudian fleet represents the insistence of the British government on securing naval supremacy at the Treaty of Utrecht, signed with the French in 1713.

38. *junto:* this represents the Whig confederacy of Ministers against the Jacobites.

41. *the Empress, conceiving the greatest abhorrence of what I had done:* this refers to Queen Anne's dislike of Swift on account of certain of his writings, despite his services to her Ministers.

Chapter VI

44. *the grandfather of the Emperor now reigning:* King James I, who ruled through favourites and by the distribution of honours.

49. *white staff:* the symbol of the office of the Lord High Treasurer of England (until 1714).

Chapter VII

52. *several Committees of Council:* Swift is here referring to the secret committee set up by Walpole in 1715 to enquire into the conduct of the negotiations for the Treaty of Utrecht, in which his enemy Bolingbroke, and other Tory leaders, had played a part. This inquiry led to the impeachment of Bolingbroke, who fled abroad. The articles of impeachment against Gulliver are a satire on Bolingbroke's impeachment.

54. *to put out both your eyes:* some of Walpole's supporters were in favour of impeaching Bolingbroke not for high treason but for lesser crimes, and punishing him, not by death, but by the loss of his titles and estates.

57. *the Emperor always made a speech . . . expressing his great lenity:* Swift may have been referring to the royal proclamation after the Jacobite rising of 1715 and the speech of George I after Atterbury's impeachment in 1722.

Chapter VIII

62. *he was very glad of my resolution:* this refers to the fact that Bolingbroke's exile in France and his intrigues with Jacobites in England were a constant source of embarrassment to the French court.

63. *ancient:* ensign.

PART II

CHAPTER I

69. *Finding it was likely to overblow:* the following page is intended as a satire on the excessive use of nautical jargon by writers of travel-books. Swift was no mariner and probably had no more notion than the average reader what these technical terms meant. The description is lifted, almost word for word, from Sturmy's *Compleat Mariner* (1669).

70. *Tartary:* the Chinese empire.
    the frozen sea: the Arctic.

72. *speaking-trumpet:* megaphone used by bo'sun of a ship.

73. *nothing is great or little:* an idea discussed in *A New Theory of Vision* (1709) by Swift's friend, George Berkeley.

74. *lappet:* flap or fold.

76. *small cyder:* light or weak cider.

79. *hanger:* short sword.

CHAPTER II

82. *nanunculus, homunceletino:* fake words in imitation of the pedantic style of learned writers of Swift's time.

85. *pumpion:* pumpkin.

CHAPTER III

89. *scrutore:* writing desk.

90. *lusus naturae:* a freak of nature.

96. *Gresham College:* a college in the city of London at which lectures were given on scientific subjects.

CHAPTER IV

97. *Geographers of Europe are in a great error:* it was a matter of controversy among geographers of Swift's time whether or not the American continent was joined to Asia.

100. *Salisbury steeple:* the spire of Salisbury Cathedral is the highest spire in England, and is 404 feet high, equivalent to about 5,000 feet in Brobdingnag.

Chapter V

102. *tennis-balls:* in those days these were hard.
104. *espalier:* trellis.

Chapter VI

113. *spinet:* harpsichord.
116. *compliers with the times:* time-servers, opportunists, careerists.
118. *how a kingdom could run out of its estate:* the National Debt had only recently been instituted, and gave general cause for uneasiness in Swift's time.

    a mercenary standing army: this also was a cause of alarm in Swift's time and was the occasion of much criticism of the Whig government.

Chapter VII

120. *Dionysius Halicarnassensis:* or Halicarnassus, was a naturalised Roman of the late first century B.C., who wrote a patriotic history of Rome.
123. *mercurial:* sophisticated, ingenious.
126. *a general composition:* a general settlement, terms of peace.

Chapter VIII

136. *Phaeton:* in Greek mythology Phaeton presumptuously drove the chariot of the sun, but his incompetence threatened to burn up the earth, and he was brought down into the river Eridanus by a thunderbolt from Zeus.

PART III

Chapter I

141. *Fort St. George:* Madras.
142. *a Dutchman:* the cruelty of the Dutch towards other traders in the East was notorious.

CHAPTER II

146. *the minds of these people are so taken up with intense speculations:* the satire is here directed against scientists and mathematicians, whom Swift especially despised, notably Sir Isaac Newton.

147. *kennel:* gutter (canal).

149. *the true etymology:* the following passage is directed against what Swift considered the pedantry of grammarians.

151. *bevil:* at an angle, or sloping.

CHAPTER III

159. *About three years before . . . entirely change the government:* These paragraphs were first printed in 1896 (from manuscript additions in a copy of the first edition, owned by Swift's friend, Ford). Early publishers for their own safety refused to publish them.

161. *neither the king . . . are permitted to leave the island:* George I was often criticised for his repeated visits to Hanover.

CHAPTER IV

This chapter refers to the widespread poverty which resulted from the madness of 1720 known as the South Sea Bubble. Projectors—or, as we should call them, company promoters—advertised wild and foolish schemes for making money quickly, and many people of wealth invested in them, to the ruin of their own estates and the impoverishment of their tenants. It has been suggested that Munodi was intended as a portrait of Bolingbroke, but it seems more likely that he was an imaginary figure, intended to stand for good sense and a belief in tradition.

CHAPTER V

168. *This Academy:* Swift's contemporaries would be familiar with reports of experiments by members of the Royal Society. A detailed account of Swift's satirical treatment of such experiments is to be found in *The Scientific Background of Swift's "Voyage to Laputa"* in *The Annals of Science*, Vol. II, No. 3.

168. *calcine:* burn.

16

169. *all hung round with cobwebs:* in 1710 a French inventor had actually made stockings and gloves from threads spun by spiders.

175. *cephalic tincture:* brain fluid.

success hath not hitherto been answerable: results have not so far come up to expectation.

Chapter VI

175. *chimæras:* extravagant fantasies (from the name of a mythological beast).

176. *redundant, ebullient, and other peccant humours:* excessive, explosive, and other harmful disorders.

spleen, flatus, vertigos, and deliriums: ill-temper, pride, giddiness, and disordered imagination.

scrofulous: having a tendency to feverish swelling of the glands.

foetid: evil-smelling.

purulent: poisoned.

ructations: belchings.

177. *occiput:* the back of the head.

178. *plots and conspiracies against the government:* the following passage alludes to the methods used to obtain evidence of treason against the Bishop of Rochester, Atterbury, whose banishment aroused the anger of the Tory party against Walpole's government.

Chapter VII

184. *not a drop of vinegar in his camp:* tradition relates that Hannibal split a rock by saturating it with vinegar after wood had been burnt on it to heat it.

Chapter VIII

185. *his eyes were the most quick and piercing:* Swift will have nothing to do with the tradition that the greatest poet of antiquity was blind.

Didymus and Eustathius: commentators on Homer.

185. *Scotus and Ramus:* Renaissance critics of Aristotle.

186. *Descartes:* 17th century French philosopher.

Gassendi: a contemporary of Descartes, opposed to the ideas of both Descartes and Aristotle.

attraction: the theory of magnetic attraction, upheld by Newton, whom Swift hated.

187. *Polydore Vergil:* an Italian scholar of the 16th century who settled in England.

Nec vir fortis, nec femina casta: Neither strong man nor chaste woman.

188. *three kings:* possibly Charles II, James II, and William III.

Chapter XI

204. *trampling upon the crucifix:* trampling upon a picture of the Cross was one of the inflictions imposed upon suspected Christian converts in Japan during the persecutions of the seventeenth century.

205. *an absence of five years and six months:* this is a mistake. The voyage had actually lasted about three years and eight months.

REVISION QUESTIONS

PART I

Chapter I

1. Mention six or eight details in the account of Gulliver's life before he travels to Lilliput which show Swift's care in making his story convincing and circumstantial.

2. What is the first detail suggesting that Lilliput is a country out of the ordinary? (N.B.—It occurs before Gulliver wakes up.)

3. Explain briefly the sentence: "But fortune disposed otherwise of me."

4. What impressions does Gulliver gather of the characte of the Lilliputians during his first day with them?

Chapter II

5. Give a brief account of (*a*) the appearance of the Emperor, (*b*) Gulliver's bedding, (*c*) Gulliver's progress in learning the Lilliputian language, (*d*) the effect of Gulliver's weapons on the King and his subjects.

6. Give an account of Gulliver's clemency to his six attackers, and the effect it had on his subsequent treatment.

7. Write an account of some of the contents of a lady's handbag of the present day in the same style as that of the Lilliputians' inventory of the contents of Gulliver's pockets.

CHAPTER III

8. Give a brief account of (*a*) the military exercises performed on Gulliver's handkerchief, and of the accident which put an end to them, (*b*) the recovery of Gulliver's hat, (*c*) the military parade under Gulliver's legs.

9. What examples of political satire are to be found in *Gulliver's Travels* up to this point?

10. Summarise briefly the conditions of Gulliver's release. Were these conditions, in your opinion, wise and just?

CHAPTER IV

11. Part of the attraction which *Gulliver's Travels* has had for readers ever since it first appeared is its striking verisimilitude —that is, its appearance of truth. Mention a dozen details of Gulliver's account of the principal city which illustrate this quality.

12. Give a brief account of the cause of the dispute between Lilliput and Blefuscu.

CHAPTER V

13. Summarise Gulliver's account of the capture of the Blefuscudian fleet.

14. How did Gulliver incur the King's displeasure?

15. Describe in a few lines Gulliver's interview with the Blefuscudian ambassadors.

CHAPTER VI

16. Comment on the superiority of Lilliputian law over English law.

17. Mention the good and bad points of the Lilliputian educational system.

18. Describe briefly the methods used to measure Gulliver for his clothes.

CHAPTER VII

19. State briefly the circumstances in which Gulliver got to know of the intrigues against him.

20. Summarise the arguments for and against Gulliver put forward by Flimnap, Bolgolam, and Reldresal in the secret committee.

21. Re-write in simple language the passage on pp. 57–58 beginning "And as to myself" down to "and against such powerful enemies."

CHAPTER VIII

22. Describe Gulliver's reception in the Kingdom of Blefuscu.

23. Give an account of the circumstances in which Gulliver left Blefuscu.

24. What details in the description of the voyage home maintain the air of verisimilitude?

PART II

CHAPTER I

25. "That which first surprised me was the length of the grass " (p. 71). What does this recall in the story of the voyage to Lilliput?

26. Mention half a dozen of the details which do most to bring vividly to the reader's eye the smallness of Gulliver in proportion to the Brobdingnagians.

27. It is part of Swift's aim in this book to puncture human vanity by lowering his own dignity as a man. Point out several instances in this chapter in which Gulliver is reduced to an undignified situation.

CHAPTER II

28. Give a short account of:
(*a*) Gulliver's treatment by Glumdalclitch.
(*b*) The visit of the neighbouring farmer with the spectacles.
(*c*) The exhibiting of Gulliver at the near-by market town.

CHAPTER III

29. Explain and expand the following quotations:
(*a*) The Queen observed my coldness.
(*b*) The King conceived I might be a piece of clockwork.
(*c*) The Queen rallied me upon my fearfulness.

30. Write a paragraph on:
(*a*) Gulliver's bedchamber.
(*b*) The King of Brobdingnag's opinion of humanity.
(*c*) The Brobdingnagian scientists' views on Gulliver.

31. Describe briefly Gulliver's treatment by the Queen's dwarf.

Chapter IV

32. Describe briefly:
(*a*) Gulliver's travelling box.
(*b*) The temple at Lorbrulgrud.
(*c*) The King's kitchen.

33. What reference does Swift make in this chapter to writers of travel books?

Chapter V

34. At the beginning of this chapter Gulliver speaks of "several ridiculous accidents" which happened to him. Describe briefly any three of these, excluding the adventure of the monkey.

35. Give a brief account of Gulliver's exhibition of his skill in navigation.

36. Describe in detail the incident of the monkey.

37. Illustrate from this chapter the statement that in his account of Gulliver in Brobdingnag Swift endeavours to place humanity in as ridiculous and unpleasant a light as possible.

Chapter VI

38. Mention several examples of Gulliver's ingenuity as a craftsman.

39. Refer the following passages to their context:
(*a*) It was the most violent exercise I ever underwent.
(*b*) How often I then wished for the tongue of Demosthenes or Cicero.
(*c*) He desired to know at what age this entertainment was usually taken up.

40. Show how Swift puts the ideal view of the British constitution in the mouth of Gulliver, and his own satirical view of it in the mouth of the King.

CHAPTER VII

41. "I shall here insert a passage which will hardly obtain belief." What passage does this sentence introduce? Summarise it briefly.

42. Learn by heart the sentence on p. 123 beginning: "And he gave it for his opinion" and ending ". . . the whole race of politicians put together."

CHAPTER VIII

43. By what means does Swift contrive to keep up the reader's interest to the very end, even after he has left Brobdingnag?

44. Why did the ship's captain, as well as Gulliver's wife and family, at first imagine that he had lost his wits?

45. Read the final sentence of this chapter. What does it recall in Part I?

PART III

CHAPTER I

46. How does Swift achieve variety in introducing this his third adventure?

47. Write out in your own words the passage on p. 145 beginning "But at the same time the reader can hardly conceive . . ." and ending " . . . it seemed for a while to stand still."

CHAPTER II

48. Describe briefly (*a*) the appearance of the men of quality in Laputa, (*b*) Gulliver's first meal in the King's palace, (*c*) the method of measuring for a suit of clothes, (*d*) the character of the women of Laputa.

49. " These people are under continual disquietude." What was the nature and cause of these disquietudes?

CHAPTER III

50. Describe briefly either (*a*) how Laputa moved through the air, or (*b*) the efficiency of the Laputians in the use of the telescope.

51. How did the King keep his dependant territories in subjection?

CHAPTER IV

52. Why did Gulliver wish to leave Laputa?

53. Give an outline of the character and views of Munodi, and explain the cause of his unpopularity at Court.

CHAPTER V

54. Outline briefly three of the most absurd projects undertaken by the Academy at Lagado.

55. Give details of the project for conversing without language.

56. Describe in Swift's style a project for (*a*) the invention of television, *or* (*b*) the invention of the atomic bomb, *or* (*c*) the invention of the electronic brain.

CHAPTER VI

57. Illustrate from this chapter Swift's extreme bitterness in political matters.

58. What were Swift's opinions concerning military honour and hereditary nobility?

CHAPTER VII and VIII

59. For what reason do you suppose Swift introduced the visit to the island of Glubbdubdrib?

CHAPTER IX

60. Describe briefly the method adopted by the King of Luggnagg for disposing of his enemies.

CHAPTER X

61. Give a brief account of Gulliver's notions about immortality before he hears the account of the Struldbrugs.

62. Give a brief account of the Struldbrugs as they actually were.

ADDITIONAL QUESTIONS

A. PART I

1. How does Swift suggest that a Lilliput crowd is very much like an English one?

2. Which incidents seem to justify calling Gulliver "a *good-natured* giant?

3. "The personal possessions which Gulliver handed over to the inspectors are matter for mirth; those which he secreted are essential to his preservation." Discuss and illustrate.

4. Why were the people of *both* islands glad to see the last of Gulliver?

B. PART II

5. How does Swift help the reader to feel that to the people of Brobdingnag Gulliver is a strange *animal*?

6. What use does Swift make of (*a*) the dwarf, (*b*) Glumdalclitch?

7. Gulliver is frequently sorry for himself. Give an account of one incident where this self-pity seems justified, one where it does not.

8. Show that after Gulliver had disappeared the King would miss him for reasons different from those explaining the regret of the Queen.

9. What suggests that Brobdingnag is a picture of England as it might have been?

C. PARTS I and II

10. How far is it true to say that Part I deals with what Gulliver did, Part II with what he felt? Why?

11. Show how the differences between Gulliver's position in Part I and that in Part II are illustrated by:

(*a*) the use of a handkerchief;

(*b*) attempts to provide bedding for Gulliver.

12. Compare Swift's devices to get Gulliver away from Lilliput and Brobdingnag in respect of (*a*) amusement, (*b*) excitement, and (*c*) ingenuity.

13. Show from both Parts Swift's skill in anticipating objections (e.g. How could Gulliver see *inside* the house in Lilliput? How could Gulliver in Brobdingnag talk to creatures whose ears were sixty feet from the ground?)

D. PART III

14. What impressions of himself would Gulliver make on the different sets of inhabitants because of the questions he asked?

15. In what ways are Gulliver's ideas *changed* by what he sees and hears?

16. What use does Swift make of *contrast*?

E. ALL PARTS

17. What evidence is there for thinking that Swift despised those who showed no gratitude for services rendered?

18. Dr. Johnson said of *Gulliver's Travels*, "When once you have thought of big men and little men, it is very easy to do the rest." Show that this fails to do justice to Swift's skill.

19. "The chief end I propose to myself in all my labours is to vex the world rather than divert it," wrote Swift. What justification is there for saying that Swift succeeds in vexing the readers of his own age and diverting those of later ages?

20. What makes Swift's way of telling Gulliver's stories right for his purpose?

21. An Irish Bishop is reported to have said that this book was full of improbable lies. Show that the use of "improbable" is *or* is not justified.

22. Show that it can be said of each voyage that it left Gulliver "a sadder and a wiser man."

F. STYLE AND METHOD

23. What does each quotation illustrate of Swift's skill?

(*a*) I have been chiefly studious of truth without affecting any ornaments of learning or of style.

(*b*) They all agreed that I could not be produced according to the regular laws of nature, because I was not framed with a capacity of preserving my life, either by swiftness, or climbing of trees, or digging holes in the earth.

(c) . . . my colour came and went several times with indignation to hear our noble country, the mistress of arts and arms, the scourge of France, the arbitress of Europe, the seat of virtue, piety, honour, and truth, the pride and envy of the world, so contemptuously treated.

(d) It is in length three *Glonglungs* (which make about fifty-four English miles) and two and a half in breadth, as I measured it myself in the royal map made by the King's order, which was laid on the ground on purpose for me, and extended an hundred feet; I paced the diameter and circumference several times barefoot, and computing by the scale, measured it pretty exactly.

(e) When I had done, Glumdalclitch always carried my boat into her closet, and hung it on a nail to dry.

(f) A strange effect of narrow principles and short views! that a prince possessed of every quality which procures veneration, love, and esteem; of strong parts, great wisdom and profound learning, endued with admirable talents for government, and almost adored by his subjects, should from a nice unnecessary scruple, whereof in Europe we can have no conception, let slip an opportunity put into his hands, that would have made him absolute master of the lives, the liberties, and the fortunes of his people.

(g) I hired a horse and guide for five shillings, which I borrowed of the Captain.

(h) For upon my admittance two days after my arrival, I was commanded to crawl on my belly, and lick the floor as I advanced; but on account of my being a stranger, care was taken to have it made so clean that the dust was not offensive.

G. CONTEXT QUESTIONS

24. I now heard a trampling over my head, and somebody calling through the hole with a loud voice in the English tongue; if there be any body below let them speak. I answered, I was an Englishman, drawn by ill fortune into the greatest calamity that ever any creature underwent, and begged, by all that was moving, to be delivered out of the dungeon I was in. The voice replied, I was safe, for my box was fastened to their ship; and the carpenter should immediately come, and saw an hole in the cover, large enough

to pull me out. I answered, that was needless, and would take up too much time, for there was no more to be done, but let one of the crew put his finger into the ring, and take the box out of the sea into the ship, and so into the Captain's cabin.

(*a*) What features of the construction of the box justified Gulliver's calling it a dungeon?

(*b*) Why was Gulliver's reply so sensible to himself but so ludicrous to the listeners?

(*c*) To what uses had this ring previously been put?

25. Those to whom the King had entrusted me, observing how ill I was clad, ordered a tailor to come next morning and take my measure for a suit of clothes. This operator did his office after a different manner from those of his trade in Europe. He first took my altitude by a quadrant, and then with a rule and compasses, described the dimensions and outlines of my whole body, all which he entered upon paper, and in six days brought my clothes very ill made, and quite out of shape, by happening to mistake a figure in the calculation. But my comfort was that I observed such accidents very frequent and little regarded.

(*a*) Apart from being "a good fit" or not, what would Gulliver's new clothes have that his old ones did not have?

(*b*) What does Swift expect readers to think or feel about a land where this could happen?

(*c*) Give an account of how new clothes were made for Gulliver in one of the other strange lands.

SWIFT'S LIFE AND TIMES

Principal Dates

SWIFT		*BACKGROUND*
Born in Dublin	1667	
Leaves Trinity College, Dublin	1685	
Leaves Ireland for Leicester	1688	William III succeeds James II
Becomes Secretary to Sir William Temple	1689	War declared on France
		Bill of Rights shows objections to a standing army
Takes Holy Orders	1694	
First important prose writings	1697	
Accepts living of Laracor (on death of Temple)	1699	
	1701	Act of Settlement restricts King's freedom to leave England
	1702	Queen Anne succeeds William III
Published *The Battle of the Books* and *A Tale of a Tub*	1704	
	1705	Walpole [Flimnap] made 1st Lord of the Treasury and Chancellor of the Exchequer
	1707	Grand Alliance against France
Swift openly a Tory. Edits *The Examiner*. Advises Tory leaders (Oxford, Bolingbroke)	1710	Whigs out of Office; Tories in office.
		The Royal Society holds its meetings at Crane Court
Writes *Journal to Stella*		
Writes *The Conduct of the Allies*	1711	

Member of Scriblerus Club	1713	Peace of Utrecht ends War of Spanish Succession and orders demolition of Dunkirk (i.e. blow at enemy's fleet)
Appointed Dean of St. Patrick's (Dublin)		
Swift leaves England for Ireland	1714	George I succeeds Queen Anne
		Fall of Tories. Beginning of Whig ascendancy
	1715	Bolingbroke takes refuge in France
		Whig Committee of Secrecy enquires into Peace of Utrecht
	1717	Dampier's *New Voyage Round the World* increases interest in travel books
	1719	Defoe's *Robinson Crusoe*
	1720	South Sea Bubble
	1721	Walpole back in power through influence of Duchess of Kendal
	1722	Trial of Atterbury, using intercepted papers and letters as evidence
Death of Vanessa	1723	
Published (anonymously) *The Drapier's Letters*	1724	Cartaret [Reldresal] sent to Ireland
		As Lord Lieutenant offers £300 reward for discovery of authorship of *The Drapier's Letters*
Published *Gulliver's Travels*	1726	
Last visit to England	1727	George II succeeds George I
Mental breakdown	1741	
Death at the Deanery, Dublin	1745	
Buried in St. Patrick's Cathedral		

CHANGES IN USE OR MEANING OF WORDS

[Words are given in the order in which they appear in *Gulliver's Travels*, with modern equivalents at the right-hand side.]

PART I

admiration	strong wonder, astonishment.
periods	carefully constructed sentences.
habits	garments.
allowed	acknowledged.
presently	immediately
complexion	disposition
condition	place in the social scale
sensible	aware of
censure	opinion (without hint of condemnation)
particular	in detail

PART II

hand	handle
nicely	fastidiously
fopperies	foolish tricks
parts	accomplishments
artist	skilled mechanic
nice (workman)	accurate
injuries	insults
artificially	ingeniously
seasonable supply	timely provision
genius	gift
plantations	colonies
issues	payments, expenditure
Institution	Constitution
evil genius	spirit with power to harm
refinement	subtlety
foot	footing
conceit	notion, idea
passages	happenings
freight	passage

PART III

glass	telescope
parallel	level
motions	feelings
progressive	horizontal
prevent	anticipate
antic	grotesque
in good intelligence	on good terms
determined	completed, brought to an end
managing	using corrupt practices
skipper	ship's boy